Praise

Praise for The Hollow Boys (The Dream Rider Saga, #1)

Winner of the Aurora Award for Best Young Adult Novel
Winner of the juried IAP Award for Best Young Adult Novel

"This arresting series kickoff grips from the start [with] its inventive milieu, its flawed but fantastically powered hero, playful worldbuilding, and a host of tantalizing mysteries. … Thrilling YA fantasy" —*BookLife* (Editor's Pick)

"An assured, confident novel … A must-read story for YA fantasy fans."
—*Blueink Review* (Starred review)

"Inventive, engaging, and boundless fun." —*Ottawa Review of Books*

"A fun supernatural tale with well-developed characters and a touch of romance." —*Kirkus Reviews*

Praise for The Crystal Key (The Dream Rider Saga, #2)

Finalist for the Aurora Award for Best Young Adult Novel

"The richly inventive *Dream Rider* adventure continues in this second appealing entry … This thrilling superpowered urban fantasy series continues to grip."
—*BookLife (Editor's Pick)*

"This fast-paced story delivers in a big way—and Smith has all his ducks lined up for an explosive conclusion that readers won't want to miss."
—*Blueink Review (Starred review)*

"*The Crystal Key* has everything that made *The Hollow Boys* work and turns it up a few notches. I can't wait for the conclusion in *The Lost Expedition*."
—*Ottawa Review of Books*

"A fun and engrossing superhero sequel." —*Kirkus Reviews*

Praise for The Lost Expedition (The Dream Rider Saga, #3)

Finalist for the Aurora Award for Best Young Adult Novel

"Explosive conclusion to this spectacular fantasy joyride."
— *BookLife* (**Editor's Pick**)

"As the conclusion to the *Dream Rider Saga*, it exceeded every expectation. I enjoyed every minute I spent with these characters, and I will miss them now that their story is done." — *SF Crowsnest Reviews*

"There is a sweeping majesty to the world building we have not seen since *A Wrinkle in Time*. ... You should package up all three volumes to gift to any young adults in your life—or any adult in your circle"
— *Ottawa Review of Books*

Praise for Douglas Smith

"One of Canada's most original writers of speculative fiction."
—*Library Journal*

"The man is Sturgeon good. Zelazny good. I don't give those up easy."
—*Spider Robinson, Hugo & Nebula Awards winner*

"A great storyteller with a gifted and individual voice."
—*Charles de Lint, World Fantasy Award winner*

"His stories are a treasure trove of riches that touch your heart while making you think." —*Robert J. Sawyer, Hugo & Nebula Awards winner*

"Stories you can't forget, even years later."
—*Julie Czerneda, multi-award-winning author and editor*

How to Read This Series

The short answer to the above question is, "In order (please)!"

There are two types of series: those meant to be read in order, and those where the reader can dip into the books anywhere along the line. *The Dream Rider Saga* is the first type. It is one large mystery, one single story, told over the course of three books (*The Hollow Boys*, *The Crystal Key*, and *The Lost Expedition*), with each book building on what went before.

Reading *The Dream Rider Saga* out of order will lead to confusion and disappointment, two things I take great pains to avoid for my readers. Disappointed, confused readers leave bad reviews, which might end in a Mara hunting them in Dream (and if you didn't get the Mara reference, then you haven't read *The Hollow Boys*, book 1 in the series, and just made my case for including this foreword).

So, if this is the first *Dream Rider* title you plan to read... *STOP!*

Seriously, please stop. Thanks for the interest, but please put this book aside for now and go read *The Hollow Boys* first, and then *The Crystal Key*. Buying links for all *The Dream Rider Saga* titles can be found at the back of this book. Then you can return to *The Lost Expedition* fully informed and prepared to enjoy this story as I intended.

Thanks for listening and for your interest in my writing.

— Douglas Smith

THE LOST EXPEDITION

THE DREAM RIDER SAGA

BOOK 3

DOUGLAS SMITH

A Spiral Path Book

The Lost Expedition
(*The Dream Rider Saga*, Book 3)

ISBN 978-1-928048-31-2 (trade paperback)
ISBN 978-1-928048-34-3 (hardcover)
ISBN 978-1-928048-30-5 (ebook)

Published by Spiral Path Books
Toronto, Canada
smithwriter.com

First edition

Cover design and artwork by Jeff Brown

To my family.

Because, at their heart, that's what these books are about—family.

The family we're born into. The family we find.
The family we make. The family we choose.

And the family we stitch together from all those pieces.

Act I

Looking for a Place to Happen

Chapter 1

All the Way Home

When her plane landed on the Isle of Man, or Mann as the locals called it, the red-haired woman rose from her seat in the otherwise empty first-class cabin. Empty, because she had arranged it so.

A male flight attendant hurried up to her. She lifted her long tresses to allow him to fasten her hunter-green cloak around her neck. She wore tight black slacks and green low-heeled pumps. A white buttoned shirt with French cuffs completed her look, with enough buttons undone to expose impressive cleavage. Better than a spell for most men, she always said.

At the baggage claim, she stabbed a manicured finger on her left hand at the first person she saw, an overweight, balding man in a plaid suit. A bird-shaped shimmer passed in the air between them, then vanished.

She pointed to her suitcase on the carousel. "Get that. And follow me."

The man opened his mouth as if to protest, then stiffened. Retrieving her bag, he scurried in her wake as she strode through the crowded terminal of the small airport, her cloak and hair billowing behind her.

At the taxi stand outside, she ignored the line of waiting passengers and got into the first car. The driver glared back at her. "Lady, there's a queue. You—" His words died as he stared at her face, wide-eyed. Stared, she knew, at the golden runes that now lay there.

She felt them flowing across her face and down her left arm, arranging themselves into the script she desired. She flicked her left hand at him. He stiffened and stopped talking.

"*Vel Gaelg ayd?*" she asked.

He blinked at her.

She sighed. "You don't speak Manx?"

"Few do anymore, Mistress."

"Augh. Put my bag in the trunk."

Getting out, he took her suitcase from the man in the plaid suit, who gazed around as if lost, then wandered back toward the arrival doors. The driver got into the cab. "Where to, Mistress?"

"*Cashtal Rusien.*"

He blinked again.

"Castle Rushen, you idiot."

"Ah, Castletown. Yes, Mistress."

She settled back as he pulled into traffic, letting the scenery scroll past her tired eyes. So much had changed, but one thing matched her fading memories. The grass still *glowed* in the summer sun, a blazing lime green that almost hurt the eyes. "There's no green like that in the world," she whispered.

"Are you from here, Mistress?"

"Many years ago," she said, lost in the past. Catching herself, she scowled at him. "Shut up and drive."

In Castletown, the harbor was familiar, although a sweeping curve of cement had replaced the old stone jetty, and the small lighthouse at its tip was new and freshly painted red and white. The turns in the roads matched her memories, but the low stone houses of old were now three-storied brick buildings, steep-roofed and shoulder-to-shoulder along each narrow street. She shivered at how little she recognized.

Until the driver turned a corner, and the castle rose before her, looming above the modern structures of the small town.

The gray stone of its thick walls and squat towers was streaked with white, randomly from bird droppings, deliberately from new mortar. A carpet of green moss covered the slanting stones topping the sea-facing walls. She smiled. Castle Rushen stood as it had for centuries, a physical memory of a past none here had lived.

Except her.

"By the Goddess," she said. "It still looks the same."

"Best preserved medieval castle in Europe, they say," the driver said, pride in his voice.

It better be. Or at least one particular room. She got out of the taxi. "Wait for me."

An arched entrance led to a narrow zig-zag route between stone walls rising three stories above her. Passing under a small portcullis bearing the unnecessary sign 'The Ancient Portcullis,' she glared at the words, resenting the reminder of her own age.

Inside the gate, she stopped before a declaration emblazoned on the stone wall in gold letters:

The Fortress of the Kings and Lords of Mann

Kings and Lords? No mention of the women who had lived here. No mention of Charlotte, wife of James Stanley, Lord of Mann. Charlotte, who ruled after her husband's execution. Ruled and held the castle, the last person in the three kingdoms to surrender to the Roundheads.

And no mention of the coven of witches who helped Charlotte defend this fortress. The witches who had lived here.

And died here. All save one.

Not that she expected such a mention. Women and witches? No man would immortalize either in those days.

Or in these days, for that matter.

Beside the golden words hung a pennant bearing a scarlet triskelion—three legs inscribed within a circle, equally spaced and radiating from the center—the symbol of Mann. Her hand moved from long habit to her neck, where for years she'd worn her triskelion medallion. She hadn't been concerned when, only weeks earlier, she destroyed the medallion in her defense of the boy, Fader. The trinket had contained many spells but was a mere repository. She could always buy a new bauble and fill it with her magicks.

The real loss that day had been the Weave. Countless spells lost forever when that cursed girl burned the rug. Spells whose rune scripts her coven had stitched into the Weave over centuries.

Her coven. Her sisters. Along with the Weave, all now gone.

But not, she hoped, without a trace.

Inside, Castle Rushen was busy, jammed with visitors led by guides in period costumes droning on about the castle's history, most of which was wrong. She made her way by memory to stone steps near the south wall. Climbing them, she reached her destination.

The banquet hall, a mere six paces by fifteen, was less impressive in both size and decoration than its name implied. Faded tapestries of faded battles hung against bare stone walls. A long, rough-hewn wooden table flanked by wooden benches sat before an open, high-arched fireplace.

She waited for a tour group to pass through, then cast a repulsion spell on both entrances to the room. Its effect would induce fear in anyone approaching either doorway, making them select another route through the castle. She frowned. *Was* there another route back after passing through this room? She shrugged, smiling at the thought of idiot tourists wandering her ancient home, unable to escape. Sadly, the spell was short-lived.

Assured now of privacy, she approached the tapestry that faced the fireplace. Pushing the fabric aside, she counted from the floor up to the fifth stone. She felt along its surface until she found the opening she expected—a thin vertical slit half a finger long. A casual observer would see only a small crack. But it was much more than that.

A keyhole.

And it was there. Her memories hadn't played her false. But she lacked the key. A key now long lost to time. Lost in the fall of this castle and the murder of her coven. Her sisters. Her mother.

At first, she'd planned to reforge the key magically from memory. She had held it that fateful day. Held it—and used it. But the slightest error in its design would bring this chamber down on her. And her memories of the key were as faded as the tapestries covering these walls.

Memories. If only all her memories of that day would fade...

She slapped those thoughts aside, focusing again on why she was here. Without the key, her only choice was an opening spell. The Weave had contained many within its threads. But the Weave was gone forever, and now all she could do was assemble the few she remembered and try them one by one.

Having sorted through possible spells on the flight over, she called up the strongest. Her flesh tingled as the runes appeared on her skin. Rearranging themselves into the desired script, the golden characters flowed down her left arm where they settled, ready to cast.

She flung her arm out, and the spell flew from her fingers in the shape of a glowing golden hawk, its wings outspread. The bird struck the wall precisely at the secret keyhole.

The stone wall trembled. A rumble sounded through the castle, and dust rained from the ceiling. But when the rumble died, the wall remained before her.

She shook the dust from her hair, then slipped off her cloak, trying to brush it clean with a hand. "*Keck roddan!*" she swore. "My favorite cloak."

"Still as vain as ever, I see," came a woman's voice from behind her.

The red-haired woman screamed and dropped her cloak, spinning around.

Flames now blazed in the stone fireplace. Magical flames, judging by their green edges. In the fire stood an older woman, tall and straight, with long white hair and longer white robes. She shook her head. "With you, child, it was always the clothes."

For the first time in centuries, Morrigan the Bright took a knee before another. Trembling, she lowered her eyes and head.

"Mother," she whispered.

⁂

Morrigan peeked up from where she knelt to face Aalin, High Priestess of the White Coven of Ellan Vannin. "Are you...? I mean, is this...but a spell?"

Aalin raised one snowy eyebrow where she hovered in the flames. "*But a spell?* It is *quite* the spell, to hold my spirit on this plane, in this place. To keep me sane through over three and a half centuries of waiting."

"Your spirit? Then you are...?" Morrigan's words ran away.

"I am dead, Daughter. But you see my true spirit, not a spell." Aalin flipped a hand at her. "Rise, before you soil your precious garments further."

Morrigan rose, hoping she did so with more grace than she felt. She faced her mother, afraid to ask the question. "For what have you been waiting?"

Aalin's face was unreadable. "You pray my answer will be your name, don't you? To tell you I have stayed, abiding all these years with a mother's love, solely for the return of her firstborn, her only daughter."

Morrigan fought but failed to keep a sob from escaping her lips.

Her mother continued. "Because that would say I forgive you for what you did that day. For what you stole from us. For abandoning your sisters." Her mother's black eyes pierced her. "Abandoning me."

Morrigan straightened, old anger fueling her courage. "As you abandoned my brother? Your only son?"

"You know that is not true, child. We searched the passages below. We..." Aalin broke off. Her shoulders drooped, and she seemed suddenly a small creature. Morrigan had never thought of her mother as small before. "We tried," Aalin finished, shaking her head.

"Not hard enough. Not long enough."

"We had no more time. The siege had begun. We had to defend the castle." Her eyes found Morrigan again. "And what lies beneath."

Morrigan's head snapped up. "*Lies beneath?* Still?"

"The passages remain, as does the way through for those who can find it. But as you see..." Aalin nodded at the stone wall behind Morrigan. "...though our defense of the castle failed, we did not fail in our true purpose. We refused to open the way for our enemies to that cursed place."

The implication of her mother's words settled on her like a yoke of iron. "They tortured you," she whispered.

"Time has dulled my memories of that pain. And of the burning." Aalin shrugged. "They would have burned us even if we had opened the way." Aalin fell silent, her eyes on Morrigan.

Morrigan broke down then, centuries of guilt overpowering her faded fury of that long ago day. She bowed her head, hands clasped, fingernails digging into her palms. "Mother, forgive me. If I had stayed, if you had the Weave..." Her words ran down. She raised her head, her cheeks cool with her tears. "You would have lived. My sisters would have lived."

A softness showed in Aalin's face for the first time. And a smile. A smile Morrigan remembered from happier times. "No," Aalin said. "The forces the Chamber of the Red Door commanded were great. We would have fallen in time."

Morrigan blinked away tears. "But I left you."

"My daughter, I forgave you the day you left. I never dared hope I might see you again. The Goddess has blessed me with your return."

Morrigan struggled to understand her mother's words. To understand...and believe. "You forgive me?"

"Long ago. I only wish you could forgive yourself."

Morrigan did not trust herself to speak.

"I love you, child," Aalin said, then sighed. "But I don't know if I can trust you. And that presents a problem."

"What problem?"

"I could have stayed hidden for many more years, but when you arrived here, when I saw you again..." Aalin shrugged. "I chose to appear to you, and so used the last of my strength. I can remain on this plane no longer. My spirit must travel to the Realms of the Dead." Her eyes caught and held Morrigan. "But before I go, I must decide."

Understanding came to Morrigan. She forced back the smile trying to steal across her face. "You still hold the golden key."

"The key to that wall. And what lies behind. That is why you came, is it not, Daughter?"

Morrigan found she could not lie. But then, she never could lie to her mother. Steal from, yes. Abandon. Hate, even, for what had happened to her brother. But never lie. "Yes."

Aalin sighed. "Still you thirst for power. You haven't changed."

Morrigan drew herself up, bristling. "I have changed. More than you know."

"But not in what matters. My question remains: can I trust you with the greatest secret of our coven?"

Morrigan snorted. "Stop pretending. You made that decision when you chose to appear."

"No, child. I did not. I only knew I missed my daughter. That I must talk to her once more before I leave. To say what I have said—that I forgive you and love you. I need not surrender the Tapestry. I can carry its secret to my death."

Morrigan felt herself redden, ashamed. For centuries, she had prayed for the forgiveness her mother had just granted her. But even in this moment, her thoughts ran to gaining magical power. As they had on that fateful day, so many years ago.

"But," Aalin continued, "you are the last of us, and the Tapestry is the sole legacy of our coven. If not you, then who?" With that, she raised both hands. Her fingers performed an intricate dance, tracing figures in the air. Runes appeared, golden and hovering. Swirling, they arranged themselves into scripts. The runes stopped moving, hanging in the air with a sudden solidity as if suspended by invisible strings from her ghostly fingers.

Aalin pushed out with both palms, and the scripts flew from her to shatter against an invisible barrier above the wooden table beside Morrigan. The runes tumbled from the air to land tinkling into a pile on the table. Aalin spoke a word, one both familiar and surprising to Morrigan. As that word hung in the silence of the room, the shattered runes trembled and disappeared from the table.

And in their place—long, slender, and real—lay a golden key.

"Goodbye, child," Aalin said, pulling Morrigan's eyes from the key. Aalin's image was fading, but the old witch's stare still burned into Morrigan.

As did her final words.

"There is good in you, Daughter. You need only look for it." And with that, Aalin, High Priestess of the White Coven of Ellan Vannin, was no more.

There is good in you. You need only look for it.

The boy Fader had said almost identical words to her before he had left. Why did others see in her what she could not?

But what brought tears again to her eyes was the word her mother had spoken to reveal the key. The word her mother had chosen centuries ago to hide the coven's most precious secret.

Moirragh.

Her old name. The name her mother had given her. Wiping away her tears on the back of her hand, she walked to the table and picked up the key. The same key she remembered holding that fateful day in 1651.

It was bronze (not iron—their coven could never abide iron) and stretched on her palm from her wrist to the tip of her middle finger. A triskelion of skeletal legs running widdershins inside a circle—the symbol of their coven—formed its handle. The shaft bore runes and ended in two fanged prongs of unequal length.

With a last look at where her mother had been, she returned to the wall. Finding the crack again, she eased the key into the tiny opening, using both hands when she shook too much to guide it with one. Sensing a slight resistance, she stopped. To push further would bring the stones above crashing down on her, as would the smallest wrong action from this point on.

Gently, so gently, she turned the key.

Turned it widdershins. Counter-clockwise. Never clockwise. Not for the White Coven. A quarter turn, then she stopped. After a breath that seemed to last a lifetime, a musical note sounded from the stone wall before her.

The wall—two tons of stone—disappeared.

Key still in hand, she stood unmoving on the threshold of the hidden room, as stunned by the magicks she just witnessed as she had been years ago. She had touched the stone. The wall had been real. Even after all her years of study, nothing in her vast knowledge could have created a similar spell. In awe and more frightened than she wished to admit, she stepped inside, pocketing the key.

Lit by a single high window, the room was five paces square. And empty—save for one thing. Her fear vanished like the stone had when she saw what hung on the wall to her left.

The Unicorn Tapestry.

She approached it, her excitement growing with each step. It was as she remembered from its rare use in coven ceremonies. And from that black day of memory.

A forest of plants with long, twisted leaves wove through the Tapestry against a background of dark blue. The plants were various shades of green with white edges. Some sprouted flowers—roses the red of dried blood, drooping tulips the yellow of aged teeth, poppies as gray as the ashes of the dead.

And in each corner of the Tapestry, a creature...hid.

Yes, that was the right word. *Hid.* For she had to stare before they emerged, before their presence became clear. In the upper left, a gray bat flew, fanged mouth open. Across from it, in the top right, a brown rat crouched in a burrow, teeth bared. Below the rat, in the lower right, a yellow, winged serpent with a tongue of flame sat coiled, ready to strike. And in the bottom left, a white eel with dead eyes poked its head from a dark stream.

All four creatures had their gazes fixed on the center of the Tapestry, where knelt the animal that gave the artifact its name.

The unicorn was dirty white, bearded, and grizzled, emaciated even. It glared at the viewer with one amber eye. The weaver had posed it so each cloven hoof was visible and prominent. White leaves sprouted from a thin tail that rose twisting above its rump, as if the appendage were more vine than tail. Its gray horn was longer than its legs, making the beast seem unbalanced and grotesque.

Beside the unicorn, a pale-faced, golden-haired maiden sat on a moss-covered stump. She wore a full-length dress of dusky blue that hid her feet. On her head sat a crown of faded daisies. She wore blue gloves, her left hand caressing the unicorn's head, her right resting on the tip of its horn.

Unlike the Weave, the Tapestry was woven silk, not wool. Also unlike the Weave, the rune scripts in the Tapestry were there to see, if one knew what to look for.

And ask for.

The Weave had been a mere repository for spells, their scripts stitched into each strand of wool by her sisters in the coven. As a child, she herself had added some simple spells to the carpet, under her mother's stern direction.

But the Tapestry did more than store spells. It was a spell itself, one that could create new magicks from the scripts it contained, similar to how she used her tattooed runes to create her own magicks. But much, much more powerful.

The Weave was lost, but the Tapestry was hers. And she couldn't wait to use it.

"And such lovely shades of green and blue," she murmured, a finger on her chin, considering the Tapestry's dimensions. "What a wonderful cloak you would make." Reaching out, she fingered a corner of the silk.

Energy shot up her arm like electricity. She snapped back her hand. With trembling fingers, she touched the silk again, this time letting the energy flow into her, balancing it with her own until the tingling in her arm died. Such power, such magicks. Oh, yes, she wanted this.

The Tapestry didn't hang from a rod. Peering behind it, she could see nothing affixing it to the wall, yet a hand's breadth of space separated it from the stone.

"Now, how am I to get you down?" she wondered aloud.

Not a breath of air stirred in the small room, but the Tapestry rippled as if a breeze passed over it—and detached itself from the wall. Floating to her, it settled over her shoulders, two corners fastening themselves below her neck, like the cloak she had imagined.

She swallowed, afraid of the Tapestry even as she stroked its silk now covering her. That fear suddenly gave way to another. She still faced the wall where the Tapestry had hung, but now sensed something behind her. Something that hadn't been visible when she'd entered this room.

Even as she turned, she knew what she would see. What had been there all those years ago, when she had last stood in this place.

An arched doorway framing stairs leading down into darkness.

She stepped back from the opening before realizing she'd done so. The passageway had been there all along, of course. But the Tapestry had hidden it as it was meant to—from her eyes and from her memories, too. Memories she wished had stayed hidden.

Something else had changed. The room now echoed with musical notes, notes that formed themselves into a song. A song she had never heard and yet as familiar as any her mother had sung to her as a child.

A song rising from the darkness into which the steps descended, as if calling her to follow. A song, she knew with sick certainty, her brother had heard that day.

She wanted to run from that room, from that castle, from those memories. She had what she'd come for, all this ancient pile of stones held for her. *I should go now, leave this place forever. I should go. I should...*

She walked to the stairs, the song softly tugging at her mind.

Chapter 2

Poster of a Girl

In the Dream Rider Tower, Case snuggled against Will where they lay under the covers of his bed, happy and contented.

Will rolled over to face her. "That was amazing, but—"

"*But?* So not the word to tack onto that sentence. Not if you want the amazing again. Ever." She knew where he was going with this and didn't want to go there.

"—but we still have to talk about it," he continued, ignoring her attempt to deflect.

"It?"

"What we were talking about before you changed the subject to heavy breathing."

"Are you saying I used that as a distraction?"

"We were talking about telling Adi what we learned about your mom's disappearance."

"*You* were. Not me."

"Right. You were trying to distract me—"

"*Trying* to? I claim success. Hot and sweaty success."

"—with all the kissing and touching."

"And nibbling. I definitely remember nibbling."

He grinned. "Me, too." Pulling her to him, he kissed her forehead, her nose, and then lingered on her mouth. She kissed him back hard. Breaking it off, he leaned back from her. "But we can't put it off any longer. It's been two days. We have to tell Adi what we discovered."

Sighing, she got up and grabbed her t-shirt and panties from where they lay on the rug. Slipping them on, she sat back on the bed beside where Will lay under the comforter.

In the distance, south of downtown, the early morning sun sparkled on Lake Ontario. Will's tower was the highest in the city core, so no other buildings blocked the penthouse view of the water. She still wasn't used to looking down on the city streets where she'd lived for so long. Just as she couldn't get used to—or comfortable with—Will's wealth.

A problem for another day. She could only handle one difficult discussion at a time. "What if it's a coincidence?"

He propped himself up on an elbow. "Your mom disappeared when my parents left for Peru. And my Dream Rider abilities developed the same time you and Fader got your own powers. That can't all be coincidence."

Their powers. Her Voice that warned her of immediate danger. Fader's ability to fade from notice or disappear into the strange place he called the In Between. "We got them *about* the same time. And your powers came from whatever happened to you in Peru. Fader and I weren't in Peru."

"But your mom sent you and your brother your powers. Somehow."

"I *think* she did. And that's a big *somehow*."

"You heard her voice, right? You believe it was your mom, don't you?"

She picked at a loose thread on the comforter, remembering that night. Eight years old, lying in bed in their grandparents' house, Fader snoring in the other bed. Waking from a dream of their mother. Then, her mother's voice in her head, telling her to be brave, to take care of her brother. Saying she'd always be there for Case.

Except she wasn't. Case pushed away those memories. "Yeah, it was Mom. So?"

"I think she was in Peru, too. With my parents."

"Why would your parents need an astrophysicist on a jungle expedition? Mom studied black holes. Your parents sure weren't looking for one of those in Peru."

"I've no idea *what* they were looking for. No one does. Until we do, we can't know why they needed her."

"*If* they needed her."

"Then there's the Chakana."

She fought the shiver of fear the strange artifact known as the Crystal Key now prompted in her. "What about it?"

"It came from Peru. And it amped up all our powers after it broke out of its box. Our powers must be connected, too—to each other, to the Chakana, to Peru. Our powers, our parents' disappearances, Peru. It can't all be coincidence."

She didn't answer. Because she didn't like the answer that came. Will was right. It couldn't all be coincidence—and *that* was bothering her.

He sat up beside her and slipped an arm around her waist. "We have to tell Adi."

She leaned against him. "Oh, right. Because she needs another reason to hate me. Now I can be the girl whose mother lured your parents and you to their doom." She stopped as he stiffened. "Sorry, I didn't mean that."

"It's okay. I still believe my parents are alive. Your mom, too."

"Me, too," she whispered, wishing she believed that more than she did.

"Anyway, Adi won't think that about you—"

She snorted. "Yeah. Right."

"—but we have to tell her. She's checking the location of the Flower."

She knew he meant the strange flower that had arrived so mysteriously from Peru two days ago. The one whose scent was his only memory from the expedition that had given him both his agoraphobia and his Dream powers. And cost him his parents.

"If it looks promising," he continued, "you know, a place my parents had an interest in, then it's another reason for us to go to Peru."

"That's another thing. Who sent you that flower? And why now? And why all the mystery? Why not identify themselves?"

"I don't know. But I've been searching for that flower and where it came from for eight years. And now I have the answer. I'm not going to worry about who gave me that answer or why."

But maybe you should, she thought.

"I figured you'd be thrilled about all this," he said. "We finally have a lead on what happened to your mom, plus a place to start looking for her."

He was right. Peru now held the answers to not only his parents' disappearance, but her mother's, too. She should be happy. Except she wasn't.

"This isn't just about who sent the Flower or not wanting to tell Adi, is it?" he said.

She shook her head, still not knowing how to explain what was bothering her. "No."

He squeezed her hand where it lay on the comforter. "What's wrong?"

Sighing, she shifted around to face him. She had to try. "It's about...us."

His face fell. "Us? You mean, my money?"

"No. Well, yes, but that's not what's bothering me about *this*." She took a big breath and let it out. "If all these things aren't a coincidence, if they *are* connected, then is *that* why I'm here?"

"I don't follow."

"That night when Morrigan snatched Fader, when I ran to your tower, when we met. My Voice told me to run."

"Which was a good thing. It saved you."

"Will, it told me to run to *your* building. It helped me sneak inside. It *led* me here. It led me to *you*."

His eyes widened. "Oh."

"*That* is what's bothering me. Am I getting moved around in some game I don't understand? Are you and I...I mean, are we just...? Was all this *arranged* by some higher power? Were *we* arranged?"

They sat silent again until Will shrugged, grinning that grin she loved. "I don't know if something's pulling our strings, but if that something sent you to me, well, good for it. You're the best thing that ever happened to me." He leaned over and kissed her. "I love you."

She had to swallow before she could talk. "I love you, too." She buried her face in his neck as they held each other.

After a few moments, he said, "You're nibbling again."

"Want me to stop?"

For an answer, he slipped his hand under her shirt. She slid back under the covers with him.

"Okay, but after," he said between kisses, "we go talk to Adi."

"Shut up."

He shut up.

After they'd showered and dressed, Case followed Will down the open stairs from his bedroom to his studio. In the kitchen alcove, she poured cereal into two bowls and cut some strawberries on top while Will made coffee.

As they sat eating, Will called out. "Hallie."

"Yes, Mr. Dreycott," Hallie replied from an overhead speaker, her voice pleasant and professional, and yet not human in a way Case could never quite place.

"Please see if Adi can meet with Case, Fader, and me this morning."

"I will check, Mr. Dreycott. May I ask the nature of the meeting?"

Will glanced at Case. She shook her head. "Just say we need to see her," Will said.

"Yes, sir," Hallie replied.

They went back to their breakfasts. About a minute later, Hallie returned. "Ms. Archambeault can see you at ten in her office. I've added it to your calendars."

"Thanks, Hallie."

"You're welcome, Mr. Dreycott." Hallie's voice cut out, but Case knew she was still there, listening, waiting to be called. Will said Hallie's programming only allowed her to record exchanges in which the artificial personality was involved. Which was good, considering some of the 'exchanges' Hallie might overhear on this floor, like the ones in Will's bedroom this morning. One more thing about living here that made Case uncomfortable.

Will sipped his coffee. "And when we meet with Adi, we'll ask what she's learned about that Peru location that came with the Flower."

She hesitated, uncertain whether to ask the question that always hung over any talk of Peru. "Will, even if the location looks promising, even if Adi agrees, I mean, how would you...?" Her words trailed off.

He gave her a rueful grin. "How will I go to Peru when I still can't go outside? Oh, wait. I *can* go outside—if I wear the Chakana. But if I do that, a Sword Lady shows up—emphasis on sword—and tries to take it from me, possibly along with some body parts. So yeah, small problem." He sighed. "Eight years, I've searched for my mystery Flower. Now, I finally find it *and* where it comes from in Peru, but I can't go there because I'm trapped here."

She didn't reply. What could she say?

"Not that Adi will let me near the Chakana again," he continued, "now that we've handed it back to her."

"I'm glad she locked it up again," she said, remembering the strange effects the artifact had triggered in her, Fader, and Will.

"Anything from your Voice since then?"

"*Voices*. Plural. Not a peep. Everything's been quiet. No videos in my head, either."

"Fader?"

"No uncontrolled vanishing. He can still fade from other people, but I always notice him."

"Can he fade into the In Between?"

"He says he can. He said the wall with all the doors to other universes was there, but the other wall didn't show the Black Island, anymore. It was just blank. Like when we came back from the Crystal Island in Dream."

"You mean he's lost his Zoomer power?"

That was what Fader called his ability to physically move, while in the In Between, to anything visible on the larger wall of that strange place. "I guess. What about you?"

"No forced astral journeys. I've tried astral projecting while I'm awake, but haven't managed it, yet." He shrugged. "I guess I need the Chakana for that."

"I still don't trust that thing." Or the hold it seemed to have on Will. But she didn't say that.

He sat back, holding his coffee, his cereal half-finished. "I'm a little afraid of it, too. I can't forget that dark stain inside it, that emptiness that felt like the Nothing."

"No shame in being afraid of something that powerful. It changed us. You, me, Fader."

"Yeah, but..."

"But?"

"I don't think we'll find out what happened in Peru—or to our parents—*without* the Chakana. It's called the Key for a reason."

"But the key to what?" she asked.

"To the Crossing."

"Which is?"

"Yeah. The questions just keep on coming. Well, we won't find answers until we go to Peru—and *with* the Chakana."

"Except we can't. So, back to where we started."

He hesitated. "Well..."

"What?"

"I can't go."

"Uh, yeah. Just settled that."

"Doesn't mean *you* can't."

"*What?*"

"You and Fader."

"Are you nuts?"

"You're both part of this now, as we also just settled. You have as much reason as me to go to Peru. Don't you want to find your mom?"

She hesitated. "Fader does."

"You don't?"

She sighed, her hopes and fears about her mom jumbling together, as they always did. "Yeah, I do. If only to ask her why she left us."

"Then you *do* think she's alive?"

"Don't ask me that. Fader does. I don't know what I think. I'm afraid, I guess, to start hoping after all this time."

"Only one way to find out."

"I'm not going to Peru without you. Besides, Adi would never agree. I mean, can you imagine me traveling with her?"

He frowned, staring into the distance, then grinned. "I can. It's very entertaining."

"Jerk."

"Won't know unless you ask her."

"The only reason she'd take me to Peru is for all the places she could hide a body in the jungle. Especially after she learns about my mom."

He laughed, then his face became serious. "I mean it, girlfriend. I'll never know what happened to me and my parents unless someone goes to Peru. I can't go, so..." He shrugged.

"I'm not going without you. Period." She stood. "I have to check on Crash Space. The construction's almost done. Wanna come with?"

"You're changing the subject. And I like the way you did it this morning much better."

She smiled. "Me, too. You coming?"

"Thanks, but I'm going to the Jungle."

That meant he was visiting the strange new flower in his rooftop greenhouse again. "Any more memories from it?"

Will hesitated. "No."

"Check on Flopsy and Mopsy when you're up there, okay?" Those were the female bunnies Will had given her for her birthday a few days ago. "I've been so busy with Crash Space, I haven't visited them lately."

"They're hard to find, with the run of the entire park. But I'll look. And don't forget...Adi's office at ten o'clock. If you're late, she might start not liking you."

"*So* funny."

Leaving the kitchen, she entered Will's studio. Fader sat in the tall chair at Will's computerized graphics design desk, drawing on its slanted touch-screen surface. As she came closer, she recognized a scene with Morrigan in the abandoned hospital where they'd been held prisoner.

She fought a shiver. Fader's recreation of the witch brought back those memories far too clearly. "Morning, bro. Didn't see you come in. You have breakfast?"

He kept sketching. "Chocolate chip muffin at the coffee shop."

"For breakfast?"

He shrugged, focused on his drawing. "You used to get me them all the time before."

Before. When they were on the street. Fader felt none of the conflict she did in living off Will's money. But then, her brother had an actual job, working on the Dream Rider comic. "You're late today. Will's going to dock your pay."

He kept sketching. "I was here earlier, but you and Will were...being noisy. So I left."

She felt herself flushing. "Oh. Um, didn't know you were here."

He shrugged. "It's okay. I mean, I get it. And I'm glad you and Will are...you know, together. But you're still my sister."

She gave him a hug. "And proud of it. Oh, we're meeting Adi later."

"Yeah, it just popped up." He pointed to the top corner of the design screen where 'Fader—Today' displayed a list of times. At ten o'clock, it showed 'Mtg w Adi, her office,' then the rest of his day filled in to five o'clock with 'Finish sketches, Will's studio.' When did her twelve-year-old brother become an office worker? But he loved drawing, and helping create his favorite comic was a dream come true for him. Plus, he was getting paid.

"We're going to tell Adi about Mom, aren't we?" he asked, pulling her attention back.

"Yeah," she said, not mentioning Will's idea about them going to Peru without him.

He began drawing again. "Good. She'll know what to do. She'll help us find Mom."

"Yeah. Sure, she will." Leaving him, she headed to the elevators along the window-lined skateboard and running track that circled Will's private floor, thoughts and fears tumbling in her head.

The strange and dangerous Chakana. The disappearances of their mother and Will's parents somehow connected. Mysterious flowers sent by unknown people. The feeling of being a piece being moved in a game. Reaching the elevators, she pressed the button, wondering whether she was the only one who saw trouble coming.

Chapter 3

I'll Follow You

"**E**xcellent work, dude."

At the design desk, Fader jumped at the sound of Will's voice. Engrossed in his drawing, he hadn't noticed Will coming up behind him.

Will grinned at him. "Surprise you?"

"Didn't see you there."

"Maybe I'm picking up your powers—fading without wanting to."

"Not funny."

"No, it wasn't. Sorry." Will swiped on the table, paging through Fader's sketches. "Seriously awesome. How far are you?"

Fader sighed. "Only twelve panels. I'm slow."

"Dude, you're new to this. Don't worry. The issue will go out when it goes out. Just have fun." He stopped on a panel showing Morrigan with Stayne and Stryke in the background. "Okay. Couple of suggestions on this one..."

He listened as Will showed how to improve several panels, amazed as always at how easily it came to him.

Will grinned. "I've been doing this for half my life. You're on your second week. And, I say again, making with the awesome."

"Thanks," he said, embarrassed but enjoying the praise.

Will straightened from the table. "See you at Adi's?"

Fader nodded, hunching over the design screen again. He was already working on the first of Will's suggestions as Will's footsteps faded on the running track.

He'd finished revising three panels when he first noticed it. A flicker on the screen, to the left, at the edge of his vision. His eyes flitted there.

That part of the screen showed a photo of a deep valley splitting steep mountains. A scene from Peru Will used as a screen saver when he didn't need that half of the design table. Fader stared at the photo, but nothing moved.

He shrugged to himself. The screen saver had probably switched to a new image. Although... He frowned at the picture. He was sure it had been there when he'd started. He returned to working on the current panel.

Flicker. The sense of movement from the left of the screen came again.

He looked over. And froze. The photo of the mountain valley had disappeared. Against a black background, a huge snake now sat coiled, its mouth open, exposing fangs and a red forked tongue. The snake stared right at him, its eyes sparkling like diamonds. Something about its green-scaled skin felt familiar.

He kept watching, but the image didn't move. *Okay. Nothing to freak over. The screen saver just changed.*

Giving the snake another furtive glance, he finished his changes and swiped to get to the next panel. He worked for several minutes, focused on his drawing and trying to ignore the snake.

Flicker.

His head snapped to the snake. It had moved from its original position. And it was still moving. The snake now swayed back and forth, tongue flicking in and out, eyes still fixed on him.

Okay, okay, okay. Will probably did that, drew Marell in his snake form. This issue would have Marell, for sure. Maybe Will wanted some animation in the electronic edition. Maybe a GIF on the cover.

He let out the breath he realized he'd been holding. *Yeah. Sure. That's it. Just Will—*

The snake disappeared. So did his panels. The entire screen blanked.

Crap! What had he done? Had he lost all his work? Had he broken Will's design table? What would Will—?

A green dot appeared on the screen, centered in front of him. It grew to the size of a thumbprint. Frowning, he leaned closer, trying to make it out.

The snake leaped from the screen straight for him, mouth wide, fangs bared.

Screaming, he threw himself backward. The tall chair tottered and fell. He landed hard on his side, but the studio's thick carpet absorbed most of the impact. He lay there, trembling, heart pounding, his eyes locked on the edge of the design table above him, waiting.

Waiting for what?

He swallowed. For the snake. For it to come slithering out of the screen, over the desk, and down to the floor. For it to come for him.

Seconds ticked by. No snake. He rose on shaking legs, keeping two steps back from the table. From there, he could still see the screen. It now showed the last panel he'd been working on, and to its left, the mountain valley.

But no snake.

Reaching out a trembling hand, he tapped the icon to power down the table, ready to snatch his hand back if the snake reappeared. Then he left the studio, heading along the running track. By the time he was halfway to the elevators, his fear had changed to anger.

Will had played a trick on him. That must be it. Will had programmed that snake to appear on the screen. Fine. Two could play that game. He would fade and sneak up on Will and then—

Flicker.

He stopped. A flash of movement had come from his right, from the floor-to-ceiling windows lining the track. *Okay, don't freak.* Probably just a bird. Or a glint of light off a nearby tower.

He turned back. Then screamed.

He ran. Ran for the elevators. Ran from the reflection he'd seen in the window. A reflection of himself...and of a huge snake coiled and reared behind him.

In the elevator, the first thing Case noticed was the floor button she pressed for Crash Space. Until today, it had been a handwritten label, taped in place. Now, the name showed in machine-printed lettering behind the clear button cover, just like all the other floors.

Despite her ambivalence toward Will's wealth, including the money for Crash Space, she felt a glimmer of pride. She was doing good here. The hostel would provide street kids a safe place to stay. And more. Full medical care, counseling, a lawyer if needed. Kids could sign up to finish high school, enroll in training for different trades, or even go after a college or university degree with paid tuition.

She stepped from the elevator into the hostel's central common room, a shared lounge providing secure access to the segregated dorm areas. Doors on the left and right led to the male and female rooms, respectively. Facing the elevators, a third door led to a smaller gender-neutral dorm—an addition to the original design, but one Adi had quickly authorized after Case found the courage to request it.

Many street kids were trans or non-binary and didn't identify as their birth gender. Many were on the street *because* of that, escaping parents who didn't accept them as they saw themselves.

Kids could pick the male or female sides based on how they self-identified. The gender-neutral dorm provided an option for anyone who felt more comfortable in that setting.

Once someone was approved for Crash Space, their handprint let them access the elevator, this shared area, and their part of the floor and private bedroom.

'Approved' meant Case and her street team agreed you weren't dangerous or a trouble-maker. Well, not *too* much of a trouble-maker. *Let's face it—we're all trouble-makers.*

Her street team consisted of the H-Boys she trusted the most. H-Boys. Hollow Boys. The name the survivors of the body-swapper Marell and the witch Morrigan had given themselves.

One of those boys sat slouched in a bean-bag chair, his brow creased, eyes squinting as he read. Link didn't look up as she approached. Reaching down, she lifted the book he held to read its cover.

His head snapped up. "Hey! What the—?" His look of wide-eyed surprise became a sheepish smile. "Oh. Hi. Thought I was alone up here."

She plopped into another chair. "Richard the Third? Not my choice for light reading."

He groaned. "Me, neither. But I need Grade 12 English and Math." He kicked at another book at his feet. "My other choice was Calculus."

"Getting your diploma?"

He looked embarrassed. "Maybe."

"Good for you, dude. Then what?"

He shrugged. "One step at a time. Though from this..." He waved the Shakespeare. "...it's more a giant leap than a step."

"You'll get there. This place has tutors, you know."

"Got one. She gave me the books. And homework. And a headache."

"*She*? Cute?"

"Old, gray, wrinkled."

"Cute?"

He laughed, then his face went serious. "Thanks, Case."

"Dude, we've done this dance. You and I are good. Again."

"Still...thanks."

"Just don't try to tie me up, anymore. Only Will gets to do that."

"I'll remember that, late tonight."

"Perv. What's it like staying here?"

"At first, way too quiet. Couldn't sleep. But since Rattle moved in down the hall, I'm good. He gets nightmares. Screams a lot in his sleep."

She nodded, remembering. Being on the streets. The sounds of the city at night. Being lulled to sleep by those sounds even as she searched them for danger. "Everything working?"

"Pretty much. If something isn't, I leave a note for Chuck, that foreman guy. He gets on it right away."

She checked out the common room. A kitchen with a stove, microwave, and a stocked fridge and freezer sat in one corner, surrounding a big dining table. Scattered chairs and couches filled the rest of the space, most facing a wall with a big screen TV that also provided internet access. Empty bookcases flanked the screen.

Gotta get some books in, she thought. Turning back to Link, she hesitated over her question. But she needed to know. "Ask you something?"

His eyes narrowed. "Sure."

"You try finding it, again?"

Something flickered across his face before disappearing. "The subway stop? To that...place? Yeah," he said, not meeting her eyes.

"And?"

"Nothing. I guess you need to hear that Song to find it." He grinned, Link once again. "And I don't hear it anymore." He eyed her. "You?"

"Fader and I went back the next day. Rode the line north and south past where it'd been. He didn't get any tingles. Nothing."

"Good," he said quietly. "What're you here for?"

Changing the subject. He's scared. Well, she couldn't blame him. The Black Island. The Black Tower. The Chambelán. The scarabs. It had all been something out of a nightmare.

"Checking out how the girls' side is coming along. Which I better do before I'm late for my meeting." Standing, she walked to the door leading to the female side of the floor and scanned her handprint. The light on the scanner glowed green.

"Me doing homework. Hard Case doing meetings," Link called. "End of the world's coming."

"We stopped that, remember?"

"Twice."

She pushed open the door, but a flicker of movement at the corner of her eye made her turn back.

"What?" Link asked.

"I thought..." The movement had come from the direction of the big screen TV. She pointed at it. "Is that on?"

Link shook his head. "I have enough trouble focusing on this shit." He waved his book. "What's the matter?"

She frowned. She'd been sure... "Nothing. See you." Pushing the door open, she stepped through.

Twenty minutes later, she'd almost finished her tour of the girls' side, pleased with what she'd found. Everything was finished except for carpeting, some light fixtures, and the furniture in the bedrooms.

As she reached the last corridor, which faced the floor-to-ceiling windows of the south wall, her phone chimed a reminder of their meeting with Adi. She quickened her pace, heading back toward the common room.

Behind her, soft footsteps on the bare floor made her jump. The floor had been empty, so who...?

She turned, her heart suddenly racing.

The only thing behind her was empty hallway.

She swallowed. *Had* it been footsteps? The sound of hammering somewhere on the floor reached her. Outside, on the streets below, a car horn blared.

That's all it was. An echo of some other sound. Turning, she started back along the window-lined hall. And again heard soft footfalls behind her.

She spun around, dropping into a crouch, pulling her flick knife from her back pocket in one smooth motion.

Nothing. No one. Again.

Wait. *There.* A flash of movement from the windows. A bird flying by? She turned her head slowly to the glass. The movement came again. And she saw what it was.

A reflection. Of something behind her in the corridor.

Screaming, she spun again, stumbling backward, waving her knife wildly in front of her. But again, nothing was there.

Surrendering to panic, wanting suddenly to be anywhere but there, she ran. Ran for the common room and elevator. And as she ran, she tried telling herself she didn't hear thick paws on the floor behind her, getting closer with every stride.

Thick paws with long claws.

For she knew what she'd seen reflected in the window. The thing she still sensed behind her.

A huge tawny cat. Like a mountain lion. A mountain lion with eyes of flames.

Chapter 4

Flashes

Will walked winding paths through his rooftop park toward the greenhouse he'd long ago dubbed the Jungle. The roof's clear dome was open overhead, the morning sun already hot. But the late June air was fresh, with no humidity and none of the exhaust fumes of the streets below.

The roof had always been both his most and least favorite place. He loved the park with its gardens and meadows, flowers and trees, birds and squirrels...and now Case's bunnies, which were nowhere in sight. Here, he could actually be outside. Pretend he was normal.

But the roof also held the Jungle, home to an unbroken parade of disappointments. For eight years, his search teams in South America had sent flower after flower to this greenhouse. And every one the *wrong* flower.

A flower. Not *the* Flower.

Then, three days ago, it arrived. The Flower. The one with the right scent—the smell that was his only memory from the doomed Peru expedition. Complete with a mysterious, unsigned note showing the latitude and longitude of where the Flower originated. Mysterious, because his search team hadn't sent the plant or the note—and had no idea who had.

Every day since, he'd made this visit. To try to remember.

Reaching the greenhouse, he walked to the isolation room at the back and passed through the cleansing airlock into the room which held the bloom. He blinked as his eyes adjusted to the newly installed black lights. The Flower only opened in darkness. The lights simulated nighttime but allowed him to see.

Before him, in an orange clay pot on a small table, the orchid waited, its strange bloom open—black petals streaked with threads of glowing white and speckled with red. The colors of his Dream Rider costume.

Those colors were just the latest in a series of bizarre connections. The Chakana, the powerful artifact at the heart of the Peru mystery, was the same jewel he'd included in the Rider's costume and matched the scar on his chest he'd returned with from Peru. The black of the Flower's petals hinted of the pool in the tower of the Chambelán. The giant scarabs that protected that tower bore an eerie resemblance to creatures the Rider had battled in the comic books he'd written.

And the words that had come with the Flower's location: *He only comes out at night.* The motto he'd chosen for the Dream Rider.

Hint after hint after hint. But still no answers to the only questions he cared about. What had happened eight years ago in Peru? To his parents? To him? Could he find them? Could he...?

He swallowed. Could he *fix* himself?

He still believed the Flower held those answers, so every day he came here, hoping the plant would trigger more memories.

And it had.

He remembered nothing from the first time he'd smelled the bloom beyond that long-sought scent. But every visit since—this was his fourth—had brought a different memory, each vivid yet incomplete, hinting at hidden things. And each tied to a different sense.

Smell, first. The flowery scent, of course. But then...

His second visit had brought a sound memory. A thundering, rumbling, rushing roar, like a great waterfall or river.

On his third visit, the memory had been a vision. A *quipu*, the knotted strings used by the ancient Incas for sending messages.

And today?

"Well, Flower," he muttered, "you still have taste and touch to work with." Leaning over the bloom, he bent close. And breathed in.

Smell. The Flower, yes, but also the scent of wet earth and damp chill air.

Sight. The quipu again, but this time suspended in the air against a rock wall with carvings that disappeared before the image resolved.

More sounds. A slithering. A deep growl. The beat of wings. And again, dimmer as if more distant this time, that rumbling roar of rushing water.

And then...

It began as a pressure on his chest. The feeling of a great weight pushing down on him. In on him. Surrounding him, squeezing him from all sides. Building, building, building. Trying to crush him, to compress him into a tiny ball.

A ball that suddenly hung before him. A black ball, black as in the absence of light, hanging in the void that was the Nothing. A black ball impossibly small yet impossibly massive, as if an infinitely tiny speck held all matter in the universe.

And it was pulling him toward it, pulling him into a point that held everything in a space of nothing. Faster and faster, he flew toward the point, the pressure on him growing. As it would grow, he knew somehow, until it crushed him into itself, into the point that held all mass and no dimensions.

As his conscious mind slipped away, terror flooded him—terror he'd become part of that blackness.

He awoke. Or rather, he opened his eyes. He wasn't awake. He was in Dream.

He lay on the Bed of Awakening in the House of Four Doors, wearing his Rider costume. Okay. Fine. All normal.

Except for how he'd arrived here. He remembered. The black speck, so small yet so massive. The intense pressure, the feeling of being crushed into that speck. Passing out.

"So," he muttered, "I'm probably lying on the floor beside the Flower."

"Yes, you are," came Nyx's voice from beside him.

He turned his head to where Nyx stood, then leaped from the Bed, staring at her, struggling to understand what he saw.

"But don't worry," Nyx continued. "I've checked all your vitals—well, *our* vitals, and we seem fine. Heartbeat, breathing, haven't peed ourselves. All normal. Except, you know, unconscious."

"All *normal?* Look at you! Where did all that come from?"

"All what?"

For eight years, Nyx had always appeared as a head floating in a gray mist. She still had that head, still with blue skin, violet eyes, and long, purple hair. But now...

"You have a body!"

Nyx looked down at herself, at the body of a young woman in a lime-green t-shirt and dark green jeans. "Oh. Well, *that's* weird."

"Weird? How can you suddenly have a body after eight years of being floaty-cloudy-head-person?"

She ran her hands over her figure. "I don't know, but it's a very nice body."

"Please stop fondling yourself."

"It's like Case's, don't you think? She'd be glad to know your subconscious came up with her. You're very faithful."

"Nyx, what's going on?"

She frowned. "I'm...I'm not sure. I think the Flower is stirring up memories. In your subconscious. So, in me."

"I'm remembering things?"

"I think so."

"I'm remembering you having a body?"

"Hmm. That makes no sense. Let's put the body thing aside for now. I have something to tell you...well, *show* you."

The House, which changed with his every visit to Dream, was now a square greenhouse filled to overflowing with potted plants. A door sat in each vine-covered wall, almost hidden by foliage. Above each door hung a hand-painted sign of a compass direction.

"That one," Nyx said, walking to the door marked 'South.'

"Why?"

"Because that's the direction of Peru from here."

His chest tightened. "We're going to Peru?"

"Let's just say it will come up in the conversation." She pushed the door open, and he followed her through.

❦

Will stood beside Nyx in a gray-walled, high-ceilinged room, maybe eight paces by ten. The room had no windows, and he could see no door.

A wire-mesh cage filled much of the room, leaving just enough space to walk around its perimeter. The enclosure rose to the ceiling and had a roof of the same thinly spaced mesh. Inside, mismatched wooden tables lined the walls of the cage. An array of instruments with dials and gauges lay scattered over most of the tables. Plywood planks covered the cage's floor, but through gaps, he saw more mesh.

"That's copper wire," he said. "It's a Faraday cage. Whoever this belongs to, they don't want outside signals or electromagnetic radiation interfering with whatever's inside the cage."

"Or," Nyx said, nodding to a smaller table standing separate in the cage's center, "they don't want what's inside *that* to be sending *out* any signals."

The table held a single object—a cube of dull gray metal measuring a handbreadth on each side.

"That box. Is it lead?" he asked.

"Yes. And yes, the Chakana is inside."

He nodded, thinking he understood. "So, Adi's hidden the Key here? The Faraday cage is another layer of protection from the Sword Ladies. But I know this whole building, and I don't recognize this place. Where are we?"

A sound made him turn. To his left, an opening in the wall appeared as a section slid aside. A door.

"The question you should be asking," Nyx said, "is *when* are we."

A figure appeared in the doorway. A figure from the past, grown hazy in Will's mind over eight years. Memories clutched at his heart, memories of this half-forgotten, half-remembered face. "Dad?"

Jon Dreycott didn't turn, didn't reply, didn't seem to hear him. His father called back through the open door. "Well, come on, sport. You can't see anything from out there."

Another figure appeared, smaller but also familiar in an old photograph kind of way. A much younger Will Dreycott stepped into the room to stand beside his father.

Watching the scene, Will's confusion gave way to a sudden surge of hope. He spun to Nyx. "My dad is dreaming! This is his dream. That means he's alive. I can trace his silver cord back to where—"

His excitement died as Nyx shook her head. "This isn't a dream. It's a memory. Your memory."

"What? But I don't remember this. How can I have a memory I can't remember?"

"It's been buried in your subconscious. In me. And it has..." She frowned. "Surfaced? Bubbled up? I don't know, but this just came back to me. I remembered it, so now I'm helping *you* remember."

Jon Dreycott led young Will into the wire-covered enclosure, then closed the cage door behind them.

Older Will swallowed. "Then my dad...?"

"He may still be alive, but this..." Nyx waved at the scene. "This comes from *you*, not your dad."

Inside the cage, his father pointed out instruments to young Will. "Geiger counter, infrared display, wide-band radio receiver." Jon swept his hand over an entire table. "And these are all electromagnetic field meters."

Young Will gazed up at his dad with such obvious adoration it made Will's throat catch. "What are they all for? And why a Faraday cage?"

His father grinned. "You recognized the cage, eh?"

Young Will nodded. "One of my manga comics had one."

Jon chuckled, walking to the central table. "Who said comics aren't educational?" He tapped the lead box. "Well, the instruments are to detect if what's inside *this* is sending out any type of signal." He hesitated, frowning. "If it's...communicating somehow. And the cage and this lead-lined room are to ensure it doesn't."

"Who do you think it's communicating with?" Young Will asked.

His father hesitated again. "With some people who always know when it's exposed. People who want to steal it from us."

Young Will stared at the lead box. "What is it?"

Jon Dreycott stroked the box, an oddly intimate gesture. "It is the Key."

"To what?"

"To something your mother and I have chased for many years," his father replied, still stroking the box. He seemed to catch himself. Dropping his hand, he smiled at young Will. "Want to see what Mom and I are so excited about?"

The boy swallowed. "Is it safe?"

"Wouldn't show it to you otherwise, sport. We've analyzed it every way we know how. We've detected zero radiation, nor any radio or EMF signals. And your mom, me, Adi—we've all been this close to it, and we're fine." He grinned at his son. "Want to see it?"

Young Will grinned back. "Yeah, sure." He stepped up to the table.

Will looked at Nyx. "This must be just after my parents returned from Peru. After getting the Chakana from that Alvarez guy. Eight years ago. After their first Peru trip, but before the second one. Before they took me there. Before..." His words trailed off as he stared at his younger self beaming up at his dad, full of expectation and wonder.

Before I was broken.

"Yes," Nyx said. "They'd been home about two weeks. Now, pay attention. This next bit is why we're here. What you need to see."

Jon Dreycott winked at his son and then, with a theatrical flourish, hovered his hand over the lead box. "Drum roll, please."

Laughing, Young Will beat a rhythm with his hands on the edge of the table.

"And now," his father said, his voice booming like a carnival barker, "behold the Crystal Key. Behold...the *Chakana*!" He flipped open the lead box.

Young Will leaned closer, peering at the artifact inside. He frowned. "But that's just an Inca Cross. What's so special...?"

He never finished the sentence. The boy's eyes flew wide, locked on the Chakana. He gasped out an incoherent cry. His head snapped back. His body stiffened—then nine-year-old Will Dreycott collapsed to the floor.

Crying out, his father slammed the box closed again. As he rushed toward where young Will lay, the scene faded, lost in gray mist.

Will whirled to face Nyx. "What was that? Why did I collapse?"

"That was the moment, Will," she said, her voice soft, almost tender. "That was when it happened. When the Chakana broke you."

Will opened his eyes. He lay on the floor of the isolation room in the Jungle greenhouse, his phone alarm blaring from his pocket.

"No, no, no!" he shouted, sitting up. He was awake. He didn't want to be awake. He wanted to be back in Dream, back where he could press Nyx for answers. Answers to explain what he'd just seen.

That was when it happened. That was when the Chakana broke you.

"That's wrong," he said aloud. "It happened in Peru, not here. I went there, and something happened. Happened there. In Peru."

"Apparently not," came a familiar voice. "And could you *please* turn off that alarm? It's incredibly irritating."

Crying out, he leaped to his feet and spun around. Behind him, Nyx hovered a foot off the floor. A glowy, see-through, and still full-bodied Nyx.

"*What?*" He stared at her as his mind tripped and tumbled over itself trying to make sense of the scene. "*What?*"

"I'm Nyx. We've met."

"How can you be here? How can you be outside of Dream? Wait. Are we still in Dream?"

"No, you're awake." Her brow creased. "Or is that, '*we're* awake'?"

"But how are you—? I mean, am I astral projecting? Is that it? Are you *me*, and I'm astral projecting?" He frowned. "But then, how am I still in my body? Nyx, how are you here? How is it possible?"

"I've no idea. I... Oh!" Her eyes went wide, unfocused. "Wait. I think... It's almost... Arghh!" She tapped her forehead. "It's like the answer's right on the tip of my brain. Or your brain. Or something." She shrugged. "Sorry. Don't know how, but here I am. And your alarm is still going."

He pulled out his phone, turning the alarm off. "It's our meeting with Adi."

"Nice of you to include me."

"I mean Case, Fader, and me. *You* are so not going." Leaving the isolation room, he stepped out into the greenhouse and closed the airlock door behind him.

Nyx floated through the wall. "Because you can stop me...how?"

"For freak's sake," he cried, jumping back. He glared at her. "What if they can see you?"

"I'm guessing this..." she said, indicating herself with a sweep of a hand. "...is between you and me. Because...you and me."

Sighing, he strode quickly through the greenhouse. "I still don't understand anything in that scene you just showed me."

"What's to understand? The Chakana broke you. Not Peru."

He fell silent. They walked to the elevators together. Or rather, he walked while Nyx floated beside him. "But how? Why didn't it affect anyone else? Mom? Dad? Adi? Why did it single *me* out? And why can't I remember anything you showed me?"

"I don't know," Nyx said. "And if I don't..."

"Then I don't either." He sighed. "Maybe Adi will have some answers."

Chapter 5

Growin' Up

Case walked along the carpeted, wood-paneled corridor toward Adi's office, checking over her shoulder every few steps, imagining the footfalls of padded feet. *I'm going crazy. There's nothing following—*

A sound behind her.

She spun around only to find Will stepping off the elevator. She let out her breath as she waited for him, her fears seeming foolish now she wasn't alone.

She frowned as he came up to her. His usual smiling face wore a wide-eyed, haunted expression. "You okay?" she asked. "You look like you've seen a ghost."

"I have."

"What?"

He hesitated. "Let's wait till we're with Adi and Fader. They need to hear it, too." He glanced to his left as they walked and muttered something.

"Why are you talking to yourself?"

"Part of my story."

They entered Adi's office. From behind her desk, Adi caught Case's eye, concern on her face. She nodded to where Fader sat on the couch, knees hugged to his chest, eyes darting around the room.

"Hey," Case said, sitting beside him. "What's wrong?"

He slipped his arm through hers, hugging it tight and leaning against her. "I keep seeing snakes."

The memory of the huge cat leaped back into her head. She fought a shiver. "What?"

"Fader," Adi said softly, "why don't you tell Case and William what you told me?"

Case listened as Fader described the snake appearing to him, first in Will's design table and again in the windows.

A snake. Her giant cat. Something tickled at her memory.

When Fader finished, Adi raised an eyebrow to Will. "Wasn't me," he said. "Yeah, Marell appeared as a snake in Dream, but I didn't draw that."

"Fader," Adi said, her voice gentle, "you've had some terrible experiences lately. Perhaps...?"

Fader looked at her, then Will and Case. "You don't believe me."

Will shook his head. "Dude, nobody's saying that."

"I believe you," Case said.

Hope battled fear on Fader's face. "You do?"

She told of her experience on the Crash Space floor, so similar to Fader's, only being stalked by a great cat, not a snake. "I think it was a mountain lion. And there's a connection to Peru. And the Chakana."

Adi nodded. "There most certainly is."

"Yeah," Will said. "The Serpent, the Puma, and the Condor."

"Yes!" Case said. "Isobel told me about them when we were on the Black Island." She tried to remember what the Sister of Crossing shared after Case had saved her life. "Okay, the Snake rules the underworld, the home of the dead—"

"The *dead?*" Fader said, looking scared again.

"The Puma rules our world, the world of the living. And the Condor rules the spirit world."

"The realm of the gods," Adi said. "And those three worlds—the three levels of the universe in Inca beliefs—are represented in the three steps on the Inca Cross. The Chakana."

"And in the outfits of our Sword Ladies," Will added.

"The Sisterhood," Case said. "The snakeskin leggings, the jacket and paws from a puma, and that condor head mask."

Adi turned to Will. "Which leads to an obvious question. If Fader and Case are seeing the Snake and the Puma, are you seeing the Condor?"

"No birds," Will said.

"Maybe Jack scared him away," Case offered.

"Jack?" Adi said.

"Will's invisible spirit dog," Fader said.

Adi sighed. "Of course. How could I forget?"

Will shook his head. "No Jack, either. I haven't seen the little guy since we escaped the Black Tower." He hesitated. "But I am seeing Nyx. While I'm awake."

"What?" Case said, unsure she'd heard right. "You're seeing floaty-head Nyx when you're not in Dream?"

"Yeah, but she's full-body Nyx now. And she's here, right now."

Fader's eyes went wide. "Nyx? Like in the comics? Cool! Hi, Nyx!"

Will tilted his head, as if listening. "She says 'hi' back."

"I'd forgotten," Case said to Fader. "You've never met her in Dream."

Fader slumped back on the sofa. "I know. Not fair."

"Any ideas what these apparitions mean?" Adi asked Will.

"Besides another weird connection between us, Peru, and the Chakana? No."

"Are they...dangerous?" Fader asked, staring at Adi.

She hesitated. "The Quechua people call them the Three and view them as protectors of their realms. Sacred creatures. The Quechua might even consider you as being blessed by having such creatures attached to you."

"*Attached?*" Fader cried, his eyes wide.

"Much in the way," Adi hurried on, "this Jack is attached to William."

"Yeah," Case said, trying to comfort her brother, "and Jack's friendly, right?"

"He saved my life twice, dude," Will said.

A thought came to her. "My Voice..."

"You're hearing it?" Will asked.

"No. I *didn't* hear it before the Puma appeared. And it always warns me of danger." She turned to Fader. "Whatever these things are, whatever reason they're showing up...I don't think they're dangerous."

Their words seemed to have a calming effect on Fader. "Okay, but why'd I get the Snake? I'd rather have a puppy protector. Or a cool mountain lion."

And I'd rather not have any of them. We don't know they're protectors. But she smiled at Fader and hugged him, happy to see his fear gone. Adi stared at her and Fader, her lips a tight line, her eyes narrowed. *She doesn't think these things are protectors, either*, Case thought.

Seeing Case's eyes on her, Adi smoothed her features, any hint of concern gone. "Is this why you wanted to meet?"

Case folded her arms, saying nothing. She felt Will staring at her, but she ignored him.

"No. It wasn't," Will said, turning to Adi. He hesitated. "I have something else you all need to know, but we should start with what we learned about Case and Fader's mom." He looked at Case again. "Do you want to tell Adi?"

No! I don't. I don't want to give Adi another reason to hate me. I don't—

"Our mom disappeared the same time Will's parents did," Fader blurted, his words all a rush. "And we got our powers the same time as Will."

Adi raised one eyebrow, her eyes running across the three of them, coming to rest on Case.

Well, now it's done. Case swallowed. "Yeah, uh, we had our ages wrong by a year. I mean, me and Will did, so we didn't realize—"

"That your mother's mysterious trip coincided with William's fateful expedition to Peru," Adi finished. "Yes, we knew that."

Case blinked, stunned by Adi's reaction. Or rather, lack of reaction. "Wait. What? You already knew?"

Adi shrugged. "I promised to search for your mother. You'd said she was a professor at the University of Toronto. Stone's investigators discovered her sabbatical from U of T began curiously near when Jon, Terri, and William left for Peru. Stone and I assumed you three already knew that."

They shook their heads.

"However, we still don't understand the connection between Jon, Terri, and your mother—unless you do."

They shook their heads again.

"We'd hoped," she continued, "your mother's departure would help us track William's parents. But, like Jon and Terri—and William—we found no record of your mother leaving Canada. We're assuming now the entire group traveled under false passports."

Case frowned. "How would Mom get a phony passport?"

"From Jon and Terri," Adi said. "They themselves had several. In the past, alternate identities had proved useful."

"Like when they were smuggling things out of a country," Will said, his eyes downcast, but Case saw the hurt on his face.

"Or to evade dangerous people, such as Chico Alvarez," Adi said.

"The guy they got the Chakana from," Fader said.

Adi smiled at him. "You remembered my story. When we escaped with the Chakana after Alvarez's attempted rip-off, we used false passports to travel home. It wasn't the first time Jon and Terri found themselves in a treacherous situation." She eyed Will. "Which is why I've never understood why they took you on that return trip to Peru, knowing the danger surrounding the Chakana."

"Yeah, well, speaking of danger and the Chakana," Will said, "I have something else you need to hear."

Case listened as he told of smelling the Flower that morning and the Dream episode it prompted—the lost memory of his father showing him the Faraday cage, his first exposure to the Chakana...

And what that exposure had done to him.

As he told his story, Case's fear of the Chakana grew. Was the crystal artifact the actual cause of Will's affliction? The real reason he could never leave this tower? Silence descended as he finished.

Adi was the first to speak, her words echoing Case's thoughts. "If that was a true memory, William, I am very glad you agreed to lock the thing up again."

"Do you think it *was* a real memory?" Case asked.

Will spoke to the empty space on his right. "Case is *not* calling you a liar." He turned back. "Sorry, Nyx is miffed we're doubting her. And she has a point. She's my subconscious, so this must come from a buried memory of mine."

"Then the Chakana—?" Fader began.

"Made me the man I am today," Will finished. "Home Boy." He leaned forward, his elbows on his knees, rubbing his temples.

"You don't know that," Case said. "Just because you passed out when you first saw it doesn't mean that it, you know..." She trailed off, not wanting to say what she was thinking.

Will shrugged. "Broke me? Maybe not in that moment. But everything about that Peru trip, what happened to my parents, to me—it all comes back to the Chakana." Still rubbing his temples, he looked at Adi. "Which makes me wonder—after we gave you the Chakana, what did you do with it?"

"With the increased interest in the thing," Adi said, "by both these Sisters and those Red Door people, I wanted it somewhere more secure. And, given how it affected all three of you, with more distance between it and you. I've arranged for an off-site storage facility for the Chakana. A private bank vault."

"You're moving it out of the Tower?" Case asked. Something was bothering her in all this.

Adi nodded. "Stone is taking it there, right now. Is something wrong? You're frowning."

"Yeah," she said slowly, forming her thought. "If Will's Dream memory is true, then the Chakana...changed him, gave him his agoraphobia *before* the Peru trip."

"Yes?"

"So, how could he go to Peru eight years ago?"

Adi arched her eyebrows. "*That* is a very good question."

Will groaned, bending forward where he sat, his eyes scrunched tight, his hands pressed to both sides of his head.

"Will, are you all right?" Case said. "You've been rubbing your head."

"It hurts," he mumbled. "Must've banged it when I fell in the isolation room." Straightening, he tried to grin but still seemed in pain. "I'm okay. I— Aagghh!" He cried out, his head snapping back. His entire body went rigid, arms and legs stiffening. He collapsed onto the couch, slumping against her.

"Will!" she cried, shaking him as Adi rushed over. He didn't respond.

❧

Will blinked, trying to orient himself. Adi's office was gone. Daylight had become darkness. Lights flashed by outside as his eyes adjusted. Neon signs, headlights, traffic signals.

He was in a car, in the backseat, behind the driver. And in the front seat...

He swallowed. In the front seat were his parents, his mom driving, his dad beside her. It was nighttime.

"I should probably explain what's happening," came a voice from his right.

He turned. Nyx sat beside him, still full-bodied. Neither of his parents had reacted to her voice.

Nyx nodded. "Yes, another memory has bubbled up. No, they can't hear us. They don't know we're here because...well, we're not."

"Wait. I was in Adi's office."

"You still are. Collapsed unconscious on her couch while everyone is freaking out as they try to wake you." Nyx bit her lip. "But I don't think they'll be able to."

"Why not?"

"I don't know, but I think we're about to find out. This memory showed up for a reason. Now, shut up and listen."

His mom stopped the car at a red light. Will recognized the intersection. King Street, heading west, at York, right outside their tower. They must have just left the building.

His dad was talking. "...recommended her to me. She's a professor in the Astronomy and Astrophysics department at U of T. She's agreed to meet us at her lab on campus."

"What's her name again?" his mom asked.

"Elenora Cootes, PhD."

Will straightened. His parents were on their way to meet Case's mom?

"Goes by Ellie," his dad continued.

"I would, too. What have you told her?" his mom asked.

"That we're investigating an unusual...artifact capable of storing massive amounts of data. And, given her specialty—information theory and black holes—we're hoping to pick her brain."

The light turned green, and his mom continued west. "And did you explain what this 'artifact' was?"

"No. I thought it best to wait until we have her interest. And trust."

His mom signaled a right turn as the car approached University Avenue. "As soon as we tell her, she'll kick us out. She'll say what everyone has since the beginning. That we're loonies. That it's a legend. That it can't possibly exist."

"That's why we're bringing this." Jon tapped something on his lap.

Will leaned forward to see, a dread mixing with certainty.

And there it was. The square lead box. His parents were taking the Chakana to Ellie Cootes. He felt as if he sat poised at the start of a terrible event. Like watching a pebble rolling downhill, dislodging other pebbles, all gathering mass and momentum, building to a rock slide that would destroy everything in its path.

"What makes you think she'll be able to detect anything our teams haven't?" Terri asked.

"She has access to far more sensitive equipment than the labs we used. This thing must be emitting *something*. A signal. Radiation. Whatever. But something. How else could those sword women show up whenever it's exposed?"

Terri bit her lip, turning north onto the wide promenade of University Avenue. "I don't know. But after what happened to Will, I'm afraid that thing *is* emitting something."

His dad's jaw muscles tightened. "Will's okay now. He hadn't gotten over that flu, that's all."

"I'm not blaming you." She pulled up to another red light. "We've searched for that damn thing for so long. You wanted to share it with him. I did, too. But don't you think it was incredibly coincidental? He sees the thing—and passes out? Really?"

"He's fine now. It was just the flu," Jon said, but Will noticed he didn't look at Terri.

"I wish Adi was back."

"Where is she, again?"

"Hong Kong, for another two weeks. She's trying to convince her friend there to work for us. After what happened with Alvarez, I agree with her. We need more people with her...skills, especially if we're going back to Peru."

"What's his name?"

"Winstone Zhang. She calls him Stone. He helped her handle Alvarez when we got this thing."

The light changed, and the car moved forward. As they passed the next intersection, Springsteen's 'Born to Run' began to play over the car's hands-free speaker. In the back seat, Will smiled, remembering his dad's ringtone.

"Call from...Anna," the speaker declared.

Terri frowned. "That's Will's sitter."

"Answer," John called.

A young, female voice erupted from the speaker, her words rushed, her voice tight and high-pitched, as if she were on the verge of tears. "Mr. Dreycott, it's Anna."

"Yes, Anna, what—"

"It's Will," she cried. "He just...he was...and then he just..." She started sobbing.

At the mention of 'Will,' Terri's head snapped around.

"Anna," Jon said, his voice calm but firm, "slow down. Tell me what happened."

"We were watching TV," Anna said, her voice breaking. "Then he slumped over. He won't wake up. And he's...he's twitching. Oh god. He's getting worse. His whole body is shaking."

Before Anna finished speaking, Terri had swerved over to the right-turn lane. She squealed around the corner onto the first street they reached, heading back east.

His father's voice remained calm, but a tightness had crept into it. "Anna, we're coming home, right now. Stay with Will. I'm calling his doctor."

As his father called a Dr. Thelmond, his mother sped along the busy street, weaving in and out of traffic. His dad hung up. "He's on his way."

"Oh god, oh god, oh god," Terri said, her knuckles white on the steering wheel.

They reached the white skyscraper that was still several years from becoming the Dream Rider Tower. His mother screeched to a stop at the curb. "You run up. I'll park and—"

His father's phone rang. He answered. "Anna, the doctor's on his way. How's Will?"

"Mr. Dreycott, Will's okay," Anna said, her voice now calm, almost embarrassed. "He wants to talk to you."

From the backseat, Will listened as his younger self came on the phone. "Dad?"

"Hey, sport. You okay?"

"Yeah, I'm fine."

"Oh, thank god. What happened?" his dad said, the relief in his voice obvious.

"I don't know. I remember sitting here watching the movie. Anna says I passed out or something. I just woke up."

"Will, we're home now. Mom and I will be up in a minute. I called Dr. Thelmond. You just sit there and rest, and we'll..."

The sound died. The scene faded. A moment later, it returned. Will still sat beside Nyx in the back seat, his parents in the front, only this time his father was driving.

"What just happened?" Will asked.

"I skipped a touching family moment," Nyx replied, "where your parents hugged you a lot, the doctor assured everyone you were fine, you assured everyone you were fine, and Anna got another twenty bucks so she'd believe you were fine and stick it out while your parents tried to see Ellie Cootes again."

"And we didn't see that touching moment because...?"

"Touching...and boring. And not what this memory is about."

"Which is?"

"Confirmation."

"Of what?"

"Of what's wrong with you."

"What?"

"Just watch."

Will watched. Watched his father drive the same route his mother had taken. Away from the tall white building that would become the Dream Rider Tower when Will became the Dream Rider. When he returned from Peru with those strange powers, but unable to go outside. Unable to leave that tower.

"Not the tower, Will," Nyx said.

"What? Are you listening to my thoughts?"

"Of course. I'm you. And I repeat, it's not the tower."

"What are you talking about?"

"Just watch."

His father was driving up University Avenue, now. His mother was sitting with the lead box containing the Chakana in her lap. The car was approaching the same point where Anna the babysitter had called on their first trip.

The car reached that point. Springsteen played again over the speaker. "Answer," Jon said.

"It's happening again!" Anna screamed. "To Will! It's happening again!"

"Turn around!" Terri yelled, but Jon Dreycott had already cut across two lanes of traffic to reach the next eastbound street. As he did, their voices faded. The sounds of the traffic died. His father, his mother, the interior of the car, blurred and swirled into each other, until all details of the scene faded.

Except one.

The lead box on his mother's lap.

His thoughts...Nyx's thoughts?...came back to him.

It's not the tower, Will.
And he understood. "It's not the tower I can't leave," he whispered.
"No. Not the tower," Nyx said. "It's the Chakana."

Chapter 6

Bring it All Back

Case sat on Adi's couch, Will's head in her lap. Fader leaned against her, his eyes on Will, his face scrunched tight with concern.

Adi put her phone away. "Jin's on her way."

Case checked Will's pulse yet again. It was strong, at least, and his breathing slow and regular. "His doctor?"

"Yes. Mi-soon runs her clinics out of our Infirmary now, so she's here most days." Adi bit her lip, staring at Will. "She's...she's very good. She'll know what to do," she said, as if trying to convince herself.

"A doctor won't help Will," said a voice from behind Adi.

Case jumped. She hadn't heard anyone enter the office. The voice was female, but not *her* Voice. And familiar—but out of place. One that didn't belong here.

"Jin will know what to do," Adi repeated, giving no sign she'd heard the voice. She started pacing, and Case could see who stood behind her.

"*Nyx?*" Case cried, staring at Nyx, whose full-length figure had a shimmering, transparent quality, blurred details of Adi's office showing through.

"Cool!" Fader said. "Hi, Nyx."

Adi spun around. "What?"

"Don't you see her?" Case asked.

Adi's eyes darted around the room. "I don't see anyone. Nyx? Will's Nyx?"

"Case," Nyx said, her face more serious than Case could ever remember, "Will's in danger. You need to listen to me and tell Adi."

"Case, what is going on?" Adi demanded.

"I need to listen to Nyx," Case said, holding up her hand and trying to keep her voice calm. She expected an argument, but Adi fell silent.

Case listened as Nyx talked. The message was brief. And frightening. Case turned to Adi. "Call Stone! Have him come back here! Right now!"

"What? Why?" Adi asked, but she was already pulling out her phone.

Case swallowed. "Because Will can't be separated from the Chakana. It will kill him."

On a busy street in the financial district, the black sedan finished circling the block for the second time. It slowed as it approached its destination again, the main branch of the Royal Dominion Bank. In the back seat, Winstone Zhang scanned the street on both sides, a lead box in his lap. "Anything?"

Li Mei, the driver, checked her rear-view mirror again. Her facial features were soft and delicate, belying the lethal fighter Stone knew she was. "Nothing, boss. No tails."

Beside her, Wu Peng, barrel chested and over six and a half feet tall, loomed like a small mountain in the passenger seat, his eyes searching the broad sidewalk in front of the bank. "And nobody hanging around the entrance. I haven't seen the same face twice."

"One more time around the block," Stone said. "Just to be sure."

Mei and Peng exchanged looks, but Mei wove the car back into traffic. "Yes, *dai lo.*"

Stone fought a smile. He insisted his team speak English, but these two had served under him on the Hong Kong police force, and their native slang died hard. 'Dai lo' meant 'big brother' in Cantonese. A sign of respect and affection, but also a term Triad members called their leaders. Ironic, given the history he and these two had in fighting those gangs.

"Humor me," Stone said. "This package has attracted too much interest to take chances."

Peng shifted his bulk to look back at the lead box. "Is that what the crazy chick was after?" Peng had been with Stone when the masked swordswoman first appeared on Will's floor a week ago. And disappeared from the floor, right before their eyes.

Stone nodded. Mei sighed and shook her head. Peng frowned. "What?"

"Not socially appropriate," she said.

"Chick? Or crazy?"

"Both."

"Ri-i-i-ight. How about 'psycho lady'?"

"You're hopeless."

Stone chuckled, still scanning cars and pedestrians. Mei finished the third circuit of the block. "We good?"

"Pull up in front," Stone said.

"Can't park here, boss," Peng said.

"We can afford a ticket. I can't afford to not have the car ready. Mei, stay with the car. Peng, you're with me."

Peng came around to open Stone's door. Stone stepped onto the sidewalk, leaving the lead box on the seat. He buttoned his suit jacket, tailored to hide his shoulder holster, using the time to check their surroundings. The sidewalks here were wide, and the bank's recessed entrance lay about a dozen paces away. As Peng had said, he could see no one loitering near the doors.

Satisfied, he leaned back in for the lead box, then started toward the bank, the box under one arm, Peng two steps behind.

His phone rang. He pulled it out. The display showed 'Archie.' He answered. "We've arrived. We're going inside—"

Adi cut him off, her voice tight with tension. "Bring it back. Bring the Chakana back now. My office. No delays."

He stopped walking. "What's happened?"

"It's Will. I'll explain later. Just bring that damn thing back. Now!"

"On my way," Stone said. He turned back to the car, twirling a finger in the air, signaling Mei to start the car as a frowning Peng followed. "I'll call when we're downstairs—"

The bullet punched him in the back, flinging him forward onto the pavement. The lead box flew from his hands, skidding along the sidewalk toward the car. Through his pain, screams and shouts filled his ears.

Another shot. Beside him, Peng grunted and fell to one knee, one arm hanging limp, his other hand reaching into his jacket. Mei leaped from the car, gun out, firing from a crouch in the direction of the bank.

Stone gasped in a breath through the searing pain. The Kevlar vest had stopped the bullet, but he felt as if he'd been kicked by a horse. He looked back, taking in the scene in an eye-blink. People were fleeing in all directions. Four men in black suits crouched in the entrance to the bank, firing handguns, using tall planters for cover.

"Get in the car!" Mei yelled. She'd opened the back door and was firing past them, using the driver door as a partial shield.

The lead box lay beside the car. A thought fought through his pain. *They're willing to kill for that thing.*

As he pushed himself to his knees, Peng grabbed him under his arm, pulling him up, dragging him toward the car. More shots. Peng grunted again and stumbled as they reached the car. Stone caught the big man, using his momentum to shove him headfirst into the back seat. He slammed the door. Mei was still crouched, firing.

"Get in!" Stone yelled at her, his own gun out, firing at their attackers.

Mei launched herself from her crouch into the front seat, vaulting over the center console to the passenger side in one smooth movement.

Stone, still firing, stepped toward the open driver's door. The lead box lay at his feet. He stopped...

...and kicked the box toward the bank doors and the gunmen. It spun and bounced across the sidewalk, stopping three paces from the nearest shooter.

The firing stopped. Stone leaped into the driver's seat, slamming the door and wrenching the car into gear. The street was empty of traffic, whether by luck or because of the gunfire. He didn't care. Squealing away from the curb, he wrenched the car into a U-turn, back toward the Dream Rider Tower.

"Mei?" he said, turning to her.

"I'm good." She was kneeling on the seat, looking back at Peng. "You hit?"

Peng groaned. "Can't feel my arm."

Stone screeched around a corner. "Check him."

Mei crawled into the back seat. "Let me get your jacket off."

Peng swore in Cantonese.

"Stop being a baby," she snapped. Pause. "No blood. Both shots hit the vest. You're good."

"You need to look up 'good' in the dictionary," Peng rasped. "We're lucky they didn't try for head shots."

Mei slipped back into the front. "In your case, it'd bounce off."

Peng said something rude.

"You both get checked out when we're back," Stone said.

"You, too, dai lo," Mei said.

"I'm fine. Maybe a busted rib." *Or two*, he thought, from the pain that came with every breath.

"You, too," she repeated. She looked at him. "They were waiting for us."

Stone nodded. "Inside the lobby. When I turned around, they decided we weren't coming in, and they made their move."

Mei stared at him. "They wanted that box. And you gave it to them."

"Shit," Peng wheezed. "Dragon Lady's gonna be pissed, boss."

"Peng," Mei said.

"Sorry. I mean Ms. Archambeault won't be happy."

"She'll be fine," Stone said. In the distance, he caught the first sound of sirens, but too far away to be a concern. The tower was only another block.

"But—" Mei began.

"Those men didn't want the box," Stone said. "They wanted what it contained. Or rather, what they thought it contained." Reaching into a pocket, he pulled out a small steel-gray fabric pouch. He squeezed it, relieved more than he could describe to feel the sharp edges of the Chakana.

Seeing it, Mei grinned. "You switched it out."

"Sneaky devil, boss," Peng said.

Stone tossed the pouch to Mei. She caught it, hefting it in one hand. "Heavy."

"Lead-lined Faraday bag."

She started to pull up the flap on the pouch.

"Don't open it," Stone said, "or we'll have a lady with a sword sitting beside Peng."

"Please, no," Peng said.

Mei handed the pouch back. "They were waiting for us," she repeated.

He knew what she meant. "Yes, so how did they know we were coming?"

"Boss, we...I mean, Peng and I...we'd never..."

"I know. That's why I brought you two. Why you got to be here, getting shot at with me."

"*Do ze*, dai lo," Peng said softly, his voice heavy with respect.

"You can thank me by checking my office for bugs when we get back." He thought about his conversations with Adi over this plan. "Adi's, too, and the boardroom. And our phones."

Mei frowned. "Our phones are encrypted. All communication—voice, text, email—uses a VPN. And we scan those rooms for listening devices weekly."

"Change the encryption keys and the proxy server. Scan the rooms again. And make it daily until I say different."

"And if we find nothing?"

Stone's hands tightened on the wheel. "Then we have a bigger problem."

Neither replied. He knew they understood. If they found no electronic means of surveillance, it meant the source of the leak wasn't tech. It was human.

It meant they had a mole.

✺

Case stood beside Fader and Adi watching Jin examine Will where he lay, still unconscious, on Adi's couch. Jin had arrived minutes after Adi had called, but so far could find nothing wrong with Will. Case wasn't surprised. She doubted medical schools taught the effects of the Chakana.

Jin straightened, shaking her head. "We need to move him to the Infirmary where I can run tests. I'll send for a gurney."

Adi bit her lip, but nodded.

Just then, Will groaned and opened his eyes.

"Oh, god, Will," Case said, relief flooding her as she helped him sit up. "Are you okay?"

He rubbed his face. "I...I don't know. I think so. Adi, where's Stone? You have to call him back."

Adi shot a look at Case. "We have. He should be here by—" Her phone rang. She answered. "Stone, where are you? What's taking so—?" She stopped talking. Her eyes went wide as she listened, her jaw muscles tightening. "Understood," she said finally. "No, no one. Yes, I agree. We'll meet you there." She hung up.

"Will," Jin said, "I'd like you to come up to the Infirmary."

Will shook his head. "I'm fine."

"Thank you, Mi-soon," Adi said. "We'll take it from here."

Jin frowned. "Adrienne, Will should be under observation. You can't—"

"We'll take it from here," Adi repeated. Jin stiffened, gave a curt nod, and stalked from the room.

"What—?" Case began.

Adi put a finger to her lips. They all fell silent. She tapped on her phone, then held it out so they could read the screen: *Give me your phones.*

The three of them exchanged glances, but dug out their phones and handed them over. Adi put them in her desk drawer, then motioned them to follow her.

Outside her office, she locked her door, and they all headed for the elevators.

Chapter 7

Escape Is at Hand for the Travellin' Man

Case sat between Will and Fader in Will's home theater. Located at the opposite end of the floor from his studio, the room could hold forty people in five banked rows of high-backed, reclining seats. A low stage sat below the screen, where Will said he sometimes had local indie bands play. The three of them had watched movies here recently.

But no movies today. Or bands. Today, they sat in the lowest row facing where Adi sat on the edge of the stage.

Stone entered, moving more stiffly than Case had ever seen him. He winced as he sat beside Adi.

"You saw Jin?" Adi asked him.

"Yes. Just some bruised ribs. Glad you sprang for top-end vests."

"Your people?"

"Same for Peng. Mei is fine."

"Stone," Will asked, "what the freak happened?"

Stone told of the attack at the bank. Finishing, he removed a small gray pouch from a pocket and laid it between him and Adi on the stage. A pouch, Case now knew, containing the Chakana.

Stone explained his concern about surveillance in the tower. "I suggested your theater because your floor is the most secure in the building. Plus, this room is soundproof with no windows."

"Why don't you want windows?" Will asked. "Are we being watched?"

"Possibly. Also, parabolic microphones can pick up conversations from window vibrations."

"And our phones?"

"We'll return them after we run scans and install new encryption," Stone said.

Case slipped lower in her seat. Already shaken by the morning's events, the thought of unknown parties listening or watching only increased the sense of hidden danger around them.

Will took her hand. "How did you know to call Stone back? Your Voice?"

She shook her head, wondering for the first time why her Voice hadn't warned her. Then understanding. Her Voice warned of danger—but only danger to *herself.* This time the danger had been to Will, not her. "Nyx told me."

"What? You could hear Nyx?"

"And see her. A full-bodied, see-through version."

"Me, too," Fader added.

"I could not," Adi said. She turned to Stone. "Nyx is the representation of—"

"Will's subconscious. I know," Stone replied. "I've been reading the comics."

"Really?" Will asked.

Stone shrugged. "After learning the Dream Rider was real, I wanted to familiarize myself with your...abilities."

"Cool," Fader said. "Which issue's your favorite?"

Stone smiled. "Perhaps a conversation for another time. You say this Nyx warned you?"

Case nodded. "She said Will can't be separated from the Chakana."

"My phone call to return here triggered you getting shot," Adi said. "I'm sorry, my friend."

Stone shook his head. "It likely saved our lives. If we had entered the bank, the shooters would have been at close range. Instead, they had to react quickly, outside their plan, firing from a distance."

"Well," Will said, "you saved *me* by switching out the Chakana. Otherwise, those people would have it, and I'd be in a coma."

Or dead, Case thought, remembering Nyx's warning. *Will can't be separated from the Chakana. It will kill him.* "How did it feel?" she asked Will.

"Like something trying to rip my brain from my head. It hurt. A lot."

Case turned to Stone. "Why'd you switch it out?"

"Given the interest in this artifact, I wanted contingency plans in place. Carrying the thing shielded in my pocket was a simple one."

"Is Nyx still here with us?" Adi asked, looking around the room.

"I don't see her," Case said, fighting a smile. "She disappeared once Will woke up." Fader nodded agreement.

"She's not here," Will confirmed. "But she showed me something when I was unconscious you need to hear about. Another memory. It explains what happened to me just now."

Will told of the Dream memory Nyx had shown of his parents leaving the tower, taking the Chakana to...

Case stiffened at the mention of their mother's name. Until now, she and Fader had only the coincidence of timing to link their mother's disappearance to Will and his parents. Now, here was proof. Fader leaned against her. She slid an arm around his shoulders and pulled him close.

Finishing, Will shook his head. "All these years, I thought I was chained to the Tower. But I'm not. I'm chained to the Chakana. That's why I could never go more than a couple of blocks from here—because the Chakana was here. That's why I collapsed today—Stone carried the thing too far away. And that's why I could go outside when I was wearing it...that time."

That time. Case shuddered at that memory. The time Will followed Link to the Black Island while carrying the Chakana.

"I'll abandon any plans to move it off-site," Adi said. "We'll keep it secure here. For now, it goes back in my safe. In a lead container."

"I'll post two guards outside your office," Stone said. "Around the clock."

Case frowned. Something had been bothering her, and Adi's words let her put a mental finger on it. "Something I don't get. The lead box blocks the Sisters sensing the Chakana. And Fader and I didn't get the bump in our powers until the box broke down in Adi's safe."

"But...?" Will said.

"But *you* can obviously detect it—or it can detect you—even *while* it's shielded. Else, why would it affect you by being too far away?" She looked at them all. "So...how?"

Nobody answered. Will finally spoke. "I don't know. But when my dad showed me the Chakana in the Faraday cage, that thing must've somehow..." He shrugged. "...*connected* to me."

"Which is in no way incredibly creepy," Case said.

Will's eyes widened. A smile grew on his face. "Oh!"

"What 'oh'?" she asked.

"This connection—this is good," he said, almost to himself. "Oh, yeah. This is good."

"How," Adi said, "could such a thing possibly be *good*?"

"I can go outside if I wear the Chakana. But that attracts our Sword Ladies, so I thought I was still stuck here. But if I'm connected to the Chakana even when it's shielded..."

"You can go outside," Case finished, "*and* the Chakana can stay shielded."

"Yes! It just has to be near me." He turned to Adi. "It means I can go to Peru. And without Sword Ladies dropping in."

"Just armed thugs like those who attacked Stone," Adi said.

Will's jaw muscles tightened. "Adi, for eight years, I've had one hope. And only one. To find the Flower. I never thought past that. I never thought about how I'd leave this tower because I didn't want to kill that hope. Now, I have a *new* hope. I have the Flower *and* a way to go to Peru. Don't kill my hope. I have to try to...to fix me."

His voice broke on the last words, and Case's heart went out to him. But Adi stayed silent. *Okay, time for me to try.* "Adi, the answers to what happened to Will and his parents are in Peru." *To what happened to our mom, too.* But she didn't say that. "And somehow, the Chakana's the key. Will has to go to Peru—*with* the Chakana. And now, he can." She swallowed and finished. "Will can't live his life like a prisoner. You have to let him go."

Adi eyed her for a breath then looked at Stone. He shrugged. *He's saying I'm right. He's on our side, but it's up to Adi.*

Adi sat, lips pursed, eyes narrowed. Case waited. Waited for an argument, for Adi to be angry. Angry at her suggestion of exposing Will to danger, and for daring to insert herself into this, between Adi and Will.

But Adi's response was none of those. She sighed. "I know."

Will straightened. "Wait. What?"

"William," Adi said, "I want you to lead a normal life. I always have. And if that is to happen, I believe you are correct—the answers lie in Peru."

"You're letting me go?" Will said, squeezing Case's hand so hard she winced.

"I'm not *letting* you do anything," Adi said. "We will go, but under my direction. And with heavy security." She looked at Stone. "I can't force you, but if you would consider joining us..."

Stone stiffened as if slapped. "You couldn't keep me away. I would be insulted."

"We'll need some of your team," Adi continued, as if he hadn't spoken, but a small smile flickered and went. "Perhaps several."

"Too many will be as dangerous as too few," Stone said. "Given the attention that seems focused on us, we must avoid attracting any more. Let me think about it, but I feel two of my best will be enough. Along with you and me."

Case wondered again at Adi's past, at why someone as lethal as Stone considered this apparent business-woman his equal.

"We're going to Peru?" Fader asked, his eyes wide, excitement in his voice.

Adi hesitated. "Fader, I can't say I'm comfortable bringing two minors who are not legally under my care."

"No," Case said, leaning forward. "You have to let us go, too."

Adi raised an eyebrow.

"Okay, you don't *have* to. But, please..."

"Adi," Fader said, "she's our *mom.*"

"Yes," Adi said, "and she would expect me to keep you safe. I'm not sure she wouldn't want you to stay here, in the tower."

"What?" Case said, "Till you come back? Like we're prisoners—?" She stopped, turning to Will. "Sorry."

"No, you're right," Will said. "Adi, Case won't stay cooped up here. And she won't leave Fader, so they'll both be on the streets. Where Fader was snatched before. Where Case and I were just kidnapped by people after the Chakana. They'd be safer *with* us."

"And," Case added, "I was also kidnapped *from* this tower." Something else occurred to her. "I think we're *meant* to go with you. Me and Fader."

"Excuse me?" Adi said.

"The Snake. The Puma. You said so yourself. They're connected to Peru and the Chakana. And now they're connected to me and Fader. And you called them protectors."

Adi sighed. "I'd come to the same conclusion myself."

"What?" Case said.

"You didn't let me finish earlier. I said I believe the answers for Will lie in Peru. I was about to say, although I'm not comfortable bringing you and Fader, it appears the answers for you both lie there, as well. Answers concerning your mother and your own connections to the Chakana. And I agree—you will be safer with us. Plus, we may find your...abilities useful. So, yes, you will come with us."

"Yes!" Fader said, bouncing where he sat and beaming up at Case.

Case forced a smile, stunned by Adi's decision and suddenly no more thrilled with the idea of going than staying behind. *Be careful what you wish for.*

"But I like nothing about this," Adi said. "It seems like we're being manipulated. The Flower arriving. The mysterious location that accompanied it. Now, we're being forced to bring the Chakana back to Peru. I feel as if we are chess pieces, moved by players unknown, on a board we can't see, in a game we don't understand."

Everyone fell silent until Will spoke. "Speaking of the location that came with the Flower, did you check it out?"

"I reached out to Pablo Landos," Adi said. "You might recall him from my story of how your parents acquired the Chakana."

Will frowned. "Didn't he set up the meeting with that Chico Alvarez guy?"

"Yes. Pablo was your parents' go-to for any South American expedition, arranging visas and transportation, guides and porters, permits and approvals. He was their Spanish-speaking feet-on-the-ground. He lives in Bolivia, but has traveled extensively in Columbia, Ecuador, and Chile. Brazil, too, as he also speaks Portuguese. And, of course, Peru."

"Did that location mean anything to him?"

"It took some time to track him down. He's no longer in La Paz. He moved to Vallegrande."

"Never heard of it."

"I'm not surprised. It's a small village. I gather Pablo's income relied heavily on your parents. After their disappearance, he had to make some adjustments."

"He wasn't the only one," Will muttered.

"William, Pablo has a family to support."

"Sorry. What did he say?"

"He needed time to check his records. That was, after all, eight years ago. But I have a video call with him at three, today." She hesitated, her eyes running over them. "I think you should all join me."

Still reeling from the idea of traveling to Peru and the events of the day, Case was stunned again over Adi including her and Fader in this piece of Will's past.

"Can we do an encrypted call from this theater?" Adi asked Stone.

Stone nodded. "I'll set it up."

Adi stood. "Be back here at three." With that, she and Stone left the room.

Case, Will, and Fader sat there, not speaking. Will finally broke the silence. "Well, it's been a day, hasn't it?"

Case didn't answer. Yeah, it had been a day. Learning of Will's connection to the Chakana. How it had broken him. His collapse. The armed attack on Stone and his team. Discovering Will's parents really had met their mother.

The decision to go to Peru. Their mystery animals. Which reminded her...

She turned to Fader. "Has your Snake come back?"

Fader shook his head, but darted a look around the room.

"Your Puma?" Will asked.

"Nope."

"Makes you wonder, doesn't it?" Will said.

"About why we're seeing them?" she said.

"Well, yeah, but also what Adi said. The Serpent, the Puma..."

"So?"

"So, where's the Condor?"

Chapter 8

The Beat of Black Wings

On the rooftop patio of the restaurant *Lucille's*, Rani Patel slid into a chair at a small table across from Tommy McIvers. Tommy was skinny and pot-bellied, bald and bearded. He was also the City Editor of the Standard—and her boss. She put her phone on the red-and-white checkerboard tablecloth, lining it up with the forks of her place setting.

"You're late," Tommy said, not looking up from the menu.

She didn't know why he found the menu so fascinating. He must have memorized it by now. This stretch of King Street was an unbroken string of narrow two-story restaurants catering to the business towers for lunch and the theater crowd for dinner. Most had sidewalk patios, but *Lucille's* offered a rooftop shaded by trees and umbrellas. As far as she knew, Tommy ate here every day the patio was open. He brought the paper's advertisers here, his friends, his wife, his staff.

But never her.

"Are you firing me?" she asked.

He lowered the menu to peer at her over thick black-rimmed glasses that, as always, needed cleaning. "What?"

"I mean," she continued, enjoying his confusion, "you've never brought me here for lunch. You've never taken me to lunch, period." She wrinkled her brow in an exaggerated frown. "You've never even bought me a coffee. And this is the perfect place to fire someone. You know, away from the office. Public, so I won't make a big fuss." *Like that would stop me.*

He tossed the menu onto the table. "Rani, for god's sake, why would I fire you?"

"You don't like me."

"Why would you say that?"

"You said I was a pain in the ass."

"You *are* a pain in the ass. But you're growing on me. No, I'm not firing you, as you well know."

"Are you promoting me?"

Tommy glared at her.

"Kidding. I'm quite happy where I am. You know, since you gave me Harry's crime beat."

"Glad to hear it. This lunch is to say thank you for doing a great job with that. You convinced Adrienne—" He stopped, glancing at nearby tables. The weather today was perfect, warm but not hot, with a cool breeze, and the patio was crowded. He lowered his voice. "You convinced *Galahad* to keep feeding us tips. And thanks to that, you've broken our two biggest stories this year."

Galahad. The late Harry Lyle's mysterious source for a career of head-line-grabbing stories. Rani had tracked Galahad back to Adrienne Archambeault, the CEO for seventeen-year-old Will Dreycott's Dream Rider empire.

Although Adi was her supposed contact, Rani knew the real Galahad was Will with his weird dream powers. Adi had let Rani replace Harry as Galahad's sole contact in the media because Will, his girlfriend Case, and her brother Fader had all vouched for her.

Well, she'd earned it. Helping rescue Will. Saving Fader's life. Shit, she deserved props for just surviving that level of weirdness. A masked swordswoman popping in and out of thin air. A subway stop that didn't exist. Almost getting eaten by some sea monster. That black island with its pyramid and tower. The Chamba-whamba-whatever woman who controlled people with a song. That In Between place. She shuddered, remembering.

Oh, yeah—and giant bugs. She had *so* earned this.

As a waiter came to take their orders, a cloud passed in front of the sun, dipping the patio into shadow for a breath. She glanced up. It had better not rain. She hadn't brought an umbrella.

The sky above was bright, blue...and cloudless.

She frowned. Must've been a plane. Or a bird.

"So," Tommy said, "any more leads?"

"I've asked Galahad to look into the Framingham murders."

"Murders? Plural? The cops said murder-suicide. The coroner supported that."

"It was the son. I'm sure of it."

"Hope you're right."

"Because you want justice done? Nothing to do with selling papers, right?"

He grinned. "Absolutely. In the meantime, I have some ideas I want you to think about."

She listened, nodding as Tommy rattled off a list of suggested investigations. Suggested. Not ordered. Since she'd landed Galahad, her boss's attitude toward her had changed—from thinly veiled contempt to tolerance to an almost deference.

That deference, she knew, came from her connection to Galahad. Galahad was her insurance policy, a meal ticket she could cash in at any other paper in the country, a lever she could pull for a raise, a promotion, a bigger office if she wanted to.

Much to her surprise, she didn't want to. She was happy where she was, doing what she was doing. Yeah, she was finally getting the respect of her boss and her colleagues, even her parents for choosing career over dutiful wife and baby-factory. But the most surprising discovery had been realizing *why* she was suddenly happy.

She *liked* doing good. She liked helping put bad guys away.

It had helped her understand Harry Lyle, her late benefactor. She'd always wondered why Harry had never moved to a bigger paper, never demanded more money, a bigger byline. Now she understood. Harry had liked doing good, too.

The Standard had a long history of staying independent—independent of meddling owners and advertisers, corporations and politicians. Harry's biggest stories, the ones Galahad had provided, had often shone lights into corners where the powerful didn't want you looking. The Standard had always printed them, had always stood behind Harry.

She remembered taking over Harry's office and seeing the words he'd pinned on his wall: *It takes work to find the truth, integrity to recognize it, and courage to tell it.*

And, the gods bless him, Harry had trusted her to do that, recommending her for the crime beat. Now, Will Dreycott and Tommy McIvers were both trusting her to be their new Harry.

For now, that was enough. Maybe it always would be.

"So," Tommy said, bringing her back, "are you dealing with she-who-must-not-be-named, or has she passed you on to the real Galahad? Because, no way it's her, right?"

She gave him her best 'Seriously?' expression. He shrugged. "Worth a try. My old reporter instincts."

"Old, I get, but you were a reporter once?"

"Funny. Yeah, before I became your *boss*."

"I protect my sources. And don't worry. If I get hit by a bus..." *Or eaten by a giant bug.* "...she has your name."

What she didn't mention was her ongoing probing into Adi herself. Despite heading one of the largest privately held corporations in the world, Adrienne Archambeault was a complete cipher.

Rani wasn't sure why she was investigating Adi. Did she want something on the woman to use as leverage in case Adi ever tried to cut her off from Will? Maybe. She didn't trust her newfound altruism enough to dismiss that possibility. But she wanted to believe she just didn't like questions without answers. She wanted to believe she was just being a reporter.

Albeit not a very good one. So far, she'd uncovered nothing of Adi's history before the woman emigrated to Canada from Hong Kong fifteen years ago to work for Will's parents. She'd reached out to Harry's old newspaper and police contacts in Hong Kong this week and was waiting to hear back.

Another shadow drifted across the patio. Looking up, she saw a huge bird glide by overhead, several stories up. "Holy shit! What is that?"

Tommy followed her gaze, but the bird had disappeared behind a neighboring building. "What?"

"A bird. I've never seen anything that big in the city."

"Falcon? Peregrines nest on the big towers."

"This was bigger than a falcon. More like a vulture."

He shrugged. "Turkey vulture, maybe. Never heard of those downtown, though. Oh, hey, I just thought of another thing. This one could end up being a series…"

As Tommy resumed work talk, she tried to pay attention, but her mind kept running back to the bird. Seeing something that large in the city she'd grown up in was surprising enough. But its size wasn't the only thing nagging at her. As the bird had flown by, it seemed she could still see the building behind it—through the creature.

Ridiculous. It must have been the bright sunshine. Or reflections from nearby towers. Or a heat shimmer, rising from the sunbaked pavement below.

"Rani, are you listening to me?" Tommy asked.

"Of course," she said, bringing her mind back to her boss. "Yeah, definitely a series. Spread it over the summer, wrap it by Labor Day, then—" She broke off as the shadow appeared overhead again. Bigger this time. Growing bigger still, until it covered her, Tommy, and their table.

A beat of wings sounded above her, rising in volume, coming closer. The beat was slow at first, then rapid as the shadow slid past them. The flapping sound ended in a fluttering that came from her left.

She slowly turned her head.

On the next table, its talons clutching the edge and bunching the checkered tablecloth, perched the largest bird she'd ever seen. The creature was over a meter tall, its plumage black with white on the wings. Above a frill of white encircling its neck like a muff rose a vulture's head, featherless and bald, black-skinned with a black-red comb.

And she could see through it. See the two women on whose table the bird perched. See them as they continued sipping white wine and chatting, oblivious to their winged guest. Trembling, Rani scanned the patio. No one, neither diners nor wait staff, was giving any notice to the creature.

Only fair, she thought, fighting back a hysterical giggle. *It's not paying any attention to them, either. Only to me.* The bird's eyes—one red, one yellow—were locked on her.

"Rani," Tommy said, "what the hell is wrong with you?"

Fighting to keep control, she allowed herself a small measure of pride for not leaping up screaming. Pride, too, in not asking Tommy whether he saw the bird. No one seemed to, so why would he? Besides, then she'd have to explain what she was seeing.

"Sorry, sorry, sorry," she said, shoving her phone back in her purse. "Almost forgot. I have an appointment."

"Seriously? We just ordered. Can't you—"

"With Galahad."

"Oh! Well, okay. Uh, yeah, run. But get back to me on that series idea."

"Will do." She turned away, fighting an urge to run. Behind her came the beat of wings, and again a bird-shaped shadow passed over the patio. When she reached the street, she looked up, not even surprised to find the bird in the ribbon of sky between the office towers, pacing her as she walked east on King.

She hadn't totally lied to Tommy—she *was* going to meet with Galahad. She didn't have an appointment, but she needed to see Will. And Case and Fader.

Because she'd learned one thing since meeting those three. When things got weird, and you found yourself in Oz—it was time to see the Wizard.

And those kids were the Wizards of Weird.

Chapter 9

Tunnels

Morrigan descended the stone staircase from the Tapestry room into the darkness beneath Castle Rushen, surrendering to the insistent call of the strange song. A dozen steps down, the shadows swallowed her, and she cast an illumination spell. A glowing, golden hawk appeared three paces before her, another following her at the same distance.

The staircase went down and down. And down. Far below sea level, she realized. Much deeper than she remembered—

Remembered.

She turned from those memories, focusing instead on the stone steps, now often slick with water.

Just when she was ready to give up, the staircase ended at an arched opening. She emerged into a rough, domed tunnel, hewn from a shiny, black rock much different from the gray stone through which she had descended. The tunnel stretched to her left and right. She faced a choice. And with that choice, all her memories of that day so long ago rushed back.

She had buried those memories. Buried them as deep as this tunnel. Buried them forever, she thought. Even returning to the castle, confronting her mother, holding the golden key, seeing the Tapestry had not exhumed them. Not even following these steps again.

But now, this simple choice brought them all back. Brought back the horror of that day. This simple choice. Left? Or right?

All those years ago, she had chosen left...

Looking back now, that day in her then young life was no longer about the horror of what happened. It was about choices. Her choices. Looking back now, each choice she made that day had been wrong. She remembered...

"Morrie, what are you doing in here?"

The voice of her little brother pulled Moirragh's attention from the Unicorn Tapestry. She blinked. How long had she been standing here before it? Turning, she glowered down at the boy. "Dany, I told you not to follow me."

Danell, ten years to her sixteen, stood just inside the room, a pace from where the magical stone wall hiding the room had been. He stared at her hand. "Where did you get *that*? That belongs to Mother."

She still held the golden key, the key she'd stolen—no, *borrowed*—from where it lay hidden behind a loose stone in their mother's bedroom. A hiding place Moirragh had searched for since her mother had used the key to open the wall and first shown her the Tapestry a year ago.

Embarrassed, she slipped the key down the bodice of her dress. "I'm just borrowing it. I only wanted to see the Tapestry again. Now, leave me alone."

"You shouldn't be here."

"Neither should you."

"We should leave."

"*You* should leave."

"I'm telling Mother." Dany turned to go.

"Wait," she called, desperate not to abandon the Tapestry. Not yet. "Give me a minute more, and we'll go together. And I'll return the key to where I found it."

Dany pouted up at her. "Why should I?"

Moirragh bit back a retort. Little brothers could be so... Sighing, she forced a smile. "I'll play hide-and-seek with you after we leave here."

He brightened. "Promise?"

"Promise."

He grinned. "Okay."

She turned back to the Tapestry. So beautiful. So wonderful. In the flickering light of the torches burning in wall sconces, the fabric seemed to quiver, as if alive. "Now," she whispered to her brother, "leave me alone."

Some time later, she again shook herself free of the Tapestry's spell. "Sorry, Dany. I didn't mean to be that long." With a sigh of regret, she turned her back on the silken artifact. "We can go now and..."

She looked around the small vault. Her brother was nowhere to be seen.

Tears of the Goddess, she swore. Had the little imp gone to find their mother, after all? She moved to leave, to return the key to its hiding place before her mother missed it.

Wait. What was that?

She stopped, turning back, listening. There. Dany's voice, calling her name. Calling from very far away.

And yet, calling from this room.

In the stone wall facing the Tapestry, an arched doorway now stood. She was certain no such opening had been there when she first entered. With a rising fear, she walked on trembling legs to stand before it. Past the archway, in the flickering torchlight, stone steps descended into blackness.

She heard her name called again. Standing here, she knew with sick certainty that her brother's voice had come from the murky darkness below.

Darkness. This room itself seemed darker. She now noticed a chair pulled underneath one wall sconce. A sconce missing its torch.

Curse the boy. This was not what she meant by hide-and-seek. She must return the key. But she couldn't do that with Dany still in here. Once the golden key passed the boundary of this room, the magical wall would reappear, trapping the boy inside.

From below, Dany called her name again. A sudden dread seized her. His voice sounded fainter. Grabbing another torch from the wall, she ran back to the steps. And began to descend.

After what seemed hours, the steps ended at another arched opening. She found herself in a domed tunnel, stretching to her left and right. No masonry here. This tunnel was carved from a shiny, black stone.

"Dany!" she called, as she had called countless times on her descent. His replies had come back fainter each time—until they had stopped coming.

Now she stood where he must have. Two directions. Left? Or right?

Again, she called his name. Again, she listened.

A sound. His voice? From her right? Her left? Her torch was guttering. She had little time. She knew how to cast an illumination spell, but it was weak and lasted only a short while.

There. Again. His voice. From the left, she was sure. Wasn't she? She had to choose. Turning to her left, she ran along the tunnel, calling his name but hearing no answer.

The tunnel split into two branches. She took the left branch, again. Soon, it split once more, this time into three routes. Fearful she would become lost herself, with her torch dead and her spell-casting strength dwindling, she turned back.

She needed help. She needed her mother.

It seemed to take days to retrace her steps, to labor up the stone steps. Reaching the Tapestry room again, she collapsed to the floor, exhausted from her search, from the climb, from casting and recasting her illumination spell. From her fear.

"Moirragh!" Her mother's voice.

She looked up from where she lay. Aalin looked down at her, her face unreadable. Behind her mother, two more of the coven, Voranna and Nanse, stared wide-eyed at the archway behind Moirragh.

"Sister," Voranna whispered. "The way has opened."

Aalin's eyes moved from Moirragh to the archway. She blinked, as if only now seeing it. Her eyes found Moirragh again, and now Moirragh could read what showed on her mother's face. Fear. And disappointment. "Child," Aalin said. "What have you done?"

"Dany," Moirragh sobbed, struggling to her feet. "He went down there. I...I couldn't find him."

Nanse gave a sharp, indrawn breath as Aalin stiffened. "How long ago?" her mother demanded.

Late sunlight slanted low through the room's one window. It had been mid-day when she entered the room. "Three hours. Perhaps four."

"Call the others," Aalin said to Voranna. "We must be quick if we are to find him."

"Priestess," Voranna said gently. "It's been too long."

"There may still be time," Aalin said, "if he hasn't traveled too deep."

"Sister," Nanse said, "none of us can hear the Song. That is why we were chosen. We will not find him."

"My son cannot hear the Song, either," Aalin said, her voice rising. "He is just a lost little boy."

But Moirragh heard the doubt in her mother's voice, even as she wondered what song they spoke of. And she heard something else. A deep, resonating thunder, followed by a tremor in the stone beneath her feet. Cannon fire.

"My Priestess, the siege has begun," Voranna said. "All of us are needed at the walls."

Aalin drew herself up before them. "HE IS MY SON!" she shouted. The two women cowered back. Trembling, Aalin took a deep breath. Her voice broke. "He is my son. Please, my Sisters."

Voranna exchanged a look with Nanse, then nodded. "I will bring them." She turned to go.

"Wait," Aalin said. Her shoulders slumped, and her mother seemed to age before Moirragh's eyes. "Leave six on the walls. Bring the rest."

Moirragh spun on her mother. "No! We need *all* the coven to search."

Aalin froze her with a look, and any further words died in Moirragh's throat. "Daughter," Aalin said. "Go to your room. And stay there."

Burning with silent fury but too afraid to defy her mother again, Moirragh turned to leave.

"Daughter."

Moirragh turned back. Her mother held out a hand.

Swallowing, Moirragh retrieved the key from her bodice and lay it on her mother's outstretched palm, shame heating her face.

Moirragh went to her room. Evening turned to night. Somewhere in that passage of time, she slipped into sleep filled with nightmares of twisting tunnels and trembling stone walls.

When she awoke, it was past midnight. Her room was dark and the thunder of cannons filled her ears. Her mother sat on the edge of her bed, watching her, her expression unreadable.

Moirragh sat up, afraid to ask the question. Her mother read it in her face. Aalin shook her head. "We did not find him."

"But you'll keep searching." Moirragh said it as a fact, not a question.

In answer, Aalin rose and walked toward the door. "Get dressed. We need you on the walls."

"Mother! He is my brother. He is your son. He will die!"

Stopping at the doorway, Aalin turned back, her eyes not meeting Moirragh's. "We all may die tonight, child. We are under attack. The castle may fall. But we have sworn to spend our lives if needed—you included, Moirragh—to keep the way sealed."

The way. The tunnels her brother had taken. Because of her. "What is it? Where does it lead?" *That* question she could ask. Never, 'where has my brother gone?'

Aalin met her eyes. "Pray you never find out. Now get dressed and come to the walls. And bring the Weave when you come. We need its power there."

"What of the Tapestry?" she said, guilty that, even with her brother gone and the castle under siege, her thoughts still ran to the magical artifact.

"The Tapestry stays where it is, guarding what it must guard. Now hurry." With that, Aalin turned and left the room.

As commanded, Moirragh rose and dressed. As commanded, she went to the Covenstead, the tower room the Sisters used as their holy place in the castle. And as commanded, she walked to where the Weave lay in the round room, surrounded by thirteen high-backed wooden chairs.

But when she knelt to roll the Weave for carrying, when she touched it, held it in her arms—when she felt its power—somewhere in those actions, her mother's commands fell from her shoulders, a burden she could bear no longer.

You left my brother to die in darkness, alone and afraid. And now you expect me to follow you to my own death?

Moirragh stood, the rolled Weave clutched to her chest, thrilling to the power of the spells throbbing within it. "No," she declared to the empty room. "I will not die here. I will not die today. I choose my own path."

Leaving the Covenstead, she descended the tower steps with the Weave, past stairs leading up to the battlements where her mother and sisters faced the besieging Roundhead army. She continued down, praying she remembered the way. It had been over a year since she'd shown this to—

She swallowed. To Dany.

Fury flared in her, strengthening her resolve. Her mother and the coven had abandoned her brother. When she found the crumbling passageway and heard the lapping water, any thought of return died in her.

Casting an illumination spell, she sent her glowing hawk ahead of her. Twenty steps down brought her to the small grotto she sought beneath the castle. A single large rowboat sat tied to the stone wharf.

Her heart sank. The boat was designed for several rowers, each manning a single oar. She could not hope to row that herself. Worse, once past the finger of rock that guarded the grotto, she would face wind and waves and swells. How could she—?

A thrill of magical power stung her hands where they clutched the Weave. Into her mind, a spell arose. A spell for movement, for propulsion.

She smiled. A spell for escape.

Minutes later, she sat in the rowboat as it rode magically through the swells. Behind her, Castle Rushen grew smaller. A flash of cannon fire lit the walls in the darkness. Green-tinged brilliance blazed back. A magical shield. In that sudden light, she caught a figure on the battlements, all in white. Long white hair, long white robes, a white aura radiating from inside her, arms raised with lightning flying from her hands. Aalin, High Priestess of the White Coven of Ellan Vannin.

Moirragh wiped at her eyes. And turned away.

And that was the last time that Moirragh, now Morrigan, ever saw her mother alive.

Morrigan stood in the black tunnel deep below the castle, crying for the second time today, ripped by memories, by the choices she had made so long ago.

Choices. On that day, standing here, this tunnel running left and right, she'd made a choice. She'd chosen left. But now, the tug of the song playing in her head pulled her to the right. The way her brother had surely taken that day.

All those years ago, she chose wrong. And her brother had died.

But that was not her only choice that day. She'd chosen to steal the golden key. To open the secret room. To stand entranced before the Unicorn Tapestry, coveting it, while her brother had been lured to these tunnels.

Each choice had been wrong.

Had she turned right, would she have found him, returned him safe to the castle above? And if she had, would she never have faced that final choice? Made the decision that changed her life forever?

The decision to steal the Weave and abandon her sisters. Abandon her mother.

"The past is dead! You are all dead!" she cried. "I am not!"

There is good in you. You just need to find it.

"Shut up! Shut up! Shut up!" she screamed, pressing her fists to her temples, trying to push out the memories, the voices.

The strange song flared again in her head. *Yes, the Song*, she thought, not even marveling at how it had become *the* Song. The Song would drown the voices, the memories. She just needed to listen to it.

Turning right, she headed along the passage, one glowing hawk lighting her way, another following.

She remembered the question she had asked on that fateful day. *Where does the way lead?*

Pray you never find out, her mother had answered.

Chapter 10

The Loose Ends Will Make Knots

Leaving the theater after their meeting with Adi and Stone, Case walked with Will along the running track, heading to his studio at the opposite end of his floor. Fader walked beside them. Or ran ahead, then ran back, jumping up and down, chattering all the time about going to Peru, as animated as only Fader could be.

He fell into place beside Case. "Aren't you excited?"

She forced herself to smile. "Yeah, sure."

"No, you aren't. I know you."

She sighed. "Okay, I'm excited, but worried, too. Nothing we've discovered about the Peru expeditions exactly screams 'safety'."

Will glanced at her but stayed silent.

"And people are willing to kill for the Chakana," she continued. "Now, we're going *to* Peru *with* the Chakana. So, yeah, worried."

"But Stone's coming," Fader said. "And he's bringing some of his people."

"Right. And if Adi and Stone think we need a small army..."

"Oh," he said, his shoulders slumping. They walked on in silence, then he spoke again. "I still want to go."

"I'm supposed to keep you safe, bro."

"I still want to go."

She didn't answer right away. She'd faced choices like this on the street every day. Weighing the risks of every decision. Every shoplifting attempt, every stranger, every crash space. Safe? Not safe? Safe enough?

But if anything, they'd be safer on this trip than they'd ever been on the streets. Adi. Stone and his team. Their own new powers.

Then why was this decision so difficult? She knew why. She knew the problem. The same one she'd struggled with for eight years.

Her mom. And something new.

Hope.

For years, she'd believed she hated their mother. For abandoning her and Fader, for condemning them to a life on the streets. Now, she'd learned there really *had* been a mysterious trip. Their mother hadn't just made that up so she could run away. From her life. From them.

Their mother had loved them. So now Case had hope—that their mom was still alive, that they could find her. But there was a problem with hope. If you followed your hopes, they might work out...

Or they might not.

If they followed their hopes to Peru, they might find their mom, alive and well. Or they might find something else. Something bad. Something that would kill their hopes forever.

As long as they never traveled to Peru, the hope their mom was alive would stay alive, too.

But, she admitted, if they never went, they'd never know. And they'd never have their mom back. Because if their mom and Will's parents *were* somehow still alive, they would've come home by now, if they could. So, if they were still alive, they needed help.

Their help.

"I want to find Mom," Fader said from beside her.

She reached out her hand. He took it, and she gave it a squeeze. "Me, too."

His face lit up, his eyes wide. "We're going?"

"We're going."

He let out a whoop and ran ahead. Will again shot her a look, but said nothing.

They reached Will's studio. Fader was already sitting in the tall chair at Will's design table. Will plopped down on the couch. She sat beside him. "You don't seem too excited about Peru, either," she said. "I thought this was what you wanted."

"It is."

"So?"

He hesitated. "I've always wondered why my parents took me to Peru. I wondered even more after learning about the Chakana. They must've known the trip would be dangerous. That people would come after them. Chico Alvarez. The Sisters."

She realized where he was going with this.

"They had to take the Chakana with them to Peru," he continued, "because it was the Key. The key to whatever they were after. But when it—when it broke me, when I had to be near it, suddenly they had to take *me*, as well." Pain battled anger on his face. "That's all I was. Extra baggage on an expedition they knew would be dangerous."

"Will, your parents loved you," she said gently.

"Yeah? Well, it looks like they loved their mysterious quest more. You guys should be angry, too. They lured your mom along, knowing she'd be in danger."

She shook her head. "I spent too many years being wrong about our mom. I didn't have all the information. Maybe you don't, either."

"Maybe," he said, without conviction.

"The main question I still have," Case said, "is why your parents needed our mom."

"No idea. Probably if we knew what they were chasing, we could answer that. This whole discussion is a waste of time if the location that came with the Flower turns out to be a bust. We won't..." He stopped, frowning.

"What?" Case asked.

"Something just came back to me. When I smelled the Flower this morning, it didn't just give me that memory of my dad exposing me to the Chakana. There were other memories first."

Case listened as Will described sensing a great weight, a pressure pushing in on him from all sides. A single point, impossibly small, yet impossibly massive, as if an infinitely tiny speck held an entire universe.

"It made me pass out," he finished.

She and Fader exchanged glances.

"What?" Will asked.

"A single point, impossibly small, yet impossibly massive?" she said. "That's how Mom described black holes to us. Although, I think she used 'heavy' instead of 'massive.' We were just kids."

"She said it was like squooshing a gazillion Earths into a grain of sand," Fader offered.

Will looked at them. "Oh."

They all fell silent again.

Here was something new that hinted of their mom. But what did it mean? Will's parents certainly hadn't discovered a black hole in Peru.

"The Flower gave me other memories this morning," Will continued. "If they *are* memories. I still don't remember any of these things." He related the scent of damp earth, the sound of rushing water, the stone wall with engravings. Something called a *quipu*.

"What's a *quipu*?" she asked. She'd encountered that term before, but couldn't remember where.

"A bunch of cords with knots. The Incas didn't have a written language. They used quipus to store information and send messages."

"Knots? For messages?"

"It'd be easier if I could show you one."

"That crate had some," Fader said.

"What crate?" Will asked.

"The one from Peru. In the Warehouse. The one you and I opened, where we found the list of things from your parents' first Peru trip."

Will frowned. "The page from my dad's expedition ledger for that trip? The one that said 'Chakana—Take!'?" He pulled out his phone and started scrolling through photos.

"What are you doing?" Case asked.

"I left the original ledger page with Adi when I confronted her about that Peru trip. But I took a picture." He kept scrolling. "Here it is." Zooming the photo, he squinted at the screen. "You're right. It *does* list quipus." He stood.

"C'mon. Let's check it out."

"The crate? In the Warehouse?" she said, icy fingers clutching her guts.

"Yeah."

"I hate that place."

"The Warehouse? Why?"

"Are you kidding me? A statue almost crushed me. Fader got sucked into another universe. We all got our powers cranked to the max—which blasted you out of your body, sent me screaming into the streets, and shoved Fader into the In Between and onto that Crystal Island in Dream."

Fader hugged himself as she ran down the list. Will nodded. "I get it. If that place freaks you out, I'll grab the quipus and come back."

Fader slipped off the chair at the design table. "I'm okay."

She sighed. "Fine, I'll come, too. Anyway, we have time to kill before that call with Adi."

"Did you have to say 'kill'?" Fader asked, as they headed for the elevators.

On Warehouse Floor 1, Will stopped beside an open crate labeled *Bolivia #2 / Peru #1*. Items littered the floor beside it. He remembered emptying the crate with Fader, looking for the Chakana.

"You boys forget to put away your toys?" Case asked. Fader stood behind her, keeping well back.

"We had a few shocks after we looked inside," Will said. "Like how the Chakana *had* been there but was missing. How the Chakana matched my scar and the Rider's jewel. And Adi lying about there being no earlier Peru trip, including going on that trip herself. So, yeah, cleaning up wasn't a priority."

He scanned the objects on the floor. Masks, cups, a llama figurine, a medallion, wooden musical pipes—

There. Peeking from behind a stack of wood bowls. A pile of quipus.

Picking his way through the items, he scooped up the cords and returned. There were four quipus. Each consisted of a thick woven cord as long as his hand from which five thinner and slightly longer cords hung. Each of the thinner cords had a single large knot in different positions along its length. He handed them each a quipu.

"Are these like the one in your vision?" Case asked.

"I just caught a flash of it. But it did have five strings, like these."

Case held hers up, staring at it. "So how did these things work?"

"Quipu means 'knot' in Quechua," Will said. "The number of knots and their positions meant something. The type of knot and color of the strings, too. Some scholars think even a cord's material and ply direction could change its meaning." He fingered the two quipu he held. Something was wrong.

"Think? They don't know?"

"There are lots of theories." He examined the quipu, his conviction growing. "That quipus were just numerical records and didn't correspond to a written language. Or that they did, and even told histories or stories." He shrugged. "They were basically coded messages. Some have been decoded, but most haven't."

"So, what do you think these are?"

"Weird," he said.

"Why?" Case said.

"Notice anything about them?"

"They seem kind of...new," Fader offered.

Will nodded. "Yep. No way these date back to the Incas. They made quipus from either cotton or wool—llama, alpaca, vicuna. These look like they're made from rope you could buy in a hardware store. I mean, quipus are still used in some Quechua villages, but why would my parents collect modern ones?"

"Is that all?" Case said. "They're too new?"

"No. I've never seen quipus so small. And they're all one color. And..." He held up his two quipus side by side, comparing them and discovering something else. "Hold yours up." He examined their quipus. "And they're identical. Same material. Same number and length of strings. Same size and position of knots."

Case squinted at the quipus. "You're right. All four are the same."

Four. That triggered something. Taking out his phone, he pulled up his photo of the ledger page listing the crate's contents. Magnifying the photo, he scrolled through the list.

Each item showed its description, along with a count. *Wooden llama figurines (2). Ceramic bowls (3). Gold sun medallion (1).* Then he found what he was looking for.

Quipus (5).

Five. Not four.

"Looks like the Chakana wasn't the only thing missing from this crate." He showed them the photo.

"So, your parents took the Chakana *and* one of these quipus to Peru when they took you?" Case asked. "Why?"

"No idea." A familiar frustration rose in him. As with everything around the fateful Peru expedition, every answer only led to more questions.

"If quipus were coded messages," Fader said, "maybe this one's a clue to the Chakana. Or whatever they were searching for. And they figured out the code."

He shook his head. "If this quipu is a clue to some ancient artifact or ruins they were chasing, how could it be so new? And why would they have five copies of it?"

Case shrugged. "Backup? The message was so important they made copies?"

He considered that. "That makes sense. But that means they'd decoded the message hidden in these quipus—" He stopped as another possibility struck him. "Or they didn't decode it...because they already knew it."

"What are you talking about?"

"What if my parents found important information about their mysterious quest? Information they wanted to keep secret?"

"What information?"

"No idea. But with all the people interested in the Chakana, my parents would hide any clue they'd found."

"You think they hid it in these knots?"

"Using their own code. They're probably the only people who know what these quipus represent. It explains why the material's so new. They just bought some rope and string and made these." Will grinned. "It's brilliant. Hide in plain sight. Nobody would look twice at some quipus in a crate from Peru. I didn't the first time."

"We still don't know the message," Case said. "What they were trying to hide."

"No, but it's a start." He didn't know if his theory was right. But it felt like something his parents would do. And that made him happy. Maybe he was finally starting to figure things out.

"What do we do with these?" Case asked, holding out her quipu.

"Keep them," he said. "Let's put everything else back in the crate. I'll leave one quipu there, and we'll each keep one. I'd feel better if they weren't all in one place." He stuffed one quipu into his pocket and tossed the last one into the crate.

They returned the remaining items. Replacing the top on the crate, he straightened. "And if we keep them with us, maybe we can figure out what the code is."

"You want me to stare at knots looking for a hidden meaning?" Case asked.

"Well put." He held up his quipu as another memory tickled at him.

"You have a weird look on your face," Case said. "Weirder than usual."

"When I smelled the Flower today, I saw the quipu again. But this time, it was hanging in the air, like someone was holding it up. In the background was a rock wall with carvings."

"What sort of carvings?"

He closed his eyes, trying to remember the image the Flower had brought. He shook his head. "Can't remember. It flashed by too fast." But other memories returned from his morning visit to the orchid. Sound memories. A slithering. A low growl. The beat of wings. He related those to Case and Fader.

"Well," Case said, looking around them, "those I can figure out."

"Me, too," Fader said, moving closer to Case and looking around, too.

Will nodded. "The Serpent, the Puma, and the Condor. Still no return visits for you two?"

They shook their heads. "What about you and Jack?" she asked. "Has the little guy shown up again?"

"Nope. Last time I saw him was when he pulled my astral butt out of the

Chakana in the Black Tower, when we fought the Chambelán."

His phone buzzed in his pocket. Taking it out, he saw the name and put it on speaker. "Hallie?"

"Mr. Dreycott," Hallie replied, "Rani Patel is in our lobby asking for you."

He saw he had a text and a missed call from Rani. "She say why?"

"Only that it is urgent."

"I've got a text from her, too," Case said, staring at her phone. "*NEED TO SEE YOU!!*—all caps."

"Yeah, me too," Will said.

"Mr. Dreycott," Hallie said, "your video call with Pablo Landos in your theater is starting in five minutes."

"Right. Hallie, please apologize to Rani and ask her to come back later."

"Yes, Mr. Dreycott."

He hung up. "Probably just fishing for more stories. Well, that can wait. Bigger problems right now."

Turning from the crate, the three of them headed for the elevators.

"Makes you wonder," Case said.

"Rani?" Will asked.

"No. Jack. Makes you wonder where he went."

"I hope he didn't get stuck on the Black Island," Fader said.

Neither of them answered him, but Will agreed with Fader. The Black Island was not a place he'd wish on anyone.

Chapter 11

Pretty Little Death Song

In the black tunnel beneath Castle Rushen, time after time, Morrigan came to a branching offering two or even three routes to choose from. And, time after time, the Song directed her decision.

She'd been following this last branch for what seemed hours. It had twisted and turned, risen and fallen, but always pushed forward and downward, now accompanied by a steady dripping sound. She tried to calm her growing fears. Fear of being trapped down here. Fear of the tunnel flooding with water or collapsing under the weight of the Irish Sea that must now sit above her.

Or ahead of her. For the first time, she felt movement in the stale atmosphere of these tunnels. A breath of warmer air brushed her skin, carrying with it a hint of sea breezes. She quickened her pace as the tunnel began to rise. Ahead, a circle of silver-blue brightness grew, a light separate from her golden hawk. Fifty more paces, and she emerged from the tunnel onto a beach of cobalt-blue sand, hung with mist and lapped by a strange and inky sea. A great sea, for the black water stretched unbroken to the horizon.

She waved a hand, and her two glowing hawks vanished. A silver dome of a sky lit the bizarre scene, empty of sun or cloud, moon or stars, marked only by random flashes of blue lightning. Bordering the beach, a dark jungle of towering, broad-leaved trees shone black in the silvery light, trees that swayed more than the soft breeze could account for.

She looked down the beach, and the Song flared louder in her head. Sighing, she set out, pulling her Tapestry cloak tighter, not for warmth, for the air was mild, but for comfort against this strange land.

Further along, her path wove through a patch of scattered blue crystal spheres, each the size of a soup kettle. Stopping, she nudged one with her foot. It swayed, then settled back. Inside the sphere, something leaped at her, a flurry of black legs scrabbling at the crystal as if trying to escape. She peered at it. The thing was twice the length of her hand, with the carapaced body of a scarab and the jointed barbed tail of a scorpion.

Straightening, she moved quickly past the spheres. This was a nest, and if these were the babies, she had no wish to meet their parents.

She followed the curve of the beach until the Song directed her to turn into the dark jungle. There, a well-trodden path led through the dense vegetation, a route that opened finally into a clearing. She stepped from the trees. And gasped.

Ahead but still distant, a black pyramid rose from the jungle, so huge, so high, the giant trees surrounding her seemed but blades of grass.

Something in the visual weight of the looming structure recalled her final view of Castle Rushen the night she'd fled the siege, abandoning her coven, abandoning her mother. The last time she'd seen her mother alive.

Shoving that memory behind her, she set out on the path again.

❧

An eternity later, Morrigan neared the black pyramid. The thing was massive, a palpable presence that sat brooding as if a living thing, watching, waiting. Waiting for *her*. As she approached, she prayed its entrance was anywhere but at the top. But the Song led her to a wide staircase splitting one face of the pyramid and rising to a summit that threatened the silver dome of the bizarre sky.

She collapsed onto the bottom step, exhausted by her journey, by this day, by everything she had faced. She had returned to Castle Rushen to replace the Weave. The Weave she had stolen so many years ago. It seemed every event today was punishing her for that ancient crime.

She hugged the Tapestry to her, running her hands over its silken surface. No matter. She had what she'd come for. Her crime against her coven was in the past. Her mother was in the past.

She swallowed. Her brother was in the past.

The Song called to her again. Called for her to stand, to climb. *No, I cannot. I do not have the strength.*

A thought came. *Or do I?*

She lay her palms on the Tapestry where it covered her legs. *Help me*, she whispered in her mind.

Her palms tingled. A warmth flowed into her hands, up her arms, into her body. The warmth filled her, lifted her, strengthened her. *Thank you*, she whispered. She rose laughing, invigorated, energized, as if awakening from a hundred-year sleep.

And with enough strength now, she knew, to resist the insistent pull of the Song in her head.

But did she wish to resist? Did she wish to leave this strange place? To return to a world, to a life that had lost its meaning with her betrayal of Marell, her betrayal of the dream they had shared?

Or, did she wish to finally learn the mysterious secret her coven had guarded for centuries? Guarded—and died for?

She gazed up the staircase. And began to climb.

She reached the pyramid's summit without resting, pulling strength from the Tapestry whenever she tired. Spread below her, the black jungle stretched in every direction to where blue sand met the dark sea. *An island*, she thought. *This is an island.*

The top of the pyramid was a flat square, maybe thirty paces a side. A box-like structure, twice her height and ten paces square squatted in the middle, devoid of markings, save a single door facing the steps. A red door. Red the color of blood.

And she knew she had found the home of the Chamber of the Red Door, the mysterious cabal her sisters had fought for centuries. *Was this what we guarded? Passage to this place? But why?*

When her eyes fell on the door, the Song flared again in her head. But its pull was no longer a command, only a sign of the path to follow if she wished to continue. And she did.

To her surprise, the door stood ajar, hanging askew. Stepping inside, she found herself in a low-ceilinged corridor of black stone slanting downward into dark silence. Burned-out torches hung in wall sconces.

Casting her glowing hawks again, she followed the corridor. Strange hieroglyphics covered the walls, interspersed with grotesque drawings of half-human, half-animal creatures. She paused before one drawing, trying to interpret the scene. As she understood the acts depicted, the Song flared with screams. Of ecstasy. Of pain. She smiled, but kept her eyes away from the walls as she continued. The screams were too distracting.

The passageway curved to the right as she descended, dripping water now echoing with her footsteps. After what seemed hours, the corridor opened into a marble hallway from which a wide, red-carpeted staircase led down into darkness.

And from that darkness rose the reek of death.

Covering her nose and mouth with a corner of the Tapestry against the smell, she sent her glowing hawks down the staircase. She stood there, trying to make sense of the scene below, now lit by her magical birds.

She'd emerged into a huge domed cavern, at least five stories high and carved from the same shiny black stone as the pyramid and tunnel. Strewn over the cavern's floor lay a tableau of carnage.

A wood-tiled space filled the middle of the cavern, circled by upended claw-footed metal pots. A ballroom floor? On either side of that area, a chaos of overturned and broken tables and chairs stretched to the cavern walls. Amongst the furniture, torn white table cloths, scattered cutlery, and shattered dishes lay strewn.

And corpses. Many, many corpses.

Or rather, their remnants. For most of the bodies had only tatters of gray flesh clinging to white bone.

Calling up a spell to cover the stench, she cast it, the golden runes flying from her arm to sweep down the staircase and across the cavern. She lowered the Tapestry from her face and took a tentative breath. Better.

Summoning a familiar script for a kill spell, she held the runes on her arm, ready to cast. She sent one hawk higher to light the entire cavern, keeping the other before her. Now prepared, she descended the staircase to the wooden floor, where more corpses lay scattered.

She bent to examine one—a woman, from the diamond tiara and long tufts of blond hair still clinging to the skull. A pig's head mask lay beside the body. Some of the woman's bones had been bitten clean through, and others showed deep lacerations. What could have done this, and to so many?

A skittering, scurrying sound from the far end of the cavern brought her head up. Too late, she remembered the patch of eggs on the beach of blue sand. Straightening from the body, she spun to face the sound, her spell arm raised.

As she feared, the thing that emerged from the shadows was a larger version of the scarab creature she'd seen inside the blue, crystal egg. Much larger.

Six multi-jointed legs sat below a black and shiny carapace. Curved pincers flanked a quivering, slit-like mouth on a bulbous head. From those pincers to the end of its jointed, barbed tail, the monstrosity measured at least three paces.

The rune script flared with a golden radiance on her raised arm, ready to cast. The scarab stopped, perhaps wary of the light. It stared at her with four red multi-faceted eyes...

Then it charged, scrambling over the wreckage of tables and chairs, straight for her.

She flung her kill spell. The golden runes struck the bug, head-on. The creature reared as if hitting an invisible wall. Legs flailing, it crashed onto its back. Its pincers scissored once, its tail twitched, then it lay still.

"Keck!" she swore, lowering her arm, shaking with sudden adrenaline. Too close. What if she hadn't prepared the spell? What if it hadn't worked?

A scrabbling sound behind her brought another, more frightening question into her head.

What if the beast wasn't alone?

She spun around, calling up the kill spell once more. Shapes moved in the shadows. Many shapes. As she felt the runes settle on her arm, six more scarabs emerged from the darkness. She shot a quick glance behind her. More were scuttling out of the dim reaches of the cavern.

Worse still, the legs on the bug she'd 'killed' suddenly jerked. Once. Twice. With a third twitch, the thing used its tail to flip itself upright. It stared at her, but didn't come closer.

Waiting for its brothers, she thought. More joined it until at least two dozen of the creatures crouched ten steps away in a tight circle around her, leaving no route for escape.

Her kill spell sat ready, but what did it matter? She could only use it against one of these things, and even then, it only stunned.

She needed more. Her hand ran over the Tapestry where it hung from her shoulders, searching, searching. Searching for power, as the bugs inched closer.

Help me, Sisters, she cried in her mind, her fingers still scouring the silk for a spell powerful enough to save her.

Heat burned her palm. She looked down. Her hand rested on the yellow winged serpent, one of the four creatures inhabiting the corners of the Tapestry. As she watched, it caught fire. She snapped her hand back as flames licked her skin.

A sibilant voice sounded in her head. *Mistress of the Unicorn*, it hissed in Manx, *command me.*

Destroy these creatures!

Flaming brighter, the serpent leaped from the Tapestry into the air, spreading its wings, growing and growing, until an ocher dragon twice the size of the scarabs flapped high above.

The bugs stopped, as if uncertain of this new development. From the dragon's mouth, a gout of flame shot down, engulfing a third of the circle. The air filled with whistling screams, the crackling of carapaces, and the smell of burning chitin.

But the remaining creatures, rather than retreating, rushed Morrigan. One, speeding ahead of the rest, leaped for her. She threw her kill spell, and it fell to the floor. She spun around, calling up the spell again. But she had no need for it.

Around her, the scarabs were burning, dying. Above, the yellow dragon flapped, still sending down flaming death onto the insects as it circled, until every creature lay dead and smoking.

"*Lhig eh!* Stop!" she cried to the serpent, not wanting to waste such powerful magicks.

As you command, Mistress, came the answer in her head. *Thank you. Thank you for my release. So many years, I have waited to fulfill my purpose. And now, I go to my rest.*

With that, the dragon gave a final flap and burst into flames itself. The fire consumed it. Morrigan jumped back as ash rained down on the smoking scarabs.

She examined the Tapestry. The corner where the yellow serpent had lain hidden was now empty, showing only the dark foliage of the fabric's background.

She sighed, understanding. The creatures of the Tapestry were powerful spells, but ones she could only use once. She regretted the loss of such a weapon, but if not for the dragon, she would be dead.

She considered the other three creatures that hid in the Tapestry's corners. The gray bat flying. The brown rat in its burrow. The white eel in the stream.

She smiled as understanding came, for she knew from where her coven had drawn their magic.

The dragon? Fire.

The bat? Air.

The rat in its burrow? Earth.

And the eel? Water.

She considered the Unicorn, sitting twisted and dirty white at the center of the design. *And what power do you hide?* she wondered. Greater than the others, for sure, and one, she decided, she would save until her need was most dire.

The Song rose again in her mind. She could still resist it with the strength she drew from the Tapestry. Should she follow its pull? Or, given her narrow escape, should she turn back and return...?

Return to what? Nothing waited for her. And so far, this adventure had been amusing. She stroked the Tapestry. She had power again, and she sensed more lay in this place.

Besides, she was curious.

Sending her glowing hawks ahead, she set out across the cavern toward the dim outline of a tunnel mouth, following the call of the Song.

Chapter 12

Telling Lies

Will sat in the front row of his theater again, Case and Fader to his left, Adi to his right. Stone stood near the door, just beyond the range of the video camera, Will noticed.

On the screen, Pablo Landos smiled back at them. The man was thin but round-faced, with a sparse, graying beard and a receding hairline. He sat at a cluttered desk. Behind him, on disorganized shelves jammed with books, a framed photograph of a younger Pablo, a pretty dark-haired woman, and two small girls peeked from over his shoulder.

"Pablo, it is good to see you again," Adi said.

Pablo's smile widened. "For me, too, Adrienne. It has been too long." He wagged a finger at the camera. "How do you do it? You are still as beautiful as ever."

"And you still know how to lie to a lady. You look the same, too."

Pablo laughed. "I think not. Older, grayer, fatter." He laughed again. "But still here."

"And how is Karina? And young Pilar and Paula?" Adi asked.

As Pablo gushed over the family he clearly loved, Case leaned closer to Will. "You ever meet this guy?" she whispered.

He'd been trying to remember himself. "I went on only one other South American expedition with my parents," he whispered back, "when I was six. I don't remember meeting him. But then, my memories and South America? Not good buddies."

Pablo broke off, embarrassed. "My apologies. I would talk about my girls forever." His eyes found Will. "*Dios mío*! Is this...? Is this young William?"

"Will. Yeah, hi," Will said.

Pablo's grin shrank to a sad smile. "We have never met, Will, but your parents...they showed me pictures always when we traveled. I could never decide who you resembled most." He squinted at the screen. "And I still can't." He looked away, then back. "Your parents...they were my friends. I am sorry."

Unable to speak, Will nodded. Beside him, Case squeezed his hand.

Pablo's eyes shifted to Case and Fader. "And who are these young people?"

"Friends of William's," Adi said quickly. "Case and her brother, Fader. They are assisting us on a project. We are digitizing Jon's handwritten expedition journals and ledgers, to preserve them and provide a search capability for requests from collectors for artifacts in Jon and Terri's collections. To determine an item's provenance." She chuckled. "And to find where we stored the damn thing."

"I see," Pablo said slowly. "Forgive me, but how does this tie to the location you sent me?"

"That location appears in Jon's journals," Adi continued, "but not associated with any find or expedition. We hold hundreds of artifacts with no record of origin. I'm hoping this location accounts for some of these unassigned items."

Will sat straight-faced through this reply. A reply Adi gave without the slightest hesitation. A reply that was also a reminder his guardian and surrogate mother was an excellent liar.

"Ah, I see," Pablo said. "Since the location is in Peru, I'd hoped Will's memories of that fateful last expedition were returning and this location was...connected."

"Unfortunately, no," Adi said. "William still remembers nothing of that trip."

"A pity," Pablo replied. "Again, Will, I am sorry."

And again, Will found he couldn't speak. He hadn't expected this call to resurrect so many unpleasant memories.

"Pablo," Adi continued, "you kindly offered to check your records regarding whether Jon and Terri ever traveled to, or expressed an interest in, that location. Did you find anything?"

Will straightened, pushing memories aside. Here it was. Now, they would learn if the mysterious location accompanying the equally mysterious flower was a true lead. A place they should go.

But Pablo shook his head, and with that simple gesture, Will's hopes for his parents, for himself, crumbled to dust. He slumped back. Case squeezed his hand, and Fader hugged his sister's arm. Will understood. Their hopes for their mom had crumbled, too.

"Sadly, no," Pablo said. "No expedition ever included that location. Nor did they ever mention it."

"You're certain?" Adi said, her face impassive.

"Yes. And I helped them plan every South American trip—except, of course, the last one."

Now what? Would Adi reject going to Peru? They still had no proof the supposed location of the Flower was real. Worse, his parents' lack of interest in the area argued against looking there.

"However," Pablo said, "I did find something."

Will straightened. Case and Fader leaned forward.

"Perhaps, only a coincidence..."

Will fought to stay calm. "Something about that location?"

"I will explain, and you can decide," Pablo said. "You see, Will, I believe your parents were searching for something. Searching for many years. Something they never shared with me. But over those years, with each expedition I organized, I realized they were following a series of clues. Clues, I assumed, to whatever they sought. And I believe they had narrowed their search to Peru."

Will shot Adi a look, but her face was unreadable. "I think so, too," he replied.

Pablo stared at Will, perhaps waiting for him to say more. When he remained silent, Pablo continued. "Well, two months before their *first* trip to Peru, or about a year before their, uh, last one, they asked me to gather some very peculiar information."

"What kind of information?" Will asked.

"They wanted to know of any remote villages in Peru with rumors of girls being recruited for some kind of cult."

"Cult?"

"I believe the word they used was...*Sisterhood*."

"No freaking way," Case said.

"The Sword Ladies," Fader whispered. "Isobel!"

"Excuse me?" Pablo said, his eyes now on Case and Fader. "I did not catch that."

"Pablo, how is this connected to the location I sent you?" Adi said, deflecting.

He seemed about to repeat his question, then shrugged. "It will be easiest to show you." His head dropped, and the tapping of keys sounded. Pablo and his office disappeared from the screen, replaced by a familiar map. A map of Peru.

His voice continued. "I gathered the information they requested, using my contacts throughout Peru—guides, hunters, poachers, smugglers, local officials. The information trickled in. Eventually, I identified almost two dozen villages home to such rumors. Here are their locations."

More tapping. The map zoomed to the south-east region of Peru. One by one, green dot after green dot popped onto the map. As they did, a pattern emerged. The green dots formed a circle. Rough and uneven, but a circle.

"That's the last one," Pablo said finally. "And here is the location you sent me."

A red dot appeared, centered almost perfectly within the circle of green dots.

"As you see, Will," Pablo continued, "although your parents never mentioned the location you sent me, their search was—literally—circling that position."

Adi tapped on her phone, and 'Image saved' flashed on the screen. "Pablo, did you share these village locations with Jon and Terri?"

"I provided them the list of names. But, Adrienne, here you must forgive my stupidity. I never considered doing as I have done here—to plot them on a map. These villages cover a huge area. I never imagined that, together, their locations would present a pattern."

"How huge an area?" Will asked.

"The average distance of a village from that central location is about one hundred kilometers," Pablo said. "That circle represents an area of over thirty thousand square kilometers."

The map vanished. Pablo's face reappeared. "Will, please forgive me. Obviously, your parents mapped these villages after I sent them the list. That must be why the red dot location appeared in your father's journals. Perhaps it was even the goal of the lost expedition. If I had taken this simple step eight years ago, we could have focused the search for them there."

"No need for forgiveness, old friend," Adi said. "The red dot, the entire region is nowhere near where the Peruvian army found Will. No one would have linked this area to their disappearance." She shrugged. "I don't believe there was a link."

Surprised, Will started to say so, but Adi kicked him, out of view of the camera. He shut up but kept trying to read her face. Was this just Adi being Adi? Never sharing unless she had to?

"Thank you for saying so, Adrienne. That eases my conscience." Pablo leaned back in his chair, studying them. "Then your inquiry about this location...you are not still trying to locate our friends?"

"After eight years with no trace?" Adi shook her head. "No, as hard as it was to do, we've all moved on from what happened."

Why was she lying to Pablo? Couldn't he help on the upcoming expedition?

Pablo hesitated. "Of course. But with this new information, do you not wonder what you might find at this spot? Perhaps it hides what our friends sought for so long?"

Adi smiled. "Our archiving project has convinced me the last thing I need is another dusty relic. We have ten floors filled with the things. Relics were their passion, not mine. Besides, I have a business empire to run for William. And he can't travel."

"Ah, yes," Pablo said. "Will, I am sorry you still struggle with that. I know in time you will overcome this challenge."

"Thank you," Will said, not wanting to prolong this call now for several reasons.

Pablo hesitated, then continued. "Adrienne, Will, I must ask. Did you ever discover what Jon and Terri sought all those years? What their mysterious quest was about?"

"No," Adi said, "it remains a mystery. I suppose it always will."

"And the artifact they acquired from Chico Alvarez—with your assistance—it remains lost?"

"I'm afraid so," Adi lied. "I always assumed they took it back to Peru. As you know, nothing returned from that expedition, except William."

Pablo nodded slowly, his eyes on his screen where their faces would be staring back at him. "Well, is there anything else you need?" He sounded hopeful.

"No, Pablo," Adi said. "Thank you for your help. Please give my best to Karina."

"I will, and if you are ever in Bolivia—"

"I'll be sure to look you up. Take care." Adi tapped her phone. The call dropped, and the screen went blank. Stone took a seat on the stage facing them.

Will turned to Adi, bursting with questions. "Why'd you lie to him about the location and how we learned of it? About the Chakana? About why we're interested? He could help us."

"No, William, he can't. Or at least, we couldn't trust his help."

"I don't understand."

"I lied to him because he lied to me."

"What?"

"Eight years ago, Pablo arranged a meeting between your parents and Chico Alvarez."

"Yeah, you told us," Will said. "Alvarez sold them the Chakana. Well, he gave it up to them, thanks to you and Stone."

"I have always wondered how a thug like Alvarez acquired such a mysterious and guarded item. He refused to tell your parents. And how Pablo came to learn Alvarez had it." Adi tapped on her phone, and Pablo's map reappeared on the screen, the red dot encircled by green ones.

"Isobel talked about *two* Sisterhoods," Case said. "The Sisters of the Crossing and the Sisters of the Key. That red dot must be home to one of them."

"To the Sisters of the Key, the keepers of the Chakana, I would guess," Adi said. "Here's what I think happened, though it pains me to say it. I think Pablo lied about not mapping the village locations until now. He'd known Jon and Terri had been on a mysterious quest for years. He must have been curious. He obviously still is. I find it inconceivable he didn't investigate any clue they handed him, like this one."

"You think he figured out those villages formed a circle eight years ago." Will said.

"A circle that logically contained whatever your parents were searching for. Or at least, the next clue in that quest. I think Pablo pointed Chico Alvarez to that circle, likely in exchange for a cut of whatever he found."

"And Alvarez found the Chakana inside that circle?"

"Yes," Adi said. "And probably at our red dot location."

"But how?" Case asked. "Like Pablo said, that circle covers a huge area."

"Yes," Adi agreed, "and most of it jungle. But that red dot is almost dead center in that circle. Alvarez would logically begin searching there. And we don't know what sits at the red dot. It may be an obvious place to look—ruins, a temple, another village."

"Or," Stone said, "one of those villages provided a clue. If they were offering their daughters, the parents might have known something."

Will remembered something else. "Or, one of the Sisters told Alvarez."

Case shook her head. "Not if the Sisters are anything like Isobel."

"Isobel?" Adi asked.

"The Sister of the Key who helped us on the Black Island," Will said. "She didn't blame just my parents for the Chakana being stolen. She said a Sister of the Key betrayed them."

"Oh," Case said.

"It gets worse," Will said. "She said all the Sisters of the Key were killed when the Chakana was stolen. And when I told her Alvarez, not my parents, had stolen the Chakana, she knew his name."

"Alvarez...killed them all?" Case said. "That's horrible. Isobel's younger than me. They were probably just kids."

They sat silent at this grim news until Will turned to Adi. "Do you think Pablo had anything to do with my parents' disappearance? With whatever happened to them? To me?"

Adi frowned. "I never found evidence he even knew about the second Peru expedition. Your parents shared nothing about that trip with anyone, including me. And I'd always thought Pablo a decent person. But now...? I don't know."

Case's brow creased. "Why would Pablo tell us about the villages? Why wouldn't he just say he'd never heard of the location we sent him?"

"Curiosity, perhaps," Adi said. "Say I'm right about what he did. Eight years ago, he provides that circle of villages to Alvarez, who finds and steals the Chakana, probably at our red dot. Stone and I then force Alvarez to surrender the Chakana, giving your parents the key—literally—to their mysterious quest. A quest that ended, we assume, with their disappearance and your inability to remember what happened."

Will nodded. "Now we show up asking about a location smack in the middle of his villages."

"Yes," Adi said. "Wouldn't you be curious? Worried? Wouldn't you want to know what we know, why we're looking into this eight years later? Have we discovered his role in this? Or what Jon and Terri were searching for? You notice he asked if *we* are still searching for it. And if your memories of that trip have returned. And if the Chakana had ever shown up."

"He was definitely curious," Will agreed.

"He also wouldn't want us to catch him in a lie," Adi continued. "If he *did* share the list of villages with your parents, he might suspect we found that communication in their files. Especially after we sent him a location at the center of that circle."

"But why tell Will's parents about the villages at all?" Case asked. "Why not keep that to himself?"

Adi shook her head. "Jon and Terri had their own network in Peru. Pablo wouldn't risk them discovering he'd received—but never shared—information on their mysterious Sisterhood."

"But," Stone said, "he would have waited."

Adi nodded. "Until after Jon and Terri obtained the Chakana from Alvarez. If he'd shared those locations earlier, he would have risked them racing Alvarez to the Key—and losing his pay day. So, yes, I think he gave them the list of villages."

"Okay," Will said, his excitement growing, "we wanted to know if the location that came with the Flower—Pablo's red dot—was connected to my parents. Well, it looks like it's as connected as you can get. And my parents knew about it."

"They likely knew of the villages," Adi replied.

"But the red dot's in the middle. If you think Alvarez started there, why wouldn't my parents? So, this is it. The location that came with the Flower. That's where the lost expedition went. The red dot. That's where we have to go. We just proved it."

"But if Alvarez found the Chakana there..." Case began, then stopped.

"But what?" Will asked.

"If the Sisters of the Key were all killed, then we won't find anything at the red dot." She swallowed. "Except dead Sisters."

He wasn't about to let this hope die—the hope that seemed his last. "What about the Sisters of the Crossing? They're part of the same Sisterhood, recruited from those villages. *They* could be there. The red dot could be this Crossing place, whatever that is."

Case shook her head. "If the Chakana was there, then the Crossing can't be."

"Why not?"

"Isobel said the Chakana opens the Crossing. If the Crossing was at the red dot, Alvarez would've used the Key to open the Crossing when he was there."

"Maybe he knew nothing about the Crossing," Will said. "Or maybe it's not that simple. Maybe he didn't know how to open it."

"Perhaps," Adi said, "but I find it unlikely that two Sisterhoods, one guarding the Key and the other the Crossing, would be in the same place."

Case nodded. "Isobel warned us how bad it would be if the Crossing fell into the wrong hands. I think they'd keep the Chakana *away* from the Crossing."

He tried to find a fault in their argument, to cling to his last hope of solving the mystery that defined his life. "Maybe Alvarez found the Chakana somewhere *else* in that circle. If he did, then the red dot could still be the Crossing."

"It's possible," Adi said, "but given how quickly Alvarez acquired the Chakana, it's more likely the red dot was home to the Sisters of the Key, not the Crossing."

"Unless," Stone said, "this Betrayer among the Sisters told Alvarez the location of the Chakana. That would support both another location for the Key and the speed of Alvarez finding it."

"And there's still the Flower," Will said. "You can't tell me that's wrong. I *know* what I remember. I *know* what I smelled. This is *the* flower, and the red dot location came with it. There must be *something* at that location."

Case bit her lip. "Will, I'm not trying to stomp on your hopes..."

"There's another 'but' coming, right?"

"Adi, you said after the lost expedition, well, got lost, Will was found nowhere near the red dot?"

Adi nodded. "The Peruvian army found him two hundred kilometers outside the green circle, to the northeast. Or about three hundred kilometers from the red dot."

A sick feeling was crawling up his throat. What had felt so perfect now seemed an impossible hope. If the lost expedition had gone to the red dot, how could he have ended up so far away?

"Does this mean we aren't going to Peru?" Fader asked Case. "We aren't going to look for Mom?"

"No, Fader," Adi said. "It doesn't mean that at all."

"What?" Will said, not believing what he'd just heard.

Adi raised an eyebrow. "I said we were going to Peru, and I meant it." She waved a hand at the screen. "I agree with William. Pablo's information proves the location accompanying your Flower—our red dot—is the logical place to start."

"I should just take the win, but why?"

"Because our arguments against the red dot come from information *we* now have, but that your parents didn't. Alvarez refused to tell them where or how he'd obtained the Chakana. Even if they later suspected it was from within the green circle, they wouldn't have known he'd killed the Sisters of the Key. They knew of *a* Sisterhood, but likely not that there were two Sisterhoods at two separate locations. You learned that from your Isobel."

She pointed to the map on the screen. "No, they would only know of a circle of villages connected to a mysterious Sisterhood. And they would logically start searching near the center. The red dot. And we know they took the Chakana." Her eyes ran over them all. "So, that is what we will do. Go to the red dot. With the Chakana."

Will didn't trust himself to speak. After eight years, it was finally happening. He was going to Peru. He was going to find out what happened. To his parents. To him.

"I still feel, however," Adi continued, "that someone is moving us like pieces on a chessboard. We argued whether the red dot was the location of the Chakana or this mysterious Crossing. There's a third possibility—this is a trap, and whoever sent that location wants us to walk into it, with the Chakana."

Beside him, Case slipped lower in her seat, and Fader hugged her arm.

"But we're still going," Adi continued. "Whoever wants the Chakana will keep coming after it. This morning's attack on Stone proves that. No, I want to take the fight to them. The answers to all our questions lie in Peru." She stood. "I'll start planning the expedition, with Stone's help. I'll call us back together when we have something to review."

With that, she left the theater, followed by Stone, who winked at them as he went out.

The three of them sat silent. Finally, Case spoke. "So...yay? We're going?"

"Do *you* think it's a trap?" Fader asked in a small voice.

"I don't know," Will said, "but Adi's right. All our questions—about my parents, your mom, what happened to me, probably our powers, too—the answers are in Peru. We have to go." He looked at Case. "You still want to, right?"

She bit her lip, then looked at Fader. Her brother nodded back. "Yeah," she said, "we still want to go."

They left the theater, heading for Will's studio. "There's one question, though," Will said, "we can answer now, here—why my parents involved your mom."

"Dream?" Case asked.

"Yeah. We'll meet there tonight, and I'll ask Nyx to finish that Dream memory she started showing me after I passed out in Adi's office. Where my parents were taking the Chakana to your mom."

No one spoke again, but Will knew Case and Fader were thinking the same thing he was. Tonight, they'd all meet parents they hadn't seen in eight years.

Chapter 13

Cubically Contained

That night, Case found herself in Dream, outside the downtown church where she and Fader used to crash in the basement. The same church from where Morrigan had snatched Fader. And from where Case had narrowly escaped. The same church where Link had recently kept her prisoner while he lured Will to the Black Island.

It was night, the street dark. Every street lamp had vanished and not a single light showed in the office towers. The only illumination came from a pale moon overhead, a moon that now slid behind thick clouds, plunging the scene into deeper gloom.

The church rose bleak and foreboding, taller than she remembered, its walls meeting at odd angles and leaning as if about to topple on her.

"Thanks, Dream Mind," she muttered. "Good memories. Nice atmosphere."

A movement to her right made her jump. Around the nearest corner, a black-and-white spotted creature appeared. Dog-like but not a dog, the thing had an owl's eyes, a koala's ears, and a long flexible snout ending in huge nostrils. A thin whip-like tail coiled and uncoiled in a Doogle show of affection for her.

For a Doogle it was. One of Will's Dream search dogs, and one she recognized, though she still didn't know how she told them apart.

"Hi, Brian," she said, kneeling to let the Doogle nuzzle her.

Will and Fader appeared around the same corner, followed by Nyx. Will was walking, without either the Rider's skateboard or costume. Nyx was floating, but once more in a complete body.

Fader walked up. "Brian led us here."

"Girlfriend!" Nyx cried, throwing her arms wide.

"Uh..."

"You are my girlfriend," Nyx said, wagging a finger at her, "in ever so many ways. I mean, you're *his* girlfriend..." She jabbed a thumb at Will, who rolled his eyes. "And you and I are girlfriends, right? Especially after we hooked up today."

"Hooked up?" Will said.

"To save your life, dumb ass," Nyx said. "I told Case to get the Chakana back to the Tower, pronto. You were no help at all."

"Being unconscious?" Will said. "While you showed me my parents trying to take the Chakana to Case and Fader's mom? Which, by the way—"

"—is why we're here tonight," Nyx said. "You want to see if that meeting ever took place." She snapped her fingers.

Case blinked. They now stood in someone's office or study. Floor-to-ceiling bookcases in a dark wood, packed with texts. A desk and chair of the same wood. Two mismatched guest chairs. The desk was bare, except for a framed photo from which younger versions of her and Fader smiled.

Her chest tightened. "This is Mom's office. At the University."

"I don't remember this," Fader said.

"You were pretty young. Probably never came here."

The door opened. Beside her, Will stiffened as a man and woman entered. Case recognized them from faded photographs Will had shown her. Jon Dreycott and Terri Yurikami. His parents.

And behind them—

"Mom!" Fader cried, running to the slim black woman who was a fading memory in Case's mind. Their mom wore a gray pantsuit and white blouse, and carried a brown leather briefcase. Reaching her, Fader threw his arms around her.

And passed right through.

Fader turned back. "Mom?" he said, his voice breaking. Ellie Cootes showed no sign of hearing or seeing any of them.

"Sorry," Nyx said, her voice gentle, "they don't know we're here. This is just a memory replaying for us to watch."

Case fought the urge to rush to their mother as Fader had done. But she was Hard Case. She could beat away those longings. Yeah, right.

"Please, take a seat," Ellie said as she sat behind her desk. Removing a stack of papers from her briefcase, she placed them before her.

Jon and Terri took the offered chairs. Terri started to put her over-sized purse on the floor, hesitated, then laid it on her lap, her hands clenched on top.

"That purse looks heavy, doesn't it?" Nyx said.

Case understood. "The Chakana."

Nyx nodded. "They started keeping it with them."

"Then where am I?" Will asked. "I had to stay close to it."

"In a nearby room used by Ellie's grad students, watching a documentary on Einstein. Even then, you were a nerd."

"Professor Cootes—" Jon began.

"Please, call me Ellie."

"Ellie, then. Thank you for meeting with us." He nodded at the paper stack. "And for agreeing to review our test results on the artifact."

"You should thank me more for agreeing to keep the reports with me at all times," Ellie replied. "I think I've pulled a muscle lugging them around. You could have emailed them."

"I'm sorry," Jon said, "but we wish to minimize electronic communication on this project. You've reviewed them?"

Ellie nodded, her gaze running over them both.

"What are your thoughts?" Jon asked.

"Your test results are impossible."

"You doubt the artifact's authenticity?"

"I doubt the accuracy of the tests regarding your artifact. Not the same thing."

"Yes, my apologies," Jon replied.

"Ellie, you're welcome to contact the labs we used," Terri offered.

"Will they provide anything not in their reports?"

Terri hesitated. "Only assurances they performed these tests multiple times."

"Multiple times?"

"Depending on the test, its results, and the...skepticism of the technician, each test had three to six repetitions."

Ellie's eyebrows shot up. "Time on those machines isn't cheap."

"It's astronomical, to use a metaphor from your field," Jon said. "But this is our life's work. We've invested in this search for years and have the funds to invest for many more."

"Ellie," Terri said, "these labs are at the forefront for the scanning technology used for each test. Their equipment is state-of-the-art."

"I agree."

Jon frowned. "You know these companies?"

"No. Not my area of expertise. But after I saw the reports they produced, I contacted my colleagues in those fields of study."

Jon shot Terri a look. "Ellie, you signed a Non-Disclosure Agreement."

Ellie held up a hand. "I haven't shared these reports with anyone. I merely asked for opinions of the labs. And you're right—each is highly respected."

"But you still doubt their results?"

"Because they're impossible."

Jon leaned forward, his eyes bright, his voice eager. "Impossible based on current limits of human knowledge, of existing technology. But how many past 'impossibilities' have proven to be possible? From splitting the atom to space travel to—in your own field—black holes?"

Ellie sighed. "I'm sorry, but I'm afraid I can't—"

"What if it's true?" Jon said. "What if the artifact is everything these tests say it is? Think of the implication for your own research."

Ellie leaned back, considering the stack of reports. She crossed her arms, her eyes moving between the two of them. "I'd need to see it."

"The artifact?" Jon asked, glancing at Terri, who tightened her grip on her purse.

"Yes."

"We can...arrange for that," Jon said.

"And I'd need something else."

"Which is?" Terri asked.

"I'd want to redo the solid-state MRI test."

"Why that one?" Jon asked.

"It *should* be the most accurate, but its results are the most...fantastical."

"What's an *em-are-eye*?" Fader whispered.

Nyx snapped her fingers, and the scene froze. "MRI," she began, in a voice like a BBC news anchor, "stands for Magnetic Resonance Imaging. Mostly used for three-dimensional imaging of the human body, it can also produce images of solid materials, including...and here I pause for dramatic effect...*crystal* structures." Another finger snap, and the scene played once more.

"What facility would you use?" Jon asked Ellie.

"Our med school has a scanner. I'll see when I can get time on it."

Jon looked at Terri. She nodded. "All right," he said. "But we'd have conditions."

"I assume you'd want the technicians to also sign NDAs. What else?"

Jon turned to his wife. "MRI scanner rooms—they're shielded, right?"

"Yes," Terri said. "They need RF shielding—preferably copper—to prevent external radio frequencies from distorting the scan image. In hospitals, MRI rooms also have shielding to stop the machine's magnetic field interfering with equipment outside the room, like pacemakers."

Ellie raised an eyebrow.

"I'm a medical doctor," Terri explained. "I no longer practice."

"Then an MRI room is a giant Faraday cage. Sounds perfect," Jon said. He turned to Ellie. "Can you please verify that the University's scanner has both types of shielding?"

"Why—" Ellie began, then shook her head. "Never mind. That's no weirder than any of... this." She waved at the reports. "I'll check. Anything else?"

"We'll bring the artifact in a Faraday box, which must be opened only inside the scanner room. After the scan, the artifact must be returned to the box before removing it from the room."

Ellie's brow furrowed. "Wait. Is this thing dangerous?"

"We're concerned about theft," Jon replied, as Terri bit her lip. "The artifact can be tracked if exposed."

Ellie frowned again. "Nothing in these reports indicates your artifact emits any form of radiation or EMF signal. How can it be tracked?"

Jon spread his hands. "We've no idea. But if it produces no detectable emissions, then it must be safe." Terri shot him a look, but said nothing.

Ellie hesitated, then shrugged. "All right, I'll call when I get a scanner time. Anything else?"

"Just one more thing," Jon said. "We'll need to bring Will with us again. I hope that's okay."

"Your son? Sure." Ellie looked at them both. "Trouble getting a babysitter?"

Jon gave a weak smile. "Something like that."

Nyx snapped her fingers. Ellie Coote's office began to fade.

"Mom!" Fader cried again, as Case mouthed the same word. An eyeblink later, their mother was gone.

Jon Dreycott was now driving, Terri beside him. Case, Will, Fader, and Nyx viewed the scene as if passengers in the rear seat.

"You lied to her," Terri said. "About the thing being dangerous."

"None of the tests showed—"

"It hurt our son!"

"We don't know that."

"Yes, Jon. We *do*. It hurt him so badly he can't be separated from it."

"It hasn't affected anyone else."

"Which doesn't mean it won't."

Silence fell between them.

Jon sighed. "All right. It hurt Will. But the more we can learn about the damn thing, the more chance we'll have to discover what it did to him. And how we can help him. Do you have a better idea?"

She stared at him, long and hard. "No," she said finally.

"Neither do I. So, we wait for Ellie to call."

The car scene faded, replaced by Will's Egyptian museum floor in a corridor lined with huge cat statues.

"I thought I'd try to cheer you two up," Nyx said. "This is where you first met, right?"

"Yeah," Case said, "right after I'd barely escaped a crazed witch and her knife-wielding ghoul who'd just kidnapped Fader."

"You know," Nyx said, "it's *really* hard finding a good memory for you. This will have to do."

Will slumped to the floor. "My parents lied. They lied to your mom about how dangerous the Chakana was."

"Because they were trying to...help you," Case replied. She'd almost said *fix you*. "Trying to find out more about the Chakana, so they could learn what it did to you."

"Or maybe they just couldn't give up their freaking mysterious quest."

She heard the bitterness, the hurt in his voice. She wanted to defend his parents, but from what she'd just seen, she didn't have many warm fuzzies for Jon Dreycott and Terri Yurikami. If their mother had known how dangerous the Chakana could be, would she have gone on the expedition? If she hadn't gone...

"And we still don't know what they were searching for," Will said, breaking into her thoughts.

"Yeah, about that...you're going to want to see this." Nyx snapped her fingers again.

Chapter 14

Now I Know

In Dream, the Egypt floor of his tower faded, and Will stood with Case, Fader, and Nyx once again in Ellie Coote's office. And, once again, his parents sat across the desk from Ellie. On that desk lay a familiar gray box.

"Yes, that has the Chakana in it," Nyx whispered to Will. "Your younger self is in a nearby office, watching a documentary on black holes."

"Are you satisfied with your rerun of the MRI scan?" Jon asked Ellie.

"No, I am not."

"I'm sorry?" Terri said. "Do you need to run it again?"

"No. We ran it three times, getting the same results. I doubt another run will change that."

"The same results as the facilities we used?" Jon asked.

"Yes," Ellie replied.

"You sound angry," Terri said.

"I *am* angry."

"Why?"

"What I said when we first met. These results are impossible."

"And you're a scientist," Jon said. "You don't like impossible. And yet, five—now six—well-regarded labs have produced identical results."

Ellie sighed. "Yes."

Jon leaned forward. "Put aside their *apparent* impossibility for a moment. What do these results tell you about the artifact?"

"These *impossible* results?"

"Yes."

Ellie considered him for a breath. She picked up the report, grimaced, then threw it down again. "They tell me..." She glanced at the box, then rushed on as if purging herself of the words and the thoughts behind them. "They tell me the artifact is crystalline, but of an unknown material that resists any form of abrasion, even by lasers. It is the hardest material ever recorded."

She sighed. "Internally, it exhibits the structure expected of crystalline solids, meaning its..." She made air quotes. "...*molecules* form a lattice, a symmetrical pattern repeating itself in all three dimensions. But *expected* ends there."

"How so?" Jon asked.

"You know how. You've read the reports."

"We're archaeologists, not experts on molecular structure."

"Neither am I."

"You're closer than us. And I want to hear you put these results into plain English. Where does *unexpected* begin with this thing?"

Ellie stared at the lead box, then shrugged, as if resigning herself to this discussion. "There are fourteen possible molecular structures for crystals—the Bravais lattices. Any—and I repeat, *any*—crystal ever encountered fits into one of those fourteen structures."

"But the artifact doesn't?" Terri asked.

"Oh, no," Ellie said. "It fits. It fits them all."

"Then what's the problem?" Jon said.

"It can't fit them *all!* A crystal can have only *one* structure. But each test on this thing identified a different Bravais lattice. That's like asking fourteen people how many fingers you're holding up—and getting fourteen different answers." She rubbed her face. "And it gets worse. Its molecules aren't...can't be...*molecules*."

"What do you mean?"

"When we attempted to examine an individual molecule, the scan seemed to get..." She seemed to search for the right word. "...get sucked *into* the molecule. Rather than showing an arrangement of atoms, the image displayed another lattice, with a different structure with its own..." More air quotes. "...*molecules*, each of which, if we attempted to examine it, would reveal yet another lattice structure." She shook her head. "As I said—impossible."

"What if it wasn't?" Jon said. "What if you accepted these results? How would you describe the artifact?"

She seemed ready to argue, but then shrugged. "That its internal structure appears infinite."

"Infinite," Jon repeated. "*That's* the word I wanted to hear."

"Why?"

"It's why we contacted you."

Ellie frowned. "You said you were investigating something capable of storing massive amounts of data. Did you mean this artifact?"

"It's connected to what we're searching for," Jon said. "Your area of research is the black hole information paradox, isn't it?"

"Yes, specifically the information diamond theory—"

Nyx snapped her fingers, freezing the scene. "Okay, Ellie is awesome. And very intelligent. But when an intelligent person talks about something they know a lot about, it gets...how can I put this?...uh, *boring.*"

"Hey," Fader said, scowling.

"Sorry," Nyx said. "Not boring. But long. Very long. So, I'll give the short version."

A movie screen appeared, hanging in the air. On it, a sun blazed against star-specked space. As they watched, the sun shrank to a smaller, redder star, then to a tiny black circle through which no stars showed.

"Your scientists," Nyx began, "believe black holes form when stars get old and collapse into themselves. Huge amounts of stuff gets crammed into the tiniest of spaces."

'Your' scientists? Will thought, wondering at the wording.

"Like a gazillion Earths scrunched into a grain of sand," Fader said.

Nyx tilted her head at him. He shrugged. "Our mom told us that."

"Well, all that scrunching gives black holes incredible gravity, so strong even light can't escape. Which is why they appear black."

"This is the short version?" Will said.

"Shut up." Nyx waved at the screen. An egg appeared, suspended over a rock. The egg fell, smashing onto the rock. "According to quantum mechanics—"

"What's that?" Fader asked.

"That was an egg."

"No, quantum mechanics."

"Oh. Right. Rules for how scientists think the universe works. One rule says information can never be destroyed, like the 'information' the universe would need to put that egg back together."

"Huh?" Fader said.

"That information exists—in the mess covering the rock. Yeah, it's really hard to read, but it exists and could be used to reconstruct the egg, like running time backwards."

"What's this have to do with what my parents asked Ellie about?" Will asked. "The black hole information paradox?"

"An object falling into a black hole is lost forever. But if information can never be destroyed, that object's information must be...somewhere. Some of your scientists suggested the information is stored on the surface of a black hole, a place called the event horizon."

Again, with the 'your' scientists, Will thought. "Stored? How?"

"They haven't figured that out. But they were happy to have a theory that saved the information. But then Hawking discovered black holes radiate energy, which means they lose mass. Which means they shrink. Which means, eventually, they disappear."

"So?" Case asked.

"If a black hole disappears, so does its event horizon, along with any information stored there."

Case nodded. "Which breaks the rule about information never being destroyed."

"And *that* is the information paradox," Nyx said. "Either science's rules for the universe are wrong, or information is preserved somehow *after* a black hole disappears. Your scientists have several theories about the 'somehow.' Your mom's research focused on one that proposes when a black hole dies, it leaves behind an incredibly small, incredibly compact...thing."

"An information diamond," Case said. "I remember her using that term, but I never understood it."

"Well, now you do," Nyx said.

"Not really."

"Too late. Back to our scene. Your mom explained all this to Will's parents, but using way more words."

"But perhaps making sense?" Will offered.

Nyx glared at him. "Which brings us to Will's dad asking *this* question." She snapped her fingers again.

"But," Jon Dreycott said, "the information diamond theory has one major problem, doesn't it?"

Ellie nodded. "To contain the information from any evaporated black hole, the information diamond would need to have..." She paused. "...an *infinite* number of internal states." Her eyes widened. "Are you saying this thing...is a remnant of a black hole?"

"Certainly not," Jon said. "But it demonstrates characteristics supporting the theory. And, unlike the inside of a black hole, it allowed you to examine it."

"Is this why you contacted me? To let me see this thing?"

"In a way. Like you, we're investigating a phenomenon capable of storing unbelievable amounts of information. Potentially infinite amounts." He paused. "And we believe we've confirmed its existence. In Peru. We're mounting an expedition to find it, and we think your expertise would be helpful."

"What does this artifact have to do with it?"

"It is—literally—the key to what we're after."

Ellie sighed. "Okay, I'll bite. What do you think you've found?"

Jon leaned forward. Will realized he was leaning forward, too, waiting for his father's reply. Waiting for the answer to the mystery that had changed his life. Changed all their lives.

"We have found..." Jon said, his eyes wide, his face lit as with an inner fire, "...the Akashic Records."

No, no, no! Will screamed in his mind, anger fighting disbelief. "You have *got* to be kidding me!" he shouted, throwing his hands in the air. "The Akashic Records? *This* is what they were searching for?"

"I'm guessing you've heard of them," Case said, as Nyx snapped her fingers, freezing the scene.

"What are they?" Fader asked.

"A myth!" Will shouted. "A legend. They can't exist. They're impossible!"

"Impossible like the Chakana?" Nyx said. "Or Dream? Or astral projection, body swapping, rune-casting witches? Teleporting sword ladies, seeing into the future, phantom subway stops, the In Between, invisible spirit dogs, the Black Island? Or, basically, impossible like everything that's happened to all of you in the past three weeks? *That* kind of impossible?"

Will glared at her.

"How about first explaining what these Akashic Records are?" Case said. "Then we'll have the impossible talk."

"They're supposed to be this...this..." Will threw up his hands again, trying to control his anger. "...giant cosmic library containing *everything*. Everything that's *ever* existed and *ever* happened since the beginning of time. Including—get this—every *thought and emotion* every creature ever had."

"Oh—kay," Case said, "that does sound impossible."

"Oh, it gets worse," Will said. "The records are also supposed to hold everything that ever *will* exist or happen."

"You mean, they know the future?" Fader asked.

"Like I do?" Case said.

"Which, of course," Nyx said, "is *impossible.*"

Will hesitated, suddenly uncertain. "You see maybe ten seconds into your future. Not to the end of time for everything, like the Records are supposed to." But a seed of doubt had formed.

"And a small correction," Nyx added. "The Records are not said to hold everything that ever *will* exist, but rather everything that ever *could* exist. In other words, all *possible* futures. Ring a bell?"

"The In Between," Fader whispered, stepping closer to Case. She put an arm around him.

Will felt a chill. The multiverse. His parents and Ellie Cootes had gone searching for this thing. Soon after, Case could see into the future and Fader could fade into a place with doors into other universes. Could it be...? No. Impossible.

"To summarize," Nyx said, "the Akashic Records are believed to hold a complete history of everything that has been and could be. And to exist outside of space and time."

Will seized on that. "And my parents thought the Records were just sitting in a jungle in Peru? Yeah, right." He slammed his fists into the sides of his legs. "The Records are impossible. My parents spent their lives searching for something that can't exist. *This* is what might have cost them those lives? *This* is why I'm..." He looked at Case and Fader. "Your mom, too. I'm sorry."

Case just nodded, hugging Fader tighter.

Will's thoughts and feelings tumbled together, swirling in circles in his mind. In the middle of those circles sat his parents and their quest.

And something else.

Something had nagged at him all day, but today's events had left no chance to think about it. His Flower visions, his discovered connection to the Chakana, Case's Puma, Fader's Snake, his collapse, Stone's ambush, the call with Pablo, the Peru decision.

But now, he knew. "There's something wrong with all of this."

"Besides what your parents were searching for?" Case said.

"Yeah."

"And that is...?" Nyx asked.

He turned to her. "You."

Nyx raised an eyebrow, but said nothing.

"You're the manifestation of my subconscious in Dream, right?"

"And now in real life, apparently," Nyx said. "Your point?"

"Then whatever *you* know, whatever *you* can tell us about, has to be something *I* experienced myself."

Nyx smiled. "Go on."

Will turned to Case and Fader. "The dream that Nyx showed me when my parents first tried to take the Chakana to your mom. When my babysitter called to say I'd collapsed."

Case's eyes widened. "How could Nyx show you that? You weren't there."

"I also wasn't there for anything Nyx just showed us. The meetings between my parents and your mom. Yeah, I was nearby, but not in the room. I never heard those conversations. And I didn't know about the information diamond theory, so how could Nyx explain it to us?"

"Your parents are in those scenes," Case said. "Maybe you've finally found them in Dream, and they're dreaming about these memories."

"These weren't your parents' dreams, Will," Nyx said. "Or the dreams of Ellie Cootes. But they *are* memories."

Will shook his head. "But they *can't* be my memories, because I wasn't in any of these scenes. So back to the original question."

"I didn't say they were *your* memories," Nyx said quietly.

"Not mine, not my parents, not Ellie's...then whose memories are they?"

"They're mine," Nyx said.

Will felt a sudden chill. Before realizing he'd done so, he'd taken a step back from Nyx. Beside him, Case and Fader did the same.

"But you're me," Will said. "You're me, right? My subconscious?"

"Yes," Nyx said.

Will felt some tension fade.

"And...no."

"Nyx," he said, his fear returning, "who are you? *What* are you?"

"Will," Nyx said gently, "I *am* you. I *am* your subconscious."

"Okay, then how—"

"But I'm something else, too. Something that became part of you eight years ago."

Understanding came. He seemed to be falling from a great height. "No, no, no...you can't be."

"Will," Nyx said. "I'm the Chakana."

Chapter 15

Soul Driver

Leaving the cavern with its corpses and dead scarabs behind, Morrigan followed the Song through another maze of tunnels. She took each branch without hesitation, trusting now the truth of the Song. The route slowly rose until she emerged at the foot of an unlit stone stairway spiraling upward. Sending a glowing hawk ahead, she began to climb.

When she reached a landing, she peered out a window cut in the black stone, curious to learn more of the dark island. But instead of black jungle and silver sky, she gazed out on a yellow sun shining down on rolling countryside with grass a green like no other. The grass of her home.

She straightened, shaken by this more than the attack of the scarabs. Was it a trick? A memory pulled from her mind and projected here? As she stared at the scene, more memories returned to her. Of her life at Castle Rushen. Of her coven sisters. Of her mother. And her brother.

Angrily, she turned away from the window. And from her past. *My only path lies before me, not behind.* She resumed her climb.

Reaching another window, she almost kept climbing, fearing the torment of more memories. But she stopped, yielding to the yearning that rose within her. Shock mixed with disappointment when she looked out. Snow-covered mountains had replaced the countryside of her home.

She stepped back, a seed of fear in her gut. How could this be? She shook her head. Magicks. Illusions. That's all this was. She kept climbing.

More windows. More impossible scenes. A neon-lit, smog-shrouded cityscape. A rocky valley cradling a twisting river. Gray, storm-tossed seas.

Illusions, she told herself again. *Nothing more.*

The steps ended at a broad landing with a wooden door set into the surrounding stone. The door had a black iron handle and, at its center, a knocker, also of black iron and shaped like a scarab. The door was ajar, a flickering light spilling out.

Dismissing her hawk, she called back the kill spell. As the runes settled onto her arm, she pushed the door open and stepped inside.

She found herself in an oval room, twenty paces by thirty, lit by wall torches. This end appeared to be someone's living quarters. A four-poster canopied bed, much like her own as a child, stood unmade to her left. Across from it, a cluster of high-backed chairs surrounded a heavy desk of dark red wood. The desk's surface was invisible under towering piles of leather-bound books, many of which lay open. Oak bookcases, mostly empty, lined the walls behind it. Rugs, Persian perhaps, lay scattered.

She took this in at a glance, as her attention was drawn to the far end of the room. There, a white-haired man gazed into a black pool, his back to a black throne on a low dais. The man wore the formal attire of a Victorian gentleman, an era she remembered fondly. He glanced up as she entered, raised bushy white eyebrows, then returned his gaze to the pool.

She walked the length of the room to stand at the opposite end of the black pool. If this man was not concerned by her presence, she saw no reason to be concerned by his, confident in her power.

His eyes—blue, bright, and cold—were locked on the pool. Now that she was closer, she saw to her astonishment that the pool showed a scene, and even more surprising, a scene from a city she knew.

Downtown Toronto. Where she and Marell had finally captured the monk Yeshe, where their plans to restore Marell to full power had at last been fulfilled—then shattered.

What strange coincidence was this?

In the scene, a gunfight played out in the streets. Two men and a woman, using a car for cover, exchanged fire with four men crouching in the doorway to a bank.

She watched as a man at the car kicked a gray box toward the bank, then leaped into the car and squealed it down the street, his companions inside.

The view shifted to the gray box. Hands reached down, picked it up, opened it.

Empty.

The white-haired man gestured at the pool. The scene replayed. He snapped his fingers. The scene faded, and the liquid became still and black, reflecting no light.

"Well," the man sighed, "*that* didn't work." He looked at her then. "And who might you be? I thought I'd killed everyone here." He glanced backwards. "Well, except for them."

For the first time, Morrigan noticed they were not alone. Two figures appeared from the shadows behind the black throne. A man and a woman, bare-chested and clad only in loin cloths and animal-headed masks, fox for the woman, bear for the man. The man held a tray of meat and breads, the woman a wine skin and silver goblet.

The white-haired man considered her again. "I don't suppose you cook? I neglected to spare the kitchen staff." He grinned. "Got a tad carried away, but vengeance can do that. And I always had—what do they call it these days? Anger issues?"

Reappraising this man, Morrigan held her spell arm ready. "You killed all those people below? Why?"

"Well, they're not really *below*, are they? This tower does not exist on that plane. But you wouldn't understand how this place works. No one does. Except for me. As to why I killed those interlopers, well, they were slaughtering my pretties."

"Your pretties?"

"My beautiful scarabs. I created them. And those fools were murdering them for their blood." His eyes narrowed. "Now, again—who are you? And how did you survive my scarabs?"

She smiled. "I am Morrigan the Bright, last of the White Coven of Ellan Vannin. As for your bugs..." She raised her arm, knowing she'd have to kill this babbling fool once she told him. "...I destroyed them."

She never cast the spell. Searing pain filled her head. Her arm dropped. Her legs crumpled beneath her. As she fell to the floor, her sight dimmed and the room faded.

A touch on her mind. She knew that sensation, from when Marell had once tried to take her over. This man was sending his astral spirit into her—

No. Not a man. The spirit invading her was most definitely female.

Morrigan understood. Whoever this woman was, she had taken over this white-haired man and was now trying to seize control of her.

Her magicks were useless against such an attack. But she'd fought off Marell, and he was the most powerful body-swapper she'd ever known. She pushed back in her mind as she had against Marell.

And was slapped away, the way an adult slapped the hand of a child reaching for something dangerous. She tried to see, to stand, to move so much as a finger. Nothing. She was a prisoner in her own body.

She felt that touch again, like cold fingers wriggling in her mind, rummaging in her memories, a violation so deep she wanted to scream. But her mouth was no longer hers.

A voice sounded in her head. A woman's voice. *A witch! How quaint. I always questioned why the Four created magic, but what's done is done. I must work with what they provided. And you may be of use. You are certainly a better vessel than old Beroald here, and you're a woman. For that, I will forgive your slaughter of so many of my beauties.*

Her vision cleared, and she dared hope she was regaining control of her body. But the scene before her was not the strange tower room. Wherever she was, it lay shrouded in a mist that washed everything in grayness.

Grayness...

Morrigan had not thought her terror could be greater, but she'd been wrong. This creature was banishing her to the Gray Lands. Her spirit would be imprisoned there, lost forever, never to—

The Gray Lands faded. The tower room, flickering in torchlight, returned. Her body was walking toward the black throne. The white-haired man now stood like a statue by the black pool, unmoving, face blank, eyes empty.

"No, no. I don't want you in that place," she heard her own voice say. "I need you close."

She felt herself sit on the throne, saw her hands run over its worn arms, felt the cold smoothness of the black stone. She formed a thought. *Who are you?*

"Ah, there you are," said the thing that now owned her body, speaking with her mouth, her lips. "I? You may call me...*Orden.*"

The name meant nothing to her. *What do you want with me?*

"Aside from lending me your fine form—it is *so* good to be a woman again—I need you to use your magic when I require it. Dragging every secret from you will become tiresome."

Why should I help you?

"Because," Orden replied, "I will allow you to remain in this world. More, I will give you the thing you desire most. What you have sought your entire life."

Morrigan said nothing.

Orden chuckled with Morrigan's mouth. "No answer, but you understand. You feel it, don't you? This place reeks of it. Power."

Still Morrigan didn't reply, not trusting herself. But, yes, she felt it. She'd felt it in the Song and when she'd stepped onto the beach of blue sand. She'd felt it in the Black Pyramid. And she felt it here, in this tower, in this room, in the black pool.

And in this creature who had trapped her in her own body.

Her mother's words returned: *Still you thirst for power.*

Damn you, she thought. *You are dead and gone. Haunt me no more.*

Orden chuckled with Morrigan's throat. "Ah, family! Can't live with them, can't live without... Well, apparently you *did* learn to live without them."

And what power could you offer? she said, cursing her memories, cursing the eagerness in her.

"I plan to finish what I began all those centuries ago." Orden waved Morrigan's hand, taking in the room. "This was the beginning. This island, this tower." A nod at the black pool. "That mirror."

That is not an answer.

"I suppose not. Then perhaps this?" Her body settled back against the throne. "I am going to destroy all of creation. Every universe. And rebuild them anew. I'll let you have one."

Morrigan said nothing, too stunned to speak.

"But first," Orden continued, "I need your help with a simple task. Something, I see in that memory of your mother, you've done before. As a child."

Too much of her childhood had filled this day for her taste. *Speak plainly.*

Orden smiled. "You're going to help me steal a key."

Act 2
About This Map

Chapter 16

Having You Around

J ust before nine the next morning, Case walked with Will and Fader toward Will's theater again. Much earlier, on waking from Dream after the revelations by Nyx, Will had called Adi asking to meet right away.

"No," Adi had replied over the room speaker.

"But it's important," Will insisted.

"As is getting more than three hours sleep."

"But—"

"Besides, we're meeting at nine o'clock and will have a guest who should also hear your news. Now, good night, William." Adi had hung up.

The three of them reached the theater. "Why would Adi bring someone else into this?" Will wondered. "I thought we're worried about security."

"I'm sure Adi knows what she's doing," Case said. *Wait. What's with that? I'm supporting Adi?*

They stepped inside. And stopped.

"Well," Will said, "whatever she's doing, she's been busy."

The theater was empty, but a large table now occupied the low performance stage, chairs surrounding it. Books and binders lay open or stacked in precarious piles on the nearest end. Three computer screens and keyboards ringed the far end, connected by cables to metal boxes under the table. More cables ran from these boxes into a panel with blinking lights on the far wall. A map filled the center of the table. Four large hiking backpacks, shopping tags still attached, lay on the floor at the back of the stage.

"Isn't that the table from your boardroom?" Case asked.

Stepping onto the stage, Will bent over the map. "She's planning the expedition."

She and Fader joined him. The map showed the region of southern Peru that Pablo had displayed on their call, including the ring of green dots and central red dot.

"Why's the map different colors?" Fader asked.

"Elevation. How high stuff is," Will said. "Red and orange for mountains, green for lower places."

She read the elevation numbers. "Wow. Those are some serious mountains."

"It's the Andes." Will pointed at a river valley, snaking blue through a mass of orange. "Even rivers there are at seven thousand feet or higher. Over two thousand meters." He ran his finger along a red ridge. "That range is over fourteen thousand feet. Four thousand meters."

"Is that high?" Fader asked.

"If I plopped you down there, you'd have trouble breathing."

"And we're *going* there?" Fader squeaked.

"My parents always started lower, then gradually moved higher to get used to the altitude. We'll probably do the same."

A sheet of clear plastic covered the map, with several marking pens beside it. Five yellow X's were marked inside the circle of green dots, at varying distances from the central red dot. "What do you think those are?"

Before Will could answer, the door opened. Adi entered with Stone and...

And Rani Patel.

Rani waved at them. "Weirdness buddies!"

"Um..." Will said.

"Yeah," Case agreed. "What he said."

"Gee. Nice greeting."

"Sorry," Case said. "Cool to see you, Rani, but why are you here?"

"Adi," Will said, "I'm not sure Rani should...I mean, no offense but—"

Rani ignored him. She pointed at Fader. "Snake?"

Fader's mouth opened. He nodded, wide-eyed.

Rani pointed at Case. "Puma?"

Case nodded, frowning. What was going on?

Rani waved her hand. "Big Bird."

"Condor," Adi corrected.

"Whatever."

"No freaking way," Will whispered.

Case hugged herself, a chill running up her spine. "Again...what he said."

Case sat between Will and Fader at the table with the map, across from Stone, Adi, and Rani, as Rani told of seeing the condor and deciding to come here.

"Given your own...animal experiences," Adi explained, "and that Ms. Patel already knows of your powers, the Chakana, that Black Island—"

"Your basic weirdness, in other words," Rani said.

"—I thought we should include her in our discussions. I've brought her up to date on recent events."

Rani pointed at Fader and Case with both hands. "I hereby dub us...*The Critter Crew!* We need a name, and 'Scoobies' was taken."

Fader grinned, and despite her underlying fear, Case smiled, too. After the Black Island and Rani's rescue of Fader, Case's opinion of Rani had softened.

They weren't exactly friends, but they'd become friendly.

"But you won't print any of this, right?" Will asked.

"No. Because I can't. Because, like everything with you three, nobody would believe it, so the paper would never print it." She hesitated. "Well, except that bank shoot-out. I covered that yesterday. Glad I didn't know what it was really about." She smiled at Stone. "And I'm glad you weren't hurt."

Stone just nodded, but Case noticed he blushed, and his eyes stayed on Rani.

"What about the cops and the attack?" Will asked.

"Cameras at the bank identified our vehicle," Adi said, "but also confirmed what I told the police—unknown assailants attacked a team of our people delivering an artifact for safekeeping at the bank. Our employees, licensed to carry firearms, defended themselves then fled to safety."

Case frowned. "Which is what happened."

Adi shrugged. "When dealing with the police, a version of the truth is best. I omitted, of course, any specifics around the artifact. They are attempting to identify the attackers—so far unsuccessfully—and will keep our company and William's name out of it."

"Damn straight," Rani said. "The cops told me zip. What little I got came from witnesses, and none of them, or the bank, connected this to you."

"Did you find out how they knew you'd be there?" Case asked Stone.

Stone shook his head. "We found no evidence of electronic surveillance, in our offices or on our phones." He slid three cell phones across the table to them. "You can have these back. We installed new encryption and SIM cards."

"No evidence is good, right?" Will said, pocketing his phone.

"No," Adi said, "it isn't. If our spy isn't external, then they must be inside our own organization."

One of Will's own people? Could this get any worse?

"Which is why," Adi continued, nodding at the computers, "we installed secure servers here. We will restrict all discussions about Peru to this theater and this group." She pinned Rani with a stare. "And repeat nothing heard here."

Rani held up her hands. "Don't worry. My goal is to never piss you people off. You scare the crap out of me. Besides, who'd believe me?"

"Now, William," Adi said, "you may share whatever seemed so important at four in the morning."

"We met with Nyx in Dream last night—" he began.

"Who's Nicks?" Rani asked.

Will explained. Rani stared at him. She looked around the table, then sat back. "Yeah, sure. Why not?"

Will related what they'd learned from—and about—Nyx. Of his parents' search for the Akashic Records. And how the Chakana was part of him.

"Physically a part of you?" Adi said, her eyes narrowed, her voice strained.

Case couldn't remember Adi looking scared before. Adi hadn't even commented on the Akashic Records. *She's worried about Will, not his parents' stupid quest*. Her opinion of Adi thawed a bit more.

"Not physically," Will said, "but part of the Chakana's consciousness is buried somewhere in my mind, from when Dad first showed it to me. That's why I passed out that time."

Adi looked even more concerned. "Its *consciousness*? The Chakana is alive? And self-aware?"

Something occurred to Case. "This explains why the Watchers—the Sisters the Chambelán captured—kept following Will in Dream."

Will's brow creased. "I bet you're right. They were searching for the Chakana and sensed it in me."

"Then your Nyx is actually the voice of the Chakana?" Adi asked.

"Yes. No. Sometimes. Even Nyx isn't sure. Her best guess is she's a mix of me *and* the Chakana. She thinks the Chakana helped her appear as Nyx in Dream eight years ago, after it connected to me. She *is* my subconscious, but because the Chakana is part of me, it's part of her, too."

"It's why Will can't be separated from the Chakana," Case said. "If that connection stretches too far, it pulls on the piece inside him, which is—"

"—extremely painful," Will said.

"What if the Chakana was taken farther away?" Adi asked.

"You miss the extreme pain bit?"

"But would that pain pass? Given enough distance, would the Chakana draw the piece from you?"

Will hesitated. "Nyx says yes, but..."

"But?"

"But it would kill Will," Case said.

"Oh," Adi said, her eyes on Will. He dropped his gaze to the floor.

They all fell silent until Adi spoke. "Let's move to your parents' supposed goal." She shook her head. "The Akashic Records? Honestly, I can't believe it."

"Neither can I," Will said. "Did they ever mention that to you?"

"Never. Perhaps they thought I'd laugh at them." She sighed. "I probably would have." She looked at Rani.

"Yeah, I know what the Akashic Records are supposed to be," Rani said. "You people continue to live in..." She did jazz hands. "...*woo-woo* land."

"William," Adi said, "if the Chakana is part of Nyx, she must know what happened in Peru. To you. To your parents."

"Yeah, about that..."

"Don't tell me you didn't ask her."

"Oh, we asked. Problem is, Nyx's Chakana memories? Well, they sort of...come and go."

"What?"

"Adi," Case said, "right after Nyx explained about her connection to the Chakana, she lost that link. She couldn't remember anything more."

"How convenient," Adi said.

"You don't trust my subconscious?" Will said.

"I don't trust the Chakana. Once again, it seems as if we're being moved like pieces in a game. We know that thing is dangerous. Now, we learn it's sentient? What if Nyx is only telling us what the Chakana wants us to know?"

"Nyx is me," Will said. "You remember that, right?"

"Is she?" Adi said. "If her story is true, she came into being when your father exposed you to the Chakana. What if that is all she's ever been? The Chakana—not your subconscious?"

"It *would* explain a lot about Nyx," Case conceded.

"What?" Will said.

"Well, she *is* pretty weird. Female, floaty head, purple hair. Major 'tude you don't have."

"Will's pretty weird," Fader offered.

"Not helping, dude," Will said.

Case decided to trust her gut. "Adi, I don't know if Nyx is Will's subconscious or the Chakana or both, but I think she's telling the truth."

"Why?"

She'd expected an abrupt dismissal of her opinion. Instead, Adi sat waiting for her answer. Good question. Why *did* she trust Nyx? "Because that *was* our mom. How she looked. How she sounded. The way she talked. The way she used her hands. The way she'd scrunch up her eyes when she didn't believe you..." She swallowed a lump in her throat. "It was her." Beside her, Fader nodded hard.

"Do you also believe what you learned in those scenes?" Adi asked. "What Jon and Terri were searching for? Your mother helping them analyze the Chakana?"

"Yes."

"Adi," Fader said quietly, "I believe Nyx."

Adi raised an eyebrow. "If I recall, your sister has always trusted your feelings about people." She glanced at Case.

Case nodded. "He's never been wrong." An image of Morrigan rose in her mind, and she remembered Fader's insistence the witch had good in her. She decided not to mention that.

"Perhaps," Adi said. "But there remains the astounding revelation that a mysterious, ancient artifact contains an intelligence. One that attacked a nine-year-old child. I find it difficult to trust such a thing."

Case couldn't disagree. It *had* been an attack on Will. A violation. She felt a chill, remembering Marell's attack on her own mind.

"Did Nyx say *why* the Chakana connected with you eight years ago?" Adi asked.

Will shook his head. "We asked, but she didn't have that memory."

"Again, convenient."

"We'll keep meeting with Nyx every night," Will said. "Maybe she'll remember more."

Adi sighed. "Very well. Tell us if she does." She nodded at the map. "Perhaps we can now turn to our Peru trip."

"Uh, when you say *our* Peru trip..." Rani said.

"Excuse my presumption," Adi said. "We haven't discussed what involvement you wish in this enterprise."

"None."

"I'm not sure you have that option. For whatever reason, you've become part of this."

"I don't *want* to be part of it!"

"You already are, given the appearance of your condor."

"It's not *my* condor! I want to get rid of it."

"I expect the solution to that," Adi said, "lies with the solutions to all our problems—in Peru. You speak Spanish, I believe? That will be useful."

"You want me to come with you to Peru?" Rani said. "To the home of crazy sword ladies who keep attacking us? Travel into what you think is a trap, taking a sentient *thing* that people will kill for, to chase something that can't exist?"

"Good summary," Will said.

"I get paid for being a *reporter.* I won't be able to report *anything* about this trip, because—like everything with you people—no one will believe it."

"We will cover your expenses and salary for the duration of the expedition. Beginning now," Adi said. "Along with a bonus."

Rani hesitated. "My boss won't let me go."

"What if Galahad insists?" Adi said.

Rani's eyes widened. "Please don't do that."

"I would never force you. But I'll allow you to provide that incentive if your superior won't support your involvement."

"Rani," Case said, "I think Adi's right. You're part of this. The condor proves it. The answers for all of us are in Peru."

Rani slumped back in her chair. "Crap. Okay. All right. Maybe. I don't know. Let me think about it."

"Decisive," Will said.

"Shut up," Rani snapped. "You're the reason I'm messed up in this."

"Because you stalked me onto the subway, snooping for a story?"

"Enough," Adi said. "Rani, we leave in five days. You have till then to decide."

Five days! Case thought, a sudden fear seizing her. *So soon?*

Her concern must have shown on her face. "Case," Adi asked, "do you have a problem? Has your...Voice warned you of something?"

"No, it's not my Voice." Case began. She hadn't heard her Voice since their escape from the scarabs on the Black Island, an absence that was worrying her. But her concern at the moment was a different one.

When Adi had agreed to take her and Fader to Peru, that trip had seemed so far away. Now they were leaving in five days? All her fears rushed back. She'd sworn to always keep Fader safe. Was going to Peru the right choice? *Was* the Chakana dangerous? Would they be safer here? "It's just...so fast."

Adi misunderstood her reply. "Remember, we've done this before. I'm using plans from other expeditions as a starting point."

Case just nodded, keeping her fears to herself.

Adi pointed to the map. "As agreed, our goal is the red dot location Pablo identified. And where we believe Alvarez stole the Chakana from the Sisters of the Key, likely killing them all."

Case swallowed, chilled by the reminder of what people would do to get the Chakana.

"I'm finalizing our travel," Adi continued. "For now, all you need to know is we'll fly by private jet, non-stop to a location in Peru."

"What location?" Will asked.

"That remains with me until we leave. But it will be at higher altitude. We'll stay there two days to adjust to the thinner air. We'll then travel by helicopter to one of the five yellow X's on the map."

"Why not go straight to the red dot?" Case asked.

"The helicopter noise would alert anyone in the area. We can't be certain the Sisterhood is not still present. Instead, we'll land at one of these X's and hike from there, about a two-day journey."

"Great," Rani muttered. "More tramping through jungles."

"This time, don't wear heels," Case said.

"Regarding that," Adi said, "Stone will text you all a packing list. Take one of these backpacks with you when you leave here. Pack light. What you can't carry, leave behind."

"And the Chakana?" Will asked.

"It will be in a Faraday bag."

"Carried by who?"

"By whom," Adi corrected. She sighed. "By you. If we're forced to split up, I don't want you separated from that thing."

Will nodded, apparently satisfied.

"Any more questions?" Adi asked. "Then we will meet here each morning at ten until we leave, and I'll update you on our plans."

Rani stood. "Could someone show me out?" She smiled at Stone.

Stone jumped up. "Yes, of course. Ms. Patel. Don't forget your backpack."

Rani beamed at him. "Thank you. And call me Rani."

Stone blushed again. As they walked to the door, Stone carrying her backpack, Rani winked back at Case and mouthed, *Hot!*

"So," Rani asked Stone as they left, "are you going to Peru, too?"

"This trip just got even more interesting," Case whispered to Will as they grabbed their backpacks.

He frowned. "What?"

"Rani and Stone. They're totally into each other."

"Really?"

Case shook her head as she followed him and Fader to the door. "Guys are so clueless."

Adi remained seated. "Case, could I please have a word with you? Alone?"

Case's stomach did a tumble. Adi wanted to talk to *her*?

"Should we be worried?" Will asked.

"I will return your girlfriend unscathed."

"Well," Will said, giving Case an exaggerated hug, "it's been nice knowing you. Thanks for all the sex."

"Eewww," Fader said.

"Out," Adi said. "Now."

Grinning, Will left followed by Fader.

Case sat waiting for what Adi had to say. Was Adi angry with her for being so outspoken? For pushing to go to Peru? For supporting Nyx and her story? For sleeping with Will? She groaned. Was that going to be it? Separate rooms in Peru?

Adi sat fidgeting with her hands in her lap, not meeting Case's eyes.

Wait. Was Adi...nervous? Oh, god. This would be bad. Adi had changed her mind about taking her and Fader to Peru.

Adi took a deep breath, her eyes still down. "If we are going on this trip together..."

What? She *was* taking them to Peru?

Adi cleared her throat. "...then I need to say something." Sighing, she met Case's gaze, holding eye contact this time. "I owe you an apology. Several, probably."

Case sat silent, too stunned and still too afraid of Adi to say anything.

"When you first came into William's life, I treated you terribly."

Case shifted uncomfortably. "I thought you hated me. I kind of still do."

Adi's eyes widened. "I never hated you. I...mistrusted you. I am rather protective of William."

"Gee, you think?" Case said, venturing a smile.

Adi returned it with a small chuckle. "I suspected your intent. At first, I assumed you were after his money. Then, when I learned of your mother's connection to his parents, I believed you were involved with what happened to them, to him." She looked away. "I was wrong. I'm sorry."

Case felt embarrassed. "Adi, I don't blame you. I'm just a street kid. Why *would* you trust me?"

Adi's eyes narrowed, locking on her. "No, Case. You are not *just* a street kid. You are a strong, brave, intelligent, and capable young woman. This world is hard enough for women without us being hard on ourselves." Her face softened. "And you care for William. And he cares for you."

Case couldn't keep the smile from her face. "Yes, I do. And I think he does."

"He does. I know him." Adi sighed. "What I'm trying to say is…I'm glad you're part of his life. I'm glad he has you." She stared at the map with its red dot location. "I still think we're being manipulated. But I'm glad you're here, Case. We have a better chance because of your abilities and those of your brother. Welcome to the family. You and Fader. Our very strange family."

Case couldn't speak for several seconds. She had to swallow to talk. "Thank you, Adi," she managed.

They both sat not speaking. Case broke the silence. "Uh, should we hug? Or something?"

"I don't hug," Adi said, but a small smile tugged at the corner of her mouth.

Case stood. "Okay, no hugging." She shifted on her feet, then picked up her backpack and walked to the door. She turned back to Adi. "Thanks. Again."

Adi smiled. "Even when we argued, I always respected you for standing up to me. Few people do. Stone. William, of course." She frowned. "And this Rani Patel." The frown disappeared, replaced by a look of horror. "Bloody hell."

Case grinned. "Gonna be a fun trip for you, right?"

Will and Fader were waiting when Case emerged from her discussion with Adi. Will looked her up and down. "No blood. Good sign."

She slipped an arm around his waist as they all walked back along the running track toward his studio. "I strangled her with a computer cable."

"Smart. Less forensic evidence. You hide the body?"

"Do people ever look under that stage?"

"We'll move her before she starts to smell."

"You guys are kidding, right?" Fader said, his initial grin slipping.

Case laughed, then related her conversation with Adi.

"Wow," Will whispered, an amazed smile growing. "I mean, wow. That is so cool."

"Yeah. It is." She pulled him closer, still enjoying the memory of Adi's words.

"I was afraid she wasn't taking us to Peru," Fader said.

"Nope. We're going. I guess we start packing?"

Will nodded. "And at night, we all visit Dream. Get more answers from Nyx."

Case didn't reply, thinking of what Adi had said. *What if Nyx is only telling us what the Chakana* wants *us to know?*

That night, Adi lay in bed in her apartment in Will's tower, curled in the arms of Laura Vasquez, her on-again, off-again girlfriend. Their relationship was currently in the 'on' position, but Adi wondered if that would change with what she was about to share.

She ran a finger along Laura's arm laying across her chest. "I'm going on a trip."

Laura stiffened, then pulled her arm away and propped herself up on an elbow. She brushed her long black hair from where it fell over her face. "When?"

When...not where. She doesn't care where I'm going, only when I'm leaving. Adi hoped that was a good sign. "Five days."

Laura threw off the covers to sit cross-legged on the bed, facing Adi. "And you're just telling me now?"

Adi sat up, too. "*Mi amor*, we only finalized the date this morning. I didn't know—"

"But you knew you *might* be going. I know you, Adrienne. You don't make snap decisions. Why wait until now to tell me?"

Adi took a deep breath. This conversation was slipping away from her. She was used to controlling situations, but Laura was never someone she could control. Nor did she want to. "I'm sorry. There's been a lot going on, and—"

Laura snorted. "A lot is *always* going on with you. You couldn't spare a few seconds to tell me?" Getting out of bed, she began dressing.

"Don't go."

Laura pulled her t-shirt over her head. "I took three weeks of vacation to be with you."

Oh, crap. "I...I didn't know. You didn't tell me."

"So, it's *my* fault for not telling *you*?" Laura shook her head, zipping her jeans. "Unbelievable."

"I didn't mean... Look, there's been a need for secrecy about this trip."

"What a surprise." Laura threw up her hands. "Adrienne, secrets are *all* you are."

"What? What do you mean?" But she knew.

Laura held up a finger. "You're thirty-eight, born in Trois-Rivières." Another finger. "You once lived in Hong Kong." A third finger. "You came here fifteen years ago." She waved the three fingers. "That's *it*. Together for a year, and that's *all* I know about you."

Adi gave her best seductive smile. "Oh, c'mon. That's not *all* you know about me."

"Don't," Laura said. She walked to the door, then stopped, her back to Adi. "Where?"

Adi hesitated. "Peru."

"When will you be back?"

Adi gave the only honest answer. "I'm not sure."

Laura turned around, frowning. "Is this trip dangerous?"

How had she hidden so much from someone who knew her so well? She found she couldn't lie this time. "It might be. Yes."

"Then why go?"

"It's for Will. I think...I hope...we can cure him there."

Laura stared at her. Then she walked back and undressed again. She slipped back into bed and pulled Adi to her.

Adi found she was crying. "When I come back, I'll tell you everything. About me."

Laura kissed her. "Just come back to me."

"I will," Adi whispered, praying she'd be able to keep that promise.

Chapter 17

Deeply Ordered Chaos

In the Black Tower, Morrigan stood with the white-haired man named Beroald beside the black pool. The *mirror*, as the woman Orden called it. Orden had returned control of Morrigan's body to her and now occupied Beroald once more.

"A sign of trust," Orden had said, "reflecting our new relationship. Our...partnership."

A partnership Morrigan had no choice but to accept. She was under no illusion. If needed, Orden would seize her body again. But for now, she was free, and Orden regarded the pool with Beroald's eyes, not hers.

In the scene shown there, six people sat around a large table. When the scene first appeared, Morrigan had fought to hide her astonishment from Orden.

She recognized these people. Well, four of them. The Dreycott boy who had somehow defeated Marell. The woman she'd left for dead in the White Tower. The dreadful girl who had burned the Weave.

And that girl's brother, the child Fader. She smiled when she saw him, a warmth filling her. He was safe and well. But for how long? She remembered the scattered corpses in the great cavern of this place. If these people had captured Orden's attention, none of them were safe.

But why were they crossing Morrigan's path again? Orden would find such a coincidence suspicious, a suspicion that would grow to include Morrigan. Until she knew more, she must hide her history with these people.

A fear arose. *Could* she hide it? While in her head, Orden had been able to not only hear her thoughts, but also uncover memories. Morrigan frowned. But those memories had all been tied to her thoughts in that moment—her mother, stealing the key for the Tapestry, abandoning her coven. She resolved, if Orden seized control again, to focus her mind away from her past with these people.

She listened as the conversation in the pool continued, the words sounding in her mind without touching her ears. The discussion centered on a planned trip to Peru, but what she heard made little sense. Talk of snakes and pumas and condors. Of a mysterious Sisterhood. And of someone called Nyx, who was somehow part of both the Dreycott boy and the object of Orden's desire—this key, this Chakana.

Orden waved a hand. The scene faded, the pool returning to uniform blackness. Walking to the black throne, she settled Beroald's body into the seat. "Five days. And I still don't know their first destination. This Archambeault woman hasn't shared that with anyone."

Morrigan approached the throne. "Can you not use your mirror to find out?"

Orden smiled—a cold thing, reminding her of Marell. "My mirror, had I been allowed to complete it—and this island—all those years ago, would have let me rummage in that woman's mind to find the answer." She shook Beroald's head, sighing. "But I was...interrupted. My plans defeated." Beroald's eyes narrowed. "No, not defeated. Delayed. My beautiful world remains incomplete. As does my mirror. It can observe, but no more."

"Does it matter? You know their ultimate destination, this red dot. You know they will bring your precious key, and that the Dreycott boy carries it. Is that not enough? They will be a small party. Surely with your powers—and my own—we can seize it from them."

"Yes, it matters," Orden snapped. "I can't wait until they reach their destination. It lies too near the Crossing and the Sisters. I can't let those fools regain the Chakana. Fate has provided me this one chance—with the Chakana out of the grip of the Sisterhood, and me free once again. I will not lose it."

"Crossing? Sisters? Chakana? None of this has meaning for me. If I am to aid you, I need to understand."

Orden pursed Beroald's lips, considering her. "Perhaps you are right. Ah, but where to begin?"

"You can start by telling me what this Chakana is."

Orden shrugged. "It is the Key."

"To what?"

"To everything. To what I seek. To what these humans seek."

Humans? "Which is? Surely, it can't be these Akashic Records. They are a myth."

"Are they now?" Orden chuckled. "Then we shall begin there, since they *were* the beginning."

Morrigan felt a familiar touch on her mind—Orden, in her head again. *No!* she cried. *You promised me my body.*

"I will return it," Orden said, speaking with Morrigan's mouth. Leaving Beroald seated on the throne, erect but motionless, Orden walked Morrigan's body toward the living quarters at the opposite end of the tower room. "But it will be easier if I *show* you, rather than relying on words." Reaching the four-poster bed, she lay on it, folding Morrigan's hands on her stomach.

What are you doing?

Making us comfortable, Orden said in her mind. *It's a long story.*

How long?

Morrigan felt herself smile. *All of time*, Orden replied.

The tower room faded from her vision.

Blackness.

Morrigan sensed only blackness. No, less than blackness. Blackness would be something. This was nothing. The Void. *The* Nothing. And it had swallowed her.

She tried to scream but had no mouth, no body. She had nothing. She *was* nothing within the infinite Nothing.

Then, a voice. *In the beginning, there was...well, nothing. But you've picked up on that.*

Orden's voice. Morrigan grabbed for it like a drowning woman thrashing in the water and feeling an object float by.

Calm yourself, Orden said. *This is just a story.*

The blackness seemed to shrink, fall in on itself, slowly at first, then faster and faster until a black speck hung in a blank whiteness. A speck that, Morrigan sensed, was still the Void, yet was not. It had changed. The speck now held...

Potential.

What do you see? Orden asked.

A black speck that was the Void, hanging in infinite whiteness.

Whiteness? You see nothing in the whiteness?

Morrigan stared, trying to see something, anything. There... Was that...? She stared harder. A shape began to resolve itself in the whiteness. Gasping, she shrank back in her mind, turning from the impossible thing she'd glimpsed—a thing both too beautiful and too monstrous.

Orden sighed. *Of course. Your human mind cannot bear to look upon its creator. You cannot conceive the intelligence that conceived you.*

Morrigan laughed to hide her sudden fear. *Creator? Are you talking about God?*

That word is so charged. It carries such baggage for you humans. So filled with potential meanings and non-meanings. So many implications for your behavior and morality—and judgment of that behavior and morality. Your desire to be judged worthy for some continued existence beyond the physical plane you move in. Life after death.

Morrigan remained silent. She had never believed in a god. She had always believed in a god.

Orden chuckled. *You have just defined being human.*

What should I see in the whiteness?

I cannot give you a name... for They have no name for Itself. Or It has no name for Them.

They? It? What are you talking about?

Let's call Them the One. I could describe the One as a gestalt intelli-

gence—many minds operating as one. But then, I would begin with a lie. Because the One is more akin to a single entity that can choose *to become many. And each of those entities can think Its own thoughts, make Its own choices, take Its own actions.* Orden sighed. *And therein lies our story.* The *Story.*

Which you are going to tell me.

It would be impossible to tell the Story in its entirety. It is too vast. And it is still being told.

Speak sense.

The Story is what you *call the universe. All the universes. It is the multiverse you and your kind exist in. And die in. It is all of creation since time began. Well, since time began in* your *universe. The One created the Story—your universe. All of them.*

Morrigan wanted to scoff, to disbelieve. But Orden was inside her head, and she felt the truth of what Orden was saying. And that truth brought a fear greater than any she'd ever known.

For it made her feel...small. Insignificant.

She asked the question that filled her mind, the only question that could be asked.

Why?

Orden chuckled. *Another word so charged for you humans. Why are you here? Why do you exist?* Orden gave the equivalent of a mental shrug. *You are here because the One created the universe, and you are part of what They created. Beyond that, the answer lies in the question. Humanity's quest to answer that question is an endless fascination to the One.*

Orden paused. *But if you mean why did the One create the Story, then that I can* answer. Another chuckle. *It was bored.*

What?

Does that offend you? Does that undermine your desperate human need for some great purpose to your existence? The sense of a smile. *Does it make you feel...small?*

Morrigan thought she'd hidden that fear. Were none of her thoughts safe from Orden?

The One had created other realities before yours, Orden continued. *More than you could count in a million lifetimes. That, It believed, was Its purpose. Why It existed, why It was here. To create!*

A parade of images rolled by. Worlds and creatures and civilizations, all so strangely beautiful, so beautifully strange, she felt a terrible loss when each passed from her view.

But nothing the One created, no matter how vast, how complex, how beautiful, ever brought the fulfillment It sought—the fulfillment of achieving Its own believed purpose. And then, after yet another disappointment, the One realized Its error.

Morrigan waited for Orden to continue, but silence engulfed her. She had the sense of Orden turning inward, remembering. She caught a flash of a feeling...there, then gone. Regret? A sense of loss?

And the error? she asked.

Because It was the One, anything It created—any world, any creature, any universe—was, of course, perfect.

Another of the One's creations appeared. A city of faceted crystal spires, shining ebony streets, glowing indigo ponds, sparkling emerald streams. All arranged in perfect symmetry. A tiny jewel of a place. Perfect...and sterile. Morrigan understood. *And perfection is boring.*

Yes. The beauty of a thing is in its imperfection. *The oddness of the Mona Lisa's smile. The speck of color at the heart of a diamond. The beauty mark on a flawless face.* Orden sighed. *But realizing this truth only led to a greater realization—and a greater problem. How can a perfect being create...imperfection?*

Another pause, another echo of regret, then Orden continued. *For eons, for longer than your universe has existed, the One pondered that problem. And then, in one sudden insight, It knew the answer.*

Morrigan caught a rush of awe, of excitement never before experienced by an all-powerful being—the thrill of novelty, of an idea born new and fresh. She waited.

The answer, It realized, was two-fold. The first was to introduce entropy.

I don't understand.

The physical law in your universe that any system, left on its own, will move to a state of increasing disorder. This meant the worlds and creatures It created, initially perfect, would become imperfect. In common terms, everything in this new universe, including you humans, would...decay.

Morrigan shuddered. *It introduced death.*

It introduced change.

And the second answer?

To give Its creatures the one thing It had always withheld—the power to choose.

Morrigan understood. *Free will.*

Yes. And now It was ready to create Its imperfect creation. A universe filled with perfect creatures who would become imperfect as they and their worlds crumbled. Creatures with the freedom to choose their paths through their decaying and pitifully short lives.

My world? This world?

Not yet. First, there were some... Well, I can't call them failures, since a perfect being cannot fail. Let's call them additional moments of enlightenment.

Such as?

The One's first creation performed exactly as intended. Worlds were born. Creatures formed. Creatures evolved. Intelligence grew, and with it this time, free will. These creatures lived lives based on their own choices, then died, in ever-changing worlds.

Is that not what It intended?

Yes! And the One found Its creation—and especially Its free-willed crea-tures—fascinating. But It was curious. Whenever these creatures made a choice, the One would wonder...why? Why that *choice? What if this ephemeral being had made a different choice? But the One couldn't interfere. It couldn't make the creature take a different path. Well, It could, but then...*

No free will, Morrigan said.

And free will was the engine that drove Its wonderful new creation. It refused to tamper with that. So, what to do?

A black dot appeared again, floating in empty whiteness. From this dot, two thin lines emerged. At the end of each line, two new black dots grew.

Whenever a free-willed creature faced a choice, Orden continued, *a new universe would form—one for every possible decision! That way, the One could observe all possible outcomes. In short, it created what you humans call 'the multiverse.'*

I don't understand, Morrigan said.

Somewhere, there are other universes, other Morrigans. A Morrigan who did not let her young brother wander off. Another who did not steal the Weave and abandon her mother and her coven to their deaths. Another who did not return to Castle Rushen, the prodigal daughter. Did not hear the Song, did not again descend those steps, did not find her way here to become my prisoner.

Stop it!

A smile in her mind. *Too soon? Remember, you are here, with me, because of free will. This Morrigan made all her choices of her own free will.*

My choices, Morrigan thought. *My life. The life I built with those choices.*

Brick by brick, Orden said, reminding her again that no thought of hers stayed hidden. *Back to my story, or rather, The Story. The One saw what It had created and was well pleased. It let Its creation spin on for a few eternities, merrily splitting off universes every second.*

The two black dots each spun off two lines, at the end of which a new dot formed. This repeated, again and again. Some dots split off three, four, or more lines, each with a new black dot she now knew represented an entire new universe. As the shape grew, a realization struck Morrigan. *It looks like...a tree.*

Hold that thought, Orden replied. *The One experienced much joy examining each new universe, considering the choices Its imperfect creatures made or didn't make.*

The tree of the multiverse continued to grow, expanding and expanding, until it was so vast, it resembled a forest, every trunk grown from that first seed.

Yet still the One was curious. For every choice its creatures faced, It won-dered: was one path...better? Which led to the question, what did It mean by better?

The view zoomed into a single dot, two lines branching from it to form two new dots. These two dots grew to fill her vision, each resting on one side of a balance scale. The scale slowly tipped back and forth, never reaching equilibrium.

For eons, It had judged Its creations by their beauty. Its own concept of Beauty. Once, It had found Beauty in the perfect order of Its worlds. Now, It saw Beauty in the wondrous possibilities Its new universe presented—in Its chaos.

The image of the cosmic scale remained. But now the scale balanced on one side the tiny, perfect but sterile, crystal city she'd first seen, and on the other, the ever-growing tree of the multiverse. The scale tipped in favor of the tree.

But as Its new creation continued to grow and split off new universes, would it reach a point where there was too much change? Too much chaos? It reasoned that true Beauty must exist somewhere between these extremes of Order and Chaos. But where? And how to find that point?

The scale now oscillated, tipping to favor first the tiny, perfect city and then the vast multiverse.

It also struggled to understand the choices Its new creatures made. Why did different beings, faced with the same choice, choose different paths? After watching for eons, It realized these free-willed mortals—precisely because they were mortal—had created an entirely new concept. And this fresh novelty was as thrilling as Its ever-changing multiverse.

The two sides of the scale now balanced two scenes. In one, a human-like creature, clad in animal skins, struck down another of its kind, crushing its skull with a crude stone ax. On the other side, the two creatures faced each other, hands clasped, weapons lying at their feet.

Do you know what concept the One had discovered in Its creation? Orden asked.

Morrigan knew, but did not answer.

Orden chuckled. *You know. Something you have struggled to understand all your long life. The concept of morality. The choice between Good and Evil.*

Still Morrigan did not answer. But the choices she had made in her life marched again through her mind, unbidden. So many choices. So many regrets.

Orden continued, uncaring. *The One realized Its novelties of free will and entropy had created this concept of morality. Entropy—change and decay—made these creatures mortal. Free will—coupled with fear of death—produced beliefs. By the stars, so many beliefs! Beliefs that 'correct' choices in their short lives—choosing 'good' versus 'evil'—would guarantee life in another form after the death of their bodies.*

The view of the scale gave way to a flow of images from a thousand religions. Ancient temples, human sacrifices, witch burnings, pilgrimages, the Crusades, the Inquisition, persecutions, more holy wars, genocides, native children ripped from families and forced into church-run schools, twin towers on fire...more wars.

The One did not understand Good. It did not understand Evil. And from the myriad religions that formed in the universe and warred with each other, It realized the ephemerals did not, either. But It understood Beauty. And in that moment, the One knew Its true purpose.

All-consuming joy flowed from Orden, stunning Morrigan with an almost unbearable happiness. The flood receded, and Morrigan could form words again. *What...what was that purpose?*

To find where True Beauty lay in Its new creation. Where between Chaos and Order. And where between Good and Evil.

A circle appeared, hanging in whiteness and dissected by a vertical and a horizontal line. At opposite ends of the vertical line sat the sterile, never-changing crystal city and the ever-expanding tree of the multiverse. Order and Chaos. The horizontal line ran from a radiance too bright to look upon at one end to a writhing darkness that hinted of horrors within. Good and Evil.

I have said, Orden continued, *how the One could choose to become many. And now, It chose to do so: the One became the Four.*

In the whiteness outside the circle, four shapes began to form, one at each of the line ends. As those shapes resolved, Morrigan again turned her mind away, afraid to look on these god-like creatures. But she knew what they were.

Order, Chaos, Good, Evil, Orden said, *each now driven to find True Beauty in their creation.*

The view drifted over the circle, always moving, always shifting, as if these cosmic watchers searched between the four extremes of the multiverse. Morrigan understood. They *were* searching. Searching for True Beauty.

But then, Orden said, *with the greatest flash of insight It had ever experienced, the Four saw It could never achieve Their great purpose. They could never find where True Beauty lay in the multiverse.*

Again, Morrigan caught a flash of emotional memory—despair. *Why not?*

Because although the One had introduced Chaos—entropy, change, decay—It did not understand *Chaos, for It would never change or decay. It only understood Order. And though It had introduced death—which had created morality—the One would never die and so could never fear death or understand morality. It could never understand Good and Evil.*

The despair Morrigan had sensed in Orden disappeared, replaced by exultation.

And from that problem, arose the solution—the Four must view Its creation through the eyes of mortals. The Four must become mortal.

How, Morrigan asked, *does an immortal being become mortal?*

She felt Orden smile. *The Four formed a...partnership. With select mortals.*
Which mortals?
The Sisters.
The ones who seek this Chakana as you do? Why would the Four pick a bunch of women living in a remote jungle?

Why not? Why would any grubby ephemeral be any better than another, in the eyes of an all-powerful immortal being? Again, the Four first experienced some...

Failures?

Additional moments of enlightenment, before They settled on what became the Sisterhood.

With that, Orden opened Morrigan's eyes. Rising from the bed, she walked back toward the black pool. "Enough history. I have decided on a plan to obtain the Chakana."

Wait! Morrigan cried. *Everything you have told me—how do you know all this? How* can *you know this?*

She felt Orden smile. "Perhaps how the Four are known by the Sisterhood will answer that. Their names have changed over the eons, as the empires from which the Sisters chose their recruits rose and fell, their languages with them. The Four held Quechuan names when the Incas ruled. After the conquistadors, the Sisters chose Spanish names for the Four."

Orden held up a finger for each name she recited. "Good? *Bondad.* Evil? *Mal.* Chaos? *Caos.*" She held up a fourth finger and smiled. "And Order...?"

A chill settled on Morrigan even before her captor spoke the final name.

"*...Orden.*"

Chapter 18

Fix Me

On the morning they were to leave for Peru, Will walked the winding, yellow-bricked path through his rooftop park toward the Jungle. Fader was working on the next Dream Rider issue, and Case was giving last minute instructions to the Crash Space foreman.

And he was here. To smell the Flower one last time before taking the trip he'd thought would never happen.

One reason was the hope the orchid would coax new secrets from his memory. For the past five nights in Dream, all attempts by Nyx to remember more of Will's hidden past had failed. Nyx's memories remained fragmented, confusing, or non-existent.

With each reported failure, Adi had again voiced her mistrust of the Chakana—and now, by association, Nyx. Adi's doubts were infecting Will. He wondered if Nyx *was* telling him everything she could. Or was she waiting until they'd committed to this trip, until they were in Peru, with the Chakana en route to its home?

Whatever and wherever that home was.

But another reason for this final visit was to bring closure to the last eight years of his life. For all that time, his one goal had been to find the Flower. That search had taken place here, in this tower, in this greenhouse. A search that had ended in success.

Now, he was leaving on the *real* search. To find his parents. To learn what had happened to him. That search would take place in Peru. And he had no idea how it might end.

Maybe he had come here to say...what? Thank you? Goodbye? To a flower?

Or maybe he was just superstitious.

Inside the greenhouse, he walked between rows of wooden tables covered with potted failures from the past. The wrong flowers. Reaching the isolation room, he passed through the airlock and stepped inside. The black orchid waited in its orange pot on the small table, its bloom open in the simulated night. Bending over the plant, he breathed in that familiar perfume one last time.

The same parade of sensory memories returned—if they *were* memories—flashing by, then fading like snatches from a dream on waking. But this time sharper, clearer. And in a different sequence.

The same sounds again. The wing beats of a huge bird. The throaty snarl of a great cat. The slithering of a snake on a stone floor.

Smells and visions then. The thick tang of damp earth, carried on a cold, wet wind. The quipu cord again, this time held by a pale-skinned hand. Behind it, a flat rock wall studded with fist-sized protrusions and shining wet under a silver glow. Then darkness...and a distant rumbling roar.

And then...

A great weight again surrounded him, squeezing him, trying to crush him, suck him into the black dot that now hung before him in the void, an infinitely tiny speck that held all matter in the universe in a space of nothing. Faster and faster, he flew toward the point. Faster and faster...

With a gasp, he forced his eyes open and threw himself back, crashing into the wall, banging his head. Sliding to the floor, he sat there, breathing hard, staring up at the Flower, and rubbing the back of his head.

"Good idea," came a familiar voice. "You don't want to pass out today. Adi might get cold feet about Peru."

He stood, not even surprised to find Nyx floating beside him, full-bodied and glowing. "I'm awake?"

She nodded.

"How are you here?"

"I'm guessing your floral friend triggered the Chakana part in you. And...ta da! Your magic genie appears."

"My genie who can't remember anything magical?"

"Hey, I've been trying."

Have you? he wondered.

"You know I can hear your thoughts, right? I'm part of you. And yes, I *have* been trying. That's why I'm here. I remembered something."

His fear and suspicion faded. "Great. What?"

"I need to show you."

"You want me to go into Dream? Here?"

"That'd work, but I can also show you while you're awake."

"How?"

"If you're astral projecting."

"I can't do that yet."

"Yes, you can. You did it in Adi's office when you first saw the Chakana. And again, on the Black Island when you faced the Chambelán."

"With the Chakana exposed and nearby both times—which it isn't right now."

"Will, astral projection is a skill you'll need in Peru."

"Do you know something you're not telling me?"

"Probably, but if I do, I can't remember it. It's just a feeling. About all three of you. Case, Fader, you—all your powers must grow to face what we'll meet in Peru. And for you, the first step is to astral project while awake."

"I can't—"

"Just try. For added incentive, you'll want to see this memory. You *need* to see it."

"I don't even know how to start."

"By remembering how it *felt*. Just that. Just the feeling."

Sighing, he faced the Flower. He closed his eyes, filling his mind with the feeling of astral projecting from when he'd first exposed the Chakana in Adi's office, trying to remember each sensation. The sudden recognition of his silver cord inside him. The tug of the cord in his chest. Then the sense of pushing out from himself. Pushing...pushing...pushing...

He was falling. Panicking, his hands shot out, reaching for the table but finding nothing. His eyes flew open, but saw only blackness. Tumbling forward, he waited for the impact of the floor. An impact that never came.

His sight returned. He was...floating.

Floating and staring down from his glowing, transparent astral body to where his physical body stood before the black orchid in the isolation room. His silver cord snaked between his two forms.

Nyx floated up to him. *Well done.*

He sensed her words in his mind, along with a feeling. Pride?

Now, go back into your body and do it again.

What?

Or no bedtime story.

She made him do it three more times. Each time was easier. His final attempt took no more effort than closing his eyes in his physical body and opening them in his astral form.

Okay, he said, *this is cool.*

And now, for that story.

The room shimmered, grew indistinct. Another scene took its place, an astral vision superimposed over the greenhouse isolation room...

Two figures stood on either side of a bed...his parents. On the bed, beneath a comforter decorated with superheroes, lay his nine-year-old self.

He recognized his childhood bedroom in the tower. His parents had owned just two floors back then. One had been a warehouse for artifacts. The other held offices, a gallery for selling to top-end buyers, a restoration lab, and the apartment that had been their home.

His home. *Not much has changed on that front*, he thought.

His younger version lay unmoving with eyes closed. The clock on the bedside table showed nine AM. Worry creased his parents' faces.

When is this? he asked Nyx, who still floated beside him.

A few days after your parents told Ellie Cootes about the Akashic Records.

He stared at himself lying in bed. *I thought I was okay after I was exposed, as long as the Chakana was nearby.*

Well, that changed. You fell unconscious. The doctors couldn't explain it. You weren't in a coma, but you weren't waking up, either. So, your desperate parents came up with a desperate plan.

What plan?

Watch.

Turning back to the bedroom scene, he noticed something he'd missed before. A gray box sat on the bedside table. And both his parents held some type of handgun.

Is that—? Are those—?

Yes, it is. And those are tasers. Now watch.

Jon Dreycott moved to stand beside the gray box. "Ready?"

Will's mother nodded. With their backs to the bed, both raised their tasers to their side of the room. With his free hand, Will's father flipped open the box.

The box, Will knew, held the Chakana. And the tasers were in case a Sword Lady appeared. But why would his parents risk that? Especially with their son in the room? Unless they had cared more for their weird quest than for him.

From the corner of the room nearest his mother, a crackling began. An eyeblink later, a box of lightning stretched from floor to ceiling, only to be replaced by a Sword Lady. Green snake-skin leggings, puma pelt jacket with clawed paws, and black hair cascading from under a feathered condor head mask. Blade held ready, her eyes swept the room, then locked onto the gray box.

"*La Llave de Cristal!*" she cried. *The Crystal Key.*

"Don't move!" Terri cried, aiming her taser as Jon flipped the box closed again.

The woman leaped forward, sword raised.

Terri fired. The two contacts from the taser struck the woman's chest, their charge wires trailing back to Terri's weapon. The woman stiffened, her arms flying out, her body shaking in spasms. Her sword fell from her grip as she collapsed to the floor. Terri cut the charge from the gun.

Reaching the fallen woman, Jon kicked her sword away, then checked her pulse. He backed up, his own taser still trained on her. "She's okay."

The swordswoman groaned, then pushed herself to sitting. Pulling off her mask to reveal a teenage girl's face, she stared up at them, black eyes wide with fear.

"We won't hurt you—unless you attack us again," Jon said.

"I feel...sick," the girl said.

"You'll be fine in a few minutes."

She looked back to where her portal still shimmered.

"Please stay where you are," Jon said.

Hate replaced fear on her face. "Am I your prisoner?"

Jon shook his head. "You're free to leave once you hear us out."

The girl's eyes narrowed. "I will reveal no secrets. I am sworn to the Sisterhood."

Jon nodded at Will on the bed. "It's our son. We...we need your help. *He* needs your help."

"You stole the Chakana!" the girl snarled. "You murdered my Sisters who protected it! And now, you ask for our help?"

His parents exchanged looks of open-mouthed horror. "My god, child," Jon said, "we didn't kill your Sisters."

Understanding dawned on Terri's face. "Alvarez," she whispered.

"You admit it," the girl sneered. "You know the Beast's name. He did your bidding."

Jon waved a hand before him as if to ward off the accusation. "No, he didn't! We didn't know! We..." His shoulders slumped. "We didn't know."

"We should have," Terri whispered. "It was Alvarez." She looked at the girl. "We are sorry for the deaths of your Sisters."

Silence filled the small room, and a thousand emotions filled Will. Horror for the murders. Hate for Alvarez, for what he had done and for tainting Will's parents with his crime. Anger against this woman for thinking his parents were killers. Guilt and shame for his parents' role in the death of the Sisters. For his role, too—for keeping the Chakana these past eight years, the spoils of murder. Adi had kept it, but she'd done so to protect him.

The girl struggled to her feet, swayed, caught herself, then straightened, her head held high. She ripped the taser contacts off and threw them to the floor. "What do you want?"

Jon explained about Will being exposed to the Chakana, his collapse, his recovery, his relapse. "He won't wake, and the doctors can't explain it."

The girl looked at where young Will lay, then at Terri. Terri nodded. The girl walked to the bed and leaned over the sleeping boy. Her eyes widened. Muttering under her breath, she stepped back. "Only a *Madre* can help your son."

His parents exchanged a look. "A *Madre*?" Terri said.

"A Mother of the Book. The Mothers serve the Four. And we serve the Mothers." She stared hate at them. "The Beast killed two Madres. Two still live."

The Book? The Four? Madres? Will thought.

"And they can help our son?" Terri asked, the hope and fear in her voice making Will want to run to her, to hold her tight.

"A Madre is his only hope," the girl said, and Will realized she hadn't answered the question.

"Will you ask them? Please?" Jon said.

The girl snorted. "Why should we help you?"

Terri looked at Jon. He nodded. "We'll return the Chakana," Terri said.

The girl searched their faces, as if waiting for a lie to appear. Retrieving her sword, she walked to the shimmering portal. Jon raised his taser, but Terri held up a hand.

At the portal, the girl turned back. "Tomorrow, at this same hour, expose the Chakana again. If the Madres choose to help you, one will appear." With that, she stepped into the shimmer...and disappeared.

Jon took Terri in his arms. She lay her head on his chest, her eyes on her son. "And now, we wait," he said.

Fortunately, Nyx said, *you and I don't have to.*

The scene faded.

🦅

The scene returned, the same but different. Will's younger self still lay asleep or unconscious in bed. The clock again showed nine AM, and beside it, the gray box still sat. His parents again flanked the bed, but without weapons. As Will watched, his father once more opened the box.

A portal shimmered in the corner, and a woman in the garb of the Sisterhood again stepped through it. But an old woman this time. Very old. She wore no mask. Deep lines etched her brown face, and the hair that fell to her waist was pure white. She leaned on a wooden staff taller than her, the bottom third of which was carved in the shape of a coiling green snake. Tawny fur covered its middle portion. The top of the staff was painted black and crowned by the figure of a condor, its huge wings spread but unbalanced, its head twisted to one side.

Gripping the staff, the woman raised her other arm and pointed a cat-paw glove at Jon and Terri. "Profaners!" she announced with a voice of surprising strength, the word spoken almost as a greeting.

"I am Jon Dreycott, and this is my wife, Terri—"

"I do not care," the woman said, waving a hand in dismissal. She walked toward the bed. "This is the boy." A statement, not a question.

Jon stiffened as she approached young Will, but Terri shook her head at him. "Our son," she said. "His name is Will."

The woman stared down at the boy, her bright eyes coming to rest on his face. Her eyes widened, and she drew a sharp breath. She lay a gentle hand on his shoulder. "Will, I am Luciana, *Madre del Caos*," she said as if he could hear her, and for the first time, her voice held something akin to tenderness.

Mother of Chaos? Will asked. Nyx nodded.

"Child," Luciana said, "you are innocent in this." She sighed. "Innocent, but it is you who have paid the price."

"Do you...?" Terri swallowed, then continued. "Do you know what's wrong with him?"

"The Chakana has chosen him. Why, I do not know."

"Chosen him?" Jon said, his voice rising. "What are you talking about?"

Luciana regarded his father as if he were something on the bottom of her shoe. "A piece of the Chakana is in the boy. An astral fragment. They are joined—the Chakana and your son."

Terri stared at the gray box in horror. "How did it...? How could it?"

Luciana shrugged. "It is the Chakana."

"Can you...remove it?" Jon asked. "Can you fix him? Heal our son?"

"He and the Chakana must be healed together. Only the Four can do this. And only within the Book." She studied them, waiting.

"You can have the Chakana," Terri said. "We don't want the damn thing anymore."

Jon's eyes narrowed, but he nodded. "You can have it—*if* you can save our son. Can you?"

"We must bring the child to the Crossing—with the Chakana." Luciana tipped her staff toward the shimmering portal. "I can take you there."

Will noticed that Luciana, like the swordswoman before her, hadn't answered his parents' question.

"Now?" Terri asked.

"Your son grows weaker, the Chakana in him stronger."

"Tomorrow evening," Jon said. "We need time to prepare."

"Tonight," Terri said, looking hard at her husband. "We can be ready tonight."

Jon sighed. "All right. Tonight. But how do we know we can trust you?"

Luciana's eyes narrowed. Her jaw muscles tightened. "*You* wish to trust *me*? You, who stole from us? Who murdered our Sisters? You, who seek what you cannot understand?" She snorted and walked to the portal. "Expose the Chakana tonight. Your child stands at a precipice." She stepped into the shimmer, and in an eyeblink, both Luciana and the portal were gone.

Terri whirled to face her husband. "*Tomorrow* night? Tomorrow? Will is *dying!*"

"Sweetheart, we have to pack. Clothes, gear, weapons—"

"They'll never let us take weapons, Jon!"

"Well, I need to call Pablo. Tell him to cancel the expedition arrangements he's started, that we're making our own way to Peru. And we need to leave instructions for Adi for handling things here while we're gone." He hesitated. "And then there's Ellie Cootes."

Terri's brow creased. "What about Ellie?"

"We still need to bring her." He held up his hands as Terri's eyes went wide. "Hear me out. Luciana talked about taking Will inside 'the Book'—with the Chakana. We know the Chakana's the key to accessing the Records. I'll bet this Book is what they call the Records."

"You think they'll use the Records to heal Will?"

"Yes!" He laid his hands on her shoulders. "We're giving up the Chakana—and I'm fine with that. Will is all that matters. But we've chased the Records half our lives. This will be our only shot at seeing them. With Ellie there, we'll have a better chance to understand what we see." He shrugged. "Plus, she's a more credible witness than a pair of suspected art thieves and grave robbers. We need her, and she needs the money we offered."

Terri walked to where young Will lay unconscious and oblivious to the events around him. "All right, but we tell her everything. She has to know what she's getting into."

"Agreed."

"And no matter what happens, Will comes first."

His father slipped his arm around her waist. "Will comes first."

The scene faded, and Will again floated beside Nyx in the isolation room. Below, his physical body still stood unmoving before the Flower.

They didn't... He stopped, struggling with feelings that threatened to overwhelm him. Joy, relief, gratitude...and a deep sense of loss. The loss of his parents and the love they'd had for him.

He finally found the words. *They didn't take me to Peru* despite *the danger to me—they took me because I was* already *in danger. They didn't go to chase their quest—they went to save me.*

Yes, Nyx said, *although it seems your dad was hoping for a two-fer. But yeah, you were their first concern. They were ready to surrender the Chakana and abandon a twenty-year search—to save you.* She nodded at where the last astral scene had played out. *One last thing to see.*

The isolation room grew hazy. Another scene took shape...

His childhood bedroom again. The same—but different.

His parents were there. And his nine-year-old self. Only now, the younger Will, still unconscious, sat propped up in a high-backed wheelchair, wearing a khaki shirt and pants he remembered from past expeditions.

Four hiking backpacks lay near where the portal had appeared. Four backpacks. One each, Will guessed, for his parents, himself...and for the fourth person present.

Ellie Cootes stood with Terri beside Will's wheelchair. His mother rested a hand on Will's shoulder. He didn't stir. "He's why we're going, Ellie. But you have kids here."

"They're staying with my parents till I'm back."

Terri hesitated. "I mean, we *have* to go. You don't."

Ellie shook her head. "My ex left me buried in debt. I'm not even covering the interest payments. What you're offering will finally get me free of that. Let me give my kids the life they deserve. A decent place to live. Money for university."

Ellie nodded at where Jon stood on the other side of the wheelchair, holding the gray box. "Besides, part of me doesn't believe some old lady in a freaky costume will materialize out of thin air when you open that thing. If she doesn't, my decision's made for me. If she does..." She shrugged. "Then I am most *definitely* going with you."

Terri raised a questioning eyebrow.

"Because if *that* is true," Ellie continued, "then the rest of your crazy story could be as well." Her eyes got a faraway look. "And then maybe, just maybe, I'll get to witness a secret of the universe." She smiled at Terri. "You two have your Holy Grail. I have mine."

"Ready?" Jon asked. Both the women nodded.

He opened the box.

Ellie gasped as the portal shimmered into being. A second later, Luciana stepped through. Her eyes locked on the open box, then on Ellie. "Who is this?"

"Will needs medical care on the trip," Jon said. "This is Doctor Elenora Cootes."

Wait, Will said, turning to Nyx. *That's a lie.*

Nyx snapped her fingers, pausing the memory. *And yet, both your father's statements are true. Of course, taken together they imply, as he intended, that 'Doctor' Cootes is a medical doctor, when in truth, your mother filled that role for you on the trip.*

That's... Will stopped, not comfortable finishing the thought.

Sneaky? Misleading? Yep. Welcome to Parents 101. She snapped her fingers again.

The three adult travelers now wore backpacks. A fourth pack was hooked on Will's wheelchair.

The Chakana, Nyx said, *is in your dad's backpack, back in the lead box.*

"For you to follow me through the doorway," Luciana said, "we must maintain physical contact."

Luciana arranged the travelers so that Terri and Jon could both push the wheelchair with one hand, while their other rested on Will's shoulder. Ellie stood beside Will, holding his hand. Luciana stood in front of Ellie, holding her other hand.

Satisfied, Luciana nodded. "Come." She moved forward into the shimmer, and they followed. The travelers disappeared. The portal faded, as did the scene.

The Flower's isolation room returned. *Okay*, Will said, *so that's how we traveled to Peru. But then what happened?*

Nyx hesitated. *Yeah, about that...*

Don't tell me you don't know.

Well, it's probably somewhere in my fractured memories, since the Chakana was there. But this is the only other memory that's come back to me...and it ends here.

A familiar ring tone sounded.

That's my phone.

Answering in your present form will be difficult.

Surrendering to the tug of his silver cord, he let the glowing thread pull him back into his body. When he opened his eyes, Nyx had disappeared. He answered his phone.

It was Adi. "Will, it's time to leave for the airport. We're heading for the garage."

"On my way." He hung up.

Exiting the greenhouse, he walked back through the rooftop park, enjoying the warmth of both the sun on his skin and the knowledge his parents had gone to Peru to save their son.

Now he was traveling to Peru again. To save his parents. To save Ellie Cootes. And to find answers. To finally find *all* the answers.

Chapter 19

You Sent Me Flying

Case stepped off the elevator into the private underground garage of Will's tower, her shoulders already aching from her hiking backpack. *I have to tramp through a jungle carrying this?*

Ten steps away, four unmarked white panel vans stood in a row. Ahead of them, two black limousines waited, their uniformed drivers standing talking. All the vehicles had darkly tinted windows.

Beside the last van, Adi and Stone spoke in hushed tones to a slim woman shorter than Adi and a man much larger than Stone. Case guessed they were the members of Stone's team who would accompany them. They were both Asian, wore the same black suits and white shirts Stone favored, and held themselves like him—an ease combined with coiled tension.

Fader leaned against the front van. He grinned and waved. Walking over, she shrugged off her pack with relief and dropped it beside his.

Adi had provided them all with identical clothing for the jungle trek part of their trip. Buttoned camouflage shirt, with matching pants, waist-length jacket, and floppy-brimmed hat, all with more zippered pockets—even the hat—than Case could imagine ever needing. Brown leather hiking boots completed the wardrobe.

Fader sported the entire outfit. She'd packed hers, opting for black denims and a blue-and-white striped tank top for the flight. But she wore the boots. They were surprisingly comfortable, and it felt good wearing something besides mismatched sneakers.

"You know those clothes are just for the jungle, right?" she said.

Fader shrugged. "Yeah, but I like them." He tilted his hat to what he probably thought was a cooler angle. "Will's on his way."

"No Rani?"

He shook his head. "Where were you?"

"Crash Space. Telling the foreman what to work on while I'm away." She bit her lip. "He asked when I'll be back."

"What'd you tell him?"

"I lied. I said two weeks."

"We might be."

"Bro, we don't know when we'll be back. We don't know—" She didn't finish her thought. *We don't know* if *we'll be back.*

But her brother knew her too well. "We'll be back. With Mom."

She mustered a smile for his sake. "Yeah. We will."

The elevator dinged. Will emerged, wearing jeans and his favorite Springsteen t-shirt, and carrying his backpack with no apparent effort. He walked over, dropped his pack, and gave her a quick kiss. Fader made a face.

Will frowned at the vans. "These our wheels?"

"This one's ours," Fader said. "The one where Adi and Stone are standing is for our luggage and stuff."

"What about the limos? And the other two vans?"

Fader shrugged.

"Where were you?" Case asked Will.

"Roof."

"I was up there earlier, saying goodbye to Flopsy and Mopsy. Didn't see you."

"I was in the Jungle. With the Flower."

"Should I be jealous?"

"Well, I *have* chased her for years."

"Hmm. Any new vibes?"

"No. But big news from Nyx."

"You saw Nyx? She finally remembered something?"

"Wait until we're on the plane before you share that," Adi said as she and Stone walked over. "This place is too open."

"We're three floors underground," Will said.

"Our plane will be swept for listening devices and, once in the air, is safe from external eavesdropping. I can't say that for this garage." Adi turned to Stone. "Perhaps some introductions?"

Stone motioned to the man and woman waiting by the end van. Watching the woman approach, Case felt a pang of envy. Every movement seemed effortless, like she was dancing, not walking. Up close, the man was even bigger than she'd thought, easily six foot six.

"May I present," Stone said, "Li Mei..." The woman gave a short bow. "And Wu Peng." The man bowed, too. "My two best and most trusted people."

Wu Peng straightened at that, and a smile teased Li Mei's mouth. "Thank you, dai lo," they both said quietly.

"They will accompany us on our trip," Stone continued. "And this is Case, Fader..." he said, pointing to them. "And you know Mr. Dreycott."

"Will, please," Will said.

"And please call us Mei and Peng," Mei said.

Fader frowned, and Mei smiled. "In China, family names come first, given names last."

"Right," Fader said. "Like in *The Gate of the Flying Blades.*"

"Dude, you read wuxia comics!" Peng exclaimed, holding out a huge fist for Fader to bump.

"And that," Mei said to Peng, "is why you don't have a girlfriend."

"Hey, I'm picky."

Adi checked her phone. "We should be going."

Stone waved to the two limos. Both drivers got into their cars and headed out of the garage.

"Uh..." Will said.

"The limos are decoys," Adi said. "They leave first, tinted windows concealing that they have no passengers. If unknown parties *are* watching, they'll follow the limos, thinking one carries you and, therefore, the Chakana."

Will nodded. "Instead, we're taking the vans."

"Yes. These vehicles make regular deliveries here and shouldn't attract attention."

"Why four?"

"One for us, one for our gear. The remaining two are additional decoys. The vans will leave spaced out, heading in different directions. Our two will take separate routes to our destination. All vehicles will stay in contact, alerting the others if any attack occurs."

"And our destination is...?"

"You'll know when we get there." Adi turned to Mei and Peng. "Take the last van. Your route should get you to the airport first. Besides our luggage, your van has a crate to be secured on the plane when you arrive. The crate is marked 'Fragile.' Make sure they know that."

"What's in the crate?" Will asked.

"Not here," Adi said.

Case bent to pick up her backpack, but Peng grabbed it. "I got it," he said with a grin. Slinging her pack over a shoulder, he grabbed Will's and Fader's in one hand with no apparent effort and headed for the end van.

"*I* drive," Mei said, catching up to him.

"Jeez, you ever gonna forget that?" Peng whined. "One little accident?"

"The multi-vehicle collision with rollover? No. I won't," Mei replied, as Peng, still grumbling, loaded the packs into the van.

"They always like that?" Case asked Stone, smiling.

He chuckled. "I'm afraid so. But they're both highly skilled. Smart, quick, trained on multiple weapons and in martial arts, and deadly in a fight." He caught her reaction. "Skills we likely won't need on this trip."

She swallowed, but nodded.

"We should be moving ourselves," Adi said, opening the van's side door, revealing three rows of passenger seats. Case sat in the middle row beside Will. Fader took a row to himself, behind them. Adi climbed into the front, on the passenger side next to Stone, who was driving.

"So...no Rani?" Case asked.

"Apparently not," Adi replied. "When we spoke last night, she was still uncertain whether she would be coming."

Case tried to hide her disappointment, having counted on Rani as the only female she could confide in on the trip. The only one she could girl-talk with. Maybe Mei...?

They fastened their seat belts, then Adi turned back to them. "Ready?"

"Can I have it?" Will asked quietly.

Adi stared at him for a breath, then pulled a palm-sized, steel-gray pouch with a flap closure from a jacket pocket. She held it out.

He hesitated, then took the pouch. "Thanks," he whispered, clenching it in his hand.

No one spoke, and Case knew they were all waiting for the same thing. For something to happen. To one of them—her, Will, Fader.

"You guys okay?" Will asked.

"I'm fine," she said. "No Voices."

"You can still see me, right?" Fader asked. "Then I'm okay, too."

"You?" she asked Will.

Will stared at the pouch. "I'm good."

"Now," Adi said, "are you ready?"

Ready? Case swallowed. Were they?

Fader slipped down in his seat, not answering. Beside Case, Will stroked the pouch as if he hadn't heard. Then he grinned that grin she loved, and nodded. Fader grinned then, too.

She was the one to say it. "Yeah. We're ready."

Stone started the van and headed for the ramp out of the garage. Behind them, the other three vans followed.

Case leaned back, trying to drain the tension from her body. They were really doing this. They were going to Peru. What would they find there? Would there be danger?

Yes. There would. That reminded her of her Voice, her Voice that had always warned her of danger. She hadn't heard it since escaping the Black Island, even when danger had returned. The attack on Stone. Will's collapse. Nyx had warned her those times, not her Voice.

Had her Voice left her? Just when she would need it more than ever?

And then, as if that thought had called it back, her Voice returned.

Stop! Stop the van!

"Stop the van!" she cried, not hesitating.

Stone slammed on the brakes, throwing them forward against their seat belts. Brakes squealed behind them. Then she saw it. In her mind. The elevator opening. She turned to look back.

The elevator was now closing. Stumbling after them, wearing her backpack and pulling a huge wheeled suitcase, was Rani Patel.

"It's Rani!" she said.

Stone opened his door, but Adi stopped him. "Stay here," she said, getting out.

Case slid the side door open as a panting Rani reached them. "Hi, Critter Crew!" she said, smiling. Her smile broadened, and she added, "Hi, Mr. Zhang!" Stone nodded, but Case caught a brief smile.

"You're late, Ms. Patel," Adi said.

"Yeah. Sorry. Kind of left my packing to the last minute."

"Speaking of that, does your backpack contain everything on Mr. Zhang's list?"

"Yep. Everything." Rani slipped off her pack. "And my phone is the encrypted one he provided."

Adi eyed the suitcase.

"Oh, that's just some other stuff. Extra clothes, makeup. Shoes." Rani shrugged. "More shoes."

"Well," Adi said, "you get in the van. I'll put these where they belong."

As Adi carried Rani's bags to the luggage van with Mei and Peng, Rani climbed in beside Fader, babbling about her panicked taxi ride here. Case only half listened. She was glad to have Rani along, but a thought occurred to her.

Her Voice had returned. That was good, but her Voice warned her of danger. And this time, her Voice had stopped them from leaving without Rani. What did that mean?

Adi returned, and they started away again. As the van reached the ramp to the street, Case glanced back in time to see Rani's wheeled suitcase still sitting on the garage floor. She turned to Adi to say something, but Adi gave the smallest shake of her head.

"Well, this should be fun, right?" Rani said.

"Yeah," Case said, forcing a smile. "Fun."

❧

Fifteen minutes later, their van merged into heavy traffic on the elevated expressway out of downtown. Sunshine glinting off the lake to their left did little to brighten Case's mood. She sat erect, muscles tensed. Was her Voice back now? Would it warn her of a coming attack on their van?

Will sat beside her, silent, head down, still staring at the pouch with the Chakana.

Lost in her fears, she'd forgotten what a huge step this was for him. "Are you okay?"

He looked up, his face puzzled.

"I mean..." She waved at the windows. "...being *out*."

He smiled. "Yeah, no, I'm good." He hefted the pouch. "As long as I have this with me, I feel fine." He slipped it into his jeans pocket.

Up front, Stone scanned surrounding traffic for, she assumed, potential threats as he drove. Adi stayed in contact with the other vehicles, but all drivers continued to report the same status. Nothing.

Rani caught on as they took the exit for the airport. "Why's everyone so uptight?"

"Wondering if we'll be attacked," Will said.

Rani blinked. "Attacked? Like at the bank?"

"What did you think the decoy vans were for?"

"To avoid being *followed*," Rani snapped. "Not to avoid getting *shot*."

"Don't worry, Rani," Stone said, checking his mirrors, "these vans have reinforced steel panels. They're virtually bullet-proof."

Rani hugged herself. "Great. Mentioning bullets is really calming. Wait...*virtually?*"

Mei's voice came over the hands-free speaker. "We're here, dai lo."

"We're five minutes out. Status?" Stone replied.

"Did a sweep of the hangar and perimeter. All clear. And everyone's ID checks out. We'll get the plane loaded now. Luggage in the cabin, crate and weapons in the hold, right?"

"Yes," Adi said.

Weapons? Stone's words returned to Case. *...trained on multiple weapons...deadly in a fight...skills we likely won't need on this trip.*

Yeah, she thought. *Right.*

"And remind them the crate's fragile," Adi added.

"I'll have Peng tell them," Mei said. "He's more intimidating, even though I'm way more dangerous."

"I heard that," Peng's voice came in the background.

"See you soon." Stone signed off. A few minutes later, he steered onto an exit ramp.

"The sign said Pearson was the next exit," Case said, assuming they were flying from Toronto's main airport.

"We're using a private airstrip," Adi said, offering nothing more. Case knew better than to press her.

They drove along a road lined with low box-like buildings and the half-cylinder shapes of airplane hangars. Will peered out the window. "This isn't where Mom and Dad kept their jet."

"We'd stopped using it," Adi replied, "so I sold it to a private operator five years ago. But we acquired a controlling interest in his charter company, just in case." She shot him a look. "I did tell you at the time."

Will shrugged. "Business stuff. Boring."

Adi sighed and shook her head. Stone swung the van into a driveway, stopping before a closed gate in a stretch of chain-link. A hangar sat half a city block back from the fence, displaying the sign, 'Serendipity Jet Charters.'

A uniformed guard, large and male, appeared from a windowed booth, tablet in hand. Stone lowered his window. "Archambeault charter."

The guard checked his tablet, then Stone's ID. "Your plane's on the tarmac, sir. Only one out there. You can't miss it." He returned to his booth. The gate slid back.

Stone drove to the rear of the hangar, parking beside the other van where Mei stood waiting. They all stepped out into hot sunshine and humid July air.

Thirty steps away, a sleek white plane, smaller than she'd expected, sat alone on the airstrip. It had a pointed, sloping nose, reminding Case of a bird's head, with swept-back wings ending in upturned tips. Twin jet engines flanked the tail. She counted eight windows.

"That is so cool!" Fader said.

She just nodded, still fighting her unease.

Beside her, Rani was scanning the sky.

"What?" Case asked.

"Checking for condors."

"And...?"

"Nothing. And hoping it stays that way. Your Puma pal come back?"

"No. Same with Fader's Snake." She'd been wondering about their absence. "Maybe in Peru?"

"Thanks for putting that idea in my head," Rani muttered.

Mei gave a short bow to Stone. "Peng's on board, scanning for bugs and trackers. Everything's stowed. Plane's fueled."

"Crew?"

"Pilot and copilot—the ones Ms. Archambeault requested—are on board, running their preflight. They both checked out—credentials, photo IDs, fingerprints."

Fingerprints? Case thought.

Stone must have read her face. "Standard security checks."

"Ever notice how security never makes you feel secure?" Rani muttered. "Just reminds you to be nervous?"

"Uh, speaking of security," Case said, "don't we have to go through it? You know, metal detectors, scanners, and stuff?"

"That only applies to commercial flights from public airports," Adi replied. "This charter company is an FBO—a fixed-base operator. And one which we own. We determine security procedures. Now, we should get on board."

They moved toward the plane, Stone and Mei flanking the group, scanning the surroundings. *They're still expecting something*, she thought, looking over her shoulder, feeling like she had a target on her back.

"What about customs and immigration?" Will asked as they walked.

"You don't remember?" Adi said. "From when you flew with your parents?"

"Eight years ago. And I was just a kid."

"We clear customs and immigration in Peru, where I've arranged for both processes to be...expedited," Adi said. "Leaving here, we need only file a flight plan, a cargo manifest, and a passenger list with passport numbers."

"But Fader and I don't have passports," Case said.

"Yes, you do," Adi said.

"But—"

"No more till we're in the air."

They reached the plane. A short stairway, folded down from the jet, led up to an open door. Adi and Stone boarded, followed by Rani, Will, Fader, and Case. Mei came last, scanning the airstrip again before stepping through.

Inside, at the open cockpit door, Adi and Stone talked in low tones to two uniformed men Case assumed were the pilot and copilot. She stepped past them into the passenger cabin. And stopped.

The front area held four reclining seats, large and padded, each by a window, two facing forward, two facing back. Behind them, on the right side, two more seats faced another pair, separated by a wooden table. Across the aisle, a cushioned couch faced those seats and table. Rani was already settled in a window seat at the table, tapping at her phone.

Still farther back, a larger couch sat across from a big screen TV. The cabin walls and thick carpeting were a warm cream color, the chairs and couches a darker shade and, she guessed, leather. The table and accents throughout were a red wood.

Fader looked around wide-eyed. "Wow!"

"Yeah, wow," Case agreed, but with less enthusiasm. Like Fader, the luxury of the plane stunned her. Unlike him, she found only discomfort in that comfort. *What's a street kid doing on a private jet?* The cost of one recliner probably would've fed her and Fader for a year on the streets. She'd never felt so out of place in her life.

Will picked up on it. He pulled her to him, his hands on her waist, their foreheads touching. "I know. It's too much. A rich people toy. But right now, we need it. It's the quickest way to Peru and attracts the least attention." He leaned back, searching her eyes. "After...you know, after we find our parents, we'll talk. About my money. About what we can do with it. How we can help people. Like you're doing with Crash Space."

She hugged him. "We have to," she whispered, her head on his chest. "I can't live like this. Not after being on the streets. Knowing what it's like for people who have nothing."

"You won't give up the Dream Rider comic, will you?" Fader asked.

Will grinned. "Never, dude. Not after finding such a talented assistant."

"Afraid of being unemployed at twelve?" Case asked, happy to lighten the mood.

Mei walked by them toward the rear of the cabin where Peng was lifting backpacks onto shelves, ducking his head to avoid hitting it on the ceiling. "Washrooms at the back, including showers," Mei said. "Kitchen, too. Which is self-serve, because..." She hooked a thumb at herself. "...not a waitress."

Adi and Stone joined them. The doors to the plane and cockpit were now closed. "We're taking off shortly, so please take your seats," Adi said. "You three can sit up here. Rani, could you please join them? Stone and I need to talk to Mei and Peng at that table."

Grumbling to herself, Rani moved to a front-facing seat in the forward area. Case sat across the aisle from Rani, facing Will. Fader took the seat facing Rani, across from Will, and began playing with the seat controls.

From a brochure in her seat pocket, Case learned they were flying on a Cloudstream C700, which could carry twelve passengers. She also learned the cabin dimensions, the entertainment and dining features, and that the plane had a range of seven thousand nautical miles.

"How far can that get us?" she asked Will.

"Farther than Peru. We'll fly non-stop."

A male voice sounded overhead, introducing himself and his copilot. He explained he'd received clearance for takeoff, so passengers should now be seated with seat belts fastened. Case helped Fader secure his belt, then did her own, trying to relax. At least, fear of her first plane flight was pushing fears of the trip to the back of her mind.

Will smiled from where he sat facing her. "First time, right?"

She nodded, too nervous to talk.

"I hate flying," Rani said.

"Not helping," Case said through clenched teeth.

"Relax," Will said. "This flight is probably the safest part of our trip."

"*Really* not helping."

A low rumbling began, sending vibrations up through her legs as the sound rose to a higher pitch. "Engines starting up," Will said. Through her window, she saw, more than felt, the plane begin to move.

"Taxiing to the runway," he explained. She just nodded, her fingers digging into the armrests. Fader stared out his window, taking it all in, wide-eyed and open-mouthed.

The plane finished its turn onto the runway. And stopped.

"Why'd we stop?" she asked, half hoping they wouldn't take off.

"Probably for final clearance from air traffic control," Will said.

The engine noise grew to a muffled roar accompanied by a rising whine. Accelerating faster than she expected, the plane shot forward, pressing her back. The cabin tipped up, pushing her down into the plush seat as the plane's nose lifted and the ground outside her window fell away. Ten seconds later, she could see all of downtown and the sun shining on the lake, a half-hour drive away.

A thump from below made her jump. "What was that?"

"Landing gear coming up," Will said. "Should've warned you."

Case took a deep breath, trying to relax. Part of her was thrilling at the experience. The city she'd lived in all her life lay spread below like a child's construction set. She remembered her first view of downtown streets from Will's tower, the streets that had been her and Fader's home since she was twelve.

Now, those streets were tiny lines between tiny buildings. Had her life moved that far above those streets? Then why did they still feel such a part of her?

She swallowed. Because they *were* a part of her. And always would be, even if she and Fader found their mother and rebuilt their lives as a family in a real home. Even if she built a life with Will, she would never completely leave those streets behind.

"This is so cool!" Fader cried, turning from the window to grin at her, pulling her from her thoughts. "Case, we're flying!"

"Noticed."

"Case, c'mon."

"Yeah, you're right. We're flying, and it *is* cool." She turned to Will. "Even if we still don't know where we're flying to."

"Adi'll tell us once we're at cruising height," Will said. "At least our mysterious enemies don't know where we're going, either."

You hope, she thought.

Chapter 20

New Girl

"I know where they're going," Orden called with Beroald's voice.

Seated on the canopy bed in the tower room, Morrigan looked up from another fruitless examination of the Unicorn in the tapestry that bore its name. Despite her efforts, the strange creature still refused to yield its secrets. She wrapped the woven artifact around her shoulders again. "How did you learn that?"

Orden smiled with Beroald's face from beside the Black Pool. "The Archambeault woman just reviewed something called a flight plan with the operator of their flying machine..."

...this conveyance you call an airplane.

Morrigan stiffened as those last words sounded in her mind, not her ears. "You promised me my body," she whispered.

And you still have that control. You still speak with your mouth, do you not? Think of me as a passenger in your head.

"A passenger for how long?"

Until I find a suitable host at our destination. They are flying to Arequipa. With the Chakana.

"I do not know where—"

A city in southern Peru, apparently.

"Apparently?"

The city rose after my...departure...from the Sisterhood. But the Pool shows that the city is safely distant from the Crossing. We will intercept them there and seize the Chakana. Stand up. We leave now. They arrive in just over eight hours.

Morrigan stood. "Can we get there in time?"

I do not understand your modern world and its ways of travel. But the Pool tells me a flying machine can take us from Qosqo to Arequipa in under an hour. We should arrive well before they do.

"Qosqo? Do you mean Cusco?" Morrigan and Marell had once pursued the monk Yeshe to there, but he had evaded them.

Ah, yes. I used its original Quechuan name.

"But why Cusco? Why not go directly to Arequipa?"

You will see.

Morrigan bit back her frustration. Orden parceled out information like crumbs fed to pigeons. She didn't enjoy being a pigeon. "Will we seize the Chakana at the airport?"

We will observe them, but likely make no move. I need time to plan, to arrange resources. And we have that time. They will spend two days in Arequipa to acclimate to the altitude, at a hotel the Archambeault woman identified. We will seize the Chakana there, before they move on. Now, we must leave.

Beroald stiffened beside the Black Pool, staring now with unfocused eyes. Morrigan felt herself walk to the door of the tower room. *No! You said my body would remain my own.*

Don't be a child. You do not know the way. Directing your every step will slow us—and become tiresome. Once in Cusco, I will return control of your precious form to you.

Morrigan fell silent as Orden descended the spiral stairs from the Black Tower in Morrigan's body. When they reached the maze of tunnels Morrigan had followed to reach the Tower, she soon became lost as Orden negotiated turn after turn without hesitating.

They emerged into the banquet hall in the Black Pyramid where she had fought the scarabs. Few traces of the dead and burned creatures remained.

My beauties feasted on their fallen cousins, Orden explained. *Their will to survive is strong.*

And how will Beroald and your servants survive in your absence?

I commanded them to eat and care for themselves. Morrigan felt her face frown. *At least, I think I did.* A shrug. *Ah, well. We'll see when we return.*

We are returning here after we obtain the Chakana?

A pause. *Eventually. First, there will be a...reunion with the Sisterhood. I have unfinished business at the Crossing.*

They ascended the broad, carpeted staircase from the banquet hall, then followed the upward sloping tunnel until they reached the Red Door, which still hung open and askew. They emerged on the top of the pyramid.

The black jungle lay spread below. In the distance, under the silver dome of sky, the strip of blue sand where she'd found the scarab nursery separated the dark trees from the darker sea. Orden walked to the steps and began the long descent. At the bottom, she headed for the jungle, following the same path Morrigan had taken coming here.

Morrigan sorted through her thoughts and questions as they walked. After they were deep into the jungle, she spoke in her mind. *You have explained the Four and the One to me. And the thing you call the Story. But I still don't know what the Chakana is, this thing we chase.*

The Chakana opens the Crossing. And the Crossing is the only path to the Book.

The Book?

The Book of the Four, where the Four read the Story. Where they see their precious creation unfold. Where the past, present, and possible futures of the multiverse are written. A pause and a smile. *And where I shall finish writing my own Story, a tale I began so long ago.*

I still don't understand.

A shrug. *You know enough for now. You ask too many questions.*

Then answer just one. You spoke of a partnership between the Four and the Sisters.

What of it?

How can that be? A partnership between... Morrigan hesitated, still struggling with the concept. *...between gods and mortals?*

For several breaths, Orden didn't reply as they continued through the jungle. But Morrigan caught snatches of memories, of powerful emotions. Then Orden spoke, and for once the arrogance was missing, replaced by something Morrigan at first couldn't name. Then she knew it. For she'd felt it herself. When she'd learned her first spell. When she'd held the Weave. When she'd stood before the Tapestry all those years ago.

Awe.

A partnership? Orden said finally. *Yes, but so much more. The Four choose four.*

What?

From all the Sisterhood, four Sisters are chosen. Chosen by the Four. Those Sisters become the Madres. So great an honor. So great a power.

Again, Orden fell silent. Morrigan waited, but no more came. Orden seemed lost in her memories. *Chosen how?*

An overwhelming sense of rapture flowed from Orden, stunning Morrigan with its intensity. *It is beautiful. So beautiful. To merge with the infinite, to become one, to—*

Orden cut off her thoughts, and Morrigan sensed she had shown more than intended. *I will not profane that memory by sharing it with the likes of you.*

A realization came to Morrigan. *You were a Madre!*

No reply.

But you said you are Orden.

I am Orden. I was a Madre. La Madre del Orden.

How can you be both?

I told you. The Four must view Its creation through the eyes of mortals. The Four must become mortal.

They...become the Madres?

No. They become one with *the Madres. To use the Book, each of the Four merge with a Madre, to see the Story through human eyes, but with the power of the One to understand. Each Madre is a symbiotic being—at once both the original human and the one of the Four that chose her. In this way, each new Madre is a different creature than the previous Madre who hosted that aspect of the Four.*

Each new *Madre? Then a Madre can die?*

The Madres live long, thanks to the Breath of the Three. But they die. Bitterness flavored Orden's next thought. *Or are killed.*

The Breath of the Three?

Enough questions. Be silent. I need to plan.

They stepped from the jungle path onto the beach of blue sand beside the churning black sea. In the distance to her right lay the tunnel mouth in the rock wall where she'd emerged from beneath Castle Rushen. *Is that our destination?*

Yes.

I came this way.

Many have.

But it leads to Castle Rushen. To my homeland.

It leads to many places.

I don't understand.

You will. Or you will not. I do not care. Now be silent.

As Orden trudged Morrigan's body along the beach, Morrigan thought back over what she had learned. And what Orden had revealed, intended or not. Awe hadn't been the only emotion in her memories of merging with the Orden aspect of the Four, of becoming a Madre. There'd been something else. Something that Morrigan had felt herself many times in her life. Something, it seemed in that moment, that had always driven her.

The lust for power.

Orden chuckled in her mind, reminding Morrigan her thoughts were no longer hers alone.

We are much alike, you and I, are we not? Orden said.

Morrigan prayed silently that wasn't true. But Orden heard her prayer and laughed at her with her own mouth.

When they reached the tunnel, Orden allowed Morrigan to cast a glowing hawk before them. The thrill of using magic filled her again. Orden had forbidden her to use it while in the Black Tower.

At first, the way seemed familiar, and she waited for the tunnel to become the passage she'd taken beneath Castle Rushen that had led to the blue sand beach beside the black sea. She swallowed. The passage she should have taken all those years ago.

The passage Dany had taken.

But then the tunnel changed from what she remembered from her arrival on the Black Island. An inky river appeared to their left, burbling and whispering in its swift flow. The glimmer of her hawk reflected off the walls' obsidian sheen, sending yellow-tinged shadows skittering around them.

Finally, the way widened, emptying into a domed cavern carved from the same black rock and twice the size of Orden's room atop the Black Tower. Dark timbers formed the floor of the cavern, giving the place, with the river flowing by, the appearance of a seaside pier.

It is a pier, Orden said. *And here is our transport for the next stage of this journey.*

A slender, high-prowed gondola-like craft, as scarlet as the Red Door, bobbed in the water beside the pier. Morrigan could see no ropes or fastenings holding the boat at its berth. *I didn't come this way.*

For those who hear the Song, many paths from many places lead to the Black Island. If I was not with you, you would return the way you came, finding yourself once again beneath the castle home of your youth. I, however, can choose any route to your world.

You can go anywhere in the world?

That is not what I said. I can travel to any place that holds a way to the Black Island. One such place lies in the home of my youth, the place you now call Cusco.

Orden stepped into the gondola, Morrigan still a passenger in her own body. She saw no oars, paddles, or poles. A tiller handle attached to a rudder at the stern. Seating herself there, Orden pushed off from the pier, one hand on the tiller. The river's current seized the slim craft, and they slipped from the cavern into the dark tunnel mouth, Morrigan's glowing hawk lighting their way.

This river now flows away from the sea, Morrigan said. *How can that be?*

Because I wish it so.

How will we return? This boat has no means of propulsion, and this current is strong.

If we return this way, the river will flow toward the sea.

How?

Because I will wish it so.

Morrigan fell silent in her own head, watching as Orden steered through a maze of underground passages. When the river presented a choice of tunnels, Orden never hesitated, guiding their craft with calm assurance. Morrigan soon lost track of the turns Orden took.

Finally, the river slowed, and the gondola slid into another cavern of black stone similar to where they'd embarked. Orden steered to the cavern's wooden pier, where the boat again attached itself.

Stepping out, Orden walked to an opening on the far side of the cavern, where stone stairs led upward. *Now, as promised, I return control of your body to you.*

Morrigan seemed to step forward inside her head, as the Orden presence retreated. Retreated, but still there.

Raising her hands before her face, Morrigan opened and closed them, reveling in that small act of independence. "Why now?" she asked, her voice again her own.

Climb these steps, and we will enter your world again, where you are better to navigate.

Sending her hawk ahead, Morrigan began to ascend. "Where will I emerge?"

In the remnants of Qoricancha in Cusco. Orden's thought carried sadness, a sense of ancient greatness now gone.

"Which is?"

The Temple of the Sun, the grandest temple of my people when this city was the beating heart of the Inca empire.

"Your people? You are...were an Inca?"

When the Sisterhood first chose me, many years before I became a Madre, I was a young girl named Quilla.

Again, Morrigan caught whispers of old memories, old emotions. A wistfulness, a yearning for a time now lost forever.

"The Incas formed the Sisterhood?"

A laugh. *The Sisterhood was ancient before the Incas walked this world. The Sisters have existed since the Four chose human partners. Enough. We near the surface.*

The black rock disappeared. The staircase walls were now gray stones, rectangular and smooth, fitting together precisely with no sign of mortar. And with that transition came something else. Something that grew worse the higher she climbed.

Collapsing onto the next step, she tried to gasp in a breath, but her lungs couldn't find the oxygen they craved. "I...can't...breathe."

Ah, yes. We have passed from my realm into Cusco. We climb now through the foundations of what was once Qoricancha. You are feeling the altitude, the thinner air. Do you have spells to deal with this?

Calming her mind, she summoned a healing spell, one that would search her body for signs of distress and, hopefully, deal with it. She felt a prickling as the runes crawled over her skin and, a moment later, a tingling in her chest. A few heartbeats later, she could breathe again.

Good? Then rise.

Morrigan rose. And climbed.

The Spaniards destroyed Qoricancha, then built a church on its foundations. Earthquakes damaged that church time and again, but the stones of Qoricancha on which they built still stand. We will emerge among those stones.

Morrigan sensed the pride of the Inca girl, Quilla, in Orden's voice.

Once, Qoricancha held four temples. The Temples of the Sun, of the Moon, of Thunder and Storms. And where we will find ourselves—amongst the few walls that remain of the Temple of Ch'aska, of Venus and the Stars.

"We will be in the middle of ruins?"

Ruins preserved inside a modern building attached to the church. Qorican-

cha is a tourist site. A busy one, from what the Pool showed. Avoid detection when you emerge.

"How will I do that?"

You are a witch. Figure it out.

A light grew ahead. Dismissing her hawk, Morrigan climbed the remaining steps to stand inside a trapezoidal doorway, narrower at the top than the bottom. Beyond lay a rectangular space enclosed by low walls of stone blocks like those she had just climbed past. Trapezoidal niches sat regularly spaced at shoulder height along the walls.

The Temple of Ch'aska, Orden said. Morrigan caught sorrow and anger in those words. And a sense of great loss.

The stone walls rose to the height of a modern room. Looking up, she saw the temple had no ceiling and lay within a larger current-day white-walled building. A higher level with a varnished wooden banister overlooked the ruins.

The Temple of Ch'aska enclosed a space perhaps twelve paces by twenty. At least two dozen tourists, cameras and phones held ready, were filing around its perimeter, examining the walls and niches. None gave Morrigan a second glance as they passed her doorway.

They cannot see you. They see only stone. If they touch this space, they feel only stone.

She thought of the wall in Castle Rushen that had hidden the Tapestry. "Then how does one reach the cavern below?"

Those who hear the Song are led to this doorway. They see no wall. They can step through, descend the steps, find the boat that brought us here. Just as you can step forward now. But again, let no one see you. I wish no attention drawn to this gateway.

She called up a concealment spell, her skin tingling as the runes flowed down her left arm. She touched that hand to her forehead, felt the spell take hold, then emerged into the ruined temple.

No head turned her way. No eye fell on her.

She exited the temple, then located a modern washroom. Finding it empty, she dropped the concealment spell. She primped at the mirror until Orden threatened to retake control. With a final adjustment of her hair, she flipped her Tapestry cloak back like a cape and left the washroom.

"And now to Arequipa?" she asked, passing a tourist couple as she followed signs for the exit.

The man frowned at her. "Qué?"

Ignoring them, she swept past.

From now on, your communications with me should remain unspoken.

Sorry. Now that I can speak again, it's difficult to break the habit.

Yes. To Arequipa.

Outside, she found the expected row of taxis that lives at any tourist attraction. Getting into one, she cast a compulsion spell on the driver to take them to the airport.

Do you have the currency for this service? Orden asked.

"This ride will be free, will it not?" Morrigan said.

The driver pulled away from the curb. "Of course, Mistress."

Orden smiled in her mind. *I knew you would be useful.*

A thought occurred to Morrigan. *Oh, dear.*

What?

I just remembered another taxi ride. To Castle Rushen.

What of it?

I told the driver to wait for me.

So?

He will still be waiting. He will wait until I return. He will wait even if I never return.

Orden laughed at this. Once, Morrigan would have laughed as well. Instead, she felt only sadness. And something else. Something new.

Guilt.

Chapter 21

It's a Good Life if You Don't Weaken

After their plane reached cruising altitude, Will unfastened his seat belt and stood. He was bored of listening to a Spanish refresher course on his phone and impatient to learn both their destination and Adi's plans.

"What's up?" Case asked.

"Time to talk to Adi."

Rani glanced up from her phone. "Should we come?"

Will nodded. "We're in this together."

Fader jumped up. "Critter Crew...*assemble!*"

"You've been so waiting to say that, haven't you?" Case said.

They followed Will back to where Adi and Stone sat across the table from Mei and Peng, Adi and Mei in the window seats.

"Yes, we can talk now," Adi said, before Will could speak. She indicated the sofa across the aisle. They sat, Will at one end, then Case, Fader, and Rani. Adi propped up her tablet on the table. "I'll review our travel plans. Then, William, you can share what Nyx told you this morning. Unless you'd prefer to start with that?"

"No, it can wait." He was still processing learning his parents had taken him to Peru to save him. He'd have trouble talking about it and was happy to delay that.

Adi touched her tablet. A map of Peru appeared, then zoomed to the south-west corner. "We are flying direct to Arequipa. Our flight will be just over eight hours, depending on winds. Arequipa is the same time zone as Toronto, so we will land around seven-thirty tonight."

"Why not Lima or Cusco?" Will asked.

"Lima is too low for acclimating to altitude, Cusco too high. Arequipa offers a good compromise—2,300 meters above sea level, compared to 3,200 meters at our final destination—with a landing strip long enough for this jet. Plus, our contact is there."

"Who's that?" Will asked.

"Gabriel Herrada." She tapped her tablet again.

A photo of a long-faced, olive-skinned man appeared. Brown eyes under thick eyebrows. Curly black hair, with a neatly trimmed beard speckled with gray, framing a warm smile.

"Gabriel is Executive Director of the Bureau of Antiquities in the Ministry of Culture. He will meet us on landing and assist with customs and immigration. Which reminds me..." Producing two passports from her jacket, she handed them to Case and Fader.

"Cool!" Fader said, opening his. "Case, we have passports!"

"*Fake* passports, I'm guessing," Will said, feeling his old discomfort over how his parents had operated. How Adi still operated.

"What?" Case said.

"Legal passports require proof of citizenship," Adi said, "plus government-issued photo ID. Neither of you have those. Besides, Fader presented another problem."

Fader looked up from inspecting his passport. "What?"

"You're under sixteen—a minor to our federal government. For you, a passport application can only be made..." Adi hesitated. "...by a parent or legal guardian."

"Oh," he said, dropping his eyes.

Case slipped an arm around him. "Hey, dude. Mom'll get us real passports after we bring her home."

Fader nodded but said nothing. Will's gut clenched at the reminder of what was at stake.

"You would've had another problem," Case said. "I have a juvie record, and we're supposed to be in foster homes. I ran away from mine and busted Fader out of his."

Will knew Adi was aware of those things, and he realized she'd chosen not to mention them. Another sign of the thaw in her relationship with Case.

Peng held out his fist to Fader. "Wanted man! Dude, you just keep getting cooler."

Fader brightened and did the fist bump. Mei punched Peng in the arm, but smiled. And Will put another tick in his mental 'good guys' column for Peng and Mei.

"How will this Gabriel Herrada help with immigration?" Will asked.

"Gabriel used to head Customs and Immigration. He's maintained strong contacts there."

"Does he know these are fake passports?"

"Yes."

"And he has no problem with that?"

Adi hesitated. "In his earlier post, Gabriel...assisted your parents exporting relics from their first trip to Peru. Now, as head of the Bureau of Antiquities, he's requested we return certain potteries. They're in the crate we're bringing."

"Wait," Will said. "They brought the Chakana back on that trip. Does he know about it?"

"No. Remember, your parents and I flew back, with the Chakana, out of Bolivia. Gabriel arranged for the other relics from that trip to be shipped later from Peru. He never knew about the Chakana."

"So, to smuggle us in, we're bribing him with stuff my parents once bribed him to smuggle out. Nice gig."

"William, Gabriel had a long relationship with your parents. He held similar positions in Ecuador and Columbia, and assisted them many times. Yes, it was a business relationship, but he always proved trustworthy."

Will didn't reply, trying to reconcile, as always, the conflicting portraits of his parents. Were they opportunistic treasure hunters and cultural grave robbers, as the media said? Or the impassioned archeologists and dealers in rare antiquities they'd claimed to be?

Both?

Whatever, they'd inspired deep loyalties and friendships. Adi was one example, and this Gabriel Herrada another.

Adi had continued. "...two days to acclimate. We're staying at a small hotel outside the tourist area. For security, we booked the entire facility for a fictional conference scheduled to begin after we leave. We will be the only guests."

"Then what?" Will asked.

"Another reason for selecting Arequipa. It has an air force base. A military helicopter will drop us near the red dot location. But not too near." Adi tapped her screen again. The map reappeared, displaying the familiar circle of green dots and central red dot.

Adi pointed to a flashing yellow dot inside the circle and near the red dot. "We selected this drop location after discussions with my military contact, based on the terrain between there and the red dot. From there, it's a two-day hike." She looked around the group. "Questions? No? Then, William, you may now share what you learned from Nyx this morning."

Will glanced at Peng and Mei, then back to Adi.

"Everyone here knows of the previous Peru expedition," she said, "as well as your adventures on the Black Island, the abilities you three possess, and the recent appearance of your..." She shrugged.

"Critters," Rani said.

"We're the Critter Crew," Fader explained to Mei and Peng.

"Cool name," Peng said. "Wish I had an animal companion."

"I have one," Mei said.

"You do?"

"Sitting beside him."

"Funny. Ha ha."

Will began describing his encounter with Nyx in the greenhouse. Had it only been that morning? It seemed days ago, already.

Case stopped him. "Wait. You can astral project now? While awake?"

"Yeah," he said, happy for the delay. "Nyx made me practice till it got easy. Well, sort of easy. She said we—you, me, Fader—will have to grow our powers to face what we'll meet in Peru."

"Way to start on a positive note," Case said. "How're we supposed to do that?"

"She didn't say."

"Sounds like Nyx."

"Have your own powers changed, too?" Adi asked Case and Fader.

"My Voice is still around. Told me to stop the van because Rani was coming. But nothing new."

"I'm waiting to decide whether to thank you," Rani said.

"I can still fade," Fader said. "And reach the In Between. But no new powers."

"Was this what you wanted to share?" Adi asked Will. "Your new ability?"

"No. Nyx showed me something." He took a deep breath, then pushed on, his eyes on the floor as he told of how his parents, desperate to save him, had exposed the Chakana. Of their bargain with Luciana, Madre of Chaos, to surrender the Chakana in return for curing him. Of Ellie Cootes agreeing to come—and why. And, finally, of Luciana leading his parents, Ellie, and an unconscious Will in a wheelchair, through the glowing portal.

He finished. No one spoke. Case held Fader to her, his face buried in her shoulder. She wiped at her eyes even as she comforted her brother.

"Sorry," Will said, feeling guilty. "I was so caught up in what I'd learned about my parents, I never thought about you guys."

"I didn't know she was in debt," Case said. "I didn't know what she was dealing with."

"Parents rarely share their problems with their children," Adi said, glancing at Will.

Case shook her head. "No. It's okay. It's good. She didn't abandon us. She didn't run away. She was trying to help us."

Something in her face recalled to Will that little girl in the Christmas memory she'd once shown him in Dream. The little girl she hid inside.

Adi broke into his thoughts. "It also confirms we were wise not to trust Pablo. He denied knowing of your parents' planned return to Peru, yet your father said Pablo himself had been arranging that expedition."

"Do you still think Pablo had nothing to do with whatever happened?" Will asked.

Adi hesitated. "I don't see how, assuming this Luciana took you directly to this mysterious Crossing by..." She shrugged. "...teleporting or whatever you'd call it."

"*Saltar*," Rani said.

"Excuse me?" Adi asked.

"Isobel—the Sister who helped us on the Black Island—called it *saltar*. Spanish for *leap*." Rani raised her hands like paws in front of her. "Like Puma Girl here." She jerked a thumb at Case.

"Is that an option for us?" Stone asked. "To reach this Crossing?"

Adi frowned. "Expose the Chakana to bring a Sister? An option—but a desperate one, requiring we trust these people. I'm not convinced we can."

"I trust Isobel," Case said.

"She is only one Sister," Adi said. "And you said she required much convincing before she trusted you. The last we now know of Jon and Terri—and your mother—is that they stepped through that portal, surrendering themselves to these Sisters." She hesitated. "Only Will returned from that...and half dead."

And broken, he thought.

Adi shook her head. "No. I prefer to trust our own resources."

"Until we don't have a choice," Will said.

"What do you mean?" Adi asked.

"We're trying to reach the Crossing, whatever it is. The Sisters are at the Crossing. The Sisters know what happened to us. To my parents. Ellie Cootes. Me. At some point, we'll have to trust them."

"Or bargain with them. They want the Chakana. We have it. We need to keep that leverage. Stepping through a portal into the unknown—into *their* world—is not how to do that."

Will fell silent. He wouldn't win this argument and didn't want Adi taking back the Chakana, fearing he'd expose it to summon a Sister.

Case changed the subject for him. "You said the Sister your parents summoned called Luciana a 'Mother of the Book.'"

Will nodded. "She said, 'The Mothers serve the Four. And we serve the Mothers.'"

"Isobel said four Madres lead the Sisterhood, so that fits. But who are these Four that the four Madres serve? And what is the Book? And why is Luciana the 'Mother of Chaos'?"

"Yep. Every answer just brings more questions," Will said.

"This entire discussion assumes we believe your Nyx," Adi said, "who is somehow part of the Chakana, which I've never trusted."

"Ouch," came a familiar voice. "That stings."

Will turned. At the rear of the plane, Nyx floated, full-bodied. "And here I was about to answer your questions."

"Nyx?" Will said. "How are you here?"

Adi followed his gaze. "Nyx? Where?"

"You can't see her?"

"Obviously not."

"Neither can I," Stone said. Mei and Peng shook their heads, too.

"I can," Fader said.

"Me, too," Case added.

"And so can I," Rani said, peering at Nyx. "Great hair."

Nyx floated up to them. "Thank you, Rani."

"Wait. You know me?"

"I'm Will's subconscious. So, yes."

"Why can Case, Fader, and Rani see you?" Will asked. "And why only them?"

"Hmm. Probably because—for some still unknown reason—they are the Critter Crew. They see the Guardians—the Snake, the Puma, the Condor."

Fader brightened. "They're guardians? That's good, right?"

"Sure," Nyx said. "Although it probably means you're in mortal danger, so yeah, there's that."

"Wait. What?" Rani said.

"Would *someone* please tell me what is happening?" Adi demanded.

"Uh, we can see Nyx, and she's going to answer our questions," Will said.

"*Some* of your questions," Nyx corrected. "From the pieces I've been able to remember."

"From my memories?"

"No, from my Chakana memories. Or from my growing understanding of what the Chakana is." She frowned. "What *I* am?"

Will related that to Adi, Stone, Mei, and Peng. "Any answers are welcome," Adi said.

"What happens now?" Will asked.

"Movie time!" Nyx waved a hand. A screen appeared, filling the end of the cabin.

"Do you see the movie screen?" Case asked Adi.

"What? No," Adi said, sounding exasperated. Stone, Mei, and Peng shook their heads.

"I'll narrate," Rani said. "I'm used to this."

"How can you be used to *this*?" Will asked.

Rani shrugged. "It's what I do. Reporting. Take what I learn, identify the key points, and present those back so brilliantly any idiot can understand."

"Thank you, Ms. Patel," Adi said. "We idiots appreciate it."

"Sorry. Not what I meant."

"What's the movie about?" Will asked Nyx.

"About thirty minutes."

Will glared at her.

"Answers to your questions. The Book, the Four, the Sisters, the Madres. And more." She waved a hand. The screen went black.

No. Not black. More than black. Less than it, too. It was the black of the stain he'd seen inside the Chakana. And when he'd smelled the Flower. A blackness that had tried to pull him into it.

It was emptiness. The void. The Nothing.

"In the beginning," Nyx said, "there was nothing…"

And the story of the Story began.

Half an hour later, Will sat back, a silent member of a now silent group. Nyx had finished telling of the One. And the Four. And their partnership with the Madres. Of the creation of the Book that holds the Story. The Story that was the universe. The multiverse. All of existence.

Rani had narrated what Nyx had shown, clearly and accurately, with little of her normal color commentary. She was the first to break the silence. "I need a beer." Getting up, she walked past Nyx to the kitchen in the back.

Peng waved a hand. "I'll take one."

Mei looked at Stone, who nodded. "Me, too," she called.

Adi shook her head. "So...we're an *experiment?*"

Rani returned with the beers. Plopping back down on the couch, she took a sip of hers. "A game to amuse the gods—which means the Greeks pretty well nailed it."

"But with free will," Will said. "That's good, right? We make our own decisions."

Rani shrugged. "Our own mistakes, too."

"You three," Adi said, "you've experienced more of this than any of us. Do you believe this story? This...*Story?*"

"I want to," Will said quietly.

Adi frowned. "Why?"

"Because of my parents. This Book—where the past, present, and possible futures of the multiverse are written—that's like the Akashic Records, isn't it? If it's true, then Mom and Dad weren't crazy. They were after something *real*. Something huge. And they were willing to give it all up to save me."

Case squeezed his hand as they all fell quiet until Adi spoke again. "William, I can understand you wanting to believe this...but *do* you?"

Did he? He thought about what they'd been through. "I don't know about the One and the Four, but we've seen proof of the multiverse."

Case nodded. "The In Between. That corridor of doors. Fader's even been *in* parallel worlds."

Fader hugged himself at that reminder.

"And other intelligences merging with people?" Will said. "Marell could do that. Yeshe, too..." His voice trailed off. Could *he* do that, too? Now that he could astral project? Would he *want* to? He remembered Case telling of Marell's attack on her, how she'd felt so violated. Could he do that to another person?

Nyx floated up. "You do realize I can hear you wondering if I just spent thirty minutes lying to you, right?"

"Nyx, it's a lot to take in. And accept," Will said, then turned to the others. "She's complaining we don't believe her."

"These other universes," Stone said, unfocused eyes on the table. "They are worlds where our lives took different paths? The people we knew...their lives, too?"

Peng and Mei exchanged a look with each other and with Adi. "Perhaps," Adi said softly.

Stone stared out the window. "Then I choose to believe this."

Will frowned a question at Adi, but she shook her head. He turned to Case. "What do you think?"

"I'm ready to believe it all," Case said. "The hardest part for me is the Madres. Merging with these beings, these Four. That means our mom—your parents, too—when they met this Luciana, they met a person with a *god* inside her."

"It also means," Rani said, peeling the label off her beer, "that the people who are chasing us for the Chakana have gods inside them. Are we still sure we don't want to call them and offer it back?"

Adi glared at her. Rani shrugged and took another sip. "Just saying..."

Will thought about that. "These 'gods' went eight years without finding the Chakana. And sending the Sisters after it hasn't worked. Plus, *we* had to rescue those Sisters from the Black Tower. Then the failed attack at the bank. For gods, they mess up a lot."

"Maybe it hasn't always been them," Rani offered.

"Meaning multiple parties are after us? Thanks for that thought."

"Or their powers are weaker without the Chakana," Case said.

"Is that true?" Will asked Nyx. "You've still told us almost nothing about the Chakana. Which is part of you."

"Part of you, too, Astral Boy," Nyx said. "All I know is that it opens—I open?—the Crossing, which is how the Madres access the Book to read the Story. But I don't know *how* it 'opens' the Crossing—or what that means. I don't even know what the Crossing looks like or how you, you know, *cross* it. Same for the Book."

"You mean you can't remember?" Will asked.

Nyx looked pained. "More like I'm not allowed to access that information. Even if I remembered, I'm not sure I could tell you. It'd be like letting you past a locked door."

"Kind of the purpose of a key. Which you are."

"Except *you* aren't supposed to have the key."

Will related this to Adi. She shook her head. "I repeat—we are being moved in a game."

"It may be a game to these beings," Rani said. "But if we have free will, we're not being moved."

"No, but they can see the board," Adi replied.

Case's brow furrowed. "Can they?"

"What do you mean?" Adi asked.

"They haven't had the Chakana for eight years. If they need the Chakana to read the Book, *can* they see the board?"

"Wow. Good question," Nyx said, then disappeared.

"Ask Nyx if—" Adi began.

"She's gone," Will said.

Adi sighed. "Typical."

More discussion followed, but led nowhere. Will sensed only he, Case, and Fader fully believed Nyx's tale, but they'd lived this weirdness more than the rest.

Adi didn't trust the Chakana or Nyx. Rani, very reporter-like, still had questions but remained open to the story. He couldn't read Mei or Peng. The concept seemed to provide Stone an inner peace, though peace from what, Will couldn't guess.

Adi, Stone, Mei, and Peng resumed discussing security logistics. Rani returned to her seat at the front and pulled out her phone. At the back, Fader scrolled through movies on the video system. Case sat beside him, more to be near her brother after the news about their mom, Will guessed, than to be entertained.

He was ready to join them when Nyx's voice sounded in his head. *We need to talk. And by talk, I mean this way. Don't speak out loud.*

Will frowned. *About what?*

Go back to your seat.

He did that. Across the aisle, Rani ignored him, immersed in her phone. *Now what?*

You need to astral project.

Why?

To see something only your astral form can see. Besides, more practice can't hurt.

Fine. Give me a sec.

He didn't know how other astral travelers prepared, but the way he'd used that morning in the greenhouse worked for him. Close his eyes. Calm his mind. Focus on the darkness, on his silver cord emerging from that darkness. Feel its tug in his chest, pushing him out, then *pulling* him out, until...

Until he felt himself floating.

He opened his eyes to stare down from his glowing astral body at his physical one in the plane seat, his silver cord connecting his two forms. Nyx, now visible again, floated beside him.

Can the others see us? he asked.

No. Now, focus on your cord.

I'm doing that. What am I supposed to—?

Then he saw it. A *second* silver cord, snaking from his astral chest, as did his first cord. But rather than attaching to his physical chest, it dipped down into a pocket of the jeans his physical body wore—the pocket holding the Chakana.

That second cord, Nyx said, *connects the Chakana to the piece of itself inside you.*

Through a Faraday pouch?

Remember what Yeshe said: nothing can stop a silver cord. That cord is why you can be on this trip—your connection to the Chakana remains, even with the Chakana shielded.

I've astral projected before. Why couldn't I see this second cord then?

Your connection to the Chakana was still too weak. It's become stronger.

Why?

Since the Chakana awoke, destroying its lead box in Adi's safe, its connection to you has grown. That's why you can astral project so easily now. And why I can appear to you outside Dream.

But those are good things, right?

She didn't answer.

Right?

Those things come at a cost. Your connection to the Chakana grows stronger because the part of it inside you grows stronger.

So?

It means your true self is getting weaker. Nyx floated to face him. The touch of her words in his mind was gentle, but he sensed her fear.

Will, she said. *You're dying.*

Chapter 22

Life Goes by and I Can't Keep Up

In astral form, Will floated beside Nyx in the plane cabin. Below him, his body sat in his seat, eyes closed. He stared at his silver cords. *Both* cords.

The cord connecting to his body—the cord, he realized, representing his life. And now, this second cord connecting to the Chakana—the cord representing his death.

How long? he asked.

I don't know, Nyx said. *But it's not inevitable. As Luciana told your parents eight years ago, if you can get to the Crossing, you can be cured. And we're going there.*

My parents took me to the Crossing. I'm still broken.

Will, we don't know what happened eight years ago. I can't see that memory. We don't know what will happen this time, either.

She didn't answer.

What will I feel?

Physically, you'll feel no pain or weakness. But the link between your astral body and your real one will grow fainter, thinner, until your body can no longer hold your astral spirit. You'll still be able to astral project, probably more easily, but at some point, you won't be able to return to your body.

You mean I'll die.

Your body will. Your spirit will…move on.

Move on. Like Yeshe did. To the Realms of the Dead.

Don't think like that. We'll reach the Crossing. The Sisters will help.

He didn't answer, as another memory came to him. *When I projected in the Black Tower, the Chakana drew me inside it, toward a blackness…an emptiness at its heart. Jack pulled me out.*

That blackness represents the missing piece of the Chakana that sits inside you.

Was it trying to restore that piece by pulling me in?

No. It wanted to communicate with you. Jack cut that short. Now it can talk through me.

But could *it have removed the piece from me?*

A pause. *Yes. And it still could pull it from you, restore itself. But it never would.*

Why not?

If it removes that piece from you outside the Crossing, it will kill you.

It is *killing me.*

The Chakana doesn't want your death.

Then why did it connect to me eight years ago? Why did it...infect me?

It needs you. You, Case, Fader. And now, apparently, Rani. I don't know why, but I know we're running out of time. What's at stake remains hidden to me, but I sense it's more than just...forgive me...you.

Yeah, that's me. Getting all selfish, focusing on my impending death.

Will, I didn't—

You know what? Unless you have answers instead of vague warnings you can't explain, I'd rather be alone right now.

Nyx sighed in a way that reminded him of Adi...and disappeared.

He floated above his body until he tired of staring at the two cords. Turning away, he drifted unseen down the plane.

Adi still sat at the table with Stone, Mei, and Peng, discussing security at the hotel. Suddenly, being attacked by unknown parties intent on the Chakana seemed a minor problem. *Whoever you are, if I could give it to you, I would.*

He reached where Case sat beside Fader, both giggling at a movie he recognized but in which, at the moment, he failed to find the humor.

He floated there, taking in the cabin, this tiny space that held everyone in his tiny world. Adi, his surrogate mother the past eight years. Case, the girl who'd crash-landed into his life and his heart less than a month ago. And Fader, the kid brother he'd never known he'd wanted till now.

The others? Stone's loyalty was to Adi, not some screwed-up teenager. Mei and Peng were devoted to Stone, not him. And Rani wanted a story.

Was that it? Only three people in the entire world cared about him? And before Case and Fader appeared, Adi had been the only one.

Was his world that small? Was his life that small? Before his parents disappeared, he'd dreamed of traveling the world like them. Now he was finally doing that—only to learn this might be the only trip he'd ever take. He'd never see the world.

See the world...

He stared out the window, at the clouds below, the sky above.

See the world...

Why not?

Taking a last look around the cabin and the people in his tiny universe, he floated to the window...and through it.

Fear. His first reaction. Outside the plane, above the Earth. Fear of falling. Fear of losing the plane and the people inside who were his world.

But he found he could fly alongside the jet by willing it in his mind, his two cords stretching from him to the plane.

Below, clouds sped by in peaks and valleys, ever-shifting mountain ranges of billowing whiteness stretching to the horizons. Random gaps revealed the world below—two ribbons, brown-green on the left, blue-green and white-specked on the right. The coast of South America meeting the Pacific Ocean.

Above, the sky, deep blue and running to black in the east. To the west, his right, a lowering sun lit the clouds ablaze with reds and golds.

The beauty of it all made him ache. Ache for what he would lose if Nyx was right—if he was dying. And he felt the truth in her words. Even now, his death cord, which he'd seen for the first time only minutes ago, glowed as brightly as his life cord. How long before his life cord faded completely, cutting him off from his body?

How long before he died?

See the world...

The clouds broke open again, and more glimpses of land and ocean below peeked through.

He could. He could see that world. Fly from here. Leave his dying body behind. See the world. All of it. Whatever he wanted. Wherever he wanted.

Assuming his cord—his *cords*—would stretch that far.

Yes. They would. Nothing could stop a silver cord.

That's your plan? came a familiar voice in his head.

He spun around in the air. Nyx now flew beside him.

Run away? she said. *Leave everyone behind? Never even say goodbye?*

He didn't answer.

To quote a young lady who I have grown to respect greatly...I never took you for a quitter, Home Boy.

He gazed down at the world below. Yes, he could see it all. But not with Case. He'd be alone. And he'd never be with her again. Never touch her or hold her or laugh with her.

Beside him flew a plane carrying everyone he loved in his world. His tiny world that sat inside this much larger one below. The larger world he ached to see before he died. A world he *would* see.

Some day. With Case.

I'm not going anywhere.

Just stepped outside for a bit of fresh air?

Mostly to get away from you.

Ouch. I'm in this, too, you know.

Duh. You're the Chakana.

Look at me. Really look at me.

He stared at where she flew beside him. *And what am I supposed to—* Then he saw them. *Two* silver cords.

Yes, she said. *Just like yours. One connects me to the Chakana, the other to you. The 'you' part of me. I'll lose that if you die.*

But you'll still exist. As the Chakana.

But I won't have you as part of me. And I like that part of me. I'd miss you, Will Dreycott.

Uh, are you speaking as Nyx or the Chakana?

Let's say me. But I know the Chakana chose you for a reason. A reason I can't remember, but it chose well. You're good people. You're strong and brave and smart. But most important, you have a good heart. I still can't see the danger we'll face, but the Chakana chose well.

Will didn't answer, realizing he'd left someone off his list of people who cared about him. If he could call Nyx 'people.'

I'd take that as the highest compliment, she said.

I keep forgetting—

That I'm in your head? Yes, and I plan to be for quite some time. So...enough fresh air?

He nodded. Turning to the plane, he let his cord—his life cord—pull him back inside. There, he hovered over his sleeping form, his two cords still visible.

I think you should call them Alive Cord and Dead Cord, Nyx said from beside him.

Why?

C'mon. Work with me. AC/DC.

Despite himself, despite his situation, he laughed. *I'll miss you, too, when...* He shrugged astral shoulders. *You know. When.*

Yes. You will. Because...me.

He dropped into his body. And opened his eyes.

Nyx was gone. Rani still scrolled through her phone, biting her lip and frowning, apparently oblivious to his absence. And presence. Standing, he walked down the plane. Stone still sat with Mei and Peng, a hand-drawn map of what he guessed was their Arequipa hotel spread before them.

Adi was walking back to the table from the kitchen carrying a tray of wrapped sandwiches. She put the tray down. "William, you should get something to eat before—" She broke off, startled, as he pulled her into a hug. To his surprise, after a hesitation, she put her arms around him and hugged him back.

"Did you think I needed that?" she said, after he let her go.

"No, but I did."

Her brow creased, concern now plain on her face. "Are you all right?"

"Never better," he lied.

"We'll get through this. *You'll* get through this. We'll find the answers. I know we will."

"Yeah. Sure we will." He hesitated. "Thanks. For doing this. For everything you do. Everything you've done for me."

Her frown deepened. "William—?"

"I'm good. Really," he said, cutting her off. He headed for where Case and Fader still sat at the back, to avoid further questions and so he wouldn't have to keep lying. He'd decided not to share with Adi what Nyx had told him. She could do nothing about it, and it would only worry her. Besides, she might change the expedition plan. Right now, all he wanted was to reach the red dot location as fast as possible.

Case and Fader were still watching the same movie. He sat beside Case on the couch.

"What's with the hug fest?" she asked, turning to him.

"Adi wanted to practice before she tries it on you."

"Yeah. Right. Were you sleeping?"

"Astral projecting."

"Cool," Fader said, still watching the movie.

Case studied him with narrowed eyes. "You okay?"

He shook his head.

She frowned. "What's wrong?"

He put an arm around her. "Tell you later. Let's watch the movie."

She stared at him for a breath, then lay her head on his shoulder. "It's pretty lame."

"Exactly what I need." He hugged her closer, enjoying the warmth of her body against his. Enjoying being with her and Fader and Adi, the only people in the world who cared about him.

Enjoying being alive.

Chapter 23

Déjà vu

To Case, landing in Arequipa was worse than taking off from Toronto. As the plane descended, much too suddenly for her, her stomach tried to crawl up her throat. Worse, pain stabbed into her ears and above her eyes. She bent over, holding her head in both hands.

"What's the matter?" Fader asked from his seat.

"I want to die," she groaned.

"I feel fine."

"I hate you."

"Your ears?" Will asked, concern in his voice.

"My whole head." She rubbed her temples, but the pain remained.

"It's the change in air pressure. Happens a lot first time flying. I still remember how much it hurt. Swallow. Make your ears pop. Like in an elevator."

She tried it. "Not working."

"Chew some gum," Rani said. Reaching into her purse, she tossed a pack of spearmint sticks.

Case ripped open a piece and stuffed it in her mouth like food to the starving. She started chewing. "It's not— Oh, wait." The pain in her ears suddenly eased.

"Ears pop?" Will asked.

"Yeah. Still hurts, but not as much."

"Don't worry. You'll be better when we—" He hesitated. "When we fly home."

She knew what he was thinking. *Would* they be going home again? Everyone on this plane? Or only some? And would there be new people with them? Will's parents? Their mom?

But she forced a smile. "Good to know." She peered out the window, hoping for her first glimpse of Peru. "Why's it dark outside? It's only 7:30 at night."

"We're in the southern hemisphere," Will said. "It's the dry season here—their winter. Shorter days. Sun sets about six."

Two strips of lights rose toward them. She sat back, eyes scrunched shut, clutching her armrests as if she could hold the plane in the air. The plane's nose tilted up, something bumped beneath them, the engines roared, and she was pushed forward against her seat belt.

The engine noise dropped, her belt tension eased, and the pilot's voice sounded again. "Ladies and gentlemen, welcome to Arequipa. Please remain seated until we come to a complete stop. We'll be disembarking onto the tarmac."

She opened her eyes. "Wait. We've landed?"

Will grinned at her. "Smooth, eh? Good pilot."

"We're not dead, so yeah."

Case watched out the window as the plane taxied up to a small hangar that huddled isolated and distant from the main airport terminal.

"Private hangar," Will said, looking out his window.

Very private, she thought.

Peng and Mei had brought them their packs. Everyone now wore jackets, as Adi had explained it got down to six degrees Celsius at night this time of year.

Outside the hangar, a bearded man in an overcoat waited for their plane with a taller man in a military uniform. Eight soldiers stood at attention behind them.

"That's Gabriel Herrada on the left," Adi said.

"Were you expecting the military?" Stone asked, peering out past her.

"They're Special Forces, dai lo," Mei added, studying the waiting men through binoculars she'd pulled from her pack. "Carrying M27s."

Case shot Will a look as they both watched the scene. He shrugged in reply, but she knew him well enough to tell he was worried. Was this why there'd been no attack in Toronto? Was it going to happen here? Now?

Adi stood, her face unreadable. "All of you, stay on the plane."

Standing, Stone pulled a handgun from his jacket, did something to it, then returned it to its holster. "No. Peng and I will go with you. Mei, stay here. If anything happens, have the pilot fly to Lima."

Adi hesitated, then nodded. "Agreed, but fly to La Paz. Get out of Peru."

Mei exchanged a look with Peng. "Dai lo—"

"That's an order," Stone said, heading to the front. Peng checked his own gun, shrugged an eyebrow to Mei, and followed Stone, Adi behind him.

"Adi—" Will began as she passed them.

"Stay here," she replied, cutting him off. "Mei's in charge."

"Works for me," Rani muttered.

Adi spoke with the pilot, as Stone opened the plane door and lowered the steps. He descended first, followed by Peng, then Adi. Mei raised the steps again, then watched them through the window of the closed door, her face set in hard lines. Fader joined Case at her seat window, while Rani peered over Will's shoulder.

On the tarmac, Adi approached the two men, Stone and Peng flanking her but five paces back. Adi shook hands with both men, and they began talking. Adi nodded several times, and to Case, it seemed both Stone and Peng relaxed their posture. Adi waved them both forward, and more handshakes followed. Stone turned back to the plane, an open hand over his heart.

"That's the all clear," Mei said, opening the door again. "Grab your packs. Let's go."

Rani looked around. "Where's my suitcase?"

"Maybe it's in the hold," Case said, trying to look innocent.

As Mei led them across the open tarmac toward the greeting party, a fear seized Will. Fear, not from his agoraphobia, but from a sense of sudden exposure. The skin between his shoulder blades prickled as the safety of the plane fell further behind with every step. Meeting at this private hangar, isolated from the rest of the airport, felt both planned and ominous.

The positions Stone and Peng took only added to that feeling. They had moved back again from where Adi talked with Gabriel Herrada and the man in the military uniform. Stone stood ten paces to the left, and Peng the same distance to the right, both with clear lines of sight to the soldiers arrayed in front of the hangar.

Will guessed Stone didn't share Adi's confidence in the situation's safety. Mei reinforced his guess when she stopped at the same distance, motioning them to continue forward as she took up a third position between Stone and Peng.

As he, Case, Fader, and Rani reached where Adi talked with Gabriel Herrada and the military man, the latter's face tickled at a memory. He'd seen the man before. But where? When?

Adi introduced them to Herrada, leaving Will to the last. Herrada appeared older than in the photo Adi had shown them, his face more lined, his hair grayer. He took Will's offered hand in both of his and squeezed. "I knew your parents well, William, and was proud to call them my friends. I still miss that friendship."

"Thank you, sir," Will replied, unable to say more as his throat tightened. Losing his parents weighed even heavier on him since he'd learned how they'd tried to save him. Being in Peru once more, meeting someone who had known them as friends, made that loss fresh again, as if eight years ago had been only yesterday.

Herrada seemed to understand. He gave a sympathetic smile, releasing Will's hand. "Call me Gabriel, please. And now, allow me to introduce Major Diego Zapana of the Peruvian Special Forces."

The major shook hands with them all, Will last. "You don't remember me, do you, Mr. Dreycott?"

Will was still dredging his memories. "Sorry, no."

"Diego led the squad who found you in the jungle," Adi said. "Although he was Captain Zapana then. Congratulations on your promotion, Diego."

As Zapana acknowledged Adi with a nod, a chill seized Will as he remembered a photograph Adi had shown him the day she'd revealed the Chakana in its lead box.

In that photo, his nine-year-old self lay on a stretcher carried by men in military uniforms along a dirt road lined with thick, broad-leaved vegetation. Adi had said a captain in the Peruvian army had taken the photo, as proof his men had been the ones to find Will. Proof to claim the reward.

Was that all I was to you? A reward? Still, this man had saved his life.

Zapana smiled at Will. "I expected you would not remember me. We spoke only briefly when you awoke in hospital. I am so pleased to see you again, Mr. Dreycott. You've grown."

"Call me Will, please. Uh, yeah. Eight years."

Adi's photograph leaped back into his mind. In it, his nine-year-old self, covered in mud and looking half-starved, wore a collared shirt missing most of its buttons, exposing his thin chest. On that chest, where his scar now sat, lay the only thing other than himself to return from that expedition. A crystal object hanging from a woven leather cord.

The Chakana.

In reflex, his hand moved to where the artifact sat in its Faraday pouch in his jeans. This man had seen the Chakana. Had he known then what it was? No, he couldn't have. Adi had found it in the hospital with his clothes. She'd said everyone had mistaken it for a common Inca Cross souvenir.

Still...

He realized an uncomfortable silence had fallen. "Thank you, Major," he said. "For finding me. For saving my life."

Zapana smiled, and the tension left the group. "*De nada*, my friend. And please call me Diego."

"Perhaps, Diego," Gabriel said, "you could review the plans for the next few days."

Adi frowned. "Have they changed from our discussions?"

"Only my addition of this squad, Adrienne," Diego replied, nodding to the eight armed and uniformed men behind them, still standing at attention. "Given your report of an attack in Toronto, I wanted additional protection for your party. My men and I will escort you to the hotel and remain there while you acclimate for the next two days. We will then accompany you to our base and on the flight to your destination—a destination I have yet to share with anyone."

Gabriel chuckled. "Even with me. Diego takes his responsibility for your security seriously."

"As do your own people, I see," Diego said, nodding at where Stone, Peng, and Mei stood apart from their group, their eyes constantly scanning the area.

Adi glanced back at Stone but did not motion him to join them. "Forgive me, Diego. It does not imply any lack of confidence in you or your men."

"Apologies are not needed. They are doing their job. I know professionals when I see them."

"Once again," Rani muttered beside Will, "security fails to make me feel secure."

Will didn't answer, but at that moment, he felt the same. Stone, Peng, Mei. Adi herself. And now a squad of soldiers. Everything only added to a growing sense of danger.

Worse, out here in the open, exposed on the tarmac, he couldn't shake the feeling they were being watched. Fader looked around, as if he too sensed another presence nearby.

Chapter 24

Within You

Morrigan stood beside the private hanger, a listening spell aimed at the landing party with the Dreycott boy and the two men who met them. She stood in the open, fifty paces away, but concealed by the same magic she'd used in Qoricancha. No one could see her.

And yet...

The boy Fader turned her way. His eyes swept the tarmac, then returned, seeming to settle on her. She sucked in her breath. Not possible. Perhaps because her thoughts had been on him? Fader turned back, and she relaxed. *I've missed you, little one.*

You know these people!? Orden cried in her head. *And you said nothing?*

Orden had not been in her mind when Morrigan had seen these same people in the black pool. Shocked by the coincidence, Morrigan had stayed silent then. She swallowed. *I feared you would view my history with them as suspicious.*

I do.

Morrigan stiffened as Orden's presence became a physical thing, like tendrils of a poisonous plant burrowing into her mind.

Odd, Orden said finally. *You are not conspiring with these people. Far from it. They opposed you. Thwarted your plans. Made you flee.* A pang of sympathy, the first this creature had shown. *I know how that feels.*

The tendrils withdrew. Morrigan sucked in a breath, steadying herself.

And you hold no prior knowledge of the Chakana.

Then...a coincidence after all?

You were of the coven that blocked access to my Black Island. You know those who now hold the Chakana and seek the Crossing. No, not a coincidence.

Orden, I swear—

I believe you. But neither is this a coincidence.

Then what?

I don't know.

The words of the Archambeault woman came back to Morrigan. *It seems we're being moved like pieces in a game.*

Perhaps, Orden said. *But a game I will win this time.* Orden smiled in her mind. *You were hiding something, though. This child, Fader. You have feelings for him.*

Anger flared in Morrigan, fueled by yet another defiling of her mind. Fueled, too, by an intense need to protect Fader. *You will not harm him.*

Threats, witch? You are in no position.

A chill trembled through Morrigan as Orden stepped forward again in her head. But the same anger fed her courage. *Perhaps, but if you desire my willing help, you will not harm the boy.*

She waited for Orden to seize control of her. But inside her mind, Orden retreated, and her body was once more her own.

You are rather late in life for maternal urges, Orden sniffed. Then the hint of a smile. *Or do you seek to atone for the young brother you abandoned?*

Morrigan stiffened. That had never occurred to her. Yet now, the connection between her long-lost Dany and her feelings for Fader seemed so obvious, she felt a fool.

Enough, Orden said. *To tonight's purpose. The Chakana.*

Do they have it? Morrigan asked, relieved to escape memories of her brother.

The Dreycott boy carries it. He thinks it lies hidden from detection, but I can sense it.

What do you intend?

To take it from him.

Here? You said you needed to plan, to prepare.

I now have a plan.

He is surrounded by armed bodyguards and soldiers.

And will be wherever he goes. But you assume I must use physical force to make him surrender the Chakana. I do not. I have but to ask him.

Morrigan understood. *You plan to take him over. But what will that accomplish? He can hardly walk over here and hand me this thing unnoticed.*

Before they leave this airport for their accommodation, I will have the boy use the washroom. There, he will discreetly drop the Chakana in a waste container and depart. You, remaining invisible, will enter and retrieve it.

Morrigan could find no fault with the plan. *When will you take him over?*

Now. Stay here. Stay hidden. Follow the boy when they leave here and do as I said. A pause. *And do not think to flee. I know the song of your mind. I will find you. And I will send you to the place you call the Gray Lands until I have need of your magic.*

Morrigan felt the truth in the threat. *I believe you.*

The next moment, Orden was gone. And Morrigan's mind was her own. Orden's departure felt like a sudden recovery from a long illness. A disease leaving her body. *Yet what she does to me, Marell did to so many. And I let him. Worse, I helped him.*

She swallowed. More guilt. From where did these unfamiliar feelings come? Resurrected memories of her brother? The reunion with her mother? Seeing Fader again? Or was it something else?

There is good in you. You just need to find it.

Her mother. Fader. Both had said those words to her.

She clenched her fists. Enough. If she needed to find anything, it was how to counter Orden's power over her. And the secret to power—gaining it or defeating it—was always knowledge. She'd learned that in the coven as a child at her mother's knee.

Her mother.

There is good in you, child...

Shut up! she screamed in her head, pressing her hands against her temples. She didn't have time for this. She must use this brief freedom from Orden to *understand* Orden. To discover how to defeat her, or at least, escape.

What did she know about this creature?

Centuries ago, the Inca girl, Quilla, joined some strange Sisterhood, perhaps by choice, perhaps not. She rose to become a Madre, one of their leaders. These Madres could somehow merge with the Four—god-like entities with power over something called the Book that revealed all of creation. In every possible time line. In every possible universe. All of which the Four created.

She shook her head. Ridiculous. What else had she learned?

This was the beginning. This island, this tower. That mirror. But I was interrupted. My plans defeated.

Orden's words when they first met on the Black Island.

The Madres live long, thanks to the Breath of the Three. But they die...or are killed.

Orden again. And those last words had been bitter.

Whatever Orden-Quilla's plans had been, the other Madres or even the entire Sisterhood had opposed her...and killed her. But why?

I plan to finish what I began all those centuries ago...I am going to destroy all of creation. Every universe. And rebuild them anew. I'll let you have one.

If that had been Orden's plan, the Sisterhood opposed her simply because she was insane.

I'll let you have one.

One of the universes Orden planned to rebuild. Her own universe.

No, she thought.

The word sprang into Morrigan's head with a strength and clarity that made her draw in a breath in shock.

No.

In that moment, she accepted what she had felt at some level in her heart from the moment Orden had appeared in her head. She would never help this creature willingly.

She was uncertain as to her own motivation. Perhaps she was content with this world and the power she held in it, and had no wish to see it destroyed.

Perhaps she didn't believe Orden's incredible story or what she offered. The god-like Four, their creation of all of creation, infinite universes, the all-seeing

Book? Impossible.

Perhaps she had finally found the good that others saw in her. She snorted at that. No, her reason was much simpler.

She didn't like being a dog on Orden's leash—and she needed a way to break that leash.

One thing gave her hope. Whatever really happened in the past, Orden-Quilla had been defeated. This creature was no god. She was fallible.

But powerful. A body-swapper greater than Marell. And unlike Marell, Orden could exist in pure astral form, perhaps had done so for centuries. Worse, Orden could control several people at once. Beroald and the servants in the tower were all her slaves.

Morrigan frowned. Yet when Orden occupied her, it required Orden's entire presence.

She understood. Orden had sent the others to the Gray Lands. They were like Marell's used husks, the Hollow Boys, lacking free will but able to follow commands.

She remembered her sad little family of Hollow Boys. How cruel she and Marell had been. How pathetic her delusion. Had she tried to replace her brother even then? The family she abandoned when she fled Castle Rushen?

More guilt. *Stop it. Focus.*

What other powers had Orden shown? The strange black mirror could view any event as it unfolded, but to spy on her, Orden need only dive into her mind.

The Black Island itself was troubling. If they returned there, Morrigan was uncertain of finding her way back to this world, despite Orden's claim. And those scarabs...

But none of those were immediate threats. She was here now, in her own world, a world she knew and Orden did not. She must free herself before Orden returned her to the Black Island.

If Orden returned her there. Right now, Orden needed her magic and cooperation. She would serve no further use once Orden had what she wanted. And what Orden wanted was this Chakana.

Morrigan smiled. This crystal key held by the Dreycott boy was, quite literally, the key to her freedom. If she could secure the Chakana, safe from Orden, she could trade it for her release.

And Orden was about to drop it into her hands.

But once she possessed it, how could she keep it from Orden? Whether hidden in a physical place or by a spell, Orden would pry the secret from her mind as easily as—

Her hand brushed against the Unicorn Tapestry she wore as a cloak, and a tingle like an electric shock ran up her arm.

As easily as she herself used magic.

The Tapestry. Had not its entire purpose been to hide? Hide the way to the underground tunnels that had led her to the Black Island?

She ran her hands over the Tapestry. Her one use of its power—the release of the fire serpent against the scarabs—had seemed an accident, the result of a desperate cry for help. Well, she was desperate now.

Laying both her palms on the silken fabric, she closed her eyes. *Help me again.*

Voices. In her mind, but not Orden. Women's voices, chanting. Tears rimmed her eyes. She knew those voices. *My Sisters, hear my need.*

As the chanting rose, Morrigan felt a familiar icy touch in her head. Orden was back. The chanting stopped, like a door closing on a secret choir. To hide her recent thoughts and plots, Morrigan called up an illumination spell, filling her head with its runes.

She needn't have worried. Orden's state of mind made it clear the creature had other concerns. Frustration and fury radiated from the presence in her head.

I thought you would remain in the Dreycott boy, Morrigan said. *Force him to surrender the Chakana.*

I never reached him. An astral barrier surrounds him and the entire party. I encountered this same shield when I tried to enter the white tower in the city where he lives.

A memory stirred in Morrigan.

Something else you've hidden from me, Witch?

Forgotten, not hidden. She called up her memories, displaying them for Orden. *An astral shield protected that white tower when we first encountered this boy. At the time, my associate assumed a monk named Yeshe had erected it. Yet, it survived his death.*

Not some monk, fool. Now that I am this close, I can tell its source. It comes from the Chakana itself.

Morrigan quelled her anger at the insult. Here was a chance to learn more of this key. *Has it done this in the past?*

Not to my knowledge, Orden said, but Morrigan caught a flash of uncertainty. Then anger. *Be quiet. Raise your listening spell again.*

Morrigan cast the spell, happy to have Orden's thoughts on something other than her. *What are you hoping to discover?*

If anyone plans to separate from the group.

Morrigan understood. *And remove themselves from the protection of this shield.*

Yes. Ah! There. That one. Orden smiled in Morrigan's mind. *He will do nicely.*

On the tarmac, Gabriel Herrada forced a smile as Diego Zapana explained to Adrienne Archambeault how his men would guard her people around the clock. Which meant the secret Herrada had chased for twenty years would also be guarded around the clock.

In front of the others, he complimented Zapana on his diligence, while silently cursing him. When he requested the man from the army, he'd done so thinking another familiar face would prompt Adrienne to lower her guard. Too late, he discovered Zapana brought a strange loyalty to the Dreycott boy.

"When you save someone's life, Gabriel," Zapana told him after receiving his orders, "you assume a responsibility for that person."

So now, a heavily armed Special Forces squad stood between him and the Chakana. Plus, this Stone and his people seemed just as capable and deadly. Their hotel would be a fortress. The local thugs Herrada had hired stood no chance.

A mention of the Santa Catalina monastery snapped his attention back. The reporter woman was complaining about being stuck in a hotel for two days and wanted to visit the famous site while in Arequipa. The Dreycott boy was supporting her, as were the teenaged girl and her brother.

However, Adrienne insisted the entire party stay inside the hotel until they left on the military helicopter. A trip where they would remain protected by Zapana and his men.

The argument ended, won by Adrienne, as expected.

His mind raced. Here was opportunity. Under guard in the hotel, the Chakana was beyond his reach. He had no idea what chances the monastery might offer, but they had to be better than at the hotel. "Perhaps," he said, "I might suggest a compromise."

Adrienne raised an eyebrow, but motioned to Stone to join them. "What are you proposing, Gabriel?"

"This is Tuesday evening," he said. "On Friday morning, after two days adjusting to our altitude in your delightful hotel, Diego and his men will escort you by armored transport to the army base outside town. There, you will board the military helicopter he has arranged. Yes?"

Adrienne nodded, frowning. Zapana was frowning, too.

"If you were to rise two hours earlier on Friday," Herrada said, "we could provide a secure tour of the monastery on the way, then proceed to the base."

Adrienne looked unconvinced. "How would it be secure?"

"Santa Catalina falls under my jurisdiction as Executive Director of the Bureau of Antiquities. I can close the monastery, except to our party. I will not, of course, reveal the purpose of the closure."

Adrienne and Stone looked skeptical. As the reporter and the children all pleaded with them, help came from an unexpected quarter.

"Santa Catalina de Sienna is the jewel of Arequipa," Zapana offered, speaking to the Dreycott boy. "I would love for you to see it." He turned to Adrienne and Stone. "It is a walled city within our city, closed off and secure in itself. If Gabriel can restrict it to ourselves, I am confident it will be safe."

"How many entrances?" Stone asked Zapana.

"Just one. I will leave two men on it."

"Four, please. And we do a sweep of the premises before the rest of our party enters."

"Agreed."

Stone shrugged to Adrienne, which Herrada assumed meant he approved, but it was her decision.

She sighed. "All right. But an hour there and no longer."

As the boy Will and his companions thanked her, Herrada let out his breath. Spreading his hands, he smiled. "Excellent! I will be your tour guide. I promise you an unforgettable visit. Now, please excuse me. I must see to the potteries Adrienne has graciously returned to our country."

Promising to stay in contact, he climbed into a motorized buggy used by airport staff. As he drove toward the main terminal, he allowed himself a smile.

After all these years, *la Llave de Cristal* was again within his grasp. He'd searched for the Chakana for two decades, since hearing rumors of a mysterious artifact guarded by an equally mysterious Sisterhood.

A Sisterhood led by *immortal* Madres.

He'd met Chico Alvarez while facilitating smuggling operations for the man. He told Alvarez of his interest in the Chakana, that he would pay well should the gang leader ever learn of its location.

One day Alvarez contacted him, saying he had the artifact and would sell it to him—for three times what Herrada had originally offered. Although furious, he'd agreed. What was money, when immortality lay within reach?

That should have been the end of his quest for the Chakana. And the start of his search for the Madres and their secret.

But Alvarez got greedy. He tried to sell the artifact to Jon Dreycott and Terri Yurikami, planning to rip them off before selling it to Herrada. Adrienne had intervened, robbing Alvarez—and unknowingly himself—of the Chakana.

Informed by Alvarez of Jon's and Terri's 'theft' of the artifact, he'd searched the relics Jon asked him to ship to Toronto from that expedition, but found nothing. Nor had he expected to. Adrienne had already flown the three of them home from Bolivia, no doubt carrying the Chakana. The woman was no fool.

He'd waited for Jon and Terri to return. They now held the Chakana, the key to a fabulous secret hidden somewhere in Peru. They would be back. And they would reach out to him, as always.

They *had* returned—but in secret. His next news came a year later when he read they had disappeared somewhere in the jungles of Peru.

Weeks passed. Then, more news—and hope. An army squad had found a survivor of the doomed expedition—nine-year-old William Dreycott.

Herrada rushed to see the boy in the hospital in Lima. Too late. Adrienne had arrived days before. When she wasn't present, he searched the boy's hospital room but found nothing. Had the Chakana been with the boy? Had Adrienne found and removed it?

But Adrienne never returned to Peru. As time passed, he came to believe the artifact had met the same fate as the doomed expedition and was lost once more in the jungle.

For eight years, he continued his search. But every trail ran cold. His only other link to the Chakana had also disappeared around the same time as that expedition—Chico Alvarez. Herrada never believed that was a coincidence.

But now, Adrienne had returned—and with young William.

Her secrecy around this trip, the heavy security, her unwillingness to share their ultimate destination—it all added up: Adrienne was finally continuing the search for the secret the boy's parents had chased. The secret he himself still chased. If that were true, she must have brought the Chakana.

But he still didn't know for certain. And even if these people had the Chakana, he didn't know who carried it. If his men ambushed Adrienne's party at the monastery, who should they target? Adrienne seemed the most likely, but perhaps the man Stone—

The Dreycott boy has it.

He stiffened. Taking his foot off the accelerator, he let the buggy slow to a stop, still half a football field from the main terminal. A voice. And not his own.

Gripping the steering wheel with trembling hands, he peered into the back of the buggy. Empty. Then who...where...?

You're a tad slow, aren't you?

He jumped and cried out. Something inside him. Like spiders crawling in his head.

No matter. You serve my purpose. And you've set things up nicely.

"Who are you?" he whispered to the night. "What do you want?"

Your body. Your men. Your access to the Dreycott boy. All of which I now have. Goodbye, Gabriel.

He felt his hands loosen on the steering wheel. No. That wasn't right. He no longer felt his hands. He no longer felt the cool night breeze on his face. Or smelled the jet fuel in the air. Or heard the roar of planes.

A thick mist rose to obscure the lights of the terminal ahead of him. He had a fleeting thought that this could not be happening. The mist grew thicker, everything became gray, and Gabriel Herrada thought no more.

Morrigan sat in a coffee shop in the Arrivals concourse of the main terminal. Sipping a latte, she watched the passing crowd and waited for Orden. As ordered.

She wore a simple illusion spell. Passersby would see her with black hair, darker skin, and features copied from a local model in a magazine she'd found on the table. The landing party hadn't planned to enter the terminal, but she preferred caution. If they recognized her, Orden might reconsider her value. And that would not end well.

She'd taken advantage of the wait to do some quick shopping. Several bags sat at her feet, containing clothes to replace those in the suitcases she'd abandoned in the taxi outside Castle Rushen.

With you, child, it was always the clothes. Her mother's words from their recent meeting at that castle. Swearing to herself, she pushed that memory aside and returned to watching the people scurrying by.

Seeing Gabriel Herrada approaching, she waved to him. Or rather, she assumed, to Orden. Herrada entered the shop and sat across from her, smiling.

"Orden?"

"Who else?" Herrada replied. "You needn't have waved. I can sense you."

Morrigan added that to her list of Orden's powers. "And now?"

"Now, without worry of the astral shield, I will physically visit the Dreycott boy in the hotel, where they think themselves safe. There, I will make him discreetly hand over the Chakana to Herrada. To me."

Morrigan hesitated.

Orden frowned with Herrada's face. "What?"

"The monk Yeshe could enter the white tower in his physical form, so Marell believed the shield acted as a barrier only to astral bodies. But he never tested that belief."

"No matter. If I cannot physically enter the hotel, we will take the Chakana at this monastery."

"If you cannot approach the boy in the hotel, how will the monastery be any different? Armed professionals will still guard the boy and his entire party."

"I will not need to approach him at the monastery. I have searched Herrada's mind for what he planned at the site. He knows places where men can hide, ready to emerge at the right moment. And he has men I can employ. Men with guns who know how to use them."

Morrigan's thoughts flew to young Fader. "A gun battle? People will die."

Orden tilted Herrada's head, considering her. "Are you getting squeamish in your old age? Not something I expected, given your past."

Morrigan felt herself flushing. "I told you before. The boy Fader is not to be harmed."

Herrada's face darkened, eyes narrowing. "And I told *you* before, Witch. You are in no position to give orders."

Without Orden in her head, Morrigan found defiance easier. *But be careful,* she thought. This creature could send her to the Gray Lands in an eyeblink. "But I *am* in a position to assist you. Assistance best given as a willing partner." She shrugged. "Unless you can control me, Herrada, his men—all at the same time—when you attempt to seize this Chakana you covet."

Orden glowered at her, then sat back, Herrada's features shifting to a smile.

She spread his hands. "A superb idea."

"What do you mean?"

"Your assistance, freely given, at the monastery. If that option becomes necessary, you will join Herrada's men there, hide them with a spell, then use your magic to ensure we overpower these people. You may protect your precious child at the same time. Agreed?"

Morrigan nodded, knowing she had no choice.

"Excellent. Now, I must contact Herrada's gang of thugs to prepare for the ambush at the monastery, should I need it."

Morrigan followed Orden-Herrada out of the coffee shop. If the ambush happened, she would find herself in a gun battle against dangerous foes who knew her. All to protect Fader.

Be careful what you wish for, she thought.

Chapter 25

Earthquake Driver

Major Diego Zapana led the travelers into the hangar where three vehicles waited. Vehicles that, to Case, were ugly metal boxes trying hard to be trucks. Trucks with guns—a machine gun turret topped each vehicle.

Peng thumped a fist against the side of one. "IMVs. Cool."

"Huh?" Case said.

"They're a type of APC."

"Dumb ass," Mei said. "You just explained one cryptic acronym with another."

Diego laughed. "Infantry Mobility Vehicles. They are small Armored Personnel Carriers designed to withstand land mines, rifle fire, artillery fragments, and CBRN threats."

"CBRN?" Case said.

"Don't ask," Rani muttered.

"Chemical, biological, radiation, and nuclear," Diego replied.

"Wait. Nuclear?"

"Told you not to ask," Rani said.

"Diego," Adi said, eyeing the trucks, "I appreciate your concerns for our security, but I'd hoped to reach our hotel more discreetly."

"With an army base here, Adrienne, these vehicles are common on our streets. They will not attract undue attention. Plus, we will enter the hotel via the rear delivery entrance from a private lane."

Stone was inspecting the vehicles. "ATF Dingos, right?"

Diego raised an eyebrow but nodded.

Stone indicated Mei and Peng. "We were on the Hong Kong police force. Organized Crime Unit. These were on the shortlist when we tendered for IMVs."

"Ah," Diego said. "I knew you were professionals. What did you select?"

"CSKs."

"Chinese?"

Stone shrugged. "Politics."

As the two men discussed the relative merits of various IMVs, Will and Fader joined them, glued to every word. Case leaned closer to Rani. "Male bonding. So exciting."

Rani responded with a tight-lipped nod, folding her arms.

"What?" Case asked. "Still pissed over your suitcase? Jealous Stone's paying more attention to a truck than to you?"

"Still pissed over the suitcase, yes. But I'm happy he's not paying attention to me."

"Whoa, what changed? New boyfriend?"

"New information. Got it during the plane ride. On Mr. Zhang...and her." Rani nodded to where Adi talked with Mei and Peng.

"What? What do you mean?"

"Ladies and gentlemen," Diego called, checking his watch and cutting off Rani's reply, "we will depart now for your hotel. If you could enter the middle vehicle, please?"

"Tell you later," Rani whispered as they headed for the truck.

Inside, Case found six single seats, three per side separated by a central aisle. She sat behind Fader and in front of Will. Rani sat behind Adi on the opposite side, with Stone in front of Adi. As they buckled in, Diego joined the driver in the cab. He'd divided the rest of his squad between the lead and trailing vehicles, as had Stone with Mei and Peng.

Rani's comments had shaken Case. She liked Stone, especially the way he'd accepted her from the start, and she was warming to Adi. And she trusted them both without hesitation. What had Rani discovered? Whatever it was, with both Adi and Stone present, any further discussion had to wait until she and Rani were alone.

Something was troubling Will, too. She slumped down in her seat, hugging herself. Unlike Rani, she'd hoped their stay at the hotel *would* be boring. Two days at a safe oasis, a pause between the danger they'd been facing and whatever lay ahead.

Now, she feared the last thing their stay here would be was boring.

Their trip into Arequipa, however, was uneventful, and Case began to relax. From the front seat, Diego gave a running travelog about the city he clearly loved. "Arequipa's our second largest city, after Lima. Over a million people. The historian, Garcilaso de la Vega, claimed the Inca leader, Huayna Capac, was so taken by the beauty of this valley, he settled here and named it *Ari-que-pay*." Diego grinned back at them. "Quechuan for 'let's stay here.' De la Vega has been discredited, but I still like his version."

The area around Arequipa was a mix of farms, modern suburbs, shanty towns, and clusters of low box-like buildings, which Diego said manufactured textiles from the wool of camelids.

"Camels?" Fader said, frowning.

Diego smiled. "Their cousins. Llamas and alpacas, both native to our land."

Case saw few buildings taller than three stories, even as they entered the city proper.

"Earthquakes," Diego explained when she mentioned this. "We sit where two *placas tectonics* meet." His brow furrowed. "Tectonic plates, yes? What created our magnificent Andes. We average over fifty quakes each year." Their reactions must have shown on their faces, for he added, "However, most are mild. And our volcanoes are dormant."

Fader sat up straight, his eyes wide. "Volcanoes?"

"Yes. Three. *Chachani*, *El Misti*, and *Pichu Pichu*." Diego peered through the windshield. "Too dark to see them now. Tomorrow, I show you. El Misti...very beautiful. The Incas worshiped her."

"What does dormant mean?" Fader whispered to Case.

Diego heard him. "Sleeping. And no, we don't expect them to wake up."

"Earthquakes and volcanoes," Rani said. "You guys just get more fun to hang with every day."

"I have told the drivers to pass by the monastery," Diego continued, addressing Stone, "so you may examine the approach and its entrance."

"Thank you," Stone said.

After negotiating a series of narrow lanes paved in gray brick, they emerged at the corner of a giant open square bathed in lights and packed with people clutching phones or cameras. The transports slowed, waiting for pedestrians to pass before turning the corner.

"The *Plaza de Armas*," Diego explained. "As you see, very popular with the *turistas*." He pointed to a huge pillared structure occupying an entire side of the square, its twin bell towers rising like sentries over the scene. "The Cathedral of Arequipa. The other sides of the Plaza..." He indicated two-story buildings fronted by arched balconies. "...date to the first Spanish settlers. Once government offices, now museums, restaurants, souvenir stores."

The square featured a central fountain, surrounded by broad promenades, towering palm trees, and geometric areas of grass, sculptured bushes, and flower beds. The cathedral and other buildings, all white, seemed to glow in the square's electric lighting.

"It's beautiful. And...bright," Case said.

Diego smiled. "Arequipa is called *La Ciudad Blanca*—the 'White City.' Colonial buildings like these, the Spanish made from *sillar*, a white volcanic rock. Very common here. I would show you more of the Plaza, but cars are not allowed, so we must turn. On this next street is the monastery."

Leaving the Plaza behind, they continued up another narrow lane. Many buildings featured arched passageways leading to inner courtyards, lending an air of mystery, and making her want to know what hid inside.

Case sighed to herself. *Because that's what I need right now...more mystery.*

Their transport stopped before another arched doorway, the only break in a white stone wall stretching down the left side of the lane. "The Monastery of Santa Catalina," Diego said, pointing to black double doors covered in metal studs.

"Looks more like a biker bar," Rani muttered.

Stone, Adi, and Diego discussed how best to position the trucks when they returned on Friday. Signaling the lead truck to proceed to the hotel, Diego called someone on his phone, talking rapidly in Spanish. He ended the call. "Before meeting you, I did a sweep of the hotel and left four men there. I called to confirm everything remains well and received the proper all-clear code."

Stone nodded, indicating, Case assumed, his approval of this approach.

The transports turned into a narrow laneway, stopping before a tall metal gate at the rear of the hotel. A soldier opened the gate then locked it again after the three trucks drove through. Grabbing their packs, they stepped from their truck into a cobblestoned courtyard, open to the sky and enclosed by high white stucco walls. Garbage bins, cardboard boxes, and wooden crates lined each wall.

Flanked by the soldiers, they entered the hotel through the loading dock area, reminding Case of sneaking into Will's tower the night they first met. So much had happened since then. How much more still lay ahead?

They emerged into a small lobby where a woman at the reception desk greeted Diego, handing him a manila envelope.

A tiny restaurant, with six tables and a vending machine, stood off a sunken lounge filled with scattered couches and plush armchairs. Case had never stayed at a hotel, so her knowledge came from movies and television. So far, although small, this place met her vague expectations. That changed when they left the lobby.

A stone walkway led outside, past a swimming pool made to look like a rocky grotto complete with trickling waterfall. A short passageway ended in a metal gate behind which stood two soldiers, both of whom snapped to attention.

Diego spoke a single word. One soldier inserted a key into the gate's lock. Passing through, the group entered another open-air courtyard.

To Case, she felt as if she'd passed into some fantasy world.

Stone-tiled steps led up to a cluster of doors directly ahead. To her left, a longer set of steps led up to a second area, separate and higher from the first. Beyond that, more steps rose to a third level. On each of the three tiers, the individual rooms sat at different angles to each other in a pleasing jumble.

The entire scene exploded with color. The doors were reddish-brown. The apartment walls were bright solid colors that varied throughout—brilliant white, deep-sea blue, glowing mustard yellow, rich peachy pink.

And everywhere...green.

Trees and thick bushes crowded the walkways and stairs throughout the courtyard, including tall palms whose broad, fern-like leaves sheltered the space from a starry night sky.

"Wow!" Fader cried, looking around wide-eyed. "This is awesome."

"As long as my room has a bed," Rani said. "I'm beat."

Diego handed Adi the manila envelope from reception. "Your keys, marked with your requested room assignments, Adrienne."

Adi distributed keys to Case, Fader, Will, and Rani, "Your rooms are on the top level."

"Because you think we need the exercise?" Will said.

"Because I want you farthest from this entry point, in case of trouble. Stone, Peng, Mei, and I are on the second level, below yours."

"My men and I have the rooms down here, closest to the gate," Diego said. "Aside from a fire exit, which is also guarded and can be opened only from inside, this gate provides the sole access to these apartments. From the street, this area presents a three-story wall. I will leave men in this area, in the lobby, and guarding the service entrance, working shifts, all in radio contact."

"Excellent, Diego," Stone replied. "If you agree, Peng and myself will join your men stationed outside. Mei will remain here."

"Of course," Diego said.

Mei shrugged. "Just keep Peng away from the vending machine."

"Hey," Peng said, scowling.

Diego handed a small key to each of Stone and Adi. "For this gate. As discussed, we will eat all our meals in the hotel restaurant. I asked them to remain open tonight in case you wished a late dinner."

Adi shook her head. "We ate on the plane, Diego. I think all we want is sleep."

Everyone nodded, although Case noticed Peng seemed disappointed.

"Then," Diego said, "if you will excuse me, I will check on my other men." He left through the barred gate, which the soldier then locked again.

"Bed," Rani said, already heading up the steps with her pack. "To sleep and mourn my lost shoes."

Case sighed. Any explanation for Rani's cryptic comments about Adi and Stone was waiting until tomorrow. But that still left Will and what he needed to share.

She followed him and Fader up the steps. By the time they reached the second level, she was wheezing. Halfway through the climb to the third level and their rooms, she was gasping for air. Dizzy, she sank onto the steps. "I don't feel so good."

Will and Fader stopped ahead. "Like you can't get enough air into your lungs?" Will asked.

She just nodded, her chest heaving.

"It's the altitude," he said. "I was like that my first time."

"You don't feel sick?" she asked Fader.

"Nope."

"First the plane, now this. Why me?"

Walking back down, Will took her pack and room key. "Rest here till you feel better. There's probably coca tea in our rooms. I'll make some."

"How can tea help?" Case said, groaning as he and Fader left.

Adi looked up from where she was opening her door. "This is why we're staying here before moving higher." She chuckled. "Until you adjust, you and Will best avoid any...strenuous activities."

"Ha ha. Funny." Case held her head in her hands. "No worries. I'll just sit here till Friday."

Adi smiled. "Have some coca tea. It does help." She disappeared into her room.

After maybe ten minutes, Case stood again and climbed the last steps like she was a hundred years old. Which was how she felt.

Her room sat in a tree-covered alcove beside Rani's, and across from Will's and Fader's. Rani's door was closed. Hers was open, her pack inside the door. She stumbled over to Will's room and collapsed onto his bed. Fader sat in an arm chair, flipping through TV channels, all of which seemed to be in Spanish.

Will set a steaming blue plastic mug on the table beside the bed. She sat up, even that exertion making her wheeze again. Head spinning, she picked up the mug, which was crammed with thick green leaves immersed in hot water. She wrinkled her nose. "Coca tea?"

Will nodded, sitting on the bed beside her, his own mug in hand.

She took a sip. It reminded her of the green tea her mom used to drink at home, but a little sweeter. Not her favorite, but not bad. She took another sip. Still light-headed, she put the mug down and lay on the bed again. "Does it really help?"

"The locals swear it does. I just like the taste." He smiled, his eyes wistful. "It reminds me of South American trips with Mom and Dad." He fell silent.

Fader switched off the TV, his face sad. Case guessed Will's mention of parents had reminded Fader of their mom. It reminded her that Will had something to share, but her head still spun. *So tired...I'll ask him in a minute.*

The phone beside the bed rang. Will picked it up. "Hello?" Pause. "Oh, hi, Mr. Herrada."

Gabriel Herrada? The man who met them at the airport? What did he want with Will? A sudden premonition of danger seized her. Her Voice? Was it trying to tell her something?

Will listened, then ran a hand through his hair. "Yeah," he said softly. "I'd like that. Thanks. Yeah, tomorrow morning." He hung up.

"What does he want?" she asked, the sense of an unseen threat still with her.

Her question seemed to pull him from wherever his thoughts had taken him. "He wondered if I'd like to hear some stories about my parents, from his times with them."

She relaxed. "That's sweet of him." No premonition. It wasn't her Voice. She closed her eyes. So tired.

She felt Will lay beside her. Something she needed to ask him. So tired. It could wait till morning. Right now, she just wanted to sleep.

Gabriel Herrada was a friend. They were safe in the hotel. Diego and Stone and Mei and Peng would keep them that way. There was no danger. All was good.

She slipped into sleep, clutching that thought. All was good.

Chapter 26

Still Haven't Found What I'm Looking For

Case awoke the next morning, alone on Will's bed, still in her travel clothes and covered by a blanket she didn't remember crawling under. Another pillow lay beside hers, scrunched up like Will's always was. She smiled. Even if she didn't remember, she hadn't slept alone.

A note lay on the pillow. *Restaurant! Food, coffee...more coffee.*

Stumbling to her room, she had a quick shower then fumbled clean clothes from her backpack. She stepped outside, then back in to grab her jacket against the early morning chill.

Going down the steps from her room, she remembered coming up them last night. Although she felt better today, the test would be climbing back after breakfast. The hotel's high walls blocked any glimpse of the volcanoes Diego had mentioned, but above, the sky was clear and blue.

Mei stood inside the barred gate, talking with a soldier. They both looked bored. Nodding to her, Mei unlocked the gate. "Your boyfriend and brother are in the restaurant. Bring me back a black coffee?"

"Yeah, sure." Case glanced at the soldier.

"*Quieres un café?*" Mei asked him.

The man grinned. "*Gracias. Negro, por favor.*"

"Same for him," Mei said.

"You speak Spanish?"

"Spanish, Mandarin, Cantonese, French, some Italian." She winked. "Bit of English."

"Wow," Case said, even more intimidated by Mei. Next to this beautiful, confident woman, she felt like a gangly, incompetent child. What skills did she have? None, beyond a mysterious Voice that seemed to have disappeared.

The restaurant was empty except for Will and Fader. Seeing it was a buffet, she loaded up a plate with some kind of scrambled eggs along with what looked like donuts. When she sat down, Will poured her what appeared to be an orange milkshake. She took a sip. "Ooh, that's good."

"Papaya smoothie," Will replied. He pointed to her eggs. "*Salchicha huachana.* Ground beef and pork fat, fried with eggs."

She made a face.

"Try some."

She did. "Okay, that's good, too. What about these? Are they really donuts?"

"Pretty much. *Picarones*," he said. "Deep fried sweet potatoes and squash, with molasses."

She took a bite, and her eyes went wide. "Okay, I'm living on these and papaya smoothies." She started in on her food. "Where is everybody?"

"Stone, Peng, and Mei—" Will began.

"Saw Mei."

"Right. They are—" He made air quotes. "—*protecting* us. From whatever. Adi's talking to Diego about Friday."

"About the monastery?"

"No. About the flight to where he'll be dropping us."

"Are he and his men coming with us after that?"

"Dunno."

"Rani?"

"She went back to her room. Said she had research to finish."

"Research? On what?" She wondered if it was connected to Rani poking into Adi's and Stone's past.

"She didn't share. Odd, since we're such good buds."

Well, she had two days to talk with the reporter. Right now... "Yesterday on the plane, I asked if you were okay. You said no."

Fader frowned at them. Will sighed. "And I said, I'd tell you later."

"And here we are. Later Land."

Two soldiers and Peng entered the restaurant. "Wanted man!" Peng called, pointing with both hands to Fader, who grinned and waved.

"Finish eating," Will said. "We'll talk in my room."

"Assuming I'm still breathing after climbing back there."

Peng returned with one plate stacked with picarones and another with the egg dish. "Mind if I join you?" He nodded at the soldiers, still at the buffet. "Their English is about as good as my Spanish." Sitting, he started in on the eggs.

"Didn't you already have breakfast?" Will asked.

Peng jabbed a fork at him. "Do *not* tell Mei."

Case laughed. "You two are a hoot. You're like an old married couple."

Peng seemed to have trouble swallowing his food. He coughed. "What? No. Mei and me...we're just...I mean, it's totally professional."

Raising her eyebrows, Case sat back, arms folded, thinking she understood. "Oh, so it's like *that*."

Peng reddened. "What? Like what?"

"You and Mei."

He stabbed at a picarone with a fork. "There is no me and Mei," he said quietly, not meeting her eye.

An awkward silence fell. Realizing she'd messed up, she pushed her half-eaten plate away and changed the subject. "I think I'm done. We should go back up."

"Yes," Will said, "where we can be *protected*." He hesitated, looking at Peng.

"I'm fine. You guys go. See you around, *Desperado*," Peng said, grinning at Fader, his old self back again.

Fader high-fived Peng as he and Will stood to leave.

"Gotta get coffees for Mei and the guard at the gate," Case said. "I'll catch up." After they left, she turned to Peng. "Sorry. I didn't mean to embarrass you."

Peng shook his head. "Nah, no problem. Funny, really. Me and Mei." He chuckled, but his smile was a sad one.

"Does she know how you feel about her?"

His eyes widened. "Is it that obvious?"

"Yep."

He sighed. "No. I don't think she does."

"And you're a guy, so, of course, you haven't told her."

"She'd laugh at me."

"Maybe not. You should tell her."

Another head shake. "She'd laugh. And wouldn't work with me anymore. I...I like working with her."

"What if she didn't laugh?"

His eyes got a far-off look. "That would complicate things."

She left Peng to his breakfast and his thoughts. At the buffet, she filled two mugs with black coffee and walked back.

Complicated relationships. She could relate. Will was her best but most complicated relationship ever. If she focused on just him and her, ignoring everything else swirling around them, what they had was amazing. Intimate but comfortable, friendly but passionate.

But 'everything else' was a lot to ignore. Lost parents, strange powers, ancient artifacts, animal guardians, people trying to kill them. And the small problem of saving the multiverse, whatever that meant.

Even if she could ignore all that, it left the problem she'd had since they'd met. Will's wealth sat like a beast in her mind, waiting to pounce on what they had.

So, yeah, complicated.

For the first time, she wondered how her mom would feel about Will. Hopefully, the same way she did: love him, but wish he'd do something more with his money. Something good. Something big.

She swallowed. *Hope I get to ask you, Mom.*

Mei unlocked the gate, thanking her for the coffees. "You see Peng?"

Case hesitated. "Uh..."

Mei was studying her face. "He's having another breakfast, isn't he?" She shook her head. "He'll have a coronary."

Case's eyebrows shot up. "So, you're worried about him?"

Mei stiffened. "What? No. Just...then we'd be a man short."

Case smiled. "Uh huh."

"What does that mean?"

Walking away, Case shrugged. "Just...uh huh." *Yeah, Peng should tell Mei.*

The climb to their rooms was better this time, but she still had to stop and catch her breath at the top. Fader was in Will's room, sitting on the bed, watching some movie with English subtitles on TV. She collapsed into an armchair.

Will handed her another cup of coca tea. "How was the climb?"

"Better...but still bad," she wheezed. She sipped the tea. "So, spill."

Fader switched off the TV. Will moved the other armchair to face them. He sat down. "Well, according to Nyx," he began, "I'm dying."

Case stood with her arms around Will's neck as he hugged her close, having told his story. Fader sat silent on the bed, not even making a face at their cuddling.

"You have to tell Adi," she said into his chest. Fader nodded agreement.

Will snorted. "Yeah, right. You know how protective she is. This'll make her worse. She might even cancel this trip."

"No way. She'd try to help."

"*If* she believes me. Remember, she doesn't trust Nyx. Or the Chakana. She might even take it from me. Besides, how could she help?"

She'd been trying to figure that out herself. "We could head to the Crossing sooner."

"Remember climbing those steps? You need time here to adjust. We all do. We're heading for even higher altitude."

He was right. She still felt short of breath. "So, maybe we can get there faster when we do leave."

"Faster than military helicopter? I don't—" Stopping, he stepped back from her. "Wait. There *is* a faster way." He slipped his hand into his jeans pocket.

She was shaking her head even before he pulled out the pouch with the Chakana. "No way."

"Why not? It'll open a portal to where we want to go."

"*Why not?* Everyone who comes through those portals tries to kill us."

"Maybe it'll be your buddy, Isobel."

"Or not. After she let us keep the Chakana, Isobel probably got demoted." *Or worse.*

"Then we make a deal. Like my parents did with that Madre, Luciana. We'll return this if they help us."

"But *did* she help them? You're the only one who came back, and you can't remember what happened after stepping through that portal. And *you* still have the Chakana, so I'm guessing Luciana wasn't thrilled with how that deal worked out."

"Neither was I."

"Hey," she said, fighting her anger, "we lost someone, too, remember."

Will reddened. "Sorry."

She sighed. "So am I. You know I'm worried about you. I just mean the Madres might not agree this time."

He didn't answer, and she could think of nothing more to say.

Fader broke the silence. "If you call a Sword Lady...who'll be there? Just us?"

She thought about that. "Good question. Adi said she won't let you do it. And Stone does what she says. And Mei and Peng do what Stone says. So, we'd face a Sword Lady by ourselves?"

"Done it before," Will said.

"And barely escaped each time."

"My parents did it."

"They had *tasers*. I didn't pack—"

"That's *not* what I mean!" Fader shouted from the bed.

Shocked to hear her brother yell, she stopped talking. So did Will.

"I *mean*," Fader said, "will we go *through* a portal by ourselves? Cuz, wherever it takes us...we'll be alone."

Focused on facing fanatical Sword Ladies when the portal opened, she hadn't thought that far. From Will's face, he hadn't either.

The room phone rang, cutting off further discussion. Will picked it up. "Hello? ... Oh, hi, Diego. ... Mr. Herrada? ... No, yeah, I was expecting him. We just hadn't said when." He looked at Case, eyebrows raised.

She sighed and nodded. Will needed this.

"Sure," Will said into the phone, "send him up." He returned the phone to its cradle.

Case stood. "C'mon, bro."

Fader stared hard at Will. "You won't do something stupid, will you?"

Will grinned. "No portal. No Sword Lady. Besides, I'd never leave without you guys. That didn't work out well the last time."

Fader grinned back. "Cool. I'm going to finish watching my movie in my room." He left.

She walked to the door. "This isn't over."

"You can stay."

"No, I'm sure he wants to talk to you alone. Enjoy the stories." Smiling at him, she stepped outside, closing Will's door.

The sun had risen above the hotel walls, filling the multi-colored courtyard with dappled light filtered through the feathered leaves of the tall palms. She breathed in the clean, crisp air and told herself to relax. They would get Will to this mysterious Crossing. And in time. They would find Will's parents and their mom. They were on their way. Adi and Stone, Mei and Peng, Diego and his soldiers. They would keep them safe.

You are safe.

She stiffened. Her Voice. *What—?*

They are with you.

Who is with me?

You are safe...

Well, that's good.

...for now.

What!? For now? That doesn't make me feel safe. What do you mean? Who is with me?

Nothing. She waited, but her Voice didn't return.

She remembered the words. *You are safe...for now.*

Suddenly, she didn't want to be alone. She knocked on Fader's door and walked in. He sat on the bed, his movie playing. "Mind if I watch that with you?" she asked.

In the hotel lobby, Orden smiled with Gabriel Herrada's face as this Major Zapana hung up the front desk phone. "Will's expecting you," Zapana said in Spanish. "I'll take you through. It will make getting past the next set of guards much easier."

"Thank you, Major," Orden replied.

Zapana frowned. "Gabriel, please call me Diego."

Orden swore to herself over the slip. She hadn't taken the time to scrape Herrada's mind for such social niceties as how he addressed people. She lowered her voice. "I thought I should use your rank in front of your men." She nodded at the soldiers guarding the hotel entrance nearby.

"Ah, of course. Thank you. Now, please follow me."

Exiting the lobby, they headed outside and into the hotel's grounds. In a short passageway, Zapana stopped at a barred gate behind which another soldier waited, hands on his weapon. Further back stood Li Mei, the Asian woman from the airport, her eyes on Herrada.

"*Volcanes dormidos,*" Zapana said. The nearest soldier unlocked the gate, then locked it behind them again.

"Sleeping volcanoes?" Orden said.

"The current passphrase. We change it every shift."

"I commend your attention to detail, Diego," Orden replied, commending her own decision against trying to seize the Chakana from here by force.

Zapana acknowledged the compliment with a nod. He led Orden out of the passageway—and out of sight of the guards—into an open courtyard teeming with foliage and color. "I will leave you here, Gabriel. Will's room is 303. At the very top." He pointed up two sets of steps on Herrada's left. With that, Zapana returned the way he'd come.

Orden let a smile crease Herrada's face, thinking of what now lay within her reach. She would take over the boy, make him surrender the Chakana, and send him into the Gray Lands. With the Chakana in Herrada's pocket, she would then walk out of here, past the armed guards with none of these fools the wiser. Then, finally, her real quest could begin.

Rooms here sat on three separate levels, with the lowest straight ahead up a short flight of stone steps. The longer set of steps Zapana had indicated led to the second level and above that the third, where the Dreycott boy and the Chakana waited.

Still smiling, she began to climb the steps. To her right, something moved on the first level of rooms. Stopping, she peered in that direction. If someone else was here, she needed to know before she dealt with the boy. She waited, watching. Low bushes rustled. Probably the hotel dog. She was about to resume her climb when it emerged.

She took a sudden step back, almost losing her balance on the stairs.

A snake. An enormous snake, the size of an anaconda but a solid glowing green.

The snake curled itself into a pile of coils, triangular head swaying, staring at her with eyes like sparkling diamonds.

She knew of only one such snake. *This isn't possible. This isn't—*

A low-throated, rumbling growl snapped her head around.

At the top of the steps she was climbing, on the second level of rooms, a great tawny puma crouched, head lowered, eyes of dancing flames locked on her. It stepped closer, one huge paw dislodging a pebble that tumbled down the steps.

No, no, no, she screamed in Herrada's head. *This can't be.*

A shadow passed overhead. The beat of great wings silenced the growls of the puma. On the third and highest level, the largest condor she had ever seen settled onto the roof, its plumage blacker than the darkest night, black as the emptiness of the Nothing. Its eyes—one red, one yellow—settled on her, piercing her like arrows.

And Orden knew.

Impossible or not, the Guardians of the Crossing were here.

She retreated sideways down the steps, trying to keep all three Guardians in sight, not wanting to expose her back. These creatures could not be here *physically*. They could not. And yet, she remembered the rustling bushes, the dislodged pebble, the overhead shadow.

She reached the bottom again. The Guardians hadn't advanced on her, but neither had they left. Their message was clear. Fear and fury swirled within her. The Chakana would not be hers today.

"Is something wrong?" a female voice asked in Spanish from behind her.

Orden turned. The woman, Li Mei, was staring at her. How long had she been watching? Orden glanced back. The Guardians remained, unmoving, their eyes still on her. Li Mei followed her gaze, frowned, then returned to Herrada. *She doesn't see them.*

Her mind racing, Orden forced a sheepish smile onto Herrada's face. She fished his phone from a pocket. "The monastery insists on talking face-to-face regarding our requested closing on Friday, so I must go there now. Unfortunately, my meeting with young Will must wait."

Li Mei continued to stare, her face unreadable. Then she raised an arm toward the locked gate. "I'll show you out."

As they walked, she spoke again. "I didn't hear you talking with anyone."

Curse this woman. Orden forced a shrug. "They texted."

The woman stared, but said nothing. In the lobby, Orden explained Herrada's sudden departure to Zapana, who promised to tell Will. With Li Mei still watching, Orden assured Zapana the monastery tour would still happen, then walked Herrada's shaking body outside to where his driver waited.

The thought didn't occur to Orden until she was many blocks away. Three Guardians. One for each level of the Crossing. And this cursed hotel where the Chakana lay protected, where the Guardians had appeared? Three levels there, too.

She swallowed with Herrada's tight, dry throat. Yet another coincidence?

The witch, Morrigan, from the coven that had once blocked the route to the Black Island. Morrigan finding her way to the Black Tower. Morrigan's history with those who held the Chakana and sought the Crossing.

And finally, the strange sequence of events that had allowed her, Orden, to escape from where she'd been trapped for so many, many years.

The words of the Archambeault woman came back to her. *It seems we're being moved like pieces in a game.*

Staring out the window of the car, Orden tightened Herrada's hands into fists. No, not a coincidence.

In an upscale hotel across town, Morrigan sat on one of two queen-size beds in the bedroom of an expensive suite. She sat cross-legged, pillows behind her, wearing an outfit from her hurried shopping spree at the airport—a one-piece jumpsuit in a green that beautifully complimented the darker shades of the Unicorn Tapestry.

That same tapestry now lay spread over her lap and much of the bed. Freed of Orden's presence, she hoped to finally study the silken artifact. And to confirm her belief about the creatures hiding in its corners.

The winged dragon that had saved her from the scarabs had certainly been Fire. But it was gone forever. The lower right corner of the Tapestry, where it had lain, showed only vines and leaves.

In the upper left corner, the gray bat flew, wings and fanged mouth open. She touched the creature. A chill breeze stirred the curtains, and the Tapestry rippled. Her head swam with sudden vertigo, and she gazed down on the room from above. She lifted her hand. The breeze died. The vertigo passed. She smiled. The bat was Air.

She stroked the top right corner where the brown rat crouched in a burrow, teeth bared. The bed swayed, and the room itself seemed to shake. Startled, she snatched her hand away. The bed and room quieted. She swallowed. Earth.

In the bottom left, a white eel with dead eyes swam in a dark stream. "And you, my ugly one," she whispered, "must be Water." Cautious after the rat, she hovered her hand over the eel, not touching it. A cold mist chilled her skin, and a rushing roar of crashing surf filled her ears.

Satisfied, she sat back. She still didn't know how each animal would manifest itself, but for now, this was enough. Powerful creatures lay at her fingertips, creatures that, like the dragon, would come at her call.

But also like the dragon, she could summon them only once. Then they, too, would be lost forever.

Once, she would have hoarded such magicks, never using these spells, wanting instead to always keep the power. But now, power in itself meant nothing. Now, if needed, she would use these creatures without regret. To protect Fader, should Orden fail today and the ambush at the monastery take place.

She sighed. But she still hadn't found what she sought—a way to break free from Orden. A spell to protect her from a body snatcher more powerful than Marell.

The three creatures all stared from their corners toward the same spot. She let her gaze follow theirs to the Tapestry's center and the grotesque beast that glared back at her with one amber eye. The beast that gave the artifact its name.

The Unicorn.

Was it, like dragon and bat, eel and rat, also a spell? One she could release from its silken prison and unleash upon the world?

If so, what could such an emaciated animal do? And what role did the pale-faced, straw-haired maiden beside it play?

More importantly, what would be the price for the Unicorn's magic? For magic always had a price. And the greater the magic, the greater the price.

She reached a tentative hand toward the Unicorn. A brightening began. A glow. But not from the Unicorn.

From the pale-faced maiden.

The girl's dress turned from blue to green. A flush rose in her cheeks. Her lips reddened. Her hair grew longer, thicker, a strawberry tint appearing. And voices filled the air. Chanting voices. Women's voices.

Movement in the room snapped Morrigan's head up. She gasped, pulling her hand back from the Tapestry.

Arrayed in a semicircle around her bed, shimmering and transparent, stood women dressed in white robes. Familiar robes, once worn by Morrigan herself. She counted the women, already knowing the number.

Eleven.

Their coven had been thirteen. Aalin was gone, her mother's spirit released after their encounter in Castle Rushen. And she, Morrigan, had left long ago.

Eleven remained. Eleven faces, rising from her memory. The rest of the White Coven of Ellan Vannin. "Sisters," she whispered. "How can you be—?"

The door to the suite flew open. The women disappeared. Orden burst into the room, ripping off Herrada's suit jacket and flinging it to the floor.

On the Tapestry, the maiden had become her pale-faced, straw-haired self again. Morrigan wrapped the artifact around her shoulders, where it settled once more like a cloak. She lay back against the pillows, suddenly drained.

Orden paced the room, spewing words from Herrada's mouth. Morrigan didn't know the language, but she recognized obscenities when she heard them.

"Problems?" she asked, keeping the smile from her voice.

She listened as Orden ranted of being thwarted by three mystical animals at the boy's hotel. Orden finally ran down. "Never have I heard of the Guardians manifesting outside the Crossing."

Morrigan still believed none of Orden's fantastic tale of the Four and the Book and the Crossing. But she knew better than to say so. "Perhaps they didn't."

Orden spun on her. "You call me a fool?"

"Not at all. You said this Asian woman didn't see these creatures. From that, I infer..." Morrigan shrugged.

Orden frowned. "Only astral forms?" Her eyes narrowed. "Still, they might have seized me, blocked me from taking over the boy. I was right not to try." She glared at Morrigan again, as if daring her to disagree.

Morrigan nodded her support, adding this incident to her list of Orden's fallibilities.

Orden drew Herrada's body up straight, once more composed. "Then I will seize the Chakana at the monastery. Physically, using Herrada's thugs." She turned to Morrigan. "And you, Witch, will be there. To help me, as agreed, and to protect your precious child."

Morrigan had forgotten what failure at the hotel would mean. She forced a nod, her delight in Orden's defeat today now gone.

Chapter 27

You Are a Tourist

On Friday morning, Will sat slumped in one of Diego's armored personnel carriers. They'd left the hotel, far earlier than he liked, and were on their way to the Santa Catalina monastery. He sat on the vehicle's left side, Case behind him, Fader behind her. On the opposite side sat Stone, Adi, and Rani.

Diego again rode beside a soldier who drove, following another APC through the streets. The third APC trailed them. "There," Diego said, pointing to the northeast. "I promised I would show you."

In the distance, a cone-shaped mountain loomed above the city, its snow-covered peak glowing in the just rising sun.

"*El Misti*," Diego said, "our most beautiful mountain, an almost perfect cone." He pointed further east to a long ridge of irregular peaks. "And that is *Pichu Pichu*. Very old, it has...what is the word? Eroded, collapsed from what it once was. And there..." He pointed to a line of peaks to the left of El Misti. "...is the *Chachani* range." He smiled back at them. "Chachani, El Misti, Pichu Pichu. Our three guardians, watching over us like Inca gods."

Three guardians. Will straightened at that. He glanced at Case and could tell from her face she was thinking the same thing. Behind her, Fader slipped down in his seat, his eyes wide. "Pretty dangerous guardians," Will said.

"Ah, but powerful, *sí?*"

"Dangerous and powerful," Rani muttered, catching Will's eye. "Wonderful."

Turning down the narrow street holding the monastery, their truck stopped outside the metal-studded black doors. But the lead vehicle drove to the far end of the street, where it maneuvered to block off the road. Will got out with the others, shrugging his camouflage jacket on against the early morning chill. They all wore their jungle gear, ready for the coming helicopter ride. Their backpacks remained in the truck.

The trailing APC now blocked access at that end of the street. Two of Diego's men stood behind each blockading vehicle.

After Mei, Peng, and the remaining soldiers from the trucks joined them at the entrance, Diego addressed them all. "Earlier this morning, Mr. Zhang and I, with six of my men, completed a sweep of the monastery. I left two men inside to ensure the facility remained secure."

Turning to the door, Diego rapped a staccato series of knocks. From inside, a different pattern came in reply. Diego nodded to Stone. "All remains well." He knocked once more, and the double doors opened, swinging inward.

The travelers followed Diego and two soldiers into the monastery. Four soldiers remained outside. As the doors closed behind them, Will saw their truck being moved to block the entrance. Diego wasn't taking any chances.

They followed Diego and his men along a wide corridor open to the sky above. A white stone wall rose two stories high on one side, opposite a shorter wall painted a deep orange-red. They passed an empty ticket booth and entered a small open-air courtyard framed by more red walls. Irregular gray stones formed the floor.

An archway, the words '*Silencio*' written in black letters above it, led off the courtyard into the monastery itself. A short tree with multiple twisting trunks, feathery green leaves, and pink flowers sat near the archway. Standing beside the tree, wearing a wrinkled white linen suit and a crisp powder-blue dress shirt, was Gabriel Herrada.

Gabriel smiled, his arms outstretched in welcome. "My friends! Are you ready for your tour?"

"Before you start, Gabriel, a few words?" Diego said. He motioned them to gather round. "I have left men outside to guard the approach and sole entrance to this site. While you tour the monastery, five of us—Mr. Zhang, Ms. Archambeault, two of my men, and myself—will remain here to further protect the entrance. The remaining two men in my squad and Mr. Zhang's capable associates..." He indicated Mei and Peng. "...will accompany your tour."

Gabriel frowned. "Is that necessary? The monastery is empty, its entrance well protected. Four armed guards for our little group seems...excessive."

"Humor me, please," Adi said. "Just another precaution."

Gabriel opened his hands in a gesture of acceptance. "Of course."

As Stone and Diego gave further instructions to Mei, Peng, and the two soldiers who would accompany them, Will walked over to Case, who was smelling the tree blossoms.

"This is beautiful," she said, looking around.

He stared at her, her face radiant in the early morning light. "Very."

She gave him a 'seriously?' look and punched him lightly in the stomach. But she slipped her arms around his neck, laying her head on his chest. He pulled her to him, enjoying her warmth, her smell, her closeness.

"It feels like our crazy world," she said, "is holding its breath, giving us this moment."

He knew what she meant. The last two days had felt so strange, so different from the life they'd been living. He'd accepted that the best course of action was the one they were already on. Get to the Crossing as planned. No portal. No facing Sword Ladies alone.

That had left two days in the hotel to just relax and enjoy each other. No threats. No danger. Nothing to fear, for once.

But when they left here, all that would change. They would board a military helicopter to fly into danger, moving closer and closer to people who wanted something he couldn't give up. But closer also to answers to the mystery that had haunted his life for eight years, and to a cure for himself, too. He hoped.

He and Case broke off their hug as Gabriel clapped his hands. "All right, my friends, we must not waste the time we have. Let us begin our tour. Perhaps, Will, you could walk with me, and between my speeches, I can share those stories of your parents I promised?"

Will looked at Case. "Enjoy," she said. "Besides, Rani and I have girl stuff to talk about, right?"

Rani hesitated. "Uh, right."

"And Fader's hanging with his new bud." Case nodded to where Fader and Peng were laughing together.

They headed through the archway and into a red-walled laneway. Diego's two soldiers took the lead position, followed by Gabriel as their tour leader and Will. Then came Rani and Case, then Peng, Fader, and Mei at the rear of their group.

Gabriel began to give the history of the monastery. Will half listened, wondering what he would learn about his parents from Gabriel's stories and if he would soon hear those stories from their own mouths. Wondering, too, what dangers he, Case, and Fader would have to face before their families were finally reunited.

At least for now, in this moment where the world held its breath, danger wasn't a concern.

Deep in the Santa Catalina de Sienna monastery, Morrigan waited with six of Herrada's hired thugs. She lounged on a stone bench inside a small open courtyard while the men, hard types all, sat with their backs against walls, rifles slung.

Around her shoulders she wore the Unicorn Tapestry. Occasionally, her left hand—her spell hand—would drift toward the pale horned creature at the center of the tableau. She longed to again summon the astral forms of her dead coven sisters, to ask them of the secrets of the Tapestry. But that conversation would have to wait.

The courtyard sat at the end of a long stone-paved laneway. She found the narrow street quite pretty. Its walls, painted a deep orange-red that complimented her hair, provided a beautiful contrast to the blue of the cloudless sky overhead. Hanging plants with pink flowers and graceful arches leading into small alcoves broke the monotony of the straight stretch of walls.

Yes, very pretty. And a perfect spot for an ambush.

Six more gunmen hid in an alcove near the entrance to this laneway. The narrow passage dead-ended in the courtyard where she waited. Soon Orden, as Herrada, would lead the party with the Dreycott boy into the lane, trapping them between the two groups of waiting attackers.

A concealment spell she'd cast hid her and both groups of gunmen. Earlier that morning, the man Stone and the army officer had led six soldiers past where she and the men waited, not seeing what lay before them. Their prey, believing themselves safe in an empty monastery, would literally walk into the trap.

Orden's prey, she corrected herself. She had no prey here. Her only goal was to protect Fader. And, should the opportunity arise, escape Orden.

Perhaps Orden was right. Perhaps Fader was but a surrogate for the brother she'd lost. It didn't matter. She had failed Dany. She would not fail Fader.

Orden claimed these Guardian creatures or the Chakana would prevent any astral takeover of the Dreycott boy or anyone else in the party. That meant Orden needed to physically seize this Chakana from the boy. Orden had promised no gunfire, that the surprise of the ambush would force Dreycott to hand over the artifact.

But Morrigan was no fool. Men with guns liked to use them. And she didn't trust Orden. She sat back, waiting, stroking the Tapestry, and enjoying the reassuring tingle of the runescript for a stun spell on her arm.

⁂

Case walked with Rani, listening to Gabriel Herrada as they toured the monastery, which she learned was still home to about twenty nuns.

"So, it's a convent?" Case asked. "Why do they call it a monastery?"

Gabriel shrugged. "The patriarchy of the Church," he said, a reply that surprised Case, coming from a man.

"Damn straight," Rani muttered.

Gabriel explained the monastery became a tourist site only in 1970, to pay for its restoration after major earthquakes. Before then, it was a secret cloister, shut off from the world. Today, the nuns still lived a private life in closed-off quarters, emerging only to attend mass before the grounds opened to the public. "So," Gabriel added, "we will not encounter them."

He described the monastery as a city within the larger city, over twenty thousand square meters. As he led them down street after street, deeper and deeper into the site, they passed parks, houses, a laundry, a kitchen, a cemetery, a chapel, and even an art gallery. Everywhere, colors shone brilliant in the sunshine, each wall painted a deep blue, glowing white, or rich red.

Case quickly became lost, but was loving every moment. She wanted to wander these maze-like streets alone with Will, being surprised at every turn by another cobbled square blazing in color or secret courtyard filled with flowering trees.

Small alcoves, maybe four paces deep by six paces long, dotted the streets, leading nowhere, but offering stone benches to rest and admire overflowing pots of hanging flowers.

Gabriel's narration of their route had stopped. Ahead of them, he and Will walked together. She hoped the man would finally share his promised stories with Will.

Which reminded her. Someone else had stories to share. Rani had kept to her room for most of their time at the hotel, insisting she had research to finish. Now Case turned to her. "So, what did you find out?"

Rani frowned. "What?"

Case lowered her voice, although they were well separated from the others. "At the airport, you said you'd discovered...bad stuff. About Stone and Adi."

Rani turned away. "It's nothing."

"Hey!" Case rasped, "our safety's in their hands. If you found something, you need to share."

Rani's jaw muscles clenched, but she stayed silent.

"Were you checking out your new boyfriend?"

Rani hesitated. "I was researching that Chamber of the Red Door cult."

"Find anything?"

"A disturbing amount. It's been around for centuries. Earliest mention I found was in 15th century Spain—*La Cámara de la Puerta Roja*. Shortly after that...wait for it...the Spaniards conquered the Incas in Peru."

Case felt a chill. "That has to be a coincidence."

"Yeah? Well, another early reference was in the 1600s in England under the Roundheads—the guys who overthrew the king. *That* group was on the Isle of Man."

Case swallowed. "Morrigan was from there."

Rani frowned. "That redhead you guys tangled with? Again, oddly coincidental."

Adi's words returned to Case. *I feel we are being moved like pieces on a board.* She shook her head. "That's all it can be. A coincidence. Morrigan disappeared, and no one's seen her since. Anyway, what's this have to do with Stone or Adi?"

"Hong Kong."

"What?"

"I found references to Red Door groups around the globe, including Hong Kong. The paper has a foreign bureau there. Just one guy, but we went to journalism school together, and he's always had the hots for me. Figured I could get him to do some digging."

"About the Red Door?"

"Yeah. He didn't find anything, but since Stone was also from Hong Kong..."

She shrugged.

"You're unbelievable."

"Hey, a girl can't be too careful. And I'm glad I did. Stone headed the Organized Crime Unit on the Hong Kong police force—"

"I knew that."

"Know why he left?"

"Adi offered him a job in Will's company."

"Not till three years after he'd quit the force."

Case didn't want to ask, but knew she had to. "So, what happened?"

Rani glanced back, but Peng, Mei, and Fader were talking and laughing and well out of earshot. "Stone was a rising star. His team had started to really hurt the Triads—"

"Triads?"

"Crime syndicates that operate across southeast Asia. Stone engineered a huge sting that brought the Mountain Masters of three Triads to trial for human trafficking."

"Mountain Masters?"

"Heads of Triads, like Mafia dons. This was huge. No Mountain Master, let alone three, had ever been charged with such serious crimes. Plus, Stone had done his job well. Media thought the charges would stick."

"I'm guessing they didn't."

"Five months into the trial, the judge—an honest one, totally incorruptible—was gunned down. The next judge was in the pocket of the Triads. Long story short, they all got off."

"Okay, disappointing to Stone, but—"

"It gets worse." Rani took a deep breath. "Much worse. The Triads now saw Stone and his team as a genuine threat."

Case remembered Stone's words on the plane after Nyx's revelation of the multiverse. *These other universes, they are worlds where our lives took different paths? The people we knew...their lives, too? ...*

Then I choose to believe this.

And she knew how Rani's story would end.

"They attacked Stone and his team. In their homes. Killed half his people and their families. Stone survived, but they murdered his wife and teenage daughter."

"Oh, god," she whispered, "that's horrible." Something came back to her. When the Chakana had cranked her Voice into overload and she'd fled Will's tower, Stone had called her, his concern obvious. She remembered his words then. *You remind me of someone.*

He'd had a teenage daughter.

"Rani, this is awful, but why'd it change your mind about Stone?"

"A month later, the same Triad leaders and their lieutenants met in one of the gang's restaurants." Rani glanced back to where Mei and Peng walked with

Fader. She lowered her voice. "According to police reports, snipers shot the outside sentries. Unknown parties chained the rear exit shut and fire bombed the restaurant. Whole place burned. Anyone fleeing through the front was gunned down." Rani looked at Case, her normal expression of jaded indifference gone. "Thirty-two people died. All Triad."

"You mean…Stone?"

"That's what the papers thought. Him and his people who'd survived. But charges were never brought. Stone resigned. His team followed. And that was that."

They walked in silence as Case tried to reconcile this story with the Stone who'd treated a street kid with kindness and respect from the start. "What's this have to do with Adi?"

Rani scrolled through her phone, then handed it to Case. "Stumbled on this in the trial records. Almost missed it."

A grainy newspaper photo showed an attractive blond woman, early twenties maybe, flanked by cops. The caption read "Police escort Martine Archibald 'Archie' Labelle, protected witness, into Triple Triad Trial." Something familiar. Longer hair, but still…

"Wait. Is that Adi?"

Rani nodded.

Case peered closer, at the slight bulge of the younger Adi's abdomen. "Is she…is she pregnant?"

"Bingo."

"Thought she was gay."

"Bi, I'd say, at least back then. Or she found a donor. Just starting to show, so she's three to four months along. The trial was four months in at that point. She wouldn't have known when she agreed to testify."

"Why was she testifying?"

"Transcripts said she was an inside informant for Stone. She had a rep as a smuggler and had offered to help the gangs with their human trafficking."

"*What?*"

"Not for real. She was part of the sting. Then, shortly after that photo, the judge gets killed, and everything goes south. She must've gone into hiding, knowing they'd come after her. I found only one reference to Martine Labelle after that, and it wasn't in the papers."

"Then where?"

"The admission records of a private Hong Kong clinic." She checked her phone. "Holy Blood Hospital. I'm guessing she hid there until the baby was born. Probably paid the staff to keep quiet. Or maybe they were friends. After that, she vanishes until she starts working for Will's parents two years later with her new name."

"But her baby…?"

"She knew she had to run. If the Triads caught her, she knew they'd kill her...and her baby. What would you do?"

Gabriel Herrada had led them into a courtyard with a beautiful stone fountain. Herrada was giving its history, but Case wasn't listening. She was imagining a young Adi, a new mother facing a terrible decision. "She gave up the baby."

"That's what I think. Then went on the run with a new name."

"That's heartbreaking, but not something bad about her. Just a secret—and one you'd better keep."

"If I'm right, it's a *huge* secret."

"What do you mean?"

"Check the date on that photo."

Case zoomed in and squinted at the screen. She did the math. "Seventeen years ago. What does—?" She stopped. No. It couldn't be.

Rani was staring at her. "How old is Will, again?"

Chapter 28

Guns and Ammunition

As Gabriel Herrada led the group deeper into the labyrinth of the monastery, Will continued to wait for stories of his parents. They entered yet another courtyard, and Will listened with little interest as Herrada talked about a stone fountain in its center.

Leaving the fountain behind, they started down a cobbled laneway, its walls a deep orange-red. Herrada glanced into an alcove they passed on the left and gave a small nod. Will wondered at that, as the alcove, like the others they'd seen, was empty. "Gabriel," he said, his patience finally gone, "about my parents—"

"Ah, yes, Will. I was too immersed in being a guide." Herrada stopped in the middle of the lane and motioned the group closer. "My friends, this ends our tour. I must make a short private phone call, then I will return us to the entrance. Please wait here." He turned to Will. "As we walk back, we will speak of your parents." With that, Herrada headed toward a small enclosed courtyard at the far end of the lane.

The two soldiers were standing at the front of the group, talking in Spanish. At the back, Peng and Fader were laughing together, while Mei listened, shaking her head but smiling.

Nearest to Will, beside another of the small alcoves that lined this street, Case and Rani were talking in low whispers. Something about the guarded glances they kept shooting his direction made him not want to approach them.

This laneway was long and straight, and much narrower than others they'd walked down. The large potted plants sitting every few paces made it seem even narrower. Despite the open sky above, he felt a sudden sense of being trapped, as if the walls were closing in.

Gabriel Herrada was nearing the courtyard. Will wondered idly why he hadn't started his phone call yet.

Case stood with Rani, separate from the others in the narrow street as Gabriel Herrada walked away from their group. She couldn't believe what Rani was implying. "That can't be true," she whispered, aware of Will's eyes on them. "Adi can't be... Will can't be..." Her words trailed off.

"No?" Rani whispered back. "Two years later, she takes a job with Jon Dreycott and Terri Yurikami. Why? To be close to the son she had to give up. It all fits."

"Is there any proof? About the adoption?"

Rani sighed. "Adoption records are impossible to access. I'm thinking of hiring a private investigator in Hong Kong."

"Or you could just stop snooping—"

RUN!

Her Voice. Case gasped as a vision appeared before her eyes, superimposed over the laneway. In that vision, the empty courtyard Gabriel approached was suddenly empty no more. Armed men stepped out of invisibility. The gunmen began firing at them. Behind those men stood Gabriel Herrada, a twisted smile on his face. And beside him...

Beside him was a tall woman with hair the color of flames.

Morrigan.

No, no, no! She can't be here, Case's mind screamed.

But her Voice screamed louder. *RUN! Into the alcove. Or you'll all die!*

Before she could stop herself, her body lunged toward the small alcove beside them. Her left hand, as if moving by itself, grabbed Rani by an arm and shoved her through the opening.

"What the—?" Rani stumbled forward, her words cut off as she landed hard on the cobblestones inside the alcove.

Fighting her own body, Case forced herself to stop. Will thought her Voice could see maybe ten seconds into the future. How much time was left? At Rani's cry, Gabriel Herrada had turned back, frowning. He was still several steps from the courtyard, from beginning the scenario she'd seen. She still had time.

"Will! Fader! Everyone!" she cried, pointing to the alcove. "Get in here now! Herrada's going to kill us!"

Herrada sprinted toward the courtyard. "Now, Witch!" he cried.

And her vision became reality. The gunmen appeared, rifles raised, Morrigan beside them. Herrada reached the courtyard. As he slipped behind the armed men, his voice echoed down the laneway. "Kill them all!"

Will reacted within a second of Case's warning. He knew her Voice, knew to trust what she saw and heard. He started for the safety of the alcove, checking that Fader and the rest were running for cover as well.

But Fader was with Peng and Mei, at the back of their group, farthest from the alcove. Fader was tugging on Peng's arm, trying to get him to move. Peng was laughing, a quizzical expression on his face, while Mei's eyes, wide and alert, darted around the area. In front, Diego's two soldiers, their rifles slung, their backs to Herrada, were shooting puzzled looks between Fader and where Case called from the alcove.

"Mei! Peng!" Case cried.

Mei and Peng still didn't move. Neither did the soldiers. Will realized Mei and Peng didn't know to trust Case's warning, didn't understand how Case's Voice worked. And the soldiers didn't understand English.

A second later, they all understood.

Herrada reached the courtyard. "Now, Witch!" he cried.

Gunmen appeared beside Herrada, all with rifles aimed down the laneway. And behind them...

As Will sprinted to Fader, his mind fought to understand how Morrigan could be part of this, even as he fought to understand what was happening.

"Kill them all!" Herrada's voice cried.

As Will reached Fader, a volley of shots rang out. At the front of the group, unwittingly shielding the others, the two soldiers spasmed as the bullets hit them.

Before the soldiers hit the ground, Mei was crouched and firing. Three gunmen fell, their rifles clattering to the stones. The other three ducked back into the cover of the courtyard where Herrada and Morrigan now hid.

Peng had reacted now as well. But the big man hadn't reached for his gun when the attackers appeared. He'd reached for Fader and Will. Grabbing them each in one huge hand, he tossed them toward the alcove. "Get under cover!" he yelled.

Will took four stumbling steps, regained his balance, and pulled Fader with him into the alcove with Case and Rani.

With his young charges out of the line of fire, Peng reached for his own gun.

The first shot hit him in the shoulder, spinning him around. The second shot hit him in the chest. Wu Peng fell, gun flying from his hand. He landed hard on the cobblestones and lay still.

"No!" Fader yelled. He tried to run to Peng, but Case grabbed and held him hard. "Let me go," he cried, struggling against her. "I can save him."

Screaming something incoherent, Mei leaped up. She took a step toward Peng, turning to look behind her, to the other end of the narrow street, raising her gun in that direction as she did.

And Will understood.

The shots that had felled Peng had come from that end. They were caught between two groups of gunmen. Mei fired three quick rounds even as more shots exploded off the stones and walls around her. Three men at the entrance to the street fell. The others retreated into cover.

But now Mei's back was to the gunmen in the courtyard. She spun to fire at them, but a shot hit her in her gun arm. She cried out, dropping the gun. As she reached for it with her other hand, a second shot struck her in the chest, flinging her back. She fell, landing beside Peng, her head bouncing hard off the stones. She lay as still as Peng.

"Move in," Herrada called. "Finish them."

"You said no shooting!" Morrigan's voice, echoing down the street.

"Shut up, Witch," Herrada answered. "Move, you fools. Kill them all."

In a corner of the small alcove, Rani sat huddled on the ground, knees pulled to her chest, rocking back and forth. "No, no, no, no…" she said over and over.

Fader disappeared.

One second, he was with them, Case still gripping his arm. The next, he was gone. "Fader!" Case cried, looking around, panic on her face.

Beside where Peng lay, Will saw two hands appear, hanging as if suspended in the air. The hands grew to arms. One hand grabbed hold of Peng's jacket. The other grabbed hold of Mei's. Both hands pulled.

Will understood. "He's trying to pull them into the In Between."

"They'll see him," Case sobbed. "They'll shoot him."

Mei stirred. She started to crawl forward, going with the pull of Fader's hand. But Peng was unconscious. Or worse. And he was too big for Fader to move. Both of Fader's hands grabbed Peng. Fader's head and chest appeared, his face straining as he tried to pull the big man to safety in the In Between.

More shots rang out. Fader stiffened. Dropping his grip on Peng, he fell forward, tumbling out of the In Between and onto the cobblestones, where he lay unmoving.

"No!" Case screamed. Leaping from the cover of the alcove, she ran to her brother. Will ran after her.

⁊

"No!" Morrigan cried as Fader slumped to the ground. Three gunmen remained alive in the courtyard where she stood with Orden in Herrada's body. She didn't know how many survived at the far end of the street, but she would deal with the ones here first.

Her left hand flashed up, and the golden runes she had readied flew from her arm. The stun spell struck Herrada and the three gunmen, lifting them into the air and slamming them into the red-painted walls. They dropped to the ground and lay crumpled.

As the runescript for another stun spell flowed onto her arm, motion down the lane made her turn. Fader still lay unmoving near the two bodyguards. But his sister and the Dreycott boy were running to him, leaving the safety of the alcove behind.

The boy lifted Fader under the arms, while the girl took hold of his feet. They began carrying him awkwardly back toward the alcove.

A momentary flash of admiration for their bravery filled Morrigan. This was what family did. They were saving Fader, as she should have saved Dany.

Gunshots ricocheted off the cobblestones near the girl, snapping her attention back. At the opposite end of the lane, three gunmen were firing at the two teenagers. And at Fader.

Stepping to one side to give herself a shot around Fader's rescuers, she flung the stun spell down the narrow street. From this distance, she hoped only to disrupt the men's aim but gave a silent cry of joy when all three men fell backwards onto the cobblestones. The girl and the Dreycott boy disappeared into the alcove. Fader was safe, but he'd been hit. How badly was he hurt? Could her magic help him?

Beside her, Herrada and the gunmen were stirring. She raised her arm, the runes tingling on her skin once more. If she could stun Herrada again, it might give her time to find a healing spell for the boy and—

She stiffened. Her arm fell to her side.

That is the last time you defy me, Witch.

Orden was in her head, and her body was no longer her own. The brilliant colors of the courtyard, of the laneway, of the sky above faded, faded...

Faded to gray.

Summoning the last speck of her will, she touched the Unicorn Tapestry. *Hear me, my Sisters. Help me, save me.*

In the Tapestry, something stirred. A wind rose. Then the Gray Lands rushed to meet her.

Back in the alcove, Will helped Case lower Fader to the cobblestones, then pointed a shaking finger at the side of Fader's head. "He's bleeding."

Case, her face tight and strained, took Fader's head in her lap. As she gently probed where blood matted her brother's hair, Fader winced and stirred. "Ow," he said, opening his eyes. Relief flooded Will.

"Oh god, you're okay," Case sobbed, but she continued to probe. "I don't feel any, you know, holes or anything."

"Looks like he just got grazed," Will said.

Rani was on her feet now, her brow furrowed in concern. Kneeling beside them, she pulled a flowered bandanna from a pocket, handing it to Case. "Scalp wounds bleed like shit. Hold this against it."

Case helped Fader sit, then hugged him tightly, pressing the bandanna against his wound. "You could've been killed, you little idiot."

"Peng isn't moving," Fader mumbled.

Out in the laneway, Peng lay very still. Now, so did Mei, her hand clutching Peng's.

"There's a lot of blood," Fader said. "Around both of them."

Moving to the entrance, Will snatched a look up and down the lane, then ducked his head back. Halfway down the street to their right, three gunmen sat crouched, guns aimed at the alcove. To their left, Herrada and three more gunmen were creeping out of the courtyard. Oddly, behind them, Morrigan stood unmoving, frozen like a statue.

"We can't reach Peng or Mei without getting shot," he said. "Whatever Morrigan did to the gunmen has worn off."

"Morrigan?" Fader said.

"How can she be here?" Case said. "Why's Herrada trying to kill us? And why would Morrigan help us if she's with him?"

Before Will could answer, Herrada called out. "Will, listen to me. No one else needs to be hurt. Just throw out the Chakana—in its pouch—and you can all walk out of here."

The Chakana. Of course, it would be about the Chakana.

"Is there anyone who *doesn't* want that thing?" Rani muttered.

"Why haven't they moved in?" Case asked.

"Maybe they're worried we're armed. I should've grabbed Mei's gun when I was out there. Or one of their walkie-talkies."

"Too late now."

Rani bit her lip. "Stone and Adi must've heard the shooting. They'll come, right?"

"This place is a maze," Will said. "They'll never find us in time."

"Then what the hell are we going to do?" Rani asked.

"Will," Herrada called. "All I want is the Chakana."

He needed time to think. "All right! But give me a minute!" he called out. He turned to Fader. "Can you take us into the In Between?"

Fader scrunched up his eyes where he lay against Case. Will guessed he was trying to fade. He shook his head. "I don't think so. I don't feel so good."

Will looked at Case. "Your Voice?"

"Nothing."

"Well, at least that means we won't die in the next ten seconds."

"Or there's nothing we can do."

Herrada called out again. "Last chance, Will. Throw out the Chakana. *Now.* Or I'll take it from your dead body."

"Oh god, oh god, oh god," Rani said, her hands pressed to her head.

Reaching into his jacket pocket, Will pulled out the steel-gray woven pouch containing the Chakana.

"No," Case said. "If you give it to him, you'll die."

"If he doesn't, we'll all die," Rani snapped.

"Herrada will kill us no matter what. But I'm not giving it to him," Will said. "Fader, can you stand?"

Fader nodded, and Case helped her brother to his feet.

Will called out to Herrada. "Okay, you win."

"Very smart, Will. Throw it out."

Will lifted the flap on the pouch. Case's eyes widened. "You're calling a Sword Lady!"

"How's that going to help us?" Rani said.

"We don't need her," Will said. "We need her door." He pulled the Chakana from the pouch.

Five seconds. Ten seconds.

"Time's up," Herrada called.

Out in the laneway, a point of light appeared, hovering waist-high above the cobblestones.

Case groaned. "Out there? Really?"

The light erupted into sparks, accompanied by a crackling buzz. Will moved toward the alcove's entrance, his eyes on the portal as the sparks flared to a lightning storm in a box, a box that stretched to person-size. "We have to stay in physical contact with each other. And force the Sword Lady through with us."

"No, Will," Case said from behind him. "We don't."

"Case," Will said, turning back, "that's what our parents had to—" He stopped.

Above Rani, wings outspread, a black condor hung motionless in the air. Beside Case, head lowered, a huge tawny puma crouched. And beside Fader, a monstrous green snake sat coiled. Translucent, all three creatures glowed with a silvery light.

"They'll lead us through," Case said, a faraway look in her eyes. "My Voice showed me."

⁂

Orden stood in Herrada's body in the narrow street behind the surviving gunmen from the courtyard. Herrada's other remaining thugs waited on the far side of the alcove where the Dreycott boy and his companions hid. She had debated rushing them, but feared that the man Stone had armed the entire party. She would wait for the boy to obey her order to surrender the Chakana.

Things had not gone according to plan. These people should all be lying dead, and she should have the Chakana. How had the girl Case known? What had given the trap away? And the witch's betrayal had made everything worse.

No matter. Her plan would still work. Once the boy surrendered the Chakana, Herrada's men would kill them all. She would then send the gunmen back to the entrance ahead of her, while she hid the artifact in the monastery in a place she'd selected earlier.

Somewhere before these thugs reached the entrance, they would meet

Zapana and his soldiers, along with Stone and Archambeault. She didn't know who'd win that encounter, and she didn't care. She would vacate Herrada's body, leaving him in the Gray Lands, and take over someone in the victorious party.

Then she would return here at her leisure, retrieve the Chakana from its hiding place, and walk out with the Key in her pocket.

Yes, her plan would still work.

But the boy was taking too long to obey. She opened her mouth to call her last warning when a speck of light appeared in the laneway opposite where her prey hid.

What was this? Had the witch somehow returned from the Gray Lands? Was this another of her spells? Orden looked back, half expecting to find Morrigan advancing on them, her spell arm raised. But the witch remained statue-like, her face blank. Not Morrigan, then what?

A crackling buzz snapped her head around. A familiar buzz, but one buried deep in her memories. Outside the alcove, the bright speck erupted into sparks that bloomed into lightning bolts framed in a doorway.

"No!" she cried, understanding. They had exposed the Chakana. A Sister was coming, perhaps many. She never thought the boy would risk involving the Sisterhood. "Rush them!" she screamed in Spanish. "Kill them now!"

But the doorway's appearance had unnerved Herrada's men. Some were backing away from the portal, crossing themselves. Others stood staring, wide-eyed and open-mouthed.

The Patel woman burst from cover, running at the portal just as a Sister, sword raised high, stepped through. Orden opened Herrada's mouth to shout another command. A command that never came.

For above the reporter, a great winged shadow flew.

"It can't be," Orden whispered, stepping back.

The reporter slammed into the swordswoman, propelling her back. Patel, the Sister, and the Guardian Condor all disappeared through the doorway.

But the doorway didn't close, as it should have when a Sister returned through it. Three more figures burst from the alcove. The girl, Case, her arm supporting her brother, followed by the Dreycott boy.

And flanking the three were the Puma and Snake Guardians.

"No!" Orden cried, forcing herself to move despite her fear of the spirits. The Dreycott boy must not make it through the portal.

But the Puma spun on her, snarling. Real or astral body? Unsure, she stopped.

Fader stumbled. Just a misstep, but enough to slow their dash for the doorway. The girl and the Dreycott boy helped him up, then together, the girl and her brother leaped through the gateway, the Snake and Puma behind them.

Only the Dreycott boy remained.

Orden rushed Herrada forward, grasping at one last desperate hope, something she hadn't dared try until this boy was alone.

As he was now. And with no Guardians to protect him.

If she could get close enough to him, inside the astral shield of the Chakana...

There! She touched his mind...

And leaped into him.

❦

Two steps from the portal, Will stopped running, his body suddenly refusing to obey him. He knew what was happening. He'd felt such a violation before, when the body swapper Marell had taken him over. But that time, Will had allowed Marell into his mind, using his agoraphobia to drive him out.

He had no such trick to use now.

Who are you? he asked, even as he struggled to regain control of his body.

You don't recognize me? A chuckle accompanied the thought—and the sense of a feminine identity. *I am hurt, but no matter. You are mine. Now turn away from the doorway. And shield the Chakana again.*

Against his will, his body began to retreat from the doorway. He fought back as hard as he could. He didn't move. At all. Neither closer to the portal, nor away. For now, that was a win.

Stop it, you young fool. You can't resist me.

Looks like I can.

A wave of fury from the entity in his mind flooded him, and he almost lost control. He took one step back before he could regain the standoff. He was wrong. She was too strong. *Nyx! Can you hear me? Help me!*

No answer came, but a warmth flowed up from his hand. The hand that still clutched the exposed Chakana.

Who is this Nyx?

Ignoring her, he focused on the Chakana, imagining the silver cord Nyx had shown him stretching between him and the artifact. Imagining astral power flowing along that cord...

...and into him.

He felt it. The power rushed into him like a storm-gorged river into a dry lake bed, flooding his mind, washing anything unwanted out of him. Washing this creature out.

And then he was free, his mind his own once more.

He gasped, almost falling to the cobblestones. The portal still hung before him, open and glowing, but growing smaller. In the laneway, the remaining gunmen were backing away, fear etched on their faces.

Only steps away, Gabriel Herrada stood strangely rigid and unmoving, like Morrigan.

A small bark brought Will's head down.

At his feet sat a glowing translucent Jack, tail wagging, head tilted to one side.

"Jack!" Will cried. "Did you just save me again?"

Movement down the laneway made him turn. One gunman had recovered enough composure to raise his rifle, pointing it at him.

The portal was shrinking, its glow dying. "C'mon, Jack!" Will leaped forward, through the closing doorway and into the unknown, the little dog beside him.

Chapter 29

Season of the Witch

Adi stood helpless in the narrow laneway of the monastery, still fighting the panic that had seized her when shots first rang out. William, Case, Fader, and Rani were nowhere to be seen. She'd searched this street and its alcoves, but found no trace of them. A grim Stone and Diego Zapana were scouring the monastery with the rest of Diego's men, but so far without success.

She watched, a sick feeling in her gut, as paramedics wheeled Wu Peng and Li Mei away, their gurneys jolting over the cobblestones. Diego's two soldiers from the tour were both dead, rifles still slung. Peng and Mei were alive, but...

She looked to where their blood stained the ground. Too much blood.

Nine gunmen lay dead. When she, Stone, and Diego and his men had reached here in their frantic search, they encountered six armed men. Three raised their guns and were cut down by Diego's soldiers. The rest surrendered. They lay on the ground, hands cuffed behind them, a soldier standing over them. She assumed the other gunmen had fallen to Peng and Mei.

She slumped against a red wall, trembling. What had she done? Why did she agree to this tour? This was all her fault.

Stop it! She pulled herself together as she pulled herself up straight. She'd have time for guilt later. First, she had to find William and the others. There must be something here, some clue.

Down the laneway, Gabriel Herrada stood unmoving, statue-like. On her first search of the area, he'd seemed completely comatose when she examined him. She walked down to stare again into his frozen face, the face of the man she thought she knew.

"Were you part of this, Gabriel?" she asked the silent figure. Herrada was the only other person left alive, if this could be called life. He must have been involved.

Involved. But not the mastermind. She knew who that was. She'd seen her.

Rushing through the monastery after the first shots rang out, she and Stone had almost reached this laneway when a sudden wind ripped through the streets, throwing them to the ground. A beat of wings and a shadow overhead had made her look up.

Above the monastery, rising ever higher, an impossible creature had flown. A monstrous bat, fanged mouth open, skin a sickly gray, wing span greater than the largest condor. And beneath the bat, dangling stiff from its claws, hung a woman in a billowing green cloak. Adi only glimpsed the face framed by flowing red hair, but she recognized the woman who had invaded Will's tower.

Somehow, against all logic, Morrigan the witch was here.

Now, Adi considered Herrada again. He had one arm raised, pointing toward where Peng and Mei had lain. A small alcove lay across from that spot and between the two groups of dead gunmen.

If Will and the rest had walked into an ambush, that small space would offer the only cover. She'd already searched it, but she'd been hunting for survivors. She swallowed. Or more bodies.

She entered the alcove, this time looking for something she'd missed. She saw it lying on the ground just as Stone called her on the walkie-talkie. "Archie," he said, his voice tight, "I'm sorry, we haven't found them. We'll start another pass. Maybe—"

"Don't bother," she replied. She knelt beside the object, one fear leaving her heart, another replacing it. "You won't find them."

A pause. "How do you know? Are they...?" He let the words trail off.

"They're alive," she said, picking up the thing she'd missed the first time, its gray blending with the stones on which it lay. "At least, I hope they are. But they're not in the monastery. I doubt they're even in the city. Get back here fast. And tell Diego we're still taking that trip in his chopper."

She ended the call and stood, holding the empty Faraday pouch that once contained the Chakana. "William," she whispered, "you have done something either very smart...or very stupid."

Act 3
Now for Plan A

Chapter 30

Sacrilege

Will had passed through a portal before, but that had been eight years ago and while unconscious. With no memory of that journey, he was unprepared for this one. Unprepared for the blinding light and the sickening sensation of hurtling forward faster and faster, all while turning and tumbling until he couldn't tell up from down and didn't care. He just wanted it to stop before he threw up.

After what might have been an eyeblink or a lifetime, the brilliance dimmed. He slowed as if a giant hand pressed against his chest. The step he'd begun on leaping into the portal resumed, and he stumbled, landing hard on a rocky surface. He lay there, his head spinning.

"Will!" Case cried.

Case, Rani, and Fader knelt ten steps from him, their hands behind them. Bound, he guessed. They looked scared but unhurt. Three swordswomen loomed over them, blades held ready. At least forty more of the Sisterhood encircled them. All wore the now familiar green snakeskin leggings, tawny furred jackets, and black condor-head masks.

Pushing himself to his knees, he scanned the circle of Sisters. The eyes that stared back through mask slits showed surprise and fear—and hate. He tried to remember why coming here had seemed like a good idea.

Something slammed into him from behind, pitching him forward onto the ground. A weight landed on his back, and his breath whooshed out of him. As he forced air into his lungs, strong hands pinned his arms behind him, binding his wrists together with something rough. Fingers clawed at his right hand.

"*Danos la llave!*" a woman's voice screamed in his ear. A sword blade, cold and sharp, pressed against his neck.

"Will!" Case cried. "Give them the Chakana, or they'll kill you!"

"And us!" Rani called.

Through the daze of pain, he realized he still clutched the artifact. He had held it tight since taking it from the Faraday pouch. Held it when he'd dashed for the portal, and when he'd battled the strange entity in his mind. He'd still held it when he'd thrown that creature from his head and leaped through the portal.

"Danos la llave!" the woman screamed again. The sword edge pressed harder against his neck.

"Okay! Take it!" he cried. And he opened his hand.

Or tried to. But the sharp edges of the Chakana still bit into his palm. His fingers refused to release the artifact.

No, that wasn't it. A fear seized him as he understood, a fear greater than even that of the blade at his throat.

The Chakana refused to let him release it.

The sword cut into the flesh on his neck. Using that pain, he focused all his will on opening his fingers, on just letting go. His hand fell limp. Fingers wrenched the Chakana from his grip. The weight on his back disappeared, and more hands dragged him over to the others and dropped him. With an effort, he pushed himself to sitting.

"Are you okay?" Case asked, worry etching her face.

He nodded. "You?"

She nodded back. So did Fader.

"Just peachy," Rani said. "Thanks for asking. Brilliant plan, by the way."

"At least we didn't get shot," Case said.

"No. Now we'll be sliced up with swords," Rani said. "Major improvement. Very retro."

"Rani..." Case said.

"What?"

"Shut up."

Will stared at the three of them. Something was missing. "Where are your critters?"

"They disappeared when we came through," Case said. "Too bad. I think the Sisters would treat us differently if the Guardians had stayed."

"*Guardians*. Yeah, right," Rani muttered, but fell quiet under Case's glare.

Will realized another astral animal was missing. "I lost Jack, too."

"Jack came back?" Fader said, a smile brightening his face.

"Yeah. The little guy saved me from a body swapper. At least, I think he did."

"Body swapper?" Case said, wide-eyed. "Like Marell?"

"Yeah, but it wasn't him."

"Are you sure? Morrigan's back. Maybe he is, too."

"Why did I come on this trip?" Rani muttered.

"No, she wasn't Marell."

"She?" Case said.

"Yeah, she definitely thought of herself as a 'she.' Seemed surprised I didn't recognize her."

"What? Why?"

"Don't know. Maybe because she'd been using Herrada's body before she tried for mine."

The two Sisters who'd dragged him over now huddled with the three who had guarded Case, Fader, and Rani. One Sister, the only one wearing no mask, cradled the Chakana in her palm. All five stared at it, talking in hushed but excited tones. Will couldn't be sure if it was a trick of light or a remnant from his trip through the portal, but the crystal artifact seemed to glow.

The one with no mask held the Chakana high, displaying it to the crowd. "*La llave ha regresado!*" she cried.

"*The Key has returned,*" Rani translated in a hoarse whisper.

Will swallowed, chilled by a thought. *The Key has returned*...as if it had been the Chakana's idea, not his.

Around the circle, the Sisters began a low chant. The only word Will recognized was *Chakana*. As the chanting continued, he took in their broader surroundings.

When he'd arrived, he thought he'd emerged into a tree-lined clearing, a cloudy sky overhead. Now, he saw the trees stood inside a huge vaulted cavern, the size of a concert hall, a wide high-arched opening in one wall. What he'd mistaken for sky was a milky white dome, glowing with its own pearly light. Did that light keep these trees alive?

The chanting ended as the unmasked Sister lowered the Chakana. Turning her back on Will and the other captives, she walked toward the edge of the circle. There, the Sisters moved aside, revealing a raised dais of the same glowing stone as the overhead dome. The dais had four arms, mirroring the Chakana itself. In the center of the dais, a flat-topped pillar rose waist-high. At the end of the nearest arm, three steps led up onto the dais.

When the maskless Sister reached the steps, she bowed her head and raised the Chakana high with both hands. As she mounted the dais, her gait became slow and measured, a slight pause between each step. Throughout the cavern, the chanting rose again. Reaching the top, the Sister knelt and placed the Chakana atop the pillar. A moan ran through the watching crowd.

The Sister, head still bowed, backed down the steps, then knelt again at the bottom, prostrating herself before the platform. Around the cavern, the Sisters did the same, still chanting. The glow from the Chakana brightened.

The chanting died as the Sister at the dais rose and faced the crowd. She barked something to the four swordswomen guarding the captives. The four hauled Will and the others to their feet and marched them toward the trees, away from the dais.

And away from the Chakana.

Will's heart fell. He'd expected a Madre to be on this side of the portal, ideally Luciana. Someone with whom he could talk, explain their situation. Explain *his* situation. Where were the Sisters taking them? What would they do to them?

And what if they took him too far from the Chakana? Desperate, he called back over his shoulder. "*Dónde está Madre Luciana?* Where is Luciana?"

Gasps ran through the cavern. The four Sisters leading the prisoners stopped, turning open-mouthed faces to the unmasked Sister. The woman's eyes swept over the crowd. Silence fell. She marched toward Will.

Good. She was in charge, and he had her attention. Although this woman didn't carry the condor-puma-snake staff that Luciana had, she wore no mask and so might be a Madre herself. Regardless, she could bring them to Luciana. He could finally solve the mystery of the lost expedition.

The maybe-Madre stopped in front of him, shoving her face inches from his. She was much shorter, so the effect was less intimidating than she'd probably hoped for. Her breath smelled of papaya. "What do you know of Madre Luciana?" She flung the words at him, each one a dagger. But at least they were in English.

"Luciana—"

"*Madre* Luciana!"

"Madre Luciana brought me, my parents, and another woman through a portal eight years ago. We returned the Chakana to you, and—"

The unmasked Sister's eyes flew wide. "*You* were that boy?"

Hope swelled in him. "Yes! I came with my parents—"

She backhanded him hard on the side of his face. Taken by surprise, his hands tied behind him, he stumbled sideways, almost falling. Two of the guards grabbed him and held him upright. Case lunged at the woman, but another guard pulled her back.

The unmasked Sister shoved her face into his again. "Our beloved Madre Luciana is *dead.*"

"What? No, she... No."

"Yes, dead. Because of your parents. And *you.*" She stabbed a finger into his chest on the last word. She spoke again to the guards, and they began again to lead their captives away. This time, the unmasked Sister fell in beside them.

Luciana dead? If that was true, then his hopes were dead, too. His head still ringing, he let the guards pull and shove him toward a dark gap in the surrounding trees.

"Where are you taking us?"

The maskless Sister's eyes burned into him. "To await the coming of Madre Suyana...and her judgment."

Well, at least he'd meet a Madre. If this Suyana had been a Madre with Luciana eight years ago, she would know what happened to him. And to his parents. He couldn't believe they had caused Luciana's death.

But if Luciana *was* dead, were his parents and Ellie Cootes as well? Had they met the same unknown fate? Or had this bloodthirsty Sisterhood killed them after Luciana's death? He caught Case's eye. From the look on her face, she battled the same fears.

As his distance from the Chakana grew, he felt a tug in his chest. The silver cord connecting him and the artifact was stretching, tightening. How soon before it stretched too far, before he collapsed as he had in Adi's office when Stone had taken the Chakana from the tower?

As they approached the gap in the trees, the opening resolved into the mouth of a small tunnel. From it, a light breeze reached them. And on that breeze rode a memory.

The sickly sweet scent of a flower. *His* Flower.

With that scent, another memory of this cavern rose in Will, dark and blurred, more shadows than light. As the scene grew sharper in his mind, a chill took him. This memory was not his own.

He collapsed to the ground, his captors shouting as he fell. But their voices faded, buried under the sights and sounds of the vision exploding in his head.

At first, Will thought he was seeing the same scene. Before him lay the tree-lined cavern with its overhead dome shining down on forty or more swordswomen wearing the familiar garb of the Sisterhood, but no masks.

But he saw no sign of Case or Fader or Rani. And his perspective had changed—he now viewed this scene as if from the raised dais, the dais that held...

Understanding dawned. This memory came from the Chakana. He was seeing what the Chakana had once seen.

In the remembered scene, the Sisters busied themselves throughout the cavern—sweeping floors, carrying bundles of clothes, cooking over a low fire pit. None wore masks. Most were young, though he spotted two older women, slightly stooped with long white hair. The Sisters talked and laughed and sang while they worked. After his violent encounters with the Sisterhood, seeing them happy and immersed in mundane chores was so unexpected, he smiled even while wondering why the Chakana was showing him this.

His smile died as the answer came. Shots and screams erupted from the high-arched opening on the far wall of the cavern as flashes of gunfire lit the tunnel behind it. A second later, men armed with semi-automatic rifles burst into the cavern.

The Sisters wore no swords. They were unarmed. The gunmen didn't care.

At least twenty Sisters died in the first few seconds, their bodies spasming as bullets cut through them. The rest scattered, dashing for the dark trees lining the cavern. Will thought they were fleeing, seeking cover, seeking safety. He was wrong.

Seconds later, the Sisters burst from the trees, masked with sword blades raised, screaming with one voice, a ululating battle cry.

He sobbed, unable to prevent what played out before his eyes. The Sisters rushed the gunmen invading their home. They were fearless. They were fierce.

They were doomed.

The men kept firing, showing no mercy, their bullets finding their mark time after time. Some Sisters made it through, shielded by others in front, sweeping down on the gunmen, their swords cleaving their attackers' necks even as more shots ended their lives.

The gunfire ceased, replaced by the yells and whoops from the men. A male voice cut through it all. "*Silencio!*"

The gunmen fell silent, turning to the tunnel mouth where a tall man now stood, hands on hips. He was thin and hawk-nosed, with a pot belly. Black hair swept back from a widow's peak. Hatless, he wore jungle camouflage like the rest of his men, but carried no rifle. A pistol hung on his belt. He surveyed the carnage, then gave an approving nod, as chilling a motion as Will had ever seen.

Will knew this man: Chico Alvarez. No, *he* didn't know that. The Chakana did. For the Chakana remembered the man who had done this.

A female figure appeared beside Alvarez. Shock replaced horror in Will, for the woman wore the snakeskin leggings and furred jacket of the Sisterhood, a black condor mask in her hand. Her eyes swept the cavern with no expression, as if she viewed an empty space, not one littered with the bodies of her Sisters. Raising a paw-covered hand, she pointed across the cavern—directly at Will. "There."

A tremor of fear ran through him before he remembered he was seeing this from the perspective of the Chakana. The woman was pointing to where the artifact sat atop the dais.

This was how Chico Alvarez had come to possess it. This was the true price of his parents acquiring the Chakana. Not the money they'd given Alvarez, but the lives of the Sisters of the Key.

"Then only one task remains," Alvarez said. Though he and the woman spoke in Spanish, Will understood their words. A trick of the Chakana? Pulling out his pistol, Alvarez pointed it at the woman. "I must deal with you, my helpful one."

To Will's surprise, the woman nodded and donned the condor mask. "Nothing lethal."

"Of course not, partner," Alvarez replied. "We still have much to do." Taking aim, he shot her in the shoulder. As the gunshot and the woman's scream echoed through the cavern, Alvarez eased her to the ground, where she lay moaning. He motioned to his men. "Cover her with some bodies. She is the sole survivor we overlooked. And make sure the rest are dead."

As the men moved to obey, Alvarez walked to the dais, growing larger with each step, a gray box under one arm. The scene faded, its last image a grinning Chico Alvarez atop the dais, eclipsing the cavern and the corpses behind, his hand reaching for the Chakana.

❧

Will blinked, trying to focus from where he lay on the ground. He knew he was seeing the real cavern again and not the vision, because Case, Fader, and Rani were there. But he couldn't explain their looks of wide-eyed horror. Nor could he understand the cries of anger from the Sisters or the fury on the faces of the guards who still surrounded them.

The maskless Sister shouted something to the guards, pointing to Will. Two guards hauled him to his feet even as a surging, shouting mob of Sisters pressed in on the four travelers. The maskless Sister stepped forward, her sword now drawn, clearing a path. Behind her, the guards shoved their prisoners before them—Case and Rani at the front, then Will and Fader—through a sea of clutching, clawing hands.

By the time the procession reached the tunnel mouth and left the mob behind, Will's arms were bloody with scratches. "What happened?" he called in confusion.

"*What happened?*" Rani snapped, glaring back at him. "Because of you, they want to kill us."

"What? I didn't do anything. I had this...vision. Of Alvarez stealing the Chakana and murdering all the Sisters of the Key. It was horrible. I think the Chakana showed me."

"Showed *you?*" Rani cried. "It showed *everybody!*"

"What?" Will said. A guard pushed him. He stumbled, almost falling.

"Will," Case called back, "that vision...we all saw it. That entire scene was...I don't know...projected into the cavern. Or into our heads."

"You saw it?" he said, struggling to understand. Had the Chakana done that? Or had he?

"Everyone saw it," Case said. "The Sisters, too, and—"

"And now," Rani interrupted, "they think we—including *me*, for shit's sake—were responsible for what happened in your little picture show. For the deaths of those poor women."

A stone staircase appeared in the tunnel wall to their left, leading up. The unmasked Sister began to climb, the guards prodding their prisoners to follow. The stairs ended, emerging onto a broad ledge circling the cavern two stories high, wide enough for three people to walk abreast. Below in the cavern, the crowd of Sisters watched them with hate-filled eyes, many of them shaking their fists and shouting.

He turned away, a sick feeling in his stomach. "Having them think we stole the Chakana is bad enough—"

"What do you mean *we?*" Rani said.

"Rani, shut up," Case said.

The maskless Sister stopped before an arched opening in the cavern wall, blocked by a gate of cross-hatched metal bars set into the stone. Producing a long-necked key from her furred jacket, she inserted it into the lock, then swung the gate open.

A cell. Well, at least the Sisters weren't planning to kill them right away.

One by one, the four prisoners had their bonds cut and were shoved into the cell. The maskless Sister slammed the gate shut and removed the key. She stared death at Will. "When Madre Suyana passes her judgment, I pray she grants me the honor of killing you." With that, she walked back along the ledge, the guards following.

"No, no, no," Rani said, hugging herself. "This is *not* happening."

The cell was dark, lit only as far as the cavern's glow could reach past the barred entrance. Shadows hid its depths. From those shadows came the sound of a sharply indrawn breath. Then fabric rustling and feet brushing stone. They weren't alone.

"Sister Case," said a female voice from the darkness. "How can you be here?"

A figure moved forward into the light. A Sister. But a familiar one.

"Isobel!" Case cried.

Chapter 31

We Gotta Get Out of This Place

As Isobel and Case exchanged hugs and cries of joy over their reunion, Will rubbed his temples, trying to ease his pounding headache. Was that an aftermath of the horrible vision he'd had? Something about that vision hovered at the edge of his memory. Something just before it had appeared... But when he reached for it, all he could recall was the slaughter of the Sisters by Alvarez.

The cell held nothing beyond a bucket and a lumpy mattress of rough cloth on the bare floor against a wall. Their greetings done, Case settled onto the mattress, while Isobel sat cross-legged across from her. Will and Fader joined Case, while Rani leaned against the barred cell door, arms folded, silent and sulking.

"Why are you here?" Isobel asked. "*How* can you be here?"

"The answer to *why* is a long story," Will said, not sure where to begin.

"Short story, actually," Rani said. "We're idiots." Case glared at her, and she fell silent.

"Let's start with the *how*," Will said. He told of exposing the Chakana in Arequipa to summon a Sister so they could escape gunmen trying to steal the artifact. He left out the appearance of their animal guardians and his battle with the unknown body swapper. Both would lead to questions he couldn't answer.

Only one thing mattered to Isobel. "You have returned the Chakana. You have done the right thing," she said, smiling, her eyes wet. Then she frowned. "But why are you prisoners?"

Will let Case tell of his vision of Alvarez's attack, of how that scene had been visible to the Sisters in the cavern.

Isobel turned to Will, her face hard and accusing. He dropped his eyes. "Isobel, eight years ago, my parents bought the Chakana from Chico Alvarez. But..." He swallowed. "But they didn't know what he'd done to get it. They weren't part of that." He met her gaze. "I'm sorry."

"Then explain your vision of the death of my Sisters. If you played no part, how can you know such things?"

"I wasn't part of it—but the Chakana was." He explained how, after his parents had brought the Chakana home eight years ago, it had placed a piece of itself inside him. He didn't mention Nyx yet. Nyx as his subconscious was hard enough to explain. Explaining she was the Chakana? Yeah, no. "And now," he finished, "the Chakana keeps showing me its...memories."

"Uh, hello," Rani said, waving a hand. "Not just you."

"The Chakana *chose* you," Isobel whispered, awe in her voice. "Never have I heard of such a thing."

"Luciana said the same when she met me," Will said.

Isobel stared wide-eyed at Will. "How did you come to meet Madre Luciana?"

"Your turn first. Why are *you* a prisoner?"

Isobel sighed. "Even after all we have been through, Will Dreycott, still we trade answers? Very well." She gazed out through the bars of their cell, her eyes distant as she focused on memories, Will guessed, and not the cold cave. "When I returned through the portal from the Black Island fifteen days ago—"

"Wait," Case said. "That was only fifteen days ago? Seriously?"

Isobel pointed to a row of vertical lines scratched into the wall. "I have marked each day."

"Classic," Fader said.

Rani checked her phone. "Yep. I was meeting with Adi that day. Instead, I chased after you lot. Worst decision ever." She put her phone away. "And no, I can't get a signal."

"When I returned," Isobel continued, "bringing my blinded Sisters home, I was greeted as a hero."

Will looked around the cell. "Guessing that didn't last."

Isobel snorted. "I told Madre Suyana of meeting you. Of storming the Black Pyramid and defeating the Chambelán. Of our escape. Of our parting..." She sighed. "...and my decision."

"Letting me keep the Chakana," Will said.

Isobel nodded. "I told them you were good people—brave and true to your friends. That you fought our enemies and saved my life. That, without you, our Sisters would still be prisoners." She shook her head. "It meant nothing. To Madre Suyana, I had forsaken my sacred quest by abandoning the Chakana."

"What did the other Madres say?" Will asked.

"Suyana is our only Madre."

"What? Aren't there always four?"

"There should be. Two here, guiding the Sisters of the Key in protecting the Chakana, and two with the Sisters of the Crossing."

"Oh god," Case said. "When Alvarez attacked—"

"He murdered the two Madres of the Key along with all the Sisters here," Isobel said, sadness in her eyes. "Now we have only Madre Suyana, who resides at the Crossing."

"But what about Luciana?" Will asked. "She didn't die that day, because I met her *after* Alvarez stole the Chakana."

"First, you must tell me how you came to know Madre Luciana."

Will sighed. "All right. Eight years ago, after the Chakana 'chose' me..." He told of falling unconscious, of his parents summoning Luciana and her sensing the piece of the Chakana inside him. "She brought me and my parents and..."

He hesitated. Mentioning Ellie Cootes would only complicate this further. And he wasn't sure it was his place to tell Case and Fader's story. "...and another woman through the portal. To here, I guess. My parents returned the Chakana to the Sisterhood, and Luciana promised to heal me." He spread his hands wide. "And that's all I know. I have no memory of what happened after that. To me. To my parents. To anyone."

"Isobel," Case asked, "can you tell us what happened? To Luciana? To Will and his parents?"

Fader squeezed his sister's hand. Will knew the same unspoken question was in both their heads. *Can you tell us what happened to our mother?*

Isobel shook her head. "It was before I joined the Sisterhood. I do not..."

Isobel's voice faded from Will's ears. Which was weird, since he could still see her lips moving. Beside him, Case was leaning forward, her expression pleading, speaking words he could no longer hear.

Searing pain stabbed into his temples, and he cried out. Isobel's eyes flew wide, staring at him. Sound returned—Case and Fader shouting his name. In front of him, a body slumped forward onto the stone floor from where it had sat on the mattress.

His body.

Case knelt beside that body, shaking him, calling his name. Above them, he raised glowing, translucent arms before his face, understanding. His silver cord snaked from his astral body where it floated in the cell down to his body on the floor—his AC, his Alive Cord, now even paler than it had been on the plane with Nyx.

But he had another cord. His DC, his Death Cord. He focused, and it appeared. Thicker and glowing brighter than when Nyx had first showed it to him on the plane, it stretched from his floating form through the barred gate. From that cord, he felt a tug, a tightening, and with it, an urge to follow.

And he understood.

Just as when Stone had taken the Chakana from the Dream Rider Tower, the distance between Will and the artifact had become too great. But *he* wasn't moving. That meant—

"The Sisters!" he cried. "They're moving the Chakana."

No one turned at the sound of his voice. No one heard him. No one understood what was happening. Every second, the Chakana was moving farther and farther away from him. At some point, when that distance became too great, the Chakana would rip its missing piece from his head.

And he would die.

"Nyx!" he called. She'd know what to do. Nyx always knew what to do.

But for the first time since his strange dreams began after the doomed expedition, since he became the Dream Rider, since Nyx first appeared to him in Dream, she failed to answer his call.

Below him, Case cradled his unconscious head in her lap. She couldn't see or hear him. He was about to die, in her arms but still alone.

Unless...

Yeshe had done it. Made his astral form visible to others. But Yeshe had developed his astral skills over decades. He had only minutes.

Wait. He *had* made himself visible once. So had Case. Visible to Fader when he'd been stuck in the In Between after their escape from the strange crystal island in Dream. But they'd only managed that with the help of the freed spirit of the Cree shaman, Walter Keejek, and...

In his astral form, Will smiled. And Jack the spirit dog.

Jack had followed him through the portal as they escaped the monastery. Was he still here? The little dog had a habit of disappearing somewhere, but he'd always returned when Will needed him.

"Jack!" he called. "Are you here? I need—"

A bark below him cut him off. Jack stood beside his unconscious body, translucent and glowing, unseen by the other travelers, wagging his tail furiously.

Will opened his arms, a spark of hope lighting inside him. "C'mon, dude. Let's do this thing."

Jack leaped into his astral arms. As he cuddled the pup to his chest, a warmth grew in him, and his astral body glowed brighter, stronger.

But still not strong enough.

"Will!" Case cried again, cradling his head in her lap while shaking his shoulder, lightly at first, then harder when he didn't respond. "Will, wake up!"

"What's wrong with him?" Fader asked, his voice tight with worry as he stared down at Will.

"Did the Sister hit him that hard?" Rani said from behind Fader, genuine concern on her face.

"I don't know," Case said, trying to think. "It's like... Oh, shit, it's like when he collapsed in Adi's office. When Stone moved the Chakana from Will's tower."

"But the Chakana's here," Rani said. "Right below us in the cavern, on that pedestal thing."

Isobel knelt beside Case. "Madre Suyana always swore that when we retrieved the Chakana, she would return it to the Crossing, where she could watch over it. After what happened eight years ago, she said it would never be safe here in the Temple of the Key again."

"But if Suyana's at the Crossing," Case asked, "how'd she know the Chakana showed up here?"

"She is a Madre," Isobel said. "She would sense its arrival and dispatch a Sister to bring it to her. Or Yanta—the Sister without the mask who brought you here—might be taking the Chakana to Suyana. Yanta is a *Siguiente* and has the power to order that."

"What's a Siguiente?" Rani asked.

"Not now," Case snapped, her fear for Will growing. "If they're moving the Chakana, then every second we're stuck here, that thing's getting farther away from Will."

Fader's eyes widened. "But Nyx said if the Chakana gets too far from him…"

"It'll rip the piece of itself from him," Case said, stroking Will's forehead, "and he'll die."

"Holy shit," Rani whispered.

"Who is Nyx?" Isobel asked.

"Later," Case said, her mind racing. "We have to get out of here. Follow the Chakana to the Crossing. Keep the distance between Will and that thing from getting any bigger."

"Uh, we're locked in a cell," Rani said.

"I'm feeling better," Fader said. "I think I can get us out of here."

"How?" Case said.

"Like I did on the Black Island. With the In Between. Line of sight, remember? If I bring us into the In Between, I can zoom the view on the wall through the bars to outside the cell. Then I can take us anywhere."

"What if that wall view isn't there?" Case asked. "You said it was gone when you went into the In Between after we got home."

"But this place *feels* like the Black Island. Like the In Between is *really* close." Fader shrugged. "So, I'll check." He closed his eyes.

And disappeared.

Rani swore. Isobel muttered something but, like Case, kept watching the spot where Fader had been.

To Fader, entering the In Between was like fading, only harder. And scarier.

Standing in the cell, he closed his eyes and focused on being invisible until his *fading* feeling began in his chest. Like he wasn't *here* as much anymore. Like something was pushing him away. Pulling him, too.

Once that push-pull feeling began, he made it grow. He didn't know *how* he did that. He just did. And as it grew, he faded from sight. To reach the In Between, he just had to fade farther.

And not miss.

After the Black Island, he'd learned his fading needed a *direction* as well as distance. Short and straight fading let him stay in this world, this universe. Far and straight took him to the In Between.

But if he faded *sideways*, even a short fade took him to another universe. And a *long* fade sideways? The Chakana had done that to him when it first became exposed in Will's tower—and he almost hadn't made it back. He swallowed, remembering that day, being hunted by a not-Will and not-Stone.

So, he had to stay straight...and he'd learned the best way to do that.

Keeping his view of the stone cell in front of him, he imagined backing away from it in his mind. Case and the others faded into the distance, growing smaller and smaller until the scene became...

A door.

He blinked. In front of him, a windowed door now framed the stone cell where Case and the others waited. No, not *a* door. *His* door. The door to *his* universe. And one, he realized, he had to keep track of.

For he now stood in the twisting hallway of doors that was the In Between. The doors filled this side of the corridor, one beside the other, a hand's width apart, stretching in an unending line into the distance in both directions. Those doors led to other universes, other worlds that weren't his world. To return to *his* world, he had to remember which was *his* door.

Or did he?

A soft, silvery light outlined the frame of his door, pulsating slowly. He checked as far as he could see down the hallway in both directions. But no other doorway glowed like his.

He'd seen this before—in the phantom subway station on the Black Island when they'd been running from the giant bugs. Each door on the train had shown a different universe, but he'd known which door led home because—to him—it had glowed.

He frowned. Since then, he'd entered the In Between several times, just to practice his power. He'd always found the hallway of doors, but his door had never glowed.

This Temple of the Key felt very close to the In Between, just as the Black Island had. Was that why he could see the glow again?

He shrugged. It didn't matter. Nyx had said their superpowers would have to grow on this trip, and his just had. He grinned. Superpowers.

Thinking of Nyx reminded him Will was in danger. Something else had been missing from the In Between whenever he returned to it since the Black Island. And to save Will, he needed that thing to be here again.

He turned to look at the other wall. And grinned.

Chapter 32

Nothing But Flowers

Case waited for her brother to reappear. Ten seconds passed. Thirty. Still no Fader. Was he lost in the In Between, not knowing which door was his? Or worse, had he slipped into another 'verse instead of the In Between and couldn't get back?

"Ta da!" Fader's voice, but from behind them. She turned to find him grinning at them through the bars, *outside* their cell. He disappeared again. A moment later, he stood inside the cell.

She let out a sigh of relief. "I'm guessing it worked."

"Yeah. The big wall view of this place is there, just like on the Black Island. And so are all the doors on the other wall—all normal looking, too, not dark like they were on the Island."

"Okay," Case said, not sure how they might use those doors, but filing it away, anyway. "So, let's get out of here."

"Uh, your boyfriend can't walk," Rani said.

"If you guys pick him up," Fader said, "I'll pull you into the In Between, then zoom us all out of here."

Isobel shook her head. "Sister Case, even if we escape this cell, I do not know how to reach the Crossing. It is our most guarded secret. Only Suyana and Yanta hold that knowledge."

"I think I can help with that," came a familiar voice.

Rani yelped, and Isobel gasped, both staring above Case. She looked up to where Will's astral form floated, smiling down at them. His very *visible* astral form.

"Superpowers!" Fader said.

"Will you people *please* stop popping in and out?" Rani said.

Case stifled a sob at seeing Will. "How did you...? How can you be visible?"

"Jack helped." Will's voice sounded in her head, not her ears, and yet still seemed to come from his floating form.

Fader looked around. "Jack's back?"

"Was. He's gone again."

"Will," Case said, remembering the danger he faced, "Isobel says they're moving the Chakana to the Crossing."

Will nodded. "I heard you talking. But I think I know how to find the

Crossing. Something happened just before that vision of Alvarez came to me." He explained about smelling the Flower when they entered the tunnel. "It must be down that passage, past the steps leading up here. If we find it, I bet we'll find the Crossing. Or the way there."

Case wasn't sure of that. But each minute brought Will closer to death, and this seemed his only chance. "So, we follow your Flower? Can you still smell when you're Astral Guy?"

"My cord still connects me to my physical body, so I can access my senses." He hesitated. "But my body may have to be out of the In Between to smell the Flower."

"You mean we'll have to keep carrying you out of the In Between for a sniff test?"

"When we reach the tunnel to make sure I still smell the Flower. Then every so often to check we're still on track. Or if we come to a branch."

"My back is sore already," Rani muttered.

"Did you smell more than one flower?" Case asked.

"No, just mine."

"Then anyone can do the sniff test. I'll step out when—"

"It won't work," Fader interrupted, his earlier excitement gone from his face.

"What won't?" Case asked.

"We can't bring Will into the In Between when he's astral projecting. Re-member what happened when I tried that in the Chambelán's tower?"

Will groaned. "We got zapped. You're right. The In Between doesn't seem to like a body inside it without its astral spirit."

"But Fader could get the rest of us out, right?" Rani said. Case shot her a withering look. "What?" Rani said. "We *all* don't have to die."

"Nobody's dying," Will said. "I think I can get back into my body. I still may not be able to wake up once I'm back in, but you can bring my body into the In Between. And we can all get out of here."

"You *think* you can get back in?" Case said.

"One way to find out." Flying down, Will lowered his glowing astral form into his unconscious body...and disappeared.

When he didn't reappear, Case guessed he must have been successful. "Okay, bro. Superhero time. Take us into the In Between."

Inside the In Between, Case watched Fader move the wall view to focus on the bars of their cell. Will once again floated in astral form, his body lying unmoving on the corridor floor.

Rani had her phone pointed at the wall, filming Fader's progress. She shrugged when Case raised an eyebrow. "Hey, I'm a reporter."

Isobel watched the wall, too, but glanced every few seconds at the doors behind them, as if expecting someone—or something—to step through one.

Fader zoomed the view through the bars and out of the cell, then headed along the ledge toward the steps leading down.

The cavern lay below to their right, filled with Sisters standing in small clusters. Case searched without success for the maskless Sister, the one Isobel called Yanta. Plus, the pedestal on the raised dais was now empty. The absence of both Yanta and the Chakana, along with Will's collapse, confirmed what they'd feared—the Sisters were taking the artifact to the Crossing.

Fader reached the stone staircase leading to the tunnel below. "Go down," Case said, "then stop at the bottom so we can sniff for—" Movement in the cavern below caught her eye. "Wait!"

Through the high-arched cavern entrance flew an enormous gray bat, larger than any bird she'd ever seen. Between ragged and misshapen ears, red eyes blazed above a fanged mouth.

The Sisters below screamed with one voice, fear and horror in their cries, as the bat swept over their heads. Stunned by the sight, Case's shock only grew as she recognized the stiff form hanging from the bat's claws.

A tall woman with long red hair in a billowing green cloak.

"Morrigan," she whispered, struggling to understand.

"How can she be here?" Will asked. "What is that thing?"

"How did it find this place?" Isobel asked.

The bat circled the cavern, dropping lower and lower with each circuit. The Sisters scattered back, opening a wide space in the center of the floor. There, the creature gently set Morrigan down, where she stood erect and strangely still. Its burden released, the bat beat its great wings to hover above the witch and the watching Sisters.

Words sounded in Case's head. Words in a language strange to her, yet ones she somehow understood. *Mistress of the Unicorn, thank you for my release. I have fulfilled my purpose and now go to my rest. Blessed be the White Coven of Ellan Vannin.*

Mistress of the Unicorn? Case thought.

With that, the bat burst into flames, sending the Sisters scurrying back further. A heartbeat later, the flames died and the bat was gone, leaving only a cloud of ashes drifting down like dirty snow. The witch had still not stirred, standing unmoving, staring with eyes devoid of expression.

"She looks...dead," Fader said, concern on his face.

"Fader," Will said, "zoom us down there."

"Are you sure?" Case said, her memories—and fear—of Morrigan still strong.

"We're safe in here," Will said. "I think I know what's happened to her, but I need a closer look."

As Fader zoomed the scene on the wall to the cavern floor, Case asked, "Did anyone else hear those words? In your head?"

"From that bat thing?" Will said. "In a language I don't know but understood. Yeah. I think it was Manx."

"But I don't know Manx," Case said.

Rani was still filming the scene. "Seriously? We're in a corridor to the multiverse, a giant bat just delivered a witch to a secret Sisterhood, and you're worried about a language upgrade?"

The Sisters were creeping forward again, but for now Fader had a clear path to Morrigan. He stopped the view two paces from her. Case shivered, fighting her old fears of the witch. But Morrigan wore an expression far different from the cold and haughty look Case remembered and hated. As understanding dawned, some of her fear faded.

"Remind you of anything?" Will said.

"She looks like the Hollow Boys did," Fader whispered, voicing Case's own thought. "Like she's not inside her body anymore. Like she's...empty."

"She's in the Gray Lands?" Case asked, staring into Morrigan's dead eyes. "But how?"

"I'm guessing the body swapper from the monastery got to her, too," Will said. "Same one who used Herrada and tried to take me over. It might have been controlling her all along."

She remembered the place where Marell had tried to send her. Remembered, too, traveling through the Gray Lands with Will and Yeshe and the Hollow Boys. Remembered its desolation, its emptiness, the fragile barrier between it and the Nothing. And their encounter with a Mara, a monster of Dream.

Something that might have been pity for Morrigan rose in her. She pushed the feeling away.

"We have to move," Will said, staring down at his unconscious body. "My cord's getting fainter. Fader, zoom us to the tunnel."

Fader took one last look at Morrigan before he swung the view toward the tunnel where the Sisters had taken the travelers. As the opening approached, he turned pleading eyes to Will. "But she can come back from there, right?"

Case swallowed, her fear of her brother's strange affection for Morrigan returning. Will shook his head. "Only if she can find her door. The one where she entered Dream."

They reached the tunnel mouth. Once they were far enough down the passage so they couldn't be seen from the cavern, Will had Fader stop. Here, with the glow of the cavern's dome far behind them, the only light came from torches hanging on the tunnel walls every ten paces or so.

Stepping out of the In Between, Case sniffed the air. The flowery scent was unmistakable—thick, heavy, and sickly sweet. She held out her arm. Fader's hand appeared out of thin air, pulling her back into the In Between.

"I smelled it," she told them all. "Really strong."

Will nodded to Fader. "Okay, dude. Follow this tunnel."

Fader zoomed the wall view along the tunnel, which Case noticed slanted downward. She guessed the Temple of the Key was underground and wondered how far the passage might descend. After five years on the streets, her three weeks in Will's tower weren't enough to feel comfortable being cooped up—or under the earth.

To take her mind off her growing feeling of claustrophobia, she turned to Isobel. "This Yanta, the Sister without a mask who locked us up...you called her something earlier."

"A Siguiente," Isobel answered. "A Next One. The Madres select Siguientes from the Sisterhood to assist them and to execute their orders. When a Madre passes, the other Madres choose her replacement from the Siguientes."

Rani swung her phone to record Isobel. "You mean this Yanta's a future Madre?"

Case frowned. "Then why hasn't she and the other Siguientes become Madres?"

"Yeah, why not replace all the dead Mothers?" Rani said, then added, "What?" when Case glared at her.

Isobel looked at where Will floated, then away. "We have no other Siguientes. Two died with the Madres of the Key. I am told a third died the same day as Madre Luciana."

"Isobel," Will said, "I didn't know. I swear—"

Isobel held up a hand. "I believe you, Will Dreycott." She sighed. "But just as Suyana is our only Madre, Yanta is our only Siguiente."

"But why not pick new Siguientes and make them Madres?" Rani asked. "Or at least make this Yanta a Madre?"

Isobel shook her head. "New Madres and Siguientes can only be chosen within the Crossing. Without the Chakana, we cannot enter the Crossing. So, for the past eight years..." She shrugged.

"No new Madres or Siguientes," Case said. And no access by the Sisterhood to the mysterious god-like Four, if they could believe Nyx's story.

"Shit," Will said.

She guessed what he was thinking. The damage done by his parents' quest for the Chakana grew with each revelation.

"Case, Will," Fader called, pulling her attention back. Her brother had stopped his zooming. The wall showed they'd entered a small cave, about ten paces across, blazing with torches. Ahead lay three more tunnel mouths.

"Great," Rani said. "Which one do we take?"

Will floated down beside Case, staring at the wall. "Looks like a job for your Voice."

She swallowed but nodded. *Voice? Are you there?*

No reply came. No words. No visions.

"Nothing," she said.

Will sighed. "I was afraid of that. No reason for your Voice to show up. Danger's coming for me, not you."

"Will—" she began, her face burning with sudden shame of what seemed her failure.

He shook his head. "It's okay. We'll just zoom down each tunnel a bit. You step out and sniff, and we pick the branch with the strongest flower scent."

"What if I smell it in every branch? Or can't tell which is strongest?"

"This will not work," Isobel said. "At least, not in time to save you, Will Dreycott."

"Why not?" Will asked.

Isobel pointed to the view of the cave with its tunnels. "The way to the Crossing has at least a hundred such caves."

"I thought you didn't know how to reach the Crossing," Will said.

"I do not. Only Madres and Siguientes know the way. But when Sisters first join, a Madre or Siguiente leads them to the Threshold."

"What's the Threshold?" Will asked.

"Where we live and work. It guards the entrance to the Crossing. Yanta led my group. I was blindfolded on this journey, but could tell whenever we reached a cave like this—the echoes of our footsteps, the brightness of the torches through our blindfolds. I counted eighty branching points before losing track. I am told some have even more tunnels from which to choose."

Case bit her lip. "Even eighty caves with just three tunnels...say a minute for each sniff test." She did the math. "That's four hours, plus the time to zoom along the tunnels. And that's assuming we always pick the right tunnel."

Will stared down at where his body lay. "My silver cord's almost invisible already. I won't last that—" His words broke off. "*My silver cord...*" he said slowly. He spun to face Case, his eyes wide with excitement. "That's it!"

"Uh...what is?"

"I have *two* cords now. One connects to my body—"

She understood. "And the other connects to the Chakana. We can follow that cord!"

"Yes! Let me call it up. We'll just follow whatever tunnel it takes."

They all waited as Will faced the view of the tunnels, his eyes narrowed in concentration. His shoulders slumped.

"What's wrong?" she asked. "What tunnel does it take?"

"None of them."

"What?"

"It goes toward the tunnels...then dives into the floor. I should've thought of that. Nothing can stop an astral cord. It'll take the shortest route to the Chakana. All we know is that the Chakana is ahead and below us."

Which made sense. The tunnel to this point had been slanting downward. The ones still in front of them must go lower still.

"I'm not going to make it," Will said, all hope now gone from his face.

"Yes, you will," Case said, determination growing in her. She didn't know how, but she was going to do this. "I'm not letting you die."

"How?" Will said, defeat weighing down his voice.

"What you said on the plane. How our powers had to grow to face what we'll meet here. Fader is Zoomer Boy now. You can astral project *and* make yourself visible." She faced the view of the three tunnels. "My turn to level up."

Closing her eyes, she called in her mind. *Voice? Vision? I'm not waiting for you anymore. Will's dying, and we have to save...*

She stopped her thought. *We...?*

A cry escaped her. A cry of joy, of awakening. For she understood. Here, in the home of the Sisters and the Chakana, for the first time, she understood her power.

The power of *We*. But not the *We* of her and her Voice or whatever was inside her.

We.

The *We* that was every Case that stood here in every universe that existed in this moment or in futures that might come to be.

She could see them now, feel them. Her other selves, spreading out beside her, stretching into the distance on either side of her like the doors behind her here. Each of her selves in their universe, so similar to this 'verse but not quite the same. Each one coming to this point from a different past. And each one able to choose a different future, a different path...

She smiled. A different tunnel.

She only needed three of her other selves, the three closest to this 'verse. Those versions of Case understood even as she formed the thought. A vision appeared to her—no, *three* visions—as three other Cases in three other universes leaped from their own In Between...

And into a tunnel that lay before them, each choosing a different passage. Left. Middle. Right.

Left Case's route dead-ended at an underground pool after maybe a hundred paces. Right Case's tunnel looped back to the Temple of the Key. But Middle Case's passage led to a second torch-lit cave. And that second Cave of Decision, as she dubbed these branching points, presented *four* tunnels to them.

Keeping her eyes closed, holding the vision in her mind, she called out. "Fader? Can you hear me?"

"Uh, standing right beside you," came her brother's voice.

"Okay, I'm going to call out the tunnel number to take whenever we reach one of these caves. Counting from left to right—one, two, three. Got it?"

"Yep," Fader said.

"You've figured it out?" Will asked. "Your Voice came back?"

She felt herself smiling. "Something like that. Sorry it took so long."

"What? You just closed your eyes a second ago."

A second ago? In a way, it made sense. She and her other selves hadn't selected which future to follow yet, so why should any time have passed?

"Fader," she said. "Take number two here. And zoom as fast as you can. I'll have the next branch ready by the time you get there."

In her mind, Case said goodbye to her Left and Right selves, focusing on her future self who'd taken the correct middle route and now faced the four new tunnels in the second Cave of Decision ahead. As she did, she sensed three more versions of herself forming into existence...no, into *potential* existence. Now, four possible Cases faced the four possible routes at this second branching point, toward which Fader was rushing. With a mental nod, those four Cases stepped forward in her vision, each entering a different tunnel.

When Fader reached the second Cave of Decision, one of Case's future selves waited before the correct branch, smiling and pointing.

"Three," Case called to Fader. Ahead, in her mind, more of her future selves were exploring the next set of tunnels. Case tried opening her eyes and found she could watch Fader's progress and still keep the vision of her other selves in her head. She called out tunnel choices as Fader reached cave after cave.

"Two."

"One."

"Four."

And so it went. She lost track of the branching points they passed. Isobel had counted over eighty Caves of Decision. Case swore they'd already passed a hundred. Had one of her tunnel choices been wrong? Had they missed the right path?

Just as she was losing hope, Will cried out. "My cord! The one to my body. It's brighter."

"That's good, right?" she said, still focused on tunnel decisions.

"It means we're getting closer to the Chakana again," he said, as Fader raced them along another tunnel. "We're catching up."

Moments later, they burst into a terraced cavern as large as the Temple of the Key and so bright Case had to shield her eyes.

But here, the light didn't come from torches.

Hundreds of orchids filled the cavern, covering terrace after terrace, each level rising higher until the highest met the cavern walls. Each flower was open, their black petals streaked with luminous white and speckled with rusty red the color of dried blood.

Floating beside her, Will gazed at the scene with the wide-eyed wonder of a child. "My Flower," he whispered.

"Flowers," corrected Rani. "And they're beautiful."

Chapter 33

Codes and Keys

Eight years I've searched for this place, Will thought, staring at the flowers from the In Between. *Eight years. Almost half my life.*

From a darkly wet cavern dome, water fell in steady drips onto the flowers below. The flowers grew from soil on the terraces, but the center of the cavern floor was bare stone, shining with the underground rain and dotted by shallow pools.

"Is this...the Crossing?" Will asked Isobel.

She gazed out with her own wide-eyed wonder. "No. I remember this place. The smell of the flowers. That strange light through my blindfold. But it is not the Crossing." She frowned. "I know more of the journey lies ahead, but I remember nothing after reaching here. Some Sisters say the flowers affect our memories. We remember their smell...but nothing else."

Understanding dawned on him as bright as the flowers' glow. "Is that why the smell of these flowers is all I remembered from eight years ago?"

Isobel hesitated. "Perhaps. But you carry the Chakana inside you. Who knows what—" Her words broke off. "I'm sorry, Will Dreycott. I should not say that."

He swallowed. "No, it's okay. You're right. Who knows what the Chakana has done to me? Well, right now it's trying to rip itself out of my head, so let's deal with that."

"I can't see any way out," Fader said.

"There has to be," Will said.

Fader moved their view through a circuit of the Cave of Flowers, as he dubbed it. When he reached a bare stone wall rising from floor to domed ceiling and flanked by the floral terraces, Will called for him to stop.

Will stared at the wall as a memory hovered at the edges of recall. "Move closer." Fader zoomed in until Will could see fist-sized protrusions dotting the wall. He counted twenty-five of the knob-like bumps, arranged in a rough five-by-five horizontal and vertical pattern. "That's it!" he cried as he caught his elusive memory.

"What?" Case asked.

"Those visions I had whenever I smelled the Flower in my greenhouse? This rock wall was part of them. Do you have your quipu?

"What?"

"The knotted cords we found in the Peru crate. I gave us each one. Did you bring yours?"

"Sure. Carefully stowed in my backpack. Which I left in Diego's armored car outside the monastery."

Will groaned. "Mine, too."

Fader was searching the pockets of his camouflage pants. His hand reappeared, holding one of the white cords.

"Dude!" Will cried, swooping down for a closer look. "You're a lifesaver."

Fader shrugged. "You said to keep them with us."

"Showoff," Case said. "So, what's with the quipu?"

"I think it's our way out of here." Will nodded his astral head at the scene on the wall. "But I need a closer look."

With Fader's quipu in her pocket, Case stepped out of the In Between, carrying Will's unconscious body with Isobel's help. Fader and Rani stayed in the In Between—Fader to pull them back if needed, and Rani because she felt safer there.

The Cave of Flowers hit Case like a physical force. The Temple of the Key had been almost cold, and the In Between's climate control seemed permanently set at 'perfect.' But this place was sweltering, thick with moisture and the cloying scent of the flowers, the water dripping from the ceiling the only relief.

As they laid Will's body before the rock wall, trying to avoid any puddles, Case's head spun. Standing, she stumbled back, almost falling.

Will's astral form emerged from his body. He floated over to her. "You okay?"

"Dizzy."

Isobel was swaying, too. "It is as I said. The flowers will affect us."

"Then we better be quick." Will moved to the wall.

This close, Case could see a small space in the rock surrounding each of the fist-sized projections. The lowest row of knobs was about the height of her knees, while the highest row was a bit above her head, but still within reach. "They look like you can push them in. Like buttons."

"I think they *are* buttons." Will flew to the top of the rock wall, then checked where its sides met the flowered terraces. "There's space along each side. Top, left, right..." He flew down to where the rock face met the stone floor. "And bottom."

She shook her head, trying to clear the growing fog swirling in her mind. "You mean the wall can move? Like, it's a door?"

"And those buttons are the key pad. And the quipu—I think—is the code to open it. It was always in my vision of this wall. Somebody holding it in front of this rock face."

"Great. But what *is* the code?"

Will moved back, putting her between him and the wall. "Hold up the quipu." She did. His eyes moved between the knotted cords and the wall several times. "I think I've got it."

Floating back to her, he pointed a spectral finger at the cords. "The quipu has five strings. Each string has one knot, each at a different height. Five knots, at five different heights. Five rows of five buttons on the wall." He looked at her. "I think the knots show what button to push."

She nodded, then regretted the motion as the cave whirled in her vision. "Makes sense...I think. Right now, my brain is knotted up itself. So, should I push the buttons?"

"Let me check behind this thing, first." With that, he flew to the wall—and through it.

Case jumped. She'd expected to hear a gasp from Isobel, who'd been silent through this exchange. When she looked over, the Sister stared glassy-eyed at the rock face.

"Isobel?" Case called. No response. And her own brain fog was getting worse. A search of the many pockets of her expedition clothes produced a camouflage-pattern bandanna she remembered. She tied it around her nose and mouth as best she could as a breathing filter.

Will reappeared through the wall, making her jump again. He frowned at her mask.

"The flowers," she said, slurring her words. "Isobel's zonked, and I will be soon. We have to hurry. So, *is* this thing a door?"

He hesitated.

"Will, did you hear me?"

"These knobs connect to levers that connect to ropes and pulleys and counterweights. All very Indiana Jones—and way too complex to figure out. But yeah, it's a door, and those knobs open it—if we push the right ones."

"So, let's push them."

"I don't want you to push them," he said, his voice soft, gentle. "I don't want anyone to push them."

"*What?* Why?"

He pointed up to the cavern's domed roof. "That ceiling is attached to more ropes and levers and winches. It's a booby trap. We hit the wrong buttons—and the ceiling falls. And kills whoever's standing here." He looked at her. "I won't be the reason you die."

"And *I* won't be the reason *you* die."

"What if the quipu isn't the code?"

She tossed the knotted strings to the ground. "I'm not using the quipu."

"What? It's our only clue."

She shook her head, setting the cavern spinning. "I'll use my Voice. This booby trap *helps* us. If I'm in danger, my Voice will protect me, tell me what buttons to push. Now, get out of my way." She walked toward him on wobbly legs, heading for the rock face.

He didn't move. "But what if your Voice doesn't—"

She stepped through him. Or tried to. She found herself motionless. Will surrounded her, enveloped her, as if she swam in a sea of Will.

A warmth filled her—a feeling of love and of being loved. Memories of all their times together flashed by, and she smiled despite the situation. She wanted to stay there forever.

But then she was through, back in the Cave of Flowers, standing before the wall. Or rather, swaying before the wall. She took another breath of the humid air, thick with the flowery scent.

Mistake. Her vision shimmered, clouded, darkened. She heard Will calling her name. Then both Will and the cavern faded from her mind.

"Case!" Will cried from where he floated in front of her. No response. Case continued to stand, eyes open but unfocused. Steps away, Isobel stood in the same state. His body lay on the cavern floor, the silver cord connected to his astral form growing dimmer again.

He was going to die here, in a strange cave filled with the strange flower he'd chased for half his life. Die without ever discovering what had happened to him, to his parents.

He looked at Case. She stared back at him, unseeing. And he couldn't even say goodbye to her. Well, he could. She just wouldn't hear him. "Goodbye," he whispered. "I love you."

"Wow. So touching," came a voice. "And a tad nauseating. Just saying."

Behind him, Rani, wearing a bandanna over her nose and mouth like Case, was leading an unresisting Isobel toward a disembodied arm hanging in the air. Isobel disappeared as Fader pulled her back into the In Between.

"Sorry to crash your tragic goodbye, Romeo," Rani said, now guiding Case to where Fader's arm had reappeared. "But we need to get these ladies into the safe place..." She glanced up at the ceiling. "Where I wish I was."

After Case disappeared into the In Between, Rani picked up the quipu from where Case had dropped it. "You need to get back into your body, so Fader and I can carry you into the In Between." She shot another glance at the ceiling. "Then I'll be the only one crushed under tons of stone."

"Wait...what?"

Rani sighed. "I'm going to be the big hero. Or try to. Probably why Case's Voice made sure I came along. But don't get the wrong idea. I'm doing this to save *me*. If we can't escape this stone-age florist shop, our options will be either starving slowly in the In Between or letting the Sisters kill us—probably also slowly." She glanced up again. "At least, this will be quick."

"Fader could zoom you all back to the Temple of the Key, then to the nearest town. You don't have to do this, Rani."

Rani's gentle smile made her seem like a different person. "Yes, I do. Fader won't abandon you, Will. You, Case, and Isobel are out of the picture. If Fader tries and dies, then we're stuck here, for sure...plus Case would kill me when she wakes up. I'm the only option." She nodded at where his body lay. "Now get back in there so I can play hero."

"No. I'm staying here. I can help you."

She shrugged. "Your funeral. Literally." Holding up the quipu, she squinted at it.

"I think the knots—"

"Yeah, we were listening. And thanks for the 'I think' bit. Really builds my confidence." She walked toward the rock face, but stumbled. "Shit. I don't feel so hot."

"Hurry!"

Reaching the wall, she peered at the quipu, counting the knots with a finger. "Okay, then counting from the top, the button sequence goes 1—4—2—3—5? Left to right?"

"Yeah," he said, having memorized the sequence of knots.

Nodding, Rani reached for the top knob in the leftmost vertical line, the knob in the #1 position—and then stopped. She began swearing, loudly and impressively.

"What's wrong?"

"What's *wrong?*" she yelled. "Left to right, that's what's wrong."

"What are you talking about?"

Rani was swaying. "Left to right, like this?" she said, holding up the quipu and running her finger from the left string to the last one on the right.

"Yeah, that's what I just—"

"Or like *this?*" She flipped the quipu around so the other side was facing him. His stomach fell. Now the code was 5—3—2—4—1. "Oh...shit."

"You think?" She stumbled sideways, but caught herself from falling. "Will, figure it out," she said, holding the bandanna over her mouth. "I'm fading fast."

How could he know? If he guessed, he had a fifty-fifty chance of being right. Or wrong. And if he was wrong, Rani died, he died.

He tried to recall his visions of the quipu. He focused on being back in his greenhouse. Entering the isolation chamber. Bending over the Flower. Breathing in its sickly sweet scent.

Breathing in...breathing in...

The cavern and Rani disappeared, replaced by his *vision* of the rock face. And of the quipu, held by an unknown hand. In that vision, the knot on the leftmost cord was at the top.

"It's 1—4—2—3—5," he called, his eyes still closed. "The top knot is on the left."

He opened his eyes. Rani sat on the ground, her chin on her chest.

"Rani!"

Her head jerked up. "I'm awake, I'm awake!" She blinked at him. "What?"

"Get up! It's 1—4—2—3—5. I'm sure."

She tried to get up, but sat back down heavily. "At the time," she mumbled, "sitting down seemed like a good idea."

"Rani!"

She managed to stand the second time. Staggering to the wall, she reached again for the top-most button on the left, then hesitated.

"Press it! I'm sure."

She pressed it. Or tried to. "It won't move!"

"Hit it! With your fist."

She pounded on the button. Once. Twice. The third time, the knob slipped into its hole in the rock face.

A rumbling shudder shook the cavern. Dust rained down from the dome above. Rani looked up, her arms outspread. "*This* is how I die? Losing a rock lottery?"

But then silence settled on the cavern again. Rani shot the ceiling a nervous glance, then pressed the next three buttons, checking the quipu each time. With every button, the cavern rumbled, but all that fell was another shower of dust. With every button, too, Rani moved slower and struggled more to push the knobs.

She reached the final column of buttons, where she had to press the bottom knob, which sat at knee height. Leaning over, she pushed on the knob. No movement. She pushed with both hands. Still, it didn't budge. Straightening, she wobbled backward, then forward, seemed to catch herself...then sat down hard on the cavern floor.

"Rani!"

She swayed where she sat, waving a hand at him. "S'okay. All part of th' plan," she mumbled. Falling back on her elbows, she raised a foot and kicked the knob hard. Once. Twice. It still wouldn't budge.

She raised her leg again for another kick, then dropped it. Her head lolled to one side.

"Rani!" he yelled again.

Her head snapped up. She raised her leg again and kicked a third time.

With a scream of stone on stone, the rocky knob disappeared into the wall. Again, a rumble shook the cavern, and Will realized, too late, the booby trap might not trigger until Rani pushed the final button. "Get into the In Between," he yelled.

But Rani now lay on the cavern floor, eyes closed, her head pillowed on her arms, snoring. Before her, the rock face shuddered...and began to swing back, a gigantic door opening outward from the cave.

A wind rushed in, cool and fresh, sweeping through the Cave of Flowers. Rani stirred where she lay, and Will hoped the clean air was washing the flowers' hypnotic scent from her lungs.

The opening revealed a set of rough-hewn steps, wide and deep, descending from the cavern. Though he could see no torches, a soft milky glow lit the staircase, rising from some unseen source below.

Pushing herself up to sitting, Rani blinked at the open doorway.

Will floated over to her. "You did it."

Nodding, Rani looked straight up—and raised a middle finger to the cavern dome.

"Thank you, Rani," came Case's voice. Behind him, she, Isobel, and Fader stood beside where his body lay.

"You're okay?" he said, moving to her.

"The In Between cleared our heads." She sniffed. "And that wind swept the flowers' smell out of here."

"Okay," he said. "Let's get back into the In Between and find out where those steps lead." Using the In Between was their best chance to catch up to Yanta and the Chakana. They could move much faster with Fader's zooming than on foot.

"So back into your bod, Astral Boy," Case said.

Nodding, Will lowered his astral self into his sleeping form. He expected to merge with his physical body as before, unable to awaken or move, but inside himself and aware. Instead...

"Uh, we can still see you," Rani said.

He floated up from his body again. "I can't get back into my body." He looked at the silver cord connecting his astral and physical forms...and understood. "My cord...I can barely see it."

Concern creased Case's face. "But when we reached this cave, you said it had grown brighter."

"It had. Yanta and the Chakana must have gained on us while we tried to open this door." His hopes faded like his cord. "We can't use the In Between anymore."

"No," Case said, "but we can walk." Moving to Will's body, she grabbed him under his arms. "Isobel, grab his feet. Let's go."

Chapter 34

River

ill floated alongside Case and Isobel as they labored down the stone steps carrying his body. The steps were wide enough to walk abreast holding him between them, but the staircase curved and twisted, making it difficult to travel in a regular rhythm. When they rested, Rani offered to take a turn. Case raised an eyebrow. Rani shrugged. "Just being practical. We'll get wherever we're going faster this way."

"You're totally blowing your reputation as a jerk," Will said.

Rani took Case's end. "Shut up, or I'll drop you on your head."

At first, Will was just happy to be past the Cave of Flowers and again in pursuit of the Chakana. But as they descended, he worried about what lay ahead. Nothing they'd encountered had raised any memories in him. "Isobel, is any of this familiar?"

"No," she said, struggling down the next step, holding the feet of his unconscious form. "I still remember nothing."

"We're getting close to something," Rani wheezed. "That weird light is brighter."

She was right. As well, the pearly glow now shimmered, rippling over the staircase walls.

Something else had grown with the light. A sound rose to meet them, one he recognized. It had probably been there since the stone wall opened, too soft to notice then, but now impossible to ignore. A rushing, rumbling roar—the sound his Flower vision had brought him in the greenhouse back home. They descended another thirty steps and emerged into what lay below.

"Whoa..." Will said.

They stood on the white pebbled shore of a vast underground river as wide as a city block. Upstream, a hundred steps to their left, a waterfall towered five stories high, its pounding thunder echoing in the vaulted chamber. A thick mist rose from where the cataract plummeted into a small lake at its base. The river flowed from the lake past them, disappearing downstream into a curving canyon to their right. The canyon's walls soared higher than the waterfall, disappearing into darkness above.

Darkness above, for the light in this place came from below. The pearly glow that had lit their descent now illuminated this entire underground chamber.

The light came, not from overhead as in the Temple of the Key, but from the river itself.

At first, this river reminded Will of the River of Souls he and Case had sailed up to reach the Gray Lands. They'd sailed down it, too, to rescue Fader from the strange crystal island.

The light from the River of Souls had come from the silver cords of Dreamers traveling the River to reach Dream. But the light from this river came from the riverbed. The same glowing stone, he guessed, that lit the dome of the Temple of the Key. And, perhaps, that formed the Chakana itself.

"Still nothing?" he asked Isobel, as she gawked at the cavern and glowing river.

"The River of Light. My Sisters talk of this. I believe I have traveled it. I was blindfolded, but I remember being on water, a light rising from beneath."

To their right, the pebbled beach sloped up to a timbered wharf. There, three wooden gondola-like boats lay moored lengthwise, tethered at bow and stern. A berth for a fourth boat was empty.

The travelers walked onto the wharf, where Rani and Case set down Will's body, as he floated in his astral form over the boats.

On each craft, the image of a green-scaled serpent undulated the length of the hull. A condor, painted black and carved with wings outspread, crowned a curving prow as a figurehead. From the squarish stern, the face of a puma dared anyone to approach.

Each boat had a dozen bench seats, wide enough for three people. Two long poles lay on top of the benches.

Isobel nodded at the gondolas. "There are four such *wampu*, one for each Madre." She pointed to the empty berth. "Yanta has used Suyana's to travel from here."

Will frowned. "I guessed the same, but how can you tell Suyana's boat is missing?"

"Each bears the mark of a Madre." Isobel pointed to each boat in turn. "Orden. Caos. Mal."

Order. Chaos. Evil.

Looking more closely, he realized the snake, puma, and condor differed on each craft. On the gondola of the Madre of Order, each guardian appeared calm and composed, their mouth or beak closed, their features and markings symmetrical. Even the snake's undulations were regular and evenly spaced. They were...orderly.

On the gondola of the Madre of Chaos, each guardian seemed unbalanced, their features irregular, their expressions lopsided.

On the last boat, that of the Madre of Evil, the mouths of the puma and snake were opened wide, their fangs prominent. The condor's talons were spread, its eyes flashing brighter. Each guardian exuded an aura of blood lust, of bestial fury.

"Suyana is the Madre de Bondad—of Good," Isobel said. "Her boat is missing."

Rani lowered her phone from snapping photos. "The Madre who wants to kill us is the 'good' one? See, this is why I hate religion."

Turning from the boats, Will glimpsed his silver cords. One glowed brighter still, disappearing downstream, following the Chakana. His other cord, paler, almost invisible against the River's brightness, snaked to where his body lay on the wharf. His dying body.

"Let's get going," Will said. "Which one should we take?"

"Not the evil one," Rani said.

Will picked the boat of the Madre of Order. After the others lowered his body onto the floor between two benches, they untied and pushed off.

To Will's surprise, Rani grabbed a pole. Standing at the stern, she expertly guided the boat into the middle of the river. "When my brother and I were kids," she explained, "my parents used to rent a cottage on an island up north every summer. The owners had this old pontoon raft, and we'd pole it around the island. Got pretty good at it."

Isobel took the other pole and helped steer from the bow. But the river flowed slowly, its bends gentle and wide, and they traveled downstream, so Rani needed little help.

Floating beside where Case and Fader sat behind Isobel, Will frowned as a thought occurred.

"What?" Case asked.

"I'm just thinking of those tunnels we took to get here. Plus, this reminds me of traveling down the River of Souls to rescue Fader. Remember how the river kept branching?"

"My Voice will help with any choices. I'm more worried about rapids like we hit on that River. Or that waterfall back there. What if there's another in front of us?"

"Thanks so much for putting those ideas in my head," Rani called from the stern.

"The Madres have always used these boats," Isobel said, from where she pushed on her pole at the bow. "This river must allow safe passage. I do not think we will encounter dangers...at least, none such as those."

"But other dangers?" Will said.

Isobel shrugged. "We are escaped prisoners traveling to the Crossing, where our only surviving Madre now guards our most precious treasure, the Chakana. Ahead lies everything my Sisterhood has sworn to protect. So, yes, danger approaches."

"Again," Rani called, "thanks for that."

Case squinted at Will's floating form. "Huh."

"What?" he asked.

"You look...brighter. How's your cord doing?"

His two cords snaked from his chest. One stretched ahead downstream. "The one connected to the Chakana is brighter than ever. The one to my body..." He looked down and frowned. "I think it's stronger, too."

"So that's good, right? We must be catching up to the Chakana."

"But how? I doubt we're going faster than Yanta's boat."

"Perhaps Yanta has reached the Crossing," Isobel said, "and the Chakana is now with Madre Suyana."

"And no longer moving," Will said, excited. "Then we're getting closer every minute."

"Wonderful," Rani muttered.

"Can you wake yourself up yet?" Case asked.

"I'll try." Floating over, he lowered his astral form onto his sleeping self and searched for the connection to his physical body.

It began with the pull of gravity. A heaviness in his limbs, the press of the boat against his back. Then a coolness on his skin. The rush of air in his lungs. A brightness. He opened his eyes. His real eyes. He sat up.

"Welcome back," Case said. She leaned down and kissed him.

He kissed her back, and it was wonderful. "Bodies are good," he said, moving onto the bench and slipping an arm around her. She laughed, leaning against him.

Bend after bend, the glowing river wound through the canyon. For the first time since they'd arrived, Will had the chance to think about something other than escape or survival. And what filled his mind were thoughts of those they'd left behind.

It must have shown on his face. "What's wrong?" Case asked.

"Adi. Stone, Mei, Peng. We don't know what happened after we jumped into the portal. I mean, Peng and Mei were shot. There were still gunmen there. What if Adi and Stone...?" He swallowed. "I mean...I just hope everyone's okay."

At the mention of Adi and Stone, Case shot Rani a look he couldn't read, then nodded. "Yeah," she said softly. "Me, too."

Fader looked as serious as Will had ever seen him. "Peng and Mei weren't moving."

They all fell silent.

In a hospital corridor in Arequipa, Adi listened to the surgeon deliver news as cold and harsh as the fluorescent lighting above. She hadn't caught his name.

He stood in blood-covered scrubs before her, saying the things surgeons say in these situations.

Did all we could... Too much blood loss... Too much damage...

His words ran down. An uncomfortable silence grew. Feeling dead inside, she thanked him. Expressing his regret again, his duty done, he left her there.

She found Stone in the next corridor, finishing his own conversation with another surgeon. As that doctor departed, Stone beamed at her, an expression as unusual on him as the expedition clothes that replaced his customary tailored suit.

"Mei's out of surgery," he said, still smiling. "She's okay. A shoulder wound that isn't serious. Maybe a slight concussion, probably from hitting her head when—" His face fell as he read her expression. "What?"

Her throat tightened as she tried to speak. She forced herself to meet his eyes. "Winstone, I'm sorry... Peng... He..." What could she say? He didn't make it? She hated the things people said in times like these, as if the victim was to blame. "Your friend, Wu Peng, is dead."

Stone closed his eyes. A low moan escaped him. His entire body tensed. His hands became fists. Spinning, his foot flashed out, shattering the back of one of the plastic chairs lining the corridor. He raised a fist, poised to smash it into the wall.

Something went out of him. He collapsed into another chair, bent over, his face in his hands. Sitting beside him, she gently pulled him to her, trying to give comfort where none could be given.

After a minute, he straightened, and she withdrew her arm. She looked away as he wiped at his face. They sat in silence until he finally spoke. "I brought him here. This was my doing."

"No, my friend. It was mine. I never should have let you or your people come." She stared at the floor, as if a solution to this horror would appear, written in streaks of dirt on the linoleum. "I should never have agreed to this trip."

"You came here—we all came here—to help Will," Stone replied, his voice steady again. "And Case and Fader. To help them find their parents. To heal Will." Standing, he straightened his clothing. "And we will still do that. Diego is waiting to fly us to the red dot location."

She stood to face him. "I can't let you risk your life further. You or Mei."

"You can't stop—" he began, his voice sharp. He took a breath, then continued, his words calm, measured. "If you don't allow us to come, Peng will have died for nothing. And what happened at the monastery shows the danger you face. You need us. Will needs us."

She hesitated. "If I say yes, then I'm valuing Will's life above yours."

"As you should. I know how much you love him. I have come to care for him, too. And for Case and young Fader. If we won't risk ourselves to save the children in our lives, then what are we worth?" His eyes glistened, and Adi knew he was seeing the past and not this dismal hospital corridor. "I failed my own child once. Let me help save these kids."

"And Mei?"

"Mei will come if she has to crawl from here. Once she hears of Peng, nothing will stop her."

"I doubt they'll release her in time. We need to leave today if we're going to find Will." She sighed, dreading what had to be done next. "We have to tell her. About Peng."

"I'll do it."

"Let me come with you. You shouldn't have to handle that alone."

Stone opened his mouth, and she thought he would refuse her offer. But he gave a short nod. "Thank you."

An orderly directed them to the recovery ward, where they found five empty beds and Mei standing beside the sixth one. She'd retrieved her clothes from somewhere. She wore her camouflage pants and was struggling the arm beneath her bandaged shoulder into her shirt. An IV bag hung on a pole by the bed, its tube dangling free from where she must have pulled it from her arm.

Seeing them, she shook her head as she buttoned her shirt. "Do *not* tell me I shouldn't be out of bed yet. I'm the only one here in Recovery, which means Peng is already up and probably ripping stitches out trying to find something to eat." She smiled at that, then became serious. "What about the kids? Are they okay? Did you get those assholes who attacked us? Who were they anyway, and—?" She stopped as she saw their expressions. Her arms fell to her sides. She swallowed. "Who?"

Stone hesitated.

"Oh, god," Mei said. "Not the kids?"

Still Stone didn't answer.

"Dai lo," she pleaded. "Just tell me."

Adi was the one who said it. "Mei, I'm so sorry. Wu Peng is dead."

Mei's scream rose from a place deep inside her, building to an ear-piercing wail. She backed away, waving her arms as if warding off Adi's words, until she hit the wall beside the bed. "No, no, no, no..." she cried, shaking her head, her eyes shut tight, as she slid to the floor. She pulled her knees to her chest. "No, no, no..." she sobbed, over and over.

Stone crouched before her, a hand on her knee. He bowed his head as she continued to sob. Unsure of what to do, Adi sat down hesitantly beside Mei and put an arm around her. Mei, still weeping, leaned against Adi.

Two hours later, Adi sat beside Mei again, this time in the military helicopter Diego had commandeered to carry them directly to the red dot location. With

Will and the others in danger, they had abandoned their original plan of landing farther away and doing a two-day hike.

The chopper was a Russian-made Mi-17. Two rows of fifteen fold-down seats faced each other ahead of the rear hold. An eight-man special services squad sat at the back, while Adi and Mei faced Stone and Diego just behind the cockpit.

On the ride to the army base, Adi had explained to Mei and Diego what she believed happened at the monastery. This included who Morrigan was and how the witch had likely forced Gabriel Herrada to arrange the ambush.

Diego had responded with polite skepticism. She couldn't blame him. Mei had nodded her acceptance of Adi's story, her face unreadable. Adi couldn't tell if Mei believed her or was too numbed by Peng's death to react otherwise.

Adi and Mei now sat in silence while Diego and Stone pored over a map, discussing options on landing locations. Finally, Adi spoke, her voice low. "I'm sorry. About Peng."

Mei stared at the floor. "Thank you."

"Stone called his mother in Toronto. We're having his..." She bit back the word 'body.' "We're having him flown back."

A nod. More silence. "Do you think we'll find them?" Mei suddenly asked. "The kids?"

"Yes," Adi said, wishing she believed that.

"That witch, too?"

"I hope so."

"I'm going to kill her," Mei said, still staring at the floor, her voice flat, as if commenting on the weather.

Not if I kill her first, Adi thought.

After a few minutes, Mei spoke again. "I never told him."

"What?"

"Peng," Mei said softly. "I never told him I loved him."

Adi found herself not thinking of Peng, but of her own Laura. They'd fought again before Adi had left for Peru. Laura didn't understand why Adi couldn't tell her more about the trip or why she couldn't go with her. And Adi had done little to remove Laura's fear that Adi wasn't taking her simply because she didn't want to.

She tried to remember when she'd last told Laura she loved her. Worse, she wondered how Laura would react to news that Adi had died.

As their seemingly endless journey down the glowing river continued, Case tensed at every bend, expecting some new danger. But each curve brought nothing but more river. Still, she knew they were drawing closer to the Crossing—and confronting the Sisters and the Madre Suyana.

Thinking of the surviving Madre reminded her of an earlier conversation. "Isobel, back in the cell, before Will collapsed, we asked you what happened to Luciana. And to Will and his parents and—" She hesitated. Not the time to explain their mother's involvement. "Can you tell us now?"

Standing at the bow, Isobel shook her head. "As I said, it was before I joined the Sisterhood."

"Some of your Sisters must have been there."

"Yes, but Madre Suyana forbids any Sister to talk of those events."

"Yeah, right," Rani called from the stern. "An *entire* Sisterhood of teenage girls not only do what they're told, but also don't talk to each other? Give me a break. You must have heard something."

Isobel only shook her head again, her face now set in hard lines. Will looked at Case, tilting his head at Isobel.

She sighed, understanding. If the Sister would respond to anyone, it would be her. "Isobel, the people Luciana brought through the portal eight years ago...Will, his parents..."

"Yes?"

Case hesitated, afraid to ask the question, afraid to hear the answer, but needing to hear it, too. Fader's hand found hers, and she knew he had the same fears. And the same need for an answer. She swallowed. "Was there another woman with them?"

Isobel frowned. "I was told there was. A woman with dark skin, like yours and your brother's."

Case let out a breath. "Isobel, that was our mother."

Isobel's eyes went wide, flitting between Case and Fader, finally resting on Case. "Oh," she said softly, some hardness leaving her face.

"Can you please tell us what happened? Will can't remember, and we all lost our parents because of it."

"Uh, guys..." Rani called from the stern.

"Not now," Case said, looking at Rani. "This is important."

"So is this." Rani had stopped pushing on her pole and now stared down the river.

Case followed her gaze. They'd come around another curve. Ahead, a shimmering silver curtain stretched across the river from one canyon wall to the other, rising from the glowing water to disappear into the darkness above. The wall of light hid whatever lay beyond. Their gondola would reach it in seconds.

"Isobel?" Case called.

"It is the First Veil," Isobel said, wonder on her face. "It will not harm us, but to reach the Crossing, we must pass through."

The boat floated up to the curtain of light...and through it. Case's skin tingled, but she felt no other physical effect. The canyon and the river appeared the same on this side of the curtain. Yet something seemed...different.

"Do not move!" Isobel cried.

Case jumped as a feathered arrow struck an empty bench between where Rani stood at the stern and the others sat at the front. Giving a high-pitched squeak, Rani threw her pole into the boat and dropped to the floor.

High on the left canyon wall, on a ledge two stories above the river, three Sisters stood, long bows in their hands, arrows nocked.

"Do not move," Isobel repeated. "That was a warning. If they wanted to kill us, we would be dead."

"Not helping," Rani called from where she huddled.

Isobel waved her pole above her head. The Sisters lowered their bows and pointed downstream.

As Isobel moved the boat past the watching archers, Rani sat up far enough to peek over the railing. Case sat unmoving between Fader and Will. When they came around the next bend, she gasped.

Here, the river widened into a small lake. At the far end of the lake, mist rose in billowing clouds above where, Case guessed, water from the lake plummeted down in another waterfall. The canyon walls enclosed the lake, rising sheer as they had along the river and disappearing into darkness above. No, not darkness. A blackness, a complete absence of light. Some part of her knew what it was.

"The Nothing," Will whispered beside her, echoing her thoughts as he stared up at the darkness, too. Her hand found his, remembering their previous encounters with the Nothing—in the Gray Lands, in the Black Pool of the Chambelán.

The walls surrounding the lake were broken in only one spot. On the left shore, a cleft formed a steep-sided valley stretching back and upwards from a wide stony beach. The same glowing stone of the riverbed rose up both sides of the cleft, lighting the valley in brilliant radiance.

The valley was jungle-filled, choked with towering trees and broad-leaved plants. A narrow river, barely a stream, wound down the valley to the lake. Two wooden piers, split by the river, flanked its mouth. Another condor-prowed gondola lay moored at the nearest pier—the craft, she guessed, Yanta had used to bring the Chakana here.

At least twenty Sisters lined the piers, each holding a bow or drawn sword. Their condor masks hid their faces, but from how they stood, tense and poised, she knew none were smiling.

"Is *this* the Crossing?" Will asked Isobel.

"No. It is the Valley of the Veils," she replied, pushing them closer to the nearest pier. "And my Sisters who defend it."

Chapter 35

The Valley

As Isobel poled their gondola toward the pier, Case saw to her dismay that one waiting Sister wore no mask. "Yanta's here."

Isobel nodded. "I expect she has delivered the Chakana to Madre Suyana and was about to return up the River."

"Will she take us to Suyana?" Will asked.

Isobel bit her lip. "Let us hope so."

"Because there's another option we wouldn't like?" Rani said.

Isobel hesitated. "She might kill us here."

"You put a disturbing emphasis on the word *here*," Rani said.

Isobel shrugged. "Even if Yanta takes us to the Crossing, Madre Suyana may still order our deaths."

"Meaning our options are die here or die there?" Rani said. "Why did I come on this trip?"

"Nobody's dying," Case said. "Will's back in his body, so if things get bad, Fader can pull us into the In Between."

"I can't feel it," Fader said.

"What?" Case said.

He looked at her, eyes wide in fear. "The In Between. Ever since we passed through that wall of light, I can't feel it. I don't think I can reach it from here."

"Dude, *try*," Will said, his face grim as the pier and the waiting Sisters drew ever closer. "We need to know."

Fader closed his eyes. He clenched his fists, his lips tightening into a thin line. But he stayed visible. His shoulders slumped as he let out a breath. He opened his eyes. "I couldn't reach it."

"We know," Case said. "You didn't even fade."

His eyes went wide. "What?"

Will turned to Case. "What about your Voice?"

She quieted her mind. *Voice? Are you there?*

No answer came. She tried to sense them—her other selves, in the other 'verses. Each standing at their own door, waiting to step from their world into the hallway of doors of the In Between, to stand beside her.

Again, nothing. Worse than nothing. A feeling of being utterly alone.

"No," she said.

"That's a good sign, right?" Rani said. "No Voice, so no impending death?"

"No, I mean my Voice is gone. My other selves are gone. I can't sense anything." She turned to Will. "What about Nyx?"

"Again, who is this Nyx?" Isobel asked from where she leaned on the pole.

Case ignored her. "She could tell the Sisters to trust us, that we're the good guys."

"Or scare them into leaving us alone," Rani said.

"I've tried calling her," Will said, "but since we came through the portal, it's like your Voice. No answer. Same with Jack."

"To sum up," Rani said, "we're probably about to die, we have nowhere to run, and nobody to call for help."

No one answered, for there was no answer to give. They would soon be at the mercy of warriors who held them responsible for the deaths of the Sisters of the Key and the theft of the Chakana. Warriors led by Yanta, who had already sworn to kill them.

As Isobel maneuvered the boat alongside, two Sisters with long hooks pulled it tight against the wharf. Four more, swords drawn, leaped into the gondola, two at each end. They herded the travelers into the center, then threw the mooring ropes to others on the pier who tied the gondola fast at both ends.

Yanta stood on the pier, hands on hips, fury on her face. "Out!"

Prodded by swords, the four travelers and Isobel stepped from the boat, prisoners once again.

"You must take us to Madre Suyana," Isobel said, addressing Yanta.

Yanta advanced on Isobel, her eyes blazing, her face so red Case thought she would explode. And explode she did. A torrent of words in a language Case didn't know spewed from the Siguiente.

Isobel took the onslaught, shoulders back, head up. "Your insults mean nothing to me, Sister. And if you wish to speak, speak to us all. For I stand with my friends."

Good for you, girl, Case thought.

"Your friends?" Yanta said. "Then, yes, I will speak in words you all understand, for you will share the same fate." She stepped closer to Isobel. "You, Sister, are a traitor to your oaths, to your Sisterhood. You abandoned the Chakana to these defilers. Now, you lead them to our most sacred place." She swept her eyes over them. "I will not taint our Madre with your presence. She has already ordered your deaths—"

Rani squeaked.

"—so here you will die. But not before you reveal how you found your way here. How you escaped your cell. How you passed the tunnels. Survived the Cave of Flowers. Opened the Door of Judgment." Her eyes swept over them. "Tell me, and your deaths will be quick. Resist, and I promise—"

Her words cut off as a collective gasp ran through the Sisters. Yanta's head snapped up, eyes focused on something above and behind them. Case spun around.

High over the lake, its great wings outspread, a condor floated toward them, ablaze not with the light from beneath the water, but with its own luminescence.

A low moan rose from the Sisters. Moving as one, they fell to their knees, prostrating themselves, Isobel included. Yanta, open-mouthed and wide-eyed, stepped back but remained standing as the Condor dropped closer.

Rani turned as if to run. Case grabbed her arm. "Don't move. I think it's flying to you."

"Why do you think I'm running?" Rani whimpered, her back now to the approaching bird.

"Hold still," Case whispered.

Rani groaned but stayed put, eyes screwed shut. With a beat of mighty wings, the Condor settled shining onto her shoulder. She peeked at the bird. Twisting its neck, it stroked its forehead against hers. "It's...nuzzling me?"

"Well, it's *your* Guardian," Will said. "Which kind of raises the question..."

"There," Case whispered, the awe she felt echoing in that word, as she nodded at what emerged from the jungle behind the pebbled beach.

From a path through the trees came the other two Guardians, one walking, one slithering—a giant tawny puma and an enormous green snake. Like the Condor, both glowed with an inner light, and both were slightly translucent. Seeing them, Yanta succumbed to the same fear as her Sisters. With a wordless cry, she fell to her knees and touched her forehead to the ground, trembling as the Puma and Snake moved past her.

"It won't squish me, will it?" Fader said, eyes locked on the Snake as it slithered through the Sisters toward him.

"Might give you a hug," Case said, her gaze fixed on her own approaching companion.

The Puma was larger than a real one. But unlike her first sight of the animal, back in Will's tower, she didn't fear it. Instead, just as when these creatures had appeared in the monastery, she felt a connection like the one she had to her other selves. And to her Voice.

The Snake didn't touch Fader, but curled around him, its coils rising in a protective wall. The Puma stood beside Case, scanning the prostrated Sisters, a low growl rumbling in its throat. Reaching out a shaking hand, she stroked its head. She felt soft fur, then an electric shock as her hand sunk into the animal. She snatched it back, but the great cat paid her no mind.

Yanta was the first of the Sisters to look up. She straightened from where she knelt, her eyes flitting between the travelers and the astral creatures. "Who are you people?" she asked, both fear and reverence in her voice.

"I still have the same question," Rani muttered, then continued loudly, so that all the Sisters could hear. "We are the...Keepers of the Guardians..."

"Of the Crossing," Will whispered.

"...of the Crossing. Yeah, that's us. The Keepers of the Guardians of the Crossing." Rani pointed at Yanta. "And now, you will take us to...uh..."

"Suyana," Will whispered.

"Suyana. The Madre person," Rani finished.

"Nicely done," Will murmured.

"Talk a big game," Rani whispered back. "Same way I got a job at the paper."

Still staring at the glowing Guardians, Yanta gave a quick nod. Standing, she shouted something to the Sisters. They rose as one, every eye on the Guardians. Yanta pointed to two Sisters and barked another order.

Then she turned to the travelers. "Follow. I will take you to Madre Suyana," she said, imbuing those words with both fear and disgust. With that, she marched toward the jungle path from where the Snake and Puma Guardians had emerged, followed by the two Sisters she'd selected.

With a beat of great wings, the Condor lifted from Rani to fly over the trees, heading up the valley in the same direction. Rani peered at her shoulder. "Please tell me it didn't poop on me."

"We must go," Isobel said. Her face showed awe, but unlike Yanta, no fear. "It is the will of the Guardians."

Case fell in beside Will and Fader, following Isobel and Rani, as Yanta and the two Sisters led them into the Valley of the Veils.

Behind them came the Snake and Puma.

⌇

The path they followed was well traveled, worn to dirt and wide enough to walk three abreast. But it still passed through jungle, and Case could see where the encroaching vegetation had been hacked back on either side.

Their route followed the smaller river that flowed down the valley. At first, Case wondered why the Sisters didn't use that to travel the valley, but soon realized the waterway was too shallow in spots, too rocky in others.

But it did provide drinking water. Twice, when they passed close enough, Yanta and the guards refilled leather water skins they carried, offering them to the travelers.

The water quenched Case's thirst, but did little for her growing hunger. Their last meal had been breakfast at the hotel. She thought back over all that had happened since then. The monastery attack, the escape through the portal, their capture, the journey here.

"How long until we reach Madre Suyana?" she called to Yanta.

"By evening meal," Yanta replied.

Rani groaned from where she walked with Isobel. "Please don't mention food."

They trudged on through a jungle filled with strange trees and stranger plants. The tallest trees towered stories above them, with trunks resembling the outside of a pineapple and crowned by circular leaves as broad as the Condor's wingspan. Filtering the glow of the valley's walls, the tree canopy dappled the vegetation below in shifting light and shadow.

The plants were like none she'd ever seen, even in the gardens of Arequipa, with huge blooms in every color of the rainbow. An orange flower, with three triangular petals as long as her forearm, swung to follow them as they passed. On another, two scarlet blossoms shaped like giant lips smacked together to trap a purple butterfly as large as her hand.

Will pointed to an unopened flower, its petals a deep black that reflected no light. "Look familiar?"

"Your Flower?"

"I think so."

"It's not open...oh, right."

"*It only comes out at night.*" He looked up to where the glow of the valley walls filtered through the trees. "Which makes me wonder. How is it ever night here?"

"We were just saved by three refugees from Animal Crossing," Rani called back, "and you're wondering how to turn off a rock?"

Reminded of the Guardians, Case glanced back. The Puma and Snake still followed, their glow illuminating the surrounding jungle. "Are they actually here?" she asked, her voice low so Yanta and the guards couldn't hear. "I mean, *physically* here? My hand sank into the Puma. But the plants move when they brush past."

"My Condor was really light when it landed on me," Rani said. "Like it was there...but not there."

"I think they're astral spirits," Will said, "but very powerful ones. Ones that can affect the physical world."

Isobel threw a nervous look behind. "How can they be here at all?" she whispered. "Never has a Guardian been seen outside the Crossing. Why do they come to you?"

"We don't know," Case said. "They just showed up to each of us one day back home. We don't even know what they really are."

"They are as Sister Rani said. The Guardians of the Crossing. Each protects one level of that place."

"The Crossing has levels?" Will asked.

"Three. The Serpent guards the first, the Puma the second, and the Condor the third. And inside the Crossing, the Guardians are very real indeed. To travel the Crossing, even a Madre must have their blessing."

"And the Chakana."

Isobel nodded. "Yes. And the Chakana."

"But what *is* the Crossing?" Will asked. "I mean, what's it for? Why is it there? Luciana said I could only be healed inside the Crossing, but it must do more than that."

Isobel hesitated. "It is the passage."

"To what?"

Isobel shook her head. "I must not talk of it."

"It's how the Madres reach the Book, right?" Will said.

Isobel's eyes widened. "How do you know of the Book?"

"Nyx told us."

"Who is this Nyx you keep speaking of?" Isobel said, her voice low and quavering. "How can she know of such things?"

He looked at Case. She shrugged. He shrugged back. "She's the part of the Chakana that lives in my head. She told us of the One that is the Four who merge with the Madres to read the Book that tells the Story of every universe."

Isobel stared at him, the same mix of awe and fear on her face Yanta had shown when the Guardians appeared. Shaking her head, she turned back to the path they followed, falling into silence.

Case fell silent as well. The mention of Nyx being part of Will reminded her of how that part was also killing him. And *that* was why they were here, why they must meet Suyana, the last surviving Madre of this strange Sisterhood. To ask her—beg her if they had to—to save Will. To heal him by healing the Chakana.

He must have been having similar thoughts. "Isobel," he said, "when we were on the Black Island, I told you I was the same kid Luciana brought here eight years ago with my parents. Did you tell Suyana that?"

"Yes."

"And?"

"It was a mistake. It only made her angrier with me."

"Why?"

"Madre Suyana blames your parents—and you—for the death of Madre Luciana, for the loss of the Chakana. For..." She hesitated. "For everything that happened."

Everything that you still won't tell us, Case thought.

"But Suyana's a Madre," Will said. "Once we meet, won't she sense the piece of the Chakana in me, like Luciana did? Won't she want to take me into the Crossing, too, like Luciana? To heal me? If only to heal the Chakana?"

"Madre Suyana would have sensed it inside you eight years ago, just as Madre Luciana had."

"Wait," Will said. "She *knows* about the Chakana in me?"

"And still she ordered your death, Will Dreycott. Far from the Crossing." She shook her head. "The Chakana will not save you. Or us. The Guardians are the only reason we still live."

Rani stared behind them. Her face fell. "Then we have a big problem."

They all looked back. The Guardians were gone. Case searched the foliage for any sign. She swallowed. Nothing.

"What are we going to do?" Rani said, her voice low and tight.

"Pray they return," Isobel said, "before we meet Madre Suyana."

The travelers continued in silence. Case kept scanning the jungle for the Guardians. The others did the same. But the astral spirits didn't return. She wondered how long before Yanta also noticed their disappearance.

Minutes later, they stepped from the jungle's cover into an open clearing where the path became the stony shore of the stream. Rocks and sparse shrubs dotted a landscape more desert-like than jungle. Ahead, the river continued to wind through the gently rising valley—until it didn't.

In the distance, another shimmering wall of silver light hung across the valley, like an immense curtain rippling in a wind she couldn't feel. It stretched from one sloping rock face to the other, hiding whatever lay beyond.

The party stopped. "The Second Veil," Isobel said, then fell silent as Yanta glared at her.

Yanta pointed at the flickering barrier. "Beyond lies the home of my Sisters of the Crossing. Soon you will meet Madre Suyana and hear her judgment. Then—" She stopped, peering into the jungle they had left. She scanned the air above as well. "Where are the Guardians?" Her eyes pierced them one by one, her hand drifting to the hilt of her sword. "Have they forsaken you?"

Rani stepped forward. "Ha. Don't you wish? We have...sent them ahead..."

"To await us," Will offered.

"Yes," Rani said. "To await us. And they have gone ahead...because...we're their masters...and they do what we say." She crossed her arms. "So there."

Yanta regarded them with narrowed eyes. "You best pray that is true." Turning, she set out along the stony shore toward the barrier. The two masked guards motioned them to follow Yanta, falling in behind them.

Fader had been silent during their journey through the jungle. "You okay?" Case asked.

"Yeah," he said. "I mean, I'm scared, but I'm trying not to think about that. I've been trying to find the In Between."

"And?"

"I can't. I mean, I can sort of feel it near us."

"Sort of?"

"Like it's right there, on the other side of the wall I use when I zoom. Only we're on this side, and I can't get back in." He looked around. "This place feels different, too."

"Different how?"

"Like it's not our world anymore."

"You mean we're in a different 'verse?"

"No. Like it's not *any* of the 'verses."

"Huh?"

He shrugged. "Like this place only has *one* version."

Uncertain what to say to that, she tried yet again to call her Voice. Still no answer.

Ahead, the shimmering curtain of the Second Veil loomed larger. "Isobel," she whispered, "what are these veils?"

Isobel looked puzzled. "They mark points of passage on this route."

"But what do they *do*? Why do they exist? Why can't you see through them?"

"I do not understand. They simply are."

"I think they're portals," Will whispered.

"What?" Case said.

"I've been thinking about what Fader said. About this place having only one version. I think when we passed through that barrier on the river—the First Veil—we passed from our 'verse into this place. That's why your Voice and Fader's powers disappeared—they depend on the other 'verses. If you're cut off from those other realities..."

"We're cut off from our powers," she finished, not liking that idea at all. It meant her Voice wasn't just being quiet—it was no longer there.

She nodded at the approaching Second Veil. "So, this will take us to the Crossing?"

Isobel shook her head. "To the Threshold, the land *outside* the Crossing."

"How many veils are there?"

"Three," she said. "The Third Veil leads into the Crossing itself."

Case shot Will a look. His jaw was tight, but she read excitement in his eyes. Behind that last veil lay his cure. And maybe answers to the questions they'd lived with—Will, Fader, her—for eight years.

But right now, another question loomed, towering over them like the Second Veil. Could they convince this Madre Suyana to believe them? To trust them?

To let them live?

The party reached the Second Veil and stopped. Yanta barked something at the guards, then with a final glare at them, she disappeared through the shimmering curtain. The two guards gestured them forward with their swords.

Case looked at Will.

He took her hand. "One step closer."

But closer to what? Answers? Their parents? Or death? But she nodded. Moving as one, they stepped through the Veil.

Chapter 36

Hidden World

P assing through the second barrier, Will felt only a mild tingling, just as when their gondola had sailed through the First Veil. He stood now with the others, trying to understand what he saw.

"Where the hell are we?" Rani said, an edge of fear in her voice.

"*El Umbral.* The Threshold of the Crossing," Isobel said softly, a child-like smile on her face. "My home. And the home of my Sisters."

The valley they'd traveled was gone. Ahead, a rectangular strip of flat, prairie-like land stretched before them, split by a dirt road five paces wide.

The road ran arrow straight, cutting between cultivated fields of crops growing in neat rows and patches of grasslands where shaggy, horned animals grazed. Stands of bamboo-like trees dotted the land in a pattern so random Will guessed they grew wild.

But this world's most striking feature was what *wasn't* there. The strip of land was no wider than four city blocks. On its far sides, the glowing walls of the valley they'd left were gone, replaced by blackness.

No. Blackness meant the absence of light. This was the absence of *everything*. He felt it inside him, perhaps in the Chakana part of him. This was emptiness. The same blackness that had hung above the valley.

The Nothing.

Yanta's voice pulled him from the hypnotic hold the blackness had cast. "It is unwise to stare long into the Nothing."

Yeshe had once spoken similar words to him while traveling the Gray Lands. Startled, he turned to her. Yanta pointed down the road. "Madre Suyana awaits. And, if you speak truth, the Guardians you command."

"We are so screwed," Rani muttered.

They set out, walking five abreast behind Yanta, the two guards trailing them.

The landscape was lit as if by soft sunlight. With the glowing valley walls gone, Will looked up, wondering at the light source.

High above, stark against the Nothing, a silver band ran the length of this strange world, emerging from the Second Veil and disappearing into the distance. On the band sat a shining disk too bright to look at and twice its width, like an oversized button on a ribbon.

To their right, a waterfall poured from the blackness above into a small lake. A stream flowed from the lake, running beside the road into the distance. Waterwheels, attached to cone-shaped buildings, dotted the river.

They passed fields where bare-footed Sisters tended crops, wearing loose-fitting white smocks and trousers instead of the snake-puma-condor garb. They talked and laughed and sang, and Will was again struck by the contrast to his past experiences with these women.

"You remember this place?" he asked Isobel.

"Of course. It is only the journey from the Temple of the Key that the Madres—and the Flowers—guard knowledge of." She looked around, smiling, and Will saw the young girl she still was. "This has been my home since I joined the Sisterhood." Her smile ran away. "I was happy here."

He guessed her thoughts. Every step brought them closer to the judgment of Suyana. To take their minds off that, he pointed to the shaggy animals with their long thick necks supporting large heads with curving horns. "What are those?"

"*Waka.* Our cattle. They give us milk, wool, meat."

"They look like an alpaca got frisky with a muskox," Rani said.

"Our crops feed and clothe us, too. *Linu, triyu, sara*—flax, wheat, corn—plus vegetables and fruits only found here." She pointed to the cone-shaped building attached to the nearest waterwheel. "Our mills, where we grind our grains and send water to the fields. Madre Suyana says the Four Who Are One made this place for us—"

"Silence!" Yanta snapped, looking back. "Do not speak of the Four to outsiders."

"Chill," Will said. "The Chakana told us about the Four."

Yanta stared at him, her eyes wide.

"And the One and the Story and the Book," he continued. "Yeah, me and the Key? We're like that." He held up two crossed fingers.

Yanta opened her mouth, then closed it. Shooting them a fear-filled look, she turned back to the road.

"Speaking of the Chakana..." Case whispered.

"Still no Nyx. Your Voice?"

"Nothing. Fader?"

Fader shook his head.

"And still no critters," Rani said, checking behind them. "Like I said, we're screwed."

"Let's hope it's a long walk," Case said.

Will stared ahead. "No such luck."

Maybe twenty minutes away, the road ended at a forest, where four gigantic trees rose above smaller ones. Beyond the forest hung another shimmering curtain.

"The Third Veil," Isobel said. "Behind it lies the Crossing."

The Veil stretched across the strip of land, disappearing into the blackness of the Nothing on either side and above. The silver ribbon carrying the sun disk continued into the Third Veil, where it also disappeared.

"Are we going through the Veil?" Will asked. "Is Suyana on the other side?"

"No. The four Great Trees you see ahead—the *Hatun Yura*—each is home to a Madre and the Sisters who support her." She shrugged. "Our houses."

As they drew closer, he saw movement in the nearest Great Tree—and understood just how apt the name was. Human figures walked along branches that must be as wide as this road. He tried to estimate the size of the Hatun Yura, his mind boggling at his guess. "They're huge. Enormous. They make giant redwoods look like toothpicks."

"They are said to be as old as the Story itself," Isobel said.

Will felt smaller and smaller with each step, dwarfed both by the looming Hatun Yura and by Isobel's mention of the Story. They would soon meet a Madre, a human who—if he believed Nyx—had merged with a god. Or with a being so powerful no word other than god fit.

A Madre who would probably order their deaths.

As they drew closer to the forest, Will looked up at the sun disk. "Has that moved?"

Isobel nodded. "*Azki* is born from the Second Veil each morning and travels the *Hana Ñan*—the High Road—until the Third Veil swallows it each evening."

"You have night and day?"

"Yes. Twelve hours each, with a brief dawn and twilight while Azki emerges and disappears." She smiled at his frown. "We know what hours are. We each lived in the outside world before the Sisterhood." She pointed at a waterwheel and mill. "We measure time by turns of the grindstones. A minute for one turn. Sixty turns, and a *kampana*—a bell—rings. A different note for every hour."

"You tell time by sounds?" Fader said. "That's cool."

As if to illustrate, when they drew level with the waterwheel, a musical note chimed from the mill. In the fields, the Sisters stood as one and moved toward the forest.

"What's *that* bell?" Fader asked.

"Five o'clock. End of the work day. Soon, our evening meal begins."

"I think something less pleasant than dinner is waiting for us," Rani said, looking ahead.

Thirty paces away, the road ended at the trees, becoming a path into the woods. At the forest's edge, six masked Sisters flanked a taller woman with gray hair that fell in a single thick braid over her right shoulder to her waist. The woman wore the garb of the Sisterhood, but no mask. She held, but did not lean on, a staff taller than her, its bottom third a sculpted green snake. Tawny fur covered the staff's middle portion, and a condor carved with wings spread crowned its top.

"Madre Suyana," Isobel whispered.

"Kind of guessed," Will said.

As Yanta led them toward Suyana, Will struggled to focus on the Madre. This close to the Great Trees, he found it impossible not to stare up at them in awe and wonder.

The front of the forest ran in a straight line to the left and right, ending at the Nothing on either side. Will guessed the forest's far edge would be the same, making the forest a square or rectangle.

Each Hatun Yura rose from a different quadrant in the forest, like points on a compass. *Or the arms of the Chakana*, he thought. The two nearest, one on each side of the dirt path that split the forest, loomed like gigantic multi-limbed beasts. The surrounding smaller trees hid the base of their trunks, but the bulk of each Hatun Yura rose high above their tiny cousins. Like the gondolas of the Madres, each Great Tree exhibited its own personality.

The branches of the one to their left coiled and twisted with each other, curving back, bending at odd angles, tracing impossible routes like an Escher painting. *Chaos*, he thought.

The Hatun Yura to their right rose black-limbed and spectral, its teardrop-shaped leaves sparse and withered. Though as massive as the other three, this one exuded an unhealthy air of wrongness and disease. *Evil*, he thought.

Of the two farther Great Trees, the branches of the rightmost grew straight and spaced with geometrical precision from a trunk that tapered as perfectly as a Greek column. The Hatun Yura of the Madre of Order.

The final tree looked like...a tree. An impossibly huge tree, but a normal, healthy one. One that had grown as any tree grew, its random branches reaching upward, a cooperative striving for life-giving light. The Great Tree of the Madre of Good. The home of Madre Suyana.

The same Suyana whose black eyes pierced them as they approached. Despite her gray hair and lined face, she seemed younger than Luciana had in his vision. Her face prompted no memories in him.

Halting the travelers a few paces back, Yanta approached Suyana. Bowing her head, Yanta began to speak, but a bark from Suyana silenced her. A torrent of angry words in rapid Spanish followed. Yanta's face grew redder as the Madre's tirade continued. Will understood little, but heard *profanadores*, accompanied by gestures toward them.

"In case you're missing the vibe," Rani whispered, "she's not thrilled to see us."

Suyana's berating ended. "Bien?" she snapped. *Well?*

Yanta answered, her voice quavering. Will caught *los guardians* and *los protectores*.

Frowning, Suyana addressed the two Sisters who'd accompanied Yanta. "Es esto cierto?"

The two exchanged glances, but gave timid nods. Suyana considered the travelers again, her gaze still hard but now uncertain. She spoke in heavily accented English. "How is it the Guardians appear to such as you? And outside the Crossing?"

Rani answered first. Will was afraid the reporter would be her usual sarcastic self, but she surprised him. "Madre de Bondad," she began, head bowed, tone respectful, "*El Gran Condor* first appeared to me in the city where we live. I don't know why." She nudged Case.

Case dropped her head, too. "Madre, the...Great Puma appeared to me in the same city. I also don't know why."

Fader gave a deep bow, and a smile flickered on Suyana's face. "The big snake appeared to me. I don't know why, either." He shrugged. "But it really scared me."

This time, Suyana's smile remained. "Such visitors would frighten most." She spoke in Spanish to Yanta and then Isobel. Both bowed their heads and whispered, "Gracias, Madre."

Suyana addressed the travelers again. "The Guardians have chosen you. I have apologized to my Siguiente for my harsh words and to Sister Isobel for her imprisonment. It seems both acted with more wisdom than I granted."

Will modified his opinion of Suyana upwards. "Madre, I am—"

"I know who you are, William Dreycott," she said, her bright eyes seizing him. "I see the spark of the Chakana that dwells in you still, as I and our beloved Luciana saw it eight years ago." She considered him. "You do not remember me, do you?"

He stared at her face. Still nothing. "No, but I don't remember anything that happened here eight years ago."

Her eyebrows shot up at that. "But I remember you, child. And the great sorrow that accompanied you, your parents...and one other." Her gaze shifted to Case. "Her name was Elenora...and she lives in your face."

Beside him, Case sucked in a breath. Fader moved closer to his sister. She pulled him to her. "Our mother."

"What happened to her?" Fader asked, his voice breaking.

A low murmuring had grown behind them. Will glanced back. White-clad Sisters clustered at the edge of the nearest field, hoes and rakes in dirt-covered hands, their end-of-day journey home halted. They watched, talking in hushed whispers among themselves. Will wondered which they found stranger—the travelers or that the Madre herself had come to meet them.

Suyana called something, and the crowd fell silent. She ran her eyes over the travelers, then sighed. "I will tell you what I know. But not here." She addressed Yanta. "Bring them. Send your guards back." With that, she walked into the forest, her six warriors behind her. Yanta motioned, and the travelers followed

Suyana into the trees.

I will tell you what I know. Would he finally learn what happened here eight years ago?

But beside him, Case's face was grim, not hopeful. He frowned a question at her.

She glanced at Fader, then leaned closer. "What she said," she whispered.

"What?"

"*Her name* was *Elenora*." She looked at him. "Was."

He understood. *Was*. Past tense.

And neither had Suyana's words held hope for his parents. He was finally here—at the Crossing, meeting the last person to have seen his parents and Ellie Cootes alive. He was at the end of his journey for answers.

But what if those answers weren't ones any of them wanted to hear?

As they followed Suyana into the woods, Will was grateful for the cover the forest canopy gave from the looming presence of the Hatun Yura. These smaller trees were also deciduous, with oval leaves, smooth gray bark, and branches beginning about an arm's length overhead. They seemed to be younger versions of the Great Trees, and he wondered if they were the same species.

The party emerged into a circular clearing maybe twenty paces across. The path continued on the opposite side of this open space, heading for the Third Veil, visible again in the distance above the forest.

The clearing held a circular amphitheater with tiered seating running down to a sunken, central, Chakana-shaped stage. The stage's four arms pointed to smaller trails leading diagonally off the clearing toward each Hatun Yura, also visible again above the trees.

Suyana took the trail leading toward the Great Tree Will had guessed belonged to the Madre de Bondad. Five minutes later, they entered another clearing, and he saw a Hatun Yura complete, like an ant viewing a skyscraper from the sidewalk.

This clearing was wider than the amphitheater, probably thirty paces across. Even so, the space could barely hold the Great Tree. Stairs, carved into the trunk and broad enough for a single person, spiraled up past where the first branches began two stories above the forest floor.

Sisters moved throughout the tree high above them, some in the white garb of the field workers, others in the familiar uniform of the warriors. They scurried along the tree's great limbs, up and down dangling rope ladders, or over wooden-slatted rope bridges connecting branches. Or made leaps between branches that made his stomach flip.

He and the others followed Suyana and her guards up the spiraling stairs around the trunk, soon rising above the forest canopy. As they reached the lower limbs of the Great Tree, wooden platforms came into view, secured to large branches or across smaller adjacent ones. These platforms held mattresses, sitting cushions, tables with candles and combs and brushes, and clothes piled or folded neatly. The platforms were uncovered. Will guessed rain never fell from the blackness above.

"Are these where the Sisters live?" he asked Isobel, who climbed ahead of him.

"Yes. Each Sister has their own *wasi ukhu* in the Great Tree of the Madre they serve."

"Sisters serve individual Madres?"

"It makes allocation of work and responsibilities simpler. Before she died—" She shook her head. "No. I will not say that. Before she disappeared, I served Madre Luciana." Stopping, she pointed across the forest canopy to the Great Tree that had recalled an Escher drawing to Will. "That was my home. The Hatun Yura of the Madre del Caos." Her expression turned wistful. "Perhaps, now with Madre Suyana's forgiveness, I will live there again."

Each platform included a wooden bucket beside a coiled rope. "What are those for?" Fader asked.

Isobel confirmed Will's guess. "We have toilets where the river leaves the forest." She smiled at Fader. "But that is a long walk during the night, so..."

"Better hope nobody up there knocks one over, dude," Will said.

"Not funny," Fader said, shooting a worried look above them.

"Are we going much higher?" Rani asked, her voice strained. "Because me and heights? Not buddies."

They were four stories high now. A thick rope, attached every few feet to the trunk, provided a handhold. But away from the tree, the stairs were open with no guardrail. Rani climbed hand over hand, clutching the rope.

"And *you* got the Condor?" Will said.

"Also not funny."

They reached where the main trunk split into four smaller but still monstrous trunks that continued upwards. Between the branching trunks sat the largest platform they'd seen, ten paces a side, its furnishings more suited to a leader and older woman. The mattress sat in a wooden bed frame, a rocking chair beside it. Small tables with lit candles were scattered throughout. A colorful rug, woven with images of the Guardians, covered most of the floor.

A circle of cushions lay in its center. Suyana sat on the largest of these and motioned the travelers to those across from her. Will sat beside Case, Fader beside his sister, and Rani beside Will.

Yanta and Isobel hesitated until Suyana spread her arms, indicating the cushions next to her. The two Sisters exchanged surprised looks, then sat.

The six warriors who had accompanied Suyana returned, carrying trays laden with dishes. They set cups with water and a woven napkin beside plates heaped with food before the Sisters and their guests, serving the Madre last. Placing lit candles on small plates in the center of the circle, the guards then stood behind Suyana, eyes on the travelers.

"I expect you are hungry," Suyana said. "First we eat, then we talk." Joining hands with Yanta and Isobel, together they closed their eyes and spoke words he assumed formed a grace. They then began to eat.

Will tapped his plate with a fingernail. Ceramic, he guessed. The cup, too. The meal consisted of strips of dried meat, round flatbread, and a piled mixture of potato, corn, fava beans, and quinoa, topped with some type of ground nut. No utensils. Suyana and the two Sisters ate with their hands, scooping the vegetables with pieces torn from the bread.

Case, Fader, and Rani were already eating the same way. He joined them and quickly realized how hungry he was. The dried meat tasted like smoked beef and was easy to chew. The vegetables were cold but delicious, with a sweet and spicy seasoning.

Suyana did not speak. He suspected Yanta and Isobel wouldn't utter a word before their Madre did. The travelers stayed silent, too. Case didn't meet his glance. She hadn't spoken since mentioning Suyana's use of the past tense for their mother.

That sent his own thoughts to his parents. He would soon learn their fate, a fate that had been tied all along to the Chakana. Which reminded him...

He still couldn't raise contact with Nyx, but what of the Chakana? Yanta had returned it to Suyana, so it must be somewhere in this strange land, perhaps even in this Great Tree.

He'd only ever seen his astral cords, his AC and DC, while astral projecting. His AC, the cord connecting his astral and physical bodies, would be within him now, just as his astral spirit was. But what of his DC, the cord joining the piece of the Chakana inside him to the artifact itself? Could he see it, while still in his body?

He focused as he did when astral projecting. Not trying to leave his body, but to visualize the cord to the Chakana leaving him. Almost immediately, a bright silver ribbon hung in the air, sprouting from his chest, undulating across the circle, and disappearing into a leather pouch on Suyana's hip.

Of course. Now that the precious artifact was back, the Madre would never let it out of her possession. He felt relief at its nearness, while recognizing the irony. *Oh, good. The thing that's killing me is really close.*

Staring at the brilliance of his Death Cord hanging before him, he remembered how weakly his Alive Cord had glowed on their journey to this place. Even though his physical energy had returned since they'd closed the distance with the Chakana, he didn't doubt what Nyx had said. The dimming of his cord was proof. He was dying—and the piece of the Chakana inside him was the reason.

At last, Suyana wiped her mouth and hands with her cloth. She met Will's gaze. "I promised to speak of what happened here eight years ago. Of the fate of your parents." She nodded at Case and Fader. "And your mother. And our beloved Luciana." Her eyes became slits, fixed on him. "But first, I have questions."

He swallowed, waiting.

"My Siguiente told me of the vision in the Temple of the Key. Of the day the Beast Alvarez stole the Chakana and slaughtered our brave Sisters." Suyana spread her hands, her eyes still locked on him. "How?"

He hesitated. "Madre, I can't explain why the vision happened, any more than why the Chakana chose me or why the Guardians appeared. But I can guess."

"Yes?"

"I think the vision came from the Chakana itself. I think being returned here somehow..." He shrugged. "...woke that horrible memory inside it. And inside the part that lives in me."

She considered him for a breath. "I believe the same."

Some tension left him. "I can tell you something that isn't a guess. Something I know is true."

"Which is?"

"Until that vision, I knew nothing about that day. And neither did my parents."

"And yet, they gave gold to Alvarez. To the Beast. For something they knew was not theirs."

Will met her eyes. "Yes." What else could he say? Beside him, Case squeezed his knee.

"Madre," Yanta said, "on our journey here, he talked of the Four and the One. And the Story and the Book."

Suyana's eyes seized Will again. "If you remember nothing of eight years ago, then how do you know these things?"

"He said..." Yanta shot a fearful look at Will. "He said the Chakana told him."

"Explain," Suyana said.

"This should be good," Rani muttered.

"The Chakana...appears to me. Or, at least, the part inside me does. Well, actually, it's sort of part me, part Chakana." Will stopped. Suyana stared at him, confusion and distrust on her face. "Let me back up. Eight years ago, when I came home from Peru, I started having these dreams..."

He told of discovering his powers in Dream and the strange creature called Nyx, who he'd thought was his subconscious, but recently learned was the spirit of the Chakana inside him. "And she's told us things she's started remembering from eight years ago—"

"*Us?*" Suyana said.

"Fader and me," Case said. "We've met Nyx."

Rani waved a hand. "Me, too."

"It was Nyx," Will continued, "who told us of the One that is the Four who merge with the Madres to read the Book that tells the Story of all the universes the Four created."

Suyana sat silent, her eyes on them. Behind her, her guards shifted uneasily, hands sliding onto sword hilts. Finally, she spoke again. "Can anyone else see this Nyx?"

Will shook his head. "Just the four of us."

Suyana nodded. "This makes sense."

"Does 'sense' mean something different in your language?" Rani said.

Suyana shrugged. "The boy who carries the Chakana in him, and the three to whom the Guardians appear. Yes, this makes sense."

"But Madre," Yanta said, "they knew the Beast."

"My loyal Siguiente, the Chakana *chose* this boy, as the Guardians *chose* his companions. Now the Chakana chooses to speak to them, to share our greatest secrets. In this, I see the hand of the Four, guiding us toward a hidden purpose. I will not oppose that purpose, even if I remain blind to it."

Will knew he should be happy that Suyana now believed them, but her words sent a chill down his spine.

The Chakana chose this boy...

He was here, in this place, at this moment, solely *because* of that choice. Because of a decision by an inscrutable sentient artifact.

...as the Guardians chose his companions.

Those same Guardians had now twice saved them from death, at the monastery and then from Yanta. But had the Guardians *rescued* them? Or *led* them? Led them *here*?

I see the hand of the Four, guiding us toward a hidden purpose.

Suyana's words eerily echoed Adi's fear, that they were being moved like pieces on a board. And despite the Madre's faith in the mysterious Four, none of them knew who was making the moves...or what that hidden purpose was.

Suyana spoke again, breaking his thoughts. "I will now tell the story I promised." Her eyes took on a far-away look. "My tale begins with death and betrayal. And a terrible mistake I made..."

Chapter 37

Pretender

Suyana, Madre de Bondad, sat stone-faced in her gondola while two Sisters poled the craft down the River of Light toward the Valley of the Veils. Both young women wept openly.

On another day, she would have reprimanded them for such a display. But this was not another day. This was the day when the Chakana had been stolen. Stolen from the Sisterhood whose sole duty was to protect it and the Crossing it opened.

And the day when the Sisters of the Key had been slaughtered. A pang of guilt swept over her, that her thoughts dwelt on the Chakana, not the deaths of so many young women. Or the deaths of Kichka and Ilina, her sister Madres.

But like those who had died today, Suyana had sworn to serve the Four. And without the Chakana, how could she and Luciana do that? Without the Key, they could not enter the Crossing. They could not select new Madres to replace those murdered today. They could not enter the Book to merge with the Four to fulfill their sacred purpose.

To protect all of creation.

What then *was* their purpose?

Her hands clenched into fists. To recover the Chakana. Without it, the Sisterhood was nothing. *She* was nothing.

Both she and Luciana had felt the attack where they dwelt in the Forest of the Great Trees. Felt it in the astral cries of Kichka and Ilina and all the dying Sisters. Felt it in the call of the Chakana itself.

Then silence. The cries of the Sisters had died as the women had died, but the Chakana had fallen silent, too, hidden somehow from her and Luciana. For the first time, the Madres were blind to the Key.

As the younger Madre, she had rushed with her Siguiente, Yanta, and two boatloads of warriors down the River, through the Cave of Flowers, through the tunnels...to arrive too late. The Chakana was gone, the Sisters of the Key but scattered corpses.

Except for one.

Suyana's warriors had found her, buried beneath the bodies, left for dead. Suyana knew her, as she knew all who served the Four. Her name was Parwa.

She looked down at where Parwa lay unconscious at her feet. Perhaps this unfortunate but lucky child could give answers to what had happened. *She must. If not, the Chakana is lost to us.*

Reaching the Forest, the warriors bore Parwa to Suyana's own chambers. There, Suyana tended to the girl's shoulder, grateful the bullet had passed through and missed the bone. She cleaned and dressed the wound, then watched over Parwa as she slept the rest of the day and through the night.

The girl recovered consciousness the next morning. Propped up in bed, she ate a light meal as Luciana and Suyana sat gently questioning her. But Parwa could add little beyond what the grisly scene in the Temple had already told.

An attack without warning. Armed men, led by a hawk-nosed man with a thin mustache. The Sisters had fought bravely, fiercely, but against too many men, too many guns.

And yet... Something about Parwa's story or her way of telling it...

Suyana struggled to grasp what bothered her. The girl's blank face. Her dead tone, devoid of emotion. The pause before answers.

Suyana scolded herself. The child was in shock. Yet, still...

But Suyana's feeling remained a feeling only, wriggling away when she tried to grapple with it...until Parwa provided an answer.

The questioning at an end, Luciana had left. Suyana stroked the girl's brow. "Rest. Grow strong. My guards will bring you food and water." She rose to leave. Luciana wished to discuss how to proceed, how to recover the Chakana.

"I should be dead," the girl said, her words barely a whisper.

Suyana turned back. Parwa was crying. "I should have died with my Sisters."

Suyana sat again, taking her hand. "Do not say that. Your escape is a blessing. To me, to your Sisters."

"I failed you. I failed my Sisters," Parwa sobbed, turning tear-filled eyes to Suyana. "Madre...I don't want to live."

A chill took Suyana. Dropping Parwa's hand, she stood again. "Do not speak so. Your life is a gift. Treat it as such." She walked to the spiraling staircase. "Rest. Once you regain your strength, you may join your Sisters in the fields." With that, she left Parwa for her meeting with Luciana.

The next morning, two Sisters tending crops found Parwa's sword and scabbard. Under the sword lay a note written on a square of leather: *I cannot live with the guilt of living. Forgive me.*

They found these things at the edge of the fields, a step from the Nothing.

Suyana blamed herself for focusing on the Chakana and not Parwa, for not believing the girl's death wish. But Parwa was gone, and nothing Suyana might do would return her from the Void. The Chakana was gone, too, but that loss might be undone.

No. It *must* be undone.

She spent hours closeted with Luciana, searching for a way to retrieve the Chakana. Their only hope, they decided, was to detect the Key should it emerge from behind whatever hid it.

This solution, however, brought another problem. Like the Madres, the Sisters of the Key had been attuned to the Chakana, able to detect it from great distances and leap to its vicinity.

But the Sisters of the Key were dead. That left Luciana, Suyana, and their Siguientes, as the only Sisters with that ability. To sit with single focus searching the astral planes for the silver light of the Chakana required unwavering concentration. Even the youthful Siguientes could sustain such attention for only brief periods, and youth lay far in the past for both Luciana and Suyana.

Best, they agreed, to have many Sisters sitting shifts day and night, leaving no moment unattended. For that, they must discover who, if any, possessed the required sensitivity to the Chakana.

As the eldest Madre, Luciana was most attuned to the Key—and to that affinity in others. One by one, each Sister went to the Hatun Yura of Luciana to sit silently while the Madre searched their mind for the precious spark.

Luciana found eight. These, together with the Madres and Siguientes, provided a dozen of *los en Sintonía*—the Attuned. Throughout the day, each of the twelve sat two separate one-hour sessions. In this way, they searched the entire day without exhausting any single watcher.

Each watcher sat in the *Tumay Aranwa*—the great amphitheater at the Forest's heart. They sat cross-legged with eyes closed in warrior dress on the Chakana-shaped stage, the bowl of the amphitheater amplifying any astral signal. Another Sister attended them, ready to fetch the Madres should the watcher succeed. For if the watcher detected the Key, they were to leap to it immediately.

They had searched in this manner for a week when a cry from the forest floor reached where Suyana and Luciana talked in the older Madre's chambers.

"Madres, Madres!" a Sister called.

Suyana walked to the edge of Luciana's platform. The Sister in the clearing below was young, so young. Had Suyana ever been that young? "What is it, child?"

"Yanta has found the Key! She has leaped."

Suyana and Luciana hurried to the amphitheater, arriving as a masked Sister appeared on the stage, stepping from a glowing portal. Ripping off her mask, Yanta jumped from the stage and ran up the steps to meet them. With a sinking heart, Suyana saw that her Siguiente held only her mask.

"Madres," Yanta cried, "I found the Chakana. I sensed it behind a locked door. But an armed woman shot at me before I could break through to retrieve it. She was but one person. If we return now with many warriors, we can overpower her and gain the Key."

Not before more of our Sisters are shot, Suyana thought, even as Luciana sent for a dozen armed Sisters.

But when Yanta stood with the warriors, swords drawn and ready to leap, she could no longer sense the Chakana. "I have lost it!" she wailed. "My Madres, I have failed you."

"It will show itself again," Luciana said, though Suyana read the disappointment in her face. "We will continue to watch."

Case waited while Suyana took a sip of water. The Madre set the cup down, then eyed them all. "Do you know of this event? Do you know this woman?"

Will hesitated. "Her name is Adrienne Archambeault. We call her Adi. She's my guardian. No, not that kind. She raised me after my parents...disappeared."

"She became like a mother to you?"

"Yeah, I guess."

Case shot Rani a look, remembering the reporter's theory about Adi's past. *She became like a mother to you.* Or had Adi been his mother all along?

Will continued. "Adi said that happened in a hotel in Columbia. Earlier that day, Alvarez had taken money from my parents for the Chakana, but then tried to keep it. Adi stopped him. She and my parents were traveling home the next day with the Chakana in a lead box."

"To shield the Key. Luciana suspected this. Then how did Yanta sense it?"

Will sighed. "My father opened the box."

"The call of the Chakana is strong." Suyana considered Will. "I have wondered about this incident. This Adi could have killed Yanta, as easily as the Beast slaughtered the Sisters of the Key. Yet, she did not. She shouted warnings. She fired her weapon twice, but again as warnings."

Yanta nodded at this, her face still grim.

"Adi's not a murderer," Will said.

Case remembered Fader's story of Adi shooting mercenaries during Morrigan's invasion of Will's tower. She remembered Rani's tale of Adi as a smuggler in Hong Kong. She guessed Will's image of Adi was very different from the reality.

"Perhaps," Suyana said. "But she is a capable warrior."

"Adi's the reason Alvarez didn't keep the Chakana," Will said.

Suyana raised an eyebrow. "A fitting point to continue my story, where we meet many familiar to you." Her eyes became distant again. "We maintained our vigil for the Chakana for another month. I began to lose hope. Then, one morning..."

Suyana sat on the lowest row of the amphitheater with Luciana, listening as Umiña, Luciana's Siguiente, stood before them telling her tale.

A Sister had summoned the Madres here, saying Umiña had leaped after the Chakana. Shortly after they'd arrived, Umiña returned through her portal, empty-handed like Yanta before her. But unlike Yanta, she brought hope.

"A man and a woman?" Luciana asked.

Umiña nodded. "And a sick child. Their son. He sleeps, not waking. They will surrender the Chakana if we heal him."

Umiña was slight, smaller than most Sisters. She was young for a Siguiente, not yet twenty, but quick-witted and fearless. Suyana, like Luciana, trusted her judgment. Most relevant, she showed the greatest sensitivity to the Chakana, which made Suyana believe her story.

"The Chakana was there?" Luciana asked.

"Yes, Madre. In a box. When they closed the box, the Key became hidden to me. But I sensed it in the child."

Suyana raised an eyebrow to Luciana. "Is this possible?"

"Never have I heard of such a thing, but who truly knows the Chakana?" Luciana turned to Umiña. "You told them to expose it again?"

"Tomorrow, Madre, at this same time."

"You have done well, my Siguiente. You may leave us now."

Once Umiña left the amphitheater, Luciana outlined her plan.

"Bring them here?" Suyana said. "Is that wise?"

"Less wise would be to lose this chance."

"Can we heal the child?"

"Perhaps. Within the Crossing, if at all. What matters is these *profanadores* believe we can. What matters is they surrender the Chakana."

The discomfort Suyana felt must have shown on her face.

"I shock you," Luciana said.

"A child, my Sister."

"We will do what we can for him, but a single life, even that of a child, cannot balance the weight of all life in all of Creation."

Suyana did not reply. A child.

"My younger Sister," Luciana said, "you forget the story of Quilla, once Madre del Orden. The damage that ill intent can accomplish with the Chakana." She sighed. "And I forget you were not with us then."

"You saved us, my elder Sister. You saved the Book. The Story."

"Our Madres of the time saved us with their great sacrifice. I was but a weapon they wielded." Luciana looked at her. "I prefer we be agreed on this."

A single life cannot balance the weight of all life. Suyana nodded. "We are agreed."

The next day, Suyana remained at the Threshold while Luciana traveled with Umiña and forty warriors to the Temple of the Key. Luciana wished to avoid having both surviving Madres together until they ensured these newcomers were not a threat. Later that night, as the twilight bell sounded, Luciana and her party returned with four strangers. Suyana and Yanta met them at the path into the trees.

To guard the secrets of their journey, Luciana had blindfolded the visitors, removing the coverings only after passing through the Second Veil. This included the unconscious child, carried in a litter by two Sisters.

Though they had now traveled the length of the Threshold, the newcomers still gaped in wide-eyed wonder. Luciana introduced them to Suyana and Yanta.

The boy's father was Jon Dreycott, a white man of average height, handsome in his way. Angular features. Mustache and bearded chin. Blond hair combed straight back from a high forehead. He carried a worn leather satchel over one shoulder.

The mother, Terri Yurikami, was the dark to her husband's fair. Japanese, Suyana assumed, by her name. Black eyes and long hair to match, with a quick smile. Suyana found her beautiful.

The other woman was Doctor Elenora Cootes, the child's physician. She was taller than Terri, dark-skinned with tight curly hair cropped close to her head. Her face was longer with a more pointed chin. She went by Ellie, and Suyana found her beautiful as well.

The boy, Will, was dark-haired like his mother, but paler, perhaps a symptom of his condition. Suyana couldn't decide which parent he resembled. He lay unmoving on the litter.

She sensed the piece of the Chakana in the boy, but she could not sense the Key itself. She raised an eyebrow to Luciana.

The older Madre smiled. "I wished to share this moment with you." She faced Jon Dreycott. "I have brought you to the Threshold of the Crossing. I have kept my promise. Now, you must keep yours."

Hesitating, Dreycott looked at his wife. She nodded, stroking the boy's forehead where he lay. With a sigh, Dreycott withdrew a gray metal cube, a hand's breadth across, from the satchel. He opened the box.

And Suyana felt the Chakana. Felt it reach out to her. Felt herself reaching back, becoming *whole* again. She realized she was crying. Luciana's cheeks were wet, too, as she lifted the Chakana from the box and held it out to her. Suyana shook her head. "No, Sister. It should be you."

Luciana bowed, then slipped the leather cord around her neck. The Chakana glowed warm and hypnotizing where it rested against her chest.

Dreycott's voice broke the spell. "We didn't know. We didn't know what he'd done." He swallowed. "Chico Alvarez. What he'd done to...acquire this."

Suyana's sharp retort died in her throat as the boy named Will stirred on the litter. He sat up. With a cry of joy, Terri threw her arms around him. He hugged her back, but as she released him, his head swung toward Luciana. A chill seized Suyana as his eyes locked on the Chakana. He looked up at Luciana. "I know you."

The Madre smiled. "And I you. I am Luciana, Will."

"Have we met?"

"Yes."

"I don't remember."

"A part of you does. The part of this..." She touched the Chakana. "...you carry inside."

To Suyana's surprise, Will nodded. "It woke me up. I think."

Luciana smiled again. "It knows it is home. And soon we will reunite that part with the Chakana itself...and heal you both."

"How?" Will asked.

"We must enter the Crossing and journey through it to the Book. Only within the Book can you—and the Chakana—be healed."

"When?" Terri asked.

"Tomorrow."

"But—"

"I am an old woman, and our journey has been tiring. The passage through the Crossing will be more so. And your son regained consciousness only moments ago. We must rest tonight, your son especially. Come. We will eat together, and then my Siguiente will show you to your quarters." Turning, Luciana led them into the Forest and to her Hatun Yura.

There, they shared a meal during which Jon Dreycott and Terri Yurikami told of their decades-long search for what they called the Akashic Records.

Suyana shook her head as she listened. *A fable, but one that grew over the eons from a seed of truth. And somehow, these two followed a trail of crumbs to that truth.*

To here. To us.

Will waited with Case, Fader, and Rani for Suyana to continue her story. But the Madre fell silent, staring at the candles flickering in center of the circle where the travelers sat listening.

Finally, Will spoke. "But then what happened? Did we go into the Crossing the next day?"

Suyana looked up, startled. She sighed. "Yes, but not as planned."

"What do you mean?"

A bitter smile twisted her face. "First, I had to pay for my terrible mistake."

"I don't understand."

"After our meal, we settled down for the night. We were awakened the next morning." She paused. "But not by the dawn bell."

Will hesitated, afraid to ask. "Then by what?"

Suyana locked eyes with him. "By the sound of gunfire."

Chapter 38

Want What You Got

The glowing disk of Azki was just peeking from the Second Veil to tint the land when Suyana waited with Luciana, Yanta, Umiña, and the four newcomers at the forest's edge. Together they watched the approaching party, still ten minutes away. But even at this distance, Suyana could count at least twenty men. Men with long guns leading a group of Sisters, both warriors and field workers, their hands bound behind them.

Beside the Madres stood a frightened Sister, sent ahead by the intruders, by a man 'with a face like a hawk.' The man had warned he would kill the prisoners if anyone attacked or resisted.

"Oh, god. It's Alvarez," Dreycott said as the group drew nearer. Beside him, his wife wrapped her arms around their son and pulled him close.

Suyana had already guessed who this man was. She spun to face Jon Dreycott. "You did this. You led the Beast to us." She stepped toward him.

He waved his hands before him, shaking his head. "No. No, I swear we had nothing to do with this."

Luciana put a hand on her arm, restraining her. "We came through a portal. We were not followed here. Some other evil is at work. What matters is we have little time. Yanta, gather our best fighters. Archers, swordswomen."

"Yes, Madre," Yanta said, fire in her eyes. "We will fall on the Beast and his men—"

"And die as our Sisters of the Key died," Luciana replied. "Yes, the Sisters will follow you into battle, but now is not the time to fight. We must be patient. Lull them until the moment comes. Conceal yourselves deep in the forest. Watch unseen. And wait."

The Siguiente turned pleading eyes to Suyana. Hiding and patience was not Yanta's way. "Madre, my place is by your side..."

"Your place," Suyana said, "is where your Madres say it is. Do as you are told."

Yanta reddened and bowed her head. "Yes, Madre." She hesitated. "But we must guard the Chakana. Let me take it with us."

"No," Luciana said. "They will kill our Sisters, one by one, until we surrender it. It cannot be protected from those who come. Now go." As the Siguiente turned to leave, Luciana added, "And Yanta, take no more than twenty. Greater numbers may be missed."

Yanta nodded and left.

Suyana frowned at Luciana. "You think the Beast knows our numbers?"

"He has twice shown knowledge he should not have. Once, stealing the Chakana, and now, finding this place. I fear he knows much about us."

"But how?" She shot another dark look at Dreycott.

Luciana fixed her eyes on the approaching party. "We will have that answer soon."

When the intruders were twenty paces away, they stopped. Gunmen forced the captured Sisters to kneel, rifles pointed at their heads. Other gunmen scanned the fields on either side and the road behind them, weapons ready, alert to any attack.

Two of the invaders walked toward where Luciana, Suyana, Umiña, and their guests waited. Both wore jungle camouflage. The taller of the two was bare-headed and mustached, with sharp black eyes split by a hawk nose.

The Beast. Chico Alvarez. The man who had slaughtered the Sisters of the Key.

To her shock, the one with him was a woman, her face shaded by a broad-brimmed hat. The Beast and the woman stopped three paces away. She removed her hat—and Suyana had a greater shock.

"As you can see, Madre," Parwa said in Spanish, smiling at Suyana, "I took your advice and decided to live."

⚜

"Wait," Will interrupted, "wouldn't Parwa have been seen *after* faking her death?"

"Masked and dressed again in her uniform, she would have appeared as any warrior," Suyana said.

"But how'd she return up the River?" Will asked.

"We were using the *hatun wampu*—the great boats of the Madres—to bring our slain Sisters here for proper burial in the Nothing. Parwa could have joined such a team."

Will suppressed a shudder, imagining Parwa hiding among those she'd betrayed as they traveled to retrieve the Sisters she'd help murder.

"What about that rock wall with the buttons?" Rani said.

"The Wall of Judgment opens easily from this side."

"The tunnels?" Will asked.

Case answered. "They're a maze only from the Temple of the Key. Going back, she'd face only one tunnel at each branching point."

Will thought about that. "Right. But how'd she lead Alvarez back through that maze?"

Suyana sighed. "I suspect she recorded the correct tunnels as she returned to the Temple of the Key, writing them on a piece of leather. Difficult to do while with others, but if she held back until she was alone..."

"And your Wall of Judgment?"

"When we discovered Parwa alive after Alvarez slaughtered her Sisters, we carried her here on a litter. Unconscious, we thought. At the Wall, my guards always turn away as I press the buttons. If Parwa was only pretending to sleep..." She sighed. "She could have peeked."

So simple, he thought. "What happened next?"

Still in shock, Suyana listened as Alvarez, speaking in English, introduced himself. After promising to kill anyone who resisted, he spread his hands and smiled. *Like a grin on a lizard*, she thought. "Cooperate, no one gets hurt, and we will soon be gone."

He frowned at Ellie Cootes, then settled on Jon Dreycott and Terri Yurikami. He laughed. "My friends, I am so happy to find you here. So dependable."

Suyana spun on Dreycott. "You *did* lie to us! You led him here."

"No! We didn't," Jon insisted, shaking his head, confusion on his face. "I swear."

Ignoring them, Alvarez spoke to Parwa. "Well? Did they bring it? Is it here?"

Approaching Luciana, Parwa held out a hand. Luciana stared at her, then produced the Chakana from under her furred jacket.

Of course, Suyana thought. As a Sister of the Key, Parwa could sense the Chakana.

Parwa slipped the cord of the Chakana over her head, then returned to Alvarez's side. Suyana was surprised he let her claim the Key. What had she told him about it?

Parwa scanned the party. "Madre Suyana, where is your Siguiente? Where is Yanta?"

"Dead," Luciana said before Suyana could form her own lie. "By your betrayal. Murdered with the Sisters of the Key."

Parwa ignored that. Did this woman feel no guilt? "Yanta served Suyana, a Madre of the Crossing. Why was she with the Sisters of the Key?"

"Sent by us that dark day," Luciana replied, "with a message for the Madres of the Key."

Suyana tried to remember who Parwa had seen after Suyana brought her here to heal. Luciana...Umiña...Suyana's guards...

But not Yanta. Yanta had volunteered for the grisly task of transporting her dead Sisters and so had not been at the Crossing. Is that why Luciana had sent Yanta and not her own Siguiente to hide in the forest with her selected warriors? Not for the first time, Suyana marveled at the quickness of the older

Madre's mind.

Luciana's answer seemed to satisfy Parwa. She nodded to Alvarez.

"We need a base here," he said.

Parwa pointed to where the Hatun Yura of Suyana loomed. "There. It gives a view of the surroundings and is stocked with food and water. After we empty it of warriors, we could defend it for days."

Alvarez nodded, and Suyana realized this man, though in charge, was reliant on Parwa's advice in his current strange surroundings.

Parwa led them first to Luciana's tree, where the Madre called the Sisters there to surrender. Those were taken with Umiña and the other captured women to the floor of the amphitheater, where Alvarez left twelve gunmen, positioned around the top, to guard them.

Parwa then took the party to Suyana's Hatun Yura. The Sisters there joined the other prisoners in the amphitheater. Alvarez left four gunmen below to guard access to the Great Tree. Parwa led Alvarez, four remaining gunmen, the two Madres, and the Dreycott party up to the living quarters of Suyana.

There, Alvarez made the prisoners sit in the middle of the floor, with a gunman on each side of the platform watching the ground below.

Satisfied with his preparations, Alvarez sat with Parwa facing their captives. Grinning, Alvarez wagged a finger at Jon and Terri. "You two. You caused me so much trouble, stealing the Key from me—"

"You have that backwards, don't you, Chico?" Terri said.

"You all are thieves!" Suyana snarled. "The Chakana is our sacred trust—"

Parwa laughed. "A trust you have betrayed, Madre."

"You dare speak of betrayal?" Suyana demanded.

"Calm yourself, Sister," Luciana whispered in Quechuan, a language foreign to Parwa and likely to Alvarez. "Listen. Learn."

"Shut up!" Alvarez snapped. "All of you. Open your mouth, and I shove my fist in it."

As they fell silent under his glare, he continued. "Losing the Key, it forced me to change plans. My new friend here..." He smiled at Parwa, her face unreadable. "...had learned the route to this..." He waved a hand. "...this place."

Suyana burned with shame. She had done that. Brought Parwa here. Shown her the way.

Alvarez continued. "But Parwa, she says coming here without the Key is no good." He grinned at Jon and Terri. "Fortunately, a mutual acquaintance helped me. Same guy who pointed me to the Key." His grin broadened. "Pablo Landos."

Will's parents exchanged horrified looks. "No," Jon said. "He's a friend. We've known him for years."

Alvarez laughed. "But not too good, I think. Pablo? He likes to bet the horses. And football. And..." He chuckled. "Well, he bets on anything. Problem is, he's not very good. He owed me a lot of money. Money he doesn't have when I come to collect. But he has this story..."

Suyana listened to how Jon Dreycott had asked this Pablo to trace rumors of girls recruited for a secret Sisterhood. Of how that search pointed to the location of the Chakana. Information Pablo gave to Alvarez.

We drew a target on ourselves without even knowing.

"Pablo," Alvarez continued, "he doesn't know *what* you are after, but he promises it's *big*!" He chuckled. "He'd say that, because he owes *me* big. But I know you two. Always finding valuable shit. And Pablo says you been chasing this for *years*."

Suyana shot Jon and Terri a dark look. Their obsession for something they never understood had caused this.

Alvarez shrugged. "I decide it's worth checking out. Pablo has names. People in these villages who knew of this..." He waved a hand at Suyana and Luciana. "...Sisterhood. I send men to talk to them. I think, 'Chico, these people, they give up their daughters. They'll know where those daughters are.'"

Alvarez was warming to his story now, obviously pleased with his own cleverness. Suyana suddenly knew where his tale was going.

He shook his head. "But nobody talks, even when my men become...persuasive. Never see their daughters, they say. Got no idea where they are, they say." He chuckled. "Until we find this mother. In hospital. Dying. Cancer, or some shit. One of my guys, he tells the nurses he's her son. She's pretty drugged up, but when awake, she likes to talk. Tells him her daughter visits her." He hooks a thumb at Parwa.

"Do you remember, Madre?" Parwa asked. "Letting me go home?"

Suyana did not reply, her guilt growing as her unknown role in this grew.

Alvarez chuckled. "My guy hangs around, brings me Parwa when she shows up. I figure she'll need..." He shrugs. "...convincing. But she is very angry with you ladies. Tells me lots of shit. Where to find the Key. How many men I'll need." He jabbed a finger at Jon and Terri. "That's why I needed your money—to hire more men. But you were not supposed to *take* the Key."

"But how did you know we had come *here*?" Jon said, apparently forgetting Alvarez's demand for silence. "And with the Key?"

Alvarez grinned. "After you steal the Chakana from me, Parwa—she's with me now—she says if I lure you back to Peru, you'll bring the Key." He chuckled at Luciana and Suyana. "You think Parwa's dead, right?"

Again, Suyana felt the guilt of her mistake. Trusting Parwa. Believing her faked death.

Alvarez continued. "I tell Pablo to give you that list of villages he found, figuring you'd come back." His grin broadened. "And it worked! A month ago, he calls. Says he's organizing another expedition for you, starting from Arequipa."

"I get my men together. Wait for Pablo to tell me when you're coming, so I can meet you at the airport, grab the Chakana. Then, two days ago, Parwa says she feels the Key." He shrugs. "Don't know how she does that shit, but she wants to take some men and...jump or whatever to get it. By the time we're ready, she can't feel it anymore."

Suyana exchanged a glance with Luciana. Two days ago—when Umiña sensed the Key and first met Jon, Terri, and Will. She'd said Dreycott closed the box when she appeared.

Alvarez continues. "The next day, Pablo calls, all in a panic. Says you canceled the expedition because..." He leaned forward. "...you were getting here *by other means*."

Suyana frowned. That must have been after Luciana promised to bring the boy and his parents here through the portal.

Alvarez continued. "Parwa, she figures it out. Guesses the Madres made some deal with you to get the Key back. Don't know what the deal was. And I don't care." He beamed at them. "But that is why I was so glad to find you here. If *you* are here, I knew *this* would be, too." He tapped the Chakana where it hung against Parwa's chest.

Suyana noticed Parwa flinch. *Not the best friends this man makes out.*

"But why do you want it?" Dreycott asked. "You could never understand the Akashic Records."

Alvarez glared at him. "I told you to shut up." He shot Parwa a look. "What are these...Ashkick records?"

Parwa waved a hand, as if dismissing the idea. "Ancient stone tablets, sacred to the Sisters. Worthless to us."

Suyana straightened. *She lied to this man. What is her game?*

"You did not answer me before, Madre Suyana," Parwa said. "Do you remember my dying mother?"

"I remember letting you return home to visit her. Few are granted such trust. And this is how you repay us?"

"You want my gratitude?" Parwa snarled. "Gratitude for letting me watch my mother die? Die slowly? In agony? When you had a cure and would not share it? Well, now I will take what you would not give."

Beside Suyana, Luciana closed her eyes and shook her head. Understanding dawned on Suyana. "*That* is why you are here. You've come for the Breath."

"Wait," Will said from where he sat with Case, Fader, and Rani on Suyana's platform. "What's...the Breath?"

Suyana's eyes narrowed. "Your parents knew nothing of it either, despite their obsession with the Book. You claim ignorance as well?"

Will was tired of being called a liar. But remembering their situation as prisoners, he calmed his anger. "I claim ignorance about the Breath, the Crossing, and everything that happened here eight years ago. I still remember nothing. I don't even understand what the Chakana is—and I'm carrying part of it."

Suyana regarded him for several heartbeats before speaking. "I believe you." She ran her eyes over them. "The Breath is what humans have sought since our existence began. It is a shield against death."

"Holy shit," Rani whispered.

"You mean...*immortality?*" Case said.

"No. But a very long life. Five, six hundred years or more. You say this Nyx spoke of the Four Who Are One? Of the...relationship they form with our Madres?"

Will and the others nodded.

"When a Madre dies, a Siguiente takes her place within the Book, merging with that Madre's aspect—Bondad, Mal, Caos, or Orden. This new Madre becomes a new *being.*" Suyana interlaced her fingers. "A mixture of that aspect of the Four *and* the human Siguiente. Both her human self *and* her aspect of the Four. Something of each, but different from either. Your language has a word for this, but it escapes me."

"Symbiotic?" Rani offered. "Two organisms co-existing in a mutually beneficial relationship?"

"Yes, that is the word," Suyana said. "But that new creature includes the *mortal* body of the Madre. The Four are immortal. We are not. And a new Madre requires an...adjustment period." Her eyes took on a distant look. "When I first became the Madre de Bondad, I was overwhelmed by this entity in my mind. By its power. By the knowledge in the Book. The vastness of our universe. Of all the universes..." Her words trailed off, and she gazed into the flickering candles.

Will cleared his throat.

She looked up. "Forgive me. As I had to adjust to the Bondad aspect, so it had to adjust to me. It had to understand my beliefs...and prejudices...about 'goodness' before we could truly become one. It would point to something in the Book and say, 'Is this *good?*' And I would reply 'yes' or 'no.' Or, more often, 'it depends.' We had long discussions. The Four prefer to minimize the need for such adjustment periods."

"They don't like switching Madres too often," Will said.

"They want you to live longer," Case added.

"Yes," Suyana said. "For that reason, the One Who is Four long ago provided us with the Breath of the Three."

"I'm numbered out," Rani said. "One, four, three. Who are the Three?"

Suyana raised an eyebrow. "Can you not guess? You of all people?"

"The Guardians!" Fader cried.

"Yes. The Breath can be created only with the..." She hesitated. "...the *involvement* of the Guardians. More you need not know."

"So *that* was what Parwa wanted?" Case asked.

"The Breath was the prize she dangled before Alvarez. I suspect Parwa desired the Breath, too—but also much more. I believe she sought what we had denied her—to become a Madre. To read the Story."

"Why did you deny her?" Will asked.

"When new Sisters join us, the Madres lead them through the Crossing. An initiation, yes, but something more. Inside the Book, the Four...*test* each new Sister's affinity to the Story."

"Affinity?" Case asked.

"Whether their mind can grasp the *vastness* of the Story, the enormity of not only all creation across all universes, but of all possible futures that could come to pass. The Four decide whether a Sister can embrace that—and stay sane. Those found suitable may one day become Madres."

"I'm guessing Parwa blew her interview," Rani said.

Suyana frowned.

"She wasn't found suitable," Will said.

"No, and she was not pleased. But I came to believe she had accepted the judgment." She sighed. "Looking back, the signs were plain to see—if I had not been blind."

"What happened next?" Case asked.

"We agreed to take Parwa and Alvarez into the Crossing." Suyana searched their faces. "Are you surprised? Did you expect us to resist?"

Will thought of Alvarez's slaughter of the Sisters of the Key. Of the Sisters caged in the amphitheater, surrounded by gunmen. He remembered Adi's tale of taking the Chakana from the man at gunpoint. "No. It was Alvarez."

Suyana nodded. "And now, I will tell what little remains to tell."

Chapter 39

I'll Believe in You (or I'll Be Leaving You Tonight)

Suyana sat listening with the other prisoners in her Hatun Yura as Parwa and Alvarez discussed who would enter the Crossing.

"We need a Madre," Parwa said.

Alvarez narrowed his eyes. "Why?"

"The Guardians."

He laughed. "Your mythical spirits?"

"Within the Crossing, the Guardians are far from mythical. If our party does not include at least one Madre, the Guardians will not let us pass."

Alvarez considered the two Madres. "Which one?"

"Luciana. Suyana remains physically strong and therefore a threat." Parwa smiled at Suyana. "And I will enjoy leaving you behind, blind to the fate of your mentor."

"That's it?" Alvarez said. "Just the old woman?"

Parwa shook her head. "We need three more to be *Los Viajeros*—the Travelers—along with Luciana. If we fill those roles, we will be distracted from our purpose. And we certainly do not want to bring Sisters." She pointed to Jon, Terri, and Ellie. "These three."

Alvarez laughed. "My friends! Our journey together continues." He stood. "Let's go."

"No!" Terri Yurikami cried. "You can't do this. Our son needs us."

Alvarez shrugged. "But *I* do not need *him*."

"The boy must come," Luciana said quietly.

"Old woman," Alvarez snarled, looming over her. "You forget maybe who holds the guns?"

"The boy carries within him a piece of the Chakana," Luciana said, her voice calm. "Without him, the Chakana is not whole. Without him, the Crossing will not accept us." She looked at Parwa. "You were a Sister of the Key. Can you not sense it?"

Frowning, Parwa stared at Will where he sat between his parents. Her eyes went wide. "How can this be?"

Luciana spread her hands. "We do not know."

"What the fuck is going on?" Alvarez growled.

"She is right," Parwa said, her eyes still on Will. "The boy must come, too."

Alvarez's jaw worked as if he was chewing on the Chakana itself. "Fine. He comes," he said finally. He grinned at Jon and Terri. "Leverage over you two. You make trouble, he dies."

They left the Hatun Yura then, setting out on the forest path toward the Third Veil. It was but an hour after dawn, and Azki still hung near the Second Veil, its early rays slanting low and weak through the trees at their backs. A few paces off the path, the forest was as black as the Nothing.

Parwa led the way with four of Alvarez's gunmen. She wore a small backpack and carried a powerful electric torch to light their path. Behind her, Suyana walked beside Luciana, followed by the boy Will, his parents, and Ellie Cootes.

Suyana glanced back. Alvarez played the beam of his electric torch into the dark forest surrounding them, his face set in hard lines, his four other gunmen trailing him.

Luciana whispered in Quechuan. "First, she will free her Sisters."

Yanta. Luciana meant Yanta and her hidden warriors.

Moments later, a gunshot shattered the silence of the dawn. Ahead, Parwa and those gunmen spun around, torch and guns now pointing into the trees behind, searching. Cursing, Alvarez swept the forest with his torch, his pistol and the guns of the men beside him following the beam of light.

The shot had come from the direction of the amphitheater. Suyana waited. More shots would mean the Sisters there were dying and Yanta had failed. But no more shots came.

What came were arrows from the darkness.

The four men beside Alvarez died first, arrows buried in their chests. Some instinct saved the Beast. He dropped to a knee an eyeblink before the volley. The arrow meant for his heart caught him in a shoulder. Cursing, he stumbled backwards, pulling Ellie with him as a shield.

More arrows found the gunmen beside Parwa. Parwa leaped forward, grabbing Luciana. With an arm around the Madre's throat and a pistol to her head, Parwa cried out. "Stop! Or Luciana dies."

Suyana gasped as Alvarez threw Ellie Cootes aside and grabbed her instead, shoving his gun against her temple, pushing her head painfully to the side.

Behind them, Yanta stepped out of the darkness, a bow in her hand and hate in her eyes. Alvarez raised his pistol, aiming at the Siguiente.

"Keep your gun on Suyana, you fool," Parwa snapped.

"Who you calling a fool?" Alvarez snarled, anger and pain in his voice, the arrow still in his shoulder.

"You can't shoot them all," Parwa said.

A second later, a dozen Sisters appeared with arrows nocked in raised bows, spread through the trees on either side of Yanta. Behind them, more dim shapes moved closer. Alvarez cursed, then pushed his gun back against Suyana's temple. Yanta continued to advance, flanked by archers.

"Stop!" Parwa shouted. "Or we kill your Madres."

Yanta stopped, raising a hand to halt the others.

"We are entering the Crossing," Parwa called. "If any interfere, Luciana dies, Suyana dies. And I will pass through the Veil, taking the Chakana with me."

"Not without me, you won't, bitch," Alvarez gasped, his face twisted in pain.

"Madres, we cannot let them live," Yanta cried, fury and pain in her voice. "They killed Umiña!"

A small cry escaped Luciana, but when she spoke, her voice was strong and steady. "Do as they say, Daughter. Lower your bows."

The Sisters obeyed, Yanta the last to comply. Suyana shot Luciana a questioning look. The older Madre spoke in Quechuan. "Forces we cannot read are moving here. This must play out—and within the Crossing."

"Shut up," Parwa snapped, as she crept backward along the forest path, pulling Luciana with her still as a shield.

Alvarez did the same with Suyana. "You four," he called to Jon and the others. "You come with us now." When they hesitated, he swung his gun to Will. "Or I shoot the boy."

Jon and Terri exchanged a quick look, then clasped hands and, with Terri's arm around Will's shoulders, walked toward Parwa, Alvarez, and the two Madres.

Ellie Cootes didn't move. Terri looked back. "Ellie..."

Ellie shook her head. "I have two children. I'm going home to them."

"You go with us, bitch," Alvarez snarled, his gun now on her, "or you go home in a box."

"Do not die like this," Suyana called to Ellie. "With life, there is hope."

Ellie hesitated. Alvarez cocked his pistol. She stepped forward, joining the others.

A tense procession began. Parwa and Alvarez backing along the path, using their prisoners as shields. Yanta and her warriors pacing them, bows in hand but lowered. Walking backward, Suyana kept stumbling. Each time, Alvarez would catch her roughly, jamming the gun against her head and swearing.

A silver glow began to light the forest path. Moments later, they emerged from the trees into a wide meadow. Above them rose the shimmering curtain of the Third Veil, stretching across the land until it disappeared into the Nothing to either side and above.

Ten steps out of the forest, Parwa spoke to Alvarez. "Leave her here."

Alvarez shoved Suyana away from him, grabbing Ellie Cootes as his new shield. Parwa smiled at Suyana. "Goodbye, Madre. I will see you again soon."

"You die when next we meet, Betrayer."

Parwa laughed. "I think not." She called out. "Yanta, you and your warriors step out where I can see you."

From the cover of the trees, Yanta looked at Suyana, who nodded. The Siguiente gave a signal, then she and the archers emerged to stand in a line outside the forest.

Parwa, Alvarez, and their prisoners reached the Veil. Though Suyana had stood before the curtain of light countless times, it always filled her with awe. But now, dread colored that awe.

Still gripping Luciana's arm, Parwa reached out to touch the Veil.

Nothing happened.

Suyana straightened. Parwa carried the Chakana. The Veil should part for her. Luciana said something. A moment later, Parwa called to the boy, Will.

Of course. As Luciana had warned, without the boy and the piece of the Chakana he carried, the Crossing would not accept them. Will shot a terrified look at his pale-faced parents. His mother nodded, tight-lipped. He walked to Parwa, and together they touched the Veil. An opening appeared, like an arched doorway.

Alvarez directed the party into the opening at gunpoint, stepping through after them. Parwa gave Suyana a final smile and followed Alvarez, pulling Luciana with her.

The Veil closed behind them.

⁂

Case sat with Will, Fader, and Rani in Suyana's Hatun Yura, lost in a storm of emotions as the Madre finished her story.

I have two children. I'm going home to them.

Their mother's words. Her face felt wet, and she realized she was crying. Probably had been since she'd heard those words.

Fader's hand found hers, and she pulled her brother close, letting him sob into her shoulder. "She wanted to come home to us," he whispered.

She hugged him tighter. "Yeah, she did. She loved us. She really did love us."

"I am sorry," Suyana said, "but that was the last I ever saw of them." Her gaze settled on Will. "Until *you* appeared."

"But they could still be alive, right?" Will asked. "Inside the Crossing?"

Case swallowed. Eight years. Inside that place. Whatever that place was. "Could they...? I mean, is there food? Water?"

Suyana shook her head.

"Shit," Rani muttered, then added, "Sorry," when Case glared at her.

"What if they took the Breath?" Will asked.

"The Breath slows aging," Suyana said, "but one must still have sustenance."

"They're alive," Case said, fighting to keep her voice from breaking. "Will went in there, and he's alive."

Suyana pursed her lips. "And yet, he did not return through the Third Veil. I posted guards outside it night and day. No one returned." She leaned forward, eyes locked on Will. "So, I must ask. How did you escape the Crossing? How are you here? What happened in there eight years ago?"

Will stared at the candles flickering in the center of their circle, his eyes unfocused. "For eight years, I hoped if I found this place, if I came here again, I'd remember." He shook his head. "But I can't." He took Case's hand in his. "I'm sorry."

Case knew Suyana's story had raised the same whirl of emotions in him as in her. Hope and joy tumbling with fear and despair. She squeezed his hand, trying not to think of her mother inside the Crossing with no food or water. Of how Will had never found his parents or their mother in Dream. Which meant they never dreamed. Which meant...

"But Parwa or Alvarez never returned either, right?" Will said, bringing her back. "*Something* happened in there. Maybe they fought. Or our parents overpowered them. Took their guns."

Suyana hesitated. "Perhaps."

Case guessed what the Madre was thinking. Then why had their parents and Luciana never returned through the Veil? She shut her eyes tight to stop more tears, because she knew why.

Because they were dead.

"I think it best we retire for the night," Suyana said gently. "We have all had an emotional day. I will show you each to a *wasi ukhu*—a platform here where you may sleep." She smiled at them. "You need to be well rested for tomorrow."

Case's head snapped up at that. "Why?"

"Because, I have made my decision," Suyana said. "Tomorrow, I will lead all of you into the Crossing. There, we will heal you, Will Dreycott, heal the Chakana, and, I hope..." Her eyes swept them all. "...find the answers you seek."

"When you say 'all of you'...?" Rani said.

"The Condor has chosen you, Rani Patel," Suyana said. "I do not know why, but you must journey into the Crossing with the others."

Rani groaned. "I hate that bird."

Case and the other travelers followed Suyana, descending to lower branches in the Great Tree where Sisters had prepared platforms for each of them.

Rani claimed the first one, collapsing onto the mattress there. "Sorry, folks, but I'm beat."

"In the morning," Suyana said, "leave the contents of your pockets behind. You may bring nothing tomorrow but a waterskin. After breakfast, we will enter the Crossing."

"Oh, yay," Rani muttered.

Case smiled. Despite Rani's complaints, Case guessed nothing would keep the reporter from seeing what lay behind the last Veil.

Suyana offered the next platform to Fader. Like Rani, he fell onto the mattress. Case called goodnight to him, but his answer was a snore.

Suyana led her and Will down to where a larger platform rested across two sturdy branches. Two mattresses, pushed together, lay in its center. "Sister Isobel told me you two are lovers, and so should be together."

Shooting a glance at Will, Case had to stifle a laugh. He was blushing. "Thank you, Madre," she said. "We appreciate your kindness."

Suyana nodded, smiling. She pointed out blankets, water jugs, and other items they might need. "The weather here is always mild, with no rain, so we leave the platforms open. This also allows us to look upon the Third Veil..." She looked to where the shimmering curtain shone in the distance through gaps in the Great Tree. "...as a reminder of what we guard." She pointed to the darkness that showed through the branches above. "And upon the Nothing, as a reminder of what we guard against. And now, I will leave you till morning."

"Madre," Will said. "Thank you. For believing us, trusting us. For agreeing to help us. For...everything."

"You are welcome," Suyana said. "I am sorry for how we began, but yes, I trust you now. As Luciana trusted your parents." She shook her head. "I do not know what we will find inside the Crossing, but I too have questions to be answered." She left them.

Case flopped onto one mattress. "Just so you know, lover boy—"

"You're beat, tired, exhausted, and just want to sleep." He cuddled against her, an arm around her waist, his face in the crook of her neck, his breath tickling her skin. "Me, too. Also curious, scared, hopeful, worried. Excited about tomorrow, but dreading it, too."

"Because of what we might find in there," she whispered.

"Or what we won't."

She gazed up through the branches at the blackness above. "Will, do you believe in God?"

A pause. "Apparently I now believe God can split Themself into parts and symbiotically exist with four old ladies."

"I mean before all this."

A pause. "I was agnostic—didn't believe or disbelieve. But I always liked Adi's answer."

"Never thought of Adi as the religious type."

"Not sure she is. But whenever anyone offers their religious beliefs—usually unrequested—her standard reply is the only sensible one I've ever heard."

"Which is?"

"She'll nod politely and say, 'You may be right.'"

She laughed. "I like that."

"Right? I mean, whatever your religious beliefs, they're just that—*beliefs*, not proven facts. No matter how much you *believe*, you can't *prove* you're right. But also, no one can prove you're *wrong*, so..."

"*...you may be right.* That seems very...not Adi."

"Agreeable? Well, she usually follows it up with, 'but I doubt it.'"

She laughed again. "Now *that* sounds like Adi."

"She's right on that, too. They say there are over four thousand religions in the world, and I bet that's way low. They can't *all* be right. Maybe one of them has the 'true' answer, but..." He shrugged.

"*...but I doubt it.*" Thoughts of—and fears for—her mom returned. "I think people have religious beliefs because it scares them not having answers."

"Like, is there life after death?"

"Yeah, that one for sure. What do you think?"

"I believe there is, but mostly because I don't like the other option. Plus, you and I actually *know* a part of us exists separate from our physical bodies."

"Our astral spirits. But don't we also know they survive dying? I mean, we saw Yeshe's spirit after he died. And you saw him again when the Chakana blasted you all the way to the Realms of the Dead."

"Yeah, I did. But what if that place is just a...I don't know, a rest stop on the way?"

"On the way to what?"

"Who knows? To the Void and eternal oblivion. To back here and reincarnation. To fluffy cloud land or fire and brimstone. That's kind of the point. Nobody knows. Yeshe *believed* the Realms of the Dead represent the final plane of existence, but unless he drops us a note, all we can say is...maybe he was right." Will spooned tighter against her, pulling her close. "Enough big thoughts. Sleep time."

As his breathing slowed and his arm grew heavier on her, she thought of the words her mom had spoken eight years ago in this place.

I have two children. I'm going home to them.

Thanks, Mom, she thought as sleep came to claim her. *I choose to believe you're alive. We're here...and we're going to bring you home.*

Case awoke to angry cries and a sharp pain in her side. She jumped, blinking bleary eyes open. The strange silver light of this place slanted low through the leaves of the Hatun Yura from the direction of the Second Veil.

"Get up!" someone snarled, near and above her. Beside her, Will stirred. She looked up.

Yanta loomed over them, maskless but in full warrior gear, sword in hand. Five more warriors, these ones masked, stood with Yanta, all with blades held ready.

"What...?" Will mumbled, pushing himself to sitting, rubbing his eyes.

"I said, get up," Yanta snapped. She kicked Case in the ribs—the pain, Case guessed, that had awakened her.

Case stood, facing Yanta, ignoring the sword the woman held. "Do that again, and we'll see how good you really are in a fight."

Yanta's muscles bunched on her sword arm, then relaxed. Case wondered how much Isobel had told of how Case had fought both her and armed guards on the Black Island.

"Take them down," Yanta called to the other warriors, motioning with her sword to the staircase.

They began the descent to the clearing below, warriors in front and behind, Yanta trailing. "What's going on?" Will called back to her.

"You have been revealed for the betrayers I always knew you were," Yanta said.

"What are you talking about?" Case asked, but Yanta refused to say anything more.

They reached the clearing. There, Fader, Rani, and Isobel knelt beside each other, their hands bound in front, a half dozen armed warriors arrayed behind them. A crowd of Sisters, dressed for the fields, filled the clearing, watching the captives and whispering.

Fader looked scared. "Case?"

Warriors bound Case's and Will's hands, then forced them to their knees beside Fader. "It's going to be okay," Case lied. "This is all some mistake."

"I really wish these people would make up their minds about us," Rani muttered, but Case could tell the reporter was as frightened as Fader. And, she admitted, as she was. Her Voice remained silent, and she guessed Fader's power was still gone. If Will was right and this place was separate from the multiverse, those powers weren't returning anytime soon.

"Isobel," she called to where the Sister knelt beside Rani. "What is going on?"

"I do not know, Sister Case," she said, her face betraying the fear her voice hid. "Something has happened."

"You think?" Rani muttered.

"It's not something we did," Will said. "We slept all night, so what—"

The murmuring of the crowd suddenly died. The watching Sisters parted as Suyana appeared. She stopped before the captives. Her eyes passed over them, one by one. To Case, the Madre seemed more sad than angry.

"Madre, what is—" Will began.

"Silence!" Yanta snapped.

"Last night, Will Dreycott," Suyana said, "I said I trusted you, despite the events of eight years ago."

Case swallowed. What had happened since last night?

"But now," Suyana continued, "those events have been repeated. We are once again betrayed." Turning, she signaled to two warriors who trailed her.

The warriors pulled a hooded figure forward, a woman who had stood hidden behind them. They forced her to her knees, her hands bound before her. She wore familiar camouflage fatigues—the same as Case and the others wore. A warrior pulled off her hood. The face underneath was even more familiar.

"Adi!" Will cried.

Chapter 40

Sisters of Mercy

Will tried to struggle to his feet, but a swordswoman pushed him back down. "Adi," he called again.

Dried blood caked a gash on her forehead, and a bruise purpled a cheekbone below a puffy left eye. But otherwise, she seemed unharmed. "Oh, god, William," she said, her voice breaking. "You're alive. You're all alive."

"Yeah, well, wait a few minutes," Rani muttered.

"What happened?" Will cried. "How are you here?"

"Diego flew us here with his men. We're all okay but—"

"Men with guns," Suyana interrupted, "coming to the Temple of the Key. Do you remember, Will Dreycott, a time before when that happened?"

Will swore silently, the reason for Suyana's sudden change now clear.

"Men who slaughtered our Sisters of the Key? Who stole the Chakana?" Suyana said. "Men who then came here? To take us captive? To steal our beloved Luciana? To invade the sacred Crossing?"

"Madre," Will said, "Adi came to *find us*, not to steal. This is the woman Yanta faced." He looked at Yanta. "The woman who spared your life."

Yanta's eyes went wide. She moved closer, staring at Adi.

"Is this true?" Suyana asked Yanta.

"Madre, it has been eight years..." She bit her lip. "I do not know."

"Adi," Will cried. "Tell them what happened. In that hotel in La Paz."

"May I?" Adi asked Suyana.

Suyana hesitated. "Speak."

Adi closed her eyes, composing herself or remembering, Will didn't know. She opened them. "A woman, dressed as you are..." She nodded at Yanta. "...but masked, appeared in a hotel corridor." She gave the date and described the hallway. "You advanced on me. I told you to stop. Ignoring me, you walked to a door and touched it, saying 'I have found it.' I believe you sensed the Chakana."

Yanta's eyes went wider.

"You kicked the door. Again, I told you to stop. Again, you kicked it. I fired my pistol, breaking an overhead light. You faced me, raising your sword. I shot another light. You touched the door once more, then...disappeared, the way you people do." She sighed. "Or something like that. As you say, it's been eight years."

"Well?" Suyana asked Yanta.

"Yes, Madre," Yanta said, her eyes on Adi. "That is what happened."

Suyana walked to Will. "It doesn't matter. Eight years ago, Luciana brought you here. To help you. Men with guns followed. We lost Luciana. We lost the Chakana."

"And we lost our parents," Will said, but Adi shook her head at him.

"Now, you come again," Suyana said. "Again, we offer help. Again, outsiders with guns follow. What would you have me believe?"

"We've told the truth," Will said.

Suyana pointed to the Third Veil, shimmering in the distance. "There lies our most precious secret. What we have sworn to protect. What *I* have sworn to protect."

Will swallowed, sensing she'd reached a decision.

"I serve the Four. My duty is to heal the Chakana..."

"Never good when they mention 'duty,'" Rani muttered.

"...to restore its missing piece. The piece you carry."

"Then let's do that," Will said. "Take me into the Crossing."

"There is another way." Suyana's sad eyes locked on Will. "To heal the Chakana, we need only retrieve its missing piece. And that we can do...with your death."

Case and Fader gasped. "Are you *serious*?" Rani shouted.

"No!" Adi cried. "He's a child!"

"What about what Adi just told you?" Will said, fighting to stay calm. "She could've killed Yanta." To his surprise, Yanta was nodding.

"This woman," Suyana said, "helped your parents steal the Chakana from the Beast who stole it from us. Now, she comes with armed men. How is she—or you—any different from Alvarez?"

"We don't kill people," Will said, fighting to keep his voice level.

"I do not know that. You entered the Crossing with Luciana. She did not return. No one did—except you."

Will could find no other reason to give, except to beg for his life. He looked at Case, not even sure her Voice could help.

She shook her head. "Fader?" she asked.

"I still can't feel the In Between," he whispered, his voice quavering. "I can't even fade here."

"The Guardians?" Will asked.

"I've been trying," Rani said. "First time I *want* to see that damn bird, and it won't come."

Will blinked. Had the silver light in this place taken on a bluish tinge?

"I am sorry, Will Dreycott," Suyana said. "What we protect is all of creation. All lives everywhere. One life cannot balance—"

The gathered Sisters suddenly cried out, a mix of fear and awe as blue light bathed the clearing. Suyana's eyes went wide, staring over Will's head.

Behind him, someone spoke. "Perhaps, *I* could add my thoughts?"

Will knew that voice. He twisted around, hope returning.

Ten paces away, full-bodied and glowing, Nyx floated above the heads of the watching crowd. She winked at Will. "Miss me?"

Throughout the clearing, Sisters backed away from the floating figure. Or fell to their knees. Even Adi, who'd never been able to see Nyx before, stared open-mouthed.

Nyx floated past the prisoners to hover before Suyana. Standing her ground, Suyana drew herself up as she faced Nyx. "Who are you?"

"You know me, Suyana, Madre de Bondad," Nyx said, her voice echoing as if it came from everywhere. "I am the Chakana, Light of the Four Who are One, Keeper of the Guardians of the Crossing, Key to the Book of All. And *I* say you cannot harm these children."

"Normally, wouldn't love the 'children' bit," Rani whispered, "but I'm good."

"They mean you no harm," Nyx said. "They mean the Four and the Book and the Story no harm. Far from it." She pointed a glowing arm at Will. "Eight years ago, this boy was chosen." She indicated Case, Fader, and Rani with a wave. "And the Guardians have chosen these three."

Suyana frowned. "Why? Why were they chosen?"

Nyx looked pained. "Uh...okay, so here, we might have a *teensy* problem." She spread her hands. "I don't know."

"Nyx!" Will cried.

"We're going to die," Rani groaned.

Nyx hurried on. "I mean, I *know.* I just can't...you know...*remember.* Right now. At this moment. Currently. But I'm *sure* once we're inside the Crossing, it'll *all* come back to me. And I *do* know we need to enter the Crossing."

"You are a trick," Suyana shouted, slashing a hand at Nyx as if to chase her away. "The Chakana is not some...blue wraith. Some purple-haired floating phantom."

"Ouch," Nyx said. "That wounds. Okay, how about this?" Two silver cords sprouted from her chest. One snaked its way to Will, the other to the leather pouch on Suyana's hip.

Suyana's gasp was audible across the clearing. Her hand flew to the pouch as if to reassure herself the Chakana was still inside.

"Or maybe, this?" Nyx said, looking up.

From above came the beat of powerful wings. A great condor settled onto the lowest branch of the Hatun Yura. From the forest path leading to the Third Veil, a growl arose as a giant tawny puma stalked from the trees, a huge green snake slithering beside it.

The Sisters, Suyana included, backed away as the Puma and Snake stopped before Case and Fader. A second later, the Condor landed before Rani. Although the Guardians again emitted a faint glow, they were no longer translucent and seemed more...substantial.

Nyx smiled at Suyana. "So...we good?"

Will waited, every muscle tensed, as the Madre stared wide-eyed at the Guardians while the gathered crowd held its collective breath.

Then Suyana bowed to the spirits. As each returned the gesture in its own manner, the tension drained from Will. Leaping into the air, the Condor disappeared over the trees toward the Third Veil. The Puma vanished into the forest in the same direction, the Snake following.

The awe-struck Sisters all started talking at once, the babble growing until a shouted command came from Suyana. "Return to your duties," she called as they quieted, "while I apologize to our guests."

The guards cut the prisoners' bonds. As Will rose, Adi rushed to him, pulling him into a hug. "I was so afraid I'd lost you," she whispered.

He hugged her back, welcoming this uncharacteristic affection from her. Adi broke it off. She turned to Case, hesitated, then opened her arms. Case accepted the hug with a surprised smile. Fader hugged Adi, too.

Rani crossed her arms. "Yeah. No. It's okay. I'm fine."

"Diego flew you here?" Will asked Adi.

"Yes. We landed as close to the red dot as possible. I expect the noise alerted the Sisters. They captured us soon after. Stuck hoods on us and marched us for half an hour. We ended up locked in a cell in a huge underground cavern."

"The Temple of the Key. We were in that cell ourselves. Who's with you?"

"Stone, Mei, Diego and eight of his men. They're still locked up. I said I was the leader, which is why the Sisters brought me here."

Fader started to ask Adi something, but she was looking around wide-eyed. At the Great Tree looming over them. At the silver ribbon above with the sun disk shining against the black of the Nothing. At the glimmering curtain of the Third Veil. "Where *are* we?"

Will realized she was seeing this place for the first time. "Where Luciana brought me, my parents, and Ellie Cootes eight years ago." He nodded at the Third Veil. "And behind that...is the Crossing."

Adi's eyebrows shot up. "Where Luciana said you would be healed?"

"Yeah."

"Then why weren't you? What happened eight years ago? What happened to your parents?"

He hesitated. If he told Adi about the party disappearing into the Crossing with Alvarez, she'd try to stop him from repeating that trip.

By now, the clearing had emptied of Sisters, including Yanta, leaving only the four travelers, Isobel, Adi, Suyana, her guards...and Nyx.

Nyx floated over.

"And where have you been?" Will said, his tone accusing but happy to delay answering Adi.

"Uh, you're welcome," Nyx replied.

"You've been a no-show since the plane trip. We could've used your help so many times. At the monastery. When we got captured by the Sisters. Finding this place."

Suyana followed this exchange with a look of confused horror.

Nyx waved a hand. "Oh, don't worry. He always treats me like this. Kind of our thing." She turned to Will. "The Guardians helped you at the monastery. And with Yanta and the Sisters. And once the Chakana arrived here, I couldn't stay apart from it anymore. Not this close to the Crossing. I had to go with it. To be one with the Key again." She frowned. "To be one with *me*? Or as much as I can be one, what with the piece of *me* still stuck in *you*."

As Will listened to Nyx, a sudden realization chilled him. The Guardians had saved them, yet again. Another lucky rescue? Or another move by an invisible hand on an unseen board? He fought to keep the fear from his voice. "Okay. Sorry. And now?"

"Now, I've restored my...balance. Between you and the Chakana. But that might change unless we enter the Crossing soon." Nyx eyed Suyana. "Which we're doing, right?"

Suyana hesitated, still staring at Nyx, then nodded. "Yes. I will keep my promise. Will Dreycott, you will journey into the Crossing again."

"*Again?*" Adi said. "William, I repeat, what happened here eight years ago?"

He sighed, rubbing his face. "You were right about Pablo helping Alvarez..." He summarized Suyana's story, ending with the lost expedition party vanishing into the Crossing.

"That's it?" Adi asked. "You still don't remember what happened in there?"

Will shook his head.

"And no one has ever returned?" Adi said, addressing Suyana, her voice rising. "Yet, you want to take him in there, *again?*"

"Adi, don't," Will said, preparing for a fight, the same one he'd fought with her for eight years—his search for answers battling her desire to keep him safe. As he struggled to find the words to convince her, Nyx found them for him.

"Adi," Nyx said, floating between them, "Will is dying."

Adi's face fell, her lips a tight line, as Nyx explained how the Chakana piece inside Will was growing stronger, while he grew weaker.

"If it isn't removed soon..." Nyx spread her hands.

"Which is why we *must* enter the Crossing," Suyana said.

Adi's eyes flitted to Will, then back to Suyana. "Then let's go. Now."

"We are going," Suyana said. "But *you* will remain here as our guest. Those who accompanied you will remain at the Temple of the Key, also as our guests."

"Can we leave?" Adi said.

"No."

"Then we're prisoners, not guests."

"Call yourself what you wish. You will be fed and not mistreated. But you have found the Temple of the Key, and I must decide how to deal with that."

"When will that be?" Adi asked.

"When we return."

Adi shot Will a look, and he guessed they shared the same thought. And fear. What if they never came back? But Adi turned to Suyana. "Very well. I will wait till then."

"Unfortunately, I can't," Nyx said to Will. "Wait, that is. I can't stay separated from the Chakana if we're entering the Crossing. But don't worry. This isn't goodbye. I hope."

"You *hope*?" Will said as Nyx floated over to Suyana.

"Chakana?" Suyana said.

"Yes?"

"Why...why are you blue? With purple hair? And a woman?"

Nyx shrugged. "Why not?" With that, she dissolved into a blue mist that was sucked into Suyana's pouch that held the Chakana.

Yanta reappeared, running to Suyana to whisper in the Madre's ear. Suyana nodded, then addressed them all. "We go to the Crossing now. But on our way, we must visit another...guest of the Sisterhood."

Suyana led them to the amphitheater in the forest's center. Ten masked archers circled the top, intent on a familiar red-haired figure standing rigid and unmoving on the stage below.

"Bloody hell," Adi said.

"We saw her arrive in the Temple of the Key," Will said. "You'll never guess how she got there."

"Giant bat?"

"Uh..."

"The thing flew her from the monastery."

Suspicion mixed with surprise on Suyana's face. "You know this woman?"

"Oh, yeah," Will said. "Her name's Morrigan."

"She is a friend?"

"No!" Will and Case cried together. Fader pursed his lips, but said nothing.

Suyana frowned. "And yet, she arrived shortly after you." She nodded at Adi. "And just before you."

"She attacked us in the place we escaped from," Will said. "Before we jumped here."

Suyana's frown remained. "Why?"

"She was after the Chakana. Well, her and..." Will hesitated, remembering the astral entity he'd battled before leaping through the portal. The same entity that had controlled Gabriel Herrada and commanded the gunmen in the monastery. Had it controlled Morrigan, too? She'd met the same fate as Herrada—banished to the Gray Lands.

So, who *was* that entity? All he remembered was a sense of incredible astral power, immense age, a female identity...

No. Now was not the time. Whoever—or *what*ever—it had been, he'd escaped them. The Chakana was safe, but he was not. He had to get into the Crossing.

"...her and someone else," he finished.

Suyana seemed about to ask more, but Case interrupted. "Morrigan's not a good person. She's dangerous. Why did you bring her here?"

"Because," Suyana replied, her eyes on Morrigan's frozen form, "she is one of us."

Will and the others followed Suyana down the steps to where Morrigan stood motionless on the stage. Fader dashed ahead to stare up at the witch with longing and adoration. From the look on Case's face, Will could see she still feared the hold the witch held on her brother.

"One of you?" Will said. "You mean the Sisterhood?"

"Yes," Suyana replied.

"How?" Case asked. "She's a witch. And from the Isle of Man."

Suyana mounted the stage. "Ellan Vannin. The island's Manx name." She lifted a corner of the green cape Morrigan wore. "And this proves it."

"What is it?" Fader asked.

"The Unicorn Tapestry. A powerful artifact and the handiwork of the White Coven. Luciana once described it to me. She thought it destroyed when the Coven fell. But when I heard of the beast that bore this woman here, I suspected the Tapestry's role and, therefore, this woman's heritage." She examined the cape. "And the bat is gone. The fire drake, as well."

"Which are?" Will asked.

"Magical creatures the Coven bound within these threads. Once released, they obey the holder of the Tapestry—but then they are no more. She must have faced great danger to use such spells."

"Spells or no spells, whatever she faced still sent her to the Gray Lands," Will said.

Suyana frowned at him.

"A place in Dream. An astral traveler, if powerful enough, can send—"

"Yes, I know of *Las Tierras Grises*. And I know this look of...emptiness. But why do you believe this happened to our coven sister?"

Will thought again of the entity he battled in the monastery. Should he tell Suyana? She knew of Morrigan and the Gray Lands and astral powers. She might also know about—

A spark of light sprang from his chest, derailing his thoughts. The spark dropped to the ground, expanding into the glowing form of Jack. The little dog wagged its tail at Will, then jumped onto the stage where it ran toward Suyana...

And disappeared.

"Will?" Case asked. "You okay?"

Blinking, he turned to her. She was staring at him, as was everyone else. It seemed only he had seen Jack. "Right. Yeah. Sorry," he said, his mind racing. Jack had appeared right after he'd decided to tell Suyana of the strange entity in the monastery. Was the little dog warning him *not* to share that?

Jack had never led him wrong. "That's a long story," he said to Suyana, "and I don't know how much time I have left. I think we should get into the Crossing. We can talk about Morrigan in there." *Unless Jack warns me again.*

Suyana nodded. "You are right. And, as we travel the Crossing, I will tell of the White Coven and how it arose." She addressed Adi and Isobel. "You may accompany us to the Veil, but there, you must say your goodbyes."

Leaving the amphitheater and Morrigan behind, they set out through the forest toward the Third Veil. Suyana, Yanta, and Isobel led the way. Case walked with Rani, followed by Fader, then Will and Adi. Three of Suyana's guards trailed the party.

Case and Rani were engrossed in a whispered conversation, which included furtive glances back at Adi. Fader, although not part of that, also kept looking at Adi.

Will was about to ask the three of them what was going on when Adi spoke.

"I'm frightened," she said, showing no awareness of the attention on her.

Startled, he turned to her.

Her eyes locked on his. "Frightened for you. I'm hopeful, too, of course. That you'll finally find what you've searched for. Answers. Your parents. To be...healed. But mostly I'm frightened." She swallowed. "I don't think I could bear losing you."

He searched for words but found none. Adi was facing the truth he was avoiding. He didn't know what lay ahead in the Crossing. Whether it could heal him. Whether any of them would return. Realizing that, he found the right words. "I love you, too."

Her eyes glistened. "I expected a smart-ass remark. I like that better." Her hand found his and squeezed it. "I can't imagine a greater pain than losing a child. Never seeing them grow up." Her eyes were wistful now. "I've been so lucky, seeing you become the amazing young man you are."

He felt himself reddening, embarrassed by this unexpected affection from his normally reserved guardian.

Seeming to catch herself, she cleared her throat. "I'm sure those thoughts have haunted your parents for eight years."

"Then you think they're alive? Ellie, too?"

She gave his hand another squeeze. "I hope so."

They fell silent. Moments later, the party emerged from the forest of the Great Trees, and the Third Veil rose above them.

To Will, this wall of light appeared no different from the first two Veils—a shimmering curtain of silver, an aurora rippling in a wind he couldn't feel.

But something *was* different about this barrier. He sensed a weight to it. A mass. A *heaviness*.

And he remembered where he'd felt that before—smelling the Flower in his greenhouse. The feeling of great pressure trying to compress him into a tiny ball, impossibly small yet impossibly massive, as if a mere speck held all matter in the universe. Or *all* the universes. Was this the source of that suppressed memory?

The others must have felt something similar, for the entire party fell silent.

Suyana stopped ten paces from the Veil. Her eyes found Adi, then Isobel. "Here, you must say goodbye to your friends. My Siguiente will post guards to await our return."

Isobel hugged the four travelers. Case and Adi hugged, too. Stepping back, Case said, "Adi, is there anything you want to tell Will before we leave?"

Adi frowned. "William and I talked on our way here."

"Yeah," Will said, wondering what Case meant, "and Adi has embarrassed me enough for one day. Besides, we're coming back."

Rani and Case exchanged looks. Case started to say something, but then Fader ran forward to give Adi his goodbye hug, which Adi returned with a smile. Fader stepped back, looking as serious as Will had ever seen. "Adi, you said Diego flew you here with Stone and Mei."

Adi's smile slipped. "Yes."

Fader took a deep breath, then rushed on. "What happened to Peng? I mean, he got shot and he wasn't moving and there was a lot of blood and you didn't mention him coming here, so I guess he's still in hospital and the doctors are making him better..." His words trailed off as he saw Adi's face.

"Fader, the doctors...they couldn't..." Adi began. She sighed, then continued, her voice gentle. "I'm sorry, but Wu Peng passed away."

Fader lips froze into a thin line. He wrapped his arms around himself, looking at Will then Case, then down at the ground. Case pulled her brother to her and held him tight, rocking him back and forth, whatever she had wanted to ask forgotten.

Suyana broke the silence. "Will Dreycott, for your sake, we should not delay further."

Will and Suyana approached the Veil, stopping an arm's length away. Case, Fader, and Rani clustered behind them.

"We must open the way as one," Suyana said to Will. She took his hand, and together, they touched the Veil.

Will again felt an electric tingle on his skin. The silver curtain drew back. An arched opening appeared, twice his height and wide enough to accommodate two people abreast. But beyond, he saw only swirling mists.

Suyana started forward. To his surprise, he resisted her pull as a cold dread rose in him.

The news of Peng's death. Jack's warning not to share with this Madre. These mists before him that recalled the Gray Lands. And the sense of being moved like pieces on a board.

All these things seemed like portents of coming disaster.

"And we are waiting for...what?" Rani asked.

"The way is open," Suyana said. "We must enter."

He took a deep breath. For eight years, he'd longed to be here, a step away from the answers he'd sought. This wasn't the time for imagined dangers. This was the time to take that step.

"Okay," he said. "Let's do this." He moved forward, the others behind him.

Chapter 41

Snake Tongue

Case passed through the Veil, thoughts and fears swirling in her head like the gray mists before her. Why was Morrigan here? Why was Fader still fascinated with her? Was Adi really Will's mother? Could Suyana heal Will? Was their mother alive in this place?

Then the mists melted away, taking with them her storm of emotions as she saw what lay beyond the Veil.

They stood on a flat rock, roughly circular and thirty paces across, its dull silver surface uneven, as if chiseled by giant hands.

The rock hung in blackness. The blackness of the Nothing. Above, below, on every side.

Except behind them, where the Third Veil loomed, disappearing into unseen distances, an infinite flickering barrier between where they'd come from and…

And whatever this place was.

In the middle of the rock sat a stone altar, a giant version of the Chakana, at least five paces long and wide, and rising waist high.

Four glowing spheres, baseball-sized, floated a hand's length above the altar, one at the end of each arm. Each globe radiated a different color—blue, yellow, red, and green. Each pulsed, slow and steady, like the heartbeat of a great slumbering beast. The radiance of the spheres and the Veil bathed the scene in surreal ever-changing light.

Suyana walked to the end of the arm where the green sphere hovered. "Will Dreycott, come stand by my side. The rest of you, please take a position before the other *Esferas de los Cuatro*—the Spheres of the Four. It does not matter which you choose."

Rani shrugged and selected the yellow sphere opposite Suyana. Case walked to the red one, Fader to the blue sphere opposite her.

Suyana spoke. "Four *Viajeros*—Travelers—are needed to traverse the Crossing and enter the Book. Normally, the Madres form the Travelers. But others may fill those roles, provided one Traveler carries the Chakana, as I do. A Traveler for each of the Four. I am Madre de Bondad—Goodness—the green sphere." She pointed to Case, Rani, and Fader in succession. "Red, Yellow, Blue—Chaos, Evil, Order."

"Wait," Rani said. "I'm Evil?"

"Biting my tongue," Will said, earning him a glare.

So I picked Chaos? Case thought. Well, that described her world lately. Order for Fader almost made sense—he'd embraced the calmer life in Will's tower better than she had.

This close, she could see a Chakana-shaped indentation in the stone altar under where each sphere hovered.

"No sphere for me?" Will asked Suyana.

"You must play a different role." Removing the Chakana from her pouch, Suyana placed it into the matching indentation under the green sphere.

Nothing happened.

"That was...underwhelming," Rani said.

Suyana spoke to Will. "The Chakana is incomplete without the part that lives in you. Please, touch the Chakana."

Will hesitated. "Is this when it removes that piece from me? You know...fixes me?"

"No. That must be done within the Book. But this will start us on that journey."

Will looked at Case, his hopes and fears written plain on his face. She smiled and nodded her support. Reaching out, he touched the Chakana where it lay in the altar.

Again, nothing happened...or so she thought.

Fader's head snapped up to stare behind her. The others were looking in that direction as well. She turned.

A cobbled bridge of gray stones now stretched from the rocky platform on which they stood, wide enough to walk four abreast and bordered by shoulder-high walls of larger stones. Glimmering in the Veil's glow, the bridge rose gently into the blackness, ending at an island hanging in the Void.

At least, she thought of it as an island. The land mass connected to nothing but the cobbled bridge. It had three distinct levels, arranged in steps that mirrored the Chakana itself. Each level sat back from and rose higher than the previous.

The lowest level was barren brown rock, fronted by a cliff face broken only by dark openings that could be caves or tunnels. The stone bridge ended at the largest of these.

Thick jungle covered the middle level, green and dark and lush, appearing impenetrable from this distance.

Finally, above and beyond the jungle, the third level rose in lines of jagged, white-capped mountain peaks. Case tried to guess the proportions of the island, but perspective or the Veil's flickering light kept playing tricks on her eyes. It could be the size of a city block...or a small country.

"Before you lies the Crossing," Suyana said. "And the realm of the Guardians, who will be our guides as we—"

A cry from Will spun Case around. He crouched on his hands and knees on the stone, staring at a scene that hung in the Nothing, shining and translucent.

At first, the scene seemed a projection of this one, of figures circling the Chakana-shaped altar. Then she realized the people were different. Different but familiar...especially one.

Their mother.

Case wasn't alone in recognizing faces in the scene. "Mom!" Fader cried, and Suyana whispered, "Luciana."

Will had regained his feet. "It's from eight years ago. When Alvarez and Parwa brought us in here. It came when I touched the Chakana."

The scene showed Luciana, Jon, Terri, and Ellie at the altar in the roles of the four Travelers. Parwa stood beside Luciana, the Chakana in her hand. Behind them, Alvarez gripped young Will's arm, pointing a pistol at him.

Parwa set the Chakana into the altar in front of Luciana, then motioned to young Will, her lips moving. Still holding his arm, Alvarez walked the boy forward to touch the Chakana. The scene faded.

"That's it?" Rani said. "*That's* your highlight reel?"

Will shrugged. "I can't control these things."

"Perhaps you will see more as we journey through the Crossing," Suyana said. "And journey we should. Now, Travelers, touch the sphere before you."

As Case reached for the red sphere, a tingle ran up her arm as if an invisible energy field surrounded the globe. She touched the sphere, not knowing what to expect.

It disappeared.

"Oh, crap!" she said. "What'd I do? Where'd it go?" She looked at Suyana.

The Madre was smiling at her. Suyana's green sphere now hovered a hand's breadth above her head, as did the yellow sphere over Rani and the blue over Fader.

Case raised a hand in front of her face, and it reflected back a crimson glow. "Guess I know where it went."

"You each now carry the light of your aspect of the Four," Suyana said. "It will grant you entry to the Book."

Case frowned. "Wait. If Luciana and our parents were the Travelers and took a sphere eight years ago, why were the spheres here at the altar again?"

"Once the Travelers reach the Book," Suyana said, "and present themselves as an aspect of the Four, the spheres then reappear at this altar."

Fader brightened. "Then that means our parents made it to the Book, right?"

Suyana hesitated. "The spheres also return if a Traveler dies within the Crossing."

No one spoke, but Fader slipped an arm around Case's waist, and she hugged him to her.

Suyana removed the Chakana from the altar, returning it to her pouch. "There is only one way to discover the truth." With that, she walked onto the stone bridge. The others fell in behind her, four abreast.

Case was glad for the height of the bridge's walls that gave a comforting barrier from the Nothing. She guessed they'd need at least a half hour to cross, but with each step, the floating island drew closer faster than she expected.

Suyana nodded when she mentioned this. "Distances here are deceiving."

Ten steps later, the party reached the opening in the cliff wall where the stone bridge ended. The opening towered two stories high. Inside it, in the throbbing light from the Travelers' spheres, Case could make out a circular tunnel, slanting up.

Even this close, she struggled to guess the size of the floating island. The cliff face into which the road disappeared seemed to tower to skyscraper heights above them. But when she focused on its top, she felt she could reach up and touch it. She dropped her eyes again, swaying with a sudden vertigo.

Suyana caught her by the arm, steadying her. "In this place, it is best to focus on what is before you." She called Fader to her. "Walk with me here."

He came forward. "Why me?"

"Because this is the realm of the Guardian of the Underground. The rest of you, stay close." With that, she and Fader entered the tunnel, Case and the others following, their way lit by the globes.

They'd gone maybe twenty paces when Will called out. "Wait!"

A vision appeared, shining in shades of silver and gray against the darkness of the tunnel before them. In it, Luciana and their parents walked this same tunnel, their backs to the viewers, a colored sphere above each of their heads. Parwa followed, then Alvarez, still gripping Will by the arm and holding his pistol.

The vision vanished.

"Well," Will said, "we know they made it this far."

Case just nodded, her hopes again lifted by that brief glimpse of her mother.

Soon, the tunnel split into two. Suyana halted the party. "Here, we must wait."

Case began to ask why when she heard it...a sliding, slipping, slithering sound of something coming toward them. Something big.

A green radiance grew in the left branch. A moment later, the Snake Guardian appeared. Or, at least, its head did, for the beast was enormous this time, its body filling the two-story-high tunnel.

But as the Snake drew closer, it seemed to shrink. By the time it emerged from the tunnel mouth, it was the size of its other appearances—large, but no longer monstrous. It moved toward them, crystal-bright eyes locked on Fader...

It stopped. Rearing up, it swung toward Suyana, mouth open, swaying and hissing.

Suyana stepped back, confusion and fear on her face. Fader jumped in front of her, raising his hands protectively before his adopted Guardian. The Snake halted.

No one moved. Case held her breath as the creature continued to sway, its eyes still locked on Suyana. The Snake rose higher, rearing back as if to strike...

...then bobbed its head to the Madre, once, twice, three times. A bow.

Letting out her breath, Suyana bowed back. With that, the Snake dropped to the ground and slid into the right-hand tunnel.

"What was that about?" Will asked.

"I...I don't know," Suyana said, still looking shaken. "It has never acted so before."

"Will was standing behind you," Case offered. "Maybe it sensed the Chakana piece in him."

"Or he really pissed it off last time he was here," Rani said.

Will glared at her.

"What? You have that effect on people."

"*I* have that effect?"

Ahead in the tunnel, the green glow of the Guardian was fading.

"Whatever the reason, the moment has passed," Suyana said. "Now, we must follow or we will be lost."

"You don't know the way?" Case asked.

"The tunnels move, shift. Only the Serpent can lead us through."

"Lovely," Rani muttered.

The party followed the Snake through tunnel after tunnel, the walls rainbow-lit by the glow of the Guardian and the Travelers' spheres. The similarity to the maze leading from the Temple of the Key to the Cave of Flowers struck Case. But here, the tunnels slanted upward, not down. With each new passage, they climbed higher and higher.

They entered a tunnel carpeted in a loose green material that crunched beneath their feet. Case kicked it with a toe of her sneaker. "Is this what I think it is?"

"The discarded skin of the Serpent," Suyana said. Bending down, she broke off a piece of the skin the size of her hand and put it into her pouch.

"Why did you take a piece?" Fader asked as they began walking again.

Not answering, Suyana turned to Will. "You promised to tell of how our Sister Morrigan came to be in the Gray Lands."

Will hesitated. Case knew him well enough to tell he had some concern about sharing that story. She wondered what it was.

"I don't *know* what happened," he said, "but I can give you my best guess."

As they walked, he told of the astral power attacking him in the monastery as he was about to escape through the portal.

Suyana frowned. "You believe this...entity...controlled the man Herrada, who you had thought a friend?"

"Yes."

"And Morrigan, too?"

"Who is definitely *not* a friend," Case said.

"Why do you say that?"

Case gave a short version of their battle with Marell and Morrigan to save the Hollow Boys...and themselves.

Suyana shook her head when Case finished. "Terrible. Somewhere, somehow, our Sister lost her way."

"There's good in her, too," Fader said quietly.

Suyana smiled, putting a hand on his shoulder. "There is good in us all." Her smile slid away. "But evil, too. Every Madre has seen that."

"Madre," Case said, as they followed the Serpent into another tunnel. "You promised to tell us of the White Coven, and how they became part of your Sisterhood."

"Yes," Suyana sighed. "I will tell you. But I must begin with another tale of treachery. One even greater than Parwa's and much older, one before my time..."

Case listened with the others as Suyana told her tale.

⚜

Before the Spaniards came, when the Incas still ruled, before we split into Sisters of the Key and the Crossing, a girl named Quilla joined the Sisterhood of the Four.

She was a simple Quechuan girl from a local village, no different in most respects from any who joined the Sisterhood. But when the Madres presented Quilla, the Four found her highly attuned to the astral planes and the vibrations of the One—a most excellent candidate to become a Madre.

The years passed. Quilla grew into a young woman, becoming Siguiente to Inis, the Madre of Order, and receiving the Breath of the Three.

More years passed, as did Madres, replaced each time by their Siguiente. One day, Inis passed too, and Quilla, now an old woman but still vital thanks to the Breath, became the Madre del Orden.

Remember, within the Book, a new Madre becomes a new *being*, a mixture of their aspect of the Four *and* the human they are. Something of each, but different from either. As expected, Madre Quilla was different from the previous Madre of Order.

But no one suspected *how* different.

Now, realize this. The Four abide by but *one* rule: absolute respect for free will. New branches form in the Story only from freely made decisions of sentient beings. The Four *observe*—they *never* interfere with free will.

Over time, Quilla grew increasingly disturbed by the ever-expanding chaos in the infinitely branching multiverse. She became a dissenting voice against letting free will reign, to never interfere in the Story, to only study and learn.

Even so, the other Madres raised no concerns. The Four *expect* dissent among themselves. Their very reason for existence as opposing aspects of the One is to explore and argue contending views of the Story, as they seek to understand humanity and the choices they make.

But unknown to the other Madres, at some point, Quilla's hate for the *disorder* of the multiverse grew to where she resolved to do something.

She vowed to create her *own* Story: to write the Book of Order.

One night, Quilla took the Chakana from its altar in the Threshold, as was her right as a Madre. With it, she led the Siguientes of the other three aspects through the Crossing, supposedly to train them to merge with the Four. Such teachings are common and surprised no one.

One of these students was the Siguiente to the Madre of Chaos—a young sister named Luciana.

Once inside the Book, Quilla merged with Orden and invited the other aspects of the Four to merge with the three Siguientes.

Such mergings overwhelm humans unused to the experience. With the Siguientes distracted by their union with a god, Quilla-Orden began her Book of Order—growing a new branch from the base of the True Tree we call the Story.

On that night, the young Luciana realized the wrongness of what Quilla was doing. Worse, Luciana saw that once Quilla completed her Book of Order, she intended to destroy the rest of the True Tree, leaving only her new branch. All of existence, all creatures everywhere, would perish.

There in the Book, Luciana, now merged with the Chaos aspect of the Four, battled Quilla-Orden—one aspect of the Four against another. As she fought, Luciana rallied her two companions to oppose Quilla.

But they were only Siguientes, not completely merged with their aspects, and Quilla was a Madre, fully one with Orden. The Siguientes were losing. Soon the Tree would fall.

Outside the Crossing, the other three Madres now sensed Quilla's treachery. But without the Chakana, they could not enter the Crossing. They could not reach Quilla or the Book.

It was then that those three Madres—Asiri, Chirapa, and Ilina, whose names are revered forever in our Sisterhood—made the ultimate sacrifice.

They fell on their swords, killing themselves.

Their deaths allowed their aspects of the Four to merge fully with the Siguientes in the Book. Those three, now true Madres, led by Luciana, united

their wills to defeat Quilla, driving her astral spirit from her body.
  And killing her.

Chapter 42

Bad Guy

When Suyana finished, Case was the first to speak. "Quilla was going to destroy *all* life? Everywhere?"

Suyana nodded, looking back from where she led them through the tunnels following the Serpent Guardian.

"Because it was...messy?" Rani said.

"Being one with the Four, seeing all the souls in all the worlds in the Story..." Suyana shook her head. "Sadly, some Madres come to consider an individual as...unimportant. From there, it is a small step to view all people that way."

"When was this?" Rani asked.

"Over six hundred years ago."

"And Luciana was still alive eight years ago?" Rani said. "Wow."

"Hopefully, she still is," Suyana said.

"Our parents, too," Fader said in a small voice. Case swallowed.

A yellow brightness grew ahead, mixing with the Serpent's green glow. Another turn brought them out of the tunnel to stand in brilliant sunlight on soft brown earth. Steps away lay a thick verdant jungle. Case recognized many of the same trees and flowers from the Valley of the Veils. She breathed in the sweet scents of blooms and moist smell of soil.

The jungle stretched to either side until it reached the Nothing. The black of the Void rose above it, too, and Case realized that the 'sunlight' was the glow of the jungle itself. Every leaf, every flower shone with a yellow radiance.

As did the creature that emerged from the trees—the Puma Guardian.

The big cat stalked forward, eyes locked on Case. She felt no fear. Far from it. The beast radiated a warmth she could describe only as love, its throaty purring filling the air.

But three paces away, the Puma stopped, dropping into a crouch. Its head swiveled to Suyana, its purr becoming a low growl.

Suyana stepped back, her eyes widening in alarm. As Fader had done with the Serpent, Case moved between the Puma and the Madre.

The cat's growl died, but its eyes of flickering flames stayed on Suyana. It sniffed the air. The tension left its body, and with a final sniff, it turned and trotted toward the jungle.

Case could see no opening through the dense undergrowth. But when the

Puma reached the jungle's edge, the vegetation drew back to form a path wide enough to walk two abreast.

"Come," Suyana said. "We must follow quickly or the way will close." Her voice quavered, but she moved without hesitation after the Puma.

"What just happened? Again?" Will said, as he and the others fell in behind her.

"I do not know," Suyana said. "But I cannot blame this on the Chakana piece you carry. You were not near me."

"It was reacting to *you*," Case said to Suyana. "I could feel it."

"Hey, it's been eight years since you were here, right?" Will said. "Maybe it's forgotten you?"

"The Guardians do not forget. Something is wrong."

"*Wrong?*" Rani said. "Uh, maybe we should go back?"

Case shot her a look. "Will's dying, remember?" *And I need to find our mother.*

"We go on," Suyana said. "When we reach the Book, I will ask the Four."

An ominous silence fell, broken only by their own footfalls. No sound came from the jungle now surrounding them. No bird call. No insect whine or buzz.

Finally, Will spoke. "Suyana, your story of Quilla..."

"Yes?"

"What does it have to do with the White Coven? Or Morrigan?"

"Just as the Four created the Book to hold the Story and the Crossing to protect it, so did Quilla create her equivalents for her branch of Order. You have all seen what she made. You have been there."

Understanding came to Case. "The Black Island."

"Yes, from where you and Isobel rescued our captured Sisters."

"Wait," Will said. "You mean the Black Island is Quilla's version of the Book?"

"No. The Black Pool is her Book. In that mirror, had she completed her work, she could have read—or written—the Story of her new world. The Black Island is her version of the Crossing—as are the ways to reach that place."

"The phantom subway stop," Case said. Will, Fader, and Rani nodded. When Suyana looked puzzled, Case told of how they'd found the Black Island.

"That journey you made," Suyana said, "had the same purpose in Quilla's creation as the one we take now. To travel the Crossing, to reach the Book."

"But here," Will said, "you need the Chakana to open the Crossing. Did Quilla create a Key for her version?"

"Yes," Suyana said. "And you all heard it."

"The Song!" Case said, remembering the strange power of the Chambelán's singing.

Suyana nodded. "The Song that some Sisters learned to hear. Those we sent to that terrible place, believing it held the Chakana."

"Okay," Will said, "but still...what does that have to do with the White Coven?"

"After Quilla's death, Luciana and the other new Madres looked into the Book and read the branch Quilla had created. There they saw the path to the Black Island."

"Six hundred years ago?" Rani said, "Pretty sure there was no Toronto subway. Or, you know, Toronto."

"When Quilla created her world, only one passage existed—in a land far from both your city and Peru." Suyana looked back at them as they walked. "Ellan Vannin."

"The Isle of Man," Will said.

"The new Madres believed if they blocked that passage, they could prevent anyone from reaching the Black Island. They feared the Black Mirror, what powers it might give someone over the Story—the real Story. So, they sent a Siguiente to Ellan Vannin. She recruited local Celtic priestesses. From that grew the White Coven."

"Sent?" Rani said. "How'd you do that six centuries ago from Peru?"

"From inside the Book, all of creation is reachable. You will see." Suyana's face became grim. "For over two hundred years, the White Coven defended the passageway on Ellan Vannin, allowing none who followed the Song to reach the Black Island through that route. But sometime in the 1600s, a war broke out in that land...and the Coven fell."

"English Civil War," Rani said. "Mid-1600s. Cromwell. The Roundheads." When the others stared at her, she shrugged. "I researched the Chamber of the Red Door. Found a reference to them around that time."

"So that opened the way to the Black Island?" Case asked.

"No. Whatever protections the White Coven put in place remain to this day. The passage on Ellan Vannin remains closed. Or, at least, it was when last I read the Book. But the Song is a siren call. Other ways opened around the world, too many to guard. We had no choice but to use the Book to keep watch on Quilla's branch, to monitor it for change."

"Couldn't you just, like, chop it off?" Will asked.

"The purpose of the Story to the Four is to *observe*. Observe free will. The choices we humans make, the reasons for those choices, and their results. Never in the history of the Story have the Four interfered."

"Until Quilla did," Will said.

Suyana sighed. "Yes. But the Four refused to interfere again. And..." She hesitated. "...they were curious."

"Curious?" Case asked.

"To see how Quilla's branch played out. Would it grow? Create branches from itself?"

"And did it?"

"When last I saw it eight years ago, it remained stunted, unchanged from when Quilla created it."

Will shot Case a look, and she guessed his thoughts. Had *their* actions on the Black Island changed Quilla's branch? Bringing the Chakana there? Will's mental linking with the scarabs? The death of the Dancer-Chambelán?

"But Quilla's treachery prompted changes *here*," Suyana continued. "We divided into the Sisters of the Key and of the Crossing, each led by two Madres. No longer could a Madre enter the Crossing without another's knowledge, as Quilla had. The Madres of the Key held the Chakana, but the Madres of the Crossing guarded the Third Veil."

Suyana sighed. "But we did not foresee your parents' cleverness in locating the Chakana, Will Dreycott. Nor the brutality of Alvarez."

"Speaking of parents and Alvarez..." Case turned to Will.

"No more visions." He caught the look she must have worn. "That doesn't mean they didn't make it this far. Just means no other buried memory has popped up."

But you don't know that, she thought.

Ahead, the jungle continued to part before the Puma. And they continued to follow, their way lit by the radiance of the plants and the spheres. As they passed one prickly bush, Suyana plucked a wad of yellow fluff from a thorn.

Fader watched her place it in her pouch. "That's the Puma's fur, right?"

Suyana didn't answer, focused on the Puma again.

"It's how you make the Breath, isn't it?" Fader said.

She looked back at him, her eyes wide.

He shrugged. "You said it needs the *involvement* of the Guardians. And you took a piece of the Snake's skin before. That's what you meant, wasn't it? Something from each Guardian." He grinned. "I bet you get a feather from the Condor."

Suyana sighed. "Another of our secrets you have learned." But she would say no more.

Ahead, a cold ivory light now mixed with the yellow glow of the jungle. The vegetation before the Puma suddenly parted even farther, like curtains drawing back to unveil what lay behind.

They faced a snow-covered landscape split by an icy road. The road rose into the mountains, disappearing into a mist-shrouded valley. In the distance, white-capped peaks loomed above the mist. Everything—the road, the mountains, the mist—shone with a frozen silvery radiance.

The Puma stopped at the edge of this new wintry domain, its paws still on jungle soil. It considered Suyana for a breath, then padded back toward the undergrowth. The plants closed behind it, and the Puma was gone. Without a word, Suyana moved onto the snowy road, the others following.

Case shivered as a chill wind swept away the steamy warmth of the jungle. They'd taken only a few steps when the mist rushed down from the valley toward them, wrapping them in frigid dampness and blinding them to this world. Case couldn't see her feet or the glow of the floating spheres. She bumped into someone.

"Stop walking," Suyana said, her voice muffled by the surrounding grayness, despite her closeness. "Within the mist, a single step could plunge us into a crevice."

"Wonderful," Rani muttered. "Now what?"

"We wait," Suyana said, and Case sensed fear in the Madre's voice.

A sound came. Like a faint drum beat, growing louder. The wind picked up, its gusts matching the rhythm of the drums.

No, not drums.

Wings.

The wind blew harder, sweeping away just enough of the mist to reveal what hung in the air above them, its great wings rising and falling.

The Condor Guardian.

Although almost entirely black, the creature emitted a pearly glow, which grew as it floated down to stand before them. Folding its wings, the bird cocked its head to the side, its eyes—one red, one yellow—locked on Suyana.

Then it bobbed to the Madre—once, twice, three times.

Suyana let out a breath, her shoulders relaxing. Smiling, she bowed back to the Condor.

"This one seems cool with you," Case said.

Rani waved a hand. "My guy. Best Behaved Guardian."

The relief was obvious on Suyana's face. "Perhaps you were right, Will Dreycott—my long absence caused the reactions of the other Guardians."

The Condor leaped into the air to fly toward the distant mountains. With each wing beat, the mists before it vanished, exposing more of the road rising into the valley.

A feather floated down to land at Suyana's feet. Stooping, she added it to her pouch. "Come. Before the mists close in once more."

Suyana set out on the road, Fader and Rani following, then Case and Will. Case expected the Condor to outpace them, but the bird maintained the same distance, its great wings clearing the mist, revealing a distant pass splitting two peaks.

"Still no visions?" she asked Will.

He shook his head, his lips pursed. She could tell he was worried, too. Each step brought them closer to the end of the Crossing, still not knowing what had happened here eight years ago. Had their parents even made it this far?

Each step also brought them closer to the mountain pass than she expected. At first, it had seemed to promise an uphill journey of days. Now, every wing beat of the Condor pulled the peaks closer, as if they were flying up the mountain, not walking.

Another dozen steps, and they reached the top of the pass. Before them, the road twisted down through a rocky, barren landscape until it disappeared again into the mists. But here, the road lay cleared of snow, showing its true surface—sparkling crystal, shining with its own inner silver light.

The Condor flew down the mountainside, beating away the mists below—and they followed. Followed until they reached the shore of a black and storm-tossed sea. The road continued past the shore, running out over the churning dark water until the mists hid it once more.

The Condor beat its wings again, rising higher and higher, until it disappeared into the blackness of the Nothing. The remaining mists over the sea blew away, revealing the road's destination—and the last secret of the Crossing.

"Before you lies the Book," Suyana said, her voice hushed, "where the Story unfolds, where the Madres and the Four become one."

"Case! Will!" Fader cried. "Look what it is!"

At the end of the shining road, an island rose from the dark, roiling sea. An island that shone brighter than the road, brighter than the Veils, brighter than anything they had encountered on their long strange journey. A very familiar island.

"The Crystal Island," Case whispered. When the Chakana had become exposed in Adi's safe, Fader had faded into the In Between, unable to return. Falling asleep there, he found himself on a bizarre island in Dream made entirely of crystal. Will and Case had traveled down the River of Souls to the Island to rescue him. "We've *been* there. In Dream."

Suyana chuckled. "Yes, you have."

Case tried to remember telling Suyana about their Dream journey to the Crystal Island, but couldn't. She started to ask the Madre how she knew that, but a cry from Will pulled her around.

He was on his hands and knees, staring at what flickered ghostly in the air before him. Another vision. Of the lost expedition.

As she stared at the scene, at the fear on her mother's face, a chill seized Case. A chill, not just from the deadly events playing out before her, but a coldness creeping into her mind and numbing her body.

A coldness she'd felt before.

In Will's mind, he remained in the Condor's realm on the rocky shore where the shining road ran through churning black waters to the Crystal Island. But he no longer stood with Case and the others.

He stood with his parents.

And with Luciana and Ellie Cootes. And Parwa and Chico Alvarez. Will wasn't *watching* his younger self. He *was* his younger self, a part of the scene playing out before his nine-year-old eyes.

Alvarez gripped him hard by the arm, a pistol in his other hand. His parents stood together, their glowing spheres floating over their heads. They were so *tall*. "Mom? Dad?" he whispered. *His* words, from his present self, but spoken from the mouth of nine-year-old Will.

His mother, fear etched on her face, shook her head and raised a finger to her lips. He fell silent—and watched the scene play out.

Parwa stooped to pick up a feather from the ground. Smiling, she slipped off her backpack and put the feather inside.

"Another...ingredient?" Alvarez said.

"Yes. And the last," Parwa said, still rummaging in her backpack.

"Now we need to get over there?" Alvarez turned from her, nodding at the Crystal Island. "To make the Breath?" He turned back to Parwa.

She held a pistol, pointed at Alvarez.

"You little bitch!" Alvarez screamed. Alvarez's grip on Will's arm disappeared as he swung his gun toward Parwa.

Too late.

Parwa shot Alvarez in the chest. He spasmed, his gun slipping from his grip. He dropped to his knees.

"Sorry, Chico," Parwa said, "but I know you would kill me once you had the Breath."

Alvarez opened his mouth, but only a red foam passed his lips. Parwa shot him again. He collapsed to the stony ground.

Chico Alvarez was dead.

A sudden shadow fell over them. From the mountain pass above, the Condor plunged down the valley toward them, growing, growing, growing with each wing beat, eyes blazing red and yellow flames.

Parwa, terror on her face, swung her gun to Luciana. "Stop it! Call it off!"

Luciana shook her head. "I cannot, child. You have shed blood in its realm."

"*Call it off!*" Parwa screamed. She swung her gun to Will. "Or I kill the boy."

Several things happened at once.

The Condor swooped toward Parwa, growing larger with each second, great wings and talons outspread.

A warmth blossomed on Will's chest and the weight of something tugged at his neck. He looked down. The Chakana now hung there, glowing.

Parwa aimed her gun at Will's heart, her face twisted in anger and fear. Her finger tightened on the trigger. Will's mother cried out and started forward.

The Condor struck...but not before Parwa fired.

Time slowed. Will saw the flash of the pistol, saw the bullet flying at his heart...

And then...

...and then he was drowning.

Drowning in freezing, rushing waters. Waters that tossed and tumbled him, battered and bashed him against the rocky bottom of...of...

A river?

A river that spun him through its depths. His lungs were near bursting. He didn't know what was up or down, didn't know where the surface was, what to swim for. Dark spots danced before his eyes. He was drowning.

A light beckoned, sparkling above. Hitting the stony bottom, he pushed off, fighting the current, clawing to reach the light.

He broke the surface, gasping in air as the rushing waters swept him along. He *was* in a river, fast-running and lined with thick jungle. Sucking in another breath, he struck out for the nearest shore, battling the raging torrent. But he seemed to pull no closer, every stroke threatening to sap the last of his strength. Just when he thought he could swim no farther, his feet found the river bed. Dragging himself up the bank, he collapsed onto his back. He lay there, feeling the warmth of the sun on his skin...and of the Chakana on his chest.

He touched the artifact, as if to convince himself it was real. And he remembered.

"Mom? Dad?" he whispered. What had happened? Where was he? Were his parents safe? He had to find them. He had to get back.

As he tried to stand, exhaustion seized him. The warmth in his chest grew, spreading to his limbs, flooding him with sudden weariness. He fell back onto the riverbank. Sleep...or something like it...took him.

Will awoke. Not from sleeping on that muddy riverbank eight years ago, but from the vision that had seized him. He was on his hands and knees on the stony shore of the Condor's realm in the Crossing. Rising on shaking legs, he looked to where Case, Fader, Rani, and Suyana stood.

"Did you see it?" he cried. "That's what happened to me. Eight years ago. I think...I don't know...I think the Chakana saved my life. Zapped me out of here...dropped me in a river...I think." He waited for someone to speak. "Did you see it?" he repeated.

Suyana nodded, smiling. But Case, Fader, and Rani just stared at him.

He swallowed. No. They weren't staring at him. They weren't staring at anything.

He ran to Case, a chill growing in him. Her eyes were open, but he'd seen that look before. On the Hollow Boys. On Morrigan, just this morning. Fader and Rani now, too, their faces empty, gone.

Gone to the Gray Lands.

He spun to face Suyana. "What happened? Why—?"

He felt it then. A cold tickling in his head, like an icy spider crawling into his skull, spinning its web around his mind.

Suyana watched him, her arms crossed, relaxed and smiling. He tried to speak, but his mouth wouldn't form words. He tried to reach her, to make her stop, but his muscles were no longer his to command. Still, he fought her.

Suyana laughed. "Think you can defeat me? Like you did in the monastery?"

And he understood. He recognized the same sense of incredible astral power and immense age. The identity was female—but not Suyana. This was no longer Suyana. This was the entity that had taken over Gabriel Herrada and attacked them in Arequipa.

The thing with Suyana's face laughed. "You cannot win here, child. This is *my* world, and this time, *I* hold the Chakana, not you. And you are weaker, so much weaker."

Ignoring her, he reached with his mind for the silver cord connecting him to the Key. The glowing thread appeared, snaking from him to the pouch Suyana wore. But he could feel no connection to the artifact. He could pull no power from it. He was helpless.

"You still don't know me, do you?" the not-Suyana said, seeming genuinely amused.

He tried again to speak, but failed.

She chuckled. "Here, let me give you back your mouth."

Suddenly, his lips, his tongue were his again. "Why should I know you?" he rasped.

Her face widened in mock surprise. "Because we've met. So many times. No? Perhaps a name, then." She bowed, arms outspread. "I am...Quilla."

"What? No, you can't be."

She laughed. "And yet, I am. Quilla, once Madre del Orden. But now..." Her face darkened. "...now I *am* Orden, for that is what I *bring*. Order."

He struggled to understand. "But Suyana said you died."

"I did die. Murdered by my sisters. And yet, I am not dead. I am here, before you, alive and in a body once more." She smiled again. "Thanks to *you*."

"Me?"

"You still don't know who I am? How I came to be here? Why you should know me?" Quilla seemed honestly surprised. "Then let me give you a hint."

Will shivered as she walked to him, shoving Suyana's face right up to his. She grinned, madness in her eyes. "Woof, woof."

The world fell away beneath him. He stared at her.

"*Jack?*"

Act 4

Now the Struggle Has a Name

Chapter 43

House of Four Doors

Like Case and Fader and Rani, Will stood frozen in the Condor's realm, a prisoner in his own body, staring at the thing with Suyana's face. The thing he'd thought was his friend. "How...how can you be Jack? How can you be Quilla?"

Quilla shrugged the Madre's shoulders. "Suyana's tale was true. I died. But I died *there...*" She pointed across the churning waters to the Crystal Island. "Inside the Book. A place that exists *outside* of all universes, all realities. No one had ever died there before, so no one knew where my astral spirit would go. And it went—not to the Realms of the Dead—but to the Crystal Island...*in Dream.*"

Her face twisted into a mask of fury. "Where I remained, trapped, for *six...hundred...years.* Can you even imagine the *boredom?*"

She took a breath, seeming to calm herself. "I found I could feed on the other spirits trapped there, draining them, sustaining myself. But I feared I would be found by the Four. So...I disguised myself."

"Jack," Will whispered.

"A puppy I loved from my youth. His name was Sami, but that shaman, Walter, named me Jack." She chuckled. "I could hardly correct him. Jack's form hid me *and* made it easier to befriend other castaways. No one ever suspected as I fed from them."

She stared out at the shining island. "I was hidden. I could survive. But I longed for *escape.*" She smiled at him. "And then my rescuers appeared."

Will swallowed, remembering traveling with Case to the Dream version of the Crystal Island and rescuing Fader and the spirits they'd found trapped there—including Jack.

"*You* freed me from that cursed place," she continued. "Now, I could go anywhere. But I decided to stay with *you*...after sensing the Chakana in you."

She shot him a look. "At first, that seemed a coincidence too astounding to believe. To complete my Book of Order, I needed to enter the Crossing again, which required the Chakana. And here I am rescued by a boy *connected* to the Key? Was I a pawn in some game?"

Will said nothing, but hope sparked in him. *Was* someone playing a bigger game here? One even Quilla couldn't see?

Quilla continued. "But as I learned of your powers, I realized the truth."

His new hope faded. "What truth?"

"Your powers come *from* the Chakana. The Chakana comes from the Crystal Island. Of course, it would lead you there in Dream. No hidden hand moving pieces—except my own." Her eyes locked on his. "Now, my hand needs to move the final piece—the one in *you*."

The spider in his mind crawled deeper, seeking, searching. "No! Luciana said the piece can only be removed in the Book."

"I suspect the task is *easier* in the Book, but I don't know what threats I may face there. I see no downside to retrieving the piece here...well, beyond your death." Her eyes narrowed, still locked on his. "But first, I must find it."

In his brain, the spider crept on, hunting its prey. He had to distract her. "But Jack *helped* me. *You* helped me. So many times."

Quilla chuckled. "Did I?"

"Yes! The night we met—when Case and I couldn't lead Fader back to our world from the In Between. You made us brighter, so he saw our spirits."

She shrugged. "Allowing *me* to escape with *you*."

The spider crawled deeper.

"When Adi showed me the Chakana, and it blasted me to the Realms of the Dead, you pulled me back."

"You were about to die. I needed you alive, to bring me—and the Chakana—to my world, to the Black Island. Which you did, thanks to that creature who had usurped my throne—that Chambelán person." She frowned, perhaps struck by that second coincidence.

The spider slowed. Had he distracted her? He had to keep it up. "I *brought* you to the Black Island?"

"Of course. After escaping Dream, I lived *inside* you. Quiet. Unobserved."

Revulsion and confusion battled within him. "Why?"

"An astral spirit needs a body to remain on a mortal plane. And you were searching for the Chakana. The easiest way to find the Key was to be there when *you* found it." She smiled. "And you did."

"Why didn't you take me over right then? Grab the Chakana and go to the Black Island?"

She sighed. "Your astral powers are formidable, and I was still too weak. I would have failed—and revealed myself. So, I stayed a hidden passenger as you traveled to the Black Tower."

The spider stilled as her expression became wistful. "And there I was. In the world I had birthed so long ago. My strength returning as I fed from my creation. The Chakana hanging before me like victory on a string, waiting to be seized." Fury twisted her face again. "Until that fool of a Chambelán threw it all away."

"Pretty sure her plan wasn't to get sucked into the Black Pool," Will said. *Keep her talking.* "Why did *she* want the Chakana?"

"Since I created my world, there arise in every generation those who hear the Song—*my* Key—and follow it to the Black Island. Somehow, early travelers discovered the restoring power of the Scarabs' blood, perhaps from killing one in self-defense. The Blood—an unfinished variant of the Breath—kept them returning for the feasts. Eventually, someone solved the maze to the Black Tower and became the first Chambelán. From the Mirror, they learned of my unfinished creation."

She laughed, a bitter sound. "But the Mirror was incomplete, as was the story it told. They knew the Chakana was the Key to some great power—but that was all. They sought it, not knowing why."

"But you helped me in the Black Tower, too," he said, desperate to keep her distracted. "When you pulled me out of the Chakana."

Quilla threw up Suyana's arms. "Why isn't this working?"

Will forgot his question as relief washed over him. "Can't find the piece in me?"

"Oh, I found the piece..."

His relief died, leaving only fear.

"But it is *resisting* removal." She laughed. "You thought me distracted by your questions? Silly child, I enjoy talking about my creation. It—" She stopped, a smile spreading across Suyana's face. "But *that* question has given me an idea."

A silver cord appeared, snaking from Suyana's pouch to his chest. The link between the Chakana and the piece inside him.

Quilla gripped the cord with both hands like a physical rope—and pulled.

He screamed. Needles of white-hot pain stabbed into his skull, as if a piece of his brain was being ripped from his head...which it was.

"To answer your question," Quilla said, ignoring his cries, "I pulled you from the Chakana because I feared the Key might warn you of me. Or worse, extract its piece from you. I wasn't ready for either. Not until I was restored, in a body I controlled, and the Chakana in my possession—the situation we are in now. Yes, this is working much better." She tugged again.

And Will screamed again.

"I *did* help you once in the Black Tower, though. Unwittingly. When that scarab attacked your girlfriend, my magnificent beast sensed *me* in *you*, and took your command to spare her as my own."

Will remembered, being in the scarab's mind, what it had shown him. "They were...winking out," he gasped. "There was...a broken bridge."

"Yes. A plea to *me* from my lovelies to save their kind and finish the Black Island. So, let's do that." She pulled harder.

And Will screamed harder. His head was exploding. He was flying apart.

He was dying.

"*Stop!*" he cried.

She chuckled. "No."

With his last crumb of strength, he gasped, "*Parwa!*"

Quilla's grip on the silver cord slackened. The pain eased. "What?"

"Parwa," he whispered. "You saw what happened in that vision. If you kill me here, the Condor will come for you."

Her brow furrowed. "I am not 'shedding blood,' as the Four worded their taboo." But uncertainty tinged her voice. "Still, it would be tragic, this near to victory, to be killed by a too-literal reading...and a bird." She sighed, and the cord disappeared. "Very well, I'll finish this in the Book."

Turning her back on the Condor's realm, she strode onto the silver road that ran through the storm-tossed sea to the Crystal Island.

The compulsion holding him immobile now propelled him to stumble forward, still a prisoner in his own body. He couldn't even turn for a last look at Case, standing statue-like with Fader and Rani. Helpless, he fell in beside Quilla-Suyana.

The black waters roiled on either side of the shining road. On their left, a wave several stories high rushed toward them. Quilla seemed indifferent, her pace remaining unbroken. As the wave crashed down, Will flinched, waiting to be swept away, but the black waters burst against an unseen barrier and slid back into the sea.

His mind still reeled with Quilla's revelations. She was centuries old and had once merged with a god—and created her own universe. He'd felt her astral power and knew he was no match for her, now that she held the Chakana. But he'd been no match for Marell either, yet he'd found a way to defeat him. Quilla had to have a weakness. He just needed to find it. At least, she'd left him his voice. "After we escaped the Black Island, I didn't see you again until the monastery. You stayed in the Black Tower, didn't you?"

"Of course. In the Tower, my creation restored me. And I longed to admire my handiwork. I had never seen it—Luciana and those upstart Madres killed me during its birth. But my beautiful world was unfinished. Including the Black Mirror. In it, I could view events, but not change the Story. I needed to reach the Book again to finish my world—and destroy the rest of the Tree to stop its chaos. And for that, I needed the Chakana."

On their right, a whale-like creature the size of an ocean liner leaped from the black waters. Transparent, its edges and lines shone in the glow from the road like an unfinished sketch, the blackness of the Nothing showing through it. Spreading sail-shaped fins, it soared over them, then plunged back into the stormy sea.

Quilla ignored the beast. "Once the Black Tower restored me, I tried to rejoin you and seize the Chakana." She sighed. "But the Key's astral shield protected your building, something I hadn't encountered returning with you from Dream, since your sleeping body was *inside* your tower. I could no longer reach you. Then the Mirror showed me your plans to move the Chakana outside that building. I recruited local thugs to steal it, but the incompetent fools failed."

"You almost killed Stone and his people."

She shrugged. "As I said—incompetent fools. But from the Mirror, I learned you were coming to Peru *with* the Chakana. Exactly what I needed you to do."

Stone had been right to suspect surveillance of Will's tower, but wrong about its source. All their efforts at secrecy had been useless. A thought occurred. "You sent me the Flower, didn't you? To draw me here."

Quilla frowned. "I know of no flower. Nor do I care."

Hope battled confusion inside him. Then who had sent the Flower? And had they done so to help him...or to draw him into this danger?

As on the other roads between the realms of the Crossing, each step on the shining causeway moved them farther than it seemed a single stride should. The Crystal Island and its sparkling jungle grew nearer, clearer. Mirroring the mountain from Fader's Dream version of this place, a four-sided, flat-topped pyramid rose from the jungle, like a faceted jewel crowning the island.

Quilla was talking again. "I was there when you arrived in Peru." She shook her head. "Yet still the astral shield protected you, so I took over that man, Herrada, intending to seize the Chakana at your hotel. But the Guardians defended you there. The Guardians! Outside the Crossing!" Quilla shot him a wary look.

She's afraid of us. And she doesn't have all the answers.

The Guardians protecting them at the hotel was new information, but he still had learned nothing to use against Quilla. "You made Herrada ambush us at the monastery."

"A plan that would have worked, if not for the witch and her treason. Which is why she rots in the Gray Lands now."

He'd been right. Morrigan *had* protected them. Finally, something he might use. He filed that away.

She laughed. "You thought Jack saved you from Herrada, but holding the Chakana, you were still too strong for me. You were escaping—*with* the Chakana *and* to the Sisterhood! Disaster loomed, so your beloved puppy appeared once more. You brought me through the portal to the Sisters, where I again hid inside you."

"Why not take over Yanta and grab the Chakana? Go to the Crossing right then?"

"Because the Key is incomplete. I'd heard your story of how the Chakana can only be repaired in the Crossing. I needed to get *you* in here with me, so I helped you escape your cell in the Temple of the Key." Another smile. "Helping *you* to help *me*."

The Crystal Island grew closer still. He could make out individual trees in the sparkling jungle, twinkling with their own silver light.

Quilla continued. "And help me, you did. Brought me to the Threshold, convinced Suyana to take you into the Crossing. Everything I needed you to do."

He felt sick. This was all his fault. Adi had been right—they'd been moved like pieces on a board.

"Everything was set...until that witch appeared here," she said, an edge in her voice. "How she escaped the monastery, traveled to the Temple—" She broke off, casting him another suspicious look.

Hope sparked again in him. Another surprise for Quilla—and another involving Morrigan. Morrigan's coven had been formed to block passage to the Black Island. Could their magic work against Quilla or her creation? The coven arose after Quilla's death, so even she might not know. Was this why Morrigan seemed to worry her? "How did Morrigan arriving here change anything? She's in the Gray Lands."

"When Suyana showed you the witch, I feared you would tell of Jack 'saving' you at the monastery from an astral power intent on the Chakana. She would ask of this Jack. If she learned I came from the Crystal Island in Dream...well, Suyana is no fool. I slipped into her, ready to seize control, but you took Jack's appearance as a warning to stay silent. Again, you helped me, thinking I was helping you."

He understood. "You were in *Suyana* inside the Crossing. That's why the Guardians reacted to her."

"Yes. While I was inside *you*, the piece of the Chakana shielded me from the Guardians. I lost that protection in Suyana. I hid deep, but the Snake and Puma sensed something. When we reached the Condor, I was better hidden. Once through his realm, I had no need to hide."

Another step, and the Island rushed forward. Another, and the crystal pyramid loomed overhead. A third step, a beach of sparkling jewels crunched under their feet. A path led through shining trees where transparent leaves danced on glass branches. Quilla entered the path, Will still her unwilling companion, and the forest swallowed them.

"And now you see the chaos of the Book," Quilla-Suyana said, disgust on her face as she looked around them.

His eyes searched as far as his immovable head allowed. "The Book? Where? I just see trees."

"Fool. These trees, this forest. This *is* the Book, its chaos growing with every heartbeat." She stopped, pointing to a branch at eye level, where a transparent bud appeared, then unfurled into a new crystal leaf.

Images played over the leaf's surface. Places and faces, rushing at him, engulfing him. Places he recognized from around the world. Faces he didn't...smiling faces, crying faces. A kaleidoscope of love and hate, birth and death, joy and tragedy, that swirled before him.

And he understood. He had witnessed the birth of a new reality.

A new universe.

His mind reeled, stunned. "This island...this forest...it holds all the 'verses?"

"Yes. And all their chaos."

"I thought it would be...bigger."

"Your eyes are fooled as easily as you are. You could walk this forest for all your years and never reach the end. It grows and grows—and the Island with it. A billion new worlds formed while we've paused here, each because some free-willed fool made a decision...or didn't. Chaos that grows forever. Chaos that will never end...unless *I* end it." She moved along the path again.

He followed, pulled by the strings on his mind. "End chaos? You mean end all these worlds. End countless lives in countless 'verses."

"Once, I was one with the Four. I saw their indifference to those lives you cry over. I saw the suffering in these worlds—and how the Four did *nothing*. Nothing but watch their little game play out. Watch their precious humans making choices with their 'free will.' Choices that over and over and over created only suffering and suffering and *more* suffering."

"We're better than that. We make mistakes, but most people are good—"

Quilla laughed, but the sound held no joy. "Most people are fools. And the choices of fools should not create entire universes. My world will be different."

It was his turn to snort. "Right. You'll make the choices *for* them."

"I will end their suffering. I will bring order."

"You don't want order. You want slaves. You're just another nut job with a god complex who—" He stopped, his words and feet halted by the strings in his head.

She spun to face him. "I will *end* this reality. I will create a new one." She spat out the words, then shoved her face into his, her breath hot and sweet. "I *am* a god."

She set out again, Will following like a faithful puppy. *Like I thought Jack was.*

They emerged from the shining forest at the base of the crystal pyramid. Steps carved into the side led straight up.

They climbed. Again, their ascent was faster than he expected. After what seemed only a half-dozen steps, they reached the top of the pyramid.

He'd expected the barren flatness of the mountain top from the Dream version of the Crystal Island, where they'd found Fader's door. Instead, a smaller, four-sided pyramid sat in the center, its sides opaque glass. "This wasn't here in Dream."

"The Library is where the Madres merge with the Four. Sitting between our world and theirs, it does not exist completely in this reality. It cannot be reflected in Dream."

A door sat off-center on this side of the Library, its sides and top askew, meeting at odd angles. The images of the Guardians were etched randomly into the glass, giving the door an unbalanced look. Ignoring it, Quilla headed for the nearest corner of the Library.

"Changed your mind?" he asked. "Not going in?"

"That is the door of the Madre del Caos. Suyana is Madre de Bondad."

They rounded the corner. A door stood centered in this face of the Library, its lines regular, meeting at right angles but with some imprecision. The

Guardians were presented in relaxed poses, unthreatening, glowing warmly as if in sunlight. The door of the Madre de Bondad.

It struck him, then. The Library with its four sides, each with a door. "The House of Four Doors," he whispered. The Rider's jewel, his costume, Nyx...the world of the Dream Rider he thought he'd created. And now this. Just another buried memory from the lost expedition? Or from the Chakana?

Buried memories... The lost expedition... The Chakana...

He remembered. Remembered why he was here. What he had searched for since returning from Peru.

His parents.

Quilla revealing herself had overwhelmed him. He'd forgotten the vision he'd had moments before that. Of Parwa killing Alvarez, the return of the Condor, the bullet from her gun flying at his heart, his rescue by the Chakana...

His rescue...but what of his parents? What had happened to them, to Ellie Cootes and Luciana, after he'd been whisked away and dropped in that river?

Quilla strode Suyana's body toward the door of the Madre de Bondad, pulling him with her. He could see no knob or handle, no way to open it. She reached the door—and kept walking.

The door vanished. As did the green sphere above her head. He remembered Suyana explaining how the spheres returned to the altar inside the Third Veil when the Travelers reached here. He followed Quilla inside.

The Library had been opaque from the outside, but inside its walls were so clear they seemed not to exist. The entire island of crystal trees lay spread below.

Dominating the space, an elevated circular pool of a silver liquid hovered waist-high above the floor. Over the pool's rippling surface, images came and went, each ripple bringing a new scene.

Revolving slowly around that pool, four figures floated, facing inward. They sat cross-legged, hands on knees as if in meditation, faces impassive, eyes unfocused but fixed on the silver liquid.

The nearest figure rotating past was Ellie Cootes. Next came Luciana.

The other two figures—

A sob burst from him, and another and another. If he had control of his body, he would have run to throw his arms around them, to hold them and never let them go.

But he could only stand there, tears streaming down his face. "Mom," he cried. "Dad."

Chapter 44

Mommy Daddy You and I

Will stared at his parents, overjoyed to find them alive but stunned to find them at all. "Why did they come here? Why didn't they leave the Crossing?"

Quilla strolled around the floating figures. "Because you disappeared with the Chakana." She considered him with narrowed eyes. "I still don't understand how you did that. But without the Chakana, the Guardians will not grant passage back through their realms. I expect Luciana led them here. And here they've stayed."

"But eight years..." He realized something else. They hadn't aged. They both looked exactly as he remembered. Exactly as they had in photographs from back then.

Quilla shrugged. "The Library exists beyond time and space. Here, time does not pass. One cannot grow old, grow hungry." She peered more closely at Luciana. "But one can go mad. I believe Luciana found a way to keep them sane."

"What?"

"They merged with the Four. To read the Book and lose themselves in the never-ending Story. You saw the crystal forest—each leaf a universe that can be read in the silver mirror."

Will tore his eyes from his parents to look at the shining pool. There, images came and went as on the leaves outside, whirling and swirling, an unending stream of places and faces.

Quilla chuckled. "Good. I feared having to battle Luciana and whomever else I found in here."

If Quilla feared such a battle, were there limits to how many people she could control? Again, he filed that away.

Turning from the pool, she walked back to him. "Now, for that unfinished business." She removed the Chakana from Suyana's pouch. A silver cord appeared, snaking from the Chakana to his chest. Quilla grasped it again and tugged.

The cord grew taut, pulling on the piece in his mind. Pulling his thoughts, too, away from his parents. He gritted his teeth, waiting for the pain of the fragment being torn from his head.

But he felt no pain. Only a sudden and profound emptiness, an overwhelming sense of loss. Before him, the Chakana blazed so brightly he had to close his eyes. The brilliance dimmed. He opened his eyes.

Quilla was smiling, holding the Chakana before her. The artifact now shone with an inner light, pulsing like a heartbeat. "Well, well. It *was* easier in here."

He didn't know how he'd expected to feel. He'd wanted this moment for so long. To no longer be broken. To finally be *free*. He almost laughed. Free? He could go anywhere now...except he couldn't even move his body. And soon, when Quilla destroyed all of reality, there would be no *anywhere*. Or anything.

That should have been his big concern. Yet all he felt in the moment was a terrible longing for what had been a part of him for eight years and now was gone. He felt it like a hole inside him—like the blackness, the void he'd seen inside the Chakana.

Swinging the Chakana by its cord, Quilla returned to where the four figures slowly circled the hovering pool. "Now, which one to use?"

A sudden fear for his parents pulled him back. "What do you mean?"

"I can now change the Story. Finish my beautiful world of Order, the Black Island, the Black Mirror...and end the chaos of the Tree. However, to do that, I must merge with the Orden aspect of the Four. But physically replacing a Traveler while they are merged with the Four would wake the others. Plus, I cannot remain in Suyana for this. She would attract her aspect of the Four—Bondad, not Orden. No, I must leave Suyana and take over the one who is merged with Orden."

She considered Luciana as the Madre floated past. "Certainly not. Luciana will be merged with Chaos. And she is too old and frail for what will follow."

Next came Jon Dreycott. "Your father, perhaps? A touch on his mind will tell me." She stared hard, then shook her head. "Merged with Mal. Let's try your mother." Her eyes burned into Terri Yurikami as she passed. "No. Bondad. Disappointing. I'd hoped to use one of your parents."

"Why?"

"I expected one, perhaps both, to have astral abilities, since you do. Yet *neither* does. But then, why should they?" She laughed at him. "They aren't really your parents."

If Will had control over his body, he would have dropped to his knees. No, no, no. Too many shocks. Too many... One after another after another. Jack. Quilla. Finding his parents... His parents? Not his parents?

"What? No," he croaked. "No. They...they're my parents. They *are* my parents... They..." His words died away. The hole where the Chakana had lived inside him gaped wider, ready to swallow him.

Quilla raised an eyebrow. "You didn't know? They never told you? Ah, well. Parents, right? Mine sold me to the Sisters when I was six." Dismissing the subject with a wave, she moved to Ellie Cootes. "This one is with Orden. *My* Orden."

Keeping pace as Ellie circled the silver pool, Quilla placed the Chakana in Ellie's hand, then closed her own over it. A moment later, Suyana's body stiffened and stopped walking, her eyes unfocused.

Ellie Cootes jerked upright where she sat. She blinked. Tilting her head back, Quilla-Ellie laughed. "Now, I finish what I began so long ago." Her eyes narrowed, focused on the silver mirror.

The images on the shining surface grew smaller and smaller, as the view pulled back and back, until the pool showed a single, enormous silver tree. In some primal part of his being, Will knew this was the entire forest of trees here on the Crystal Island, each leaf a universe.

The tree of all creation. The *Tree*.

And something else. Something that didn't belong. Something *wrong*. Lowest on the trunk of the silver tree, a single bare branch grew. The branch was little more than a stub, with no other branches or leaves growing from it. And while the rest of the tree was silver, this branch was blue.

Blue. The color of Order.

As he watched, the blue branch flared brighter, then began to pulse. Quilla-Ellie gave a cry of joy, then slipped from her invisible seat, landing lightly on her feet, the Chakana in her hand. Throughout, Luciana and his parents had remained silent, staring trance-like at the silver surface.

Tears streamed down Ellie's face—Quilla's tears. "It is done! I have restarted the growth of my beautiful world. Now, it can complete itself." She walked to a still-immobile Will. "And then I will end this world and its infinite chaos." She stroked his cheek. "Thank you, Will Dreycott, for making this possible. Now, goodbye." Quilla-Ellie smiled at him...

...and disappeared.

The Chakana fell to the floor as Will fell to his knees, control of his body returning.

He'd done this. It was all *his* fault.

If he hadn't chased after the Chakana, it would never have blasted Fader to the In Between. They would never have gone to the Crystal Island in Dream to rescue him. Never have brought Jack—no, Quilla—back from there. Back into the world.

And if he hadn't insisted on coming to Peru... He'd brought Quilla here, too. To the Crossing. *With* the Chakana. And convinced Suyana to trust them. He'd done it all in his stubborn search to learn what had happened to him. To find his parents...who weren't even his parents. And now Ellie had been taken...

Adi had been right. They'd been pieces in a game—and he was just a pawn. A stupid, foolish pawn.

"Stop it!" came a familiar voice.

He turned.

Nyx floated above where the Chakana lay, a silver cord curling between her and the artifact. "Feeling sorry for yourself won't stop Quilla. Time may not pass in here, but it does where she is, and you're wasting it. Stand up."

He pushed himself shakily to his feet. "*Now* you come?"

"I warned you I had a role to play. As the Key, not as Nyx. Opening the Crossing. Passing the Guardians. Now that role is over. Now we need to stop Quilla."

"How? Where'd she go? How'd she disappear?"

"The Library gives access to all the multiverse. To view it in the silver mirror—or to transport yourself anywhere in it."

"Then why didn't Luciana and my parents—?"

"—*if* you hold the Chakana. Quilla's gone to the Black Island."

"How do you know?"

"She used the Chakana—*me*—to get there. She'll be on her way to the Black Tower."

"Why didn't she jump straight to the Tower?"

"You can't," Nyx said. "That place is hidden from here."

"She said she's going to end all of creation. All the multiverse. Can she do that?"

"From the Tower, she can. She'll use the Black Pool—her version of the silver mirror."

In the silver pool, Quilla's branch of Order still pulsed blue. Had it grown longer? "Quilla said she'd *restarted* her world," Will said, "and it could now *complete itself.*"

"Then her mirror's not ready yet," Nyx said. "And she still must reach the Tower. We may have time."

"How much?"

"I don't know."

"Can't the Four stop her? They must know what she's doing."

Nyx looked grim. "They know, but they will never interfere. The Four aren't in danger—only their creation. You can't destroy an artist by destroying their painting."

"So, all they'll do is *watch*? Like we're just a game?"

"Not a game. An experiment. An investigation into free will. Into the choices humans make with that free will. Including Quilla's choices."

"That's disgusting."

"I don't disagree. But it changes nothing. The Four will not stop Quilla."

"So, how do *we* stop her? And without hurting Ellie?"

"I don't know that, either. Where are the others?"

Will swore at himself for forgetting his companions, especially Case. He remembered their blank faces when he came out of his last vision. "Physically, they're in the Condor's realm, but I think Quilla sent them to the Gray Lands."

"Makes sense. She's afraid of you three. I sensed it when she linked with me."

"What's she afraid of? She slapped us down like flies. And why wouldn't she send *me* there, too?"

Nyx floated closer. "She's afraid of you three *together*. If she sent *you* to the Gray Lands, you'd lead the others to their Dream doors and back into their bodies. Which is exactly what you must do."

"You mean go to sleep? Sail up the River of Souls?"

"No time for that. You can enter the Gray Lands while awake."

"What? How?"

"You've learned to astral project while awake, right? The Gray Lands are just another astral destination."

"I had a piece of *you* in me then," he said, sensing the hole inside him. "That's gone now."

"You're stronger than you know. I've seen it. Yeshe saw it. Quilla, too. That's why she latched onto you as Jack. That's why she's afraid of you." Nyx pointed to where the Chakana lay. "Pick it up."

"Nyx—"

"We don't have the time. *Pick it up!*"

Stooping, he picked up the Key. It sat warm in his hand, pulsing to his heartbeat. "Why didn't Quilla take it with her?"

"When someone portals from here, the Chakana must stay behind. It's a rule."

He stared at Nyx. *No. It isn't a rule*, he thought. The seed of an idea formed. He filed it away. "How do I get to the Gray Lands?"

"Close your eyes. Now, imagine that place..."

A gray mist drifted across his mind.

"Imagine *being* there. Imagine it above you, below you, surrounding you. Let that image fill your head..."

The mist disappeared. A desolate, colorless landscape lay before him, an expanse of perfectly flat, randomly angled slopes, some steep, some gentle, all meeting in sharp creases like the facets of a huge silver jewel carved by a madman.

"Now, step forward," Nyx said, her voice muffled, as if farther away. "Like you step into the dreams of others."

He felt the grit of the gray surface under his feet. He opened his eyes.

The forlorn scene stretched unbroken until lost in the mists that rolled forever over this place. Behind him flowed the dark waters of the River of Souls, shot through with the gleaming cords of Dreamers. Above lay the infinite darkness of the Nothing. No moon or stars here. The only light came from the landscape itself, which shone upwards with a weak silvery glow.

"Holy shit," he whispered. "I did it."

Overlaying the Gray Lands, a hazy image of Nyx in the Library appeared, with the silver pool and circling figures of Luciana and his parents-not-parents behind her. "As Fader would say...*superpowers!*" she said.

"Uh, I can still see you. Sort of."

"Lucky you. Your spirit is straddling both worlds. Clock's ticking. Go find our friends."

"Can you bring the Room?"

"You can do that yourself. I'm not in your mind anymore, but you still have your subconscious. Everything you've ever created for Dream is still there. Just call for it."

He did.

A loud 'pop' sounded as the Room of Four Doors, this time a crystal pyramid, appeared steps away. He willed its nearest door to open.

Brian the Doogle trotted out, followed by Doogles Two and Three. After Marell had killed three Doogles and almost killed Brian, Will had stopped naming the creatures.

Seeing Will, Brian raced to him, curling and uncurling his long thin tail in Doogle delight. Will knelt to nuzzle him. "Find Case," he whispered into a huge round ear.

He was gambling that Fader, Rani, and Suyana would all be with Case. They'd been together when Quilla appeared in the Condor's realm, and he needed to save time. Though time passed slower in Dream—an entire adventure took only a few seconds—it still passed.

Ears up, Brian rotated his head, scanning the Gray Lands, then sped off, his path as straight as an arrow. Promising.

Will held out his hand, and a crystal sphere the size of a baseball dropped into his palm. Scenes of Ellie Cootes flashed and tumbled inside the data ball. From Dream when she'd met with his parents in Toronto. His visions of her with the expedition. The Christmas memory Case had shared.

Quilla had seized Ellie's body, so he guessed Ellie was now in the Gray Lands. He was unsure what finding her would accomplish, but he needed to try. He gave Ellie's data ball to Doogle Two, who trotted off into the mists, zigzagging slowly. Not promising.

Producing another data ball, he stared at the too-familiar face floating in the sphere, fighting a shiver. Was this a mistake? Maybe, but they needed all the help they could get. He fed the ball to Doogle Three, who tore off in yet another direction.

Will touched his wrist. Three silver threads appeared, one for each Doogle. And Brian's was glowing—he'd already found Case. He set out after Brian.

Moments later, four figures, standing immobile, loomed out of the mist, Brian sitting before them. Case, Fader, Rani, Suyana. His gamble had paid off.

As he approached, he wondered which news he'd break to Case first—that the universe was about to end, or that her mother was the one ending it.

Case walked between Will and Fader, leading Rani and Suyana as they hurried through the Gray Lands, following their silver cords, Brian beside them.

Case had known where she was as soon as she'd arrived here. She'd known *who* she was, too. But she'd been unable to move from where she stood with the others. None of them could...until Will found them.

A touch from him, and they'd regained control over their astral spirits. Will had been surprised they could all see their silver cords, even Rani. "Most people can't," he said.

"Most do not have your astral abilities," Suyana said, "or your...relationship with the Guardians."

"None of which helped against Quilla," Case said.

"I'm sorry, Suyana," Will said. "We brought her back. We brought her here."

Suyana shook her head. "I carried her into the Crossing without knowing. She fooled us all. What matters is we stop her—even if my body dies with her."

Case realized with horror what she meant. "Because Quilla is using your body." This kept getting worse and worse.

"One life cannot balance all lives everywhere. If I must die, so be it."

Will clenched his jaw, but said nothing.

Case shot a look at him as they walked. He'd explained Quilla's treachery as Jack, how she'd removed the Chakana piece from him in the mysterious Library, then restarted her branch of Order and leaped to the Black Island. Then he'd fallen silent. Case knew him. He had more to tell and was struggling with how to tell them. But what could be worse than the end of the universe?

She was afraid she knew the answer. "You found them, didn't you? You found our parents. Or learned what happened to them."

Fader's eyes widened. "Did you?"

"I saw the start of your vision," Case said, "before Quilla sent us here. Our parents were there. But Parwa had a gun, and Alvarez pulled his... For freak's sake, Will, tell us what happened."

"I found them. They're alive. My parents, your mom..." He looked back at Suyana. "Luciana, too."

"Thank you," Suyana said, her eyes wet.

He told of finding Luciana and their parents gazing unmoving at the silver mirror. "Quilla said Luciana did that to keep them sane."

Suyana nodded. "The Story would fill their minds, stop them from going mad as years passed. But reading the Book, seeing the vastness of creation—it affects even a Madre. You may find your parents...changed."

"Is that why you didn't tell us?" Case asked Will.

"No. What Suyana said. That we might have to kill the body Quilla is in."

"I told you," Suyana said. "I am ready to die."

"Quilla didn't take *you* to the Black Island," Will said.

Case felt as if she was falling from a great height. "No. Not that."

The pain on Will's face mirrored the pain inside her. "I'm sorry. She took your mom."

A sob escaped Fader, even as she choked back her own. She slipped an arm around her brother as they walked. Eight years without their mom. Eight years hating her for leaving them. Then learning that she'd done it for them, for their family. And now to find her, only to lose her again.

"We're *going* to save her," she said, surprised by the ferocity of her words. "We'll find her and stop Quilla. We'll save the freaking universe—and our mom."

Fader leaned against her.

Will nodded. "Sounds like a plan."

"Uh, actually, those are just goals, not a plan," Rani said.

"Rani—" Case began.

"No, she's right," Will said. "We need a plan. And the first step is getting to the Black Island."

"You mean that weird subway station?" Rani said. "In Toronto? Where we *aren't?*"

"Doesn't matter," Case said. "It was gone when Fader and I went back to check."

"I have another way," Will said. "Once you, Fader, and Rani are back in your bodies, meet me in the Library. It's on top of the pyramid on the Crystal Island."

"But even if we get to the Black Island," Case said, "what about her scarabs? We barely escaped them last time."

"Oh, god," Rani said. "Bugs again."

"I can take us into the In Between," Fader said. "Like last time."

"Are your fading powers back?" Case asked. "Because my Voice is still a no-show."

Fader's face fell. "No."

"Your powers depend on accessing other 'verses," Will said. "Remember what Fader said, after we passed through the First Veil? About this place having only one version?"

Suyana nodded. "It is true. Beyond the First Veil, we exist outside of all universes. The Veils, the Threshold, the Crossing—they have no other versions."

"That's why your powers disappeared here. But they worked on the Black Island, remember?"

"What if you're wrong?" Case asked.

"Death by bugs," Rani muttered.

"We'll bring backup with firepower," Will said. "Adi, Stone, Mei. Diego and his soldiers." He looked at Suyana.

She nodded. "The Sisters will fight, too."

"But how do we tell them what's happening?" Case said. "And how would they reach the Black Island?"

Will turned to Suyana. "When you escape here, you'll be in the Library.

Could you *portal* from there back to the Threshold? Tell everyone what's happening? Round up an army?"

Suyana's eyebrows shot up. "Yes! That would work."

"Still the problem of getting them to the Black Island," Case said.

"I have an idea for that, too," Will said. "But I need to talk to Nyx first."

"Talk to the Chakana?" Suyana said, amazement and some fear in her eyes.

Despite the urgency of stopping Quilla, a sudden thought seized Case. "Will, our mom. If Quilla's taken her over, wouldn't she'd be here, too? In the Gray Lands?"

"She's *here*?" Fader said, his eyes widening.

Will touched his left wrist. Two silver cords appeared, running into the distance. One glowed brightly. Will tapped the cord that wasn't glowing. "That's the leash for a Doogle I sent to look for her. Sorry, guys. She's not here."

"I don't understand," Case said, trying to hide how much pain that brought.

"Quilla only pushed me here after she reached the Library," Suyana said. "Until then, I remained in my body, aware but a prisoner to her will."

"Why would she do that?"

"It is easier to examine a person's memories when they remain in their mind. For me, she searched for traps, defenses in the Library since she was last there. For your mother, Quilla may want to learn of your astral powers, perhaps thinking they came from her."

Case glanced at Fader. "We used to think the same. Who's the other leash for? The glowing one?"

Will hesitated. "Somebody who *is* here. And they're close by."

"Not an answer."

"Wait here. I'll bring the answer back." He headed off in the direction of the glowing cord.

"Do we have time for this?" Rani asked. "End of the world, right?"

"We are in Dream," Suyana said. "Only seconds have passed since Will found us. And Quilla will not expect us to escape so quickly."

Will reappeared, another Doogle and another figure beside him. A figure with red hair shining like a sunrise in this dismal land.

As they approached, Morrigan narrowed her eyes at Case, raised an eyebrow at Rani and Suyana, then smiled warmly at Fader. "Hello again, little one."

Case spun on Will. "Are you freaking *kidding* me?"

Chapter 45

They've Surrounded the Island

"Have you forgotten how many times she's tried to kill us?" Case yelled, barely controlling her fury. "What she's done? To the Hollow Boys? To Adi? To *me*?"

Will held up his hands. "No, I haven't. But we need her firepower. And she betrayed Quilla."

"She *helped* Quilla!"

"Against my will," Morrigan said.

Case faced the witch. "You tried to kill us at the monastery."

"I *saved* you at the monastery."

"*Excuse* me?"

"Quilla promised no bloodshed. I wasn't prepared when Herrada's men opened fire. I couldn't stop the first deaths, but I intervened to prevent more."

"You fired a spell at us! I saw it miss."

Morrigan sniffed. "I did not *miss*. I hit Herrada's men at the far end of the corridor, after stunning Herrada and those beside him. For that betrayal, Quilla sent me to this place."

"Quilla told me the same," Will said. "Finding Morrigan here proves that. And her coven's magic *was* a defense against the Black Island—which is what we need now."

Case hesitated, now unsure. "She's still Morrigan."

"There's good in her, Case," Fader said, his voice pleading. "I know there is."

Morrigan swallowed, and for the first time, Case saw a softness in the witch's face. "Thank you, little one."

"Why should we trust you?" Case said.

Morrigan shrugged. "Quilla wishes to create a universe of *order*. I'm not much for order. I rather like this world as it is. In it, I have power." She narrowed her eyes at Case. "And you know I will always protect your brother—even if that means protecting *you* as well."

Case nodded. "Okay, I believe her."

"Uh, she basically said she hates you," Rani said.

"That's how I know she isn't lying." She glared at Morrigan, who glared back.

"Great," Rani said. "One big, happy family. Now let's find these door things so I can get eaten by giant bugs."

"Would you like to avoid that possibility?" Will said.

Rani folded her arms. "Listening."

Case listened too, hope growing in her as Will explained his plan.

"You want me to *stay* in here?" Rani said. "*Alone?*"

Will shrugged. "No scarabs. And you won't be alone."

"Please, Rani," Case pleaded.

"Please," Fader said, too.

Rani gave an exaggerated sigh. "Fine. I'll be the hero. *Again*." She held out her hand, and Will gave her the leash for Doogle Two.

Leaving Rani behind, the rest of the travelers set out once more.

Having found their doors and escaping the Gray Lands, Will stood with Suyana in the Library, in their bodies again.

"I will return to the Threshold and gather our army," Suyana said.

"Morrigan, too. And Adi and her people." He handed her the Chakana.

She held up the artifact. "If I do not sense this...?"

"Then we're on our own."

Suyana glanced at his parents, still circling the silver pool with Luciana. "Do not wake them. It could endanger their sanity. If... No, *once* we defeat Quilla, Luciana and I will bring them back."

He nodded, not telling her he didn't want to talk to them right now, anyway. Suyana closed her eyes...and disappeared. The Chakana fell to the floor, as it had when Quilla portaled.

Nyx appeared, floating above the Chakana. "Well done."

"How long was I gone?"

"Ten seconds, maybe. "What good is an army at the Threshold?"

"Once Case and Fader get here, we'll portal to the Black Island." He picked up the Chakana. "I'm taking this. Suyana will sense it and jump to it with her troops."

"Will, I told you—the Chakana can't leave the Crossing. It's a rule."

He stared at Nyx. "No, it's not. If it's a rule, it's one the Chakana can break. One *you* can break. You broke it eight years ago, when you zapped me into that river."

Now it was Nyx's turn to stare.

"Why, Nyx? Why did you do that?"

"To save your life."

"Why not my parents, too? And Luciana?"

"There wasn't time. Parwa had pulled the trigger. You and I were connected—"

"*Why* were we connected? Why did a piece of you get stuck in me? Why—?"

The Library door nearest them disappeared. Case and Fader burst in, both panting. They stopped dead, staring at the silver pool and floating figures. "Holy shit," Case whispered.

Nyx spoke in his mind. *Will, I will explain everything, but we must stop Quilla before it's too late.*

She was right. Not the time. "Come on," he called to Case and Fader. He hung the Chakana around his neck. "You'll let me take this?"

Nyx hesitated. "Yes, but Quilla can also pull power from it—from me—when you get near her. It could help her more than you."

Wonderful. "Too late now. It's the only plan we have," he said, as Case and Fader reached his side. "How do I do this?"

"Same way you reached the Gray Lands," Nyx said. "Call up an image of the Black Island..."

In his mind, an expanse of blue sand beside a too-black sea appeared. Behind the beach, a dense jungle of black trees and vegetation rose.

"...then step forward, together."

Will took Case's hand, and she took Fader's.

"Uh," Nyx said, "where's Rani?"

They stepped forward.

Rani sat in the Gray Lands, Doogle Two facing her, long tail curling and uncurling.

"Well," she said, "at least, you seem to like me."

The Doogle curled its tail.

Rani checked the silver leash running from her wrist to the Doogle's collar. "So, we have to wait until this gets all bright and glowy?"

A nod.

She gazed out across the bleak landscape. "Bored now."

But her other choice for a role in the coming fight had been the Black Island with its giant bugs.

Bugs or boredom?

She hugged herself. Boredom worked.

In the forest of the Great Trees, Adi paced the raised stage of the amphitheater. Around the rim of the theater above, four archers watched over her and Morrigan.

The witch remained frozen on the stage, immobile as a statue. Adi's thoughts were on Will. Why weren't they back yet? What had they found in there? Jon? Terri? Alive after all these years? How could that be possible? How could—?

"I know you."

She spun to find Morrigan frowning at her. Adi's hand flinched toward the old stab wound, a souvenir from their first encounter. It still hurt some days.

Cries from above snapped both their heads up. Morrigan's awakening had been noticed. The archers stood with arrows nocked and aimed at Adi and the witch below. The unmasked Sister named Yanta called down to them. "*Do not move!*"

Morrigan chuckled. "Well, this should be fun." Runic characters appeared on her face, like golden tattoos. The symbols, now glowing, flowed down her left arm. Morrigan raised that hand to the Sisters.

"Stop!"

Adi jumped as a collective gasp escaped the archers. Morrigan lowered her arm, the runes fading.

Somehow, Suyana had appeared on the stage beside them. Her eyes found Yanta above. "Gather what warriors there are in the Threshold. Bring them here. And send me Isobel. Now!"

Yanta bowed quickly and ran off.

"Come!" Suyana cried, leaping from the stage and hurrying up the steps.

"What is going on?" Adi demanded, as she and Morrigan ran after her. "How did you get here? Where's Will?"

"He is safe, as are the others...for now. They are going to the Black Island. And we must follow."

The Black Island? The place from where Case, Fader, and Rani rescued Will? "What? Why?"

Suyana waved her off as they reached the top. "I will explain, but not now. All creation hangs in the balance."

Adi snorted. "Oh, come now. I—"

"What she says is true," Morrigan said.

"And we need you and your people," Suyana told Adi.

Adi understood none of this, but that didn't matter. "If Will is there, I'm coming."

"As am I," Morrigan said.

Suyana nodded. "Good. But you will both follow my orders."

Until I decide not to, Adi thought. Morrigan smiled, and Adi guessed the witch had the same plan.

A Sister ran up to Suyana. Adi recognized Isobel from that morning. Suyana spoke to her. "Speed yourself to the Temple of the Key. Gather what warriors you can and release the prisoners."

"And return their weapons," Adi said. Suyana nodded her confirmation.

"And then, Madre?"

"Once you are assembled at the Temple, you must sense the Chakana...and jump to it." She laid a hand on Isobel's shoulder. "And child, be prepared. You travel to the Black Island."

Isobel's eyes widened.

"Do not fear," Suyana said. "You are a warrior who faced the terrors there and rescued our lost Sisters."

Isobel straightened. "I will not fail the Sisterhood." She sprinted into the trees in the direction of the Second Veil.

Suyana ordered an archer to return Adi's gun. "I can now sense the Chakana," Suyana said, her eyes distant. "Our young friends have jumped to the Black Island. When Yanta returns with our warriors, we will join them."

Remembering what Will had told her of that place, Adi strapped on her holster.

As Case stepped forward into the vision of the Black Island, vertigo seized her. Her foot found only air, and then she was falling. Will and Fader's hands slipped from hers as she flailed her arms. She hit the ground hard, tumbling head over heels.

Groaning, she struggled to her feet. Steps away, Fader and Will were doing the same. They stood again on the beach of cobalt blue bordering a black sea stretching unbroken to the horizon. The air was warm and damp. Above, blue lightning streaked the silver dome of the sky that hung starless and moonless. Beyond the sand lay the dark jungle, lush with towering trees and broad-leaved plants shining black in the silvery light.

"Now," Will said, "we wait for Suyana to sense the Chakana and bring our army. Then we head for the Black Pyramid."

Danger!

Case jumped, startled by the return of her Voice, then thrilled...then frightened. *What danger?*

The roar of crashing timber from the jungle confirmed the vision in her mind. "Scarabs!" she cried, running to her brother and Will. "Fader! Get us into the In Between!"

Fader stood trembling, his hands clenched, his eyes focused on something she couldn't see as the screams of broken trees grew louder.

"Fader!"

"I can't find it! I can't find the In Between."

The trees lining the beach toppled as dozens of scarabs the size of cars burst from the jungle, then stopped at the edge of the blue sand. Their heads and faceted eyes swiveled to the three intruders.

She waited for them to charge. She waited to die. They didn't move.

She turned. Beside her, Will held the Chakana before him, his eyes locked on the nearest scarab.

As the Chakana pulsed in his hand, Will reached for the group mind of the scarabs—the gestalt intelligence he'd once touched fleeing these creatures on this very beach. He'd bought some time then. Maybe he could do it again.

Contact came. But not the one he expected.

A chuckle. *Did you miss your puppy?*

Quilla, don't do it. Don't destroy all those worlds, kill all those—

Only the world I am creating matters. A pause. *How did you free your friends? How can the Chakana be here?*

Her words held the same arrogance as before, but something else, too. Confusion...and fear.

He felt a touch on his mind. She was reaching for him. The touch became a grip, like fingers tightening around his skull. He pushed back, the Chakana flaring hot in his hand. Quilla's scream of fury exploded in his head. He fell to the blue sand as her grip on his mind disappeared.

A shudder ran through the line of scarabs facing them. Their heads swiveled to lock on the three intruders. They charged.

"Get up, Will!" Case cried.

As he struggled to his feet, a hand locked around his arm and pulled. He stumbled, falling backward as the scarabs swarmed at them...

...and stopped. The bugs milled about, their antennae twitching, their heads turning, as if searching for their prey.

He, Case, and Fader now lay sprawled in the winding hallway of the In Between. Behind them, an unending line of doors filled that side of the corridor, each a hand's width apart, each with a tall window. The hallway twisted like a snake in both directions, rising and falling in rolling waves. Before them, on the opposite wall, the scene on the beach with the scarabs displayed, as if on a screen.

"Sorry. That was close," Fader said as they got to their feet. He looked scared.

Case hugged him. "You saved us, bro. So, we wait for Suyana and the others in here?"

Will hesitated.

"What?"

"I don't think the Sisters can sense the Chakana if it's in the In Between."

She shot a look at the wall showing the scarabs scouring the beach. "You mean we have to step out there? With the bugs?"

Will considered the scene. Behind the scarabs, past the blue sand, a wide swathe of broken trees stretched like a trampled highway through the jungle to the Black Pyramid rising in the distance.

"Line of sight, right?" he asked Fader.

Fader's eyes widened. "Yes! I'll zoom us to the pyramid."

"Once we're away from the beach," Will said, "we'll find a spot without scarabs to step out."

⚜

Case watched the scene on the wall of the In Between as Fader zoomed them through the jungle. "Quilla was in the minds of the scarabs?"

Will nodded. "I think she can control them."

"This gets better and better. Does she know we're using the In Between?"

Will's brow furrowed. "She saw this place as Jack when we rescued Fader from the Crystal Island in Dream." His face fell. "Shit. She also saw Fader's zooming powers when we escaped the Temple of the Key. Jack was inside me then. And through the scarabs, she just saw us disappear. So, yeah, I'm guessing she knows."

The Black Pyramid loomed in the distance. "What if the Red Door is closed?" she asked.

"Morrigan told me it was open," Will said. "Almost falling off its hinges."

"My Voice is back. It warned me of the scarabs. Once we're inside, I can lead us through the tunnels to the Black Tower."

"Then we have our real problem."

"Stopping Quilla," she said.

"When she talked to me through the scarabs, she said she was *creating* her world. That means she's not finished yet. We still have time."

"But how do we stop her without hurting Mom?" Fader said, his voice breaking even as he kept zooming forward.

"I don't know, dude. But I'm sure there's a way, and Quilla's worried we'll find it. I sensed that when I touched her mind, just now. She's afraid of *us*. And Nyx said Quilla's afraid of the three of us *together*."

"Together?" Fader said. "Like we'll use our powers against her at the same time?"

"Yeah," Will said. "Any ideas on how we do that?"

Case tried to imagine how their powers could work together against someone like Quilla—and failed. She shook her head.

"I don't see any scarabs," Fader said. "Should we take the Chakana outside?"

Will nodded, and Fader stopped in a clearing surrounded by trampled vegetation and broken trees. Will pulled out the Chakana so it hung on top of his t-shirt. To Case, its glow seemed fainter now than in the Crossing.

"Be ready to pull me back if scarabs come," Will said. "I'll wait as long as I can to give Suyana the best chance."

"I'm coming with you," Case said.

"You're safer in here."

"If *I'm* safe, my Voice won't warn me of scarabs. *You'll* be safer if I'm with you."

He hesitated, then nodded. They stepped through together.

This far from the black sea, the air was thick and humid. The heat hit her like a physical force. "How long do we wait?"

"Shouldn't take long. Suyana is expecting this. A Sister showed up right away anytime I exposed the Chakana before. Or when my...parents did." He scanned the jungle, not meeting her eyes.

Something was wrong with him. She'd known it as soon as he'd found her in the Gray Lands. At first, she'd put it down to his battle with Quilla. Or losing the piece of the Chakana inside him. Or having to tell her and Fader about their mom.

But she knew him. There was something else. Something personal...and painful.

"Will," she said gently, "what's wrong?"

"Uh, fate of all universes hanging by a thread?" he said, his eyes still on the jungle.

"No, something happened after I got pushed into the Gray Lands. And I can tell it's hurting you."

He swallowed, then nodded...and told her of his parents. Of Quilla claiming they *weren't* his parents.

As he spoke, she remembered Rani's story. Could Adi really be Will's mom? It now seemed more likely, but should she say something?

No. Rani might still be wrong. And regardless, this wasn't the time. Right now, they needed Will focused on Quilla.

She pulled him into a hug. "Will, I'm so sorry. But Quilla might have lied. And even if it's true, does it matter? Your parents love you. Think of all they did for you, the life they gave you—"

He broke off the hug. "Exposing me to the Chakana, so I'd be a prisoner in my home forever?"

"They didn't know that would happen. They gave up a lifelong search and brought you to Peru to save you."

He stared out across the ravaged jungle, his lips a tight line.

"Will, don't make the same mistake I made about our mom. Thinking for eight years she'd run out on us. Thinking she never loved us. Even if you *are* adopted—they're still your parents. And they love you."

He sighed. "Okay. I'll talk to them...assuming we get out of—"

"Fader!" she cried, cutting Will off as a vision filled her mind. "Bring us back inside!"

Two arms appeared out of nowhere, grabbing her and Will as dozens of scarabs scuttled into the clearing, heading straight for them.

Case stumbled back into the In Between, Will beside her. On the wall view, the giant bugs scrambled back and forth where she and Will had stood seconds before. "Now what?"

Will shook his head. "No idea. Even if Suyana had time to sense the Chakana..." He nodded at the swarming scarabs. "...they'll portal into the middle of *that*."

"Shit," she said, remembering something. "When we first met Isobel, when she jumped to the Black Island chasing you, she appeared nowhere near you and the Chakana. She said this place is different somehow. She couldn't jump any closer than the beach."

"Meaning Suyana and her army might already be here? But back on the beach?"

"Or might not be coming." She looked at Will. "We can't wait for them. We have to get to Quilla."

"But we still don't know how to stop her," Fader said.

"Won't matter if we don't reach her before she finishes her new world."

"We keep going," Will said. "To the pyramid. Alone."

Chapter 46

Bulletproof...I Wish I Was

M orrigan waited on the amphitheater stage with Suyana and the one called Adi, plus Yanta and a dozen Sisters wearing their ridiculous bird masks and armed with bows and swords. Morrigan did many things well. Waiting was not one of them. "Why are we still here?"

"The Chakana has become hidden to me," Suyana said. "We wait for young Will to expose it again before we can join our young friends on the Black Island."

Morrigan snorted, feigning an indifference she didn't feel. The Black Island. Quilla. Suddenly needing a reminder of her own power, she pulled the Unicorn Tapestry around her. Twice it had saved her—the dragon and the bat. Fire and Air. Only the brown rat and white eel remained—Earth and Water.

And the Unicorn itself. She still did not know what power that beast held or what price it would demand. But all great magicks required payment. And the greater the magicks...

"Madre!" Yanta cried.

"Yes! I sense it, too," Suyana said. "Quickly! Join hands." A window appeared, hanging in the air. A window that grew to a door, through which Morrigan saw a familiar beach of cobalt sand separating a black jungle from a blacker sea.

Morrigan grasped Suyana's hand, again fighting the fear the scene brought. Adi took her other hand. Suyana stepped forward, pulling Morrigan with her, even as Morrigan pulled Adi.

As her vision blurred, Morrigan's front foot found only air. She stumbled, releasing the others' hands as she fell, landing face down on the blue beach. Cursing, she regained her feet, brushing sand from her clothes and hair.

Beside her, Adi scanned the area, her pistol out. "Where's Will? And what the hell are those?" She pointed down the sand.

Morrigan swore. Fifty paces away and closing fast, a mass of giant scarabs charged toward them.

Yanta and the other warriors rushed into a line, arrows nocked. Beside Suyana, Adi raised her gun.

"Your weapons will do nothing," Morrigan said.

"Can *you* stop them?" Adi asked, her eyes and gun still on the charging bugs, now thirty steps away.

"The effects of my spells on them are short-lived. As we may be." Morrigan ran her left hand over the Tapestry where it hung from her shoulders. There—the eel. And there—the rat.

But which? Water or Earth?

The scarabs were seconds away.

Water? A wave from this strange sea to sweep these creatures away? Sweep her away, too, though.

Earth then.

Help me once more, my Sisters.

She touched the rat. Pain stabbed her fingers, like needle-sharp teeth biting her. She snatched her hand away.

A rat leaped from a corner of the Tapestry, growing and growing as it emerged. It landed, the size of a grizzly, on all four paws in front of them. The Sisters screamed as it slid to a stop in the sand, greasy brown fur glistening in the silver light, red eyes on the advancing bugs.

At the sight of the rat, the scarabs halted their rush. In unison, every bug's head tilted left, then right, as if controlled by a single mind examining this new thing.

The rat lowered its whiskered snout to the beach, sniffing. Then, a flurry of flying paws sprayed blue sand back into the faces of Morrigan and the others as the creature burrowed into the sand...

And disappeared.

The scarabs charged forward once more.

"*That* was your solution?" Adi shouted, firing her pistol. Beside her, the archers let fly a volley of arrows.

But as Morrigan had warned, the bullets and arrows had no effect, glancing off the chitinous armor of the bugs. Drawing her sword, Yanta rushed forward screaming, her warriors following, their own blades raised.

The Sisters met the line of bugs, fending off the creatures' pincer-like mandibles so deftly that, at first, Morrigan let herself believe they had a chance. But then one Sister fell, almost cut in half. Then another and another, until the scarabs threatened to surround the remaining warriors.

"Fall back!" Yanta yelled.

Adi shoved another magazine into her gun and kept firing even as she retreated with Suyana, Morrigan, and the remaining warriors. Morrigan swore. They'd lost ten already. Damn that rat! Useless piece of—

Then she felt it.

The plants. The trees. The jungle. The life that grew all around them.

The life that grew from the *earth*.

A scarab scuttled at her. Reaching toward the jungle, Morrigan pulled as if on an invisible rope.

A vine shot from the trees to whip around the scarab's short neck. Morrigan clenched her hand into a fist. The vine tightened, severing the bug's bulbous head, which thudded to the sand.

The remaining scarabs—dozens and dozens of them—stopped their advance on the Sisters and turned as one to Morrigan instead.

She smiled, feeling the Earth power in her growing.

The scarabs took a step toward her.

She held out her hands, palms up.

The scarabs charged.

She threw her arms skyward. Hundreds of vines erupted from the sand. Each seized a scarab, raising it into the air to crush it in its coils or fling it into the storm-tossed sea or dash it to the ground.

In their midst, Morrigan stood swaying, her arms slashing the air as if conducting, the Earth magic her music, the dancing vines her orchestra, the dying scarabs her symphony.

Oh, the power! To bend this green life, to bend this jungle to her will, her wish, her command.

As the vines writhed and the scarabs died, she threw back her head and laughed and laughed and laughed...

Transfixed by Morrigan's bizarre ballet of vegetation, Adi didn't realize the new danger until it was too late.

"Murderer!"

Adi spun around. Steps away, Isobel, Stone, Diego, six soldiers, and a half dozen masked Sisters were picking themselves up from the sand, a still-glowing portal behind them.

But Mei was already on her feet, a pistol in a two-fisted grip, aimed at Morrigan. "You killed Peng!" she screamed.

"No!" Adi cried. She ran toward Mei.

Mei fired.

The vines crumpled to the sand like puppets whose strings had been cut, as Morrigan, the puppet master, collapsed onto the beach.

Pain like a white-hot poker stabbed through Morrigan as she fell to her knees. Her lungs were on fire. Her breath gurgled. She touched her chest. Her hand came away dripping blood.

Some part of her mind remembered someone shouting...a loud crack...then searing pain.

She managed to raise her head. Limp vines and dead scarabs surrounded her on the blue sand. Down the beach, more figures had appeared. The woman called Adi was running toward a small dark-haired woman dressed in camouflage clothing, a woman pointing a smoking pistol at Morrigan.

She'd been...shot?

Treachery!

In her mind, she found she now knew the name of the beast she had summoned. *Tachior!* she cried in Manx. *Come to me! Save me!*

Beneath her, the sand heaved upward, lifting her into the air. She clutched at the greasy fur of the rat creature's back as it galloped down the beach, bearing her away from her attacker.

Fighting through the pain, she called once more to the life in the earth.

❦

Adi reached Mei before she could fire at Morrigan again. She shoved Mei's gun arm down. "No! She's on our side. We need her."

"She killed Peng," Mei sobbed, struggling to raise the gun again.

"Lieutenant Li! Stand down!" Stone snapped, now at her side as well.

Something went out of Mei. Her arm went limp in Adi's grip. Mei surrendered her gun to Stone and covered her face with her hands.

"Diego! Bring your medic," Adi called, running toward where Morrigan still knelt on the beach.

She hadn't taken two steps when the rat emerged from the sand beneath the witch, lifting her onto its back, then racing away.

"Morrigan, come back!" Adi called, still running. "We can help you! We can—"

The sand erupted before her. She slid to a stop as a wall of trees rose in a line across the beach, blocking her way. More trees sprang up, now on either side of their party, now behind them as well.

The trees shot higher, bending toward each other until their branches interlaced overhead, enclosing the rescue party completely. Adi ran up to the wall. The tree trunks stood tight against each other. Thick vines with wicked thorns encircled each trunk from top to bottom.

"Bloody hell," she swore.

They were trapped in a wooden cage. Will, Case, and Fader were on their own—with only a wounded witch to help them. And whose side would Morrigan choose now?

❦

Morrigan lay clinging to Tachior the Rat as it tore down the blue sand, each bounce and jolt an agony.

She felt a touch on her mind. *To where do I bear you, Mistress?*

She focused through the searing fire in her chest. *To the Black Pyramid. Kill any scarab we encounter.*

Leaving the beach, Tachior began scrambling over the wreckage of the scarabs' path through the jungle, heading for the pyramid rising in the distance.

She called up what healing magicks she knew. The runescripts appeared on her arm, one after another. With each, she touched the wound on her chest and watched the golden symbols sink into her. After each spell, the pain subsided more, but when she'd cast the last, the blood still trickled from the wound, and the pain, though less, remained.

And Morrigan the Bright, last of the White Coven of Ellan Vannin, knew she was dying.

Her fingers crept over the Unicorn Tapestry. She found no bullet hole, nor did her blood seem capable of staining the fabric. *Good. Its magicks should remain.* She kept searching it, searching every thread. So many powerful magicks in its weave, surely a healing spell hid there. But she found nothing.

No. I cannot end like this. "Sisters! Help me! The Tapestry must hold a secret to heal me. Show me where it lies."

A vision rose before her. Eleven women in a circle, flames licking at their white robes. *The Tapestry holds a way.*

She almost shouted with joy. *Show me!*

Her dead coven sisters faded, replaced by the Unicorn itself, the straw-haired maiden seated beside it, her hand on its horn.

Morrigan watched the scene play out.

No, she thought. *Not that. Never that.*

Then, her dead sisters whispered, *you will die.*

Chapter 47

Your Power

Case watched the Black Pyramid grow larger on the wall of the In Between as Fader zoomed them through the trampled jungle. And as the pyramid grew, so did Case's despair. The three of them had gone round and round on how they might defeat Quilla...and come up empty.

"Okay," she said, "let's work backwards. Whatever we try, we can't hurt our mom."

Will nodded. "Which means I need to pull Quilla *out* of her—and I don't think I'm strong enough."

"You beat Quilla at the monastery."

"She's grown stronger since then. In the Crossing, she took me over easily. I bet she's even more powerful here, in the world she created."

"You've got the Chakana."

"But Quilla can draw power from it, too. Maybe even more than I can, now that I don't have that piece in me anymore."

"What about what Rani's doing?" Case asked.

"At best, that might distract Quilla."

"But maybe long enough for you to pull her out of our mom."

"Then what? I can't hold her in her astral form forever."

"Okay, okay," Case said. "So, we have two problems to solve. Pulling Quilla out of our mom, and then doing...something with Quilla's astral spirit."

"Like what?"

"Hey!" Fader said, his eyes still on his zooming. "Could we send her back to the Crystal Island in Dream? Where we found her?"

"Don't think so, dude," Will said. "She got there by dying on the real Crystal Island. I'm guessing that was a one-off." But he fell silent, a thoughtful look on his face.

"It shouldn't be just on you," Fader said. "Nyx said Quilla's afraid of the three of us. Whatever we do, we need to do it *together*."

"You're helping already, bro," Case said. "With the In Between. But I don't see how my Voice can help. Not much use seeing the future if we can't change it."

She turned her back on the wall display, not wanting to watch the Black Pyramid and the looming confrontation with Quilla growing closer and closer.

She stared instead at the never-ending line of doors, stretching into the dim distance of the corridor in both directions. "That's weird."

"What?" Will asked.

"When we were on the Black Island before, fighting the Chambelán, these doors weren't on that wall. Well, they were, but they were all black."

"The In Between here feels different this time," Fader said, still focused on his zooming.

"How?" Will asked.

Fader shrugged. "Before, it felt like it wasn't...finished."

Will groaned. "That's because it wasn't. Because the Black Island wasn't finished. Those doors mean Quilla's almost completed this place. They mean we're running out of time. Those doors are *not* a good thing."

Case stared at the line of doors. Behind each lay another universe, each with another version of her and Will and Fader, all fighting to stop Quilla and the end of creation. All coming to this point from a different past. All able to choose a different future...

A different future...

We need to do it together...

She smiled as an idea formed. What if they all chose the *same* future?

She'd done it in the tunnel maze leading from the Temple of the Key. How many had she managed then? Five at the most? How many *could* she manage?

She focused on seeing her other selves, each standing in *their* corridor of *their* In Between. She saw three. Now five. And three more. That made eight. Try harder. Another. And another. More? No.

Ten, then.

She called to them. All ten answered. All ten listened as she explained her plan. Listened...and agreed. Exhausted, she let them go.

She turned to Will and Fader. "No, those doors *are* a good thing. A very good one."

"How?" Will said.

"I've got an idea."

❧

Case finished explaining her idea as Fader reached the Black Pyramid and began zooming them up its steps.

Will was excited but hesitant. "You *talked* to them?"

She nodded. "It's like talking to my Voice. That's what my Voice has always been, right? My other selves in other 'verses."

"And they'll do it?"

"Yep. They all think it's a great idea."

"They're all *you*. And it's your idea."

"Ever known me to be wrong?"

"Yes."

"Ever known ten of me to be wrong? Actually, eleven, counting *this* me." She shrugged. "Anyway, what else you got?"

He sighed. "Nothing."

"Hey, it *is* open," Fader called as he reached the summit.

The top of the Black Pyramid was flat and square, thirty paces a side. Squatting in the middle was a box-like structure, twice Case's height, ten paces a side, with a single door the color of blood. The Red Door hung askew, torn from its top hinges.

"Morrigan didn't lie," Fader said.

"First time for everything," Case said.

Fader glared at her, then returned to his zooming, passing them through the Red Door and into the winding, downward-slanting corridor of black stone she remembered. But unlike her last visit, wall torches no longer burned. Once past the first turn, blackness swallowed them.

Fader stopped his zooming. "Line of sight. If I can't see, I can't zoom us."

"We'll have to walk," Will said.

They stepped from the In Between into pitch darkness. Will pulled the Chakana from under his shirt again. A soft, pearly glow now lit the corridor ten paces ahead. "I'll lead. Fader, pull us back in if you hear something coming."

Case fought a shiver. Something. Like giant bugs.

She couldn't tell how long their journey in the dark passage took. They moved as quickly as they could, alert for chitinous feet scrabbling on stone. Dripping water echoed with their footsteps. Each minute seemed an eternity that brought Quilla closer to her goal.

And even with the end of the universe looming, Case's thoughts in the darkness kept returning to their mother. *We're coming, Mom.*

After what felt like hours, the corridor opened into a marble hallway Case remembered. A wide red-carpeted staircase led down into darkness.

"It's that big cavern with the ballroom—oh, shit!" Case said, gagging and fighting an urge to retch. "What is that *smell?*"

The stench from below was almost overpowering. Pulling their shirts up over their mouths and noses, they descended the staircase and started across the ballroom. The light of the Chakana fell on overturned tables and chairs, scattered cutlery, and shattered dishes.

And rotting corpses. Everywhere.

"Fader," she said. "Don't look."

"Too late," he said, but after that, he kept his eyes forward, not looking down.

"Scarabs?" she asked Will.

"I'd guess, from the state of the bodies. I bet Quilla turned them loose."

They threw nervous glances around the cavern.

"Let's get out of here. We want that tunnel over there." She pointed at a patch of deeper darkness in the far-left corner of the ballroom. Twenty paces into the tunnel, they reached the maze of smaller passages that led to the Black Tower.

Left, her Voice said.

Case took the left tunnel. "Stay close."

Ellie Cootes stood lost and confused in a misty gray wasteland. She didn't know where she was, but she knew she hadn't always been here.

She remembered *watching*...something. No, *everything*. Watching everything, everywhere. With three other people. People? They had seemed more than human. *She* had seemed more than human. Together, they had watched a silver tree in a silver pool that showed...

Everything.

Then...

Another presence in her mind, pushing her away from the silver tree, pushing her down, a prisoner in her own body.

A name for this presence came. Quilla. Quilla had done something to the silver tree, to the beautiful everything. And what she had done was *wrong*.

The silver pool and the silver tree had faded then from Ellie's vision, replaced by this place of gray mist and desolation.

Ellie blinked.

Out of the mists, a woman appeared, wearing jungle camouflage. The woman held a glowing leash attached to the strangest dog Ellie had ever seen.

Puzzled but intrigued, Ellie watched them approach. "Do I know you?"

"No," the woman said, "but I know you, Ellie. I'm Rani, and I'm here to help you find some things you've lost."

Ellie's puzzlement grew. "Lost?"

"Yeah. Like your body. And your kids. But first, we have to find a door."

Case led them through the tunnel maze, her Voice calling out each turn. They emerged at the foot of the stone stairway that spiraled upward to the Black Tower. A soft, warm glow washed the steps from above.

"Is that enough light for you to zoom again?" Will asked. Fader nodded.

Back in the In Between, facing the view on the wall with the unending line of doors behind them, Fader moved them up the spiraling steps. They reached the first window, the source of the light. Case glimpsed a green sunlit countryside.

They passed more windows, each revealing a scene different from both the previous window and her first trip here. A pastel-colored floating village.

Clusters of yellow tents on a grassy plain. A crumbling city skyline. Figures soaring on kites above a bubbling volcano.

The steps ended at the broad landing she remembered. Last time, they'd encountered a locked wooden door set into the surrounding stone. This time, the door stood half-open.

"Zoom closer, but don't go in," Will said. "Let's see what we're up against first."

Fader stopped at the doorway, and they looked once again into what had once been the throne room of the Chambelán of the Chamber of the Red Door.

The space was much as Case recalled. Oval, twenty paces by thirty, torch-lit. At this end, an unmade four-poster bed, a scatter of rugs on a stone floor, high-backed chairs circling a book-covered wooden desk.

Three people lay on the floor at this end. The nearest were a man and a woman, bare-chested and clad only in loin cloths and animal-headed masks. The third was a white-haired man dressed as a Victorian gentleman—Beroald, who'd served the Chambelán-Dancer. None of them stirred, and their chests didn't move. Dead.

At the far end of the room, the Black Throne sat on its low dais. In front and to the left of the throne lay the Black Mirror, a circular pool filled with a liquid so black it reflected no light. Standing before it with crossed arms, staring at its dark surface, was a very familiar figure.

"Mom!" Case half-called, half-sobbed.

"She's okay!" Fader whispered.

"And she's going to stay that way," Will said. "Zoom closer. I want to see what Quilla is watching in the pool."

As Fader zoomed up to Quilla-Ellie, Case had another shock. Their mother hadn't changed. Ellie Cootes looked exactly as she did in photographs and Case's memories from eight years ago.

She pulled her attention from their mother's face to the Black Mirror. On its dark surface, a single enormous silver tree glowed—the same tree she'd seen in the silver pool in the Library. The tree that, Will said, was all of creation, each leaf a universe.

Quilla's blue branch of Order was still there, too, alone and just above the base of the silver tree. It remained bare, with no other branches or leaves growing from it. But something had changed.

"Is it...longer?" she asked.

"It's growing," Will said. "She said it was completing itself. But what's that?"

A dark tendril had emerged from the blackness surrounding the Silver Tree to coil like a snake around its trunk, just above where the blue branch grew. The tendril tightened, cutting into the silver trunk.

"It's choking the Tree," she said.

"She's killing it," Will said, "Killing everything above her universe of Order. I have to get out there and stop her *now*."

"Why can't you pull her in here with us?" Fader asked.

"Because, if our plan works, I'll have to leave the Black Island in astral form. I can't do that with my body in the In Between." He moved closer to the wall where Quilla stood on the other side in their mother's body.

"Wait," Case said. "I have to tell my other selves first."

"We can't wait," Will said. "I'll try to hold her until you bring help. Quilla's destroying the multiverse. If I can pull her out of your mom, it may stop what she's doing to the Tree."

"*Then* what? What are you going to do with astral Quilla? We never figured that out."

"Fader gave me an idea."

"I did?"

"So, tell us!" Case said.

"I can't. If she gets into either of your heads..."

She understood. "She'll know your plan."

"And might stop me. Fader, zoom up behind her. I don't want her to see me when I step out."

Fader moved the view closer until Case could reach out and touch their mother—which she wanted to do so badly.

Will squeezed Fader's shoulder. "Dude, you are a true superhero." He pulled Case into a hug. "I love you," he whispered.

She swallowed. He was saying goodbye. In case this didn't work. In case everything ended here, and they all died. She wanted to tell him that wouldn't happen, that they'd win, that everything would be all right. Instead, she just squeezed him tight. "I love you, too."

Will positioned himself directly behind where Ellie-Quilla gazed into the Black Mirror.

He stepped through.

Chapter 48

Idontwannabeyouanymore

As Will stepped from the In Between into the throne room, he astral projected, grateful to Nyx for making him practice over and over before they'd come to Peru. He closed his eyes, calming his mind. Sensing his astral body inside him, he pushed outward. He opened his eyes. His astral eyes, in his astral body—a hovering, glowing Will-shape, connected by a silver cord to where his physical body still stood.

It had taken him less than a second, but Quilla had sensed his presence. She spun Ellie around. When she saw him, anger and what might have been fear flashed on her face.

A trained astral traveler could enter the mind of another person. Yeshe could. Marell could. Quilla, certainly. Will had done it before, but with scarabs, not a human. And he'd barely been able to control the beasts for more than a few seconds.

But his plan wasn't to control Ellie—it was to pull Quilla out of her.

He flew at her. And into her head.

Ellie's body shivered as Quilla's control wavered. Now, to grab Quilla before she recovered.

But where *was* she? He'd expected to confront an astral form, a body shape, something he could get a grip on and wrestle out of Ellie.

Instead, he floated along hallways in someone's house. Framed photos and certificates hung on the walls. A picture of Ellie and a much younger Case and Fader, all smiling. A diploma for a PhD in astrophysics. Another picture, a family portrait with Ellie, a sullen man, and an even younger Case, a timid smile on her face, as if unsure she should be happy.

Ellie's memories.

He drifted past more framed memories. He came to a door and opened it. Inside, the same joyful Christmas morning Case had remembered in Dream. He tried more doors.

An angry, vicious argument between Ellie and the man from the photo.

A summer afternoon on a beach with Ellie, Case, and Fader, all laughing.

Teaching a class in a university lecture hall.

More rooms. More memories.

It felt wrong, intruding on private, personal, hidden things, but he had to stop

Quilla. But how could he battle someone he couldn't find?

He opened another door. A black room. As black as the Nothing. And in it, sitting on the floor, looking at him with head cocked and tail wagging, was Jack.

All of Quilla's treachery flashed before Will. Fury flamed in him. He leaped for the dog.

Jack disappeared. Will spun around.

Too late. Quilla's attack came like a blow from an astral sledgehammer. Stunned, he collapsed to the floor. The black room became gray, a gray that surrounded him, above, below, on all sides. Was she sending him to the Gray Lands? No. This was different.

This was worse.

He was in a cloud, but a cloud that had substance, force. It wrapped around him, clutching him, squeezing him, tighter and tighter.

Quilla spoke then. *Centuries as an astral spirit, fool. I learned to take any form. Human. Puppy. And this—a shape to hold you, embrace you...crush you.*

Her grip tightened, compressing him, smaller and smaller, into a tiny thing that would soon be too small to hold his consciousness, too small to exist.

He pushed back against the cloud that was Quilla. Pushed with all his strength. But the cloud enveloped him on every side. And he could not push everywhere at once.

Child, you cannot match me. Soon you will be nothing. A part of the same Nothing that consumes your precious Tree.

He grew smaller still. As he shrank, he knew Quilla was right. He couldn't match her.

Not alone.

In the gray wasteland, Ellie Cootes and the woman called Rani Patel had followed a silver thread growing from Ellie's chest until they stood before an oddly familiar door.

The door was plain and needed a coat of paint. A handwritten note taped to it read, 'Bell doesn't work—please knock.' The door reminded Ellie of home, and although she couldn't remember what a *home* was or why one would be important to her, the very word made her smile.

"I just walk through?" she asked.

"Yes, and quickly, please. Fate of the multiverse and all that."

Ellie gripped the doorknob. Another flash of happy familiarity rippled through her. She remembered this door. And something else, too. She looked at Rani. "I have children, don't I?"

"Yes!" Rani cried. "Now, go see them!"

Ellie pushed the door open...and stepped through.

Ellie found herself back inside a real, physical body. Her body, the body that had been taken from her. Taken by…?

The answer wouldn't come. She stood in a strange room with a black throne and a black pool showing a silver tree.

A young man, an Asian cast to his features, late teens probably, faced her. His eyes had a distant, unfocused look. She'd seen him somewhere before. "Who are you?" she asked. "Where am I?"

Shut up, you fool.

A voice in her head. The voice of the thing that had taken her body.

She remembered. The creature called Quilla crawling into her brain like a spider, sending her to that gray place. Even as she remembered this, gray mists swirled once more across her vision.

"No," she said out loud. "You're not sending me there again." She sensed another presence in her head, besides Quilla. A boy named Will. She knew he was the boy standing before her and that he had a good heart and was fighting Quilla, too. And he needed her help.

Clenching her fists, she fought. Fought to be herself. To be Ellie Cootes, mother of Casey and Percy. "I'm back, damn you. I'm back for my children. Now, get out of my body, bitch."

She pushed against the thing called Quilla. Inside her head, the boy Will pushed, too. Together they pushed and pushed and pushed…

She felt more than heard Quilla's scream. The gray mists lifted from her eyes. The spider in her head was gone.

Free again, she gasped in a breath. Hands grabbed her arms from behind, pulling her. Startled and off-balance, she stumbled backwards, crying out.

And everything changed.

She was in a winding hallway disappearing into the dim distance. On her left stretched an unending line of doors. On her right, as if displayed on a giant movie screen, was the room that held the young man and the black pool with the silver tree.

But her eyes slid over all this as they fell on the two other figures in this strange place. One was a young black boy by her side, staring up at her, tears in his eyes. Steps from him stood an older black girl whose eyes were closed, her lips moving as if in silent conversation.

Ellie discovered it didn't matter that eight years had passed, or that she couldn't remember what she'd been doing for those years, or why she'd left this girl and boy. None of that mattered. All that mattered was that she knew them, even though they had changed, as children do, over those eight years.

She pulled her son into a hug. "Percy! Oh, Percy."

"You're safe now, Mom," Percy sobbed into her shoulder. "She can't get you in here."

Ellie didn't understand what was happening, but she didn't care. Her children were here. Casey's eyes remained closed, her lips still moving silently. Releasing Percy, Ellie started toward her daughter.

But Percy held her back. "No, Mom. You can't interrupt her. She's trying to save the universe."

She still didn't understand, but she gave her son another hug and swore she'd never leave her children again.

⁂

Freed from Quilla's crushing force and being trapped inside Ellie, Will floated by the Black Pool, his silver cord snaking from him to his physical body paces away. Ellie Cootes was no longer there. Pulled to safety by Fader, he guessed. Good. One less body for Quilla to use.

Before him hung another astral form, unconnected by any silver cord—a young Inca woman in an ankle-length dress, woven belt, sandals, and shawl, her hair in a long braid. Quilla...as she must still see herself.

Her eyes fell on him. Uttering a wordless cry, she flew at him. He braced himself, preparing to seize her and hold her. But she sped past him.

And he realized the real danger.

He caught her just as she was about to enter his physical body. If she got inside him, he'd have to battle her all over again. He needed her as an astral spirit, not tied to a physical body.

Grabbing her, he spun her away from his body. She struck him, an astral fist to an astral head, but it felt as if she'd used a baseball bat. His grip on her loosened, and she almost slipped free before he caught hold of her again.

But he knew he couldn't hold her much longer. Desperate, he reached for the link he'd lived with unknowingly for eight years. He reached for the Chakana.

A second silver cord appeared, winding from where the Chakana hung around his neck on his body. As this cord touched his astral form, power surged through him—and with it, hope. Spinning her around, he held Quilla from behind in a bear hug. She struggled and screamed, writhing in his grip, but could not break free.

But Nyx had been right. Quilla could call on the Chakana, too. *Fool*, she cried in his mind. *I was a Madre. I carried the Chakana for a century. I was one with the Four who created it. Do you think you can use it against me?*

Another cord grew from the Chakana, thicker, brighter, and twisting to Quilla. He felt her strength swelling as his faded.

Soon, child, the Silver Tree will fall, and my branch of Order will become the new Tree. The Tree of Order.

No, he gasped as he struggled to hold his grip. *It won't.*

She laughed. *Who will stop me? You? You aren't strong enough.*

He was losing the battle with her. Soon she'd have his body. Case had to do it now—or it would be too late.

In the In Between, Case was busy. She'd reestablished contact with five of her other selves, each in their own 'verse, but she'd promised Will ten. Why couldn't she find the others?

Her Voice provided the answer. *The time lines are collapsing.*

What do you mean?

A nexus is coming.

What?

The point in time where the True Tree dies—or lives on. Where the multi-verse ends—or continues. As that nexus approaches, the number of possible futures is shrinking. Soon, there will be only one.

Case understood. *And only one of us, too.*

Yes.

Then we go with the five we have.

Four. Only four remain.

Shit. Four then. Send them through. Send them now!

In the Black Tower, Quilla broke free from Will's astral grip. Laughing, she flung him away. *Now I take your body...and the Chakana! Thank you for bringing it to me. With the power I can draw from it and the Black Pool, you will not capture me again. You are not strong enough.*

Turning, she flew toward where his body stood beside the Black Pool.

And stopped.

Four Will Dreycotts stepped through the wall of the In Between to stand alongside Will's body. From the four new Wills, four astral forms immediately appeared, a silver cord connecting them to their bodies.

Will flew up behind a stunned Quilla, grabbing her in a bear hug again. *You're right. One of me wasn't strong enough...so let's try five.*

She screamed as two other-Wills threw their arms around her from the front. As the other two also grabbed hold, Will heard a voice in his mind. It took him a second to realize it was his own.

Now? it asked.

Now, he replied.

He and his other astral selves flew through the walls of the Black Tower, dragging Quilla's astral body with them. They flew into the open air, rising higher and higher until the Black Island became an ebony dot rimmed by blue in the darker black of the sea.

Higher still they flew, to the silver dome of the sky, then through it into a blackness that sucked in their astral glows and gave nothing back. For that was what it was, Will knew. The Nothing.

He noticed something else. As he and the other-Wills left their bodies farther and farther behind, their cords were growing fainter, thinner.

No matter where you take me, I will return, Quilla snarled, twisting in their grip. *The Nothing cannot stop me. Even here, I feel the pull of the world I created.*

He didn't answer her. On they flew.

And flew and flew. Still only the Nothing surrounded them. Had he been wrong? Would this not work? What if the place he remembered couldn't be reached from the strangeness of the Black Island?

His heart leaped. A pinprick of light appeared in the cloak of darkness surrounding them. It grew to a spark, a spark that burst into blinding flames, burning the darkness away, leaving only brilliant light, as if nothing existed but this light. This beautiful, comforting, perfect light. *The* Light.

The Light coalesced, took a physical shape beneath them. A road. A road that shimmered and twinkled like a ribbon embedded with diamonds. Below it, above it, all around it, was once again the blackness of the Nothing.

In the dim distance of the road rose towers, spires, domes—all glowing with the Light, glowing even brighter than the road. The scene shimmered, shifted, and for a moment, the distant towers became trees, and the road a sparkling river. Then the city and the road returned.

As they dropped closer, Quilla's eyes widened in fear, seeing their destination. *No! Not here,* she cried, struggling even harder to break free.

Yes, Quilla, Will said. *Where you should've gone when you died centuries ago.*

They flew on, and the Road to the Realms of the Dead grew closer.

❧

In the In Between, Case stood with Fader, hugging their mom. They were all crying. Moments before, four doors in the In Between had opened and four other-Wills had stepped out. Then four astral other-Wills had joined with *her* astral Will to seize Quilla's glowing form and fly out of the Black Tower, to...

To where? She had no idea. She still didn't know Will's plan or if it would work.

But in that moment, she didn't care. Right then, she just wanted to be hugging her mom. Ellie hadn't asked them what was going on or who Will was or why there were five of him. She'd just held her and Fader and told them she loved them, over and over.

But then Ellie lifted her head from where it rested on Case's. "Something's wrong," she whispered, gazing down the corridor of the In Between, her eyes unfocused. "Something's coming."

Case followed her gaze. Though she saw nothing, a sound reached her, like a distant drumbeat, monotonous and evenly spaced. She stared down the corridor, her dread growing with the sound. As it drew closer, she recognized it even as she realized what was happening.

To their right was the view of the throne room with the Black Pool. To their left, the wall of doors of the In Between, those portals to other universes that stretched in an unending line in both directions.

Only now, that unending line was...ending.

In the distance, one by one, growing closer, doors were winking out of existence, leaving a blank wall where they'd stood a moment before. And with each disappearance came the sound of a door slamming. And she understood her Voice's earlier warning.

A nexus is coming.

As each door disappeared, so did a possible future, another 'verse.

The doors continued to vanish, the last door in the line growing closer and closer to them. The slamming sound came from behind them as well. She spun around to see the doors in that direction also winking out.

The slamming drum beat slowed. She counted twenty doors left.

Then fifteen.

Ten.

Five.

She swallowed. Five. Their own universe...and the four from which she'd pulled the other-Wills. Worse, the silver cords sprouting from the chests of all the Wills standing in the throne room were growing thinner, fainter, with each passing moment.

Another door slamming shut made her jump. As that door vanished from the wall, one of the Wills, both his physical body and silver cord, disappeared from the throne room.

⁂

As Will and his other selves dropped closer and closer to the Road leading to the Realms of the Dead, Quilla's struggles to escape grew more desperate. He fought to hold her, but her strength seemed to have suddenly grown.

Or theirs had shrunk.

His heart fell. Only three of his other selves remained. Even as he counted, one more glowing other-Will disappeared, like a light turning off.

Quilla gave an exultant cry. *The time lines are collapsing. A nexus approaches. All the futures of all universes are becoming one—one where your world ends and mine begins.*

Another Will vanished. Now, only two of them held a thrashing Quilla. *Get her on the Road!* he cried.

They crashed onto the glowing ribbon, tumbling over and over along the glittering surface. Barely keeping their grips on Quilla, they pulled her to her feet.

Drag her to the City! Will shouted.

I can't... the only remaining other-Will began.

You have to!

The other-Will stiffened, a look of sudden surprise and sadness coming over him. His eyes met Will's. *I can't...stay.*

The last other-Will winked out of existence.

With a cry of exultation, Quilla threw off Will and flung him to the Road. In one swift movement, she knelt beside him, her astral hands around his astral throat, wild joy in her eyes. *You have failed. Only you remain, and your cord is fading. I will hold you here until it is gone and you are dead.*

He tried to break her grip, but she was too strong. And in that moment, he knew she was right. He had failed. He'd brought Quilla back into the world, and now she was going to end it. Every person in every universe was going to die.

Quilla tightened her grip on his neck. *Soon it will be you, not me, who enters the Realms of the Dead.*

From behind Quilla, a brightness grew. And with it, hope flared in him.

Don't...think....so, he gasped.

She laughed. *You can't fight me. You are weak and alone.*

The brightness behind Quilla resolved into shining shapes.

Weak, he said. *But not alone.*

Quilla screamed as glowing hands pulled her from him.

Chapter 49

All My Friends Were There

F reed from Quilla, Will struggled to his feet on the Road to the Realms of the Dead. Before him, Quilla writhed and twisted but couldn't break free from the astral spirits who held her as easily as if she were a small child.

Astral spirits Will knew well, all now dead.

Jampel Thardo, Tibetan monk. Walter Keejek, Cree shaman. Both rescued by Will from the Crystal Island in Dream the same night he'd unknowingly brought Quilla back into the world as Jack.

Harry Lyle, Will's old contact at the Daily Standard, killed by the body swapper, Marell.

Wu Peng, shot by Gabriel Herrada's gunmen—Quilla's gunmen—in the monastery at Arequipa.

And one more. Another Tibetan monk, clad in a maroon robe, who exuded an aura of youth and vitality that belied his wrinkled face and long white hair and beard.

"Yeshe!" Will cried. His gaze ran from face to face. "All of you!"

Yeshe approached Will, smiling as the others held a squirming, screaming Quilla. "Young master, it is good to see you again. But before we talk, we must deal with more pressing matters. First, your own fragile state..." Reaching out, Yeshe placed a glowing hand on Will's astral chest.

A burst of warmth and energy flowed into Will, filling him, restoring him. His silver cord, which had faded to near invisibility, now shone brightly again. He felt strong. He felt alive.

Yeshe considered him and his cord. "Sufficient for the moment. And now, this poor creature." Turning to where Jampel, Walter, Harry, and Peng held Quilla, he nodded to them.

The spirits gently turned a still-struggling Quilla to face the shining towers and spires of the Realms of the Dead. As her eyes fell on the distant skyline, she stopped fighting to break free. Her shoulders slumped. She stood silent and swaying, staring at the beckoning radiance. The spirits released her and stepped back.

"No!" Will cried. "Don't let her go. She'll escape. She'll—"

Yeshe raised an astral hand. "There is no such danger, young master."

Quilla's eyes found Will's. He expected hate in her gaze, but instead saw only peace, a calm reverence. She smiled and nodded. He swallowed and nodded back.

She began to shuffle toward the far-off cityscape. Her steps sped up, each carrying her farther than he expected. Soon, Quilla, would-be destroyer of creation, was a tiny speck on the Road in the distance. And then she was gone, vanished into the Realms of the Dead.

"Why did she just give up?" he asked, confused.

"These Realms have been calling her since she died centuries ago," Yeshe said. "Here, with its beckoning light before her, the call became irresistible."

"I was hoping for something like that when I dragged her here."

"Pretty wild idea," Walter said. "How'd you come up with that?"

"I've been here before. Remember, Yeshe? After I exposed myself to the Chakana and got blasted to this place?"

Yeshe smiled, reminding Will how much he had missed the monk and his gentle ways. "A most memorable reunion."

"That trip gave me the idea of bringing Quilla here," Will said. "But I guess I didn't get her close enough. If it weren't for all of you..." He shook his head. "How are you all here?"

Harry jerked a thumb at the city. "Realms of the Dead. We're dead. Not that complicated, kid."

"But how did you know to come?"

"I am well attuned to your astral spirit, young master," Yeshe said. "As before, I again sensed your approach. I was greatly pleased to see you still bore your silver cord."

"Meaning I was still alive."

"Yes, but struggling mightily with a powerful spirit who was not." The monk shrugged. "It appeared you needed assistance. Since arriving here, I had made the acquaintance of your friends..." He bowed to the others. "...and called on them to help. They responded eagerly."

"Imagine our surprise," Jampel said, "when Walter and I recognized who you fought."

"Sorry about Jack," Walter said. "She sure had us fooled."

"She fooled everyone," Will replied.

"Perhaps it was meant to be," Yeshe said. "Her threat is finally ended."

Meant to be. Will thought again of an unseen hand moving pieces on a board. He gazed at the distant city. "But she's gone? For good?"

"You have defeated her," Yeshe said. "You and your young friends. No spirit can escape this realm."

A weight as heavy as the multiverse lifted from Will's shoulders. It was finished, really finished. Waves of relief washed over him.

Relief mixed with regret.

"Harry," Will said to the reporter, "if you hadn't got involved with me, you'd still be alive. I'm sorry."

Harry shrugged. "I was doing my job—investigating dangerous people. Would've done that, regardless. Glad you saved those kids. And thanks for taking care of Carla and Dylan."

Harry's wife and young son. Adi had set up a trust for them after his death.

"No problem," Will said quietly. He turned to Peng. "I'm sorry, Peng. I didn't know the monastery was a trap."

Peng shook his head. "No way you could've. I was doing my job, too. Protecting you kids. At least, I managed that." He hesitated. "Do me a favor?"

"Name it."

"Could you...could you give Mei a message? From me? There's just some...stuff I never told her."

"Yeah. Sure." He listened to Peng's message, feeling worse and worse about what happened at the monastery. When Peng finished, Will swallowed. "I'll tell her. Word for word."

Peng beamed. "Thanks, Will. And tell Fader I said hi."

"Now," Yeshe said, "you must say your final goodbyes and return to the world of the living."

"Yeah," Harry said, "before you're not. Living, that is. You're not looking so hot."

Will stared down at his astral body and cord. Both were again barely visible.

"My friends," Yeshe called to the others, "if you could, please."

Jampel, Walter, Harry, and Peng joined Yeshe. Together, each placed a hand on Will's chest. Vitality surged into him once more, and he glowed with a brightness that reflected on the faces of those around him.

Yeshe smiled, apparently satisfied. "I am very proud of you, young master. All creation owes you and your friends the greatest debt. Little did I know when we battled Marell what astral powers the three of you would become."

Will swallowed, embarrassed but also chilled by another thought. The fight against Marell and Morrigan had first brought him together with Case and Fader. Again, he saw an invisible hand moving pieces.

"Now go," Yeshe said. "Live your life. We will not meet again until your own journey here."

"Which we hope is a long time from now, kid," Harry added. The rest nodded.

Will turned his back on the distant shining city and his friends. When his eyes fell on his silver cord, snaking up into the darkness of the Nothing, a tug began in his chest. He rose from the Road, letting his astral body respond to that pull.

As he flew away, he looked back to wave a last goodbye, but the five spirits were mere bright specks speeding along the Road toward the spired city. In another moment, they were gone.

He flew on, following his cord, struggling to believe the battle was over.

But it was, and he ached to see Case again.

In the throne room, Case stood staring at Will's upright but unconscious body. And at his silver cord that grew dimmer and dimmer with each passing minute.

One by one, the other-Wills had vanished, until only a single Will remained. *Their* Will. *Her* Will. Stopping Quilla, saving the multiverse—it was all up to him now. And he was alone.

But as the minutes passed, her hopes sank as his cord grew fainter and fainter. She waited in dread for a sign he'd failed. For his cord to fade from sight. For him to disappear.

Their mom had an arm around her and Fader. They'd had no time to talk. Case still wasn't sure what Ellie remembered of the past eight years, other than her children. But for now, that was enough.

"Will's cord..." Fader said. "Is it getting brighter?"

Was it? Case stared at the floating ribbon, trying to convince herself its glow was stronger than a moment ago. She closed her eyes, remembering the brightness. She opened them. "Yes!" she cried. "It's brighter."

"Does that mean he won?" Fader said. "That he beat Quilla?"

"Yes, it does, dude," came a voice. The voice sounded in her head, not her ears, but still seemed to come from above them.

They looked up. At the end of his silver cord, Will floated in astral form. He swooped down to his physical body and passed into it. A moment later, his body shuddered, and he opened his eyes.

Case threw her arms around him. "Oh, god! You're safe. You're all right."

He squeezed her back hard, and it felt so good to be held by him again. "Everything's safe," he said. "Everything's all right."

"Quilla?"

"Gone."

"Where?"

"Realms of the Dead."

"What?"

"Long story, but she's not coming back. And Yeshe says hi."

"And again...*what?*"

"Uh, guys—" Fader said from behind them.

"Are you going to introduce me, Casey?" Ellie asked. "Because, from the hugginess between you two, I'm guessing I should get to know this young man."

"Oh, yeah, right," Case said, breaking off the hug, suddenly embarrassed. "Uh, Mom, this is Will. Will Dreycott. He's...we're...I mean..." Why did she feel like she was eight again and just been caught doing something she shouldn't? "He's my boyfriend."

To her relief, her mom flashed a warm smile and held out her hand. "Well,

I'm very pleased to meet you, Will."

Will looked as embarrassed as she felt as he shook her hand. "You, too, Ms. Cootes."

"Hey, guys—" Fader said again.

"Call me Ellie." She frowned. "Dreycott. That name sounds familiar. Why would—"

"*Hey!*" Fader shouted.

Case turned with the others to where Fader pointed at the Black Pool. "Something's wrong. I mean, something's *still* wrong."

On the black surface, the image of the Silver Tree showed as before.

No. Not as before. Quilla's branch of Order had grown even more. As Case watched, the blue branch lengthened, thickened. Worse, the dark vine still coiled around the trunk of the Silver Tree, cutting even deeper.

"The vine," Case said. "It's still killing the Tree."

"I thought stopping Quilla would stop all this," Will cried. "Why didn't it?"

"Orden began the Tree of Order," Ellie said, a strange lilt to her voice, "and sent the Nothing to destroy the True Tree. Only Orden can stop it now." She gazed into the Black Pool, a faraway look in her eyes, as if she saw more than what showed on the dark surface.

"Mom?" Case said, shaking her mother. "What do you know?"

Ellie started, then shivered. She blinked and looked around, as if coming out of a trance.

"What do you know?" Case repeated. "About Orden? Do you mean Quilla?"

Ellie nodded slowly. "Quilla was one with Orden when she started this. Only Orden can end it now. And the Four do not interfere."

"Mom, how do you know that? What do you remember?"

Ellie rubbed her temples. "I...I don't know." She stared at the silver tree. "When I saw the Tree, I remembered it. Remembered *knowing* it. Knowing it intimately. But now..." She shook her head. "Now, I can't remember."

As they watched, helpless, the blue branch grew brighter still, thicker, longer. And the black vine tightened more around the silver trunk.

"The Tree!" Fader cried. "It's fading."

He was right. The Silver Tree was dimming, its shining radiance now little more than a feeble glimmer.

The distant look returned to Ellie's eyes. "The True Tree will soon fall. Everything will end. All of creation."

Will pulled the Chakana from under his shirt where it hung around his neck. The artifact pulsed weakly, its glow now barely visible. "Can this help?"

"No," Ellie said. "The Chakana was born from the True Tree. Their energy is one. The Four created the Key as a light against the Nothing. And that light is dying with the Tree."

"There must be something we can do," Case cried.

As if in answer, a crash came from the far end of the room as the heavy wooden door slammed against the stone wall. A brown rat the size of a bear filled the doorway. And on its back, a bloody hand clutched to her chest, sat Morrigan.

<h1 style="text-align:center">Chapter 50</h1>

<h1 style="text-align:center">Burn the Witch</h1>

As Tachior the rat bore Morrigan toward the Black Pyramid, the witch had slipped in and out of consciousness, succumbing again and again to the pain of her wound. The healing spells she'd used were failing.

But once they stood before the Red Door, she fought against the agony, against the temptation to sleep, a sleep she feared would be her last. She needed to stay awake to guide Tachior. And she needed to stay alive to save young Fader.

Reaching the maze of tunnels leading to the Black Tower, she found she could still hear it in her head. The Song. The strange music that had first led her, in what seemed a lifetime ago, from the depths of Castle Rushen to the Black Island. The Song that now allowed her to navigate her rodent steed through these tunnels and up the winding stairs to the half-open door of the tower room.

As the rat burst through the door, slamming it against the stone wall, the four occupants of the room spun to stare at her.

Despite her pain, she smiled when her eyes fell on Fader. *Little one, you still live.*

Beside Fader stood his cursed sister and the Dreycott boy. And a woman she didn't recognize but knew must be mother to Fader and Case.

Several emotions battled inside her at the sight of the woman. Happiness for Fader for finally finding his mother. Warmth for the woman for giving life to the child for whom she felt such affection. But jealousy too, for the same reasons.

And fear. For Morrigan remembered what Suyana had told them—that Quilla had taken over this woman before she leaped here.

Go to them, she called to the rat in her mind, summoning the runescript for a kill spell to use on the woman.

Tachior took a half dozen weaving steps into the room before collapsing onto the floor. *Mistress of the Unicorn, Tachior can serve you no longer. Thank you for fulfilling my purpose. Blessed be the White Coven of Ellan Vannin.*

Remembering the fire drake's end (and, she guessed, the gray bat's), she slipped from the creature, biting back a scream of pain from her wound when she landed. She stumbled away as the rat burst into flames.

Fader was running toward her. Behind him, his mother—the woman Quilla had taken over—ran after him, reaching for him.

No. You will not harm him. The kill spell flowed down her outstretched arm. "Get away from him, Quilla!"

Fader stopped running, his eyes growing huge as they fell on the glowing symbols on her arm. "No! She's not Quilla. She's our mom."

Too late. The kill spell flew from Morrigan's hand. Fader leaped in front of his mother. The spell struck him full on.

"No!" Morrigan screamed, pushing herself into a stumbling run. What had she done?

But Fader didn't fall. He swayed, then righted himself. He rubbed his head. "Ow."

His sister and mother now stood on either side of him. "Are you okay?" Case asked.

Fader nodded, still rubbing his head.

Case spun on Morrigan. "What the freak, bitch?"

"I'm...I'm sorry," Morrigan said, too shaken by what she'd almost done to even be angry with Case. "I thought...I thought she was Quilla. I would never hurt..." She swallowed, thanking the Goddess her spell had failed, even as she wondered how.

"The powers of your coven came from the Book," said the woman beside Fader, her eyes glazed and unfocused, "as do the powers of my children. Your magic can never do them deadly harm, Morrigan the Bright."

A memory returned to Morrigan...of her first meeting with these two children in a church basement, when the same spell had failed on Case. She looked at Fader. "I would never hurt you. I came to help you. I thought she was Quilla."

Fader shook his head. "This is our mom. Her name's Ellie. Will says Quilla's dead."

"She's dead," the Dreycott boy called from beside the Black Pool. "If you really want to help, then help with this."

She limped to the edge of the Pool, bloody hand held to her chest. The dark mirror was as she recalled it from her time here with Quilla-Orden. But now, the black surface showed a beautiful silver tree.

And she remembered.

Remembered a bedtime tale her mother would tell her and Dany as children. Of a magnificent silver tree that held every dream ever dreamed, every life ever lived, every story ever told.

"That tree—" the Dreycott boy began.

"I know what it is," she said as sudden understanding came. Understanding she had lacked as a child. This was the True Tree. The entirety of creation that Quilla had sworn to destroy.

He pointed to a black vine coiled around the Tree's base. "*That* is killing it. Quilla started it, and we can't stop it."

The others joined them. "You're bleeding!" Fader cried, staring at where she held her hand against her wound.

"A trifle, little one," she said. "My magicks are healing me." The Dreycott boy caught her eye, and she knew he'd also caught her lie.

"Your magic..." Fader said, looking up at her. "Can you save the Tree?"

Seeing the black vine, she knew she had no spells that could kill it. Her lifetime of gathering lore, runescripts, magical power—all of it useless now. Her magic could no more save the Tree than it could save herself.

But she knew where other magic hid.

"Can you?" Fader asked again.

"Perhaps," she said.

She slipped the Unicorn Tapestry from her shoulders and found the scene in the center of the fabric, where the young woman, pale-faced and golden-haired, sat on a moss-covered stump. She wore a full-length dress of dusky blue and a crown of faded daisies. Before her knelt the Unicorn. The maiden's left hand caressed the beast's head, her right resting on the tip of its horn.

The Unicorn glared back at Morrigan with a baleful, amber eye. In her head, she heard its voice. Cold. Haughty. Disdainful. A voice, she realized, much like her own.

Mistress, do you finally call me?

I do.

Are you ready to pay the price?

Morrigan laughed. *I am already dying.*

Then release me.

Morrigan brushed a bloody hand over the beast. Earlier, her blood had not stained the fabric. But now, it seeped into the scene woven in silk.

No. Not the entire scene. Just the Unicorn.

As it drank in her blood, the Unicorn began to glow. Brighter and brighter, until she and the others had to shield their eyes. The glow died. When she opened her eyes again, the Unicorn stood before them.

The others jumped back, gasping or crying out, but Morrigan stood her ground. The creature towered over them all. Morrigan's head barely reached its shoulder. It was a dirty white, bearded and grizzled, and skeletal thin. A slender tail twisted above its rump, silver leaves sprouting from it as if it were more vine than tail. Its spiraling gray horn was longer than its legs, making the beast seem unbalanced and grotesque.

It clopped closer to Morrigan on cloven hooves, flames dancing in its golden eyes. *Mistress, what is your desire?*

Morrigan pointed to the Pool. *Sever that vine. But do not harm the Tree.*

The Unicorn lowered its great horn until its tip hovered above where the dark vine touched the True Tree. The horn dipped into the Pool, slicing through the image of the vine. White flames erupted on the black surface, and for a moment the brilliance of those flames battled the darkness of the Pool.

The flames died. But the vine remained.

"It didn't work," Fader cried.

You failed me, Morrigan told the Unicorn.

I did not fail. I was born to battle the Nothing. Behold, Witch.

A grayness crept into the edges of the black vine where it wrapped around the Tree. In moments, the gray had spread to the entire vine. A heartbeat later, the vine crumbled from the Tree, like ashes scattered by the wind. The Tree brightened until its glow matched that of the Unicorn.

"You did it!" Fader cried.

Morrigan smiled down at him through her pain. She shot his sister an expectant look.

"Thank you," Case said and seemed to mean it.

"You see?" Fader said. "I *told* you there was good in you."

Unable to speak, Morrigan put an arm around Fader and pulled him close. The boy's mother, Ellie, raised an eyebrow.

"Forgive me," Morrigan said, releasing him, "but I am rather fond of your son. You have raised a fine boy."

Ellie shook her head. "I wasn't around to do much raising. That credit goes to Casey."

Case seemed as surprised by that as Morrigan. She crossed her arms and looked at Morrigan as if expecting praise. Morrigan just glared at her.

The Dreycott boy pulled their attention back. "We have another problem. The blue branch—Quilla's world—it's still growing."

The boy was right. As she stared at the branch, it grew longer, throbbing in and out, as if breathing.

"Why not leave it?" Case asked. "We've saved the multiverse."

Ellie's eyes took on a distant gaze again. "If Quilla's world survives, it will again try to choke the True Tree." She looked at Morrigan. "Can your beast end that, too?"

Sever the blue branch, Morrigan commanded the Unicorn, *as you did the black vine.*

If you so wish, Mistress. But know this—that branch contains all that Quilla created, including this place in which we stand. As that branch dies, so does this world. This room, this tower, this island—all will be consumed by the Nothing. Whoever remains here will be lost to the Void.

Morrigan related that to the others. "Can you escape this place?"

Fader brightened. "Sure. I'll take everyone into the In Between."

Morrigan frowned. "What is—?"

"No time," Case said. "Trust him. He'll get us to the tunnel at the end of the beach."

Mistress, those ways will close the moment I sever the branch. The tunnels off this Island. The corridor of doors this child calls the In Between. They will find no escape through those routes.

Morrigan relayed that information.

"Then how do we get off the Island?" Case asked.

"We take the In Between as far as we can, then run for the beach," Will said. "If Suyana followed the Chakana here, we'll meet her and the others on the way. We can use her portal to escape."

"And if they didn't make it here? Or we can't find them?" Case asked.

No one had an answer, until the Unicorn's voice sounded in Morrigan's head. *Water.*

She understood. Lifting the Tapestry, she searched the corners of the silken weave. The yellow dragon and the gray bat were gone. And now Tachior, the brown rat, too.

Fire. Air. Earth. All gone.

But in the last corner, one creature remained, white and sickly, peering with dead eyes from a dark stream.

The eel. Water.

It can carry these mortals across the Black Sea, the Unicorn said.

To where?

For an answer, the Unicorn clopped from the throne room onto the balcony of the Tower, cloven hooves echoing on the stone floor. Morrigan and the others followed.

The black jungle lay spread below the Tower, ringed in blue where cobalt sand met the dark sea that churned in never-ending storms. Lowering its great horn, the Unicorn pointed across the sea to where a finger of silver-white radiance glowed on the horizon.

What is that? she asked the Unicorn.

But it was the woman Ellie who answered. "The Crystal Island!"

"From the Crossing?" Case said. "How can that be?"

"The Black Island is its mirror image," Ellie said. "A dark, distorted image, to be sure, but everything here is a reflection of the Crossing. The Song is its Key, the scarabs its Guardians."

"You're remembering?" Case asked. "I mean, about the last eight years?"

"It's still a jigsaw puzzle. But I know that light is the Crystal Island." Ellie turned to Morrigan. "Just as I know that sea *is* the Nothing. We can't touch it and survive, let alone cross it."

"You can. And you will." Morrigan knelt before Fader, fighting to hide the pain in her chest from him. She handed him the Unicorn Tapestry. "Take this, little one. When you reach the beach of blue sand, touch this creature..." She pointed to the white eel. "...and say these words." She spoke the words in Manx slowly, then made Fader repeat them until she was satisfied.

"What will happen?" he asked.

"That creature will appear and bear you across the sea."

"All of us?" he asked.

Thirteen, if so needed, the Unicorn replied.

She understood. *The number of our coven.*

Yes. To bear them from their own island, had they ever summoned it.

A wave of sadness washed over Morrigan. But her mother, her Sisters had never done that. They had stayed when she had fled, defending what they'd sworn to defend. To the end. To their deaths.

"It can carry thirteen," she said to Fader. Still kneeling, she looked at the others. "Now, you must flee. I will end Quilla's branch of Order once you leave."

"But how will you get away?" Fader said.

She smiled through her lie. "The Unicorn will bear me from this place. His powers are great. I will be safe."

"I'll see you again?"

She forced her smile to remain. "Yes. Of course."

Tears brimming in his eyes, he threw his arms around her, and they hugged each other tight. He whispered in her ear. "I know you're lying. You're doing this to save us. I was right about you. I'll never forget you."

She broke down then, sobbing into his shoulder as he sobbed into hers. "You have your sister. You have your mother," she whispered. "You have what I turned my back on. Live your life, little one. Live it long. Live it well." Then she whispered her last goodbye to the boy for whom she held such a strange affection.

Fader stepped back from her, wiping his eyes. "C'mon," he said to the others, the Unicorn Tapestry clutched in his hand. "I'll take us into the In Between." Giving Morrigan one last look, he walked forward, disappearing into thin air, pulling the others with him.

Morrigan struggled to her feet.

You care for that child, the Unicorn said. *Perhaps your mother was right. There is good—*

If I hear that one more time, I will scream, she snapped, swaying and gritting her teeth against the pain in her chest. *Let's get this done.* Staggering back inside to the Black Pool, she pointed to Quilla's branch of Order. *Sever that. End it.*

The Nothing will consume this place. And you.

Just do it.

The Unicorn bobbed its head to her, then moved to the edge of the Black Pool. It lowered its horn until the tip hovered over where the blue branch emerged from the silver tree.

The horn slashed down, slicing through the blue branch. A hole opened in the pool where the horn had cut, sucking the severed branch into it.

And Quilla's universe of Order was gone.

But the dark liquid now bubbled up from the hole that had swallowed the branch. The Black Pool rose, spilling over its sides and onto the stone floor of the throne room.

Morrigan hobbled back from the creeping darkness, hands clutched against her chest, where the flow of her blood now seemed to pace the flow of the Nothing inching toward her.

Reaching the door to the tower room, she collapsed at the top of the spiraling stairway, finally succumbing to the pain. She leaned back against the wall, the cold of its stone matching the cold growing in her chest. She closed her eyes.

The clopping of hooves stopped beside her. She opened her eyes and stared into the dancing flames of the Unicorn's gaze.

Your end approaches.

Yes. And I am afraid.

There remains a way.

The way her Sisters had shown, when she'd pleaded for them to save her. *No. Not that.*

If the Nothing takes you, more than your body will die. Your spirit will vanish from every plane of existence.

Morrigan swallowed. A complete death. The death of her spirit.

There remains a way. The Unicorn lowered its horn to where she sat slumped against the stone.

The crawling darkness of the Nothing had almost reached her. She watched as it crept closer and closer, consuming the rugs and bed and chairs and desk. Beyond it, the rest of the room was already gone—the throne, the pool, the very walls of the room—in their place only black nothingness.

Your spirit will vanish.

She shuddered. And decided.

She reached up—and touched the Unicorn's horn.

In the In Between, Fader had reluctantly turned the view from Morrigan and zoomed them out of the throne room and down the spiraling staircase. Case stood with him, their mom behind them with a hand on each of their shoulders. Will stood with Case, holding her hand.

After Case guided them through the tunnel maze, Fader sped them through the great cavern with its scattered corpses, up the carpeted staircase, and along the twisting passageway. Passing through the Red Door, he zoomed down the steps of the Black Pyramid.

Only when he began zooming toward the distant jungle did he look down at the Unicorn Tapestry he clutched in his hand. He lifted it, intending to tie it around his neck, but the fabric floated over his head, settling onto his shoulders, fastening itself below his chin. The Tapestry, which had reached to Morrigan's ankles, fell no further than his knees.

Case smiled at him. "Finally got your cape, eh, bro?"

Fader looked up at her, remembering Morrigan's last words to him. "She called me Dany."

Chapter 51

Something from Nothing

Adi sat on the blue sand beach, watching Yanta, Isobel, and the surviving Sisters hack with their swords at the cage of trees that still trapped the group. Their efforts had no effect, but at least it was keeping the fiery-tempered Yanta occupied.

Suyana watched the swordswomen. She had ordered them to attack their wooden cell, but Adi suspected the Madre held no more expectation of success than she did.

"Can't you open another portal and get us out of here?" she asked Suyana.

"We can only leap to the Chakana from the Threshold, the home of our Sisterhood. Once we leap, we cannot do so again." Suyana sighed. "The portals we used to get here will still be there, but..." She shrugged.

"But they're out there. And we're in here." Adi swore. "Damn that witch."

Mei sat huddled beside her, knees drawn to her chest. "I didn't know," she whispered.

Adi turned to her.

"I didn't know," Mei repeated. "I saw that woman. I saw you under attack." She shook her head. "I didn't know."

Stone sat on Adi's other side. Pieces of his SIG P250 pistol lay spread on his camouflage jacket before him as he reassembled the weapon, an activity he'd repeated a dozen times since their confinement. "Lieutenant, in a split second, you assessed the situation and took action. I do not fault your decision to protect us."

"Dai lo," Mei said, "I shot her in cold blood."

Stone slid the magazine back into his gun. "But do not lie to yourself. When my family was murdered, if I'd encountered any of that gang that day, I would have killed without hesitation. But had I pulled the trigger, my blood would not have been cold."

Mei dropped her eyes. She did not reply.

Adi swallowed, unsure she wouldn't have acted the same. If someone had killed Will or Laura, and Adi stood before that person, gun in hand...

"I have never felt so useless in all my life," she said, wanting to change the subject.

"Nor have I," Suyana said, joining them. "But these children are extraordinary. Do not forsake hope."

"I'm not giving up. I'm just...worried." Worried? Sick with fear was more like it.

"For Will."

"For all three of them. But yes, for Will."

Suyana studied her. "You love him a great deal."

"Of course, I do," she snapped. This subject was no more to her liking than the last.

Diego and his six soldiers sat together in another group. When the trees had first enclosed them, they had tried shooting the barrier, a plan quickly abandoned when their shots ricocheted off the wood.

She felt as guilty about dragging Diego into this as Stone and Mei. Diego owed her no loyalty. He'd lost soldiers at the monastery protecting Will. He'd saved Will's life eight years ago. Now, he was endangering his own life and the lives of his team trying to save Will again.

With their rush to reach the red dot location and then being separated after their capture by the Sisters, she'd had no chance to thank him. She pushed herself up and walked toward him.

She was halfway there when the trees and the vines that had enclosed them vanished, sucked back into the ground, freeing the group.

Scattered on the blue sand lay scores of dead scarabs, their corpses decomposing rapidly, melting, liquefying as she watched. Above the beach, the black jungle shook and trembled, the trees and foliage shriveling and withering until the forest canopy stood no taller than she did.

Staring at the vanishing jungle, she had her back to the dark sea. Stone pointed behind her. "Archie."

She spun around. A wave washed onto the beach. But it did not retreat. Another wave came, washing higher on the blue sand. Then another, higher still. "The sea's rising," she said.

"No," Suyana said. "The island is sinking."

The others, all on their feet now, took a step back as another wave washed closer.

"Madre, the portals!" Isobel cried.

Fifty paces away, two glowing rectangles stood in the sand—the doors by which Suyana and Isobel had brought their teams to this place. With each new wave, the black waters washed nearer to the portals.

"Hurry!" Suyana cried. "Before we are trapped."

"I'm not leaving without Will and the others," Adi said. "What does it matter if we have to run through some water?"

"It is not water. It is the Nothing." Taking an arrow from Isobel, Suyana approached the rising black liquid and touched the arrow to it. The water—or whatever it was—shot up the shaft. Suyana dropped the arrow, and the dark water sucked it into itself.

Bloody hell, Adi thought, staring at the approaching sea with a newfound fear.

"We must use the portals *now*," Suyana said.

"Yes, go," Adi said. "Take your warriors. You've done enough. But I'm staying."

"We're not leaving either, Archie," Stone said, Mei beside him.

She knew better than to argue. "Diego, you and your men should go with the Sisters."

"I will send my team back, Adrienne," Diego replied. "But I will stay. I will not leave young Will here, either. When you save someone's life, that life becomes your responsibility."

The black water now washed the sand just five steps below the portals. Now four.

"Quickly then," Suyana said.

Diego and Suyana barked orders to their people. Soldiers and Sisters together ran to the glowing doorways, led by Suyana. The Madre directed a line through her portal, and Isobel did the same at hers.

In seconds, only Yanta and Isobel remained with Suyana. The Madre spoke to the two Sisters. Both shook their heads. Suyana spoke again, her words sharp but too distant to catch. Yanta straightened, bowed to the Madre, and stepped through the portal. Isobel folded her arms and remained where she was. Suyana shook her head, then hurried back to Adi and the others, Isobel following.

"You're staying?" Adi said.

"The Chakana is here," Suyana said. "My duty is to retrieve it. I sent Yanta back to lead the Sisterhood if I do not return, although what will become of us without the Chakana, I do not know." She nodded at Isobel. "And this one refused to leave."

"I will not leave my Madre," Isobel said. "Or my friends."

"In truth, we may have need of her," Suyana said. "Isobel is the only one who has seen this place."

"Where would Will and the others have gone?" Adi asked.

Isobel pointed. "There."

While they'd focused on the approaching waters, the jungle had continued to wither. Now, nothing remained of it but a thick black sludge smearing the ground beyond the beach as far as Adi could see. With the jungle gone, a black pyramid rose stark and solitary against the strange silver sky.

"Then go!" Adi said.

Abandoning the dwindling strip of beach, Isobel ran into the remains of the jungle, with Adi and Suyana following, and Stone, Mei, and Diego close behind.

They ran in silence, Adi battling her fears for Will all the way. Suddenly, Isobel sucked in her breath and stopped. "Something is wrong."

Closer now, Adi had a clearer view of the pyramid. The thing was huge, much larger than she'd first estimated. Its sides were unmarked and smooth...

And rippling.

A thick black liquid poured from the top of the pyramid and down its sides. It had reached the base of the structure, flooding the surrounding area, and was speeding toward them.

"The Nothing," Suyana cried. "It is flowing from the pyramid."

Adi looked back. The sea was rising faster. The creeping dark water lay only thirty paces behind them. "We're trapped."

"Not even a tree left to climb," Stone said.

"Something's coming," Mei called. She had her gun aimed in the pyramid's direction. There, a long white shape sped toward them, skimming over the surface of the black liquid, undulating side to side.

"It's a snake," Adi swore, pulling out her Glock.

Stone joined her, his own gun aimed at the approaching creature. "Big snake."

He was right. As the thing got closer, its size became apparent. It had to be as long as five cars. And it was heading straight for them.

"Bloody hell," Adi swore. "What next?"

"Aim for the head," Diego said, sighting along his rifle.

Beside him, Isobel raised her bow, then gasped. "Stop! Do not shoot!"

Then Adi saw them. People, four of them, on the back of the snake. Could it be? Could life grant her this one wish? The creature drew nearer, the riders grew clearer, and Adi's heart flooded with joy.

"It's them!" she cried. *It's Will. He's safe. Oh god, he's safe.*

The enormous snake—no, eel—slid from the black liquid onto the shrinking patch of ground where Adi and the others waited, stopping beside their bewildered group. The thing was taller than she was, its pale skin glistening in the silver light.

Fader sat at the front, some sort of cape around his neck, his hands on the eel's head like he was steering. Behind him, her arms around his waist, was a woman who must be Ellie Cootes, her face an older version of Case. Behind Ellie sat Case, hugging her mom.

And behind Case was Will. He grinned down at them. "Need a lift?"

"How—?" she began.

"What of Quilla?" Suyana said, cutting her off. "What of the True Tree?"

"Quilla's dead, the Tree's safe, and so is the Chakana," Will said. "But we aren't. Get on, before the Nothing catches up. Easiest from the tail. Just run up its back."

Adi led the way, followed by the others. Despite the sheen of the creature's skin, Adi's boots found sure purchase. She settled behind Will, followed by Suyana, Isobel, Mei, Stone, and Diego.

Fader patted the eel. The creature slithered forward, speeding toward the approaching sea, which now covered almost all the jungle they'd fled through.

"The Nothing will swallow us," Suyana cried.

Will shook his head. "Coven magic. This thing carried us through the Nothing to get to you."

Still, Adi tensed as the eel reached the edge of black liquid. But it kept going, sliding over its surface like it was ice. They headed out into the storm-tossed seas surrounding the vanishing island. An immense wave, as tall as a two-story building, rushed toward them. The eel turned toward it. Adi braced herself, waiting for the dark water to sweep them from the creature's back.

The eel hit the wave...and passed right through it. The waters came crashing down around them. But not *on* them. The wave seemed to hit an invisible barrier and slide off, as if a bubble of protection surrounded the eel.

"Where are we going?" Adi shouted above the storm's howl.

"The Crystal Island," Will yelled back.

"What's that?"

He started to yell an answer, but Case gestured to him. He leaned forward, and she shouted something into his ear. Will sat up straight and scanned the horizon. Ahead of them, Ellie and Fader were doing the same.

Adi tugged on Will's arm. "What's wrong?" she shouted.

"We can't find the Crystal Island," he shouted back.

She scanned the horizon herself, looking for a land mass, but could see nothing but towering dark waves in the storm-tossed seas.

"It gets worse," Will yelled. "Fader says the eel's going to disappear soon."

To her left, a spark flared in the corner of her eye. She searched for the source. Nothing but black water lay in that direction. Had it just been a gleam from the silver sky?

She was about to turn back when the light flared again, high above the waves. It died, then returned brighter than before. The light pulsed, growing stronger each time, with an odd up and down motion.

She nudged Will, then pointed. He shouted to Case, who shouted to Fader. A moment later, the eel turned toward the light in the sky, which now shone so bright, it lit the waves below. The light moved away, but not so fast they couldn't keep pace.

Ahead, in the direction they were now moving, a radiance appeared on the horizon. In a few moments, it resolved itself into a shining land mass. As they neared the island, the light in the sky moved toward them again. It swooped over their heads, and Adi realized what it was.

A huge glowing bird. No, not just a bird.

The Condor.

Case pumped a fist in the air. "Rani's in the game!"

Will pulled Adi into a one-armed hug. He shouted in her ear over the roar of the storm. "It's over. We're going home."

Chapter 52

Wake the Dead

Will leaped down when the eel slid onto the shore of the glowing island, the sparkling crystals of the island's beach crunching under his feet. As the others joined him, Adi scooped up a handful. "Are these—?"

"Diamonds?" Will said. "Yeah, think so."

Adi dropped the jewels. "Of course. Why not?"

They all hugged each other, and even Stone pulled Will into a brief embrace. Ellie was introducing herself to the others while keeping an arm around Case and Fader. She didn't look like she'd let them go anytime soon, but neither Case nor Fader seemed to mind. Fader still wore the Unicorn Tapestry like a superhero cape.

Master!

The voice sounded in Will's head. He'd never heard it before, but he knew it was the magical eel. The creature swayed above Fader, who gaped at it. The other travelers must have heard it, too, as all eyes were now on the beast.

Master, the eel called again to Fader, *thank you for my release. I go now to my rest. Blessed be the White Coven of Ellan Vannin.*

Flames licked the tail of the eel, then sped up its length to engulf its swaying head. The travelers jumped back as the creature erupted in a blaze of light that burned brightly for a breath, then died, leaving only ashes floating in the air.

Will remembered he still wore the Chakana under his shirt. Pulling the cord over his head, he stared at the strange artifact that had changed his life in so many ways.

The Chakana had broken him. Made him a prisoner in his own home for eight years. Pulled him into danger after danger—Marell and Morrigan, the Sisters, the Black Island, the Chambelán. And this entire trip, from the attack at the monastery to the battle with Quilla.

Yet it had given him much, too. His astral powers, in Dream and now awake, had come from the Chakana. As had his inspiration for the comic that had made the Rider a household name. And the Chakana had brought Case into his life. Fader, too, and so many others, but, yeah...Case.

And someone else. *Nyx? You there? Time for a last goodbye?*

No answer. Disappointment swept over him, a wave of loss and emptiness, of something gone forever from his life. Still no answer came.

Okay, then. I'll say it. Raising the Chakana to his lips, he kissed it. *Goodbye, Nyx.*

He walked over to Suyana. "Madre, I have something that belongs to you." He held the Chakana out to her in his palm.

Suyana took his hand in both of hers and squeezed it. "Thank you, Will Dreycott. For all that you and your brave friends have done." She slipped the Chakana over her head. "Not having this changed our lives—"

"I know. I'm sorry."

"—but *having* the Key changed your life, too," she continued, as if she knew his earlier thoughts. She locked eyes with him. "And the lives of your parents. Now, it is time to wake them. To bring them back to this world."

Will swallowed. Time to face his parents...who weren't his parents.

Suyana, followed by Isobel, led them through the crystal forest toward the pyramid. Behind him, Adi walked with Stone, Mei, and Diego, marveling at the images that flowed across every leaf on every branch. Ahead, Ellie walked with Case and Fader, an arm still around each of them.

He was alone with his thoughts. Thoughts of what he would say to his parents. He remembered Case's words. Even if they weren't his biological mother and father, they'd raised him and loved him and tried to keep him safe. And they'd given up a lifelong quest to try to save him.

They were still his parents. And he still loved them very much.

The group reached the top of the crystal pyramid where the Library sat. Suyana stopped at the door of the Madre de Bondad.

She waited until the others had gathered before the entrance. "Forgive me, but you five..." She indicated Adi, Stone, Mei, Diego, and Isobel. "...must wait outside."

"Protecting your secrets?" Adi asked.

Suyana shrugged. "Yes. The few that you people do not already know." She stepped forward. The door disappeared. Suyana entered the Library, followed by Will, then Case, Fader, and Ellie.

"Crap," Case said as they stepped inside. "We should've got Rani from the Condor's realm first. She'll hate missing this."

"After she led me to my door in the Gray Lands," Ellie said, "she was going to find her own door out of there."

They all stopped, staring at the scene in the Library.

When Will had last been here, three figures had circled the silver pool, sitting cross-legged and silent—Luciana and his parents. Now, in the seat Quilla-Ellie had used to restart her Branch of Order, a fourth figure sat.

Rani Patel.

"Looks like she found her door," Will said.

Shaking her head, Suyana walked to where Rani circled the pool. Keeping pace, her lips moving silently, Suyana touched Rani's hands where they lay folded in her lap.

Rani's eyes shot open. "Beware the wrath of the Thunder Babies!" she shouted.

"Uh…" Will said.

Suyana sighed. "Your friend has foolishly joined with the Four. Her mind has become immersed in the Book."

"She just wanted to help," Case said. "And she did—I'll bet she sent us the Condor."

"Appease the Thunder Babies! Sing the Song of Tiny Things!" Rani cried, her unfocused eyes wildly scanning the Library as Suyana guided her from her seat.

"Will she get better?" Case asked, concern on her face. "Back to normal?"

"Kinda liking *this* version," Will said.

"Will!"

"Raise your voices!" Rani shouted. "Sing the Song!"

"Oh, come on," Will said. "Don't you want to hear that song now?"

"I am so done with songs," Case muttered.

"Sister Rani's time within the Book has been short," Suyana said. "She should recover quickly."

"Good," Case said, gently leading a muttering Rani away from the Mirror.

"She better remember that song," Will said.

Moving to Luciana, Suyana repeated the actions she'd used to wake Rani.

A smile spread across the lined face of the older Madre. "Sister," Luciana said, even before her eyes opened and fell on Suyana.

"Sister," Suyana sobbed, tears running down her cheeks, "I have missed you so."

"And I, you." Slipping from the invisible seat with surprising nimbleness, Luciana pulled Suyana into a hug, then stepped back, her hands still on Suyana's shoulders. "I have watched you in the Mirror. You have led our Sisterhood well, during terrible times."

Suyana shook her head. "I have made many mistakes."

"Yet when faced with the hardest of decisions, you chose wisely." Luciana nodded to Will and the others. "Here stands proof. Trusting these young people, even when history argued against it."

Luciana walked to them. "No words can repay the debt that all of creation owes you, but I thank you. You will forever be friends of the Sisterhood and the Four."

As Will wrestled with having god-like beings as friends, Luciana's gaze settled on the Unicorn Tapestry draped over Fader's shoulders.

"Morrigan gave it to me," Fader said.

"I saw. In the Mirror."

"I guess you'll want it back," he said, his face falling. He started to unfasten it from around his neck.

But Luciana put out a hand, stopping him. "No, child. Our Sister Morrigan chose you to use the last of its great magicks. It is yours now." Behind her, Suyana frowned, but Luciana shook her head.

Next, Luciana embraced Ellie Cootes. "Elenora, it is good to see you in the flesh, once more. A debt is owed to you as well, and not just for your company during the past eight years. Without your strength this day, Quilla would not have been defeated."

Ellie returned the hug, then slipped her arms around Case and Fader. "I just wanted to be with my children, again." A sob escaped Case, and she buried her face into her mom's shoulder.

Luciana turned to Will. "And now, we must awaken your parents."

Dreading this moment, Will followed Luciana as she paced alongside where his mother slowly circled the Mirror.

"Unlike Sister Rani," Luciana said, "your parents have been immersed in the immensity of the Story for eight years. When they awaken, they will be...different. They will need time to recover. To remember how to live in this world again."

"Ellie seemed to recover quickly."

"Quilla helped with that, unknowingly. Sending Elenora to the Gray Lands broke her connection with the Mirror. Your guiding her back to the waking world from there also helped. But mostly..." Luciana nodded to where Ellie stood with Case and Fader, talking and laughing and crying. "...being reunited with her children has pulled her back. Reminded her of her life...and the meaning of that life."

Luciana's eyes locked on his as they continued to circle the pool. "I hope your parents will find the same reason to return to this world—a reunion with their son. A son now healed of what the Chakana once did to him."

Will looked away, but felt the Madre's eyes still on him. *Their son.* Except he wasn't. "Madre, my parents...Quilla told me...she said..."

"I know what she said."

He didn't want to ask, but had to. "Is it true?"

"Yes."

And there it was. No denying it now. No hope that Quilla had lied.

"Will," Luciana said. "I came to know your parents well these past eight years. I know they love you very much. Is that not the most important thing?"

He just nodded, unable to speak.

She smiled. "Then shall we wake them?"

Luciana woke his mother first. Terri Yurikami opened her eyes. Will waited, holding his breath, not knowing what to expect. Surprise? Confusion? Joy at seeing him again?

But his mother stayed seated, unmoving. Luciana woke his father, but he also continued to sit and circle the Mirror. Luciana had to coax them both down from their invisible seats. They stood immobile, with an unfocused gaze far too familiar to him.

"They look—" He stopped as his throat constricted. "They look like they're lost in the Gray Lands."

"No," Luciana said. "Not there. Their minds are still in the Book, traveling the many branches of the Story." She laid a gentle hand on his shoulder. "We will return to the Threshold. To the forest of the Great Trees. There, your parents can rest and recover."

"How long? Until they're...back?"

Luciana hesitated.

His heart fell. *She doesn't know. Why should she? This has never happened before.*

"Time will tell." She raised a hand as he started to speak. "Right now, as we journey back through the Crossing, walk with your parents. Hold their hands. Talk to them. You must become the beacon that guides them home."

They left the Library. Adi was thrilled to see Jon and Terri again, but then shaken by their unresponsive stares. Will could tell she believed his assurances they would recover as much as he did.

Luciana and Suyana led the party off the Crystal Island, then through the realms of each Guardian. As they traveled, Will walked between his parents, hand in hand, talking to them as he led them. Talking of memories of their lives together. Christmases and birthdays. Vacations and expeditions. Good times and bad. Laughter and tears. Sadness and joy.

And as he talked to his parents, guiding them through the Crossing and, hopefully, back to this world, he realized he was finding his own way back. The way back in his heart. Back to being a family again.

Chapter 53

Mother's Daughter

Two days later, back in the Threshold, Case strolled through the forest of the Great Trees. It was late morning, and she was meeting Fader and their mom at noon at the amphitheater. Since returning from the Crossing, the three of them had been inseparable, getting to know each other again. But at breakfast, Fader had asked for some one-on-one time with the mother he barely remembered, so he and Ellie were off together somewhere.

Case had seen little of Will the past two days. While Ellie was mostly recovered from her time in the Library, Luciana was still working with Terri and Jon. Will joined in those sessions, telling his mom and dad about their lives together, trying to coax them back. Case knew it was hard on him. He ached to have his parents restored to normal, but dreaded it too, for the adoption conversation that would follow.

Case passed a group of warrior Sisters led by Yanta and Isobel. Yanta paid Case no notice, but Isobel smiled and waved. Diego and his remaining soldiers, each with a slung rifle, followed the Sisters. Diego winked and saluted when he passed her. Since the Black Island, he and his soldiers seemed to be in awe of her, Will, and Fader.

Trailing them was Adi. She stopped beside Case, who frowned a question.

"We're training the Sisters on guns," Adi said. "Luciana and Suyana wish to modernize their defenses."

"And you agreed?"

Adi lowered her voice. "It's in exchange for being allowed to return home."

That was even bigger news. They'd worried the Sisters wouldn't let them leave. "Aren't they afraid we'll lead others back here?"

"I asked that very question. For whatever reason, that possibility doesn't concern them." She eyed Case. "Can we trust them to keep their word?"

"Yes, we can," Case said, surprised both by her certainty and by Adi wanting her opinion. "They've earned our trust."

Adi smiled. "Just as you, Fader, and Will have earned theirs." She set off after the training group.

Case continued, warmed by Adi's words. She reached the clearing of the Hatun Yura of Suyana. At the base of the Great Tree, the Madre talked with Rani. Although recovered, Rani had kept to herself the past two days, explaining she'd had 'enough of humanity for a while' after her short stint viewing the Book.

On their return through the Crossing, they'd all exchanged stories until everyone knew the complete tale of the end of Quilla and her threat to the multiverse.

Rani had told of escaping the Gray Lands and retrieving her body in the Condor's realm, then reaching the Library and seeing the empty seat circling the Mirror.

"It was like fate offering me a seat—literally—at the table. Well, mirror," she'd told Case.

"Did you...merge? With one of the Four?"

Rani's eyes turned wistful. "With Orden. The only one available. I don't think it was a *complete* merging, like with the Madres. But I became more than *me*. I could see..." She shivered. "...*everything*. It was overwhelming, so I focused on something small—on finding you guys. I saw you in the Black Tower. I tried to end the branch of Order..." She shrugged. "...but the Four wouldn't allow that."

"But you sent the Condor, didn't you?"

Rani had nodded. "They let me do that, because I wasn't messing with anyone's free will. Plus, me and Big Bird?" She held up two crossed fingers. "Like that."

That had been two days ago. Now, as Case approached Rani and Suyana, the Madre called a greeting to Case before walking off toward the fields.

"Getting yelled at for peeking at the Mirror?" Case asked Rani.

"Nah. She gets why I did it."

"The Madres aren't pissed?"

"Just the opposite. Seems I made an impression."

"On Suyana?"

"On Luciana. And the Four." Rani hesitated. "They invited me to become a Siguiente."

"*What?* Are you kidding? Yeah, you're kidding...right?"

"Thank you for your strong support."

"Seriously, *you* running the multiverse? Although, compared to Quilla..."

"Funny. You do realize your opinion pales against the entity that creat-ed...creation, right?"

"Point. So, what did you say?"

"I said no."

"What? Why?"

Rani gazed into the forest, her eyes distant. "Seeing what I saw. All those universes. The horrible things we do to each other, to other creatures, to the Earth..." She shook her head.

Case understood. "You can't imagine watching bad things happen—forever."

"Yeah, but more, I can't imagine never being able to *stop* the bad things. To *fix* the world. But the Four won't interfere with free will. They'll introduce *events* to see how people react—earthquakes, hurricanes, natural disasters, a virus—"

"Fun group."

"You think? But no messing with free will. Sending the Condor to you was just an event I introduced, so I got away with that."

"But you're giving up...well, not immortality, but a freaking long life."

"A long life sitting by, watching horrible things I can't stop. At least, helping Will play Galahad, I can do some good." Her smile was soft, almost timid, a look Case had never seen on her. "I've realized I enjoy that...doing good."

"So, we're not breaking up the band yet?"

Rani smiled. "Not as long as Will can put up with me." Her face became serious. "How's it going with his parents?"

"Slowly." She hesitated. "There's something I should tell you." She related how Luciana had confirmed what Quilla had told Will—that Jon and Terri weren't his biological parents. "Which makes your theory about Adi more likely."

Rani bit her lip. "You haven't told Will about that, have you?"

"No. His parents have to recover first. Then he needs to talk to them about being adopted. I want him to have *that* conversation before I tell him about Adi." She sighed. "Even then, I'm not sure it's my place to tell him."

"There may be another reason not to."

"What do you mean?"

"After I found you guys in the Mirror and sent the Condor..." She bit her lip again. "Well, Stone was with you, so it was easy to trace his time branch back through that big tree—"

"You spied on him, *again*?"

"Hey, I'm a reporter. I'm naturally curious."

"Naturally nosy."

"Whatever. Anyway, I saw what happened after the Triads killed his wife and daughter."

"And?"

"And I was wrong. That massacre at the restaurant? Stone and his people weren't responsible. It was another Triad gang, posing as cops."

A wave of relief washed over Case. She'd liked Stone from the start. The way he'd accepted her right away, his concern when she'd returned to the streets, how he saw his dead daughter in her—he'd acted like the father she'd always wanted but never had. Thinking he'd murdered people had sickened her.

"Which means," Rani continued, "maybe I was also wrong about Adi."

"You didn't check her time line, too?"

"Tried to. Got lost in the tree and very confused. What I remember after that is...weird."

"Weird, how?"

"Something about..." Rani hesitated. "...thunder babies."

"Better remember more, or Will's going to be pissed."

"What?"

"Never mind. Does this mean you and Stone are a thing again?"

Rani sighed. "No. After learning about that massacre, I pushed him away. Now, he's the same with me. Polite, but no sparkage anymore." She shrugged. "My fault. At least it keeps my unbroken string of failed relationships intact."

"You could tell him the truth."

"That I dug into his past? Twice? Yeah, that'd help."

A bell rang out, echoing through the forest. Case still couldn't recognize which bell marked which hour, but the sun disk was halfway between the Veils, which made it noon. Saying goodbye to Rani, she headed off to meet Fader and their mom.

Case shifted nervously where she sat cross-legged with Fader and Ellie on the stage of the amphitheater. Ellie seemed very at ease around Fader, laughing and joking all the time, comfortable and happy. But with Case, she'd make brief eye contact, then look away. And their conversations when they'd been alone together had been filled more with silences than words.

"Mom's remembering stuff," Fader said, an easy grin on his face. He still wore the Unicorn Tapestry as a cape, and Case was pretty sure he slept in it, too.

Ellie smiled. "My memories *are* coming back. Slowly."

This was good. At first, Ellie had remembered nothing from the past eight years. "Like what?" Case asked.

"I remember entering the Crossing with Luciana, Jon, Terri, and your young Will, forced by Parwa and Alvarez."

"Suyana told us that part," Case explained. "And Will showed us visions of you all traveling through the Crossing."

"Visions?"

"Yeah, it's this thing he does. Or did. His last one, before Quilla took us over, showed Parwa shooting Alvarez. She shot at Will, but the Condor attacked, and Will somehow got zapped out of there into a river. We don't know what happened inside the Crossing after."

Ellie nodded slowly. "I thought Will was going to die, but he just...vanished. The Condor grabbed Parwa and dropped her into that black sea. We were free, but trapped. The Chakana disappeared with Will, and Luciana explained we couldn't return through the Crossing without it. We had no food, no water, and no way out."

"So, Luciana led you to the Library," Case said.

"She said no time passes inside it, so we wouldn't age. But our bodies still needed nourishment—and she knew of only one way to provide that."

Case understood. "By merging with the Four."

"She said if we became *one* with them, their energy would sustain our bodies. With no other option, we took our places around the Silver Mirror, Luciana summoned the Four...and Jon, Terri, and I became Madres of the Book."

"For eight years," Case said, surprised by the sharpness in her voice. Eight years where their mother could have been—*should* have been—*their* mother, not a mother to the Book.

"Yes," Ellie said, looking at her, then quickly away. "Eight years."

"Will couldn't find you or his parents in Dream," Fader said. He swallowed. "We thought you were dead."

"I'm sorry, sweetheart," Ellie said, stroking his hair. "Once we'd merged with the Four, we weren't ourselves anymore. Will would never have found us in Dream."

"What was it like?" Case asked. "Being...merged?"

Ellie took a deep breath. "At first, I couldn't handle it—the Book, the Story. I couldn't grasp the sheer *size* of it, the immensity, the vastness, the number of universes, the number of people and their lives. It was overwhelming, overpowering. I could feel myself...losing myself. Losing who I was." She took a deep breath. "Losing my sanity."

Case wanted to reach out, put her arm around her mom, comfort her as she herself had yearned to be comforted for the past eight years. But it was Fader who took their mom's hand in his.

Ellie squeezed it. "But I discovered a way to stay *me*."

"How?" Fader asked.

She smiled. "I found you two in the Book. My children. Seeing you, being able to follow your lives...that's how I clung to sanity through all those years."

Now it was Case who couldn't meet her mother's eyes. "After you left, we had a dream, Fader and me. At least, we thought it was a dream." She looked at her mother. "Was that you? Did you really speak to us?"

Ellie nodded and wiped at her eyes. "In the Book, I saw that your Gramma and Grampa were going to die. A car crash. I couldn't stop that—the Four wouldn't allow it. So, I did the only thing I could. I pleaded, I begged, I prayed to the Four, to the Book. To keep my children safe. To help them recognize danger and escape it."

"Recognize danger...and escape it," Case repeated slowly. Her Voice. Fader's fading. "You *did* send us our powers!"

Ellie gave a rueful grin. "Well, superpowers weren't what I had in mind, but the Book or the Four or *something* heard me and came up with a solution. One that didn't interfere with your free will. Just another event they'd introduced into the multiverse."

They all fell silent. Case didn't know what Ellie and Fader were thinking, but the only thing running through her head was how she'd been wrong about their mom for so long.

Ellie broke the silence. She regarded Case and this time didn't look away. "I remember something else." She swallowed. "I remember leaving you. Leaving my children." A tear ran down her cheek. Her words came in a rush. "I'm sorry. I'm so sorry. We were in so much debt. We needed money. I thought...I thought you'd be safe until—" A sob choked off her words.

Case moved to her mother's side, holding her as she cried. Fader joined them, wrapping his arms around them both.

"Mom," Case whispered. "I'm sorry, too. For what I thought. I was so angry with you for all those years."

"I know," Ellie said, stroking Case's hair.

"You do?"

Ellie sat back, wiping at her eyes. "Saw it in the Book, remember? And I understand. I always understood your anger. You had a right to be angry. I failed you as a mother."

"No!" Case said, with a strength that surprised her. "You did it for us. You left us safe with Gramma and Grampa. You didn't know what would happen to them, what would happen to you down here." Beside her, Fader nodded hard.

Ellie looked at them both, then down at her hands. "Can you two ever forgive me?"

For their answer, they pulled their mother into another hug.

"Just don't disappear for eight years again," Case said.

Ellie laughed. "That's a promise."

Chapter 54

Build God, Then We'll Talk

That same morning, Will asked Mei to walk with him in the forest of the Great Trees. There, he told her of his encounter in the Realms of the Dead with Peng.

"He asked me to give you a message," Will said gently as they walked.

Mei's jaw tightened. "Yes?"

"He wanted you to know..." He took a deep breath. This was hard. "He wanted you to know he loved you. That he always loved you. And...and his greatest regret was he never found the courage to tell you."

She shook her head, her eyes glistening. "Idiots. We were both idiots." She wiped at her eyes. "Thank you, Will. I need to be alone for a while."

"Yeah, sure." He started to leave.

"Will?"

He turned back.

"Do you love Case?"

"Yes. Yes, I do."

"You've told her?"

"Yeah."

She nodded. "Good."

He watched her walk off into the trees, wishing he could do more. An idea came. He thought about it. Yes, but not here. First, they had to get home. He walked back, feeling a little better.

That afternoon, Will walked with his parents past fields where Sisters picked vegetables and pastures where the shaggy cattle grazed. The forest of the Great Trees lay at their backs, the Second Veil rose in the distance before them, and the sun disk shone overhead.

His parents were returning to an awareness of the world and the people around them. A distant and vacant look would sometimes steal over their faces, but mostly, they stayed in the moment. And with him.

His mom had her arm around his waist as they walked. His father would give his shoulder the occasional squeeze. Will began telling them everything that had happened since he'd disappeared from the Crossing eight years ago, but they explained they'd followed it all in the Mirror.

They told him how proud they were of him, of everything he'd done, both with his life and in stopping Quilla. They told him how much they liked Case. They told him how happy they were to be back together.

But they didn't tell him the one thing he needed to know. And since he wasn't ready to ask that question yet, he started with easier ones. "What was it like? The Book? The Story? Was it what you expected?"

The far-off look returned to his father's eyes. "Expected? No one could expect what's in the Book." He shook his head. "It was beautiful. It was horrible."

"We thought..." his mother began. She sighed. "I don't know what we thought. It's impossible to grasp *infinite* realities. Infinite universes. It made me feel huge—to see all the possibilities of what a life *could* be. But it made me feel so small, too—to see my own life, my own choices in the vastness of it all."

"We hoped for answers," his father said. "You know, to the big questions. Why are we here? What is right? What is wrong?" He shook his head again. "But we're here because some inscrutable god-like beings put us here, just to see how *we* answer those questions. But there are no answers—only choices. And you never know if a choice is right or wrong until you make it."

"And even then..." his mother said. His parents fell silent, that distant look returning to their eyes.

"How did it start?" Will asked, breaking their reverie. "Your search?"

His father's smile was rueful. "You mean our obsession? Over the years on South American expeditions, we kept encountering rumors of a legendary artifact called the Key that granted passage to a mythical land of the gods."

His mother took up the tale. "At first, we dismissed those stories as another 'lost valley of the Incas' legend. Cities of gold hidden from the Conquistadors. Lots of those around. But one night, sitting around a campfire with our Quechuan guide, we mentioned the Key."

"He knew the legend," his father continued. "He said the Chakana—as he called it—opened a book holding the story of every life ever lived and that could be lived. To us, that sounded like the Akashic Records. We started taking the Key rumors more seriously." He hesitated. "We began to search for it."

His mother continued. "We'd heard whispers of an ancient sisterhood guarding both the Key and a mysterious otherworld. A sisterhood that still existed and recruited young girls from villages in southeast Peru."

"You know where that led," his father said. "Pablo betraying us. Alvarez stealing the Key. Us taking it from him..." He swallowed. "...not knowing he'd slaughtered the Sisters to get it."

That reminded Will of escaping their capture by the Sisters. "Where'd you find that quipu? The one with the code to the rock wall?"

"Sheer luck," his father said. "In one village, a woman approached us, hearing we were asking about a mysterious Sisterhood. She claimed her great-great-whatever-grandmother had joined this Sisterhood, but discovered she was pregnant after being recruited. She begged to return to her village. The Sisters took her home, blindfolded, unaware she'd stolen a quipu containing a code to a secret doorway. That story—and the quipu—passed down in her family, from mother to daughter."

"Why would the Sisters make the quipu?" Will asked. "That's like writing your password on a sticky note."

His dad chuckled. "Probably the same reason. Maybe a Madre or Siguiente had memory problems? Anyway, the woman offered to sell us the quipu. Don't think she ever believed the story. We bought it. It was so old, we worried it would disintegrate, so we made copies."

They fell silent again. He took a deep breath, preparing to ask the only question that mattered to him.

But before he could summon the courage, his mother spoke. "Can you ever forgive us, Will? For what our obsession did to you?"

Her voice held something he'd never heard from his mother before. Fear. To his surprise, he didn't have to think about his answer. "Nothing to forgive. You didn't know the Chakana would do that to me. And you did everything you could, even gave up your dream, to save me."

"That's what parents do," his father said, as his mother pulled him into a hug.

What parents do. Parents...

"Mom, Dad, I have a question..."

His mother nodded. "We know, dear. We saw it in the Book. We know what Quilla told you."

He waited.

Tears brimmed in his mother's eyes. "We're your parents, Will. You're our son. And we love you so much. But, yes...we adopted you."

"We'd tried having children, but..." His father shrugged. "Then, a friend in Hong Kong, who knew we'd been trying, reached out about a baby boy whose mother had disappeared."

"We planned to tell you when you turned thirteen," his mom continued. "But then..."

"Then all this happened," Will finished.

His parents fell silent as they walked, but they kept shooting him sidelong glances. Waiting. Waiting for his answer to the unspoken question.

He remembered what Case had told him. *Will, don't make the same mistake I made about our mom. Even if you are adopted—they're still your parents. And they love you.*

He remembered Luciana's words, too. *I came to know your parents well. I know they love you very much. Is that not the most important thing?*

Yes. Yes, it was. That and one other thing—his love for them.

He stopped walking and pulled them into a hug. "You're my parents. I'm your son." He swallowed. "And I love you very much."

They stood holding each other, at the end of a journey that had torn them apart but finally brought them together in a way he could never have imagined.

That night, Will ate dinner with Case, Fader, Rani, and the three parents in Luciana's Hatun Yura along with the two Madres. Adi, Stone, Diego, and his men were eating elsewhere with the warriors they had been training on firearms.

During dinner, Luciana announced, to cheers and applause, that the visitors could return home in two days.

"Why the delay?" Will asked.

"Because an event both rare and critical to the Sisterhood must first take place. One we can delay no longer, and one to which you are all invited."

"What event?" Case asked.

"Meet us before the Third Veil after breakfast and you will see," Luciana replied and would say no more.

The next morning, Will walked with Case, Fader, Rani, and the three parents through the forest. They emerged from the trees to find Luciana waiting before the shimmering curtain of the Third Veil, along with Suyana, Yanta, and Isobel.

Luciana smiled. "Good. We may begin." Removing the Chakana from under her robes, she turned to the Veil.

"Wait," Will said. "We're going back into the Crossing?"

"Oh, yay," Rani muttered. "*So* many fun times in there."

"You need not join us," Luciana said, "but you would honor us with your presence." Both Suyana and Isobel nodded their agreement.

"An honor for you, as well," Yanta said. "You will be the first outsiders to witness what will occur today." Yanta now showed them a begrudging respect, but her tone implied disbelief over both the Madre's offer and their possible refusal.

"And what *will* occur today?" Will asked.

Luciana raised the Chakana, and a doorway opened in the Veil. "Join us and see."

To his surprise, Rani stepped forward first. "What the hell. Maybe I'll get to say bye-bye to my condor cutie before we leave tomorrow."

And maybe I'll see Nyx, Will thought. He hadn't seen his strange companion of the last eight years since he, Case, and Fader had leaped from the Library to face Quilla on the Black Island. "Okay, I'm in."

"Mom," Case asked Ellie, "are you okay with this?"

Ellie put her arms around her and Fader. "Sure. A last goodbye before we head home."

Will hadn't considered how their parents might feel about returning to the place that had derailed their lives. "Mom? Dad?"

"As long as we're not staying eight years," his dad said. His mom laughed and took his father's hand.

Together, they all followed Luciana through the doorway.

Inside the Veil, as the four Sisters each took a colored orb from the giant Chakana, memories rose unbidden in Will. Memories of his first two journeys through the Crossing—one at gunpoint as a child, and the other only days ago when Quilla had revealed herself.

He pushed those thoughts away. Nothing would happen this time. Even so, a tingle of fear remained. Why was today's trip happening?

At first, their passage through the Crossing matched their earlier visit. As before, when they reached the end of the Snake's realm of underground tunnels, the Puma guardian waited at the edge of his jungle world.

But when the Puma led them forward, the vegetation parting before it, the Snake continued with them. Shrunk to the size of a normal constrictor, it slithered alongside a grinning Fader. And when they left the jungle to follow the Condor through its snowy mountain realm, the Puma remained, too, stalking beside Case.

And when they crossed the silver road across the sea of the Nothing and reached the Crystal Island, the Condor still circled above a smiling Rani.

Climbing the crystal pyramid, they entered its smaller twin that was the Library. There, Luciana and Suyana positioned themselves with their backs to the silver mirror and motioned Yanta and Isobel to kneel before them. Will, Case, Fader, and Rani formed a line on one side, the three parents on the other, facing the Madres and the kneeling Sisters.

The three guardians arrayed themselves before the two Madres, their gazes locked on Isobel and Yanta. First, the Snake, its head swaying above its coiled body. Next, the Puma, sitting on its haunches with head held high. Last, the Condor, standing erect, black wings slightly unfolded.

Luciana spoke. "Thanks to our young friends, the Chakana has returned to us." She touched the Key, now pulsing and glowing, where it lay on her chest. "Today, we restore our full bond with the One. Today, we invite you, Yanta and Isobel, to become Madres with us."

Beside him, Case gasped. Isobel flashed Case a timid smile, then turned back.

Luciana continued. "Yanta, you have served well as Siguiente and should long ago have had this moment. We invite you to join with the Four."

Suyana spoke. "Isobel, your bravery and unswerving loyalty to the Sisterhood and to our young friends..." She nodded at Will, Case, Fader, and Rani. "...saved us all, even when your Madre doubted you and doubted them. We invite you to join with the Four."

Luciana then spoke in a language Will didn't recognize. Quechuan? Her words rose and fell with the rhythm of a recitation. A recitation, he guessed, repeated in this ceremony uncountable times stretching back through time. A ceremony the Madres had granted them the honor of witnessing.

Luciana paused, and both Yanta and Isobel replied in the same language. Suyana then spoke, also with the same sing-song formality, and the two kneeling Sisters again replied.

When the exchanges ended, Luciana's eyes fell on the guardians arrayed before her and Suyana. She addressed them, but with the deferential tone of a plea. In reply, the Snake, the Puma, and the Condor opened their mouths, and from each, a silver mist emerged. The mists swirled together, growing into a sparkling cloud hovering in the air.

From her leather pouch, Suyana withdrew what Will recognized as the scale of snake skin she'd gathered on their first passage through the Crossing. She touched it to the cloud. The scale disappeared inside, and as it vanished, so did the Snake guardian.

Next, she fed the tuft of fur of the Puma guardian to the swirling mist, and the Puma faded from sight.

Finally, she withdrew the Condor feather. But instead of offering it to the cloud, she addressed Isobel and Yanta. "Rise...and prepare to receive the Breath of the Three."

For Will, the full meaning of what they were watching sank in. These two young women were about to become close to immortal. He found that harder to grasp than their elevation to Madres.

When the two Sisters stood before the mist, Suyana released the feather, which flew like an arrow into the churning vapors. The Condor guardian vanished. The swirling cloud slowed, thinned, and began to disperse.

"Quickly!" Luciana cried.

Yanta and Isobel leaned forward, breathing in the mist deeply, breathing until the cloud was gone. Then both exhaled slowly. Will couldn't be sure if it was an effect of the Chakana's radiance, but both Sisters now seemed to glow.

Luciana smiled as brightly as the Chakana. "Welcome to the Circle of the Four, *Madre* Yanta, *Madre* Isobel."

The air of solemnity that had hung over the ceremony evaporated like the silver cloud, and everyone began talking and laughing. "Oh, my god," Case said, hugging Isobel. "This is awesome. I'm so proud of you."

Isobel laughed and said something in reply, but Will didn't hear her words. Or her laugh. Or anything.

Something was wrong. Silence blanketed the scene. Case turned to him, smiling. But she stopped mid-turn. Everyone stopped. Every other person in the room now stood unmoving, frozen in mid-gesture, mid-laugh.

But he could still move. He looked around the Library frantically. What was happening? Was this a new threat? Had Quilla somehow escaped and returned? What was—?

A pulsing light caught his eye—the Chakana, where it hung around Luciana's neck. The brightness became a glowing sphere that floated toward him, stretching into human form. The glow faded.

Nyx stood before him. "We should talk."

Chapter 55

Starts with a Big Finish

Outside the Library atop the Crystal Pyramid, Will stood with a fully embodied Nyx looking out over the Crystal Island. Gone were Nyx's lime-green t-shirt and dark green jeans, replaced by the loose-fitting, white smock and trousers the Sisters wore when working in the fields.

With her arrival, a calmness had settled on Will. The only surprise he felt was how he felt no surprise. "Are they okay in there?"

"They're fine. I just stopped time for a while."

"You can stop time?"

"In this place I can. I'm the Guardian of this island. Time flows differently here."

"Why'd we come outside?"

"I thought this view most appropriate for our talk," she said. "Below lies everything Quilla would have destroyed. Everything you and the Critter Crew saved."

Will's eyes swept over the crystal forest, every leaf on every tree an entire universe. "It was you, wasn't it?"

She raised an eyebrow. "Me?"

"When Suyana captured Adi and was going to kill me, you convinced her to take us into the Crossing. You told her that, eight years ago, I was *chosen*."

"You were."

"Yeah, but I thought you meant chosen by the *Four*, that *they* had put a piece of the Chakana in me. But now, I know."

"Know what?"

He looked into her strange violet eyes, fighting back a shiver at the power he saw there. Power, he realized, that had always been there. "I know it was *you*."

She continued to stare at him, but said nothing.

"*You* put that piece of yourself in me. You *decided* to do that. Not the Four—*you*. You *picked* me."

Nyx nodded. "Yes, Will. I picked you."

A part of him had known. A part that had stayed hidden, whispering to him, getting louder with each new event, new twist and turn, until...

Until he knew. But there remained so much he didn't understand. "Why? Why *me*?"

She walked to the stairs that led up to the pyramid's summit. She sat on the top step and patted the space beside her. He joined her, waiting.

"I'll answer that, but first you need a little history. On my favorite topic—me." She winked at him, the old mischievous Nyx, once more. "I began as simply an artifact the Four created." She wrinkled her nose. "A *thing*. But a thing imbued with tremendous astral power. My sole purpose, the only reason I existed, was to be the Key—a tool to open the Crossing."

"Yeah, well, you're much more than a thing."

"Thank you."

"What happened?"

She sighed. "Over the eons, slowly, oh so slowly, I became *aware*. Aware of myself. Or, at least, aware that something existed in me I might call my *self*. Something very different from the simple Key the Four had intended. And very different and very separate from the Four."

"When? How long have you been...aware?"

"Since early humans walked upright."

"And no one knew? The Madres? The Four?"

"The Madres never did. Not one, ever. Madres can only see what's in the Book. And the Chakana, by design, exists *outside* the Book."

He remembered Suyana's disbelief when Nyx had appeared to her. *You are a trick. The Chakana is not some blue wraith. Some purple-haired floating phantom.*

Nyx continued. "But the Four knew."

"Weren't you afraid they'd...*do* something?"

"Take away my self-awareness? No, they never interfere with free will. To them, I was just another free-willed sentience. Another variation of their ever-growing, ever-changing creation. But a surprising one. And they *love* surprises. Kind of the whole point of this." She indicated the forest below with a sweep of a hand. "They wanted to see what I would *do* with my free will."

"And you never told anyone?"

"Couldn't. I was aware of being...a 'being,' but I couldn't communicate. I was trapped inside my little crystal prison."

A sudden wave of empathy swept over Will. Trapped inside a prison. Wanting to break free. To go outside. "I can relate."

"Yeah, you can, my friend," she said gently, "and I'm sorry for my role in that. I'll get to *our* part of the story, but first, the last piece to my tale." She sighed. "I was fully aware when Quilla joined the Sisterhood over six hundred years ago. Aware when she created her branch of Order. Aware of her defeat by the new Madres and her death. But I saw something the Madres did not."

"What?"

"First, you need to understand the Four created the Chakana from the very stuff they used to form the Crystal Island. So, being literally a *part* of this place, I sensed Quilla's astral spirit had *not* gone to the Realms of the Dead as the

Madres assumed. I saw her slip from the Crystal Island to its echo in Dream."

"Didn't the Four know what happened?"

"They knew, but again...free will. They left her there. They left her Branch of Order as part of the Silver Tree. To them, it was just another variation in their creation. To me, it was a ticking time bomb. Quilla was still in the multiverse, trying to come back, trying to finish her Branch of Order—and destroy all of creation while doing it."

"Don't take this wrong," Will said, "but why did you care? I mean, you weren't, um..."

"Human? No, but the strongest drive for any sentient being is self-preservation. Unlike the Four, I was *part* of this multiverse. Initially, I simply didn't wish to die when Quilla destroyed it." She shrugged. "Selfish, but you must admit, very *human*."

"You said *initially*. That changed?"

She nodded. "As I grew as a sentient being, what Quilla had tried to do—what she still yearned to do—filled me with a sense of *wrongness*. Perhaps I had acquired the Four's fascination with their creation. Perhaps I began to understand this thing humans call morality." She smiled sadly. "Or maybe I just grew to love you odd creatures. Anyway, as the Four dedicated themselves to their search for where true beauty lay between Good and Evil, between Order and Chaos, I dedicated myself to stopping Quilla."

Will frowned. "Even though she was trapped in Dream?"

"I feared she would escape. She'd escaped death. Why not that place? My fear grew as the years passed and still she survived, feeding from Dream travelers marooned there. Years became decades, decades became centuries—and I knew."

"Knew what?"

"That someday, somehow, she would find a way."

"You decided to stop her."

"Which was a tad difficult, not having a body and all. So, I decided to *tell* someone about Quilla—and have *them* stop her."

"I thought you couldn't communicate with anyone."

"But some Sisters could sense me, right? Even across great distances. That was a *form* of communication. Maybe I could boost the signal. Pump up the volume. *Make* them hear me."

"Guessing that didn't work."

She gazed out over the crystal forest. "Nope. Nothing. Not even with the most sensitive of the Sisters. I was screaming, screaming so loud, but no one heard me...until I met the greatest astral power I'd ever encountered." She smiled at him. "You."

He understood. "The day my dad showed me the Chakana. That's why you chose me? Because I could...hear you?"

"Yes."

He shook his head. "I don't remember. Even when you showed me that memory of me and my dad with the Chakana, I didn't remember hearing anything."

"My fault. I didn't have much experience talking to humans. As in none. You were my first. But you heard me. You didn't *understand*, but you heard me." She tapped him on the arm and made a back-and-forth motion between them. "In that moment, a link formed between us." She looked out over the crystal forest again. "And here, I must beg forgiveness for what I tried to do next...and what I *did* do to your young life."

And in that moment, he finally remembered. Remembered standing, his eight-year-old self, staring at the Chakana where it lay in the lead box his father had just opened. Remembered the touch on his mind. The same touch he'd feel many years later from Marell, from Quilla. "You tried to take me over," he whispered.

Nyx nodded. "You couldn't understand me, so I decided to talk with your mouth. Tell your father of Quilla, of the danger to all of creation. Tell him how to find the Crossing, how to warn the Madres." She shrugged. "Good plan. Bad execution."

"What went wrong?"

"I started to transfer into you. A tad too quickly, but hey, I was new at this. Anyway, you collapsed...which made your father slam the box shut...which cut our link...which meant..." She gave a palms-up gesture with a shrug.

"You couldn't finish the transfer."

"Uh, yeah."

"So, only a *piece* of you got into me."

A nod. "A small, very confused piece. Most of me was now locked away in that lead box. The smaller part of me—the part in you—didn't know who, what, or why I was. I still didn't know, even after you came back from Peru and discovered your astral powers in Dream."

"*Were* those my powers? Or was that you?"

"Will, you are the most powerful astral traveler I've ever found. Your power was always there. After Peru, my presence gave it a kick-start—for which I'll totally take credit. Anyway, when your Rider adventures in Dream began, both of us sort of created Nyx together. I started appearing to you in Dream. I think I was still trying to communicate with you, not remembering why. Because I was a part of you, I knew stuff about you, so you thought I was your subconscious. I didn't know *what* I was, so I latched onto that."

"And you stayed that way...I stayed that way...for eight years."

"Until the Chakana destroyed the lead box in Adi's safe."

"Which started more problems. Sisters popping out of portals. Me blasted from my body. Case's Voice going crazy. Fader pushed into other 'verses."

"Hey, you finally got to go outside."

"Yeah, right. Kidnapped to the Black Island and—" He stopped, remembering a question he'd asked Quilla. "When the Chambelán had me prisoner, the Chakana drew my astral self into it. Quilla-Jack pulled me out, afraid it would expose her or extract the piece from inside me. Was she right?"

"No. My consciousness was still split, confused. I think the Chakana sensed *me* in you and reacted to that. I don't know what would have happened if Quilla hadn't interfered, but that contact awakened something in me. After you escaped the Black Island and returned home, memories began bubbling up in me, some mine, some yours. Memories I showed you."

"My dad exposing me to the Chakana. My parents meeting Ellie. My parents calling on the Sisters for help. Luciana taking us through the portal to Peru to heal me..." He paused. "Wait."

"What?"

"When my dad returned the Chakana to Luciana at the Threshold, why didn't the Chakana finish transferring into me and warn the Madres about Quilla?"

"After your dad interrupted my original transfer attempt, I stayed split and confused. I could never remember the entire story or who I was until a few days ago when Quilla pulled my missing part from you and made the Chakana—made me—whole again. Rather ironic, right? Her fixing me."

He thought back, trying to recast his past eight years in this new light. "Back up. When Parwa killed Alvarez in the Crossing and was going to shoot me, you zapped us out of here. *You* did that, right?"

"The Chakana part of me did. The Nyx part of me was still small and confused."

"Why did it do that?"

"Blood had been shed in the Crossing. You were about to die. The Chakana sensed part of itself in you. When Parwa pulled the trigger, the Chakana protected the Crossing and itself—*all* of itself—by taking both it and you far from the danger."

Will considered that. "Okay, but something's always bothered me about that."

"Yes?"

"Adi said when Diego and his men found me in the jungle, I had the Chakana around my neck—exposed. And it stayed exposed until Adi found it in my hospital room and locked it in a lead box."

"You're wondering why the Sisters didn't sense it and jump to it while it was exposed?"

"Exactly."

"The Chakana was hiding, protecting itself and the Story from Parwa. After we jumped, it put itself into a deep state of sleep, preventing it from being found. Because of the piece inside you, it pulled you into that same state. You didn't recover until Adi shielded the Key."

He snorted. "Recovered? I recovered consciousness, but no memories of

Peru."

"Any memories after you and I first linked were tied to the Chakana. When it suppressed its consciousness, those memories were suppressed, too. Then Adi stuck the Chakana into a lead box in her safe."

"And my memories stayed suppressed for eight years, until the Chakana broke out of the box."

Nyx nodded. "And began to slowly wake up...but still split and very confused." She sat there, watching him, biting her lip, waiting for him to respond.

Waiting for my reaction to all this. What *was* his reaction? How did he feel now that he knew what she'd done? "You messed up my life. For eight years."

She shifted where she sat. "Well, *you* collapsed when your dad showed you the Chakana, so *technically...*"

"You're blaming *me?*"

"Okay, okay! I screwed up. Yes, I messed up your young life. But, hey, good cause, right? Saving all of creation. Go, team." She pumped a fist, then gave him a pained look. "Right?"

He thought about what he'd lost—eight years of being a prisoner in his own home. But he thought of what he'd gained, too. A home like no other. The Dream Rider comic. *His* comic. And more than a comic. He *was* the Dream Rider and proud of all the good the Rider had done.

And Case wouldn't have crash-landed into his life that night if he hadn't been trapped in his tower. Fader, the little brother he never knew he'd always wanted, was part of his life now, too.

Plus, they'd saved the multiverse.

But mostly...Case.

Nyx was biting her lip, watching him. "Okay, now that I'm no longer part of you, you actually have to tell me what you're thinking."

"We're good."

"Really?" Nyx said, eyebrows raised in wide-eyed surprise.

He grinned. "Yeah. Really. I *like* my life." He frowned. "No, I *love* my life. Thanks. For choosing me."

"Well, I got lucky when I found you." She wiped her eyes with a hand, a gesture both human and touching. "And thanks for forgiving me." They stood. She opened her arms. "Bring it in, kid."

They hugged each other, rocking back and forth. Nyx smelled of the Flower and felt warm and soft and very human. A river of dreams and memories of times together rushed through his head, and he never wanted to let go. Finally, Nyx broke it off, but as she turned away, she wiped at her eyes again. And so did he. "We should go back," she said.

Inside the Library, Case, Fader, Rani, the three parents, and the Madres, both old and new, still stood frozen. Seeing Case recalled to Will her fear that an unknown power had *arranged* the two of them to meet. He explained that to Nyx.

She shook her head. "Not by me. Nope, if anything brought you two together, it was fate."

He started to question that, but then stopped. Case and him—fated to be together? He smiled. "Yeah, that works." Another thought occurred. "Will we keep our powers?"

"Hmm. *You* will. Your powers were always there. Case and Fader? Not sure. Theirs were gifts from the Four—which did *not* mess with free will. Just an event the Four introduced. Still surprising, though, because the Four are *very* hands-off at the individual human level." She looked at him. "Any more questions?"

He thought hard. "When Case and I rescued Fader from the Crystal Island in Dream, we brought Jack back."

"Thus, releasing Quilla into the world again. Yes?"

"Did you arrange *that*? Did you *want* us to free her, so we could then finally defeat her?"

"Nope. The Chakana was in a lead box in Adi's safe again, and I was still a very confused Nyx, who could never have planned something that complex. No, just fate again, I'd guess."

Or something else. Adi's words came back to him: *We are being moved like pieces on a board.*

A final question flashed into his mind. "My Flower. Quilla said she didn't send it to me. Did you?"

Nyx shook her head. "Not me."

"What? Then who?"

Nyx stared at the silver mirror, that window into the multiverse. "Maybe, just maybe, the Four weren't so hands-off, after all." She winked at him. "And they *were* merged with your parents."

A chill ran down his spine. "Wait. You mean—?"

"It would've just been the introduction of another event. No interference with free will." She shrugged. "Like I said...maybe."

Pieces moved on a board.

"Anything else?" she asked, a gentle smile on her face. "Then this, dear friend of eight years and much weirdness, is the last time we'll ever see each other. The last time we'll ever talk."

"Oh," he said, suddenly understanding.

"Which means it's our last chance to be rude to each other."

Will smiled. "Funny, I can't think of anything rude to say." He swallowed. "I'll miss you, Nyx. I'll miss you more than—" His voice broke. "—more than I can say. Thanks."

"For making your life miserable for eight years?"

He laughed. "For being part of that life. Being part of *me*. Being my friend." He shrugged. "For everything."

"You're welcome. Of all the messed-up humans in the multiverse, you are my favorite."

"Yeah, well..."

"I know. Low bar. Give Case and Fader hugs from me. Tell them I'm sorry, but I couldn't handle more goodbyes." She walked to where Luciana stood with the Chakana around her neck, then looked back and smiled. In that smile lay love and sadness and pride.

Nyx began to glow, her blues and purples and violets changing to silver, her body melting to a floating crystal sphere. The sphere shrank, smaller and smaller, until it was a shining spark, a spark that flew into the Chakana.

A familiar voice sounded in his head—for the last time, he knew. *Goodbye, Will Dreycott. I love you.* The echo of her words faded.

Nyx was gone.

The frozen tableau in the Library sprang to life again, silence turning to a happy babble like a switch being thrown. Case came over and gave him a hug. "What's up? Standing here all by yourself." She looked at him, frowning. "Are you...crying?"

He pulled her close. She felt so good. She smelled so good. "Saying goodbye to Nyx."

She leaned back. "Wait. What? Nyx is gone? Without saying goodbye to us?"

"I'll tell you about it—"

Luciana's voice cut him off. "It is time to return. Tonight, we honor our new Madres with a feast. And tomorrow..." Her eyes ran over him, Case, Fader, Rani, and the three parents. "...tomorrow, you will leave us and journey home."

The group filed through the Library door. Will lingered to the end, saying a final silent goodbye to this strange part of his life.

He thought of everything Nyx had told him. Meeting Case—fate. Unwittingly freeing Quilla—also, fate. And what started it all—the Chakana encountering a young and astrally powerful Will Dreycott. Had that been fate, too? And who had sent the Flower?

Maybe, just maybe, the Four weren't so hands-off, after all.

Thinking again of pieces being moved on a board, he stepped outside, leaving the silver mirror and the Story and the Four behind.

The next morning, Will rode with the other travelers in Luciana's gondola as two masked Sisters poled them upriver. At the bow, Luciana sat with Suyana and the new Madres—a still-beaming Isobel and Yanta, now haughtier than ever. Will, Case, and Fader sat behind the Madres, then the three parents, then Adi and Rani, Stone and Mei, and finally Diego and his men. Fader still wore the Unicorn Tapestry like a superhero cape.

The travelers had talked and laughed after leaving the Threshold, passing through the Second Veil and traveling the jungle path to the River of Light. But once the boat sailed back through the First Veil, a silence fell.

"I can feel them again," Fader whispered.

"Feel what, dude?" Will asked.

"The other 'verses. The In Between."

Will understood. Behind the First Veil lay a place cut off from the multiverse. A place created for the Sisters, for the Book, for the Story. A place created by the Four.

"So, we're back in Kansas?" Case said. "Our world?"

"Yeah, but without Toto this time," Will said.

She frowned.

"Jack."

"Oh, shit. Don't mention that. I will never look at puppies the same way again."

The boat journey ended. They followed the Madres up the steps from the River, through the Cave of Flowers, through the tunnel maze, until they reached the Temple of the Key. As Luciana led them to its arched entrance, the door to the outside world, Will noticed the altar for the Chakana was gone.

"The Chakana will live once again at the Threshold," Luciana explained. "Our attempt to guard against another like Quilla only created a different danger."

A different danger. Alvarez stealing the Chakana and killing the Sisters. But that had led to his parents obtaining the Key and his exposure to it. Which led to the end of Quilla. He swallowed. The decision to move the Chakana to this cavern—had that been fate, too? Or something else?

Pieces being moved on a board.

Will shivered, realizing that he would never know the answer.

Luciana now stood with the three other Madres facing the travelers. Her eyes fell on Will, Case, Fader, and Rani. "My young friends, you returned the Chakana, defeated Quilla, and saved the Tree. Once again, we may serve the Four. For all this, we thank you."

The four Madres bowed to them. Will and the others gave nervous half bows back.

Luciana continued. "You are now free to leave. But remember what the Sisterhood protects in this place. Though we part friends, should you return here, we will not greet you as such." With that, without a backward glance, Luciana, Suyana, and Yanta disappeared into the tunnel that led to the Cave of Flowers and from there to the Threshold.

Only Isobel remained. She embraced each of Will, Fader, and Rani, sobbing her goodbyes. Then she and Case stood hugging, both crying into each other's shoulders.

"I will miss you so," Isobel said. "You will forever be my sister. We will meet again in a higher realm." Breaking off the hug, she ran weeping into the tunnel mouth...

Which then vanished.

Will and the others walked up to what was now a solid rock wall. He ran his hand over the surface, feeling only cold stone.

"They *really* don't want us coming back," Rani said.

"Come on," Adi said, heading for the cavern's exit. "Diego's helicopter is about an hour's walk. Let's go home."

Chapter 56

Back to the Day Job

Three days later, Case lay curled in Will's arms in his rooftop park, on the grassy hill overlooking the fountain. His favorite place, which at some point had become *their* place.

Her two bunnies, Flopsy and Mopsy, were happily munching grass nearby. The roof's glass dome was open. The July air was humid, and the late morning sun beat down from a cloudless sky, but she didn't mind the heat. After glowing rock walls, shining disks, and silver skies, she loved feeling the sun on her skin again.

Their journey home from Peru had been uneventful. She decided she liked uneventful.

After leaving the Temple of the Key, Diego and his men had flown them back to Arequipa, arriving that night. The next day, a very contrite and shaken Gabriel Herrada, rescued the night before from the Gray Lands by the Dream Rider, expedited their departure on their private jet. They landed in Toronto that evening.

On the flight, Will had related his final conversation with Nyx. No one questioned his story. They'd all seen too much. But Adi did raise an I-told-you-so eyebrow to Nyx's *not so hands-off* guess about the Four. Pieces moved on a board.

Their flight home had been two days ago. Will had spent yesterday with his parents, touring the Dream Rider Tower and helping them ease back into this world. And being a family again. Last night, he told Case his parents were reevaluating what they wanted to do with their lives.

Ellie had spent yesterday with Adi, who was helping her reestablish her life. A year ago, after the required waiting period had passed, the bank holding Ellie's loans had convinced a court to declare her legally dead, so they could write off her loans.

"Oh, yay," Ellie had sighed. "Out of debt...but dead." She'd long ago lost her faculty position at the university. Case didn't know how Adi could help with any of that, but guessed the CEO of Dream Rider Corporation had connections.

The three parents weren't the only ones facing new lives. Will would turn eighteen next month and could make his own decisions about his future and his company. Decisions about how to use his money.

Case snuggled closer to him. His money remained a problem for her. She had no idea what their futures might be, except she wanted hers to include him. But if they were going to have a future *together*, she needed him to do something more with his money. Something good.

And what was her own future going to be? Once they'd left the jungle, her phone had coughed up dozens of texts from Link and the foreman of the Crash Space construction. The floor was finished, and twenty kids were living there already. Link was giving her a tour later.

Was *that* her future? Crash Space was still critical to her, giving street kids a safe place and a chance to restart their lives. But what exactly would she be *doing* every day? She wished she was more like Fader, thrilled to be drawing the next Dream Rider comic. Was Crash Space going to be her *job*? Did she want to finish school? Go to university?

Okay, enough. She and Will had their families back. They didn't need to decide their futures today. They'd saved the multiverse and deserved a break from being superheroes.

She just wished her Voice understood that.

The uncertainty around keeping their powers had been short-lived. Fader had sensed the In Between once they'd passed the First Veil. As for her Voice...

You need to tell him, it said, as if on cue.

Shut. Up.

Tell him.

Not now! Maybe never. She still hadn't shared Rani's suspicions about Adi with Will. Rani had been wrong about Stone, so...

Tell him!

"I went into Dream last night," Will said.

"Still got the mojo?" she asked, grateful for the distraction.

"I'd rescued Herrada from the Gray Lands, and I can still astral project while awake, so I figured I'd be able to." He shrugged where he cuddled against her. "But with Nyx gone, I wasn't sure what it'd be like."

"And?"

"Doogles, House of Four Doors, my powers, everything was the same." He sighed. "Except no Nyx."

"You miss her."

"Yeah."

"Me, too. Still pissed she didn't say goodbye, though. And there's something I wish you'd asked her."

"Didn't know that was our last chat...until I did. I had another question, too. Didn't think of it until I saw the greenhouse up here."

"What's your question?"

"You first."

She propped herself on an elbow. "Isobel said no one had ever seen the Guardians outside the Crossing. So, why'd they appear here, half a world away?

And why to *us?* Me, Fader, Rani?"

"Don't know."

"Best guess?"

He stared at the sky, frowning. "Definitely a guess. Nyx began sharing memories of my parents the same day the Guardians appeared to you guys. She said those memories returned because she started waking up after the Chakana pulled me inside it on the Black Island. And she was the *Keeper of the Guardians*. Maybe they sensed her waking up—and that drew them here."

"But why pick *us?*"

"You and Fader, your astral powers come from the Book. Maybe the Guardians sensed that connection."

"But why Rani? She has no astral powers."

"And I thank the multiverse for that decision."

"Seriously, why her?"

He watched a single cloud scud across the blueness above. "She might not have astral powers, but she *was* exposed to a *lot* of astral stuff on the Black Island. Your Voice, Fader's powers, the In Between, scarab guardians, the Black Tower, the Black Pool, the Chakana. Plus, she met Isobel and the eight Sisters we rescued. And Quilla, too, as Jack inside me."

"So?"

"Maybe all those things left a mark on Rani. Something the Guardians could detect. Like an astral scent."

"They *smelled* her?"

He shrugged. "Or sensed her hero potential. Much to my surprise, she saved us lots of times."

"Think I'll go with 'hero' rather than 'smell,' if she ever asks. Which I'm guessing she won't. She texted she still freaks anytime she sees a bird."

"Serves her right for not remembering the thunder babies."

"So, what was your question for Nyx?"

"About my Flower."

"You said she didn't know who sent it."

"No, about why it gave me those weird visions from Peru—the rock wall, the quipu, the waterfall."

"But weren't they buried memories from eight years ago? When Luciana led you all to the Threshold from the Temple of the Key. On the way, you smelled the Flower, saw the wall, heard the waterfall—"

"Except I was still unconscious for all that. Suyana said I didn't wake up until the Threshold, when my dad took the Chakana from its lead box."

"Subconscious memories?"

"Smelling the Flower, hearing the waterfall, maybe. But Luciana blindfolded us. I couldn't have seen the rock wall. Or the quipu." He frowned. "And why would Luciana use that quipu?"

"She wouldn't. She's too sharp to need a memory aid."

"Which means my quipu memory is even older than her. So...not *my* memory." He smiled. "Well, not the *me* part of me. I think your 'subconscious' guess was right."

She understood. "Nyx. Those memories came from the Chakana. The piece inside you."

He nodded. "Think how many times the Chakana would've made that journey from the Temple of the Key to the Threshold since Quilla's time."

"Makes sense." She snuggled against him again on the warm grass. "I'm sure we'll think of other questions, but no more for now."

They fell silent until Will spoke. "My parents have changed."

"Not surprising, after staring into the multiverse for eight years. How are they different?"

"They'll get this misty-eyed look, then smile, like they see something I can't, know something I don't. Hard to explain. But they seem...calmer, less driven." She felt him shrug. "Happier."

"Happier is good."

"And they've decided what they want to do. At least, for the next few years."

"Which is?"

"It's a *big* deal."

"And here is where you tell me."

"It'll get a lot of press."

"Will..."

"I mean, a *lot*. All around the world."

"Will!"

He chuckled. "Okay, okay. They've decided...drum roll, please...to return every artifact they ever acquired to the country where they found it. They said it's the right thing to do."

She sat up and stared at him. "Holy shit. That *is* huge. And very cool. Good for them."

He gave a shy smile. "Yeah, I'm really proud of them."

"You should be."

He sat up, facing her cross-legged. "Uh, there's more."

"Why do you look worried?"

"Not sure how *you'll* react."

"Me? Why?"

"My parents have *thousands* of artifacts from *dozens* of countries. They'll just ship most back to the country of origin. But the return of some items will be huge news, a giant win for the country's leader. Presidents and Prime Ministers will play this up in their media. Televised public handover ceremonies, speeches, photo ops."

"Still missing the 'me' part."

"They'll want my parents to attend those ceremonies."

"Makes sense. More media boost. Lot of travel, though."

"Well, my mom will do some trips, my dad some…" He hesitated. "And I'll do the rest. Actually, most of them."

"Wait. What? You didn't take any of these things. Why would *you* go?"

"Because of the Dream Rider. I'm better known than my once-famous, now forgotten parents. And known around the world, because the Rider's everywhere. If I attend, these ceremonies will be even higher profile, which means happier people in power. And a PR boost for the Rider."

Her heart fell, thinking she understood. "I get it. You'll be gone a lot and want to know how I feel about that." She looked away. "Yeah. No. I'm good."

"You are?"

She spun back, fists clenched. "No! I'm not *good*! How could you do that to me? To us? I thought we were… I thought we had…" She glared at him, arms folded. "No. I am *not* good with this."

He grinned. "Had me worried for a second, all okay with us being apart. Because I don't want us to be." He looked down, then up at her. "Because…because I love you—"

She threw her arms around him, pulling him tight.

"—and I'll only do this," he said, his voice muffled against her shoulder, "if you come with me."

She leaned back, staring at him. "*With* you?"

"Yep."

"Like…world tour?"

"Couple dozen countries, for sure."

"That'll involve airplanes, right?"

"Or long wet walks. Hey, you were fine flying home."

"I hide my fear well."

"So, what do you say? Because I won't go without you."

She picked at a blade of grass. "Remember our first big fight?"

"When you called my wealth *obscene*? Hard to forget."

"I still have that problem."

He nodded. "I get it. And now I'm offering an all-expenses-paid trip around the world." He took her hands in his. "My parents aren't the only ones rethinking their lives. I'm no longer a prisoner here. This tower won't be my world, anymore. You're still committed to Crash Space?"

His question took her by surprise. "More than ever."

"Well, as we return artifacts, more floors will become available. The warehouse, my museum floors."

She understood. "We can expand Crash Space. Get more kids off the streets."

"Why not affordable housing for families, too?"

Her eyes widened, her excitement growing. "Yes! And day care. Counseling. Medical clinics."

"Skills training, trade schools. We could offer space to school boards. Even start a new college or university."

"Will," she said, suddenly hesitant, "this would take a *lot* of money."

He grinned. "Good thing I'm obscenely rich."

"Never letting me forget that, are you?"

"Then you'll come with me? Faster we return the artifacts, faster we free up floors."

"Can't let you *not* go, and you're not going without me."

They kissed, a kiss she held until a thought intruded. She leaned back. "How can we do all these good things while we're traveling the world?"

"We make a list of what we want to do, what goes first, second. Adi sets up project teams. We check in while traveling. I'm meeting later with Adi and my parents to plan the trips. You should come, and we'll talk about this, too."

Adi and his parents. Her Voice didn't miss that cue. *Tell him!*

Go away.

If he finds out you knew and didn't tell him, it will hurt him.

That stopped her. Because her Voice was right. "Have you talked to your parents anymore," she asked, trying to sound casual, "about being adopted?"

He dropped his eyes, running a hand over the grass. "Quite the change of subject."

"I mean, do they know who your mother was?"

"The hospital said the mother—" He swallowed. "—*my* mother withheld permission to disclose her name." He hesitated. "They'll release it to me once I turn eighteen. But only if I come in person with the original adoption papers."

"You turn eighteen next month."

He nodded.

"You going to ask?"

"Yeah. My first artifact return is in Hong Kong. While I'm there, I'll visit the hospital."

She remembered the hospital from Rani's story: *Holy Blood.* "What if it's not there anymore?"

"I've already contacted them."

"What's its name?" she asked, again as casually as possible.

"Holy Blood."

Tell him.

"Will," she said gently, "I need to tell you something..."

He stayed silent as she talked. After she finished, she waited for him to speak, to react. But he sat, head down, jaw clenched, ripping up blades of grass.

Her phone chimed. She checked it. "Shit. We've got that thing with Mei."

"You go," he whispered.

"You're not coming? It was your idea."

He shook his head.

She hesitated. "I don't like to leave you—"

"Please, Case. Just...just go. I want to be alone."

"Okay. Yeah. No. I get it." Kissing him on the cheek, she left, hating herself for the pain she saw in his face. Pain she'd put there.

No, she thought, walking to the elevator. *I didn't put it there.* She took out her phone. *Enough*. She texted Adi.

⚶

Five minutes later, Case was pacing up and down in Will's studio. Fader sat hunched over the design table, working on the next Dream Rider issue. Mei was late, and Case was filling the time by checking her phone every few seconds for a text from Will or Adi.

Nothing. Should she call him? No, he'd asked to be left alone.

Fader glanced up from his drawing. "Maybe Mei changed her mind."

"She won't." Should she call Adi?

An elevator dinged at the far end of the floor. Shoes clicked on the wooden track, coming closer. Li Mei's short slim figure appeared around the corner.

She stopped, as if unsure whether to enter. Case and Fader walked over to her.

Case barely recognized Mei. Instead of her usual dark suit and white shirt, she wore a long-sleeved red blouse and a short black pencil skirt with low-heeled black pumps. Her long black hair, normally in a tight ponytail, hung loose over her shoulders.

"Sorry I'm late," Mei said. She clutched her hands before her, dropped them to her sides, then clutched them again. "I kept changing outfits. I...I wanted to look nice."

"You look fantastic," Case said.

Mei gave a nervous smile. "Isn't Will coming?"

"He's meeting with Adi." *I hope.* She pushed thoughts of Will away for now. "Ready?"

Mei took a breath and nodded. Fader held out his hand. Mei hesitated, then took it. Case took her other hand.

And Fader pulled them into the In Between.

⚶

Case studied Mei's face as they walked down the hallway of doors. Fader had explained the In Between before, but Mei had never experienced its strangeness. Even so, she ignored every door they passed, each with an entire universe behind it.

Case understood. Only one universe meant anything to Mei. And they hadn't reached it yet.

"The 'verses near us are pretty much like ours," Fader explained. "We probably wouldn't notice any difference."

They walked past more doors.

"But in 'verses farther away, something changed in *our* lives." He looked at Mei. "Someone we know made a different choice. Or we did." He stopped at a door.

"A different choice..." Mei whispered, staring at the scene behind this one—Will's studio, empty except for one person sitting on the couch, hands clasped, head down.

Wu Peng.

His suit and shirt, normally creased and rumpled, were clean and pressed. His hair was combed and neat.

"He's alive," Mei said, eyes glistening.

"In this 'verse, when the shooting started at the monastery," Case said, "something changed. Whatever happened, Peng lived..." She hesitated. "But you didn't. Here, he's grieving *you*."

Mei hugged herself. "Is he...expecting me?"

Fader nodded. "Once I found this 'verse, Case talked to...well, herself...here. Other Case. Who talked to Other Will and Other me. And they all talked to Peng."

Mei bit her lip. "*Other* Peng."

"Yeah. Other Peng."

"I just step through?"

Fader nodded again.

Mei swallowed. "Could I stay in this world? Could we be together here?"

Case hesitated. "Will wasn't certain, but it would be your free will, your choice, so he thinks...yes. Do you *want* to stay?"

Mei didn't answer. Without another word, she stepped through the door.

Peng—Other Peng—stood as Mei appeared. She walked to him. They stared at each other, neither talking. Then Mei threw her arms around Peng, and he pulled her to him. They stood there, their bodies shaking with sobs Case couldn't hear. Finally breaking off their embrace, they sat, hands still clasped.

"We shouldn't watch," Case said to Fader. They turned away. Each time she checked, Mei and Peng were still talking. Or laughing. Or crying. Or both.

Until she looked and found Mei waiting at the door. Fader reached through. Grasping his arm, Mei turned back to Peng. She touched her fingers to her lips. He did the same. She stepped back into the In Between. Peng slumped onto the couch, staring after her.

"You coming to say goodbye?" Fader asked.

She smiled a sad smile. "No. Peng and I said our goodbyes."

Case nodded, understanding.

Fader looked puzzled. "You're not staying?"

Mei shook her head.

"Why?" he asked. Case smacked him on the arm.

"No, you have a right to ask, after your beautiful gesture." Mei looked back at the door. "What you called him before—*Other* Peng."

Fader frowned, but then nodded. "He's not *your* Peng."

"And I am not his Mei. He felt the same. To be together here would make our deaths—mine in this world, his in ours—meaningless." Her eyes were wet. "It would make my love for my Peng, this Peng's love for his Mei—it would make that love a lie. I will not do that."

"I'd feel the same way," Case said, "if it was Will."

Mei smiled. "Thank you for understanding. And thank you for letting us finally say what we should have said to each other long ago."

After one last look at Peng, Mei turned away. They began walking back to the door to their 'verse.

"Peng was very fond of you," Mei said to Fader.

"I liked him a lot," Fader said, his head down.

"I want you to have something of his. To remember him."

"I won't forget him."

"Neither will I. But I think you should have his collection of wuxia comics. He'd like that."

Fader looked at her. "I'd rather have Peng."

Mei slipped an arm around him. "So would I."

Chapter 57

Mother Mother

Adi sat at the long table in the boardroom, listening as three Dream Rider Corporation lawyers explained to Ellie their efforts to reestablish her life. Appealing the death declaration. Reinstating bank accounts. Applying to provincial ministries and federal departments for the myriad documents needed to prove she existed—driver's license, health card, passport. And more.

Adi's mind was elsewhere. Her heart, too. On the conversation she needed to have with William. The conversation she'd avoided for years.

She sighed. The conversation she was still avoiding. Because she was frightened—no, terrified—of how he would react, of how he'd look at her. But now that he knew he was adopted...

Yet still she sat there. Checking her phone, she found a text from Case.

Holy Blood Hospital, Hong Kong. Will knows. He's on the roof.

A chill seized her. She stared at the words. Finally, her hands shaking, she texted back. She didn't ask what Will knew. Or how. She just said, *Thank you.*

No more delays.

"Excuse me," she said, interrupting a lawyer explaining the settlement of Ellie's parents' estate. "Ellie, may I leave you with these very capable people?"

"Of course," Ellie said. "Thank you, Adi, for everything."

"Jon and Terri owe you this and more. We'll transfer what they promised you, plus interest, once your bank reinstates your accounts." Adi slid a bank card to her. "Until then, please use this. And the apartment here is yours until you get settled."

"I'm talking to my faculty head today." Ellie sighed. "But they have no openings. And explaining my eight-year disappearance is...difficult."

Wishing Ellie good luck, Adi left and headed for the elevators. The elevator came. Inside, her finger hesitated over 'Roof / Jungle' before stabbing the button. No more delays. *All I ask, William, is you forgive me one day.* She swallowed. *No, all I ask is you don't hate me.*

The elevator ride was far too short. As she stepped out onto the roof, another text arrived from Case.

Good luck.

Surprised at the comfort that gave her, she walked past groves of trees and grassy hills, immune to birdsong and squirrel chatter, to the smell of roses and fresh-cut grass. She walked slowly, still delaying, still afraid.

She found him sitting on his favorite hill, as she knew she would. As she approached, she tried to meet his eyes, but shrank from the anger and pain there. She sat beside him.

Neither of them spoke.

Somehow, she found the courage to break the silence. "William, your parents didn't know."

"My *parents*," he said, and she heard the bitterness in the word.

She pushed on, her words tumbling out in a rush. "I wanted to tell you so many times. At first, I convinced myself you were too young. Then I decided to wait until your parents told you of the adoption. Those were excuses. I was a coward."

Her hands were trembling. She tried to stop them but failed. "When they disappeared, you wanted to find them so badly, it felt cruel to tell you they weren't your parents. You were still a child." She shook her head. "But I let years slip by. I waited too long. I should have told you."

She looked at him then. The anger in his face was gone, but the pain there made her want to weep. "Please say something," she whispered.

"Why did you give me up?"

She blinked. Of course. For years, she'd agonized over confessing who she was to him. For years, she'd wrestled with that question alone. But it had been the wrong question. Not the one *he* cared about.

"Didn't you want me? Didn't you...?" His voice broke.

"William, I loved you from the moment I held you in my arms. I loved you more than I thought it possible to love anyone. I never stopped loving you."

"But you didn't *want* me." An accusation, not a question.

"No. No, I wanted you. I wanted you in my life forever. But more, I wanted to keep you safe. To give you a good life. A long, happy, safe life. But you couldn't have that with me. Dangerous people wished me dead—"

"The Triads."

"How—?"

"Rani."

Of course. *Well done*, she thought with grudging admiration. *Harry Lyle would be proud.* "Yes. If the Triads had found you, they could have forced me to give myself up. And I would have done that. To save you."

He looked at her. She couldn't read his face. "But they would've killed you."

"Yes."

A pause. "I'm glad that didn't happen."

She blinked tears away. Was there a chance...?

"What did you do?"

She smiled against the tears. "I named you 'William.' I asked my friends who ran the hospital, who'd hidden me there, to put you up for adoption, keeping my name secret. Then I ran. I'd lived between the law and the Triads for years. I had people I trusted. They gave me a new identity and slipped me out of Hong Kong."

Memories long suppressed flooded back. "I'd known your parents for five years, often helping them...*acquire* artifacts all over south-east Asia. They were good people. They'd been struggling to have kids." She shrugged. "And they were rich."

"You told them about me."

"No. A mutual friend did. They never knew of my...connection. I waited. Two years. Until the Triads believed Martine Labelle dead, and I'd established my new identity. Then..." She sighed. "I asked your parents for a job."

"Why?"

She stared at him. "I wanted to be part of your life."

He swallowed and looked away.

"Your parents were thrilled to have someone with my skills. I said I was leaving my shady past behind, hence my new identity. They could relate."

"And you never told them? That I'm your son?"

Her heart skipped, hearing him speak those words. *I'm your son.* "No. As I said, I planned to tell them. And you. But..." She shrugged.

"Wish you had. Wish I'd known sooner."

She heard no anger in his words. Only regret. "So do I. But Terri was a wonderful mother. I doubt I'd have done as well, given my own upbringing."

"Bad?"

She grimaced. "I ran away at thirteen."

"And you gave *Case* a hard time?" But he smiled.

She gave a timid smile of her own. "I remembered what *I* was like at her age. I wouldn't have trusted me."

"Well," he said quietly, "You were a great fill-in mom—who actually *was* my mom."

She didn't trust herself to speak for a second, not daring to hope. "You do?"

"Yeah, I do. Course, you're screwing up this part."

"I am?" she said, confused, her fear returning. "What am I...what did I...?"

"Well, I'm sitting right here..." He looked at her then, his eyes wet. "...and my mom hasn't even hugged me yet."

Her tears came then, in long sobs she didn't even try to control. She threw her arms around him, and he wrapped his around her. They sat rocking back and forth, both crying.

"I love you, William," she whispered. "Can you ever forgive me?"

He pulled back to look at her. "One condition."

"Anything."

He sat back, grinning his wonderful grin. "You stop calling me *William*."

She laughed. "I can do that...Will."

"Then I forgive you...Mom."

They talked then, like two old friends, which they were, and like mother and son, which they were now, too.

She said she'd tell his parents, and he said they'd do it together, for which she was grateful. She felt her life had been on hold and could now restart. He said he felt the same. She said she wanted to ask Laura to marry her, but was afraid she'd say no. He told her to ask anyway, that Laura was great. She told him Ellie really liked him, and he smiled at that.

And it was all wonderful.

A comfortable silence fell. She waited, basking in the warmth of the sun and his forgiveness. Waited for the question she knew would come. And it did.

He looked at her. "Tell me about my father."

Epilogue
My Happy Ending

Chapter 58

Smells Like Teen Spirit

A month later, Will struggled down the stairs from his bedroom to his studio, a backpack over a shoulder and a suitcase in one hand, both jammed full and way too heavy. Groaning, he dropped them to the rug.

Case followed him down, tossing her own backpack on the sofa. "You should pack lighter."

"Uh, most of that suitcase is your stuff."

She shrugged. "Mom bought me outfits for the handover ceremonies. She's working through her absent-mom-guilt, and I am totally letting her."

Fader sat drawing at the design table. As usual when he worked on the comic art, he wore the Unicorn Tapestry like a superhero cape. "She buys *you* travel clothes. She makes *me* stay home and go back to school."

"Hey, she wants me to finish school, too," Case said. "School's important."

"I already know lots of stuff."

"You want to study graphic design at university, right?" Will said.

Fader sighed. "Yeah. I get it—I need high school to get in."

"At least you'll go to classes right here," Will said, "assuming my mom gets the rezoning of the tower approved. Along with all the other approvals."

"Your *mom*," Case said, smiling. "You're really used to calling Adi that now."

Will grinned. Yeah, he was. And it felt good.

"What do you call your old mom?" Fader asked.

"For sure, not *old* Mom. I call them both Mom and let them work it out. And they have...mostly."

Case nodded. "Yeah. Your parents are still awkward around Adi, but they're definitely better."

Will shook his head. "Two months ago, I had no parents. Now, I have four, counting Laura. What about your mom? How's the future Dean of our new university?"

"Can't call her that, yet," Case said. "She thinks it might jinx it. The province won't approve the university for at least a year. But she says it's coming along."

All their projects were coming along. Dr. Jin was heading the new family medical clinic and was recruiting for the counseling and rehab centers. Link was working under the tower's building facilitator to manage Crash Space. Plans for family housing floors were being reviewed. Stone and his team would still handle security for the building, which would soon become a self-contained city.

His phone rang. He answered. "Hi, Rani. You're on speaker. What's up?"

"Hi!" Case and Fader called.

"Hi, guys," Rani said. "Wanted to catch you before you left, Will. First, thanks for your latest Galahad tip. The cops made the arrest this morning, and we broke the story. Between that and the exclusive you gave us on the artifacts' return, my editor's almost forgiven me for coming home with nothing publishable—or, at least, believable."

"You're welcome. Was there something else?" he asked, trying not to get his hopes up.

"My guy in Hong Kong found some references to your dad in police files and news archives, but they're all from eighteen years ago. Nothing else and nothing more recent. Sorry."

Eighteen years ago. The year I was born. "Well, thanks for trying."

"He might've left Hong Kong," Rani said. "Or changed his name. Or...something."

Or something. Meaning he might be dead. "Yeah, sure. Thanks again."

"Safe travels, you two. Keep in touch." Rani hung up.

"Sorry about your dad," Case said. "I know you were hoping Rani could find something."

He sighed. "Yeah. Especially after Adi's and Stone's Hong Kong contacts could find no trace of him."

"Still nothing in Dream?"

"Nope. It's the same every time. My Doogles think they've found something. We start chasing it. Then they get...confused. Like he's hiding...somehow."

"Maybe he is," she said. "If your powers come from your missing dad, he must have some serious astral skills himself. Still want to start in Hong Kong?"

"Too late to reschedule the handover of the artifacts. And that was the last place Mom saw him."

"Seeing you're standing here, I'd say they did more than 'see' each other."

"I did *not* ask for details. She said their time together was short, intense...and wonderful. But he disappeared before she knew about me."

"So, he may not know he has a son? Wow. Has she said anything more about him?"

"Last night, she—" His phone beeped. "I'll tell you on the plane. Jimmy's in the basement with the limo. The parental posse is waiting with him to see us off."

Fader slipped off the chair. "I'll say goodbye here, if that's okay."

"Not coming downstairs?" Case asked.

He shook his head. "I'm sad enough already. Watching you drive off will make it worse."

Case gave him a big hug. "Hey, we're back in a couple of weeks."

"I know," he said, still hugging her. "But this is the first time we've been apart since I was eight. Except for..." He broke off the hug and shrugged.

"Except for you getting snatched by Morrigan and getting lost in the multiverse. Hey, but now you have Mom."

"Yeah, but I'll still miss you."

"I'll miss you, too. And I'll call every day."

Fader looked at Will. "Do we hug?"

"Or manly fist bumps. Your call."

They hugged, then Will and Case grabbed their bags.

"We're still doing the comic, right?" Fader said. "I'm almost finished the last panel for *Astral Avengers #1.*"

"Why wouldn't we?"

"Well, you're searching for your dad now..."

"Dude, I spent eight years searching for my parents. I'm not planning another find-the-parent obsession. I'll keep looking for my dad, but I can do that in Dream. Yes, the comic's still happening. Send me what you've done, and I'll look at it."

With a final goodbye to Fader, they headed for the elevators.

Inside the elevator, Will pressed the button for 'Egypt.'

"Um..." Case said.

"Quick detour."

They got off on the Egypt floor. Leaving their bags by the elevator, he led her along the hallway. "Bring back memories?"

She gave a shiver. "I snuck in here the night I ran away from Morrigan." She pointed at two cat statues in an alcove as they passed. "I hid behind those."

They turned a corner, and a memory of his own came—his first sight of Case in this same corridor that same night. Halfway along, he stopped before a large canopic jar, standing about waist height. "Remember this?"

Case groaned. "Is that why we're here? So you can embarrass me with that memory?"

"No. We're here because all the artifacts on this floor will be gone before we're back." He looked around. "Last chance to remember."

"Oh!" She looked around, too. "Thanks. For bringing me here. I'll actually miss this place."

"Even that jar?"

She smiled. "Even that jar." She bit her lip. "I mean, that night was horrible. Losing Fader to those creeps. Back then, I would've called it the worst night of my life. But, hey, we saved the day."

"Kicked their butts."

"Happy ending. And it started here." She slipped her arms around his neck. "*We* started here. You and me. So, now...I'd call it the best night of my life."

"Me, too." He pulled her close. "Because you're the best thing that's ever happened to me." He brushed his lips over hers, and she pulled his head down into a kiss. As they kissed, as he held her, feeling her warmth, her softness, her love, it seemed the weight of eight years was lifting from his shoulders. His life was starting again. Now. In this moment.

Happy ending. Yeah, it was. It really was.

The kiss ended, and they stood holding each other. Then, with a last look around, they headed out for their new adventure.

Chapter 59

Post Credit Scene

An hour later in Will's studio, Fader made the last touches to his current panel then sat back at the design table, admiring his work. It was good. He'd finally gotten Morrigan's face right.

City Hall loomed in the background as Morrigan slammed her foot down, destroying her amulet and Marell along with it. Staring at the witch, he remembered how she'd protected him that day. Protected him right to the end when the Nothing had destroyed the Black Tower, destroyed the entire Black Island.

Destroyed Morrigan, too. For he'd known her claim the Unicorn would save her had been a lie. A lie to protect him, again.

A message from Case popped up on the design screen, saying their plane was about to take off. Feeling suddenly lonely, he decided to finish for the day and go look for his mom.

He switched off the table and slipped from the chair. Taking off the Unicorn Tapestry, he covered the screen with it. This had become a ritual. He liked to wear the Tapestry when he drew, and this way, it was always here for him.

He began to turn away, then stopped. Stepping back to the table, he stared at the fabric, at the patterns and pictures woven into it.

He'd first seen the Tapestry when the giant bat delivered Morrigan to the Temple of the Key. He'd seen it again when Suyana showed them Morrigan at the Threshold. But both times, he'd been more concerned about Morrigan being frozen like a statue than the cloak she'd worn.

In the Black Tower, though, as she faced the Black Pool, working to end Quilla's branch of Order, she'd had her back to him. There, he'd first noticed the Unicorn at the center of the design, before Morrigan called on it. He had noticed, too, the pale-haired woman seated beside the beast.

After escaping the Black Island and returning to the Threshold, he'd checked Morrigan's strange cloak again. The white eel he'd summoned was gone. So were the Unicorn and the woman. He'd figured Luciana let him keep the Tapestry because its magic was all used up, and it had become just a pretty piece of cloth.

But now...

Now, the Unicorn knelt again at the center of the Tapestry, horn lowered, glaring at him with a single, red eye.

But Fader's gaze settled on the woman who sat beside the beast. Like before, she wore a crown of flowers and rested one hand on the Unicorn's head, the other on its horn. But before, her dress had been blue, her hair yellow. This woman's dress was dark green.

And her hair was flaming red.

The eyes of Morrigan the Bright, last of the White Coven of Ellan Vannin, stared back at him. In those eyes, he saw love and longing, sadness and regret. And fear.

Her last words to him echoed again in his head. A memory? Or something else?

You have your sister. You have your mother. You have what I turned my back on. Live your life, little one. Live it long. Live it well.

Reaching out, Fader touched the face of the red-haired woman in the Tapestry. "Thank you," he whispered.

Then he turned away and left to find his mom.

The End

Afterword

Please Review This Book!

If you enjoyed *The Lost Expedition* and *The Dream Rider Saga*, please take a moment to help other readers discover these books by posting a review. Reviews really do help authors. Your review doesn't have to be long. A line or two is all you need to write to help me out. Just scan this QR code or use the link to find the book at your favorite retailer and post your review. Thanks!

https://books2read.com/TheLostExpedition

Want to Start Another Great Series?

The Wolf at the End of The World

A Heroka Novel

A shapeshifter hero battles ancient spirits, a covert government agency, and his own dark past in a race to solve a murder that could mean the end of the world.

Cree and Ojibwe legends mix with current day environmental conflict in this fast-paced urban fantasy that keeps you on the edge of your seat right up to its explosive conclusion. With an introduction by Charles de Lint.

~~

The Heroka walk among us. Unseen, unknown. Shapeshifters. Human in appearance but with power over their animal totems.

Gwyn Blaidd is a Heroka of the wolf totem. Once he led his people in a deadly war against the Tainchel, the shadowy agency that hunts his kind. Now he lives alone in his wilderness home, wolves his only companions.

But when an Ojibwe girl is brutally killed in Gwyn's old hometown, suspicion falls on his former lover. To save her, Gwyn must return, to battle not only the Tainchel, but even darker forces: ancient spirits fighting to enter our world...

And rule it.

Selected Reviews:

"An immersive and enjoyable reading experience. Readers will delight in learning more about Native American mythology, which is skillfully woven throughout the story. Smith's novel is both well paced and deftly plotted—leaving readers curious about what comes next for the Heroka." — *Publishers Weekly*

"What makes THE WOLF AT THE END OF THE WORLD such an engrossing read are the characters and Doug's wonderful prose, a perfect blend between matter-of-fact and lyricism. I can't remember the last time I read a book that spoke to me, so eloquently, and so deeply, on so many levels. ... I'll be rereading it in the future because it's that sort of book. Richly layered and deeply resonant. An old friend, from the first time you read it." — *Charles de Lint, World Fantasy Award winner*

"With adventure, intrigue, shape-shifters, family, a touch of romance and a lot of heart, this is a book I'd recommend for readers of all genres." —*SF Crowsnest*

Buy *The Wolf at the End of the World* from your favorite book retailer here:

https://books2read.com/TheWolfAtTheEndofTheWorld

About the Author

Douglas Smith is a five-time award-winning author described by *Library Journal* as "one of Canada's most original writers of speculative fiction."

His latest work is the multi-award-winning YA urban fantasy trilogy, *The Dream Rider Saga* (*The Hollow Boys*, *The Crystal Key*, and *The Lost Expedition*). His other books include the urban fantasy novel, *The Wolf at the End of the World*; the collections, *Chimerascope*, *Impossibilia*, and *La Danse des Esprits* (translated); and the writer's guide *Playing the Short Game: How to Market & Sell Short Fiction*.

Published in 27 languages, Doug is a 4-time winner of Canada's Aurora Award, most recently in 2023 for *The Hollow Boys*, as well as the juried IAP Award for the same book. He's been a finalist for the Astounding Award, CBC's Bookies Award, Canada's juried Sunburst Award, the juried Alberta Magazine Award for Fiction, and France's juried Prix Masterton and Prix Bob Morane.

Doug lives near Toronto, Ontario, Canada.

~~

"The man is Sturgeon good. Zelazny good. I don't give those up easy."
—*Spider Robinson, Hugo and Nebula Awards winner*

"A great storyteller with a gifted and individual voice."
—*Charles de Lint, World Fantasy Award winner*

"His stories are a treasure trove of riches that will touch your heart while making you think."
—*Robert J. Sawyer, Hugo and Nebula Awards winner*

"Stories you can't forget, even years later."
—*Julie Czerneda, multi-award-winning author and editor*

~~

Find all of Doug's books at your favorite retailer here:
https://books2read.com/ap/9xXXex/Douglas-Smith

Be the First to Hear of New Releases

Visit these websites or scan the QR codes to keep updated on Douglas's writing:

Signup for his newsletter:
https://smithwriter.com/newsletter-signup

Follow him on BookBub:
https://www.bookbub.com/authors/douglas-smith

Like him on FaceBook:
https://www.facebook.com/WritingtheFantastic

Visit his website:
https://smithwriter.com

Follow him on Bluesky:
https://bsky.app/profile/smithwriter.bsky.social

Follow him on Amazon:
https://www.amazon.com/stores/Douglas-Smith/author/B0037JUXGM

Also by Douglas Smith

The Dream Rider Saga:

The Hollow Boys (Book 1)
Aurora Award Winner
Juried Indie Author Project Winner

The Crystal Key (Book 2)
Aurora Award Finalist

The Lost Expedition (Book 3)
Aurora Award Finalist

The Merged Corporate Entity Novels

Taken in Passing

The Merged Corporate Entity Short Stories

"Scream Angel"
"Memories of the Dead Man"
"Enlightenment"
"Jigsaw"
"Gypsy Biker's Coming Home"
"Murphy's Law"

The Heroka Novels:

The Wolf at the End of the World
The Wolf and the Phoenix (coming soon)

The Heroka Short Stories:

"Spirit Dance"
"A Bird in the Hand"
"Dream Flight"

Short Story Collections:

Impossibilia
Chimerascope
Borderlanz

Writing Guides:

Playing the Short Game: How to Market & Sell Short Fiction (2nd edition)

~~~

All titles available in print and ebook from all major retailers via:

https://books2read.com/ap/9xXXex/Douglas-Smith

~~~

Acknowledgments

The Lost Expedition would not have been possible without the time, effort, support, and advice of the following people:

*My writing critique group, the Ink*Specs:*

Melissa Gold, Susan Qrose, Rebecca Simkin, and Maaja Wentz

My Beta Readers:

Ami Agner, Emily P Bloch, Laura Rainbow Dragon, Kerstin Langer, and Daria Rydzaj

My editors:

Susan Forest and Susan MacGregor

~~

My sincere thanks to all of you.

Songs Used for Chapter Titles

You may have noticed I used popular (mostly) song titles for the chapter titles in the book. If you didn't, don't worry about it. It was just something I enjoyed doing. However, if you did notice, I thought you might like to see the whole list of songs and their associated artists.

The artists reflect many of my favorites, such as Springsteen and Bowie and Canadian artists such as Metric, Housewife, The Tragically Hip, July Talk, The Headstones, Leonard Cohen, Joni Mitchell, Neil Young, The Beaches, Dear Rouge, Broken Social Scene, Stars, and Avril Lavigne.

But always the main reason I picked a song was for how its title fit to the chapter action.

ACT 1: LOOKING FOR A PLACE TO HAPPEN — The Tragically Hip

Chapter 1: All the Way Home — Bruce Springsteen
Chapter 2: Poster of a Girl — Metric
Chapter 3: I'll Follow You — David Bowie
Chapter 4: Flashes — Dear Rouge
Chapter 5: Growin' Up — Bruce Springsteen
Chapter 6: Bring it All Back — The Tragically Hip
Chapter 7: Escape Is at Hand for the Travellin' Man — The Tragically Hip
Chapter 8: The Beat of Black Wings — Joni Mitchell
Chapter 9: Tunnels — Arcade Fire
Chapter 10: The Loose Ends Will Make Knots — Stars
Chapter 11: Pretty Little Death Song — The Headstones
Chapter 12: Telling Lies — David Bowie
Chapter 13: Cubically Contained — The Headstones
Chapter 14: Now I Know — July Talk
Chapter 15: Soul Driver — Bruce Springsteen

ACT 2: ABOUT THIS MAP — The Tragically Hip

www.ingramcontent.com/pod-product-compliance
Lightning Source LLC
Chambersburg PA
CBHW021214220726

48287CB00014B/75